THE RIVALS OF SHERLOCK HOLMES

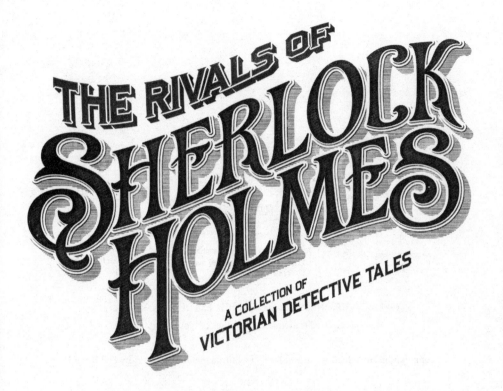

THE RIVALS OF SHERLOCK HOLMES

A COLLECTION OF VICTORIAN DETECTIVE TALES

COMPILED BY STEFAN DZIEMIANOWICZ
WITH AN INTRODUCTION BY LESLIE S. KLINGER

FALL RIVER PRESS

New York

FALL RIVER PRESS

New York

An Imprint of Sterling Publishing
1166 Avenue of the Americas
New York, NY 10036

ISBN 978-1-4351-6020-0

For information about custom editions, special sales, and premium and corporate purchases,
please contact Sterling Special Sales at 800-805-5489 or specialsales@sterlingpublishing.com.

Manufactured in the United States of America

2 4 6 8 10 9 7 5 3 1

www.sterlingpublishing.com

CONTENTS

The Female of the Species

Sherlockian Satires and Homages

INTRODUCTION

LTHOUGH CRIME WRITING—DETECTIVE OR MYSTERY STORIES—MAY BE viewed as a modern genre, its origins lie in the distant past. Dorothy Sayers, among others, traced tales in Babylonian legends, Greek myths, and the Bible that have strong elements of detection. It is also a conceit of English-language readers to believe that "detection" began (and, some say, truly ended) with Sherlock Holmes, that brilliant friend of Arthur Conan Doyle, whose detective career spanned the years 1881 through 1914. The sources of crime writing are far older and broader, and the rivals of Holmes—his mentors, competitors, and students—are many.

The English fascination with crime writing was fueled by the publication of the *Newgate Calendar* in the late 18th century. Subtitled the *Malefactors' Bloody Register* and originally no more than a monthly publication of executions, the *Calendar* was later collected in book form. It contained the stories of the criminals in startling detail and was viewed as edifying and improving. It was said to be as plentiful as the Bible in English households. From this beginning came the publications known as "broadsheets," one-page stories of trials and executions sold in the millions for a penny. This thirst for tales of crime and criminals soon led to the publication of the dime novels or "penny dreadfuls," as they were known in England. These serials started in the 1830s, originally as a cheaper alternative to mainstream fiction part-works, such as those by Charles Dickens (which cost a shilling) for working class adults.

By the 1850s the serial stories were aimed exclusively at younger readers. Although many of the stories were reprints or rewrites of Gothic thrillers, some were stories about famous criminals, such as Sweeney Todd and Spring-Heeled Jack, or had lurid titles like *The Boy Detective; or, The Crimes of London* (1865–66), *The Dance of Death; or, The Hangman's Plot. A Thrilling Romance of Two Cities* (1866; written by Brownlow, Detective, and Tuevoleur, Sergeant of the French Police), or a series like *Lives of the Most Notorious Highwaymen, Footpads and Murderers* (1836–37). Highwaymen were popular heroes: *Black Bess; or, The Knight of the Road* (1866), outlining the largely imaginary exploits of real-life highwayman Dick Turpin, continued for 254 episodes. As crime literature became popular, so did the detective story. Early popular American titles include *The Old Sleuth* and *Butts, the Boy Detective*, as well as countless stories about Sexton Blake and Nick Carter, detectives whose infallibility and invulnerability make them relatively uninteresting.

Prior to the second half of the nineteenth century, the period from which many of the stories in this volume are drawn, the concept of the detective was virtually unknown to the reading public. Short for "detective-police," a phrase appearing in *Chambers' Journal* in 1843, the official detective force was a special branch of the police, "intelligent men," in the words of the *Journal*, who attired themselves in the dress of ordinary men. The idea of an English police force was itself relatively new: The Bow Street Runners, an informal group organized in 1749 by the novelist Henry Fielding, though technically professional (they were paid by the Bow Street Court magistrates), was barely official, and an official police force was not formed until 1829, under the direction of Sir Robert Peel. In America, the first full-time police force was established by the City of Philadelphia in 1833, an outgrowth of the "night watch" that had arisen as the cities grew.

The first great writer of tales of criminal detection in any language was the Frenchman Eugène Vidocq (1775–1857), whose memoirs and novels found a ready audience. Although he was a reformed criminal, Vidocq was appointed in 1813 to be the first head of the Sûreté Nationale. This organization grew out of an informal detective force created by Vidocq and adopted by Napoleon as a supplement to the Paris police. Vidocq's memoirs told of his detection and capture of criminals, often using disguises. Later books described his criminal career, and sensational novels published under his name (probably written by others) capitalized on his reputation as a bold detective.

Vidocq's stories were more like "true crime" (in modern parlance) than detective fiction, involving little cerebral activity. The first great teller of tales about a *thinking* detective was Edgar Allan Poe (1809–1849), whose Chevalier Auguste Dupin used techniques similar to those later adopted by Sherlock Holmes. Dupin first appeared in Poe's short story "The Murders in the Rue Morgue" (1841) and subsequently in "The Mystery of Marie Rogêt" (1842) and "The Purloined Letter" (1844). Although Holmes himself derided Dupin as "a very inferior fellow," he was not above adopting Dupin's means of analysis of crime scenes and observations, and in Conan Doyle's autobiography *Memoirs and Adventures*, Doyle freely admitted his debt to Poe. Poe also introduced another staple of detective fiction, the partner and chronicler (nameless in Poe's tales) who is less intelligent than the detective but serves as a sounding-board for the detective's brilliant deductions. Doyle would bring this idea to fruition in Holmes's adventures by creating John H. Watson, M.D. as a likable narrator/companion with whom readers could identify.

In *L'Affaire Lerouge* (1866), the French writer Emile Gaboriau introduced the detective known as Monsieur Lecoq. Lecoq was a minor police detective in his first case, modeled after Vidocq, who rose to fame in six cases, appearing between 1866 and 1880. Although Sherlock Holmes describes Lecoq as a "miserable bungler," Gaboriau's works were immensely popular, and Conan Doyle knew them well. Another writer, the Englishman Fergus Hume, author of *The Mystery of a Hansom Cab* (1886), the best-selling detective novel of the century (with over 500,000 copies sold worldwide), admitted that Gaboriau's financial success inspired his own work.

Charles Dickens's works depicted a wide range of the English population, not omitting criminals and detectives. In *Bleak House* (1852–1853), Dickens introduced Inspector Bucket, the first English detective, whose image was adopted by countless other writers as prototype of the official representative of the police department: honest, diligent, stolid, and confident, albeit not very colorful, dramatic, or exciting. Wilkie Collins also contributed an official detective, Sergeant Cuff, who appears in *The Moonstone* (1868). Cuff is known as the finest police detective in England and solves his cases with perseverance and energy. Sadly, after *The Moonstone*, he was not heard from again. Mary Elizabeth Braddon, a prolific writer of sensational fiction, dabbled in detection as well; her best-known work, *Lady Audley's Secret* (1862), revolves around the efforts of the barrister Robert Audley to discover the crimes of his aunt.

Despite the Victorian emphasis on reason and intelligence and the expansion of science and invention, the detection or prevention of crime prior to the last quarter of the 19th century relied heavily on perspiration rather than inspiration. For example, in 1860, the so-called Rode Hill House murder captivated the minds of the English reading public. The "detectives" of Scotland Yard were deeply involved in the case, yet failed to solve it for many years, until the perpetrator confessed. In 1860, the Yard still relied largely on the practical training of detectives in criminal methods and techniques, personal recognition of criminals, and apprehension of criminals in the act of committing the crime. "Deductions" based on scientific observation had little place in police work. "Bertillonage," the French system of anthropometry which would later prove so useful in bringing criminals to justice, was not adopted in England until 1883; and although Francis Galton and others had recognized the usefulness of fingerprinting much earlier, it was not a serious aid in the apprehension of criminals until the 20th century, primarily because of the lack of a central database of criminals' prints.

In 1886, Arthur Conan Doyle decided to turn his hand from contemporary literary fiction to the detective story. He wrote later:

I felt now that I was capable of something fresher and crisper and more workmanlike. Gaboriau had rather attracted me by the neat dovetailing of his plots, and Poe's masterful detective, M. Dupin, had from boyhood been one of my heroes. But could I bring an addition of my own? I thought of my old teacher Joe Bell, of his eagle face, of his curious ways, of his eerie trick of spotting details. If he were a detective he would surely reduce this fascinating but unorganized business to something nearer to an exact science.

Conan Doyle's timing was excellent. In the late spring of 1891, his agent submitted two unsolicited stories to Greenough Smith, the editor of the newly-minted *Strand Magazine*. Smith recollected the day some forty years later: "I at once realised that here was the greatest short story writer since Edgar Allan Poe. I remember rushing into [the publisher] Mr. Newnes's room and thrusting the stories before his eyes. . . . Here was a new and gifted story-writer; there was no mistaking the ingenuity of the plot, the limpid clearness of the style, the perfect art of telling a story." The stories—"A Scandal in Bohemia" and "The Red-Headed League"—appeared in the July and August 1891 issues, respectively, and the success of both Conan Doyle and the *Strand Magazine* was made. Over the succeeding 36 years, 56 more stories and novellas would appear in the *Strand* in England, including what is regarded by many as the greatest mystery tale of the 20th century—*The Hound of the Baskervilles*. Holmes's adventures became a phenomenon. In America, the Holmes stories achieved great popularity as well, appearing in *Harper's Weekly*. But in 1893, Conan Doyle abruptly ceased penning tales of Sherlock Holmes and announced to the world in a story aptly titled "The Final Problem" that Holmes had died, at the hands of his archenemy Professor James Moriarty. Readers were heart-stricken, as were the publishers of the *Strand* as subscriptions plummeted.

The public vocally demanded new tales of Holmes. In the words of Conan Doyle's brother-in-law, E. W. Hornung (himself the author of the brilliant tales of gentleman-thief Raffles), they mourned, "There's no p'lice like Holmes," and Doyle told of a letter on the subject of the killing of Holmes from a lady which began, "You beast." But Doyle did not utterly abandon his readers. In an interview in *Tit-Bits* in early 1901 (probably before he began work on *The Hound of the Baskervilles*, published later that year), Doyle said, "From [the day of publication of "The Final Problem"] to this I have never for an instant regretted the course I took in killing Sherlock. That does not say, however, that because he is dead I should not write about him again if I wanted to, for there is no limit to the number of papers he left behind or the reminiscences in the brain of his biographer."

While Conan Doyle turned a deaf ear to his readers' anguish, new writers and detectives began to appear in the popular magazines, including the desperate *Strand*. Fine examples of those who rushed in to fill the gap left by Holmes's disappearance are included in this collection, including English and American writers and detectives, male and female. Some were Holmes-like, many with unique eccentricities (for example, Ernest Bramah's blind detective Max Carrados) or deep scientific knowledge (R. Austin Freeman's Dr. Thorndyke); some, like Arthur Morrison's Martin Hewitt, were as unlike Holmes as possible—smart, but colorless, business-like, and perhaps even a little shady. Holmes also was the victim of affectionate parody and satire, including pieces written by Doyle's close friends Robert Barr and James M. Barrie, and other popular writers such as O. Henry and Bret Harte. Some early examples are included here, though by now the number of stories about Holmes written by persons other than Doyle exceeds 10,000!

Although the public was somewhat appeased by the appearance of *The Hound of the Baskervilles* in the *Strand* magazines in England and America in 1901, it was plain that *The Hound* was a reminiscence of Holmes, set before his apparent death at the Reichenbach Falls. Holmes was not resuscitated until 1903, when Doyle revealed that Holmes got out of the "dreadful cauldron" by never being in it in the first place, in "The Adventure of the Empty House." This story was followed over the next 24 years by 33 more adventures of Holmes, though some readers grumbled that Holmes wasn't the man he was before he met his nemesis.

By the time of Holmes's return in 1903, however, the genie was out of the bottle—publishers and the reading public had learned to enjoy detective fiction from many hands, with a variety of detectives, as is illustrated in this volume. With Holmes's temporary disappearance from the stage, the rivals of Sherlock Holmes stepped into the spotlight, and even after his return, Holmes had to share his chosen field of "consulting detective" with other brilliant practitioners. While many are unfairly forgotten today, the stories included here are as fresh, interesting, and evocative as the enduring tales recorded by John H. Watson. Come—the game is afoot!

Leslie S. Klinger
Los Angeles, 2015

Leslie S. Klinger is the editor of *The New Annotated Sherlock Holmes: The Complete Short Stories* (2004) and *The New Annotated Sherlock Holmes: The Novels* (2005), and with Laurie R. King the anthologies *A Study In Sherlock* (2011) and *In The Company of Sherlock Holmes* (2014).

DISTINGUISHED PREDECESSORS

THE PURLOINED LETTER

Edgar Allan Poe

Nil sapientiae odiosius acumine nimio.
SENECA

A T PARIS, JUST AFTER DARK ONE GUSTY EVENING IN THE AUTUMN OF 18——, I was enjoying the twofold luxury of meditation and a meerschaum, in company with my friend C. Auguste Dupin, in his little back library, or book-closet, *au troisiême, No.* 33, *Rue Dunôt, Faubourg St. Germain.* For one hour at least we had maintained a profound silence; while each, to any casual observer, might have seemed intently and exclusively occupied with the curling eddies of smoke that oppressed the atmosphere of the chamber. For myself, however, I was mentally discussing certain topics which had formed matter for conversation between us at an earlier period of the evening; I mean the affair of the Rue Morgue, and the mystery attending the murder of Marie Rogêt. I looked upon it, therefore, as something of a coincidence, when the door of our apartment was thrown open and admitted our old acquaintance, Monsieur G——, the Prefect of the Parisian police.

We gave him a hearty welcome; for there was nearly half as much of the entertaining as of the contemptible about the man, and we had not seen him for several years. We had been sitting in the dark, and Dupin now arose for the purpose of lighting a lamp, but sat down again, without doing so, upon G.'s saying that he had called to consult us, or rather to ask the opinion of my friend, about some official business which had occasioned a great deal of trouble.

"If it is any point requiring reflection," observed Dupin, as he forebore to enkindle the wick, "we shall examine it to better purpose in the dark."

"That is another of your odd notions," said the Prefect, who had a fashion of calling every thing "odd" that was beyond his comprehension, and thus lived amid an absolute legion of "oddities."

"Very true," said Dupin, as he supplied his visiter with a pipe, and rolled towards him a comfortable chair.

"And what is the difficulty now?" I asked. "Nothing more in the assassination way, I hope?"

"Oh no; nothing of that nature. The fact is, the business is *very* simple indeed, and I make no doubt that we can manage it sufficiently well ourselves; but then I thought Dupin would like to hear the details of it, because it is so excessively *odd*."

"Simple and odd," said Dupin.

"Why, yes; and not exactly that, either. The fact is, we have all been a good deal puzzled because the affair *is* so simple, and yet baffles us altogether."

"Perhaps it is the very simplicity of the thing which puts you at fault," said my friend.

"What nonsense you *do* talk!" replied the Prefect, laughing heartily.

"Perhaps the mystery is a little *too* plain," said Dupin.

"Oh, good heavens! who ever heard of such an idea?"

"A little *too* self-evident."

"Ha! ha! ha!—ha! ha! ha!—ho! ho! ho!" roared our visiter, profoundly amused, "oh, Dupin, you will be the death of me yet!"

"And what, after all, *is* the matter on hand?" I asked.

"Why, I will tell you," replied the Prefect, as he gave a long, steady, and contemplative puff, and settled himself in his chair. "I will tell you in a few words; but, before I begin, let me caution you that this is an affair demanding the greatest secrecy, and that I should most probably lose the position I now hold, were it known that I confided it to any one."

"Proceed," said I.

"Or not," said Dupin.

"Well, then; I have received personal information, from a very high quarter, that a certain document of the last importance, has been purloined from the royal apartments. The individual who purloined it is known; this beyond a doubt; he was seen to take it. It is known, also, that it still remains in his possession."

"How is this known?" asked Dupin.

"It is clearly inferred," replied the Prefect, "from the nature of the document, and from the non-appearance of certain results which would at once arise from its passing *out* of the robber's possession;—that is to say, from his employing it as he must design in the end to employ it."

"Be a little more explicit," I said.

"Well, I may venture so far as to say that the paper gives its holder a certain power in a certain quarter where such power is immensely valuable." The Prefect was fond of the cant of diplomacy.

"Still I do not quite understand," said Dupin.

"No? Well; the disclosure of the document to a third person, who shall be nameless, would bring in question the honor of a personage of most exalted station; and this fact gives the holder of the document an ascendancy over the illustrious personage whose honor and peace are so jeopardized."

"But this ascendancy," I interposed, "would depend upon the robber's knowledge of the loser's knowledge of the robber. Who would dare——"

"The thief," said G., "is the Minister D——, who dares all things, those unbecoming as well as those becoming a man. The method of the theft was not less ingenious than bold. The document in question—a letter, to be frank—had been received by the personage robbed while alone in the royal *boudoir*. During its perusal she was suddenly interrupted by the entrance of the other exalted personage from whom especially it was her wish to conceal it. After a hurried and vain endeavor to thrust it in a drawer, she was forced to place it, open as it was, upon a table. The address, however, was uppermost, and, the contents thus unexposed, the letter escaped notice. At this juncture enters the Minister D——. His lynx eye immediately perceives the paper, recognises the handwriting of the address, observes the confusion of the personage addressed, and fathoms her secret. After some business transactions, hurried through in his ordinary manner, he produces a letter somewhat similar to the one in question, opens it, pretends to read it, and then places it in close juxtaposition to the other. Again he converses, for some fifteen minutes, upon the public affairs. At length, in taking leave, he takes also from the table the letter to which he had no claim. Its rightful owner saw, but, of course, dared not call attention to the act, in the presence of the third personage who stood at her elbow. The minister decamped; leaving his own letter—one of no importance—upon the table."

"Here, then," said Dupin to me, "you have precisely what you demand to make the ascendancy complete—the robber's knowledge of the loser's knowledge of the robber."

"Yes," replied the Prefect; "and the power thus attained has, for some months past, been wielded, for political purposes, to a very dangerous extent. The personage robbed is more thoroughly convinced, every day, of the necessity of reclaiming her letter. But this, of course, cannot be done openly. In fine, driven to despair, she has committed the matter to me."

"Than whom," said Dupin, amid a perfect whirlwind of smoke, "no more sagacious agent could, I suppose, be desired, or even imagined."

"You flatter me," replied the Prefect; "but it is possible that some such opinion may have been entertained."

"It is clear," said I, "as you observe, that the letter is still in possession of the minister; since it is this possession, and not any employment of the letter, which bestows the power. With the employment the power departs."

"True," said G.; "and upon this conviction I proceeded. My first care was to make thorough search of the minister's hotel; and here my chief embarrassment lay in the necessity of searching without his knowledge. Beyond all things, I have been warned of the danger which would result from giving him reason to suspect our design."

"But," said I, "you are quite *au fait* in these investigations. The Parisian police have done this thing often before."

"O yes; and for this reason I did not despair. The habits of the minister gave me, too, a great advantage. He is frequently absent from home all night. His servants are by no means numerous. They sleep at a distance from their master's apartment, and, being chiefly Neapolitans, are readily made drunk. I have keys, as you know, with which I can open any chamber or cabinet in Paris. For three months a night has not passed, during the greater part of which I have not been engaged, personally, in ransacking the D—— Hotel. My honor is interested, and, to mention a great secret, the reward is enormous. So I did not abandon the search until I had become fully satisfied that the thief is a more astute man than myself. I fancy that I have investigated every nook and corner of the premises in which it is possible that the paper can be concealed."

"But is it not possible," I suggested, "that although the letter may be in possession of the minister, as it unquestionably is, he may have concealed it elsewhere than upon his own premises?"

"This is barely possible," said Dupin. "The present peculiar condition of affairs at court, and especially of those intrigues in which D—— is known to be involved, would render the instant availability of the document—its susceptibility of being produced at a moment's notice—a point of nearly equal importance with its possession."

"Its susceptibility of being produced?" said I.

"That is to say, of being *destroyed*," said Dupin.

"True," I observed; "the paper is clearly then upon the premises. As for its being upon the person of the minister, we may consider that as out of the question."

"Entirely," said the Prefect. "He has been twice waylaid, as if by footpads, and his person rigorously searched under my own inspection."

"You might have spared yourself this trouble," said Dupin. "D——, I presume, is not altogether a fool, and, if not, must have anticipated these waylayings, as a matter of course."

"Not *altogether* a fool," said G., "but then he's a poet, which I take to be only one remove from a fool."

"True," said Dupin, after a long and thoughtful whiff from his meerschaum, "although I have been guilty of certain doggrel myself."

"Suppose you detail," said I, "the particulars of your search."

"Why the fact is, we took our time, and we searched *every where*. I have had long experience in these affairs. I took the entire building, room by room; devoting the nights of a whole week to each. We examined, first, the furniture of each apartment. We opened every possible drawer; and I presume you know that, to a properly trained police agent, such a thing as a *secret* drawer is impossible. Any man is a dolt who permits a 'secret' drawer to escape him in a search of this kind. The thing is *so* plain. There is a certain amount of bulk—of space—to be accounted for in every cabinet. Then we have accurate rules. The fiftieth part of a line could not escape us. After the cabinets we took the chairs. The cushions we probed with the fine long needles you have seen me employ. From the tables we removed the tops."

"Why so?"

"Sometimes the top of a table, or other similarly arranged piece of furniture, is removed by the person wishing to conceal an article; then the leg is excavated, the article deposited within the cavity, and the top replaced. The bottoms and tops of bedposts are employed in the same way."

"But could not the cavity be detected by sounding?" I asked.

"By no means, if, when the article is deposited, a sufficient wadding of cotton be placed around it. Besides, in our case, we were obliged to proceed without noise."

"But you could not have removed—you could not have taken to pieces *all* articles of furniture in which it would have been possible to make a deposit in the manner you mention. A letter may be compressed into a thin spiral roll, not differing much in shape or bulk from a large knitting-needle, and in this form it might be inserted into the rung of a chair, for example. You did not take to pieces all the chairs?"

"Certainly not; but we did better—we examined the rungs of every chair in the hotel, and, indeed the jointings of every description of furniture, by the aid of a most powerful microscope. Had there been any traces of recent disturbance we should not have failed to detect it instantly. A single grain of gimlet-dust, for example, would have been as obvious as an apple. Any disorder in the glueing—any unusual gaping in the joints—would have sufficed to insure detection."

"I presume you looked to the mirrors, between the boards and the plates, and you probed the beds and the bed-clothes, as well as the curtains and carpets."

"That of course; and when we had absolutely completed every particle of the furniture in this way, then we examined the house itself. We divided its entire surface into compartments, which we numbered, so that none might be missed; then we scrutinized each individual square inch throughout the premises, including the two houses immediately adjoining, with the microscope, as before."

"The two houses adjoining!" I exclaimed; "you must have had a great deal of trouble."

"We had; but the reward offered is prodigious."

"You include the *grounds* about the houses?"

"All the grounds are paved with brick. They gave us comparatively little trouble. We examined the moss between the bricks, and found it undisturbed."

"You looked among D——'s papers, of course, and into the books of the library?"

"Certainly; we opened every package and parcel; we not only opened every book, but we turned over every leaf in each volume, not contenting ourselves with a mere shake, according to the fashion of some of our police officers. We also measured the thickness of every book-*cover*, with the most accurate admeasurement, and applied to each the most jealous scrutiny of the microscope. Had any of the bindings been recently meddled with, it would have been utterly impossible that the fact should have escaped observation. Some five or six volumes, just from the hands of the binder, we carefully probed, longitudinally, with the needles."

"You explored the floors beneath the carpets?"

"Beyond doubt. We removed every carpet, and examined the boards with the microscope."

"And the paper on the walls?"

"Yes."

"You looked into the cellars?"

"We did."

"Then," I said, "you have been making a miscalculation, and the letter is *not* upon the premises, as you suppose."

"I fear you are right there," said the Prefect. "And now, Dupin, what would you advise me to do?"

"To make a thorough re-search of the premises."

"That is absolutely needless," replied G——. "I am not more sure that I breathe than I am that the letter is not at the Hotel."

"I have no better advice to give you," said Dupin. "You have, of course, an accurate description of the letter?"

"Oh yes!"—And here the Prefect, producing a memorandum-book proceeded to read aloud a minute account of the internal, and especially of the external appearance of the missing document. Soon after finishing the perusal of this description, he took his departure, more entirely depressed in spirits than I had ever known the good gentleman before.

In about a month afterwards he paid us another visit, and found us occupied very nearly as before. He took a pipe and a chair and entered into some ordinary conversation. At length I said,—

"Well, but G——, what of the purloined letter? I presume you have at last made up your mind that there is no such thing as overreaching the Minister?"

"Confound him, say I—yes; I made the re-examination, however, as Dupin suggested—but it was all labor lost, as I knew it would be."

"How much was the reward offered, did you say?" asked Dupin.

"Why, a very great deal—a *very* liberal reward—I don't like to say how much, precisely; but one thing I *will* say, that I wouldn't mind giving my individual check for fifty thousand francs to any one who could obtain me that letter. The fact is, it is becoming of more and more importance every day; and the reward has been lately doubled. If it were trebled, however, I could do no more than I have done."

"Why, yes," said Dupin, drawlingly, between the whiffs of his meerschaum, "I really—think, G——, you have not exerted yourself—to the utmost in this matter. You might—do a little more, I think, eh?"

"How?—in what way?'

"Why—puff, puff—you might—puff, puff—employ counsel in the matter, eh?—puff, puff, puff. Do you remember the story they tell of Abernethy?"

"No; hang Abernethy!"

"To be sure! hang him and welcome. But, once upon a time, a certain rich miser conceived the design of spunging upon this Abernethy for a medical opinion. Getting up, for this purpose, an ordinary conversation in a private company, he insinuated his case to the physician, as that of an imaginary individual.

" 'We will suppose,' said the miser, 'that his symptoms are such and such; now, doctor, what would *you* have directed him to take?'

" 'Take!' said Abernethy, 'why, take *advice*, to be sure.'"

"But," said the Prefect, a little discomposed, "*I* am *perfectly* willing to take advice, and to pay for it. I would *really* give fifty thousand francs to any one who would aid me in the matter."

"In that case," replied Dupin, opening a drawer, and producing a check-book, "you may as well fill me up a check for the amount mentioned. When you have signed it, I will hand you the letter."

I was astounded. The Prefect appeared absolutely thunder-stricken. For some minutes he remained speechless and motionless, looking incredulously at my friend with open mouth, and eyes that seemed starting from their sockets; then, apparently recovering himself in some measure, he seized a pen, and after several pauses and vacant stares, finally filled up and signed a check for fifty thousand francs, and handed it across the table to Dupin. The latter examined it carefully and deposited it in his pocket-book; then, unlocking an *escritoire*, took thence a letter and gave it to the Prefect. This functionary grasped it in a perfect agony of joy, opened it with a trembling hand, cast a rapid glance at its contents, and then, scrambling and struggling to the door, rushed at length unceremoniously from the room and from the house, without having uttered a syllable since Dupin had requested him to fill up the check.

When he had gone, my friend entered into some explanations.

"The Parisian police," he said, "are exceedingly able in their way. They are persevering, ingenious, cunning, and thoroughly versed in the knowledge which their duties seem chiefly to demand. Thus, when G—— detailed to us his mode of searching the premises at the Hotel D——, I felt entire confidence in his having made a satisfactory investigation—so far as his labors extended."

"So far as his labors extended?" said I.

"Yes," said Dupin. "The measures adopted were not only the best of their kind, but carried out to absolute perfection. Had the letter been deposited within the range of their search, these fellows would, beyond a question, have found it."

I merely laughed—but he seemed quite serious in all that he said.

"The measures, then," he continued, "were good in their kind, and well executed; their defect lay in their being inapplicable to the case, and to the man. A certain set of highly ingenious resources are, with the Prefect, a sort of Procrustean bed, to which he forcibly adapts his designs. But he perpetually errs by being too deep or too shallow, for the matter in hand; and many a schoolboy is a better reasoner than he. I knew one about eight years of age, whose success at guessing in the game of 'even and odd' attracted universal admiration. This game is simple, and is played with marbles. One player holds in his hand a number of these toys, and demands of another whether that number is even or odd. If the guess is right, the guesser wins one; if wrong, he loses one. The boy to whom I allude won all the marbles of the school. Of course he had some principle of guessing; and this lay in mere observation and admeasurement of the astuteness of his opponents. For example, an arrant simpleton is his opponent, and, holding up his closed hand, asks, 'are they even or odd?' Our schoolboy replies, 'odd,' and loses; but upon the second trial he wins, for he then says to himself, 'the simpleton had them even upon the first trial, and his amount of cunning is just sufficient to make him have them odd upon the second; I will therefore guess odd';—he guesses odd, and wins. Now, with a simpleton a degree above the first, he would have reasoned thus: 'This fellow finds that in the first instance I guessed odd, and, in the second, he will propose to himself, upon the first impulse, a simple variation from even to odd, as did the first simpleton; but then a second thought will suggest that this is too simple a variation, and finally he will decide upon putting it even as before. I will therefore guess even';—he guesses even, and wins. Now this mode of reasoning in the schoolboy, whom his fellows termed 'lucky,'—what, in its last analysis, is it?"

"It is merely," I said, "an identification of the reasoner's intellect with that of his opponent."

"It is," said Dupin; "and, upon inquiring of the boy by what means he effected the *thorough* identification in which his success consisted, I received answer as follows: 'When I wish to find out how wise, or how stupid, or how good, or how wicked is any one, or what are his thoughts at the moment, I fashion the expression of my face, as accurately as possible, in accordance with the expression of his, and then wait to see what thoughts or sentiments arise in my mind or heart, as if to match or correspond with the expression.' This response of the schoolboy lies at the bottom of all the spurious profundity which has been attributed to Rochefoucault, to La Bougive, to Machiavelli, and to Campanella."

"And the identification," I said, "of the reasoner's intellect with that of his opponent, depends, if I understand you aright, upon the accuracy with which the opponent's intellect is admeasured."

"For its practical value it depends upon this," replied Dupin; "and the Prefect and his cohort fail so frequently, first, by default of this identification, and, secondly, by ill-admeasurement, or rather through non-admeasurement, of the intellect with which they are engaged. They consider only their *own* ideas of ingenuity; and, in searching for anything hidden, advert only to the modes in which *they* would have hidden it. They are right in this much—that their own ingenuity is a faithful representative of that of *the mass;* but when the cunning of the individual felon is diverse in character from their own, the felon foils them, of course. This always happens when it is above their own, and very usually when it is below. They have no variation of principle in their investigations; at best, when urged by some unusual emergency—by some extraordinary reward—they extend or exaggerate their old modes of *practice*, without touching their principles. What, for example, in this case of D——, has been done to vary the principle of action? What is all this boring, and probing, and sounding, and scrutinizing with the microscope, and dividing the surface of the building into registered square inches—what is it all but an exaggeration *of the application* of the one principle or set of principles of search, which are based upon the one set of notions regarding human ingenuity, to which the Prefect, in the long routine of his duty, has been accustomed? Do you not see he has taken it for granted that *all* men proceed to conceal a letter,—not exactly in a gimlet-hole bored in a chair-leg—but, at least, in *some* out-of-the-way hole or corner suggested by the same tenor of thought which would urge a man to secrete a letter in a gimlet-hole bored in a chair-leg? And do you not see also, that such *recherchés* nooks for concealment are adapted only for ordinary occasions, and would be adopted only by ordinary intellects; for, in all cases of concealment, a disposal of the article concealed—a disposal of it in this *recherché* manner,—is, in the very first instance, presumable and presumed; and thus its discovery depends, not at all upon the acumen, but altogether upon the mere care, patience, and determination of the seekers; and where the case is of importance—or, what amounts to the same thing in the policial eyes, when the reward is of magnitude,—the qualities in question have *never* been known to fail. You will now understand what I meant in suggesting that, had the purloined letter been hidden any where within the limits of the Prefect's examination—in other words, had the principle of its concealment been comprehended within the principles of the Prefect—its discovery would have been a matter altogether beyond question. This functionary, however, has been thoroughly mystified; and the remote source of his defeat lies in the supposition that the Minister is a fool, because he has acquired renown as a poet. All fools are poets; this the Prefect *feels;* and he is merely guilty of a *non distributio medii* in thence inferring that all poets are fools."

"But is this really the poet?" I asked. "There are two brothers, I know; and both have attained reputation in letters. The Minister I believe has written learnedly on the Differential Calculus. He is a mathematician, and no poet."

"You are mistaken; I know him well; he is both. As poet *and* mathematician, he would reason well; as mere mathematician, he could not have reasoned at all, and thus would have been at the mercy of the Prefect."

"You surprise me," I said, "by these opinions, which have been contradicted by the voice of the world. You do not mean to set at naught the well-digested idea of centuries. The mathematical reason has long been regarded as *the* reason *par excellence*."

"'*Il y a à parièr*,'" replied Dupin, quoting from Chamfort, "'*que toute idée publique, toute convention reçue est une sottise, car elle a convenue au plus grand nombre.*' The mathematicians, I grant you, have done their best to promulgate the popular error to which you allude, and which is none the less an error for its promulgation as truth. With an art worthy a better cause, for example, they have insinuated the term 'analysis' into application to algebra. The French are the originators of this particular deception; but if a term is of any importance—if words derive any value from applicability—then 'analysis' conveys 'algebra' about as much as, in Latin, '*ambitus*' implies 'ambition,' '*religio*' 'religion,' or '*homines honesti*,' a set of *honorable* men."

"You have a quarrel on hand, I see," said I, "with some of the algebraists of Paris; but proceed."

"I dispute the availability, and thus the value, of that reason which is cultivated in any especial form other than the abstractly logical. I dispute, in particular, the reason educed by mathematical study. The mathematics are the science of form and quantity; mathematical reasoning is merely logic applied to observation upon form and quantity. The great error lies in supposing that even the truths of what is called *pure* algebra, are abstract or general truths. And this error is so egregious that I am confounded at the universality with which it has been received. Mathematical axioms are *not* axioms of general truth. What is true of *relation*—of form and quantity—is often grossly false in regard to morals, for example. In this latter science it is very usually *un*true that the aggregated parts are equal to the whole. In chemistry also the axiom fails. In the consideration of motive it fails; for two motives, each of a given value, have not, necessarily, a value when united, equal to the sum of their values apart. There are numerous other mathematical truths which are only truths within the limits of *relation*. But the mathematician argues, from his *finite truths*, through habit, as if they were of an absolutely general applicability—as the world indeed imagines them to be. Bryant, in his very learned 'Mythology,' mentions an analogous source of error, when he says that 'although the Pagan fables are not believed, yet we forget ourselves continually, and make inferences from them as existing realities.' With the algebraists, however, who are Pagans themselves, the 'Pagan fables' *are* believed, and the inferences are made, not so much through lapse of memory, as through an unaccountable addling of the brains. In short, I never yet encountered the mere mathematician who could be trusted out of equal roots, or one who did not clandestinely hold it as a point of his faith that $x^2 + px$ was absolutely and unconditionally equal to q. Say to one of these gentlemen, by way of experiment, if you please, that you believe occasions may occur where $x^2 + px$ is *not* altogether equal to q, and, having made him understand what you mean, get out of his reach as speedily as convenient, for, beyond doubt, he will endeavor to knock you down.

"I mean to say," continued Dupin, while I merely laughed at his last observations, "that if the Minister had been no more than a mathematician, the Prefect would have been under no necessity of giving me this check. I knew him, however, as both mathematician and poet, and my measures were adapted to his capacity, with reference to the circumstances by which he was surrounded. I knew him as a courtier, too, and as a bold *intriguant*. Such a man, I considered, could not fail to be aware of the ordinary policial modes of action. He could not have failed to anticipate— and events have proved that he did not fail to anticipate—the waylayings to which he was subjected. He must have foreseen, I reflected, the secret investigations of his premises. His frequent absences from home at night, which were hailed by the Prefect as certain aids to his success, I regarded only as *ruses*, to afford opportunity for thorough search to the police, and thus the sooner to impress them with the conviction to which G——, in fact, did finally arrive—the conviction that the letter was not upon the premises. I felt, also, that the whole train of thought, which I was at some pains in detailing to you just now, concerning the invariable principle of policial action in searches for articles concealed—I felt that this whole train of thought would necessarily pass through the mind of the Minister. It would imperatively lead him to despise all the ordinary *nooks* of concealment. *He* could not, I reflected, be so weak as not to see that the most intricate and remote recess of his hotel would be as open as his commonest closets to the eyes, to the probes, to the gimlets, and to the microscopes of the Prefect. I saw, in fine, that he would be driven, as a matter of course, to *simplicity*, if not deliberately induced to it as a matter of choice. You will remember, perhaps, how desperately the Prefect laughed when I suggested, upon our first interview, that it was just possible this mystery troubled him so much on account of its being so *very* self-evident."

"Yes," said I, "I remember his merriment well. I really thought he would have fallen into convulsions."

"The material world," continued Dupin, "abounds with very strict analogies to the immaterial; and thus some color of truth has been given to the rhetorical dogma, that metaphor, or simile, may be made to strengthen an argument, as well as to embellish a description. The principle of the *vis inertiæ*, for example, seems to be identical in physics and metaphysics. It is not more true in the former, that a large body is with more difficulty set in motion than a smaller one, and that its subsequent *momentum* is commensurate with this difficulty, than it is, in the latter, that intellects of the vaster capacity, while more forcible, more constant, and more eventful in their movements than those of inferior grade, are yet the less readily moved, and more embarrassed and full of hesitation in the first few steps of their progress. Again: have you ever noticed which of the street signs, over the shop-doors, are the most attractive of attention?"

"I have never given the matter a thought," I said.

"There is a game of puzzles," he resumed, "which is played upon a map. One party playing requires another to find a given word—the name of town, river, state or empire—any word, in short, upon the motley and perplexed surface of the chart. A novice in the game generally seeks to embarrass his opponents by giving them the most minutely lettered names; but the adept selects such words as stretch, in large characters, from one end of the chart to the other. These, like the over-largely lettered signs and placards of the street, escape observation by dint of being excessively obvious; and here the physical oversight is precisely analogous with the moral inapprehension by which the intellect suffers to pass unnoticed those considerations which are too obtrusively and too palpably self-evident. But this is a point, it appears, somewhat above or beneath the understanding of the Prefect. He never once thought it probable, or possible, that the Minister had deposited the letter immediately beneath the nose of the whole world, by way of best preventing any portion of that world from perceiving it.

"But the more I reflected upon the daring, dashing, and discriminating ingenuity of D——; upon the fact that the document must always have been *at hand*, if he intended to use it to good purpose; and upon the decisive evidence, obtained by the Prefect, that it was not hidden within the limits of that dignitary's ordinary search—the more satisfied I became that, to conceal this letter, the Minister had resorted to the comprehensive and sagacious expedient of not attempting to conceal it at all.

"Full of these ideas, I prepared myself with a pair of green spectacles, and called one fine morning, quite by accident, at the Ministerial hotel. I found D—— at home, yawning, lounging, and dawdling, as usual, and pretending to be in the last extremity of *ennui*. He is, perhaps, the most really energetic human being now alive—but that is only when nobody sees him.

"To be even with him, I complained of my weak eyes, and lamented the necessity of the spectacles, under cover of which I cautiously and thoroughly surveyed the apartment, while seemingly intent only upon the conversation of my host.

"I paid especial attention to a large writing-table near which he sat, and upon which lay confusedly, some miscellaneous letters and other papers, with one or two musical instruments and a few books. Here, however, after a long and very deliberate scrutiny, I saw nothing to excite particular suspicion.

"At length my eyes, in going the circuit of the room, fell upon a trumpery fillagree card-rack of pasteboard, that hung dangling by a dirty blue ribbon, from a little brass knob just beneath the middle of the mantel-piece. In this rack, which had three or four compartments, were five or six visiting cards and a solitary letter. This last was much soiled and crumpled. It was torn nearly in two, across the middle—as if a design, in the first instance, to tear it entirely up as worthless, had been altered, or stayed, in the second. It had a large black seal, bearing the D—— cipher *very* conspicuously, and was addressed, in a diminutive female hand, to D——, the minister, himself. It was thrust carelessly, and even, as it seemed, contemptuously, into one of the upper divisions of the rack.

"No sooner had I glanced at this letter, than I concluded it to be that of which I was in search. To be sure, it was, to all appearance, radically different from the one of which the Prefect had read us so minute a description. Here the seal was large and black, with the D—— cipher; there it was small and red, with the ducal arms of the S—— family. Here, the address, to the Minister, was diminutive and feminine; there the superscription, to a certain royal personage, was markedly bold and decided; the size alone formed a point of correspondence. But, then, the *radicalness* of these differences, which was excessive; the dirt; the soiled and torn condition of the paper, so inconsistent with the *true* methodical habits of D——, and so suggestive of a design to delude the beholder into an idea of the worthlessness of the document; these things, together with the hyper-obtrusive situation of this document, full in the view of every visiter, and thus exactly in accordance with the conclusions to which I had previously arrived; these things, I say, were strongly corroborative of suspicion, in one who came with the intention to suspect.

"I protracted my visit as long as possible, and, while I maintained a most animated discussion with the Minister, on a topic which I knew well had never failed to interest and excite him, I kept my attention really riveted upon the letter. In this examination, I committed to memory its external appearance and arrangement in the rack; and also fell, at length, upon a discovery which set at rest whatever trivial doubt I might have entertained. In scrutinizing the edges of the paper, I observed them to be more *chafed* than seemed necessary. They presented the *broken* appearance which is manifested when a stiff paper, having been once folded and pressed with a folder, is refolded in a reversed direction, in the same creases or edges which had formed the original fold. This discovery was sufficient. It was clear to me that the letter had been turned, as a glove, inside out, re-directed, and re-sealed. I bade the Minister good morning, and took my departure at once, leaving a gold snuff-box upon the table.

"The next morning I called for the snuff-box, when we resumed, quite eagerly, the conversation of the preceding day. While thus engaged, however, a loud report, as if of a pistol, was heard immediately beneath the windows of the hotel, and was succeeded by a series of fearful screams, and the shoutings of a mob. D—— rushed to a casement, threw it open, and looked out. In the meantime, I stepped to the card-rack, took the letter, put it in my pocket, and replaced it by a *fac-simile*, (so far as regards externals,) which I had carefully prepared at my lodgings; imitating the D—— cipher, very readily, by means of a seal formed of bread.

"The disturbance in the street had been occasioned by the frantic behavior of a man with a musket. He had fired it among a crowd of women and children. It proved, however, to have been without ball, and the fellow was suffered to go his way as a lunatic or a drunkard. When he had gone, D—— came from the window, whither I had followed him immediately upon securing the object in view. Soon afterwards I bade him farewell. The pretended lunatic was a man in my own pay."

"But what purpose had you," I asked, "in replacing the letter by a *fac-simile?* Would it not have been better, at the first visit, to have seized it openly, and departed?"

"D——," replied Dupin, "is a desperate man, and a man of nerve. His hotel, too, is not without attendants devoted to his interests. Had I made the wild attempt you suggest, I might never have left the Ministerial presence alive. The good people of Paris might have heard of me no more. But I had an object apart from these considerations. You know my political prepossessions. In this matter, I act as a partisan of the lady concerned. For eighteen months the Minister has had her in his power. She has now him in hers—since, being unaware that the letter is not in his possession, he will proceed with his exactions as if it was. Thus will he inevitably commit himself, at once, to his political destruction. His downfall, too, will not be more precipitate than awkward. It is all very well to talk about the *facilis descensus Averni;* but in all kinds of climbing, as Catalani said of singing, it is far more easy to get up than to come down. In the present instance I have no sympathy—at least no pity—for him who descends. He is that *monstrum horrendum*, an unprincipled man of genius. I confess, however, that I should like very well to know the precise character of his thoughts, when, being defied by her whom the Prefect terms 'a certain personage,' he is reduced to opening the letter which I left for him in the card-rack."

"How? did you put any thing particular in it?"

"Why—it did not seem altogether right to leave the interior blank—that would have been insulting. D——, at Vienna once, did me an evil turn, which I told him, quite good-humoredly, that I should remember. So, as I knew he would feel some curiosity in regard to the identity of the person who had outwitted him, I thought it a pity not to give him a clue. He is well acquainted with my MS., and I just copied into the middle of the blank sheet the words—

—Un dessein si funeste,
S'il n'est digne d'Atrée, est digne de Thyeste.

They are to be found in Crébillon's 'Atrée.'"

THREE "DETECTIVE" ANECDOTES

Charles Dickens

The Pair of Gloves

It's a singler story, Sir," said Inspector Wield, of the Detective Police, who, in company with Sergeants Dornton and Mith, paid us another twilight visit, one July evening; "and I've been thinking you might like to know it.

"It's concerning the murder of the young woman, Eliza Grimwood, some years ago, over in the Waterloo Road. She was commonly called The Countess, because of her handsome appearance and her proud way of carrying of herself; and when I saw the poor Countess (I had known her well to speak to), lying dead, with her throat cut, on the floor of her bed-room, you'll believe me that a variety of reflections calculated to make a man rather low in his spirits, came into my head.

"That's neither here nor there. I went to the house the morning after the murder, and examined the body, and made a general observation of the bed-room where it was. Turning down the pillow of the bed with my hand, I found, underneath it, a pair of gloves. A pair of gentleman's dress gloves, very dirty; and inside the lining, the letters TR, and a cross.

"Well, Sir, I took them gloves away, and I showed 'em to the magistrate, over at Union Hall, before whom the case was. He says 'Wield,' he says, 'there's no doubt this is a discovery that may lead to something very important; and what you have got to do, Wield, is, to find out the owner of these gloves.'

"I was of the same opinion, of course, and I went at it immediately. I looked at the gloves pretty narrowly, and it was my opinion that they had been cleaned. There was a smell of sulphur and rosin about 'em, you know, which cleaned gloves usually have, more or less. I took 'em over to a friend of mine at Kennington, who was in that line, and I put it to him. 'What do you say now? Have these gloves been cleaned?' 'These gloves have been cleaned,' says he. 'Have you any idea who cleaned them?' says I. 'Not at all,' says he; 'I've a very distinct idea who *didn't* clean 'em, and that's myself. But I'll tell you what, Wield, there ain't above eight or nine reg'lar glove cleaners in London,'—there were not, at that time, it seems—'and I think I can give you their addresses, and you may find out, by that means, who did clean 'em.' Accordingly, he gave me the directions, and I went here, and I went there, and I looked up this man, and I looked up that man; but, though they all agreed that the gloves had been cleaned, I couldn't find the man, woman, or child, that had cleaned that aforesaid pair of gloves.

"What with this person not being at home, and that person being expected home in the afternoon, and so forth, the inquiry took me three days. On the evening of the third day, coming over Waterloo Bridge from the Surry side of the river, quite beat, and very much vexed and disappointed, I thought I'd have a shilling's worth of entertainment at the Lyceum Theatre to freshen myself up. So I went into the Pit, at half-price, and I sat myself down next to a very quiet, modest sort of a young man. Seeing I was a stranger (which I thought it just as well to appear to be) he told me the names of the actors on the stage, and we got into conversation. When the play was over, we came out together, and I said, 'We've been very companionable and agreeable, and perhaps you wouldn't object to a drain?' 'Well, you're good,' says he; 'I *shouldn't* object to a drain.' Accordingly, we went to a public-house, near the Theatre, sat ourselves down in a quiet room up stairs on the first floor, and called for a pint of half-and-half, apiece, and a pipe.

"Well, Sir, we put our pipes aboard, and we drank our half-and-half, and sat a talking, very sociably, when the young man says, 'You must excuse me stopping very long,' he says, 'because I'm forced to go home in good time. I must be at work all night.' 'At work all night?' says I. 'You ain't a Baker?' 'No,' he says, laughing, 'I ain't a baker.' 'I thought not,' says I, 'you haven't the looks of a baker.' 'No,' says he, 'I'm a glove-cleaner.'

"I never was more astonished in my life, than when I heard them words come out of his lips. 'You're a glove-cleaner, are you?' says I. 'Yes,' he says, 'I am.' 'Then, perhaps,' says I, taking the gloves out of my pocket, 'you can tell me who cleaned this pair of gloves? It's a rum story,' I says. 'I was dining over at Lambeth, the other day, at a free-and-easy—quite promiscuous—with a public company when some gentleman, he left these gloves behind him! Another gentleman and me, you see, we laid a wager of a sovereign, that I wouldn't find out who they belong to. I've spent as much as seven shillings already, in trying to discover; but, if you could help me, I'd stand another seven and welcome. You see there's TR and a cross, inside.' '*I* see,' he says. 'Bless you, *I* know these gloves very well! I've seen dozens of pairs belonging to the same party.' 'No?' says I. 'Yes,' says he. 'Then you know who cleaned 'em?' says I. 'Rather so,' says he. 'My father cleaned 'em.'

"'Where does your father live?' says I. 'Just round the corner,' says the young man, 'near Exeter Street, here. He'll tell you who they belong to, directly.' 'Would you come round with me now?' says I. 'Certainly,' says he, ' but you needn't tell my father that you found me at the play, you know, because he mightn't like it.' 'All right!' We went round to the place, and there we found an old man in a white apron, with two or three daughters, all rubbing and cleaning away at lots of gloves, in a front parlor. 'Oh, Father!' says the young man, 'here's a person been and made a bet about the ownership of a pair of gloves, and I've told him you can settle it.' 'Good-evening, Sir,' says I to the old gentleman. 'Here's the gloves your son speaks of. Letters TR, you see, and a cross.' 'Oh yes,' he says, 'I know these gloves very well; I've cleaned dozens of pairs of 'em. They belong to Mr. Trinkle, the great upholsterer in Cheapside.' 'Did you get 'em from Mr. Trinkle, direct,' says I, 'if you'll excuse my asking the question?' 'No,' says he; 'Mr. Trinkle always sends 'em to Mr. Phibbs's, the haberdasher's, opposite his shop, and the haberdasher sends 'em to me.' 'Perhaps *you* wouldn't object to a drain?' says I. 'Not in the least!' says he. So I took the old gentleman out, and had a little more talk with him and his son, over a glass, and we parted excellent friends.

"This was late on a Saturday night. First thing on the Monday morning, I went to the haberdasher's shop, opposite Mr. Trinkle's the great upholsterer's in Cheapside. 'Mr. Phibbs in the way?' 'My name is Phibbs.' 'Oh! I believe you sent this pair of gloves to be cleaned?' 'Yes, I did, for young Mr. Trinkle over the way. There he is, in the shop!' 'Oh I that's him in the shop, is it? Him in the green coat?' 'The same individual.' 'Well, Mr. Phibbs, this is an unpleasant affair; but the fact is, I am Inspector Wield of the Detective Police, and I found these gloves under the pillow of the young woman that was murdered the other day, over in the Waterloo Road!' 'Good Heaven!' says he. 'He's a most respectable young man, and if his father was to hear of it, it would be the ruin of him!' 'I'm very sorry for it,' says I, 'but I must take him into custody.' 'Good Heaven!' says Mr. Phibbs, again; 'can nothing he done?' 'Nothing,' says I. 'Will you allow me to call him over here,' says he, 'that his father may not see it done?" 'I don't object to that,' says I; 'but unfortunately, Mr. Phibbs, I can't allow of any communication between you. If any was attempted, I should have to interfere directly. Perhaps you'll beckon him over here?' Mr. Phibbs went to the door and beckoned, and the young fellow came across the street directly; a smart, brisk young fellow.

"'Good-morning, Sir,' says I. 'Good-morning, Sir,' says he. 'Would you allow me to inquire, Sir,' says I, 'if you ever had any acquaintance with a party of the name of Grimwood?' 'Grimwood! Grimwood!' says he, 'No!' 'You know the Waterloo Road?' 'Oh! of course I know the Waterloo Road!' 'Happen to have heard of a young woman being murdered there?' 'Yes, I read it in the paper, and very sorry I was to read it.' 'Here's a pair of gloves belonging to you, that I found under her pillow the morning afterward!'

"He was in a dreadful state, Sir; a dreadful state! 'Mr. Wield,' he says, 'upon my solemn oath I never was there. I never so much as saw her, to my knowledge, in my life!' 'I am very sorry,' says I. 'To tell you the truth, I don't think you *are* the murderer; but I must take you to Union Hall in a cab. However, I think it's a case of that sort, that, at present, at all events, the magistrate will hear it in private.'

"A private examination took place, and then it came out that this young man was acquainted with a cousin of the unfortunate Eliza Grimwood, and that, calling to see this cousin a day or two before the murder, he left these gloves upon the table. Who should come in, shortly afterward, but Eliza Grimwoodl 'Whose gloves are these?' she says, taking 'em up. 'Those are Mr. Trinkle's gloves,' says' her cousin. 'Oh!' says she, 'they are very dirty, and of no use to him, I am sure. I shall take 'em away for my girl to clean the stoves with.' And she put 'em in her pocket. The girl had used 'em to clean the stoves, and, I have no doubt, had left 'em lying on the bed-room mantle-piece, or on the drawers, or somewhere; and her mistress, looking round to see that the room was tidy, had caught 'em up and put 'em under the pillow where I found 'em.

"That's the story, Sir."

The Artful Touch

O ne of the most *beautiful* things that ever was done, perhaps," said Inspector Wield, emphasizing the adjective, as preparing us to expect dexterity or ingenuity rather than strong interest, "was a move of Sergeant Witchem's. It was a lovely idea!

"Witchem and me were down at Epsom one Derby Day, waiting at the station for the Swell Mob. As I mentioned, when we were talking about these things before, we are ready at the station when there's races, or an Agricultural Show, or a Chancellor sworn in for an university, or Jenny Lind, or anything of that sort; and as the Swell Mob come down, we send 'em back again by the next train. But some of the Swell Mob, on the occasion of this Derby that I refer to, so far kiddied us as to hire a horse and shay; start away from London by Whitechapel, and miles round; come into Epsom from the opposite direction; and go to work, right and left, on the course, while we were waiting for 'em at the Rail. That, however, ain't the point of what I'm going to tell you.

"While Witchem and me were waiting at the station, there comes up one Mr. Tatt; a gentleman formerly in the public line, quite an amateur Detective in his way, and very much respected. 'Halloa, Charley Wield,' he says. 'What are you doing here? On the look out for some of your old friends?' 'Yes, the old move, Mr. Tatt.' 'Come along,' he says, 'you and Witchem, and have a glass of sherry.' 'We can't stir from the place,' says I, 'till the next train comes in; but after that, we will with pleasure.' Mr. Tatt waits, and the train comes in, and then Witchem and me go off with him to the Hotel. Mr. Tatt he's got up quite regardless of expense for the occasion; and in his shirt-front there's a beautiful diamond prop, cost him fifteen or twenty pound—a very handsome pin indeed. We drink our sherry at the bar, and have had our three or four glasses, when Witchem cries suddenly, 'Look out Mr. Wield! stand fast!' and a dash is made into the place by the swell mob—four of 'em—that have come down as I tell you, and in a moment Mr. Tatt's prop is gone! Witchem, he cuts 'em off at the door, I lay about me as hard as I can, Mr. Tatt shows fight like a good 'un, and there we are, all down together, heads and heels, knocking about on the floor of the bar—perhaps you never see such a scene of confusion! However, we stick to our men (Mr. Tatt being as good as any officer), and we take 'em all, and carry 'em off to the station. The station's full of people, who have been took on the course; and it's a precious piece of work to get 'em secured. However, we do it at last, and we search 'em; but nothing's found upon 'em, and they're locked up; and a pretty state of heat we are in by that time, I assure you!

"I was very blank over it, myself, to think that the prop had been passed away; and I said to Witchem, when we had set 'em to rights, and were cooling ourselves along with Mr. Tatt, 'we don't take much by *this* move, anyway, for nothing's found upon 'em, and it's only the bruggadocia[1] after all.' 'What do you mean, Mr. Wield,' says Witchem. 'Here's the diamond pin!' and in the palm of his hand there it was, safe and sound! 'Why, in the name of wonder,' says me and Mr. Tatt, in astonishment, 'how did you come by that?' 'I'll tell you how I come by it,' says he. 'I saw which of 'em took it; and when we were all down on the floor together, knocking about, I just gave him a little touch on the back of his hand, as I knew his pal would; and he thought it was his pal; and gave it me!' It was beautiful, beau-ti-ful!

"Even that was hardly the best of the case, for that chap was tried at the Quarter Sessions at Guilford. You know what Quarter Sessions are, Sir. Well, if you'll believe me, while them slow justices were looking over the Acts of Parliament, to see what they could do to him, I'm blowed if he didn't cut out of the dock before their faces! He cut out of the dock, Sir, then and there; swam across a river; and got up into a tree to dry himself. In the tree he was took—an old woman having seen him climb up—and Witchem's artful touch transported him!"

THE SOFA

W hat young men will do, sometimes, to ruin themselves and break their friends' hearts," said Sergeant Dornton, "it's surprising! I had a case at Saint Blank's Hospital which was of this sort. A bad case, indeed, with a bad end!

"The Secretary, and the House-Surgeon, and the Treasurer, of Saint Blank's Hospital, came to Scotland Yard to give information of numerous robberies having

---

1. Three months' imprisonment as reputed thieves.

been committed on the students. The students could leave nothing in the pockets of their great-coats, while the great-coats were hanging at the hospital, but it was almost certain to be stolen. Property of various descriptions was constantly being lost; and the gentlemen were naturally uneasy about it, and anxious, for the credit of the institution, that the thief or thieves should be discovered. The case was entrusted to me, and I went to the hospital.

"'Now, gentlemen,' said I, after we had talked it over; 'I understand this property is usually lost from one room.'

"Yes, they said. It was.

"'I should wish, if you please,' said I, 'to see the room.'

"It was a good-sized bare room downstairs, with a few tables and forms in it, and a row of pegs, all round, for bats and coats.

"'Next, gentlemen,' said I, 'do you suspect anybody?'

"Yes, they said. They did suspect somebody. They were sorry to say, they suspected one of the porters.

"'I should like,' said I, 'to have that man pointed out to me, and have a little time to look after him.'

"He was pointed out, and I looked after him, and then I went back to the hospital, and said, 'Now, gentlemen, it's not the porter. He's, unfortunately for himself, a little too fond of drink, but he's nothing worse. My suspicion is, that these robberies are committed by one of the students; and if you'll put me a sofa into that room where the pegs are—as there's no closet—I think I shall be able to detect the thief. I wish the sofa, if you please, to be covered with chintz, or something of that sort, so that I may lie on my chest, underneath it, without being seen.'

"The sofa was provided, and next day at eleven o'clock, before any of the students came, I went there, with those gentlemen, to get underneath it. It turned out to be one of those old-fashioned sofas with a great cross-beam at the bottom, that would have broken my back in no time if I could ever have got below it. We had quite a job to break all this away in time; however, I fell to work, and they fell to work, and we broke it out, and made a clear place for me. I got under the sofa, lay down on my chest, took out my knife, and made a convenient hole in the chintz to look through. It was then settled between me and the gentlemen that when the students were all up in the wards, one of the gentlemen should come in, and hang up a great-coat on one of the pegs. And that that great-coat should have, in one of the pockets, a pocket-book containing marked money.

"After I had been there some time, the students began to drop into the room, by ones, and twos, and threes, and to talk about all sorts of things, little thinking there was anybody under the sofa—and then go upstairs. At last there came in one who remained until he was alone in the room by himself. A tallish, good-looking young man of one or two and twenty, with a light whisker. He went to a particular hat-peg, took off a good hat that was hanging there, tried it on, hung his own but in its place, and hung that hat on another peg, nearly opposite to me. I then felt quite certain that he was the thief, and would come back by-and-bye.

"When they were all upstairs, the gentleman came in with the great-coat. I showed him where to hang it, so that I might have a good view of it; and he went away; and I lay under the sofa on my chest, for a couple of hours or so, waiting.

"At last, the same young man came down. He walked across the room, whistling—stopped and listened—took another walk and whistled—stopped again and listened—then began to go regularly round the pegs, feeling in the pockets of all the coats. When he came to THE great-coat, and felt the pocket-book, he was so eager and so hurried that he broke the strap in tearing it open. As he began to put the money in his pocket, I crawled out from under the sofa, and his eyes met mine.

"My face, as you may perceive, is brown now, but it was pale at that time, my health not being good; and looked as long as a horse's. Besides which, there was a great draught of air from the door, underneath the sofa, and I had tied a handkerchief round my head; so what I looked like, altogether, I don't know. He turned blue—literally blue—when he saw me crawling put, and I couldn't feel surprised at it.

" 'I am an officer of the Detective Police,' said I, 'and have been lying here, since you first came in this morning. I regret, for the sake of yourself and your friends, that you should have done what you have; but this case is complete. You have the pocket-book in your hand and the money upon you; and I must take you into custody.'

"It was impossible to make out any case in his behalf, and on his trial he pleaded guilty. How or when he got the means I don't know; but while he was awaiting his sentence, he poisoned himself in Newgate."

We inquired of this officer, on the conclusion of the foregoing anecdote, whether the time appeared long, or short, when he lay in that constrained position under the sofa?

"Why, you see, sir," he replied, "if he hadn't come in, the first time, and I had not been quite sure he was the thief, and would return, the time would have seemed long. But, as it was, I being dead-certain of my man, the time seemed pretty short."

THE LITTLE OLD MAN
OF BATIGNOLLES

A CHAPTER OF A DETECTIVE'S MEMOIRS

Émile Gaboriau

SOME YEARS AGO A MAN DRESSED IN BLACK, AND APPARENTLY IN THE PRIME OF life, presented himself at the office of the popular Parisian newspaper, *Le Petit Journal*, bringing with him a manuscript of such exquisite penmanship that even Brard, the prince of caligraphic artists, would have deemed it worthy of his talent. "I will call again in a fortnight," said the stranger, "to know what you think of my work."

The manuscript, like many and many of its predecessors, was at once stored away in a box labelled, "MS. to be read," without the editor, the reader, or any of the staff evincing the least curiosity concerning its contents. Time passed by, and its author failed to return; but at last the reader was in duty bound compelled to glance through the box's contents, and one day, strange to relate, he burst into the office with a beaming face. "I have just read something most extraordinary," said he; "the manuscript which that strange looking fellow in black left with us, and without joking it is really a clever performance." Now the readers attached to publishing firms or newspaper offices are not as a rule enthusiastic beings: rather the reverse, for they spend their lives wading through pages and pages of trash, and penning the laconic mention, "Declined with thanks" on the margin of amateur copy. Thus when the reader of the *Petit Journal* expressed such a high opinion of the manuscript in question a general expression of surprise escaped the various regular contributors who were present. But with unabated fervour he cut all controversy short by throwing the manuscript on the table, and exclaiming: "You doubt me, gentlemen? Well read it, your selves."

This sufficed to kindle curiosity. One of the writers on the paper immediately put the MS. in his pocket, and when by the end of the week it had made the round of the staff, there was but one opinion: "The *Petit Journal* must publish it."

At this point, however, an unforeseen difficulty arose. The manuscript bore no author's name. The man in black had merely left with it a card, on which was inscribed, "J. B. Casimir Godeuil," without any address. What was to be done? Was the MS. to be published anonymously? That was scarcely practicable at an epoch when the French press laws required each printed line to be signed by a responsible person. Besides was it certain that M. J. B. Casimir Godeuil was the author? Might he not have presented the manuscript on a friend's behalf? To decide this point the only course was to find him, and inquiries were forthwith instituted in all directions, but unfortunately without result. No one had seemingly ever heard of such a being as J. B. Casimir Godeuil.

Then it was, that all Paris was placarded with gigantic bills asking for information concerning M. Godeuil's whereabouts. The walls of Lyons, Marseilles, and other large cities were similiarly posted, and during a whole week folks asked themselves "Who can this man Godeuil be?" Several opined that he was some prodigal son, whose return to the parental roof was anxiously hoped for; others suggested that he must be the lost heir to some princely fortune; whilst others again surmised that he might be a dishonest cashier, who had absconded with the contents of his employer's strong box. But, in the meanwhile, the manager of the *Petit Journal* had attained his object. Scarcely were the first bills posted when M. J. B. Casimir Godeuil hastened in person to the office of the paper and made all necessary arrangements for the publication of his narrative: "THE LITTLE OLD MAN OF BATIGNOLLES," which constituted, he said, the first part of his memoirs. He, moreover, promised to bring other fragments of his autobiography, but in this respect he failed to keep his word, and all subsequent efforts to find him again proved unsuccessful. The following narrative (complete in itself), is therefore his only published work, but with the view of throwing some light on the author's character and object we have decided to print the subjoined preface, written by himself, and which was to have served for the whole series of his memoirs:

PREFACE

A prisoner had just been brought before an investigating magistrate, and despite his denials, his stratagems and an alleged *alibi*, it had been shown that he was guilty both of forgery and theft. Conquered by the evidence I had collected against him, he confessed his crimes, exclaiming: "Ah! If I had only known the true power of the police and how difficult it is to escape its search, I should have remained an honest man."

These words inspired me with the idea of writing my memoirs. Was it not advisable that every one should be made acquainted with the true state of affairs? Would not my revelations have a beneficial effect? Might I not strip crime of the poetry of romance and shew it as it really is: cowardly and ignoble, abject and repulsive? Would it not be useful to prove that the most wretched beings in the world, are the madmen who declare war against society? And that is what I propose doing. I will prove that everyone has an immediate, positive, mathematical interest in remaining honest—I will show that, with our social organisation, with the railroad and the electric telegraph, impunity is virtually impossible. Punishment may be deferred, but it always comes at last. And profiting by what I write, many misguided beings may reflect before allowing themselves to slide along the road of crime. Many, whom the faint murmurings of conscience would have failed to influence, may be arrested in their course by the voice of fear.

Need I speak of the nature of these memoirs? They will describe the struggles, efforts, defeats, and victories of the few devoted men to whom the security of the Parisians is virtually entrusted. To cope with all the criminals of a city, which, with its suburbs, numbers more than three millions of inhabitants, there are but two hundred detectives at the disposal of the Préfecture of Police. It is to them that I dedicate this narrative.

I

When I was completing my studies, in hopes of one day becoming a medical man—it was in the good old times when I was but three and twenty—I lived in the Rue Monsieur-le-Prince, almost at the corner of the Rue Racine. For thirty francs a month, service included, I rented a furnished room, which would cost more than three times as much now-a-days, a room of such vast proportions that I was really able to stretch out my arms when putting on my coat, without having to open the window. I rose early and I went home late; for in the morning I had my hospital to "walk," and at night time the Café Leroy possessed a seductive attraction which I was powerless to resist. Thus, it happened, that with one exception, the other dwellers in the house—mostly quiet people, living either by trade or on their incomes—were scarcely known to me, even by sight. The person I have excepted from the others was a man of medium height, with a clean shaven face, and common-place features, whom every one always deferentially called "Monsieur" Méchinet. The doorkeeper treated him with the most profound respect, and invariably took off his cap whenever he perceived him. M. Méchinet lived on the same floor as myself; in fact his door was just opposite mine, and on several occasions we had encountered each other on the landing. As a matter of course, we bowed to one another, whenever this happened, but for some time our acquaintance was confined to these rudimentary tokens of civility. One night, how ever, M. Méchinet knocked at my door to ask me to oblige him with a few lucifers; another night I borrowed some tobacco from him, and one morning we happened to leave the house at the same time and walked together down the street exchanging the usual commonplace remarks about the weather. Such was the commencement of our connection.

Although I was neither inquisitive nor suspicious—a man is seldom so at three and twenty—I nevertheless liked to know what sort of people I had to deal with, and without prying into my neighbour's life I naturally asked myself: "Who is he? what is his profession?" I knew that he was married, and to all appearances worshipped by his wife, a plump little body with fair hair, and a smiling face; and yet it seemed to me that he was a man of most irregular habits, for he would frequently leave the house before daybreak, and I often heard him come home during the small hours of the morning, after being out all night. Moreover, every now and then he would absent himself for weeks at a time—and I could not understand how pretty little Madame Méchinet could put up with such strange behaviour, and indeed show herself so loving towards a husband of such a roaming disposition. In my perplexity I bethought myself of the doorkeeper, who, under ordinary circumstances, was as garrulous as a magpie, and who, I conjectured, would readily give me the information I desired. But I made a great mistake; for scarcely had I mentioned the name of Méchinet to him, than he sent me about my business in fine style, fiercely rolling his eyes and indignantly declaring that he was not in the habit of "spying" the tenants of the house. This unwonted reception on the doorkeeper's part so fanned my curiosity, that dismissing all restraint I began to watch my neighbour in earnest.

I soon made certain discoveries which seemed to me of a most ominous character. One day I saw him come home dressed in the latest fashion, with the ribbon of the Legion of Honour displayed in his button-hole, and a couple of mornings later I met him on the stairs wearing a dirty blouse and a ragged cap, which gave him a most villainous appearance. And this was not everything, for one afternoon, just as he was going out, I perceived his wife take leave of him on the landing and kiss him with passionate fondness, exclaiming: "Take care, my dear, be prudent, think of your little wife at home." "Be prudent," indeed! Why was he to be prudent? What did this all mean? Was the wife the husband's accomplice in all these strange goings on? After this incident I was fairly stupefied, but there was even yet more to come.

One night I was in bed, asleep and dreaming. Fancy had carried me back to the Café Leroy, which I had left a few hours previously, and I was apparently absorbed in watching a most interesting game of billiards. The ivory balls sped right and leftover the green baize, now striking the bands, and now cannoning with wonderful precision and effect. One thing surprised me, that whenever they came into contact there was a loud report, and at last, indeed, there was such a constant succession of cannons and clashes that I fairly started and woke up. The problem was instantaneously explained to me. What I had taken for the clashing of the billiard balls was a loud and repeated rat-tat-tat outside my room. I immediately sprang out of bed to ascertain what was the matter, and, to my surprise, as soon as I had opened the door, who should rush in but my mysterious neighbour, Méchinet, with his clothes in tatters, his shirt-front torn apart, but a wisp of his necktie left him, his head bare, and, to complete the picture, his face besmeared with blood. "Good heavens!" cried I, in affright, "what has happened?"

"Speak lower! you might be heard," rejoined my neighbour with an imperious wave of the hand. "This wound of mine in the face may be nothing after all, but it smarts terribly, and I thought you might be able to dress it, as you are a medical student."

Without another word I made him sit down, and examined the wound he spoke of. As he had surmised, it was not serious, although it bled profusely. In point of fact, the skin of his left cheek was grazed from ear to mouth, and at different points the flesh was bare. As soon as I had washed the cheek and dressed it, M. Méchinet warmly tendered me his acknowledgments. "Well, I've escaped without much harm after all," said he. "Many thanks, M. Godeuil, I'm greatly obliged to you. Pray don't mention this little accident . . . to any one. Forgive me for disturbing you, and now, good-night!"

Good-night, indeed! As if I could sleep in peace after such an adventure. My mind was haunted with all manner of strange ideas. It was plain enough now that this man Méchinet must be a highway-robber or a burglar, possibly a cut throat, and, at all events, a villain of the deepest dye. However, he quietly called on me the next day, thanked me over again, and, to my surprise, wound up by inviting me to dinner. Such courteous behaviour was scarcely in keeping with the character I had assigned to him, and more puzzled than ever I decided to accept his invitation, hoping that it might lead to some explanation of the mystery. I was, indeed, all eyes and ears on entering my neighbour's lodgings; but, despite the most minute scrutiny and patient attention, I neither saw nor heard anything at all of a nature to enlighten me.

Still, it happened that after this dinner our acquaintance considerably improved. M. Méchinet seemed anxious to cultivate my friendship. Every now and then he would invite me to take "pot luck" with himself and his wife, and nearly every afternoon, during "the hour of absinthe," he would join me at the Café Leroy, where we habitually indulged in a game of dominoes pending dinner-time. One afternoon, in the month of July, between five and six o'clock, while we were thus engaged at the café, an ill-clad, suspicious-looking individual hurried in, and approaching my neighbour, whispered something, which I failed to master, in his ear. M. Méchinet immediately sprang to his feet with a pale face. "I'm coming!" said he. "Run and tell them I'm coming"; whereupon the messenger started off as fast as his legs could carry him. Then turning to me, and holding out his hand, my neighbour remarked: "Please excuse me, M. Godeuil, but duty before everything, you know; I must leave now, but we will resume our game to-morrow."

All aglow with curiosity, and particularly struck by his air of excitement, I could not conceal the vexation his abrupt departure caused me; and still actuated by anxiety to penetrate the seeming mystery, I made so bold as to say that I felt sorry I was not to accompany him. "Eh?" he retorted; "well, after all, why not? *Will* you come? It may be interesting?" I was too delighted and impatient to waste time in exchanging superfluous words, so that my only answer was to put on my hat and follow him out of the café.

II

In accompanying M. Méchinet, I was certainly far from thinking that such a simple act would have a most decisive influence on my own afterlife. "Well, now, I shall know what this all means," I murmured to myself, as puffed up with puerile satisfaction I trotted down the Rue Racine in my neighbour's wake. I use the word "trotted" advisedly, for in truth I had great difficulty in keeping pace with my companion, who rushed on, pushing the passers-by out of his way with a strange air of authority, and making such rapid strides that one might have imagined his fortune depended on his legs.

Just as we reached the Place de l'Odéon, an empty cab drove by. "Eh, cabman, stop!" cried M. Méchinet, and opening one of the doors he bade me get into the vehicle. "Drive as fast as you can to 39 Rue de Lécluse, at Batignolles," he added, speaking to the Jehu, and then with a bound he reached my side. The distance made the driver swear, but cutting his thin horse with a vigorous stroke of the whip he turned him in the right direction, and we rolled off, down towards the Seine.

"Ah! so we are going to Batignolles," said I, in my most winning manner— that is, with courtly deference and just an interrogative touch in my tone. But to my disappointment, M. Méchinet did not answer me and indeed, I fancy that he did not hear my remark.

A strange change had come over his demeanour. He was not precisely excited, but his pursed lips and knitted brows showed that he was greatly preoccupied. His glance, lost in space, seemed to indicate that he was studying some mysterious, intricate problem. He had drawn a snuff-box from his pocket, and incessantly drew forth enormous pinches, which, after rolling between his fore-finger and his thumb, he carried to his nose—without inhaling them, however. This was one of his little private manias which I had previously observed, and which greatly amused me. The worthy man held snuff in horror, and yet he was always provided with a huge, meretriciously adorned snuff-box, such as players use when enacting a farce upon the stage. If anything unforeseen happened to him, were it either agreeable or afflictive, he invariably drew this monster snuff-box from his pocket, and pretended to regale himself with a vast number of pinches. Later on, I learnt that the subterfuge formed part of a system he had invented with the view of concealing his impressions and diverting the attention of folks around him.

THE LITTLE OLD MAN OF BATIGNOLLES

In the meanwhile, we were rolling on. The cab climbed the precipitous Rue de Clichy, crossed the outer boulevard, turned into the Rue de Lécluse, and drew up a short distance from the number that had been given to the driver. It was materially impossible to go any further, for the street was crammed with a compact crowd. In front of No. 39, two or three hundred persons were standing with extended necks, gaping mouths, and inquisitive eyes. Their curiosity was so keen that they utterly disregarded the authoritative injunctions of half a dozen *sergents de ville* who, as they passed to and fro, kept on repeating: "Move on! move on!"

Alighting from the vehicle, we approached the house, elbowing our way through the crowd, and we were but a few steps from the door of No. 39, when one of the sergents de ville roughly bade us draw back. My companion took in the man's measure from head to foot at a single glance, and drawing himself up to his full height, exclaimed:

"Don't you know me? I am Méchinet, and this young man (pointing to myself) is with me."

"Oh, pray excuse me, sir," stammered the sergent de ville, saluting us with military precision. "I did not recognise you—I was not aware—but please walk in."

We crossed the threshold. In the hall a stalwart, middle-aged woman, with a face as red as a poppy, was perorating and gesticulating in the midst of a group of tenants belonging to the house. She was evidently the concierge or doorkeeper.

"Where is it?" roughly asked M. Méchinet, cutting her recital short.

"On the third floor, sir," she replied; "on the third floor—the door on the right hand. Oh Lord! what a misfortune! In a house like ours! And such a worthy man, too!"

I did not hear any more, for M. Méchinet had already sprung towards the staircase, up which I followed him, climbing four stairs at a time, and with my heart palpitating as if I were about to lose my breath. On the third landing, the door on the right hand side was open. We went in, crossed an ante-room, a dining-room, and a parlour, and finally reached a bed-chamber of ample size. Were I to live a thousand years, I should never forget the sight that met my eyes. At this moment even, I can still picture in my mind every particular of the scene.

Two men were leaning against the mantel-piece in front of the door. One of them, whose frock-coat was begirded with a tricolour sash, was a commissary of police; the other, an investigating magistrate. A young man, plainly the latter's clerk, was seated writing at a table on the left hand side; while on the floor in the centre of the room, lay a lifeless body—the body of a little, white-haired, old man, who was stretched on his back, with extended arms, in the midst of a pool of black, coagulated blood.

In my terror, I remained rooted on the threshold—so overcome, indeed, that to avoid falling I had to lean for support against the framework of the door. And yet, like every man of my profession, I was already familiar with death. I was accustomed to all the sickening sights which are every-day occurrences in an hospital or a medical school, but then, this was the first time that I found myself face to face with crime. For it was evident that an atrocious crime had been committed.

Less impressed than myself, my neighbour entered the room with a firm step.

"Ah, it's you, Méchinet," said the commissary of police. "I am sorry I sent for you."

"And why, pray?" asked my neighbour.

"Because we shan't need to appeal to your skill. We know the culprit, I have given the necessary orders, and he must be arrested by now."

Singularly enough, it looked as if this news sadly disappointed M. Méchinet. He drew out his snuff-box, pretended to take two or three pinches, and exclaimed: "Ah, you know the culprit!"

It was the investigating magistrate who replied: "Yes, know him certainly and positively," said he. "When the crime was accomplished the murderer fled, believing that his victim had ceased to live. But Providence was watching. The poor old man still breathed. Summoning all his energy he dipped a finger in the blood that was flowing from his wound, and there on the floor he traced his murderer's name, thus handing him over to human justice. However, look for yourself."

On hearing this I immediately glanced at the floor, on one of the oak boards of which, the letters M O N I S were traced in blood, in rough but legible fashion. "Well?" asked M. Méchinet, laconically.

"Well," replied the commissary of police; "those letters form the first two syllables of the name of Monistrol, which is that of the murdered man's nephew—a nephew of whom he was very fond."

"The d——l," ejaculated my neighbour.

"I don't fancy," resumed the investigating magistrate; "I don't fancy that the scoundrel will attempt to deny his guilt. Those five letters are terrible proof against him. And besides, he is the only man who could benefit by such a cowardly crime. He is the sole heir of this poor old fellow, who leaves, I am told, considerable wealth behind him. Moreover, the murder was committed last night, and the only person who visited the victim was his nephew Monistrol, who, according to the concierge, arrived at nine o'clock, and did not leave till nearly midnight."

"It's clear, then," rejoined M. Méchinet, "as clear as daylight. That fellow Monistrol is a perfect fool." And, shrugging his shoulders, he asked: "Did he steal anything—did he force open any article of furniture to mislead one as to the motive of the crime?"

"Up to the present," replied the commissary, "we have not noticed anything out of order. As you say, the scoundrel is not particularly ingenious. As soon as he is arrested, he will no doubt confess." Thereupon he drew M. Méchinet to the window, and spoke to him in a low voice; while the magistrate turned to give some orders to his clerk.

III

So far as M. Méchinet was concerned, my curiosity was satisfied. I had wished to know my enigmatical neighbour's profession, and now I knew it. He was simply a detective. Thus, all the incidents of his seemingly erratic life were explained—his frequent absence from home, his tardy return at night-time, his frequent change of costume, his sudden disappearances, his wife's fears and complicity, and even the wound I had dressed. But all this was of little moment now. I was far less interested in M. Méchinet than in the spectacle offered to my view. I had gradually recovered both my firmness and the faculty of reflecting; and I examined everything around me with eager curiosity. Standing beside the door, my glance took in the whole room. When scenes of murder are portrayed in illustrated periodicals they are usually invested with an exaggerated aspect of disorder. But such was far from being the case in the present instance. Everything testified to the victim's easy circumstances and habits of order and relative parsimony. Everything was in its place. The bed and the window curtains were faultlessly draped; and the woodwork of the furniture was bright with polish—a proof of daily care. It appeared evident that the conjectures of the commissary and the magistrate were correct, and that the old man had been murdered the night before, just as he was going to retire to rest. In proof of this the bed was turned down, and a night-shirt and a nightcap were spread out open on the counterpane. On the little table at the head of the bed I perceived a glass of sugared water, a box of lucifers, and an evening newspaper—the *Patrie*. On the corner of the mantel-shelf shone a weighty copper candlestick, but the candle which had lighted the crime had burnt away. The murderer had plainly fled without blowing it out, and the top of the candlestick, from which hung a few fragments of wax, like pendant icicles, was greatly soiled and blackened.

I noticed all these circumstances well nigh at the first glance. My eyes seemed to play the part of a photographic lens, and the scene of the murder fixed itself on my mind as on a prepared sheet of glass, with such precision, accuracy, and effect, that even to day I could draw from memory the bed-room occupied by the Little Old Man of Batignolles, without forgetting any single object it contained—without omitting even the green-sealed cork, which I still seem to see, lying on the ground underneath the chair of the magistrate's clerk. I was not previously aware that I possessed this power of observation—this master faculty, so suddenly revealed to me, and on the spot I was too greatly excited to be able to analyse my sensations and impressions.

Curiously enough, I was possessed of an unique, irresistible desire. I felt impelled, despite myself, towards the corpse extended in the middle of the room. At first I battled with my impulse, but it was stronger than all my other feelings; and, yielding to it at last, I approached the body. Had my presence been noticed? I do not think so. At all events, no attention was paid to me. M. Méchinet and the commissary were still talking beside the window; and the clerk was reading the minutes of the proceedings in an under tone to the magistrate. Everything, therefore, favoured my design, and besides, I was seized, as it were, with a kind of fever which made me insensible to what was going on. Under this influence, I was well nigh unconscious of the functionaries' presence, and, acting as if I were alone and free to do whatever I liked, I knelt down beside the corpse, to examine it closely and at my ease. Indeed, far from reflecting that the magistrate or the commissary might indignantly ask: "What are you about?" I acted as composedly as if I were about to discharge some pre-assigned duty.

The unfortunate old man seemed to be from seventy to seventy-five years of age. He was short and very thin, but certainly very hale for his age, acd constitutionally fitted to become well nigh a centenarian. He still possessed a fair crop of curly hair of a yellowish white tinge, and his face was covered with grey bristles, as if he had not shaved for five or six days. They had sprung forth, however, since his demise, and it is indeed curious to note how rapidly, under certain circumstances, the beard grows immediately after death. I was not surprised by this, for I had observed many similar cases among the "subjects" provided for the examination of us students in the hospital dissecting hall. What *did* surprise me was the expression of the old man's face. It was calm and, I might almost say, smiling. His lips were parted as if he had been on the point of making some friendly remark. Death must have overtaken him most suddenly and promptly, for his face to retain this good-natured look. Such was the first thought that presented itself to my mind. Ay, but then, how could one reconcile these conflicting circumstances—sudden death, and the tracing of those five letters M O N I S on the floor? To trace these letters with his own blood would require a great effort on the part of a dying man. Only the hope of vengeance could lend the requisite energy for such a task. And how enraged this poor old fellow must have been to feel the grip of death upon him before he was able to finish writing his murderer's name!

Enraged? But no, for the face of the corpse seemed positively to smile at me, and this was all the more singular as the victim had been struck at the throat with a steel weapon, which had penetrated right through his neck. This weapon must have been a dagger, or perhaps one of those formidable double-edged Catalan knives, which are pointed as finely as a needle. In all my life I had never been a prey to such strange sensations. My temples beat with extraordinary violence, and I could feel my heart swelling and almost bursting with intensity of dilation. What was I about to discover?

Still under the influence of the same mysterious, irresistible impulse which annihilated my will, I took hold of the victim's frozen, rigid hands to examine them. The right hand was quite clean, unstained; but such was not the case with the left one, the forefinger of which was red with blood! What! had the old man traced that accusatory inscription with his left hand? Was it probable? was it likely? No, a thousand times no! But then. A score of conflicting thoughts battled in my mind, and, seized as it were with vertigo, with haggard eyes and hair on end, as pale certainly as the corpse extended on the floor, I sprung to my feet, giving vent to a terrible cry: "Great God!"

My shriek must have resounded through the house. With one bound the magistrate and Méchinet, the commissary and the clerk were by my side. "What is the matter?" they asked, with eager excitement; "what is the matter?"

I tried to answer, but emotion well nigh paralysed my tongue. All I could do was to point at the dead man's hands, and stammer: "There, see there!"

M. Méchinet immediately knelt down beside the corpse. He observed the same particulars as myself, and evidently shared my opinion, for, quickly rising to his feet again, he exclaimed: "After all, it was not the old man who traced those letters." And then, as the magistrate and the commissary stared at him with gaping mouths, he showed them that the victim's left hand alone was stained with blood.

"And to think I didn't notice it!" mourned the commissary, looking very much distressed.

"Ah, it's often like that," retorted M. Méchinet, frantically pretending to inhale repeated pinches of snuff. "The things that stare us in the face are frequently those that most easily escape our view. However, the situation is now quite changed. As it is evident that the old man did not write those letters, they must have been traced by the man who killed him."

"Quite so," observed the commissary in an approving tone.

"Well," continued my neighbour, "it is plain enough that a murderer is not foolish enough to denounce himself by writing his own name beside his victim's corpse. We shall all agree on that point, and so you may draw your own conclusions."

The investigating magistrate looked thoughtful. "Yes," he muttered; "it's clear enough. We were deceived by appearances. Monistrol is not guilty. But then, who can be the culprit? It will be your business to find him, M. Méchinet."

The magistrate paused, for a police agent of subaltern rank was at that moment entering the room. "Your orders are executed, sir," said the new comer, addressing himself to the commissary; "Moistrol has been arrested, and he is now under lock and key at the Depot. He has confessed everything."

IV

The news created all the greater sensation as, by reason of my discovery, it was altogether unexpected. The magistrate and the commissary looked absolutely stupefied, and, for myself, I was overwhelmed. What, whilst we were busily seeking, by a mathematical course of reasoning, to establish Monistrol's innocence, he, on his side, had formally confessed his guilt! Was it possible? M. Méchinet was the first to recover from this hard blow. He excitedly carried his fingers from his snuff-box to his nose at least a dozen times, and then, turning to the agent, roughly remarked: "You've either been misled or else you are misleading us. There's no other alternative."

"I swear to you, Monsieur Méchinet," began the man.

"Don't swear, pray; but hold your tongue. Either you misunderstood what Monistrol said, or else you've flattered yourself with the hope of astonishing us by the news that the whole affair is explained."

The police agent, who had hitherto been most respectful in his demeanour towards the detective, now evinced signs of revolt. "Excuse me," he said, "but I'm neither a fool nor a liar, and I know what I say."

The discussion seemed so likely to turn into a dispute that the magistrate thought it advisable to intervene. "Calm yourself, M. Méchinet," said he, "and wait for information before pronouncing judgment." And turning towards the agent, he added "Now, my good fellow, just tell us what you know, and explain what you have already said."

Finding himself thus supported the agent drew himself up, gave my neighbour a glance of withering irony, and then, with an air of no little self-conceit, began: "You gentlemen instructed Inspector Goulard, my colleague, Poltin, and myself to arrest a party named Monistrol, a dealer in imitation jewellery, residing at No. 75 Rue Vivienne, and charged with the murder of his uncle here, at Batignolles."

"Quite correct," remarked the commissary, with an approving nod.

"Well, then," continued the agent, "we took a cab and drove to the Rue Vivienne. Monistrol was in a little room at the rear of his shop, and he was about to sit down to dinner with his wife—a woman of wonderful beauty, between five-and-twenty and thirty years of age. On perceiving us all three in a row, the husband at once asked us what we wanted, whereupon Inspector Goulard drew the warrant out of his pocket, and replied: 'In the name of the law I arrest you.'"

As the agent proceeded with his narrative, M. Méchinet turned and twisted with nervous impatience. "Can't you come to the point?" he suddenly asked.

But the agent took no notice of the interruption. "I have arrested a good many fellows in my time," said he, with unabated composure; "but I never saw any one experience such a shock as this man Monistrol. 'You must be joking,' he said at last, 'or else you make a mistake.' 'No,' said Goulard; 'we don't make mistakes.' 'Well then, why do you arrest me?' Goulard shrugged his shoulders. 'Don't behave like a child,' he said. 'Come, what about your uncle? His body has been found, you know, and there are convincing proofs against you.' Ah, the scamp! What a blow it was for him! He staggered and let himself fall on to a chair stammering some unintelligible reply, half the words of which remained in his throat. On seeing this, Goulard caught him by the collar of his coat, and said: 'Take my advice: the best thing you can do is to confess.' Thereupon he looked at us in an idiotic manner, and replied: 'Well, yes, I confess everything.'"

"Well done, Goulard!" quoth the commissary, approvingly.

The agent triumphed. "We were bent on getting the business over as soon as possible," he said. "We were instructed not to create a disturbance, and yet a lot of idlers had already collected in front of the shop. So Goulard caught hold of the prisoner by the arm, and said: 'Let's be off; they are waiting for us at the Préfecture.' Monistrol drew himself up as well as he could on his quaking legs, and, summoning all his courage, answered: 'Yes, let us start.' We thought the business finished after that, but we had reckoned without the wife. Up till then she had remained in her arm chair as still as if she had fainted, and without saying a word. Indeed, she scarcely seemed to understand what was going on. But when she saw that we were really going to carry her husband off, she sprung forward like a lioness, and threw herself before the door. 'You sha'n't pass,' she cried. 'Pon my word she really looked superb. But Goulard has had to deal with many similar cases. 'Come, come, my little woman,' said he, 'don't get angry. It wouldn't do any good.' But instead of moving she clung to the framework of the door, vowing that her husband was innocent, and declaring that if he were taken to prison she would follow him. At one moment she threatened us, and called us all sorts of names, and then she began to beg and pray in her softest voice. But when she perceived that nothing would prevent us from doing our duty, she let go of the door and threw her arms round her husband's neck. 'Oh my poor, dear husband!' she gasped; 'is it possible that you can be charged with such a crime? Tell these men that you are innocent.' Her grief was so great that we all felt compassion for her, but Monistrol, to our surprise, was ruffian enough to push the poor little woman back, so violently indeed that she fell all of a heap in a corner of the room behind the shop. Fortunately, that was the end of it. The woman had fainted, and we profited of the circumstance to pack the husband into the cab, which was waiting for us outside. He could scarcely stand, much less walk, and so we had literally to carry him into the vehicle. His dog—a snarling, black mongrel—wanted to jump in with us, and we had all the pains in the world to get rid of the beast. On the way Goulard tried to revive the prisoner and induce him to talk, but we couldn't get him to say a word. It was only on reaching the Préfecture that he seemed to recover his wits. When he had been properly stowed away in one of the secret cells, he flung himself on his bed, repeating 'What have I done! Good God! What have I done?' On hearing this Goulard approached him, and for the second time, asked: 'So you own that you are guilty?' Monistrol nodded his head affirmatively, and then said, in a gasping voice, 'Pray leave me alone.' We did so, after placing a superintendent outside the cell, in front ot the grating, so as to be ready in case the prisoner tried to play any tricks with his own life. Goulard and Poltin remained at the Préfecture, and I came on here to report the arrest."

"All that is very precise," muttered the commissary; "very precise indeed."

Such was also the magistrate's opinion, for he murmured, "How can any one doubt Monistrol's guilt after that?"

As for myself, I was astonished but not convinced, and I was about to open my mouth to raise an objection when M. Méchinet forestalled me. "All that's very well," said he, "only if we admit that Monistrol is the murderer, we also have to admit that he wrote his own name there on the floor, and to my mind that's rather too strong to be believed!"

"Pooh!" rejoined the commissary, "as the prisoner confesses, what is the use of troubling about a circumstance which will no doubt be explained in the course of the investigation?"

However, the detective's remark had rekindled the magistrate's perplexity. "I shall go to the Préfecture at once," he said, "and question Monistrol this very night." Then after requesting the commissary to stay and accomplish the remaining formalities, pending the arrival of the medical men who had been summoned for the post-mortem examination, he took his departure, followed by his clerk and the agent who had come to announce Monistrol's arrest.

"I only hope those doctors won't keep me waiting too long," growled the commissary, who was thinking of his dinner; and he then began to discharge his duties by sealing up sundry drawers and cupboards which contained articles of value.

Neither Méchinet nor myself answered him. My neighbour and I were standing in front of each other, evidently absorbed in the same train of thought. "After all," murmured the detective, "after all, perhaps it *was* the old man who traced those letters."

"With his left hand, then," said I. "Is it likely? And besides, the poor fellow must have died instantaneously."

"Are you sure of that?"

"Well, judging by his wound, I would swear to it. But the doctors will soon be here, and they will tell you whether I'm right or wrong. Of course I am but a student, and they will be able to speak with more authority than myself."

M. Méchinet was worrying his nose with spurious pinches of snuff in frantic style. "Perhaps," said he; "perhaps there *is* a mystery underneath all this. It is a point to be examined. We must start the inquiry afresh. And after all, why not? Well, let us begin by questioning the doorkeeper." With these words he hurried out on to the landing, and leaning over the bannister of the stairs, exclaimed, "Eh! doorkeeper, doorkeeper, just come up here, please."

V

Pending the doorkeeper's appearance, M. Méchinet devoted his time to a rapid but sagacious examination of the scene of the crime. The outer door of the apartment particularly engaged his attention. The lock was intact and the key turned in either sense without the slightest difficulty. It was therefore scarcely likely that a stranger had forced his way into the old man's rooms by means of a picklock or a false key. Whilst the detective was thus occupied I returned into the bed-room to pick up the green-sealed bottle cork which I had noticed lying on the floor. I was prompted to do this by the new instinct so suddenly born within me. On the side of the sealing-wax a circular, winding hole, plainly produced by the tip of a corkscrew, was apparent, whilst at the other end, ruddy with the stain of wine, I noticed to my surprise a deep perforation, such as might be caused by the blade of a sharp, finely-pointed weapon. Instinctively suspecting that this discovery might have its importance, I showed the cork to M. Méchinet, who on perceiving it could not repress an exclamation of delight. "Ah!" said he, "at last we are on the scent. That cork was evidently left here by the murderer. He had pricked his weapon into it—either to prevent the point from wounding him whilst he carried it in his pocket, or to keep it sharp and prevent it from breaking. So the weapon was plainly a dagger with a fixed handle, and not one of those knives that shut up. With this cork I will undertake to find the murderer, no matter who he may be."

The commissary of police was finishing the sealing-up of the cupboards in the bed-room, and M. Méchinet and I were still talking together in the parlour, when a sound of heavy breathing interrupted us. At the same moment, the portly, stalwart crone whom I had noticed in the hall perorating for the benefit of the tenants, appeared upon the threshold. Her face was ruddier than ever. "What do you desire, sir?" she asked, looking at M. Méchinet.

"Please sit down," he replied.

"But I have people waiting for me downstairs, sir."

"They can wait. Just sit down."

M. Méchinet's authoritative tone evidently impressed the old woman, and without more ado she obeyed him. "I require certain information," he began, fixing his piercing gray eyes on hers, "and I am going to question you. In your interest I advise you to answer me frankly. As you are the doorkeeper of the house you can tell me the name of this unfortunate old man who has been murdered."

"His name was Pigoreau, my good sir, but he was generally called Anténor, which was a name he formerly took in his business, as being better suited to it."

"Had he lived long in this house?"

"For more than eight years, sir."

"Where did he live before then?"

"In the Rue de Richelieu, where he had his shop, for he had been a hairdresser, and it was in that calling that he made his fortune."

"So he was rich, then?"

"Well, I've heard his niece say that he wouldn't let his throat be cut for a million francs."

The investigating magistrate was probably fully informed on this point, for during his sojourn in the house he had gone carefully through all the old man's papers.

"Now," resumed M. Méchinet, "what kind of man was this M. Pigoreau *alias* Anténor."

"Oh, the best man in the world, my good sir," replied the doorkeeper. "He was a bit eccentric and obstinate, but he wasn't proud. And when he chose, he could be so funny! One might have spent nights and nights listening to him when he was in the humour to talk, for he knew so many stories. Just fancy, he had been a hairdresser, and, as he often said, he had curled the hair of all the most beautiful women in Paris."

"How did he live?"

"Like other people—like a man living on his income, but not inclined to be prodigal."

"Can't you give me any particulars?"

"To be sure I can, sir, for it was I who cleaned his rooms and waited on him. Ah! he didn't give me much trouble, for he did a great deal himself. He was always sweeping and dusting and polishing. That was his hobby! Every day, at twelve o'clock, I used to bring him up a cup of chocolate and a roll; and on the top of them he would drink off a big glass of water at one gulp. That was his breakfast. Then he dressed himself, and that took him till two o'clock, for he was very particular about his appearance, and arrayed himself every day just as if he were going to be married. When he was dressed he went out, and strolled about Paris till six o'clock, when he used to go and dine at a table d' hôte, kept by Mlles. Gomet in the Rue de la Paix. After dinner he usually went to the café Guerbois, took his cup of coffee, and played his game at cards with some friends he used to meet there. He generally came home at about eleven o'clock. He had only one fault, poor dear man: he was dreadfully fond of the fair sex, and I often used to say to him, 'Come, Monsieur Anténor, aren't you ashamed to run after women at your age?' But then we are none of us perfect, and after all his behaviour wasn't surprising on the part of a man who had been a fashionable hairdresser, and had met with so many favours in his time."

An obsequious smile curved the portly crone's thick lips as she spoke on this point, but M. Méchinet remained as grave as ever. "Did M. Pigoreau receive many visitors?" he asked.

"Very few, sir. The person who came most frequently was his nephew, M. Monistrol, whom he used to invite to dine with him every Sunday at the restaurant of Père Lathuile?"

"And on what terms were they—the uncle and the nephew?"

"Oh, they were as friendly as two fingers of the same hand."

"And didn't they ever have any disputes together?"

"Never! Excepting that they always used to disagree about Madame Clara."

"Who is this Madame Clara?"

"Why, M. Monistrol's wife, to be sure, and a superb creature she is, too! But with all his love for the sex, M. Anténor couldn't put up with her. He used to tell his nephew that he loved his wife too much, that she led him by the nose, and deceived him just whenever she chose. He pretended that she didn't love her husband, that she had tastes above her position, and that she would end one day by doing something foolish. In fact, Madame Clara and M. Anténor had quite a quarrel last year. She wanted the old man to lend M. Monistrol a large sum, so that he might buy the 'goodwill' of a jeweller's shop in the Palais Royal; but he refused to do so, and said he didn't care what was done with his fortune when he was dead, but that in the meantime, having earned his money himself, he meant to keep it and spend it as he chose."

I thought that M. Méchinet would insist on this point, which seemed to me of high importance, but to my surprise, and despite all the signs I made him, he did not do so. "How was the crime discovered?" was his next question.

"Why, it was discovered by me, my good sir!" replied the doorkeeper. "Ah! it was frightful! Just fancy, at noon to-day I came upstairs as usual with M. Anténor's chocolate. As I waited on him I had a key of his rooms. I opened the door, came in, and, Good Heavens! what a sight I saw!" So saying, the buxom dame gave vent to a succession of unearthly whines and groans.

"Your grief shows that you have a kind heart," observed M. Méchinet gravely. "Only, as I am pressed for time, I must ask you to master it. Come, what did you think when you saw the old man lying there murdered?"

"Why, to be sure, I told every one that his rascally nephew had killed him to get hold of his fortune!"

"How is it you were so certain on the point? For it is a grave matter to charge a man with such a crime—it's sending him to the scaffold, mind."

"But who else could it be, sir? M. Monistrol came to see his uncle yesterday evening, and when he went away it was almost midnight. I thought it strange that he didn't speak to me, even when he came or when he left, for he generally wishes me good-day and good-bye. However, after he went away last night, and until I discovered everything this morning, I'm quite sure that no one else came to see M. Anténor."

This evidence fairly stupefied me. I was young then and wanting in experience, and therefore thought it really superfluous to continue the investigation. But, on the other hand, M. Méchinet could boast of very extensive experience indeed, and he moreover possessed the art of coaxing the whole truth out of a witness, no matter however unwilling. "So," said he to the doorkeeper, "you are quite certain that Monistrol came here last night?"

"Quite certain, sir."

"Then you saw him, and recognised him?"

"Ah, allow me! I didn't look him in the face, for he passed by very fast, as if he wished to hide himself, the scoundrel! And besides, the stairs are badly lighted."

I sprung from my chair on hearing this answer, which struck me as being of very great weight indeed, and, advancing towards the doorkeeper, I exclaimed, "If that is the case how can you dare to pretend that you recognised M. Monistrol?"

The portly dame looked at me from head to foot, and, with an ironical smile, replied, "If I didn't see his face, at least I saw his dog, who was with him. I always treat the animal kindly, and so he came into my room, and I was just going to give him a leg of mutton bone, when his master whistled to him from upstairs."

I looked at M. Méchinet to know what he thought of this answer, but his expression told no tales. He simply asked, "What kind of a dog is M. Monistrol's?"

"He's a watch dog, sir—quite black, with just one white spot on the top of the head. M. Monistrol calls him Pluto. He's generally very savage with strangers, but then he knows me well, for he has always been in the habit of coming here with his master, and besides, I've always been very kind to him."

M. Méchinet now rose from his chair. "That will do," said he to the doorkeeper; "you may retire. Thank you for your information." And as soon as the woman had bustled out of the room, he turned to me exclaiming, "I really think that the nephew must be the guilty party."

While the doorkeeper's interrogatory was progressing, the two medical men who had been instructed to perform a post-mortem examination of the old fellow's body, had arrived and set about their task in the bed-room. I was particularly anxious to know what would be the result of their report—the more so as, despite my own conclusions, I feared they might possibly disagree. They were certainly of very dissimilar appearance and character; for, while one of them was short and fat, with a round and jovial face, the other was lank and lean, with a grave and pompous expression of countenance. You could not look at them, indeed, without at once thinking of Molière's immortal creations, "Doctor Tant Pis" and "Doctor Tant Mieux." But, at times, extremes meet, and at least on this occasion this unmatched pair not merely met in being but in ideas and opinions as well. They both took absolutely the same view of the case, and I was delighted, as an amateur detective, and flattered, as a medical student, to find that their view exactly coincided with mine. Indeed, their report resolved itself into this: "The death of M. Pigoreau was instantaneous. He expired directly the knife or dagger penetrated his neck, and consequently he could not possibly have traced those five letters M O N I S, inscribed on the oak floor beside his body."

Thus I had not been mistaken, and I turned with satisfaction towards M. Méchinet to hear what he would have to say now. "Well, if the old man did not write those letters," he remarked at last, "who could have written them? Not Monistrol, I would take my oath to that. It would be altogether too incredible."

I myself made no rejoinder, but the commissary of police, who was delighted to be able to go away to his dinner after such a long and tiring task, overheard the words, and could not resist the pleasure of taunting the detective for his perplexity and obstinacy, which, to his mind, were all the more ridiculous as Monistrol had confessed the crime.

"Ridiculous?" ejaculated M. Méchinet; "well, yes, perhaps I am *only* a fool! However, the future will decide that point." And then, abruptly turning to me, he added: "Come, M. Godeuil, let us go together to the Préfecture of Police."

VI

W e had neither of us dined, but this puzzling affair so absorbed our minds that
we did not even think of feeling hungry. On reaching the street we walked as
far as the outer boulevard where we engaged another cab to take us to the Préfecture.
While the vehicle rolled on down the Rue de Clichy and along the Chaussée d'Antin,
crossing the grand boulevards, already all ablaze with light, and cutting through
numerous narrow thoroughfares in the direction of the Rue de Rivoli and the Quays,
M. Méchinet's fingers did not stop travelling from his empty snuff-box to his nose, and
vice versa—so great indeed was his preoccupation. Over and over again, moreover, I
heard him grumble between his teeth, "I must find out the truth; I must, I will."

All of a sudden he drew from his pocket the green-sealed cork which I had handed
to him, and turned it over and over like a young monkey, who, in possession of a nut
for the first time, asks himself how he is to get at the kernel. "And yet," he murmured,
"and yet that's a piece of evidence. That green sealing-wax must be made to tell us
something."

Comfortably ensconced in my corner, I listened to him without saying a word.
My situation was certainly very singular, and yet I did not for one moment think of
its peculiarity. My mind was entirely absorbed in this affair, the diverse contradictory
elements of which I tried to classify in my brain, turning to one after the other in hopes
that it would give me the key of the mystery which, to my idea, assuredly existed.

When our vehicle drew up on the Quai des Orfèvres all around was silent and
deserted—not a sound, not a passer-by. The few shops of the neighbourhood were all
closed, with but one solitary exception—a little tavern and eating-house, situated almost
at the corner of the famous Rue de Jérusalem, so long associated with the repression of
crime, and the name of which, synonymous, so to say, with the word "police," suffices
to chill the blood of the most hardened rogues. Against the red curtains of the tavern
windows, which shone out in the dark night with a fiery glare, I noted the shadows of
numerous customers—subordinate officials of the Préfecture, who had profited of a
spare moment to come out and refresh themselves, and detectives, who, after a long
day's arduous tramp and toil, were bent on restoring tired nature with a crust and a
glass of wine. As we walked by, M. Méchinet just gave a glance inside, more from habit
than curiosity (for, like myself, he was in no mood to loiter), and then turned swiftly
into the Rue de Jérusalem.

"Do you think they will let you see Monistrol?" I asked him, breaking once more
into a trot so as to keep up with his rapid stride.

"Certainly they will," he answered. "Am I not entrusted with following up the
affair? According to the phases of the investigation, I may require to see the prisoner

at any hour of the day or night." And then turning under the dark-arched entrance of the Préfecture, he added, "Come, come, we have no time to lose."

I did not require encouragement. A strange, vague curiosity filled my mind as I followed in his wake. This was the first time in my life that I crossed the threshold of the Préfecture de Police, against which I had hitherto been quite as prejudiced as any other Parisian. Those who study social questions may well ask how it happens that the French police are so generally hated and despised. Even the ordinary street policeman, yclept the *sergent de ville*, is an object of aversion; and the detective, the *mouchard*, is loathed as intensely as if he were some monstrous horror, in lieu of generally being a most useful servant of society. The deep-rooted prejudices that prevail among the Parisians in reference to the police are of distant origin, and are no doubt due to many causes; but the fault mainly rests with the successive governments which, turning the force from its original mission as a guarantee of public security, transformed it into a political instrument, utilising its services for the execution of the most arbitrary measures, and frequently placing it under the control of low-minded, immoral men. The unpopularity of Voyer d'Argenson duly fell on the "*exempt*" of the *ancien régime*; and besides, the hateful Bastille and the odious *lettre de cachet* would alone have sufficed to make the police an object of aversion and terror in those times. Under the Empire and the Restoration the service could not possibly hope for rehabilitation, for was it not under the control of the arch-traitor Fouché, as arrant a scoundrel as any of the criminals his subordinates were employed to track? And in the days of Vidocq, moreover, when the maxim "set a thief to catch a thief" was put into practice, and when the "security" of the Parisians was entrusted to a band of knaves, all respect for the police beame quite out of the question. Even when the force was thoroughly re-organised, the stain of former times clung to it persistently, and a new form of unpopularity awaited it when the Third Napoleon made the Préfecture the head-quarters of his system of government. The ferocity displayed by many *sergents de ville* in days of popular turmoil, the hateful practices of the political *mouchards*, the invention of spurious plots and riots, "got up" to terrify the provinces and justify acts of repression—all combined to throw odium on the force. It should be mentioned, however, that the Parisian in his aversion for the police often acts without discernment. He takes all the *sergents de ville* or *gardiens de la paix* to be of one and the same class and character, forgetting that it is mainly the Central Brigade that is employed on political duty. This Central Brigade, indeed, does not perform ordinary strict service, but is always at the préfect's disposal to be dispatched to any part of the capital where occasion may require. To the "Centrale" is assigned the sad privilege of charging the crowd, ill-treating inoffensive passers-by, and overturning women and children on days of popular effervescence. But the other brigades, to which are entrusted the protection of property and the safety of citizens, are composed of men of a very different stamp—men who behave reluctantly and with moderation when necessity compels them to assist the "Centrale" in the performance of some political task; men whose main object and desire is to prevent the perpetration of crime and to bring evil-doers to book. But then, lucklessly for them, they wear the same uniform as their colleagues of the "Centrale," and the Parisian confounds the whole force in his blind aversion. He blunders in the same way respecting the detectives—forgetting that there is the criminal service and the political service, and that the two are utterly distinct. To him the *mouchard* is invariably an unprincipled, eavesdropping knave, who earns his living by prying into other people's secrets and denouncing them to his employers. He habitually pictures the detective as a man who slinks along the boulevard trying to overhear what the promenaders are talking about, or who lingers half asleep in the corner of a café bent on listening to the conversation of the customers. The *mouchard*, to his idea, is invariably the man who questions your doorkeeper, or *concierge*, concerning your antecedents, your trade or profession, your income, and your mode of living, and who, if your opinions are not perfectly orthodox, marks a cross against your name, signifying that you are to be watched and "run in" as soon as an opportunity for political repression presents itself. The Parisian does not realise, and yet he certainly should know it, that there are other detectives of a very different stamp—men like the great Monsieur Lecoq and the eminent Monsieur Méchinet, who in their whole career never do one day's political service, but, on the contrary, spend their lives constantly tracking crime and unravelling fraud—risking incredible dangers, often wounded, and at times even killed in the performance of their duty, and yet always ready and willing to undertake any task, however perilous, to ensure the safety of society and bring offenders to book. That those men, who truly constitute the "strong arm of the law," and thanks to whose energy and enterprise Parisian crime is so swiftly and certainly punished, should be confounded with the obnoxious, political *mouchard*, is an act of utter ingratitude and injustice; but then Paris, although priding itself on its common sense, is unfortunately too impulsive, too prejudiced, and too apt to draw sweeping conclusions, to perceive the difference—vast as it may be.

As I followed M. Méchinet that night into the head-quarters of the criminal service, the main "points" of this long but I think not useless digression flashed through my mind in a twentieth part of the time it has taken me to jot them down. I realised the folly of the prejudices I had shared with so many others, and as my neighbour walked on in front of me he seemed to grow in height, importance, and dignity. Here, then, was one of those men who devote themselves to the most arduous profession that can exist, and who, for the dangers they brave, and the services they render, only reap contumely and contempt. For what is their modest stipend? It barely suffices for their every-day wants, and does not permit of laying money by, so that a scanty pension, only acquired after long, long years of toil and peril, becomes their sole resource, in their old age. I was so immersed in thought of this character, as my neighbour and I entered the Préfecture, that I forgot to look where I was walking, but a sudden stumble against a projecting angle of the pavement at last brought me back to reality. "So, here is the secret of Paris!" I muttered, glancing at the damp blank walls of the passage we had entered, "Ah, if those stones could only talk, what stories they would have to tell."

At this moment, we reached a little room where a couple of men sat playing cards, whilst three or four others lounged on a camp bedstead, smoking their pipes. M. Méchinet went inside, and I waited on the threshold. He and one of the cardplayers exchanged a few words, which did not reach me, and then he came out again, and once more bade me follow him. After crossing a courtyard and hurrying down another passage, we found ourselves in front of a formidable iron gate, with massive close-fitting bars, weighty bolts, and a huge lock. At a word from M. Méchinet a keeper opened this gate, and then, leaving on our right hand a spacious guard-room, where a number of sergents de ville and gardes de Paris were assembled, we climbed a very precipitous flight of stairs. On the landing above, at the entry of a narrow passage lined with a number of little doors, we found a tall, fat, jovial-featured individual, who in no wise resembled the gaoler usually read of in novels. "Hallo!" exclaimed this smiling colossus. "Why it's Monsieur Méchinet!" And with a self-satisfied chuckle he added, "To say the truth I half expected you; come, I bet you want to see the fellow who has been arrested for murdering the little old man of Batignolles?"

"Quite so. Is there anything new, pray?"

"No, not that I know of."

"But the investigating magistrate must have been here?"

"Oh, yes; in fact he only left a few minutes ago."

"Ah! did you hear him say anything?"

"Well, he only remained two or three minutes with the prisoner, and he looked delighted when he left the cell. He met the governor at the bottom of the stairs, and I heard him say, 'That fellow's account is as good as settled. He didn't even venture to deny his guilt.'"

On hearing this, M. Méchinet almost bounded from the floor, but the gaoler seemingly failed to notice his surprise, calmly resuming, "I wasn't particularly astonished when I heard that, for directly the fellow was brought to me, I said to myself, 'Here's a chap who won't know how to plan a defence.'"

"And what is he doing now, pray?"

"Well, he's lamenting—sobbing and crying as if he were a baby in long clothes. I was instructed to watch him, so as to prevent him from committing suicide, and as a matter of course, I perform my duty; but, between you and I, watching is quite useless, I've taken his measure properly enough. He's only crying because he's afraid of the guillotine. He's one of those chaps who are more anxious about their own skins, than about other persons'."

"Well, let's go and see him," interrupted M. Méchinet. "And above everything pray don't make a noise."

Thereupon, we all three turned round and walked on tiptoe to a door hard by. At the height of a man's head, a barred aperture had been cut in the stout oak panelling, so that the interior of the cell, badly lighted by a single gas burner, could be viewed from the passage. The gaoler gave a glance inside, M. Méchinet did the same, and then my turn followed. On a narrow iron bedstead, covered with a grey blanket with yellow stripes, I could perceive a man extended on his stomach, with his head buried in his hands. He was weeping, and his sobs were plainly audible. At times he quivered from head to foot with a kind of convulsive spasm; but otherwise he did not move.

"You may open the door now," said M. Méchinet to the keeper, after a moment's pause.

The man obeyed, and we all three walked into the cell. On hearing the key grate in the lock, the prisoner had raised himself to a sitting position, and now, with drooping arms and legs, and with his head leaning on his chest, he looked at us as if either stupefied or idotic. He was from five to eight and thirty years of age, rather above the medium height, with a broad chest, and a short apopletic neck. He was not a handsome man; far from it, for he had been grievously disfigured by the small-pox, and besides, his retreating forehead and long nose gave him altogether a simple, sheepish look. However, his blue eyes were very soft and winning, and his teeth were remarkably white and well set.

"What? monsieur Monistrol!" began my neighbour on entering the cell. "What! you are worrying yourself like that?" And he paused as if respecting a reply. But finding the unfortunate man speechless, he determined to tackle him in a different fashion. "Come, come," he accordingly resumed. "I agree that the situation isn't very lively; and yet, if I were in your place, I should like to prove that I'm a man. I should try to curb my grief, and set about proving my innocence."

"But I am not innocent," answered the prisoner, in a savage tone.

This time equivocation was out of place. There was apparently no longer any room left for doubt, for it was from Monistrol's own lips that we obtained this terrible confession. And yet M. Méchinet seemed scarcely satisfied. "What!" asked he, "was it really *you?*"

"Yes, it was I," interrupted the prisoner, springing to his feet with bloodshot eyes, and foaming mouth, as if he were seized with a sudden attack of madness. "It was I—I alone. How many more times must I repeat it? Why only a little while ago, a judge came here and I confessed everything to him, and even signed my confession. What more do you want? Oh, I know what's in store for me, and pray don't fancy that I'm afraid! Having killed, I must be killed in my turn as well; so chop off my head, and the sooner you do it, the better!"

Although, at first, somewhat disconcerted by this violent outburst, M. Méchinet promptly recovered himself. "Come, come," said he. "Wait a minute pray. People are not guillotined like that. First of all, they must be proved to be guilty. And then, justice takes due account of certain disorders of the mind, of certain sufferings and impulses—fatalities if you like—and it was indeed for that reason, that 'extenuating circumstances' were invented."

Monistrol's only reply was a long, low groan of mental agony.

"Now answer me," resumed M. Méchinet. "Did you really hate your uncle so much as all that? "

"Oh, no," promptly answered the prisoner.

"Well, then, why did you kill him?"

"I wanted his fortune," replied Monistrol in a panting voice. "My business was going to rack and ruin. You may make enquiries on that point. I needed money; and although my uncle was very rich, he wouldn't assist me."

"I understand," rejoined M. Méchinet. "And you hoped that you would escape detection?"

"Yes, I hoped so."

At this point, I began to understand why my neighbour was conducting the interrogatory in this desultory fashion, which at first had so surprised me, and I guessed what kind of trap he was preparing for the prisoner. Indeed, the very next moment he curtly asked, "By the way, where did you buy the revolver you shot your uncle with?"

I looked eagerly and anxiously at Monistrol, but he did not evince the least surprise. "Oh, I had it by me for some years," he replied.

"And what did you do with it, pray, after committing the crime?"

"I threw it away on the outer boulevard."

"Very good. I will have a search made, and no doubt we shall be able to find the person who must have picked it up."

While M. Méchinet spoke in this fashion—deliberately lying in order to arrive at the truth—his features retained an expression of imperturbable gravity. "What I can't understand," added he, after a moment's pause, "is that you should have taken your dog with you."

"What! my dog!" ejaculated the prisoner, with an air of genuine surprise.

"Ay, your dog, Pluto. The doorkeeper recognised him."

Monistrol clenched his fists, and his lips parted as if he were about to make some savage rejoinder, but at the same moment a new thought evidently darted through his mind, and he flung himself once more on his bed, exclaiming, in a tone of resolution, "That's enough torture; come, leave me to myself. At all events, I sha'n't answer any more."

As he was plainly bent on keeping his word, M. Méchinet refrained from insisting, and we left the cell together. We went silently downstairs, and crossed the passages and courtyards of the Préfecture, without exchanging a remark. But when we reached the quay, I could control my thoughts no longer. "Well, what do you think now?" I asked, catching my neighbour by the arm. "You heard what that unfortunate fellow said. He pretends to be guilty, and yet he doesn't even know how his uncle was killed. That question about the revolver was a stroke of genius on your part. How readily he fell into the trap! After that, it's plain enough that he's innocent; for, otherwise, he would have told us that he did the deed with a dagger, and not with a revolver, as you pretended."

"Perhaps so," answered the detective, and then, with a sceptical air, he added, "After all, who knows? I've met with so many actors in my time. But, at all events, that's enough for to-day. Let us go home. You must come and eat a mouthful at my place. To-morrow, when it's daylight, we'll continue our inquiry."

VII

It was ten o'clock at night when M. Méchinet, still followed by myself, rung at the door of his lodgings. "I never carry a key," he said to me, "for in our cursed trade no one knows what may happen. There are so many scoundrels who owe me a grudge, and besides, if I am not always prudent as concerns myself, I must be so for my wife."

My neighbour's explanation was superfluous, for I fully realised the dangers to which he must be exposed. And moreover, when I was previously watching him with the view of penetrating the secret of his seemingly mysterious life, I had already noticed that he rung at his door in a peculiar manner, evidently preconcerted between his wife and himself.

The bell was answered by pretty Madame Méchinet in person. With feline agility and grace, she flung her arms round her husband's neck, gave him a pair of passionate kisses, and gaily exclaimed, "Ah, so here you are at last! I don't know why, but I almost felt uneasy." But all of a sudden she paused, her bright smile died away, her brow lowered, and, loosening her hold around her husband's neck, she drew several paces back. The fact is, that she had just caught sight of me, standing close by, on the threshold. That Monsieur Méchinet and myself should return together at the same time—and so late at night—seemed to her a most suspicious circumstance. "What! have you only just left the café?" she asked, speaking as much to me as to her husband. "You have been there up till ten o'clock at night? Really, that's too bad!"

I turned to my neighbour for his reply. An indulgent smile flickered on his lips, and his attitude was that of a man who, confident in his wife's trustfulness, knows that he need only say one word to quiet her ruffled mind. "Don't be angry with us, Caroline," he exclaimed, thus associating me with his own cause. "We left the café hours ago, and we haven't been wasting our time. The fact is, I was fetched away on business—for a murder committed at Batignolles."

On hearing this, Madame Méchinet glanced suspiciously at both of us, and then, seemingly convinced that she was not being deceived, she curtly ejaculated, "Ah!"

The exclamation was brief enough, and yet it was full of meaning. It was evidently addressed to her husband, and signified, "So you have confided in that young man? You have made him acquainted with your profession, and you have revealed our secrets to him?" At least, that is how I understood the word, and my neighbour plainly construed its meaning in the same style, for he impetuously answered, "Well, yes, M. Godeuil has been with me this evening. And pray, where's the harm? If I have to fear the scoundrels whom I've handed up to justice, what need I fear from honest folks? Do you think, my dear, that I hide myself—that I am ashamed of my profession?"

"You misunderstood me, dear," objected Madame Méchinet.

But her husband did not even hear her. He had already sprung on to his favourite hobby, and, once astride, he was not easily persuaded to dismount. "Now, really," said he, "you have most singular ideas, my love. What! Here am I, a sentinel at the advanced posts of civilisation. I sacrifice my peace of mind, and risk my life to ensure the safety of society, and yet you think I ought to blush for my profession! It would be altogether too comical. You may tell me that there are a lot of foolish prejudices abroad respecting the police. No doubt there are, but what do I care for them? Oh! I know that there are a number of susceptible folks who pretend to look down on us. But, *sacrebleu*, I should like to see their faces, if my colleagues and myself were only to go on strike for a single day, leaving Paris at the mercy of the legion of scoundrels whom we keep in respect."

Madame Méchinet was no doubt accustomed to outbursts of this kind, for she did not answer a word; and indeed she acted wisely, for as soon as my neighbour perceived that there was no prospect of his being contradicted, he calmed down with surprising promptness. "Well, that'll do," said he; "just now we have a more pressing matter to deal with. We have neither of us dined, we are dying of hunger, and we should be glad to know if you have anything to give us to eat."

Plainly enough, Madame Méchinet often had to cope with similar emergencies, for, with a pleasant smile, she readily answered, "You shall be served in five minutes." And in fact, a moment later we were seated at table before a succulent joint of cold beef; while my neighbour's wife filled our glasses with one of those bright-coloured, refreshing wines, for which Macon enjoys renown. While M. Méchinet plied knife and fork with amazing earnestness, I glanced round the cosy little room, and stole a look at plump, pleasant-faced Madame Caroline, so attentive and so full of spirits— asking myself if this were really the abode of one of those "ferocious" detectives, so erroneously portrayed by ignorant novelists. However, the first requirements of hunger were soon appeased, and M. Méchinet then began to relate our expedition to his wife. He spoke with great precision, entering into the most minute particulars; and, seated beside him, she listened with an air of shrewd sagacity, interrupting him every now and then to ask for explanations on some obscure point, but without expressing any opinion of her own. However, I divined that her own views were to come, for, plainly enough, I was in presence of one of those homely Egerias, who are not merely accustomed to be consulted, but are also wont to give advice— and to see that advice followed. In fact, as soon as M. Méchinet had finished his narrative, she drew herself up, and exclaimed, "You have made one very great blunder, and, to my mind, an irreparable one."

"And what is that, pray?"

"Why, on leaving Batignolles, you ought not to have gone to the Préfecture."

"But Monistrol."

"Ah! yes, I know; you wanted to question him. But what was the use of it?"

"Well, my examination enlightened me—"

"Not at all. Instead of going to head-quarters you should have hurried to the Rue Vivienne, have seen the wife and questioned her. You would have surprised her while she was still under the effects of the emotion which her husband's arrest must necessarily have caused her; and if she was an accomplice in the crime, as must be supposed, you might, with a little skill, have easily made her confess."

On hearing this I almost sprung from my chair with surprise. "What?" cried I. "Do you really think that Monistrol is guilty, madame?"

She hesitated for a moment, and then replied, "Yes, I fancy so." On hearing that, I wished to urge my own views of the case, but she prevented me from doing so by swiftly resuming: "One thing I'm certain of—positively certain—the idea of that murder came from Monistrol's wife. Of every twenty crimes that men commit, fifteen are certainly planned or inspired by women. Just ask my husband if that is not the case. And besides, you ought to have been enlightened by the statements which the doorkeeper at Batignolles made. Who is this Madame Monistrol? You were told that she is very beautiful, very coquettish and ambitious, hankering after wealth, and wont to lead her husband by the nose. Now what was her position prior to the crime? Was it not needy, straightened, and precarious? She was greatly vexed no doubt; she suffered acutely at not being able to satisfy her tastes for expense; and we find proof of that in the fact that she asked her husband's uncle to lend them a large sum. The old man refused to do so and all her hopes were crushed. She must have hated him after that; and no doubt she often said to herself, 'If that old miser only died, we should be in comfortable circumstances.' But the old man still lived on; he was hale and hearty yet, and his fortune seemed a long way off. She no doubt asked herself, 'Is he going to live a hundred years? Why, at this rate, when he dies we shall have no teeth left, and besides, who can tell, perhaps he means to bury us.' That was undoubtedly her starting point. With such ideas in her head she was led by a natural gradation to think of committing a crime. And when she had determined in her own mind that, as the old man would not take himself off in the ordinary course of nature, he must be got rid of by foul means, she no doubt began to weigh on her husband, inspiring him with the idea of murder, and seeking to silence his qualms of conscience, till at last, when all was ripe, she virtually put the knife in his hand. Threatened with bankruptcy, maddened by his wife's lamentations, the unfortunate fellow started off, and murdered his uncle in a foolish, blundering manner no doubt, and without even thinking of the consequences that might overtake himself."

"All that is logical enough," opined M. Méchinet, when his wife, who had worked herself into a state of considerable excitement whilst speaking, at length brought her address to a close.

Logical—yes, no doubt it was; but then, what became of the various particulars we had noted? I could not forget my own observations at Batignolles; and so, turning to Madame Méchinet, I asked her, "Then you think that Monistrol was fool enough to denounce himself by writing his own name in blood, on the floor?"

"Fool enough?" she answered, with a slight shrug of the shoulders. "But come now, was it such an act of folly after all? I myself don't think so; for it is this very circumstance that constitutes your greatest argument in favour of his innocence."

This reasoning was so specious that I was for a moment disconcerted. "But he confesses his guilt," I urged, as soon as I recovered myself.

"Well, that's an excellent system to induce the police to establish his innocence."

"Oh, madame!"

"Why, you yourself are proof of that, Monsieur Godeuil."

"But the unfortunate fellow doesn't even know *how* his uncle was murdered."

"Excuse me, suppose he only *pretended* that he didn't know it—that would be a very different thing."

My discussion with Madame Méchinet was becoming heated, and no doubt it would have lasted some time longer, if at this point her husband had not thought fit to intervene. "Come, come, Caroline," said he, "you are really too romantic to-night." And speaking to me, he added, "I will knock at your door to-morrow morning, and we will go together to see Madame Monistrol. For the present, good-night. I'm quite tired and half asleep already."

He was a happy man, my neighbour, to be able to sleep in blissful forgetfulness of the problem waiting to be solved. No doubt he had only acquired this faculty of isolating his mind from his daily labours after long years of practice and experience. He had had to deal with so many crimes before, he had had. to investigate such strange, mysterious cases, and almost invariably with satisfactory results, that he probably considered it futile to rack his mind, at night-time, anent such an affair as this; knowing well enough that when he awoke refreshed on the morrow, he would be able to weigh and estimate all the accumulated items of evidence with a clear head. But then, I was very differently situated; I stood on the threshold of *terra incognita*, too absorbed and perplexed for my thoughts to allow me a moment's rest. Thus I did not close my eyes all night. A mysterious voice seemed to rise from the innermost recesses of my being and murmur, "Monistrol is innocent!" I pictured to myself the unfortunate fellow's sufferings as he lay extended on his camp bedstead at the Depot; and at the thought that his agony was perhaps undeserved my heart softened with compassion. But then, in the midst of these phases of pity, the same question invariably returned to my mind, rekindling all my perplexity, "If Monistrol were really innocent, why had he pleaded guilty?"

VIII

What lacked me in those days—as I subsequently had a hundred occasions of observing—was experience, professional practice, and exact knowledge of the means of investigation at the disposal of the police. I vaguely realised that this inquiry had been conducted in a far too haphazard, superficial manner; but I should have been greatly embarrassed had I been called upon to point out the mistakes that had been made, or to say what ought to have been done. And yet at the same time I took, as I have already said, a passionate interest in Monistrol. It indeed seemed to me as if his cause were mine;

and, after all, the feeling was but a natural one, for was not my own reputation for acumen at stake? The first doubt concerning his guilt had been occasioned by an observation I myself had made, and it seemed to me as if I were now bound to prove his innocence.

But then my discussion with Madame Méchinet, and the latter's romantic and yet not illogical theories, had so disconcerted me that I did not know what fact to select for the foundation of my defence. At each circumstance I turned to I was met by Madame Caroline's objections, and I wandered restlessly from one to the other without knowing at which to pause. As always happens when the mind is applied during too long a time to the solution of a problem, my ideas at last became as entangled as a skein in a child's hands. I could distinguish nothing clearly, and was only conscious of chaos.

It was nine o'clock in the morning, and I was still busy torturing my brain, when M. Méchinet, mindful of the promise he had made the night before, entered my room to inform me that it was time to start. "Come, come," said he; "let us be off."

I sprang to my feet at once, and followed him out of the room. We hastily went downstairs, and on reaching the street I noticed that my worthy neighbour was rather more carefully dressed than usual. He had succeeded in giving himself that well-to-do, easily-pleased air which Parisian shopkeepers delight to find among their customers; and he was, moreover, radiant with all the gaiety of a man who knows that he is marching to certain victory. "Well?" he asked, as we talked down the Rue Racine, side by side; "well, what do you think of my wife? The big guns at the Préfecture consider me to be a shrewd fellow, and yet you see I consult her; and I may add, that I have often done so with profit. After all, where's the harm? Wasn't Molière in the habit of consulting his servant? Caroline certainly has one little failing, as perhaps you may have noticed. To her mind there are no stupid crimes, and so she invests every scamp with most diabolical powers of invention. However, my failing is just of the opposite kind. While she is always hunting after romance, I am rather too much inclined to look merely at positive facts. But, by combining our two systems—taking a little of the one, and a little of the other— it generally happens that we ultimately arrive at the truth."

"What!" cried I, interrupting M. Méchinet; "do you think that you have penetrated this Monistrol mystery?"

He stopped short, drew his huge snuff-box from his pocket, took three or four imaginary pinches, according to his wont, and then, in a tone of mingled reserve and satisfaction, replied, "Well, at least I possess the means of penetrating it."

"Oh!" stammered I, wondering what this means might be, and yet deterred from further questioning by my companion's air of discretion.

But my mind was soon busy with a new train of thought. Crossing the Seine by the Pont des Arts, and traversing the court-yard of the Louvre, we had made for our destination by way of the Rue Croix des Petits Champs and the Bank of France. The streets were all alive with traffic; merchants and clerks were hurrying in and out of the bank; the neighbouring shops displayed a variety of costly wares. Signs of luxurious prosperity were indeed apparent on every side, and as I noted them I could not help remembering that surroundings often have a decisive influence on character. What indeed was Clara Monistrol, according to Mme. Méchinet's theory? An ambitious, coquettish woman, fond of display, hankering after wealth, and envious of other folks' good fortune. Even if the evil grain had not pre-existed in her mind, might not the seeds of covetousness have been sown by life in such a centre? The Rue Vivienne is no fit abode for poverty or struggling circumstances. From one end to another you can hear the jingle of specie and the rustle of flimsies. Here are the Boulevards—all life, splendour, and display; here at mid-distance is the Bourse—the Giant Temple of Mammon—crowded each afternoon with the devotees of fortune; here, at each step you take, are the offices of money-changers, stock-brokers, and bill-discounters; and even when wealth does not assert itself in the shape of bullion, notes, and shares, it is present in a thousand other forms. Here is some shop-window crowded with precious works of art; here are tantalising toilettes and bewitching bonnets; and here, at the photograph stores, are portraits upon portraits of wonderfully-adorned actresses, and elegant belles of society—all appealing to the mind of a covetous woman, eager for wealth and anxious to be admired. And note that the Bank of France, with its cellars full of millions, is but a stone's throw off; and that the Palais Royal, with its galleries scintillating with diamonds, stands at the top of the street. What a neighbourhood for such a woman as Madame Monistrol! If the portrait sketched by the doorkeeper of Batignolles were faithful to reality, and if Mme. Méchinet's deductions were correct, must not Clara Monistrol have endured unspeakable torture, living, in her comparative poverty, in the midst of this El Dorado? Must she not have been perpetually tantalised, tempted, goaded on by the every-day spectacle of all this wealth—of all these pricely wares, of all these costly adornments? She had looked no doubt with hungry eyes on many a coveted object, and the thought that there was only that little old man at Batignolles between her present envy and the attainment of her desires, had returned and returned, with increasing force, until at last she was persuaded to instigate this crime. Looking at the case in this light, and leaving my previous observations on one side, it really seemed to assume a very different aspect.

But I was unable to carry my deductions further, for, at this point, worthy M. Méchinet interrupted my reverie. We had just reached the Rue Vivienne, and stood at the corner of the National Library. "Now, follow me," said my neighbour; "keep your eyes and ears open, but don't speak unless we remain alone; and, no matter what happens, be careful not to express any surprise."

He did well to warn me, for otherwise I should not have failed to manifest my astonishment at the course he took a moment later, Abruptly crossing the street, he walked straight into an umbrella shop—one of those fashionable establishments where only the most costly articles are sold. As stiff and as grave as an Englishman, he made the mistress of the shop show him, in turn, well nigh every umbrella she had in stock. But nothing seemed to please him; he rejected even the most perfect articles, always having some objection ready to meet the praises which the shopkeeper lavished on her goods. At last, he asked her if she could not undertake to make him an umbrella on a pattern he would furnish. "It would be the simplest thing in the world," she answered; and thereupon M. Méchinet promised that he would return on the morrow with the pattern in question. The woman conducted us back to the door with many marks of deference—for, in Paris, the more fastidious a customer shows himself, the more he rises in a dealer's esteem—and the next moment we stood on the pavement outside, myself with admiration glowing on my face, and M. Méchinet with a radiant air of self-satisfaction.

The fact is, that he had good reason to be satisfied, for the half-hour spent in that shop had by no means been thrown away. Whilst examining all the umbrellas that were shown to him, he had skilfully contrived to pump the shopwoman of all she knew about the Monistrols, both man and wife. After all, it was a comparatively easy matter, for the murder of the little old man of Batignolles, and the arrest of the dealer in imitation jewellery, had caused a perfect sensation throughout the neighbourhood of the Rue Vivienne, and formed the one great topic of current gossip.

"There!" exclaimed M. Méchinet, as we proceeded slowly along the street. "There, that's how we obtain trustworthy information! If I presented myself in my real character, folks would assume a pompous air, launch forth grandiloquent phrases about vice and virtue, and then good-bye to plain, simple, unvarnished truth!"

My neighbour enacted the same little comedy in seven or eight other shops of various kinds along the street; and in one establishment, where the dealer and his wife at first showed themselves somewhat reserved and taciturn, he contrived to loosen their tongues by expending a "Napoleon" on a little purchase. To my amusement we spent a couple of hours or so in this fashion, and then M. Méchinet opined that further inquiries would be superfluous, for we now knew enough to guage the current of public opinion. In point of fact, we were very fairly acquainted with what the tradesfolk of the neighbourhood thought of M. and Madame Monistrol, who had resided in the Rue Vivienne ever since their marriage, some four years previously.

There was but one opinion concerning the husband. He was, according to general report, a very good-natured, worthy man—obliging, honest, industrious, and fairly intelligent. It was scarcely his fault, we were told, if his business had not prospered. Fortune does not always smile on those who are most deserving of her favours. Monistrol, it appeared, had acted unwisely in taking a shop which seemed fated to bankruptcy, for, within a period of fifteen years, four dealers of different trades had failed in it. The jeweller was greatly attached to his wife—every one knew it, and repeated it; but he had not unduly paraded his affection, or shown himself extravagantly uxorious and jealous. None of the people whom M. Méchinet questioned believed in Monistrol's guilt. In fact, they invariably remarked: "The police must have made a mistake, and will soon find it out."

In reference to Madame Monistrol opinions were on one point divided. Some of the neighbours considered that her tastes were of too elegant a character for her position, whilst others opined that in a shop like her husband's, it was imperative that the mistress should be fashionably attired. However, it was only on this question that our informants differed. They united in declaring that Madame Monistrol was greatly attached to her husband. Her virtue, they said, was unimpeachable. No one had ever heard of her flirting or carrying her coquetry beyond the bounds of personal adornment; and one individual naively remarked that her conduct in this respect was most meritorious, for she was remarkably beautiful, and had any number of admirers. But she had always remained deaf to their pleadings, and her reputation as a faithful wife was absolutely immaculate.

This information plainly worried M. Méchinet. "It's wonderful," said he to me. "No slander, no back-biting, no queer little stories of misconduct! I begin to think that my wife must have been mistaken. According to her idea, Madame Monistrol ought to have been one of those brazen beauties who rule the household, and who are fonder of displaying their own charms than their husband's merchandise, one of those women, indeed, whose husbands are either blind fools or else shameful accomplices. And yet I find nothing of all that. The very most that people say, is, that she is rather fond of dress, but then that's the case with wellnigh every pretty woman in the world; and because she has a few elegant whims and a little taste we've no right to brand her with infamy."

I made no reply to these remarks. To tell the truth, I was quite as disconcerted as the detective. What a difference between the fairly eulogious statements made by the neighbours and the disparaging assertions of the doorkeeper at Batignolles! However, perhaps the discrepancy might be explained; for, as it occurred to my mind just then, people in different circumstances take different views of things. And moreover, opinions vary with localities. What seems altogether scandalous and disgraceful in the

Rue de Lécluse is justifiable, seemly, and even requisite in the Rue Vivienne. The staid and quiet quarter of Batignolles, and the ostentatious easy going district of the Bourse can scarcely be expected to share the same notions of morality.

However, we had already spent too much time in prosecuting our inquiry to think of pausing to discuss our impressions and conjectures. "Now," said M. Méchinet, "Before we tackle the enemy let's have a look at his quarters." And familiar with the practise of carrying on these delicate investigations in the midst of the traffic and bustle of Paris, he drew me under an arched gateway situated just in front of Monistrol's shop.

It was a modest-looking shop indeed, almost a beggarly one, when compared with the fashionable establishments around. The weather-stained front, for instance, sadly required a coat of paint. Above the windows one could read the name of "MONISTROL," formerly traced in gilt letters, but now blackened and dingy, whilst across the panes of glass, on either side of the door, ran the inscription, "GOLD AND IMITATION." Among the articles displayed to view there were, however, but few of standard ore. The imitation goods formed nineteen-twentieths of the stock. Steel-gilt chains, jet ornaments, diadems to which Rhine stones and strass lent a fugitive subdued brilliancy, imitation coral necklets, with brooches, rings, studs, and sleeve links set with false stones of every hue, were displayed in considerable profusion, but their spurious character was altogether too evident for the passing window thief to be deceived.

"Well, let's go in," said I to M. Méchinet, after making a brief survey of the shop.

But the detective was less impatient than myself, or rather he was more expert in restraining his impatience, for catching me by the arm, he exclaimed, "One moment please. Before entering, I should just like to have a glimpse of Madame Monistrol."

However, although we remained for another twenty minutes at our post of observation under the archway, the shop remained deserted. There were no signs whatever of the beautiful Madame Clara, and indeed, we did not even perceive a shop boy or a shop girl behind the counter. "Well, well, that's enough waiting," opined my companion at last. "Come on, Monsieur Godeuil, let us chance it."

IX

To reach Monistrol's shop we had only to cross the street, a feat we performed in four strides. On hearing us open the door a slatternly looking little servant girl, of fifteen or sixteen years of age, with a dirty face and ill-combed hair, came out of a room in the rear of the shop. "What do the gentlemen require?" asked she.

"Is Madame Monistrol indoors?"

"Yes, sir, she's in the room there, and I'll run and tell her you want her, for, you see—"

But M. Méchinet did not allow the maid to finish. He roughly pushed her aside, and exclaimed: "That'll do; as she's there, I'll go and speak to her." And the next moment he walked straight into the room at the rear of the shop.

I followed close behind him on the tiptoe of curiosity and expectation, feeling as it were a kind of presentiment that this visit would result in an explanation of the mystery. I required some little energy to preserve an appearance of calmness, for to tell the truth, my mind was terribly excited, and I could hear my temples throb, and my heart beat pit-a-pat, with most unwonted violence.

The apartment in the rear of the shop was a dreary looking chamber, which apparently did joint duty, as dining-room, drawing-room and bed-room. It was in a state of considerable disorder, and its appointments were such as are common to the abodes of people in straightened circumstances who wish to appear rich. At the further end stood a bedstead partially concealed by pretentiously draped curtains of blue damask. The pillow cases were fringed round with lace and embroidered with huge initial letters, and the rug at the foot of the bed was a flowery imitation of the Aubusson style. In striking contrast with this attempted display of magnificence, appeared the table in the centre of the room. Its greasy oil cloth covering was bestrewn with the remnants of what could not have been a particularly appetising breakfast, served in crockery of the commonest kind. Reclining beside this table in a capacious arm chair, I perceived a young woman, with fair hair and blue eyes, who held between her fingers a legal document on stamped paper. This then was the beautiful Madame Monistrol. Her charms had certainly not been exaggerated. She was slightly above the average height, but admirably proportioned, as with my professional knowledge of anatomy I easily perceived, despite her somewhat recumbent position. Her nose would have done honour to a Grecian beauty, and her lips—although somewhat deficient in colour, a circumstance no doubt due to emotion—offered the graceful curves of Cupid's bow. Her ears were particularly tiny and well-shaped, and her bowed neck, on which lingered the wavy curls of her back hair, seemed as white and as smooth as polished alabaster. Her feet could not be seen from where I stood; but no doubt they were as exquisitely modelled as her hands, which with their fair white skin, their network of pale blue veins, and their tapering fingers tipped with glistening pink nails, would have fairly sent an artist into raptures.

It would be futile to conceal it. I was at first fairly dazzled by this woman's amazing beauty, and reversing all Madame Méchinet's theories anent her culpability, I decided in my own mind, that it was quite impossible such a lovely creature could have instigated the heinous crime of the Rue de Lécluse. But this impression only lasted for a moment, so contradictory and so versatile indeed were my ideas at that prefatory epoch of my career as a detective. It was her dress that made me change my mind. She was in deep mourning, wearing a robe of black crape, cut slightly low at the neck. Now black is admirably adapted to set off fair complexions, and naturally enough this toilette greatly enhanced Mademoiselle Clara's charms. But on reflection, it seemed to me that a person labouring under deep grief, a prey in fact to harrowing sorrow, would scarcely have had the requisite presence of mind to array herself in this preposessing style; and I could not help asking myself, if Madame Monistrol were not, after all, an actress who had deliberately assumed the costume of the part she meant to play.

On perceiving us enter the room, she sprang to her feet like a frightened doe, and asked in a tearful voice: "What do you desire, gentlemen?"

From the gleam in M. Méchinet's eyes I could judge that he had mentally made the same remarks as myself. "Madame," he answered, sternly, "I am sent here by the judicial authorities. I am an agent of the detective police."

At this announcement she sunk back into her arm-chair, sobbing, and to all appearance overcome; but suddenly, inflamed as it were with nervous enthusiasm, with bright eyes and quivering lips, she rose once more to her feet, exclaiming in impassioned tones: "Do you come to arrest me, then? Ah! I could bless you for it. Come, I am ready. Lead me away! Let me join the honest man whom you arrested last night! Whatever may be his fate I wish to share it. He is as guiltless as I am myself; but no matter, if he is fated to be the victim of a judicial error, it will be a last joy for me to die beside him!"

She was interrupted by a prolonged growl, coming from one of the corners of the room. I looked up and perceived a black dog, who showed his teeth and glared at us as if he meant mischief. "Down, Pluto, down!" exclaimed Madame Monistrol. "Come, go to bed and keep quiet. These gentlemen don't mean me any harm."

At first the animal seemed disinclined to obey his mistress's command, but at last, without once averting his glaring gaze, he slowly backed under the bedstead, where in the shadow I could still distinguish his bright eyes fixed upon us.

"You are right in saying that we don't mean you any harm, madame," remarked M. Méchinet. "We have not come to arrest you." He no doubt trusted that this intelligence would draw from her some expression of feeling indicative of her hopes or fears; but he was mistaken, for she did not seem to heed it.

"This morning," she resumed, glancing at the paper in her hand, "I received this summons, which orders me to be at the office of an investigating magistrate at the Palace of Justice, at three o'clock this afternoon. What can be wanted of me, good heavens! what can be wanted of me?"

"Why, information, madame," promptly answered M. Méchinet. "Information that may enlighten justice, and, as I hope, prove your husband's innocence. Pray don't look on me as an enemy. Indeed, so far as my professional character allows, I sincerely sympathise with you in your misfortune. My only object, my only ambition is to arrive at the truth." So saying my neighbour drew forth his snuff-box and took a score or so of imaginary pinches. "You will therefore understand, madame," he resumed, in a solemn tone which I had never heard him employ before; "you will understand how important may prove your answers to the questions I shall have the honour of asking you. And so may I beg you to answer me frankly!"

For fully half a minute Madame Clara fixed her big blue eyes on my neighbour and gazed at him through her tears. "Question me, monsieur," she said at last.

For the third time I must repeat it; I was altogether without experience, and yet the manner in which M. Méchinet had initiated this interrogatory caused me intense dissatisfaction. It seemed to me that he betrayed all his perplexity and wandered on in hap-hazard fashion, instead of marching straight towards a pre-determined object. Ah! how my tongue itched! Howl should have liked to intervene. If I had only dared. But then, of course, I was no one; I had no *locus standi*, and was merely there on sufferance. However, during the last few minutes, my worthy neighbour had greatly fallen in my estimation. I forgot the clever manner in which he had questioned Monistrol the night before; and it seemed to me that if he were well up in the routine of his profession, he was, at all events, quite deficient in that analytical, investigative genius, without which a man cannot hope to become a great detective. Indeed, it really seemed to me that I was his superior in the latter respect, despite my comparative youth and imperfect knowledge of men and things; and hence I suffered all the more acutely at having to stand still and listen to what I considered his blunders, without any right to intervene and repair them.

My worthy neighbour was, of course, blissfully ignorant of what was passing in my mind. Seating himself on a chair in front of Madame Monistrol, he began as follows: "As no doubt you are aware, madame, it was after nine o'clock on the night before last that Monsieur Pigoreau, or Anténor, as some people called him—in one word—your husband's uncle—was murdered at Batignolles."

"Alas! yes; so I have been told," answered Madame Clara.

"Now can you tell me," continued the detective, "where Monsieur Monistrol was between nine o'clock and midnight?"

"Ah, Lord!" groaned the jeweller's wife, clasping her hands with anguish. "What a fatality!"

M. Méchinet paid no heed to the exclamation. "Excuse me," he resumed; "you must be able to tell us where your husband was on the evening before last?"

It was some little time before Madame Monistrol was able to reply, for sobs were rising in her throat and seemed to choke her utterance. At last, mastering her grief, she murmured: "On the day before yester-day my husband spent the evening away from home."

"Do you know where he was?"

"Ah, yes, I can tell you that. One of our work-people, living at Montrouge, was engaged on a set of false pearls, and had failed to deliver them as promised. We were afraid that the person who had ordered them of us would leave them on our hands, which would have been very annoying, for we are far from rich, and business is bad enough already. So, while we were at dinner that evening, my husband said to me: 'I think I had better go to Montrouge and see if those pearls are not ready yet.' And sure enough, after dinner—rather before nine o'clock—he went out, and I accompanied him as far as the corner of the Rue de Richelieu, where I saw him take the omnibus myself."

I began to breathe again. My original idea had been the right one, and Monistrol was innocent; for surely his wife's reply meant an unimpeachable *alibi*. M. Méchinet no doubt had the same thought, for he continued in a softer tone. "If that is the case, your workman could state that M. Monistrol was with him somewhere about eleven o'clock?"

"Ah! unfortunately no."

"No? And why not pray?"

"Because he was not at home. My husband did not see him."

"That is a great misfortune. But still the doorkeeper of the house must have known of M. Monistrol's visit."

"No, monsieur. In fact there is no doorkeeper in the house where our workman lives."

This might be the truth. Similar things have been heard of before; and yet the judicial authorities would undoubtedly consider the circumstance as a most suspicious one, indeed as an additional indication of the prisoner's guilt. At all events, with such glaring absence of proof, the plea of an *alibi* became quite untenable. Was it this, then, that had impelled Monistrol to plead guilty? Had he realised that this improbable story of a journey to Montrouge, to a workman who was not at home, and who lived in a house where there was no doorkeeper, would only cause both judge and jury to shrug their shoulders with contempt? Perhaps he had. He had very likely said to himself, "I am the victim of a fatal combination of circumstances. My statements would be set down as a parcel of lies, concocted in the vain hope of saving myself from the guillotine. I should be doubly branded with infamy; and so it is best that I should accept my fate and bow my head to the last stroke of that ill luck which has so persistently followed me through life."

Whilst I was pursuing this train of thought, M. Méchinet had resumed his interrogatory. "At what time did your husband come home?" he asked.

"At sometime after midnight."

"Didn't you think he had been a long while gone."

"Oh yes! Indeed, I spoke to him about it, but he said he had come back on foot, and loitered on his way. If I recollect rightly, he had rested in a café and drunk a glass of beer."

"And pray what did he look like when he came home?"

"Well, he looked annoyed, but that was only natural."

"What clothes was he wearing?"

"The same as when he was arrested."

"And you didn't notice anything extraordinary about his manner or appearance."

"No, nothing."

X

Standing, at a few paces behind M. Méchinet, I was able to watch Madame Monistrol's features at leisure, and take due note of her slightest change of expression. She seemed to be overcome with deep grief, and big tears streamed down her pale cheeks. And yet at certain moments I fancied I could detect something like a suppressed gleam of joy in the depths of her big, blue eyes. "Is she guilty then?" I asked myself. This was not the first time that the idea had occurred to me, and now, as I stood there watching the jeweller's wife, it returned and returned with such obstinate persistency, that at last I could control myself no longer. Forgetful of M. Méchinet's recommendations, oblivious of the fact that I had no right to interfere in the proceedings, I took a few steps forward, and roughly asked: "But you, madame, where were you on that fatal evening, while your husband was uselessly journeying to Montrouge, to see his workman?"

She raised her blue eyes to mine, gave me a long look of surprise, and then softly answered: "I was here, monsieur, as witnesses can prove to you."

"Witnesses!"

"Yes, monsieur. It was so very warm that evening, that I felt I should like an ice. As it worried me to take it alone, I sent my servant to invite two of my neighbours, Madame Dorstrich, the boot-maker's wife, next door, and Madame Rivaille, who keeps the glove shop over the way. They both accepted my invitation, and remained here with me till half-past eleven o'clock. You may question them, and they will tell you that such was the case. In the midst of all these cruel trials, this accidental circumstance is really a favour from on high."

Was the circumstance of such a purely accidental character as Madame Monistrol pretended? This is what we asked each other, M. Méchinet and myself, by means of a rapid questioning glance. When chance acts so appropriately, it may well have been assisted. At least, this is what I thought, and the swift gleam that shot from my neighbour's eyes in my direction seemed to imply that his opinion was the same. However, this was scarcely the moment for an exchange of observations, which would assuredly have proved suspicious to Madame Monistrol.

"You have never been suspected, madame," declared M. Méchinet, with rare effrontery. "The worst that was supposed was that your husband might perhaps have said something to you before committing this crime."

"Ah! monsieur!" ejaculated Madame Monistrol. "Ah! if you only knew us!"

"One moment, pray. We have been told that your husband's business was not a prosperous one, that he was in needy circumstances."

"Yes, lately, it is true; trade has not been very bright."

"Now your husband must have been very worried and anxious on account of his precarious position. He must have particularly suffered on thinking of you, his wife, to whom he was so attached. For your sake, more than for himself, your husband must have longed to attain a position of ease and fortune."

"Ah! monsieur, I can only repeat it, he is innocent."

M. Méchinet assumed a pensive air, and pretended to fill his nose with snuff; but suddenly raising his head again he exclaimed: "Then, *sacrebleu*, how do you explain his confession? For an innocent man to plead guilty as soon as the crime he stands accused of is mentioned to him is most singular, madame—singular, and indeed astounding."

A fleeting blush coloured Madame Méchinet's cheeks, and for the first time, since the beginning of the interrogatory, her glance wavered. Was this to be interpreted as a sign of guilt? "I suppose," she answered in a low voice, which a fresh fit of sobbing rendered almost inaudible; "I suppose that my poor husband was so frightened and stupified at finding himself accused of such a frightful crime, that he fairly lost his head."

M. Méchinet shrugged his shoulders. "At the very most," said he, "the idea of passing delirium might be entertained; but after a long night's reflection, M. Monistrol has this very morning persisted in his original avowals."

Was this true? Had my worthy neighbour been to the Préfecture before calling me, or had he deemed it useful to make this statement without authority? At all events, the news had a crushing effect on Madame Monistrol. She turned ashy white, and I really thought that she was going to faint. We were both looking at her intently, and it seemed as if she could not bear our gaze, for suddenly she hid her face in her hands and murmured, "O Lord, Lord, my poor husband has gone mad."

Such was certainly not *my* opinion. In fact, I had very different views. I was becoming more and more convinced that this scene, so far as Madame Clara was concerned, was merely so much pure comedy. Her great despair was to my mind so much affectation, and I asked myself if she were not in some fashion or other the cause of her husband's singular attitude, and if she were not also acquainted with the true culprit. Whilst I was thinking, however, M. Méchinet continued to talk. He endeavoured to console Madame Monistrol by a few set phrases which could not possibly compromise him, and then gave her to understand that she might silence a great many suspicions by allowing him to make a minute perquisition throughout the establishment. She accepted the suggestion with unfeigned alacrity and pleasure. "Everything is at your disposal, gentlemen," said she. "Examine everything. I shall really feel obliged by your doing so; and besides it won't take you very long, for we only rent the shop, this room, our servant's room on the top floor, and a little cellar. Here are the keys of everything!"

To my very great astonishment, M. Méchinet expressed his readiness to make a search at once; and forthwith he began ferreting round the room, examining everything with the greatest attention. What could be his object? I wondered. Surely he must have some secret motive; for was it likely that such a perquisition—so readily authorised—would lead to any important discovery? After exploring the shop and the room with as much care as if he had expected to light upon the missing link in our chain of evidence, he turned to Madame Monistrol and remarked: "Well, there's only the cellar left for us to look at now."

"I'll show you the way, monsieur," she answered; and taking a candlestick and a box of lucifers from off the mantelpiece, she conducted us out of the room into a courtyard behind.

We descended a score of slippery stone steps by the light of the flickering candle, and halted in front of an old door covered with cobwebs and mildew. "Here's the cellar," observed Madame Monistrol, unfastening the padlock; and the next moment pushing back the door she led the way inside. It was a damp, ill-kept vault, and its contents were in keeping with the Monistrols' needy circumstances. In one corner was a little barrel of beer, and just in front a cask of wine, more or less securely perched on a few logs of wood. Taps were affixed both to the beer barrel and the wine cask, showing that they were both on draught. On the right hand side were three or four dozen bottles of wine, probably of a superior kind, ranged on lathes; and in a third corner an equal number of empty bottles could be perceived. I was now beginning to realise M. Méchinet's object. He scarcely glanced at the casks, but taking the candle from Madame Monistrol, he scrutinised the full and the empty bottles with equal attention. I carefully followed his inspection, and like himself I noted that not one of these bottles was sealed with green wax. Thus the inference was, that the cork discovered on the floor in the bed-room at Batignolles, and in which the murderer had evidently imbedded his dagger's point, had not come from Monistrol's cellar. As M. Méchinet was almost as prepossessed as myself in favour of the jeweller's innocence, this result ought to have delighted him; but whatever may have been his secret feelings, he thought fit to assume a look of intense disappointment and remarked, "Well, I find nothing—nothing at all; so I think we may go upstairs again."

I walked the first on this occasion, and thus reached the room in the rear of the shop before the others. Scarcely had I opened the door when Pluto, the black dog with the glaring eyes and ferocious growl, sprang from his resting place under the bed in such a threatening manner that I instinctively retreated a few paces back.

"He seems to be an unpleasant customer that dog of yours," said M. Méchinet to Madame Monistrol.

"No, no," she answered with a wave of the hand, which calmed Pluto as if by magic. " He's a good fellow, but then, you know, he's a watchdog. We jewellers have so many thieves to fear; and so we have trained him to keep a sharp look out."

The animal was quiet enough now that his mistress was beside him; and wishing to coax him into a more friendly disposition, I called him by his name: "Here, Pluto, here!"

"Oh, it's quite useless for you to call him," carelessly remarked Madame Monistrol. "He won't obey you."

"Indeed! Why not?"

"Why, like all dogs of his breed, he's very faithful. He only knows his master and me."

Many people would have considered such an answer to be altogether insignificant, and yet to me it was as a ray of light shed on the mystery we were investigating. Without pausing to reflect, yielding to the first impulse that entered my head, I eagerly asked: "And pray, madame, where was this faithful dog on the night of the crime?"

So great was Madame Monistrol's emotion and surprise at being asked this question, point blank, that she started back and almost let her candlestick fall from her hand. "I don't know," she stammered; "I don't recollect—"

"Perhaps he followed your husband," I resumed.

"Yes—now I think of it. I fancy he did."

"So you have trained him to follow vehicles then; for you told us that you saw your husband get on the 'bus."

She made no rejoinder, and I was about to continue when M. Méchinet forestalled me. Far from seeking to profit by Madame Monistrol's confusion, he did everything he could to set her mind at ease, and after advising her in her own interest to comply with the summons she had received from the investigating magistrate, he bade her good morning, and led me away.

"Have you lost your head?" he asked, when we had walked a few yards down the street.

Lost my head, indeed! Such a remark was fairly an insult. "You are really too hard on me, M. Méchinet," said I. "Few people in their senses could have done more than I have just accomplished. For if I haven't solved the problem, at all events I've shown how it may be solved. Monistrol's dog will lead us to the truth."

This outburst made my worthy neighbour smile. "You are right," said he in a paternal tone; "I quite understood your question about the dog. Only I fear you put it too abruptly. If Madame Monistrol has divined your suspicions, you may be sure that the animal will be dead, or have disappeared before the day is over."

XI

Yes, I had certainly been most imprudent. There could be no doubt of that. But on the other hand, I had discovered the weak point in the enemy's armour, the flaw which would enable us to penetrate a most artful system of defence. My worthy neighbour was fairly bowled over. Here was he, a celebrity so to say in his profession, possessed of vast experience, and said to be most shrewd. Now, what result had he arrived at during this long interrogatory? Just none at all. He had wandered through and through the maze without finding the smallest outlet, whilst I, a mere apprentice, had discovered the right road at my very first venture. Another man might have shown himself jealous of my success, but M. Méchinet was not given to envious thoughts. His only desire was to utilise my discovery to the very best advantage; and accordingly we decided to hold council at a neighbouring restaurant, one of the best places for a *déjeuner à la fourchette* in this part of Paris.

Without neglecting to ply our knives and forks, for our morning's labours had whetted our appetites to the right degree, we began by establishing the exact position of the problem, so as to arrive more readily at the required solution. To our minds Monistrol's innocence was a moral certainty; and we thought we could guess why he had pleaded guilty. However, for the time being, this was a question of secondary importance. As regards Madame Monistrol we were equally certain that she had not left her neighbourhood on the night of the crime; for it was no doubt perfectly true that she had merely accompanied her husband as far as the omnibus in the Rue de Richelieu, and that she had then returned home and spent the whole evening, as she said, in the company of two of her acquaintances. But although it might be proved that she could not possibly have taken any material part in the perpetration of the crime, there remained the charge of moral complicity, in respect of which a logical sequence of deductions seemed to prove her guilt. To our minds she had been fully acquainted with the crime—even if she had not indeed advised and prepared it—and consequently she knew the murderer.

Now, who could the murderer be? Must he not be some man whom Pluto, the black dog, was accustomed to obey quite as readily as he obeyed his master and mistress? For we had unimpeachable evidence that the dog had accompanied the assassin to Batignolles. It is true that, before Madame Monistrol was formally questioned on the subject of the dog, she had casually stated that he only obeyed his master and herself; but her subsequent embarrassment pointed to a very different conclusion. Plainly enough Pluto was in the habit of obeying some third person, with whose name we were so far unacquainted. This person must, however, be a very frequent visitor to the Monistrols' shop, for we ourselves had seen how the dog was in the habit of receiving strangers. And yet, although a frequent visitor, he could scarcely be a friend (at least so far as Monsieur Monistrol was concerned), for the crime at Batignolles had been perpetrated in such a manner as to make the jeweller's guilt seem certain. The murderer must therefore be one of M. Monistrol's bitter enemies, for hatred alone could have inspired such fiendish cunning. But on the other hand he must be very dear indeed to *Madame* Monistrol; for, although she knew his name as was morally proven, she refrained from denouncing him, preferring to abandon her husband to the cruel fate he did not deserve.

This course of reasoning could have but one conclusion: Madame Monistrol must have a favoured lover, and that lover must be the murderer of Batignolles. Her neighbours of the Rue Vivienne had no doubt given her a certificate of virtue, but under the circumstances their assurances were insufficient. Women who enjoy the very highest reputations often carry on some shameful secret intrigue for years and years, and are honoured as models of faithfulness and virtue, whereas, if their sin were known, they would be turned from with horror and loathing. Some faithless women possess extraordinary powers of deception, and go to the grave without having been once detected. When started on the road of error, their minds prove fertile in all the resources of hypocrisy and cunning, and although the hundred eyes of Argus may be on them, their secret remains safe. Now, might not Madame Monistrol be one of these women—who are not merely expert in deceiving their husbands, bat in deceiving the world as well?

We discussed this question at length, M. Méchinet and I, and our deductions were so fully in keeping with our original theory, that we could not fail to accept them. On the one hand this system proved Monistrol's innocence, even if it did not explain his plea of guilty; and on the other, it was in keeping with a great deal of what Madame Méchinet had said at supper the night before. Clara Monistrol had certainly instigated the crime, but in lieu of entrusting its perpetration to her husband, she had confided it to her lover, hoping to enjoy this ill-gotten wealth in his company, after the unfortunate jeweller had perished on the scaffold, a victim of judicial error, like Lesurques in the famous case of the Lyons mail. But then, accepting these premises, who could this lover of hers be, and how could we discover him?

After torturing my mind for some time, I at length ventured to expound a plan. "It seems to me," said I to M. Méchinet, "that the murderer can be easily found out. He and Madame Monistrol must have agreed not to see each other for some little time after the crime. The most elementary rules of prudence must have impelled them to take that course. The man will no doubt remain quiet enough. He must know that a false move would cost him his head, and so he will not dare to show himself in the Rue Vivienne; but, on the other hand, the woman will probably become impatient. She will be anxious to see her accomplice, and fancying that she has diverted all suspicion from herself, she will not hesitate to go and meet him somewhere. I would therefore suggest that you should employ one of your colleagues to dog her steps, to follow her wherever she may go; and, if this is only done, properly, why, we shall have caught the murderer before another forty-eight hours are over our heads."

M. Méchinet was grumbling unintelligibly between his teeth, and dipping his fingers into his empty snuff-box with all his wonted persistency. At first he gave me no answer, but suddenly leaning forward he exclaimed: "That won't do, my dear fellow. We musn't let the bird slip through our fingers. We must rather strike the iron while it's hot. No doubt you possess the genius requisite for the profession—in fact, I'm sure you do; but you are wanting in experience and practice. However, fortunately I'm here. Now, listen to me. A single phrase put you on the right track, and yet you don't follow up your advantage."

"I don't understand you."

"Don't understand me? But that dog, we must turn him to account."

"How so?"

"Well, wait and you shall see. In an hour's time or so Madame Monistrol will leave her shop, for she has to be at the Palais de Justice by three o'clock; and the little servant girl will remain behind alone. That will be the time for action, and you will see how I shall settle the whole business."

I did everything I could to induce M. Méchinet to explain himself properly; but in spite of all my prayers and exhortations he refused to say another word on the subject. He carried me off to the nearest café, and compelled me to play him a game at dominoes, which, as a matter of course, I lost; for my mind was too pre-occupied to allow me to engage successfully in such a frivolous pastime, whereas M. Méchinet possessed the happy gift of being able to dismiss business from his thoughts at a moment's notice. Two o'clock was striking when at last he pushed back the dominoes and exclaimed: "To work! to work."

We paid the score and left the café, and a moment later we were standing once more under the arched gateway in front of Monistrol's shop. We had only waited there a few minutes when we saw the door open and the jeweller's wife appear upon the threshold. She wore the same black dress as during the morning, and a long crape veil hang from her bonnet, giving her the appearance of a widow. "She's a clever wench," grumbled M. Méchinet between his teeth; "she means to excite the magistrate's compassion and sympathy."

Whilst he was speaking she walked swiftly down the street, and soon disappeared from view in the direction of the Palais Royal. However, M. Méchinet decided to wait another five minutes under the archway, and then catching me by the arm he led me towards the shop. As he had opined, the little servant girl was quite alone. She was sitting behind the counter, munching a piece of sugar she had purloined from her mistress. As soon as we entered she recognised us, and rose to her feet with a flushed face and rather frightened air. Before she could open her mouth, however, M. Méchinet roughly asked her: "Where is Madame Monistrol?"

"She has gone out, monsieur."

"Gone out! That can't be. You must be deceiving me. She must be in the room there, behind the shop."

"Oh no, monsieur; she has really gone out, and if you don't believe me, you may look yourself."

M. Méchinet struck his forehead, as if he were grievously disappointed. "What a pity, what a pity!" he repeated. "How disappointed poor Madame Monistrol will be!" And as the girl gazed at him, with gaping mouth and astonished eyes, he continued: "But perhaps you might be able to tell me what I want to know, my good girl. I have only come back because I have lost the address of the person your mistress asked me to visit."

"What person, monsieur?"

"Ah! you know him. Monsieur ——. Confound it! Why, I've even forgotten his name now! Monsieur ——. Monsieur ——. But surely you'll recollect him. He's the person that your dog Pluto obeys so readily."

"Ah yes, monsieur! I know who you mean; it's Monsieur Victor."

"Yes, that's it, to a T. Monsieur Victor! I mustn't forget again. By the way, what does he do, this Monsieur Victor?"

"He's a working jeweller, monsieur. He was a great friend of Monsieur Monistrol's, and they used to work together before M. Monistrol set up in business. That's why M. Victor can do anything he likes with Pluto."

"Ah! Then, if that's the case, perhaps you can tell me where this Monsieur Victor lives?"

"Certainly I can, monsieur; he lives at No. 23 Rue du Roi Doré, in the Marais."

The poor girl was seemingly delighted to be able to furnish all this information; but it was not without a pang that I heard her answer in this trusting manner, unconsciously betraying the secret which her mistress must hold as dear as life itself. M. Méchinet's was a more hardened nature, however; and, far from being touched by this involuntary treachery, he grimly indulged in a stroke of sarcasm. "Thanks," said he, as he turned to leave the shop. "Thanks; you have just rendered your mistress a very great service indeed, and she will be exceedingly pleased with you." Then, with a chuckle, he opened the door, and we walked out into the street.

XII

My first impulse was to hurry off to the Rue du Roi Doré, and apprehend this fellow Victor, who, plainly enough, was the real murderer; but M. Méchinet damped my enthusiasm with the remark: "And the law! Don't you know that we are powerless to act, so long as we are without a warrant? We must, first of all, go to the Palais de Justice, and interview the investigating magistrate."

"But suppose we meet Madame Monistrol there?" I asked. "If she sees us, she will certainly warn her accomplice."

"Perhaps so," retorted M. Méchinet, with undisguised bitterness; "perhaps so. The culprit may escape, simply because we have to go through so many irksome formalities. Still, I might perchance parry the blow. However, let us make haste. Come, stretch out your legs."

Anxiety and hope of success lent unparalleled speed to both of us, and a quarter of an hour afterwards we were scrambling up the staircase of the Palais de Justice. The offices occupied by the investigating magistrates communicate with a long gallery, where several attendants are invariably stationed to answer all inquiries. "Can you tell me?" asked M. Méchinet, in a breathless voice; " can you tell me if the magistrate who has to deal with the murder of the little old man of Batignolles is in his office?"

"Yes, he is," answered one of the attendants; "but he has a witness with him just now—a young woman dressed in black."

"That must be Madame Monistrol," whispered the detective in my ear; and then, turning again to the attendant, he added aloud: "You know who I am, so just give me a pen and a slip of paper, that I may write a word to the magistrate. Take it to him, and bring me back the answer."

The attendant started off, dragging his shoes along the dusty floor of the gallery, and soon returned to say that the magistrate was waiting for us in an adjoining room. To receive M. Méchinet, he had indeed left Madame Monistrol in his own office with his clerk, and had borrowed the use of one of his colleagues' rooms.

"What is the matter?" he asked, in a tone which allowed me to estimate the immense difference between an investigating magistrate and a humble detective.

In a clear, brief manner, M. Méchinet related what we had accomplished, what he had learnt, and what we hoped for. But the magistrate scarcely seemed inclined to share our views. "All that is very interesting," said he; "but Monistrol confesses." And, with an obstinacy that well nigh maddened me, he kept on repeating: "He confesses, he confesses." However, after another series of protracted explanations, he at last consented to sign a warrant, authorising my neighbour to apprehend Madame Monistrol's presumed lover—M. Victor.

As soon as the detective was in possession of this indispensable document, he hurriedly bowed to the magistrate, and bounded out of the room, along the passage, and down the stairs. It was as much as I could do to keep up with him, and in less than a quarter of an hour we covered the whole distance, from the Palace of Justice to the Rue du Roi Doré—one of those narrow unkempt streets in the heart of the Marais, where each tenement is a busy hive of industry, and whence *articles de Paris*, in all varieties, go forth to the entire world.

On reaching the corner of the street, M. Méchinet paused to draw breath. "Now," said he, "attention!" And with an air of complete composure, he entered the narrow alley of the house bearing the number 23. "M. Victor, if you please?" he asked of the doorkeeper.

"On the fourth floor, monsieur—the door on the right hand as you reach the landing."

"Is he at home?"

"Oh, yes; he must be at work."

M. Méchinet took a step in the direction of the staircase, and then abruptly pausing, turned round again, faced the doorkeeper, and exclaimed: "I must treat my old friend, Victor, to a good bottle of wine. What wine shop does he usually go to near here?"

"To the one over the way."

We reached the shop in six strides, and with the air of an *habitué*, M. Méchinet immediately ordered: "A bottle of wine, please—something good. That wine of yours with the green seal!"

I must confess that this idea had not occurred to me, and yet it was simple enough. As soon as the bottle was brought, my companion produced the green-sealed cork which I had found in the bed-room at Batignolles, and we immediately perceived that the wax was identical in shade and appearance with that on the cork of the bottle that had just been served to us. Thus our moral certitude was reinforced by a material proof. As M. Méchinet had no intention of regaling M. Victor with the bottle of wine he had ordered, we proceeded to imbibe its contents, and then recrossed the street and climbed the stairs of "No. 23."

M. Méchinet gave a sharp rat-tat at Victor's door, and a voice with a pleasant ring immediately responded, "Come in." The key was outside, and accordingly we opened the door. At a table, placed before the window of the room we entered, sat a man wearing a black blouse, and engaged in setting a stone in a gold ring. He was a fellow of thirty or thereabouts, tall and thin, with a pale face and black hair. He was scarcely handsome, but his features were fairly regular, and his eyes were not without expression.

He seemed in no wise disconcerted by our visit. "What do you desire, gentlemen?" he asked politely, at the same time turning round on his stool.

"In the name of the law I arrest you!" exclaimed M. Méchinet, springing forward and catching the workman by the arm.

Victor turned livid, but he did not lower his eyes. "Don't play the fool," he exclaimed, in an insolent tone. "What have I done?"

M. Méchinet shrugged his shoulders. "Come, no child's play, please," said he; "your account is settled. You were seen when you left the Rue de Lécluse at Batignolles, and in my pocket I've got the cork in which you planted your dagger so as to prevent the point from breaking."

These words proved a crushing blow for the murderer, who, taken utterly by surprise, fell back against his table, stammering, "I am innocent, I am innocent!"

"You can say that to the magistrate," retorted M. Méchinet; "but I'm very much afraid that he won't believe you. Why, your accomplice, the woman Monistrol, has confessed everything."

"That's impossible!" replied Victor, springing up as if he had been touched by an electric battery. "She knew nothing about it."

"Oh! so then you planned the little game by yourself, eh? All right. That confession will do to begin with."

And turning towards me, with the air of a man who knows what he is about, M. Méchinet added: "Please just search the drawers, M. Godeuil. In one or another of them you will probably find this fine fellow's dagger, and I'm sure you'll light on his mistress's portrait and her love letters."

Victor clenched his teeth with rage, and a gleam of fury shot from his dark eyes; but he no doubt realised that all resistance would be futile against a man of M. Méchinet's muscular build, endowed with such a pair of iron wrists.

In a chest of drawers in one corner of the room I speedily found the dagger, the portrait, and the love letters, just as my companion had opined; and a quarter of an hour afterwards Victor had been securely stowed away in a cab between M. Méchinet and myself, and was rolling in the direction of the Préfecture de Police. The simplicity of the scene had well nigh stupefied me. "And so," I mused, "that's how a murderer is arrested. What, is it no more difficult than that to secure the person of a man whose crime is punishable with death?" But in later years I learnt at my own cost and peril that there are other criminals of a far more dangerous stamp.

As for Victor, as soon as he found himself in a cell at the Dépôt, he gave himself up as lost, and made a most minute confession of his crime. He told us that being one of Monistrol's friends, he had been acquainted with old M. Pigoreau for several years. His main object in murdering him had been to designate Monistrol for the punishment of the law, and for this reason he had dressed himself like the jeweller, and had taken Pluto to Batignolles. As soon as the poor old man had ceased to live, he had seized him by the hand, dipped one of his fingers in the blood that flowed from the fatal wound, and traced on the floor those five letters, M O N I S—the discovery of which had so nearly resulted in a deplorable judicial error. "Ah! it was cleverly combined," he added, with cynical effrontery; "if I had only succeeded, I killed two birds with one stone. On the one hand, I got rid of that fool Monistrol, whom I hated, and I enriched the woman I loved. No doubt I might have persuaded her to live with me, after her husband had gone either to the scaffold or the galleys. But now —"

"Ah! my fine fellow!" retorted M. Méchinet; "unfortunately for you, you lost your head at the last moment. But then, no one is perfect. When you traced those letters in blood on the floor, you made a terrible mistake, for you wrote them with one of the fingers of the old man's left hand."

Victor sprung to his feet in astonishment. "You don't mean to say that put you on my track?" he asked.

"Yes, I do."

With the gesture of a man whose genius is misjudged, Victor raised his arms to the ceiling. "Ah!" said he; "it's no use being an artist—no use remaining true to nature!" And, with a glance of mingled pity and contempt, he added: "Don't you know that old M. Pigoreau was LEFT-HANDED?"

He spoke the truth, as subsequent inquiries enabled me to ascertain. So thus, it was a mistake—a blunder perpetrated by myself—which, after all, had led us to the truth. The discovery, on which I had so particularly prided myself, was, in reality, none at all. And it was strange, indeed, that none of us had ever ventured to surmise that the little old man of Batignolles might have been in the habit of writing with his left hand. It is true that such cases are not very frequent—still they exist; but neither the magistrate nor the commissary, neither M. Méchinet nor his wife, had for one moment met my so-called discovery with such an objection—so true it is that the simplest things often escape our minds. However, the lesson was not lost to me, for I profited by it, with good result, on a subsequent occasion of my after life as a detective.

On the morrow, Monistrol was released from prison. The investigating magistrate reproached him in stringent terms, for having led justice astray; but he met all exhortations and reproaches with the same answer: "I love my wife . . . I wished to sacrifice myself for her . . . I thought that she was guilty."

He would say no more, but his conduct implied that he must have had some very serious grounds to believe in his wife's guilt. What could they have been? I decided, in my own mind, that Madame Clara must have previously tried to tempt her husband to commit this crime; but, although weak-minded, beyond a doubt, and passionately attached to her, he had nevertheless had the courage to resist her entreaties. Finding that her efforts were useless, she had, no doubt, turned to her lover, who proved to be of a more pliable character—especially when he was offered such a prize as wealth and undisputed possession of the woman he loved; for the latter contingency would, no doubt, have followed, had Monistrol been sent to the scaffold or the galleys.

It was in this manner that I explained the affair to myself. I could swear that Madame Monistrol was the instigator of the crime. And yet she escaped punishment. Juries do not content themselves with moral proof; and the discovery of her letters and her portrait in Victor's room, was not accounted sufficient evidence against her, when she appeared at the assizes by her lover's side. She was, moreover, defended by one of the most famous advocates of the Paris bar; and then, her tears, which flowed at will, no doubt, touched the hearts of her judges with compassion. Her charms, like those of Phyrné, might also have inspired them with a yet more tender sentiment. To be brief, she was acquitted; whilst Victor, in whose favour the jury saddled their verdict with an admission of "extenuating circumstances," was sentenced to hard labour for life.

After giving such proof of his conjugal attachment, it is scarcely surprising that weak-minded M. Monistrol should have taken his wife back to his home, if not entirely to his heart, when, after securing the benefit of a doubt, she was ordered to be set at liberty. As a matter of course, old M. Pigoreau's fortune was handed over to the jeweller, but, with Madame Monistrol's extravagant tastes, it could not be expected to last long. Now-a-days, the Monistrols keep an ill-famed drinking den on the Cours de Vincennes, nigh the Place du Trone, and when the barrière bullies, who are their principal customers, are in a good humour, they pay mocking court to the wife, now a corpulent woman, with a bloated face and a husky voice, and sadly addicted to brandy and absinthe. Her charms have fled long since, like old Anténor's money; and she and her weak-minded husband, whom she often beats in her fits of drunkenness, are swiftly descending the slope of degradation and misery.

J. B. CASIMIR GODEUIL

"THOU ART THE MAN"

Mary Elizabeth Braddon

I. On the Boards

Sixty years ago, two years after the battle of Waterloo had wound up the fortunes of the long war, and sent Napoleon to his rocky cage amidst the tropical seas, London was a different London from the metropolis of to-day, a city of narrower streets and more perilous alleys and by-ways, and yet a city with a certain homely comfort and snugness about it that seems to have been left behind in the march of improvement. When the century was young, London was something more than the brilliant focus of commercial enterprize. It was a city in which people lived and died. Wealthy traders were not ashamed to make their homes over their shops or their offices. Brides went forth from the narrow streets to be married in the gray old churches; children were carried to the old stone fonts; men and women worshipped in the tall pews, Sunday after Sunday. Now the stern hand of improvement is sweeping away the good old churches. Nobody wants them. Nobody lives in London.

In the London of sixty years ago, Charles Lamb's London, the Drama was a grand institution. Theatres were fewer, and ranked higher in men's minds. Every dramatic event was a great public question. An O.P. riot would be impossible now-a-days. Managers may raise or lower their prices as the humour moves them. Nobody cares. There are so many theatres that every man can find a place to suit his inclination and his pocket. People are as fond of the drama as ever, perhaps; but it is no longer a religion, a national pride. When this century was young, the play was almost as much to the Londoner as the old riotous worship of Bacchus was to the Greek when the drama was new born.

Behold the wide circle of eager faces in great Drury Lane, every eye fixed on one man, who holds the audience spellbound, watchful of his every look and every movement, breathless almost, lest a whisper of his should escape them. There is a silence as in the house of death, an oppressive dumbness, as he glides stealthily across the wide empty stage and plucks aside a curtain that veils the arched entrance to an inner chamber.

He is a small man, lithe, muscular, with closely knit frame. He has a long thin face, black eyes that glow like burning coals, long black hair which he tosses back from the high wide brow, the brow of a Caesar, as he pauses for a moment with the curtain in his hand and looks towards his audience, but not at them.

It is an attitude to be remembered, that crouching movement, as of a tiger about to spring, the hand clutching the velvet curtain, the head thrust forward, serpent like, as if a forked sting were darting from those pale parted lips. Then with a sudden spring the man stands erect, tears back the curtain, and looks within.

What does he see? A man and woman sitting at a chess table, in a Venetian chamber. The blue waters of the Adriatic, the white pinnacles of distant buildings shine through the wide window in front of which they two are seated.

They have been playing, but are playing no more. It is all earnest now. The man leans across the table, the woman's hand clasped in his. He looks up into her fair young face with an impassioned gaze, which she returns, yielding and subjugated.

The man lets fall the velvet curtain, totters a few paces forward, and then with one long despairing cry, drops to the ground like a log.

The act ends with this picture. But that last hoarse cry of the actor dwells with his audience after the curtain has gone down. It was almost too awful for human suffering. It was like the agonized howl of a tortured animal. It was the extreme expression of passion and despair in an utterly savage nature.

The play had taken the town by storm, and the actor, who within the last two years had become suddenly famous, had won new laurels in the part; but it was a tragedy not destined to immortality, and has sunk into the night of oblivion with many of its kind.

But just now this Italian story of Love, Revenge and Murder, with Michael Elyard in the principal part, was the rage. The play drew crowded houses nightly, and Elyard was declared to have surpassed himself in the character of the Italian husband, a modern version of *Othello*, without Othello's nobleness.

In the last act of the play the betrayed husband stabs his false wife in a garden at sunset, and hides the corpse among the rushes that fringe the canal. It was this scene of the murder which thrilled the audience, and sent them home rapturous and awestricken, to dream of Elyard's white face and burning eyes, the black elf locks falling over the pale forehead, the lithe compact form clad in close fitting black velvet.

To see him drag his victim from the fountain where he had slain her to the rushes that showed dark against the red light of the setting sun; to see him bend over the fair face, and in a sudden burst of passion, rain kisses upon the dead brow and cheeks; to see him lift the lifeless corpse upon his knee and try in a wild madness to charm it back to life, then fling it from him with a sudden yell of rage at the remembrance of its falsehood; and then to watch his convulsive movements, his furtive backward glances, the nervous quivering of his muscular limbs as he hid the dreadful thing among the rushes, while the sun sank lower and the red sky took an intenser red, till all the scene seemed steeped in blood; to see all this was to drink a cup of horror that gave a keener zest to the enjoyment of a convivial meeting and an oyster supper after the play.

To-night there are two men in a box near the stage, who watch the play with expression and bearing so opposite that the difference is something to be remarked. One leans with his arms folded upon the cushion of the box, his chin resting on his arms, and his eyes fixed intently on the scene. He loses not a movement nor a tone of the actors. The other lolls back in his chair, and surveys the stage through his eyeglass, attentive, discriminating, critical, but not entranced.

The first is Captain Bywater, of His Majesty's Navy, who has just come ashore after a cruise in the south seas, and has not seen a stage play for the last seven years. The second is Phillimore Dorrell, the famous criminal lawyer, who has seen this particular play five times.

The two men are old schoolfellows at the Charter House, nnd have been dining together at a snug city tavern, where the floor is sanded and the burgundy is genuine.

Not till the green curtain drops on a maddened suicide does Charles Bywater relax his gaze. Then he lifts his head, pulls himself together with a shiver, as if waking out of a bad dream, and looks absently round the house.

"Well, Charley, what do you think of Elyard in *The Venetian Husband*. A capital piece of acting, isn't it?"

"Acting," replied the other. "It's not like acting. It's like reality."

"Which all good acting must be."

"Yes; but I have seen good acting before to-night, which was not like this. I could not have believed that any man could do such things as this man does unless he were at heart a murderer."

"My dear fellow, that is to deny the possibility of consummate art. Your true artist imagines himself the being he represents. It is as easy for him to imagine himself a murderer, as to imagine himself a hero or a lover."

"Yes, in a broad, abstract way. But this man goes into the littlenesses of crime, the finest details, the most minute particulars."

"His imagination realizes these as readily as the broader outline. It is his wonderful appreciation of detail that makes his performance so masterly and so original. The fact is the man is a genius."

"Do you know him?" asked the sailor, deeply interested.

"Almost as well as I know you. He goes into the best society. He was at Oxford; and is a man of considerable refinement. I supped with him the other night."

"What!" exclaimed the Captain, "you eat with him after seeing him in this play. Did not you feel as if you were sitting down with a murderer?"

"Not the least in the world. I felt that I was sitting down with a very agreeable acquaintance. A trifle self-conscious, as most actors are; and rather too fond of talking about his art, but a perfect gentleman, notwithstanding. We had a discussion, by-the-way, after supper, which was peculiarly interesting to me, as a man whose experience has made him unhappily familiar with the physiology of crime."

"What about?"

"About murder. Elyard has an idea that a great many murders are committed in a century which never come to light, the secret of which dies and is buried with the victim of the crime. Now, I have just the opposite opinion. It is my fixed belief, founded upon long familiarity with the history of crime, that there is an inherent something in the crime of murder which makes its ultimate discovery inevitable."

"Shakespeare has expressed the same opinion rather more tersely," said Captain Bywater. "Blood will have blood."

"True," assented Mr. Dorrell, vexed at being interrupted in his preamble, "that's Shakespeare's rough and ready way of patting it. My theory is that from the moment a man becomes a criminal he becomes a blunderer. He is off the straight track, and is sure to take a wrong step. The murderer is playing the most desperate game a man can play, with all society on the other side. The odds against success are terrible. And then there is something in blood that stupefies a man. From the instant he stains his hands he begins to do idiotic things. He buries the body that he should have lelt unburied: or, he leaves it unburied when wisdom would have buried it. His crime has been hidden for a year or more, perhaps, and no finger has been pointed at him, when he takes it into his head all at once that his secret is in danger, and unearths his victim, and is caught with the ghastly proof of his crime in his arms. Or, when the deed is done, craven fear seizes hold of him, and he flies the scene of his guilt, and so betrays himself; or he keeps some shred or scrap of his victim's garments; or he overacts the part of innocence in some way. Sooner or later his distempered spirit will lead him to some act of besotted idiocy, by which the deed he has done will be made clear to men's eyes. He is never safe. Elyard seemed deeply interested in what I told him of my experience in the ways of criminals; but he was not convinced. He clings to the idea that there are murders which justice never hears of."

The afterpiece began, and Phillimore Dorrell hurried off to a convivial supper party, leaving Captain Bywater alone in the box.

"You know my chambers, old fellow," he said at parting, "I shall be glad to see you whenever you can look in."

"That will be pretty often, Phil, depend upon it," answered the other, "but I'm going down to the country for a week or so before I enjoy myself in London."

"To see your people?" inquired Dorrell.

"My people are under the sod, Phil. I shall go and have a look at their graves; and I shall hunt up an old friend or two among the few that I knew in my boyhood."

II. Loved and Lost

Captain Bywater started by coach early next morning. The scene of his birth was a quiet village among the Buckinghamshire hills, an out of the way rustic place, shut in and sheltered from cold winds and the biting breath of worldly men and women. A cluster of cottages, an old old church, with a low square tower, and a wonderful sun dial for its only ornament, two or three comfortable homesteads, a grange that had once been a grand mansion, and the good old red brick house still known as Squire Bywater's, though the squire had been laid in his grave years ago, and Charley had let the house to an alien family who were said to do nothing for the poor; an accusation which might be taken to mean that they stopped short of giving away the greater part of their substance and leaving themselves poorer than their pensioners, as the dead and gone squire had done.

It was a bright afternoon in May when the sailor alighted from the coach in front of the old inn, a cosy-looking low white house, with a golden sun for a sign, and bright red flower-pots in all the windows.

How pretty the dear old village looked in the afternoon sunshine.

What a blessed haven from the cares and struggles of the world, what a calm retreat, what an abode of innocence and peace. The gardens were all bright with blue forget-me-nots and yellow cowslips, roses just bursting into bloom. The last of the violets perfumed the air. The ruddy fire was glowing in the village forge. Hens were cackling, ducks quacking and splashing in the pond before the inn door. Rosy cheeked children looked up and grinned at the traveller, as at a being whose arrival was the next best thing to a peep show.

All this was rapture to the sailor who had been seven years at sea. He took in everything with the eager glance of his lively gray eyes, and then he turned away from the inn, and looked long and thoughtfully at the old stone mansion yonder, with its dull neglected air.

It was a good old Tudor house, standing back from the road, a wide lawn in front of its mullioned windows, two mighty cedars casting their dense shadows on the snnlit grass, clipped yew hedges, straight walks, and a garden that looked barren and uncared for.

"Old Mr. Leeworthy is still living, I hope?" asked the Captain, turning to the inn-keeper, with a certain anxiety in his tone.

"Yes, sir, the old gentleman is still alive. He must be going on for ninety—a wonderful old man! There are very few like him now-a-days. I'm very glad to see you back, sir, after so long. I hope you are going to make a stay with us, now the war's over. Shall I have your portmanteau taken up stairs, sir?"

"Yes, I shall be here for a day or two."

"John, take Captain Bywater's portmanteau to the blue room."

Charles Bywater's gaze was still fixed on the old stone house on the opposite side of the village green.

"You've dined on the road, mayhap, sir!" said his host, "and you'd like a comfortable bit of supper, or a dish of tea."

"You can get me some supper at eight or nine o'clock, eggs and bacon—anything. I am going over to see old Mr. Leeworthy. His granddaughter is as pretty as ever I suppose?" he added, with an ill-assumed carelessness.

All through the journey from London—while the heavy old coach rolled along at a rate that seemed a snail's pace to Captain Bywater's impatience—one image had been shining before the eyes of the traveller, a fair girlish face, radiant with youthful bloom. It bad been almost a child's face, when he withdrew his eyes from its fresh beauty, five years ago, after the long lingering gaze of farewell, a sweet face looking up at him in its artless grief, half drowned in tears. To have spoken of his love then would have seemed profanation. He kept his secret, and went away to sea, meaning to come back in a couple of years, or so, and plead his cause, fearing no rival in that unsophisticated village, and secure in the belief that Helen Leeworthy cared more for him than any one else in the world.

A troubled look came over the innkeeper's round face.

"Sure to goodness, Captain, you must have heard."

"What? Is she married?"

"No, sir."

"Dead!" gasped Captain Bywater, with an ashy face.

Oh, he ought to have feared this. Fate is so cruel. And beings as lovely as Helen Leeworthy are the flowers which fall earliest under death's sickle.

"No, sir, not dead—not that any one knows—but gone."

"Gone! Where and how?'

"That's more than anybody has ever been able to find out, sir. It almost broke old Mr. Leeworthy's heart. He has never been the same man since. He just crawls about the place like the ghost of himself. It's pitiful to see him. His mind is gone. And everything is neglected—the garden—the house—nobody cares."

"Tell me all—from first to last," said Captain Bywater, putting his arm through the landlord's and leading him away from the inn door to the broad high road, where there was no one to overhear them. "When did it happen? How? When did she go away? Begin at the beginning."

"Well, sir, it was two years after you left us, and summer weather, as it might be now, only a good deal later in the year. Old Mr. Leeworthy's nephew, the politician, him as you've doubtless heard about taking a leading part in public affairs up in London, he was staying at the Grange when it happened, with his secretary. They'd been there above a month—nigh upon two months I should say, counting from the closing of Parliament, and Mr. Leeworthy—I mean Mr. Thomas Leeworthy, the nephew—was studying hard, and getting up—stat—stat—well I'm bothered."

"Statistics," exclaimed the Captain impatiently. "For Heaven's sake go on. What does Mr. Leeworthy's book matter?"

"Well, it has a bearing on the case, you see, sir. All things have a bearing. Well, sir, to make a long story short, one fine September morning, when the leaves were just beginning to turn, Miss Leeworthy was missing. There was no letter—not a word—nothing—to tell anybody where she had gone, or why she had gone. There was nothing missing out of her room—not so much as a bonnet. But she was gone, and from that hour to this nobody in Clerevale has ever heard of her."

"The secretary," cried Captain Bywater. "What of him? He was young, attractive, perhaps."

"He was young," asserted the landlord, "but he wasn't attractive, least ways, not to me. I'd have gone a mile out of my way to avoid meeting him."

"A lady may have thought differently," said the Captain bitterly.

He saw in this young secretary the clue to the mystery. Lover's secrets closely kept, an elopement, first Gretna and then the King's Bench.

"Any how, Captain, the secretary could hardly have been at the bottom of it. He never budged. His master stopped at the Grange till the end of the year, and he stopped with him. I used to meet him about the village, though I didn't want to it. A lonesome young man, shut up in his own self, as close as a church on work-a-days. I never liked the cut of his jib, as you naval gentlemen say."

"Is that all you can tell me, Jarvis?"

"Every syllable."

The Captain turned from him without a word, and walked quickly back to the village green, and across the green to the gates of the Grange. That gray and rigid face told of a grief too deep for utterance, a dumb despair deep enough to overshadow a life time.

As he drew near the broad iron gate, a sigh of agony broke from those white lips of his. Oh, Heaven, how well he remembered her. It was here, by this gate, they had parted. Could it be for ever? He could see the childish face, pure as a lily, the sweet sad eyes, brimming over with tears. And she was gone—perhaps to misery—it might be to shame. Oh, rather than that let it be death. In time, doubtless, he might come to think, with resignation, of her lying at rest in some quiet churchyard. But it was madness to think of her disgraced and dishonoured; that fair flower, which he had deemed almost too lovely for earth, trampled in the gutter, flung aside to wither, like the vilest weed. He went in at the open gate, along the grass grown walk to the low door where he had been used to enter. He rang a bell that sounded dismally, as in an empty house.

The old housekeeper opened the door. She curtseyed and smiled and seemed pleased to see him. It struck him all at once that he might learn more from her than from the master of the house. She was Mr. Leeworthy's junior by a good many years. Her memory would be clearer, and he could question her more freely.

"I have come to see your old master, Mrs. Dill; but I should like to have a few minutes' talk with you first. I've only just come home from sea, and I've heard something that has taken all the joy out of my return.

"I think I know what you mean, sir. You've heard about Miss Helen. She was always a favourite with you, wasn't she? You were like a playfellow with her, though you were so much older. She loved you like a brother."

"And I loved her as I never have loved and never shall love any other woman," answered the Captain. "I tell you my secret, Mrs. Dill, because I want you to speak freely. I want you to help me to find her."

"Find her," sighed the housekeeper. "Oh, sir, who can hope for that, after five long years, and after Mr. Thomas Leeworthy doing all that could be done, and he a public man too, and so clever. Who could do more than he could?"

"Love, my good soul, true love, which is as strong as faith, and can move mountains. Mr. Thomas Leeworthy may have been a very affectionate uncle, but he never loved his niece as I love—yes, as I love her. Living or dead—lost or found — she is to me the dearest thing upon earth. And now tell me every circumstance of her disappearance—every suspicion— every conjecture."

Captain Bywater had followed the housekeeper into a little room otf the hall, a chilly disused parlour, where the very furniture had a phantasmal look, like a dream of the past.

"Lord bless your heart, sir, there is so little to tell. We went to her room one morning and found her gone—the bed had not been slept in—she must have gone over night."

"Did she go to her room that night, at the usual hour! You are early people here, I know."

"Well, sir, that's a thing that has never been quite clear to my mind. Miss Helen used to be fond of walking out alone those fine summer evenings, while her grandpapa and Mr. Thomas sat over their port. Both gentlemen are fond of a good glass of port, you know, sir. They dined at five, and they used to sit a long time, as late as nine o'clock sometimes—and then the old gentleman would go to bed, and Mr. Thomas would smoke his pipe on the lawn, all by himself, or with Mr. Elphinstone, his secretary, as it might happen. And Miss usen't always to go back to the dining-room after she came in from her walk. She'd go straight up to her room sometimes, and sit and read there before she went to bed. Now on the night before we lost her it happened that neither I nor the maid saw her go upstairs to her room. It was a lovely evening. I remember it particularly, because it was such a red sunset."

Captain Bywater shivered. It was an idle thought to come into his mind at such a moment, but there flashed upon him that picture in the theatre last night. The body hidden among the rushes. The whole scene steeped in red lights like blood.

"No, sir, nobody saw her come indoors or go upstairs to her room that night, and if I was put upon my oath I couldn't say that she ever came back to the house after she left the two gentlemen sitting at their wine."

"Where was this Mr. Elphinstone, the secretary, that night?'

"At his work in the study, copying and compiling for Mr, Thomas Leeworthy's book, so far as I know, sir."

"So far as you know. That means that he may just as easily have been any where else."

"I could take my oath as to where he was from nine to ten," said the housekeeper, somewhat offended.

"How is that?"

"Because I saw him from my sitting-room window walking up and down the lawn with Mr. Thomas Leeworthy. It was moonlight, a lovely night after a lovely evening, and the two gentlemen were walking up and down talking for an hour. The clock struck ten as they came in to go to bed."

"Mr. Elphinstone slept in the house that night?"

"Yes, sir, I'm certain of that. If you've got the notion that Mr. Elphinstone had any hand in Miss Helen's running away you're quite mistaken. If there was a lover at the bottom of it, as some folks say, it must have been some other lover. I'll take my oath it wasn't Mr. Elphinstone."

"Why are you so certain?"

"Because she hated him."

"How do you know that?"

"I could see it in all her ways. Perhaps hatred is too harsh a word to use about any one so gentle as Miss Helen. She could hardly have hated any one if she had tried ever so. But I've seen her shrink from him, and avoid him in a way that was almost cruel I've seen him stung by it, too, though he was a proud young man, that seldom let any one see what he felt. As to anything like a love affair between those two, it isn't possible."

"Who then could have lured her away? Was any one else ever suspected."

"Lord, no, sir. Mr. Elphinstone was the only young man that ever crossed this threshold, except Mr. Chipping, the doctor, with a wife and three children and a wart on his nose."

"How did Elphinstone behave when Miss Leeworthy's disappearance was discovered?" asked Captain Bywater, still harping on the secretary.

"He was the only one of us that seemed to keep his senses. He was as calm and quiet as could be, ready to make himself useful in any way. He rode over to the market town before twelve o'clock, to set the constables at work. He was riding about all over the country for the next fortnight. If Miss Helen had been his sister, he couldn't have worked harder, or have seemed more anxious; which was very good of him, considering that poor Miss Helen had never taken kindly to him."

"Was there nothing discovered, not a trace of her?'

"No, sir, nothing was ever found; nothing was ever heard. People had their fancies: some said gipsies; some said Gretna Green. But a sweet, innocent young lady of seventeen can't go off to Gretna Green by herself, can she, sir? Some talked about the river; but the poor dear wouldn't have come to harm that way unless she'd thrown herself in, and why should she do that? God bless her, there wasn't a happier young lady in the county. Ah, sir, if you could have heard her talk of you. She loved you truly. When we had stormy weather she used to come to my room looking so unhappy, and say, 'Oh! Mrs. Dill, mustn't it be dreadful for those at sea. I sha'n't sleep to-night for thinking of shipwrecks.' And I know she has spent many a wakeful night for your sake, sir, thinking of your danger and praying for you."

"And I have thought of her in storm and in calm," said the captain. "Have you told me everything, Mrs. Dill—everything?"

"Yes, sir; there isn't a word more to be said. Five long years have come and gone, and we have heard nothing about her. We've left off hoping. The old gentleman is getting a little weak in his head. You won't get much out of him."

"Do you know what became of this Elphinstone? Is he still with Mr. Leeworthy?"

"No, sir. He stayed till the end of the year, and then Mr. Leeworthy's book was finished, and Mr. Elphinstone left him. Mr. Thomas had only hired him to help with the book. He was a very learned young man, I believe. I heard say that he went abroad after he left Mr. Thomas."

Captain Bywater went to the cedar parlour to pay a duty visit to old Squire Leeworthy. He found the owner of the Grange sitting by a fire, for the fresh May breezes were sharp enough to find out the weak points in his ancient anatomy. He wore a black velvet skull cap on the top of his silver locks, and had an ivory handled cane at his side, with which to rap the floor when he wanted attendance. He was the shrunken ruin of a man who had once been handsome, commanding, and aristocratic.

"Fine weather, sir!" he exclaimed testily, in answer to the Captain's conventional remark; "what do you mean by talking about fine weather, when the wind's in the east."

"I haven't looked at the weathercock, Squire."

"Weathercock be hanged, sir; when you're half as old as I am you'll want no weathercock to tell you where the wind is. You'll be your own weathercock. The east wind finds out every joint in my body. I can feel it in my knees, in my elbows, in my wrists even. The lubricating oil is exhausted, sir. I'm dried up and shrivelled, and there's nothing left in me to resist the cold. Let me see, you're Charles Bywater, the lad that went to sea."

"Yes, sir, I am Charles."

"Didn't I tell you so," cried the old man testily. "You're Charley, and you would go to sea. They couldn't keep you at home. Your uncle was a soldier, captain in the 49th Foot. Yes, and he was killed at Corunna. Where did I tell you he was killed? Hah! at Corunna. Yes. He was killed at Corunna, you know."

The Captain tried to look grateful for this information.

"Your mother was an uncommonly pretty woman—a little fair woman. I remember her well. She was a Vernon, and had money. Yes, she had money. I remember the bells being rung when your father brought her home. Yes, foolish thing that bell-ringing. The ringers always want money and beer—lots of beer—your father gave them beer, I daresay. I remember your father, too, a fine made man, broad shouldered, straight as an arrow. You'll never be so good-looking as your father. Young men never are. The race is degenerating, sir. The human species will be hideous in a generation or two, and every way inferior. I'm glad I sha'n't be here to see 'em."

"I have heard the sad news about your granddaughter, sir," said Captain Bywater, gravely.

It pained him to hear the old man twaddling on without a thought of the lost one.

"Yes, very sad. Naughty girl. She's given us a great deal of anxiety. If it hadn't been for that estimable young man—El—El—Elphindean—"

"Elphinstone!"

"Yes, Elphinstone. I never could remember names. If it hadn't been for Elphindon we shouldn't have known what to do. But he was indefatigable—made every inquiry—searched in every direction."

"And found no trace of her."

"No, that was unfortunate. And now. let me see, it must be nearly a year since she went."

"It is five years, sir."

"Five years, bless my soul. How short the years are when we are going down-hill to our graves."

After this Captain Bywator could not endure any more of the old man's society. He took a civil leave of him and went out to explore familiar scenes. Great heaven, with what a heavy heart! Far away amidst tropical seas, under the southern cross, he had pictured to himself the joy of this return, fancied the delight of revisiting each favourite spot, with Helen by his side. He had come back, and all was gloom.

He bent his steps towards a gate that opened out of the Grange garden into a footpath that led through some meadows, park-like meadows, with good old trees overshadowing the grass, and giving beauty to the landscape. This meadow path led to the banks of a narrow winding river. The footpath and the river-bank had both been favourite walks of Helen's. How often had Charles Bywater met her there; how often had he walked with her beside the silvery unpolluted stream.

The sun was sinking as he came through the last meadow to the river side. The light was crimson behind the long line of rush, and mallow, and wild entanglement of weeds that edged the stream.

Again there flashed back upon his mind that scene in the theatre last night—the red light behind the reeds—revenge and murder.

How lonely the landscape was in that fading light. He lingered there, pacing slowly along the narrow path, till the last low streak of crimson melted into gray, and in all that time he had not met a creature, or seen a human figure in the distance, or heard any voice more human than the hoot of a far-off owl, making its melancholy moan to the swift coming night. What deed of darkness might not be done in a spot like this, unsuspected, buried in impenetrable night!

Charles Bywater left that river path with a feeling of indescribable melancholy. He could not dissociate the scene with the mystery of Helen Leeworthy's fate. It had been her favourite walk. She had come here perhaps on that last night, and some ruffian, some loathsome brute in human shape, with a wild beast's ferocity and a man's cunning, had met her in the September sunset, alone, helpless, remote from the aid of man. He fancied her in the clutches of such a wretch, like some sweet struggling bird in the talons of a hawk. Her poor little purse, with its slender stock of money, her girlish trinkets, would be enough to tempt such a brute to murder. A knife drawn quickly across the fair round throat, one faint gurgling cry, and then the splash of a body flung to the river rats, and all foul things that dwell in the nooks and crannies of the reedy bank.

"Yes, I believe she was murdered," thought Captain Bywater. "It was not in that gentle spirit to be reckless of the feelings of others. If it were possible that she could leave her home in an unmaidenly fashion, it is not possible that she could leave her poor old grandfather to grieve in ignorance of her fate. She was always thoughtful of others."

The impression was so strong upon him to-night at this spot, that it was almost as if he had seen the deed done. The picture was as vivid to his mental vision as that other picture which he had seen last night with his bodily eyes on the stage at Drury Lane.

"What comes of Dorrell's theory, that every murder is discovered?" he asked himself bitterly. "Here is some low village ruffian who has cunning enough to keep the secret of his crime. He swoops like a hawk upon his victim, and flies off like a hawk to unknown skies. A wretch, perhaps, who could not write his name, and yet had cleverness enough to cheat the gallows."

He walked slowly back to the village green, and the inn where his supper was waiting for him.

"I would give a good deal to see the secretary," he thought. "His superior intelligence might assist me. Yet if he could do nothing to unravel the mystery, while it was still fresh in men's minds, is it likely he could throw any light upon it now?"

The landlord of the Sun waited on Captain Bywater while he eat his simple supper, a meal to which he did scanty justice. He had eaten nothing since noon, yet the tender young chicken and the home cured ham were as tasteless as dust and ashes.

"You're looking very ill, sir," said the host. "I'm afraid it's been a shock to you hearing about poor Miss Leeworthy."

"It has, Jarvis. I had known her from a child, remember."

"All the village had known her from a child," said Mr. Jarvis. "I think it seemed to all of us as if we'd lost one of our own."

"You told me you would have gone out of your way to avoid meeting Mr. Elphinstone, the secretary," said the Captain, pushing away his plate, and throwing himself back in his chair. "Why was that? was there anything repulsive about the man?"

"Well, no, sir, I can't take upon myself to say he was repulsive. He looked the gentleman, he was a neat dresser, he had a good foot and ankle, carried himself well, and was civil spoken enough whenever he condescended to open his lips to any of us villagers, which wasn't often. But there was something inside mo that turned against him, somehow, just as one man's stomach will turn against a dish that another man relishes. There was something in his dark eye that gave me a chilly feeling when he looked at me."

"Should you call him a handsome man?"

"Far, from it, sir. He was small and insignificant. You could have passed him by in a crowd without taking notioe of him, if you hadn't happened to meet his eye. That would have fixed you."

"There was something serpent-like in it, perhaps."

"Yes, sir—cold, and still, and stealthy, and yet piercing."

"Did he bear a good character while he was with you?"

"I never heard any one speak against him, but he was no favourite. He was one of those well-behaved young men that nobody likes."

This was all that Captain Bywater could hear about Mr. Thomas Leeworthy's secretary. He bade good-by to Clerevale next morning, and the coach carried him back to London. The scenes of his boyhood had become hateful to him. Everything was darkened by the shadow of his irreparable loss.

III. Driven by the Furies

Charles Bywater found himself in London with a long spell of idleness before him, very few friends or even acquaintance, a well-filled purse and a broken heart. The pleasures of the town could offer him no distraction, the vices of the town could not tempt him. His grief was as honest as it was deep. The dream of his life was ended. He had nothing to look forward to beyond his profession—nothing to hope for but the distinction of an honourable career, and perchance to die in a cock-pit, like Nelson, while his sailors were fighting over his head.

He ordered a suit of black, and put crape on his hat, having no doubt that the woman he loved was dead.

A week after his return he went to see Phillimore Dorrell, who was shocked at seeing the change in his friend.

"Why, man alive, what have you been doing to yourself?" he exclaimed. "You look as if you had died and come to life again."

"That may well be," answered Captain Bywater, "for the best part of me is dead."

And then he told Dorrell his story, and asked his advice.

"You know more of the dark secrets of this wicked world than any one else," he said, in conclusion, "you may help me to unravel the mystery."

"My dear Bywater, my experience in matters of this kind has led me to take a very commonplace view of such cases. I have found that when a young lady vanishes she generally knows very well where she is going. I do not believe in mysterious disappearances, or undiscovered murders."

"You did not know Helen Leeworthy. She was little more than a child in years, and quite a child in innocence, utterly incapable of double dealing. It is my firm belief that she was waylaid and murdered within half a mile of her home."

"And all this happened five years ago. I'm afraid, my dear Bywater, if the poor young lady did come to an untimely end at the hand of some ruffian, this will be one of those exceptional murders which go to prove my rule, that the generality of such crimes are found out. This is a case which would interest Elyard, as a probable murder that has not come to light. He was here a few nights ago discussing his favourite thesis."

"What a ghoulish temper the man must have to dwell upon such a revolting subject."

"Well, I grant that his conversation savours somewhat of the charnel house. I fancy that the hit he has made in that horrible tragedy, *The Venetian Husband*, has given his mind a twist in that direction. He sups full of horrors. But the man is interesting, and he exercises a powerful fascination over me. Not altogether a pleasant influence I admit. There is something snaky in his eye that chills me when I am most familiar with him. But he is no lump of common clay. He is a being of light and tire."

"So is Lucifer," said Captain Bywater, "but I shouldn't consider him an agreeable acquaintance."

"Oh, my dear Charley, this world is so given over to humdrum, so thickly peopled with a kind of human vegetable, that any man who has intellect and courage enough to be original affords an agreeable variety, no matter what turn his eccentricity takes."

"You might say that of the man who picks your pocket."

"Why, no, Charley, there is nothing ecceutric in pocketpicking. It is the commonest thing in life, a recognized profession. Come and sup with me to-night. I have asked Elyard, and one or two others. Cast aside care for a couple of hours. Rely upon it, my dear friend, the young lady is safe and sound, and that black suit of yours is an anachronism."

"I wish to Heaven it were so. I'll accept your invitation, though I shall be no better company than the skeleton at an Egyptian feast. I feel interested in this Elyard."

"Naturally. The man is a genius; and genius is too rare not to be interesting."

Captain Bywater had called at Mr. Thomas Leeworthy's house, in Bryanstone Square, and had been informed that the politician was in Paris, and not expected home for a week or ten days. He was not likely to be away longer than the latter period, his butler told the Captain, as there was a bill coming before the house in which he was keenly interested.

Captain Bywater had set his heart upon seeing Mr. Leeworthy, though there seemed little hope that Helen's uncle could help him to discover the secret of her fate, having failed in discovering it himself. But then, the Captain argued, an uncle's love and a lover's love are as different as lamp-light and forked lightning. The darkness which the feeble glimmer of affection had failed to penetrate might be illuminated to its nethermost depth by the piercing radiance of a passionate love.

It was nearly midnight when Captain Bywater presented himself at his friend's chambers in Gray's Inn, spacious handsome rooms, with the gloomy grandeur of a departed age. A dozen or so of wax candles lightened the supper table, and a circle round it, and left the dark oak walls in profound shadow.

The party consisted of the famous actor, and two intellectual nonentities, one a sprouting barrister, whom the great criminal lawyer had taken under his wing, the other a critic on an evening paper.

There was a good deal of conversation at supper, but the host and the critic were the chief talkers. The young barrister habitually agreed with his patron, and always laughed in the right place. Captain Bywater looked on and said nothing. The actor leaned back in his chair, with his thin white hand pushed through his long black hair, and his shining eyes fixed on space. He might be listening intently to the conversation; or his thoughts might be hundreds of miles away. It was impossible to determine which.

"What a wretched supper you have eaten, Elyard," exclaimed the lawyer, with a vexed air. "Yet that spatchcock with mushrooms was not bad. And you have hardly tasted my Chateau Yquem. Do you never eat or drink?"

"I am not a voracious eater," answered Elyard, in his deep and subdued voice.

Presently, when the dishes had been cleared away, and the guests had drawn closer together over their wine, Michael Elyard folded his arms upon the table, and looked steadfastly at his host.

Phillimore Dorrell touched the sailor's foot under the table, as much as to say, "Look out for what's coming now."

"Dorrell, did you read that case of a mysterious disappearance in to-day's *Chronicle?*"

"Yes, I saw it."

"And do you still say there are very few murders—none even—that are not eventually found out?"

"Yes, I stick to my colours. But remember, I say 'eventually.' In the statistics of crime—"

"Oh, pray don't talk to me about statistics," cried the actor impatiently. "I think I know as much about statistics as any man; the statistics of disease, of drunkenness, of crime, of mortality. I went very deeply into statistics at one time of my life."

Charles Bywater held his breath. He sat like a man of stone, and waited for what was coming.

"When you were at the University?" asked Dorrell.

"After I left the University. I assisted in the preparation, nay, I may go so far as to say that I was the chief author of a very important statistical work: Leeworthy's 'Facts and Figures for the People.'"

"I understand," said the lawyer, "you did all the work and Mr. Leeworthy had all the credit, and the profit, if there was any, which I should think was doubtful. 'Facts and Figures for the People' is exactly the kind of work I should expect to find uncut in the sixpenny box at a bookstall. But what a clever fellow you must be, Elyard, to change from such dull drudgery as bookmaking to the glorious triumphs of a famous tragedian."

"Yes, it is a change for the better," assented Mr. Elyard, with a dismal look, and then he leaned his elbows on the table, and fixed his snaky gaze upon Phillimore Dorrell, and went back to his favourite subject, murder, as one of the fine arts. De Quincey had not then written his wonderful essay upon this theme. Burke and Hare, and even the Katcliffe Highway murderers were still among the great men of the future. Indeed, the art of murder was just then suffering one of those intervals of mediocrity and decadence which are common to all great arts.

Mr. Dorrell warmed with the discussion. His experience was wide in the dark and winding ways of crime. He had many curious anecdotes to tell, and told them magnificently. The timepiece behind him struck half hours and hours, and still Michael Elyard listened, with his steadfast eyes rooted on the speaker, and led him on at every pause with some apposite question. The critic yawned, dozed, waked himself, and took his leave. The young stuff-gown listened, and approved and drank burgundy till his eyes began to blink and grow watery, and at last his chin fell comfortably forward on his breast, his head began to roll starboard and larboard, and his deep and steady breathing to sound like the soothing cadence of summer waves. In all this time Charles Bywater never relaxed his attention.

Just at the close of a thrilling anecdote the clock struck four, and Phillimore Dorrell started up from his chair.

"My dear fellow, I have to be in court at ten to-morrow morning," he exclaimed, "and here's Brunton getting absolutely apoplectic. Do you *ever* sleep, Elyard?"

"Sometimes," answered the tragedian in his dreary voice, "but I don't care much about it. Good night. Thank you for a most interesting evening. I shall go and have a walk upon the bridges. I am very fond of the Thames at sunrise."

"I shall go to bed," said Dorrell, "and I recommend you to do the same."

Mr. Elyard shook hands with his host, saluted Captain Bywater and the newly awakened barrister with a stately bow, and retired. Phillimore Dorrell drew aside the dark moreen curtain and let the grey daylight into the room.

The candles had burned low in the old silver candelabra. The empty bottles and scattered fragments of the feast had a melancholy look in the chilly morning. The barrister made his adieu and hurried off; the sailor lingered.

"What do you think of him?" asked Dorrell, when he found himself alone with his old school fellow.

"What do I think of him? I think he bears the brand of Cain upon his forehead. I know that he murdered Helen Leeworthy."

"My dear Charlie, this is midsummer madness."

"Is it? I tell you this man is a murderer—no other than a murderer would thus harp upon the horrid theme—gloating on the knowledge of his iniquity, or else so oppressed by the weight of his guilty secret that he must talk of it, must drag it out to the light of day, must parade it in some form or other before the eyes of his fellow men. It is demoniac possession, the possession of a monomaniac driven mad by the ever present vision of one hideous crisis in his past life. He is a man of one idea. Could you not see it in the play? It is all murder from the first scene to the last—a murder contemplated—a murder done. He looks and moves like the shedder of blood."

"If you will speak more calmly, I may be able to get at your meaning," urged Dorrell, as the sailor paced the room, violently agitated.

"Yes, I will tell you all. I want your help."

He explained how from that admission about the volume of statistics he had identified Elphinstone, the secretary, in Elyard the actor.

"That proves nothing against him," said Dorrell, "you, yourself told me that nobody suspected this Elphinstone; that he was active in the endeavour to trace the missing girl.

"A blind to baffle suspicion. I suspect him. I saw in him from the first the possible murderer. I see in him to-night the actual murderer. His own looks, his own lips confess it. He is a man tormented by the furies."

"Upon my honour," ejaculated Dorrell solemnly, "I begin to think that a murder has been done, and that it is going to be found out. That goes to establish my theory."

"Promise me one thing," urged the Captain. "Don't let that man know who I am. He must have heard of me at Clerevale as an intimate friend of the family, and he would be on his guard before me. When I next meet him you can call me—anything you like—Bedford—Browning."

"But I introduced you to him as Captain Bywater."

"You said the name with the usual indistinctness, and there was some little confusion in the room just then. Elyard and your friend the barrister came in together, if you remember. You addressed me as Charley all the evening. No, I don't think he heard my name. So for the future you can talk of me as Captain Browning."

"So be it—I would do more than that to oblige you."

IV. In the Red Sunset

The long vacation had begun, the courts were closed, and Phillimore Dorrell was taking his summer holiday up the river, between Henley and Reading. He had hired a furnished cottage, was doing a little reading and a great deal of boating, and keeping open house in a jovial bachelor fashion for his chosen friends.

Among these was Charles Bywater, not the liveliest companion in the world, but too much a gentleman to pester his friend with his own particular grief, and too well-informed, unselfish and true-hearted ever to degenerate into a bore.

He was passionately fond of the Thames, and spent most of his time in the solicitor's wherry, between banks which were even lovelier then than they are now, the perky Cockney villa not having yet intruded on the sylvan serenity of the shore.

At the cottage Charles Bywater was known as Captain Browning. He had a room kept for him always, and came and went as he pleased.

"News for you, Charley," said Dorrell, one afternoon, when his friend entered the shady little river-side garden, with the dust of the mail coach road upon his garments. "Elyard is to be here this evening."

"I'm very glad of that. I have been waiting my opportunity."

"The theatre closed last night, after a season of remarkable prosperity. The managers have presented him with a diamond snuff-box. He will be in high feather, no doubt."

"Do you think his triumphs will make any difference in him? I don't. He is tormented by memories that make happiness impossible."

They were to dine at five, and at a few minutes before the hour Mr. Elyard arrived, looking just as he had looked that night in Gray's Inn, and very much as he looked in *The Venetian Husband*. He shook hands with his host, gave the Captain a gloomy nod, and before they were half way through the dinner, at which he eat hardly anything, began to talk about murder.

A remarkable trial had just taken place at the Lancaste assizes.

Four men had been condemned to death for the brutal murder of an old woman and a beautiful girl of twenty. The outrage had been committed at mid-day, in a house at Pendleton, near Manchester—a house within ear-shot and eye-shot of other houses. The murderers had been seen leaving the house with their booty, they had spent their afternoon at various village taverns, and one of them had made an idiotic display of his plunder on the evening after the crime.

"With common prudence those creatures might easily have escaped the gallows," said Elyard. "It was their own folly that put the rope round their neck."

"The jury felt a natural indignation against the murderers of a feeble old woman and a lovely and innocent girl," said Dorrell. "Had the evidence been less conclusive than it was the verdict would have been the same. Men's hearts are stronger than their heads in a case of that kind."

"Ay," sighed the tragedian, "young, lovely, innocent, and foully murdered. A hard fate. And in this case, passion could plead no excuse. It was not the madness of a despised love that impelled the murderous stroke. The beautiful Hannah Partington was no victim to a revengeful lover. Such a fate would have been euthanasia as compared with here. A sordid villain, flushed with greed of gain, wanting money to squander in a village tap-room, a wretch without passion or tenderness, without even the capacity for remorse, struck the blow. I would hang such vulgar ruffians high as Haman."

"Would you argue that a despised and rejected love could excuse an assassin?" asked Dorrell.

"The tragedy of passion is sublime, even in its darkest depths," answered the actor. "Who ever thinks of Othello as of a common murderer?"

After dinner the three gentlemen strolled out upon the lawn. Phillimore Dorrell ordered the wine to be carried to a table under a willow that dipped its long green tresses into the stream, but Michael Elyard seemed in too restless a humour to enjoy the quiet of the scene.

"You do not appear to appreciate the tranquillity of your first leisure evening," said Dorrell, "I should have thought it would have been an infinite relief to you to find yourself a free man."

"I miss the excitement of the theatre," answered Elyard with a dreary sigh. "The country is pretty enough to look at in a picture, but the reality is somewhat oppressive."

"Yet you endured a long residence in one of the quietest nooks in all England," said the Captain.

"What do yon mean?" asked the actor, startled.

"When you were writing your book of statistics at Clerevale."

"Who told you that?"

"Why, man alive, don't look so scared," cried the lawyer. "It was you yourself who told us the other night at my chambers."

"Aye, to be sure," assented Elyard, "but I did not think I had mentioned the name of the place. It is no matter though. There is no secret in it."

He passed his long thin hand across his brow, and for a minute or so seemed quite lost. Then his eye wandered slowly round the scene, as if he were striving to bring his distracted thoughts back to the present.

"You have a boat, I see," he said, glancing at the wherry moored a little way from the tree.

"Yes, I spend all my leisure upon the river. Would you like a row this evening? There will be a lovely sunset."

"I should like it of all things."

"Then Captain Browning shall row you. I have a post-bag of letters to write; but he's a better sculler than I am."

Elyard gave the captain an uneasy glance, as if he hardly cared for his company, but recovered himself the next moment.

"I shall be much beholden to Captain Browning," he said, in his stately way.

Half an hour later the captain and the tragedian were sitting in the boat gliding quietly upon the placid river, the slow dip of the oars falling with a musical rhythm, both men curiously silent, as if the stillness of the summer evening, and the loveliness of the landscape had given a melancholy colour to their thoughts.

There was a rosy glow in the west as the sun went down, which gradually deepened to a warm crimson, and intensified with every moment. They had reached a point where the stream narrowed. On the western bank there was a long fringe of reeds, behind which burned the red fires of the setting sun.

Suddenly, Charles Bywater left off rowing, and leaned forward upon his sculls.

"A picturesque bit of the river this?" he said, interrogatively.

The tragedian surveyed the landscape slowly, with his cold, dark eye.

"To my mind neither so picturesque nor so pleasing as other spots we have passed," he answered. "The shores are flat and dull—poorly wooded too—there is no relief for the eye, no variety."

"But that long line of rushes, with the crimson glow behind it," urged the captain, pointing to the western bank, "surely that in itself is a subject for a painter."

"I see no interest in it," said the other coldly.

"That is strange, for it must recall the scene in your tragedy. Do you not see the resemblance?"

"Yes, now you call my attention to it. There is as much likeness as there can be between a stage play and reality, between the formal bank of a canal and the unsophisticated shore of a river."

"Does it bring back to your mind no other scene, one which it resembles more closely—the banks of a river in Buckinghamshire, just the same reedy shore, the same red sunset. Does it not conjure up before your eye the river-bank at Clerevale, the spot where you murdered Helen Leeworthy?"

Michael Elyard started np in the boat like a man distraught. He stood gazing at his accuser, dumbfounded, horror-stricken, while the light wherry reeled with the jerk he had given it.

"You would plead that you are not as the murderers of Hannah Partington. Helen Leeworthy had rejected, perhaps even scorned your love. Secretly, stealthily, you had persecuted her with a suit that was odious to her. She threatened, it may be, to inform her relatives of your pursuit, but her gentle nature revolted against doing you this injury. Instead of doing battle with your passion, as a man or a gentleman, and conquering it, you let your passion conquer you, you abandoned yourself wholly to its sway. You let the devil get possession of you. And then one night you urged for the last time your hopeless unavailing love. You knelt, you entreated, you wept, and she remained cold as marble. And then the devil within you burst his bonds, and you slew her."

"I did," shrieked Elyard, "these hands slaughtered her. I can feel the white round throat now in their grip. How the muscles quivered under my clutch, how the fair young form writhed in that brief agony, the strained blue eyes staring at me all the while. God! do you think they have ever ceased to haunt me with that awful stare. Day and night, waking and sleeping, I have seen them."

He sank down in a heap at the bottom of the boat, and crouched there, looking straight before him at the swiftly darkening landscape, and muttering to himself, as if unconscious of any other presence than his own.

"When have I ceased to see her?" he groaned. "She has walked beside me in the crowded streets; she has come between me and the faces in the theatre. Oh, heaven! if there were any spot upon this earth where she could not come, any arid desert or hill-side cavern or snow-clad mountain where her image could not follow me, I would go and live there upon bread and water, and let the rain beat upon me, and the sun scorch me, and deem such a life happiness compared with the never ending agony of the world where she is!'

Charles Bywater turned the boat, and began to row slowly back.

Elyard never stirred. For an hour there was dead silence. At last, when they were within sight of the lighted windows of the cottage, he seemed to recover his self-possession. He raised himself from his crouching attitude at the bottom of the boat, and quietly resumed his seat.

"What is your motive for ferreting out the secret of my life, and what use are you going to make of it?" he asked.

"I'll answer your last question first. The use I mean to make of my knowledge is to bring you to the gallows. I have a warrant for your apprehension in my pocket."

"And not a vestige of evidence against me," said the other, with a diabolical coolness.

"I will find evidence somehow, now that I have found my man," said the captain. "As for my motive, you will understand that, I dare say, when I tell you my name. I am Charles Bywater!"

"Great heaven!" cried Elyard. "Then it was instinct that made me hate you from the hour we first met."

"No doubt. A prophetic instinct, which told you I was Helen's avenger. You leave this boat my prisoner."

"What if I resist?"

"It would be worse than useless. I have been face to face with mutiny more than once in my life, and should not recoil from violence in a case of necessity. You are unarmed, I daresay, while I have a brace of loaded pistols in my pockets. You will be wise to come with me quietly."

"Ay," answered the other, lapsing into an indifferent tone. "I can afford to let you hector it over me for a few hours. You have not a tittle of evidence against me."

"That will be found hereafter."

"Hereafter will not do. The first magistrate before whom you take me will dismiss your accusation with contempt. You are unduly interfering with the liberty of a fellow subject upon the strength of an unfounded suspicion. My raving just now was a little bit of acting got up on the spur of the moment to deceive you. I wonder you let yourself be taken in so easily."

He rose with a mocking laugh as the nose of the boat ground against the grassy shore by the willow. As his foot touched the shore a strong hand was laid upon his arm, and before he could recover himself from the surprise of that sudden grip, he found himself standing between two burly men, with both his wrists fettered.

"What does it mean?" he gasped.

"I arrest you on suspicion of being concerned in the murder of Helen Leeworthy, whose body was found last week in a hole in the river bank at Clerevale, with your handkerchief tied round her neck."

"I told you that evidence would be forthcoming," said Charles Bywater.

A week later Michael Elyard was found dead in his cell in the jail at Aylesbury, whither he had been carried after his examination before the magistrates at the market town near Clerevale. There had been an inquest upon the poor relics of Helen Leeworthy, a skeleton form, some tresses of golden hair, the rotted remnants of garments which were more easily recognised than the person they had clothed. The inquest had been followed by an examination before the magistrates, and coroner and magistrates had alike adjudged Michael Elphinstone, otherwise Elyard, to be the murderer. As Captain Bywater had foretold, evidence was not wanting. A gipsy came forward who had seen the young lady and her assassin together near the spot where those poor remains were found. Another witness had met Elphinstone coming away from the river path looking agitated, and well nigh distraught.

Strand by strand a rope was twisted, strong enough to hang him. But Michael Elphinstone did not wait for the public hangman and the gaping crowd in front of Aylesbury jail. With his own lean hands he strangled himself in the silence and solitude of his cell, and none knew the hour at which that dark soul took its lonely flight.

Rivals from the Commonwealth

THE GREAT RUBY ROBBERY

A DETECTIVE STORY

Grant Allen

I

Persis Remanet was an American heiress. As she justly remarked, this was a commonplace profession for a young woman nowadays; for almost everybody of late years has been an American and an heiress. A poor Californian, indeed, would be a charming novelty in London society. But London society, so far, has had to go without one.

Persis Remanet was on her way back from the Wilcoxes' ball. She was stopping, of course, with Sir Everard and Lady Maclure at their house at Hampstead. I say "of course" advisedly; because if you or I go to see New York, we have to put up at our own expense (five dollars a day, without wine or extras) at the Windsor or the Fifth Avenue; but whesn the pretty American comes to London (and every American girl is *ex officio* pretty, in Europe at least; I suppose they keep their ugly ones at home for domestic consumption) she is invariably the guest either of a dowager duchess or of a Royal Academician, like Sir Everard, of the first distinction. Yankees visit Europe, in fact, to see, among other things, our art and our old nobility; and by dint of native persistence they get into places that you and I could never succeed in penetrating, unless we devoted all the energies of a long and blameless life to securing an invitation.

Persis hadn't been to the Wilcoxes with Lady Maclure, however. The Maclures were too really great to know such people as the Wilcoxes, who were something tremendous in the City, but didn't buy pictures; and Academicians, you know, don't care to cultivate City people—unless they're customers. ("Patrons," the Academicians more usually call them; but I prefer the simple business word myself, as being a deal less patronizing.) So Persis had accepted an invitation from Mrs. Duncan Harrison, the wife of the well-known member for the Hackness Division of Elmetshire, to take a seat in her carriage to and from the Wilcoxes. Mrs. Harrison knew the habits and manners of American heiresses too well to offer to chaperon Persis; and indeed, Persis, as a free-born American citizen, was quite as well able to take care of herself, the wide world over, as any three ordinary married Englishwomen.

Now, Mrs. Harrison had a brother, an Irish baronet, Sir Justin O'Byrne, late of the Eighth Hussars, who had been with them to the Wilcoxes, and who accompanied them home to Hampstead on the back seat of the carriage. Sir Justin was one of those charming, ineffective, elusive Irishmen whom everybody likes and everybody disapproves of. He had been everywhere, and done everything—except to earn an honest livelihood. The total absence of rents during the sixties and seventies had never prevented his father, old Sir Terence O'Byrne, who sat so long for Connemara in the unreformed Parliament, from sending his son Justin in state to Eton, and afterwards to a fashionable college at Oxford. "He gave me the education of a gentleman," Sir Justin was wont regretfully to observe; "but he omitted to give me also the income to keep it up with."

Nevertheless, society felt O'Byrne was the sort of man who must be kept afloat somehow; and it kept him afloat accordingly in those mysterious ways that only society understands, and that you and I, who are not society, could never get to the bottom of if we tried for a century. Sir Justin himself had essayed Parliament, too, where he sat for a while behind the great Parnell without for a moment forfeiting society's regard even in those earlier days when it was held as a prime article of faith by the world that no gentleman could possibly call himself a Home-Ruler. 'Twas only one of O'Byrne's wild Irish tricks, society said, complacently, with that singular indulgence it always extends to its special favourites, and which is, in fact, the correlative of that unsparing cruelty it shows in turn to those who happen to offend against its unwritten precepts. If Sir Justin had blown up a Czar or two in a fit of political exuberance, society would only have regarded the escapade as "one of O'Byrne's eccentricities." He had also held a commission for a while in a cavalry regiment, which he left, it was understood, owing to a difference of opinion about a lady with the colonel; and he was now a gentleman-at-large on London society, supposed by those who know more about everyone than one knows about oneself, to be on the look-out for a nice girl with a little money.

Sir Justin had paid Persis a great deal of attention that particular evening; in point of fact, he had paid her a great deal of attention from the very first, whenever he met her; and on the way home from the dance he had kept his eyes fixed on Persis's face to an extent that was almost embarrassing. The pretty Californian leaned back in her place in the carriage and surveyed him languidly. She was looking her level best that night, in her pale pink dress, with the famous Remanet rubies in a cascade of red light setting off that snowy neck of hers. 'Twas a neck for a painter. Sir Justin let his eyes fall regretfully more than once on the glittering rubies. He liked and admired Persis, oh! quite immensely. Your society man who has been through seven or eight London seasons could hardly be expected to go quite so far as falling in love with any woman; his habit is rather to look about him critically among all the nice girls trotted out by their mammas for his lordly inspection, and to reflect with a faint smile that this, that, or the other one might perhaps really suit him—if it were not for—and there comes in the inevitable *But* of all human commendation. Still, Sir Justin admitted with a sigh to himself that he liked Persis ever so much; she was so fresh and original! and she talked so cleverly! As for Persis, she would have given her eyes (like every other American girl) to be made "my lady"; and she had seen no man yet, with that auxiliary title in his gift, whom she liked half so well as this delightful wild Irishman.

At the Maclures' door the carriage stopped. Sir Justin jumped out and gave his hand to Persis. You know the house well, of course; Sir Everard Maclure's; it's one of those large new artistic mansions, in red brick and old oak, on the top of the hill; and it stands a little way back from the road, discreetly retired, with a big wooden porch, very convenient for leave-taking. Sir Justin ran up the steps with Persis to ring the bell for her; he had too much of the irrepressible Irish blood in his veins to leave that pleasant task to his sister's footman. But he didn't ring it at once; at the risk of keeping Mrs. Harrison waiting outside for nothing, he stopped and talked a minute or so with the pretty American. "You looked charming to-night, Miss Remanet," he said, as she threw back her light opera wrap for a moment in the porch and displayed a single flash of that snowy neck with the famous rubies; "those stones become you so."

Persis looked at him and smiled. "You think so?" she said, a little tremulous, for even your American heiress, after all, is a woman. "Well, I'm glad you do. But it's good-bye to-night, Sir Justin, for I go next week to Paris."

Even in the gloom of the porch, just lighted by an artistic red and blue lantern in wrought iron, she could see a shade of disappointment pass quickly over his handsome face as he answered, with a little gulp, "No! you don't mean that? Oh, Miss Remanet, I'm so sorry!" Then he paused and drew back: "And yet . . . after all," he continued, "perhaps—," and there he checked himself.

Persis looked up at him hastily. "Yet, after all, what?" she asked, with evident interest.

The young man drew an almost inaudible sigh. "Yet, after all—nothing," he answered, evasively.

"That might do for an Englishwoman," Persis put in, with American frankness, "but it won't do for me. You must tell me what you mean by it." For she reflected sagely that the happiness of two lives might depend upon those two minutes; and how foolish to throw away the chance of a man you really like (with a my-ladyship to boot), all for the sake of a pure convention!

Sir Justin leaned against the woodwork of that retiring porch. She was a beautiful girl. He had hot Irish blood. . . . Well, yes; just for once—he would say the plain truth to her.

"Miss Remanet," he began, leaning forward, and bringing his face close to hers, "Miss Remanet—Persis—shall I tell you the reason why? Because I like you so much. I almost think I love you!"

Persis felt the blood quiver in her tingling cheeks. How handsome he was—and a baronet!

"And yet you're not altogether sorry," she said, reproachfully, "that I'm going to Paris!"

"No, not altogether sorry," he answered, sticking to it; "and I'll tell you why, too, Miss Remanet. I like you very much, and I think you like me. For a week or two, I've been saying to myself, 'I really believe I *must* ask her to marry me.' The temptation's been so strong I could hardly resist it."

"And why do you want to resist it?" Persis asked, all tremulous.

Sir Justin hesitated a second; then with a perfectly natural and instinctive move-ment (though only a gentleman would have ventured to make it) he lifted his hand and just touched with the tips of his fingers the ruby pendants on her necklet. "*This* is why," he answered simply, and with manly frankness. "Persis, you're so rich! I never dare ask you."

"Perhaps you don't know what my answer would be," Persis murmured very low, just to preserve her own dignity.

"Oh, yes; I think I do," the young man replied, gazing deeply into her dark eyes. "It isn't that; if it were only that, I wouldn't so much mind it. But I think you'd take me." There was moisture in her eye. He went on more boldly: "I know you'd take me, Persis, and that's why I don't ask you. You're a great deal too rich, and *these* make it impossible."

"Sir Justin," Persis answered, removing his hand gently, but with the moisture growing thicker, for she really liked him, "it's most unkind of you to say so; either you oughtn't to have told me at all, or else—if you did—" She stopped short. Womanly shame overcame her.

The man leaned forward and spoke earnestly. "Oh, don't say that!" he cried, from his heart. "I couldn't bear to offend you. But I couldn't bear, either, to let you go away—well—without having ever told you. In that case you might have thought I didn't care at all for you, and was only flirting with you. But, Persis, I've cared a great deal for you—a great, great deal—and had hard work many times to prevent myself from asking you. And I'll tell you the plain reason why I haven't asked you. I'm a man about town, not much good, I'm afraid, for anybody or anything; and everybody says I'm on the look-out for an heiress—which happens not to be true; and if I married you, everybody'd say, 'Ah, there! I told you so!' Now, I wouldn't mind that for myself; I'm a man, and I could snap my fingers at them; but I'd mind it for *you*, Persis, for I'm enough in love with you to be very, very jealous, indeed, for your honour. I couldn't bear to think people should say, 'There's that pretty American girl, Persis Remanet that was, you know; she's thrown herself away upon that good-for-nothing Irishman, Justin O'Byrne, a regular fortune-hunter, who's married her for her money.' So for your sake, Persis, I'd rather not ask you; I'd rather leave you for some better man to marry."

"But *I* wouldn't," "Oh, Sir Justin, you must believe me. You must remember——"

At that precise point, Mrs. Harrison put her head out of the carriage window and called out rather loudly:——

"Why, Justin, what's keeping you? The horses'll catch their deaths of cold; and they were clipped this morning. Come back at once, my dear boy. Besides, you know, *les convenances!*"

"All right, Nora," her brother answered; "I won't be a minute. We can't get them to answer this precious bell. I believe it don't ring! But I'll try again, anyhow." And half forgetting that his own words weren't strictly true, for he hadn't yet tried, he pressed the knob with a vengeance.

"Is that your room with the light burning, Miss Remanet?" he went on, in a fairly loud official voice, as the servant came to answer. "The one with the balcony, I mean? Quite Venetian, isn't it? Reminds one of Romeo and Juliet. But most convenient for a burglary, too! Such nice low rails! Mind you take good care of the Remanet rubies!"

"I don't want to take care of them," Persis answered, wiping her dim eyes hastily with her lace pocket-handkerchief, "if they make you feel as you say, Sir Justin. I don't mind if they go. Let the burglar take them!"

And even as she spoke, the Maclure footman, immutable, Sphinx-like, opened the door for her.

II

Persis sat long in her own room that night before she began undressing. Her head was full of Sir Justin and these mysterious hints of his. At last, however, she took her rubies off, and her pretty silk bodice. "I don't care for them at all," she thought, with a gulp, "if they keep from me the love of the man I'd like to marry."

It was late before she fell asleep; and when she did, her rest was troubled. She dreamt a great deal; in her dreams, Sir Justin, and dance music, and the rubies, and burglars were incongruously mingled. To make up for it, she slept late next morning; and Lady Maclure let her sleep on, thinking she was probably wearied out with much dancing the previous evening—as though any amount of excitement could ever weary a pretty American! About ten o'clock she woke with a start. A vague feeling oppressed her that somebody had come in during the night and stolen her rubies. She rose hastily and went to her dressing-table to look for them. The case was there all right; she opened it and looked at it. Oh, prophetic soul! the rubies were gone, and the box was empty!

Now, Persis had honestly said the night before the burglar might take her rubies if he chose, and she wouldn't mind the loss of them. But that was last night, and the rubies hadn't then as yet been taken. This morning, somehow, things seemed quite different. It would be rough on us all (especially on politicians) if we must always be bound by what we said yesterday. Persis was an American, and no American is insensible to the charms of precious stones; 'tis a savage taste which the European immigrants seem to have inherited obliquely from their Red Indian predecessors. She rushed over to the bell and rang it with feminine violence. Lady Maclure's maid answered the summons, as usual. She was a clever, demure-looking girl, this maid of Lady Maclure's; and when Persis cried to her wildly, "Send for the police at once, and tell Sir Everard my jewels are stolen!" she answered "Yes, miss," with such sober acquiescence that Persis, who was American, and therefore a bundle of nerves, turned round and stared at her as an incomprehensible mystery. No Mahatma could have been more unmoved. She seemed quite to expect those rubies would be stolen, and to take no more notice of the incident than if Persis had told her she wanted hot water.

Lady Maclure, indeed, greatly prided herself on this cultivated imperturbability of Bertha's; she regarded it as the fine flower of English domestic service. But Persis was American, and saw things otherwise; to her, the calm repose with which Bertha answered, "Yes, miss; certainly, miss; I'll go and tell Sir Everard," seemed nothing short of exasperating.

Bertha went off with the news, closing the door quite softly; and a few minutes later Lady Maclure herself appeared in the Californian's room, to console her visitor under this severe domestic affliction. She found Persis sitting up in bed, in her pretty French dressing jacket (pale blue with *revers* of fawn colour), reading a book of verses. "Why, my dear!" Lady Maclure exclaimed, "then you've found them again, I suppose? Bertha told us you'd lost your lovely rubies!"

"So I have, dear Lady Maclure," Persis answered, wiping her eyes; "they're gone. They've been stolen. I forgot to lock my door when I came home last night, and the window was open; somebody must have come in, this way or that, and taken them. But whenever I'm in trouble, I try a dose of Browning. He's splendid for the nerves. He's so consoling, you know; he brings one to anchor."

She breakfasted in bed; she wouldn't leave the room, she declared, till the police arrived. After breakfast she rose and put on her dainty Parisian morning wrap—Americans have always such pretty bed-room things for these informal receptions—and sat up in state to await the police officer. Sir Everard himself, much disturbed that such a mishap should have happened in his house, went round in person to fetch the official. While he was gone, Lady Maclure made a thorough search of the room, but couldn't find a trace of the missing rubies.

"Are you sure you put them in the case, dear?" she asked, for the honour of the household.

And Persis answered: "Quite confident, Lady Maclure; I always put them there the moment I take them off; and when I came to look for them this morning, the case was empty."

"They were very valuable, I believe?" Lady Maclure said, inquiringly.

"Six thousand pounds was the figure in your money, I guess," Persis answered, ruefully. "I don't know if you call that a lot of money in England, but we do in America."

There was a moment's pause, and then Persis spoke again:—

"Lady Maclure," she said, abruptly, "do you consider that maid of yours a Christian woman?"

Lady Maclure was startled. That was hardly the light in which she was accustomed to regard the lower classes.

"Well, I don't know about that," she said, slowly; "that's a great deal, you know, dear, to assert about *anybody*, especially one's maid. But I should think she was honest, quite decidedly honest."

"Well, that's the same thing, about, isn't it?" Persis answered, much relieved. "I'm glad you think that's so; for I was almost half afraid of her. She's too quiet for my taste, somehow; so silent, you know, and inscrutable."

"Oh, my dear," her hostess cried, "don't blame her for silence; that's just what I like about her. It's exactly what I chose her for. Such a nice, noiseless girl; moves about the room like a cat on tiptoe; knows her proper place, and never dreams of speaking unless she's spoken to."

"Well, you may like them that way in Europe," Persis responded, frankly; "but in America, we prefer them a little bit human."

Twenty minutes later the police officer arrived. He wasn't in uniform. The inspector, feeling at once the gravity of the case, and recognising that this was a Big Thing, in which there was glory to be won, and perhaps promotion, sent a detective at once, and advised that if possible nothing should be said to the household on the subject for the present, till the detective had taken a good look round the premises. That was useless, Sir Everard feared, for the lady's-maid knew; and the lady's-maid would be sure to go down, all agog with the news, to the servants' hall immediately. However, they might try; no harm in trying; and the sooner the detective got round to the house, of course, the better.

The detective accompanied him back—a keen-faced, close-shaven, irreproachable-looking man, like a vulgarized copy of Mr. John Morley. He was curt and business-like. His first question was, "Have the servants been told of this?"

Lady Maclure looked inquiringly across at Bertha. She herself had been sitting all the time with the bereaved Persis, to console her (with Browning) under this heavy affliction.

"No, my lady," Bertha answered, ever calm (invaluable servant, Bertha!), "I didn't mention it to anybody downstairs on purpose, thinking perhaps it might be decided to search the servants' boxes."

The detective pricked up his ears. He was engaged already in glancing casually round the room. He moved about it now, like a conjurer, with quiet steps and slow. "He doesn't get on one's nerves," Persis remarked, approvingly, in an undertone to her friend; then she added, aloud: "What's your name, please, Mr. Officer?"

The detective was lifting a lace handkerchief on the dressing-table at the side. He turned round softly. "Gregory, madam," he answered, hardly glancing at the girl, and going on with his occupation.

"The same as the powders!" Persis interposed, with a shudder. "I used to take them when I was a child. I never could bear them."

"We're useful, as remedies," the detective replied, with a quiet smile; "but nobody likes us." And he relapsed contentedly into his work once more, searching round the apartment.

"The first thing we have to do," he said, with a calm air of superiority, standing now by the window, with one hand in his pocket, "is to satisfy ourselves whether or not there has really, at all, been a robbery. We must look through the room well, and see you haven't left the rubies lying about loose somewhere. Such things often happen. We're constantly called in to investigate a case, when it's only a matter of a lady's carelessness."

At that Persis flared up. A daughter of the great republic isn't accustomed to be doubted like a mere European woman. "I'm quite sure I took them off," she said, "and put them back in the jewel case. Of that I'm just confident. There isn't a doubt possible."

Mr. Gregory redoubled his search in all likely and unlikely places. "I should say that settles the matter," he answered, blandly. "Our experience is that whenever a lady's perfectly certain, beyond the possibility of doubt, she put a thing away safely, it's absolutely sure to turn up where she says she didn't put it."

Persis answered him never a word. Her manners had not that repose that stamps the caste of Vere de Vere; so, to prevent an outbreak, she took refuge in Browning.

Mr. Gregory, nothing abashed, searched the room thoroughly, up and down, without the faintest regard to Persis's feelings; he was a detective, he said, and his business was first of all to unmask crime, irrespective of circumstances. Lady Maclure stood by, mean-while, with the imperturbable Bertha. Mr. Gregory investigated every hole and cranny, like a man who wishes to let the world see for itself he performs a disagreeable duty with unflinching thoroughness. When he had finished, he turned to Lady Maclure. "And now, if you please," he said, blandly, "we'll proceed to investigate the servants' boxes."

Lady Maclure looked at her maid. "Bertha," she said, "go downstairs, and see that none of the other servants come up, meanwhile, to their bed-rooms." Lady Maclure was not quite to the manner born, and had never acquired the hateful aristocratic habit of calling women servants by their surnames only.

But the detective interposed. "No, no," he said, sharply. "This young woman had better stop here with Miss Remanet—strictly under her eye—till I've searched the boxes. For if I find nothing there, it may perhaps be my disagreeable duty, by-and-by, to call in a female detective to search her."

It was Lady Maclure's turn to flare up now. "Why, this is my own maid," she said, in a chilly tone, "and I've every confidence in her."

"Very sorry for that, my lady," Mr. Gregory responded, in a most official voice; "but our experience teaches us that if there's a person in the case whom nobody ever dreams of suspecting, that person's the one who has committed the robbery."

"Why, you'll be suspecting myself next!" Lady Maclure cried, with some disgust.

"Your ladyship's just the last person in the world I should think of suspecting," the detective answered, with a deferential bow—which, after his previous speech, was to say the least of it equivocal.

Persis began to get annoyed. She didn't half like the look of that girl Bertha, herself; but still, she was there as Lady Maclure's guest, and she couldn't expose her hostess to discomfort on her account.

"The girl shall *not* be searched," she put in, growing hot. "I don't care a cent whether I lose the wretched stones or not. Compared to human dignity, what are they worth? Not five minutes' consideration."

"They're worth just seven years," Mr. Gregory answered, with professional definiteness. "And as to searching, why, that's out of your hands now. This is a criminal case. I'm here to discharge a public duty."

"I don't in the least mind being searched," Bertha put in obligingly, with an air of indifference. "You can search me if you like—when you've got a warrant for it."

The detective looked up sharply; so also did Persis. This ready acquaintance with the liberty of the subject in criminal cases impressed her unfavourably. "Ah! we'll see about that," Mr. Gregory answered, with a cool smile. "Meanwhile, Lady Maclure, I'll have a look at the boxes."

III

The search (strictly illegal) brought out nothing. Mr. Gregory returned to Persis's bed-room, disconsolate. "You can leave the room," he said to Bertha; and Bertha glided out. "I've set another man outside to keep a constant eye on her," he added in explanation.

By this time Persis had almost made her mind up as to who was the culprit; but she said nothing overt, for Lady Maclure's sake, to the detective. As for that immovable official, he began asking questions—some of them, Persis thought, almost bordering on the personal. Where had she been last night? Was she sure she had really worn the rubies? How did she come home? Was she certain she took them off? Did the maid help her undress? Who came back with her in the carriage?

To all these questions, rapidly fired off with cross-examining acuteness, Persis answered in the direct American fashion. She was sure she had the rubies on when she came home to Hampstead, because Sir Justin O'Byrne, who came back with her in his sister's carriage, had noticed them the last thing, and had told her to take care of them.

At mention of that name the detective smiled meaningly. (A meaning smile is stock-in-trade to a detective.) "Oh, Sir Justin O'Byrne!" he repeated, with quiet self-constraint. "*He* came back with you in the carriage, then? And did he sit the same side with you?"

Lady Maclure grew indignant (that was Mr. Gregory's cue). "Really, sir," she said, angrily, "if you're going to suspect gentlemen in Sir Justin's position, we shall none of us be safe from you."

"The law," Mr. Gregory replied, with an air of profound deference, "is no respecter of persons."

"But it ought to be of characters," Lady Maclure cried, warmly. "What's the good of having a blameless character, I should like to know, if—if—"

"If it doesn't allow you to commit a robbery with impunity?" the detective interposed, finishing her sentence his own way. "Well, well, that's true. That's perfectly true—but Sir Justin's character, you see, can hardly be called blameless."

"He's a gentleman," Persis cried, with flashing eyes, turning round upon the officer; "and he's quite incapable of such a mean and despicable crime as you dare to suspect him of."

"Oh, I see," the officer answered, like one to whom a welcome ray of light breaks suddenly through a great darkness. "Sir Justin's a friend of yours! Did he come into the porch with you?"

"He did," Persis answered, flushing crimson; "and if you have the insolence to bring a charge against him—"

"Calm yourself, madam," the detective replied, coolly. "I do nothing of the sort—at this stage of the proceedings. It's possible there may have been no robbery in the case at all. We must keep our minds open for the present to every possible alternative. It's—it's a delicate matter to hint at; but before we go any further—do you think, perhaps, Sir Justin may have carried the rubies away by mistake, entangled in his clothes?—say, for example, his coat-sleeve?"

It was a loophole of escape; but Persis didn't jump at it.

"He had never the opportunity," she answered, with a flash. "And I know quite well they were there on my neck when he left me, for the last thing he said to me was, looking up at this very window: 'That balcony's awfully convenient for a burglary. Mind you take good care of the Remanet rubies.' And I remembered what he'd said when I took them off last night; and that's what makes me so sure I really had them."

"*And* you slept with the window open!" the detective went on, still smiling to himself. "Well, here we have all the materials, to be sure, for a first-class mystery!"

IV

For some days more, nothing further turned up of importance about the Great Ruby Robbery. It got into the papers, of course, as everything does nowadays, and all London was talking of it. Persis found herself quite famous as the American lady who had lost her jewels. People pointed her out in the park; people stared at her hard through their opera-glasses at the theatre. Indeed, the possession of the celebrated Remanet rubies had never made her half so conspicuous in the world as the loss of them made her. It was almost worth while losing them, Persis thought, to be so much made of as she was in society in consequence. All the world knows a young lady must be somebody when she can offer a reward of five hundred pounds for the recovery of gewgaws valued at six thousand.

Sir Justin met her in the Row one day. "Then you don't go to Paris for awhile yet—until you get them back?" he inquired very low.

And Persis answered, blushing, "No, Sir Justin; not yet; and—I'm almost glad of it."

"No, you don't mean that!" the young man cried, with perfect boyish ardour. "Well, I confess, Miss Remanet, the first thing I thought myself when I read it in *The Times* was just the very same: 'Then, after all, she won't go yet to Paris!'"

Persis looked up at him from her pony with American frankness. "And I," she said, quivering, "I found anchor in Browning. For what do you think I read?

> And learn to rate a true man's heart
> Far above rubies.

The book opened at the very place; and *there* I found anchor!"

But when Sir Justin went round to his rooms that same evening his servant said to him, "A gentleman was inquiring for you here this afternoon, sir. A close-shaven gentleman. Not very prepossessin'. And it seemed to me somehow, sir, as if he was trying to pump me."

Sir Justin's face was grave. He went to his bed-room at once. He knew what that man wanted; and he turned straight to his wardrobe, looking hard at the dress coat he had worn on the eventful evening. Things may cling to a sleeve, don't you know—or be entangled in a cuff—or get casually into a pocket! Or someone may put them there.

V

For the next ten days or so Mr. Gregory was busy, constantly busy. Without doubt, he was the most active and energetic of detectives. He carried out so fully his own official principle of suspecting everybody, from China to Peru, that at last poor Persis got fairly mazed with his web of possibilities. Nobody was safe from his cultivated and highly-trained suspicion—not Sir Everard in his studio, nor Lady Maclure in her boudoir, nor the butler in his pantry, nor Sir Justin O'Byrne in his rooms in St. James's. Mr. Gregory kept an open mind against everybody and everything. He even doubted the parrot, and had views as to the intervention of rats and terriers. Persis got rather tired at last of his perverse ingenuity; especially as she had a very shrewd idea herself who had stolen the rubies. When he suggested various doubts, however, which seemed remotely to implicate Sir Justin's honesty, the sensitive American girl "felt it go on her nerves," and refused to listen to him, though Mr. Gregory never ceased to enforce upon her, by precept and example, his own pet doctrine that the last person on earth one would be likely to suspect is always the one who turns out to have done it.

A morning or two later, Persis looked out of her window as she was dressing her hair. She dressed it herself now, though she was an American heiress, and, therefore, of course, the laziest of her kind; for she had taken an unaccountable dislike, somehow, to that quiet girl Bertha. On this particular morning, however, when Persis looked out, she saw Bertha engaged in close, and apparently very intimate, conversation with the Hampstead postman. This sight disturbed the unstable equilibrium of her equanimity not a little. Why should Bertha go to the door to the postman at all? Surely it was no part of the duty of Lady Maclure's maid to take in the letters! And why should she want to go prying into the question of who wrote to Miss Remanet? For Persis, intensely conscious herself that a note from Sir Justin lay on top of the postman's bundle—she recognised it at once, even at that distance below, by the peculiar shape of the broad rough envelope—jumped to the natural feminine conclusion that Bertha must needs be influenced by some abstruse motive of which she herself, Persis, was, to say the very least, a component element. 'Tis a human fallacy. We're all of us prone to see everything from a personal standpoint; indeed, the one quality which makes a man or woman into a possible novelist, good, bad, or indifferent, is just that special power of throwing himself or herself into a great many people's personalities alternately. And this is a power possessed on an average by not one in a thousand men or not one in ten thousand women.

Persis rang the bell violently. Bertha came up, all smiles: "Did you want anything, miss?" Persis could have choked her. "Yes," she answered, plainly, taking the bull by the horns; "I want to know what you were doing down there, prying into other people's letters with the postman?"

Bertha looked up at her, ever bland; she answered at once, without a second's hesitation: "The postman's my young man, miss; and we hope before very long now to get married."

"Odious thing!" Persis thought. "A glib lie always ready on the tip of her tongue for every emergency."

But Bertha's full heart was beating violently. Beating with love and hope and deferred anxiety.

A little later in the day Persis mentioned the incident casually to Lady Maclure mainly in order to satisfy herself that the girl had been lying. Lady Maclure, however, gave a qualified assent:—

"I *believe* she's engaged to the postman," she said. "I think I've heard so; though I make it a rule, you see, my dear, to know as little as I can of these people's love affairs. They're so very uninteresting. But Bertha certainly told me she wouldn't leave me to get married for an indefinite period. That was only ten days ago. She said her young man wasn't just yet in a position to make a home for her."

"Perhaps," Persis suggested, grimly, "something has occurred meanwhile to better her position. Such strange things crop up. She may have come into a fortune!"

"Perhaps so," Lady Maclure replied, languidly. The subject bored her. "Though, if so, it must really have been very sudden; for I think it was the morning before you lost your jewels she told me so."

Persis thought that odd, but she made no comment.

Before dinner that evening she burst suddenly into Lady Maclure's room for a minute. Bertha was dressing her lady's hair. Friends were coming to dine—among them Sir Justin. "How do these pearls go with my complexion, Lady Maclure?" Persis asked rather anxiously; for she specially wished to look her best that evening, for one of the party.

"Oh, charming!" her hostess answered, with her society smile. "Never saw anything suit you better, Persis."

"Except my poor rubies!" Persis cried rather ruefully, for coloured gewgaws are dear to the savage and the woman. "I wish I could get them back! I wonder that man Gregory hasn't succeeded in finding them."

"Oh! my dear," Lady Maclure drawled out, "you may be sure by this time they're safe at Amsterdam. That's the only place in Europe now to look for them."

"Why to Amsterdam, my lady?" Bertha interposed suddenly, with a quick side-glance at Persis.

Lady Maclure threw her head back in surprise at so unwonted an intrusion. "What do you want to know that for, child?" she asked, somewhat curtly. "Why, to be cut, of course. All the diamond-cutters in the world are concentrated in Amsterdam; and the first thing a thief does when he steals big jewels is to send them across, and have them cut in new shapes so that they can't be identified."

"I shouldn't have thought," Bertha put in, calmly, "they'd have known who to send them to."

Lady Maclure turned to her sharply. "Why, these things," she said, with a calm air of knowledge, "are always done by experienced thieves, who know the ropes well, and are in league with receivers the whole world over. But Gregory has his eye on Amsterdam, I'm sure, and we'll soon hear something."

"Yes, my lady," Bertha answered, in her acquiescent tone, and relapsed into silence.

VI

Four days later, about nine at night, that hard-worked man, the posty on the beat, stood loitering outside Sir Everard Maclure's house, openly defying the rules of the department, in close conference with Bertha.

"Well, any news?" Bertha asked, trembling over with excitement, for she was a very different person outside with her lover from the demure and imperturbable model maid who waited on my lady.

"Why, yes," the posty answered, with a low laugh of triumph. "A letter from Amsterdam! And I think we've fixed it!"

Bertha almost flung herself upon him. "Oh, Harry!" she cried, all eagerness, "this is too good to be true! Then in just one other month we can really get married!"

There was a minute's pause, inarticulately filled up by sounds unrepresentable through the art of the type-founder. Then Harry spoke again. "It's an awful lot of money!" he said, musing. "A regular fortune! And what's more, Bertha, if it hadn't been for your cleverness we never should have got it!"

Bertha pressed his hand affectionately. Even ladies'-maids are human.

"Well, if I hadn't been so much in love with you," she answered, frankly, "I don't think I could ever have had the wit to manage it. But, oh! Harry, love makes one do or try anything!"

If Persis had heard those singular words, she would have felt no doubt was any longer possible.

VII

Next morning, at ten o'clock, a policeman came round, post haste, to Sir Everard's. He asked to see Miss Remanet. When Persis came down, in her morning wrap, he had but a brief message from headquarters to give her: "Your jewels are found, Miss. Will you step round and identify them?"

Persis drove back with him, all trembling. Lady Maclure accompanied her. At the police-station they left their cab, and entered the ante-room.

A little group had assembled there. The first person Persis distinctly made out in it was Sir Justin. A great terror seized her. Gregory had so poisoned her mind by this time with suspicion of everybody and everything she came across, that she was afraid of her own shadow. But next moment she saw clearly he wasn't there as prisoner, or even as witness; merely as spectator. She acknowledged him with a hasty bow, and cast her eye round again. The next person she definitely distinguished was Bertha, as calm and cool as ever, but in the very centre of the group, occupying as it were the place of honour which naturally belongs to the prisoner on all similar occasions. Persis was not surprised at that; she had known it all along; she glanced meaningly at Gregory, who stood a little behind, looking by no means triumphant. Persis found his dejection odd; but he was a proud detective, and perhaps someone else had effected the capture!

"These are your jewels, I believe," the inspector said, holding them up; and Persis admitted it.

"This is a painful case," the inspector went on. "A very painful case. We grieve to have discovered such a clue against one of our own men; but as he owns to it himself, and intends to throw himself on the mercy of the Court, it's no use talking about it. He won't attempt to defend it; indeed, with such evidence, I think he's doing what's best and wisest."

Persis stood there, all dazed. "I—I don't understand," she cried, with a swimming brain. "Who on earth are you talking about?"

The inspector pointed mutely with one hand at Gregory; and then for the first time Persis saw he was guarded. She clapped her hand to her head. In a moment it all broke in upon her. When she had called in the police, the rubies had never been stolen at all. It was Gregory who stole them!

She understood it now, at once. The real facts came back to her. She had taken her necklet off at night, laid it carelessly down on the dressing-table (too full of Sir Justin), covered it accidentally with her lace pocket-handkerchief, and straightway forgotten all about it. Next day she missed it, and jumped at conclusions. When Gregory came, he spied the rubies askance under the corner of the handkerchief—of course, being a woman, she had naturally looked everywhere except in the place where she laid them—and knowing it was a safe case he had quietly pocketed them before her very eyes, all unsuspected. He felt sure nobody could accuse him of a robbery which was committed before he came, and which he had himself been called in to investigate.

"The worst of it is," the inspector went on, "he had woven a very ingenious case against Sir Justin O'Byrne, whom we were on the very point of arresting to-day, if this young woman hadn't come in at the eleventh hour, in the very nick of time, and earned the reward by giving us the clue that led to the discovery and recovery of the jewels. They were brought over this morning by an Amsterdam detective."

Persis looked hard at Bertha. Bertha answered her look. "My young man was the postman, miss," she explained, quite simply; "and after what my lady said, I put him up to watch Mr. Gregory's delivery for a letter from Amsterdam. I'd suspected him from the very first; and when the letter came, we had him arrested at once, and found out from it who were the people at Amsterdam who had the rubies."

Persis gasped with astonishment. Her brain was reeling. But Gregory in the background put in one last word:—

"Well, I was right, after all," he said, with professional pride. "I told you the very last person you'd dream of suspecting was sure to be the one that actually did it."

Lady O'Byrne's rubies were very much admired at Monte Carlo last season. Mr. Gregory has found permanent employment for the next seven years at Her Majesty's quarries on the Isle of Portland. Bertha and her postman have retired to Canada with five hundred pounds to buy a farm. And everybody says Sir Justin O'Byrne has beaten the record, after all, even for Irish baronets, by making a marriage at once of money and affection.

THE LENTON CROFT ROBBERIES

Arthur Morrison

THOSE WHO RETAIN ANY MEMORY OF THE GREAT LAW CASES OF FIFTEEN OR twenty years back will remember, at least, the title of that extraordinary will case, "Bartley *v*. Bartley and others," which occupied the Probate Court for some weeks on end, and caused an amount of public interest rarely accorded to any but the cases considered in the other division of the same court. The case itself was noted for the large quantity of remarkable and unusual evidence presented by the plaintiff's side—evidence that took the other party completely by surprise, and overthrew their case like a house of cards. The affair will, perhaps, be more readily recalled as the occasion of the sudden rise to eminence in their profession of Messrs. Crellan, Hunt & Crellan, solicitors for the plaintiff—a result due entirely to the wonderful ability shown in this case of building up, apparently out of nothing, a smashing weight of irresistible evidence. That the firm has since maintained—indeed enhanced—the position it then won for itself need scarcely be said here; its name is familiar to everybody. But there are not many of the outside public who know that the credit of the whole performance was primarily due to a young clerk in the employ of Messrs. Crellan, who had been given charge of the seemingly desperate task of collecting evidence in the case.

This Mr. Martin Hewitt had, however, full credit and reward for his exploit from his firm and from their client, and more than one other firm of lawyers engaged in contentious work made good offers to entice Hewitt to change his employers. Instead of this, however, he determined to work independently for the future, having conceived the idea of making a regular business of doing, on behalf of such clients as might retain him, similar work to that he had just done with such conspicuous success for Messrs. Crellan, Hunt & Crellan. This was the beginning of the private detective business of Martin Hewitt, and his action at that time has been completely justified by the brilliant professional successes he has since achieved.

His business has always been conducted in the most private manner, and he has always declined the help of professional assistants, preferring to carry out himself such of the many investigations offered him as he could manage. He has always maintained that he has never lost by this policy, since the chance of his refusing a case begets competition for his services, and his fees rise by a natural process. At the same time, no man could know better how to employ casual assistance at the right time.

Some curiosity has been expressed as to Mr. Martin Hewitt's system, and, as he himself always consistently maintains that he has no system beyond a judicious use of ordinary faculties, I intend setting forth in detail a few of the more interesting of his cases in order that the public may judge for itself if I am right in estimating Mr. Hewitt's "ordinary faculties" as faculties very extraordinary indeed. He is not a man who has made many friendships (this, probably, for professional reasons), notwithstanding his genial and companionable manners. I myself first made his acquaintance as a result of an accident resulting in a fire at the old house in which Hewitt's office was situated, and in an upper floor of which I occupied bachelor chambers. I was able to help in saving a quantity of extremely important papers relating to his business, and, while repairs were being made, allowed him to lock them in an old wall-safe in one of my rooms which the fire had scarcely damaged.

The acquaintance thus begun has lasted many years, and has become a rather close friendship. I have even accompanied Hewitt on some of his expeditions, and, in a humble way, helped him. Such of the cases, however, as I personally saw nothing of I have put into narrative form from the particulars given me.

"I consider you, Brett," he said, addressing me, "the most remarkable journalist alive. Not because you're particularly clever, you know, because, between ourselves, I hope you'll admit you're not; but because you have known something of me and my doings for some years, and have never yet been guilty of giving away any of my little business secrets you may have become acquainted with. I'm afraid you're not so enterprising a journalist as some, Brett. But now, since you ask, you shall write something—if you think it worth while."

This he said, as he said most things, with a cheery, chaffing good-nature that would have been, perhaps, surprising to a stranger who thought of him only as a grim and mysterious discoverer of secrets and crimes. Indeed, the man had always as little of the aspect of the conventional detective as may be imagined. Nobody could appear more cordial or less observant in manner, although there was to be seen a certain sharpness of the eye—which might, after all, only be the twinkle of good humor.

I *did* think it worth while to write something of Martin Hewitt's investigations, and a description of one of his adventures follows.

At the head of the first flight of a dingy staircase leading up from an ever-open portal in a street by the Strand stood a door, the dusty ground-glass upper panel of which carried in its centre the single word "Hewitt," while at its right-hand lower corner, in smaller letters, "Clerk's Office" appeared. On a morning when the clerks in the ground-floor offices had barely hung up their hats, a short, well-dressed young man, wearing spectacles, hastening to open the dusty door, ran into the arms of another man who suddenly issued from it.

"I beg pardon," the first said. "Is this Hewitt's Detective Agency Office?"

"Yes, I believe you will find it so," the other replied. He was a stoutish, clean-shaven man, of middle height, and of a cheerful, round countenance. "You'd better speak to the clerk."

In the little outer office the visitor was met by a sharp lad with inky fingers, who presented him with a pen and a printed slip. The printed slip having been filled with the visitor's name and present business, and conveyed through an inner door, the lad reappeared with an invitation to the private office. There, behind a writing-table, sat the stoutish man himself, who had only just advised an appeal to the clerk.

"Good-morning, Mr. Lloyd—Mr. Vernon Lloyd," he said, affably, looking again at the slip. "You'll excuse my care to start even with my visitors—I must, you know. You come from Sir James Norris, I see."

"Yes; I am his secretary. I have only to ask you to go straight to Lenton Croft at once, if you can, on very important business. Sir James would have wired, but had not your precise address. Can you go by the next train? Eleven-thirty is the first available from Paddington."

"Quite possibly. Do you know any thing of the business?"

"It is a case of a robbery in the house, or, rather, I fancy, of several robberies. Jewelry has been stolen from rooms occupied by visitors to the Croft. The first case occurred some months ago—nearly a year ago, in fact. Last night there was another. But I think you had better get the details on the spot. Sir James has told me to telegraph if you are coming, so that he may meet you himself at the station; and I must hurry, as his drive to the station will be rather a long one. Then I take it you will go, Mr. Hewitt? Twyford is the station."

"Yes, I shall come, and by the 11:30. Are you going by that train yourself?"

"No, I have several things to attend to now I am in town. Good-morning; I shall wire at once."

Mr. Martin Hewitt locked the drawer of his table and sent his clerk for a cab.

At Twyford Station Sir James Norris was waiting with a dog-cart. Sir James was a tall, florid man of fifty or thereabout, known away from home as something of a county historian, and nearer his own parts as a great supporter of the hunt, and a gentleman much troubled with poachers. As soon as he and Hewitt had found one another the baronet hurried the detective into his dog-cart. "We've something over seven miles to drive," he said, "and I can tell you all about this wretched business as we go. That is why I came for you myself, and alone."

Hewitt nodded.

"I have sent for you, as Lloyd probably told you, because of a robbery at my place last evening. It appears, as far as I can guess, to be one of three by the same hand, or by the same gang. Late yesterday afternoon——"

"Pardon me, Sir James," Hewitt interrupted, "but I think I must ask you to begin at the first robbery and tell me the whole tale in proper order. It makes things clearer, and sets them in their proper shape."

"Very well! Eleven months ago, or thereabout, I had rather a large party of visitors, and among them Colonel Heath and Mrs. Heath—the lady being a relative of my own late wife. Colonel Heath has not been long retired, you know—used to be political resident in an Indian native state. Mrs. Heath had rather a good stock of jewelry of one sort and another, about the most valuable piece being a bracelet set with a particularly fine pearl—quite an exceptional pearl, in fact—that had been one of a heap of presents from the maharajah of his state when Heath left India.

"It was a very noticeable bracelet, the gold setting being a mere feather-weight piece of native filigree work—almost too fragile to trust on the wrist—and the pearl being, as I have said, of a size and quality not often seen. Well, Heath and his wife arrived late one evening, and after lunch the following day, most of the men being off by themselves—shooting, I think—my daughter, my sister (who is very often down here), and Mrs. Heath took it into their heads to go walking—fern-hunting, and so on. My sister was rather long dressing, and, while they waited, my daughter went into Mrs. Heath's room, where Mrs. Heath turned over all her treasures to show her, as women do, you know. When my sister was at last ready, they came straight away, leaving the things littering about the room rather than stay longer to pack them up. The bracelet, with other things, was on the dressing-table then."

"One moment. As to the door?"

"They locked it. As they came away my daughter suggested turning the key, as we had one or two new servants about."

"And the window?"

"That they left open, as I was going to tell you. Well, they went on their walk and came back, with Lloyd (whom they had met somewhere) carrying their ferns for them. It was dusk and almost dinner-time. Mrs. Heath went straight to her room, and—the bracelet was gone."

"Was the room disturbed?"

"Not a bit. Everything was precisely where it had been left, except the bracelet. The door hadn't been tampered with, but of course the window was open, as I have told you."

"You called the police, of course?"

"Yes, and had a man from Scotland Yard down in the morning. He seemed a pretty smart fellow, and the first thing he noticed on the dressing-table, within an inch or two of where the bracelet had been, was a match, which had been lit and thrown down. Now nobody about the house had had occasion to use a match in that room that day, and, if they had, certainly wouldn't have thrown it on the cover of the dressing-table. So that, presuming the thief to have used that match, the robbery must have been committed when the room was getting dark—immediately before Mrs. Heath returned, in fact. The thief had evidently struck the match, passed it hurriedly over the various trinkets lying about, and taken the most valuable."

"Nothing else was even moved?"

"Nothing at all. Then the thief must have escaped by the window, although it was not quite clear how. The walking party approached the house with a full view of the window, but saw nothing, although the robbery must have been actually taking place a moment or two before they turned up."

"There was no water-pipe within any practicable distance of the window, but a ladder usually kept in the stable-yard was found lying along the edge of the lawn. The gardener explained, however, that he had put the ladder there after using it himself early in the afternoon."

"Of course it might easily have been used again after that and put back."

"Just what the Scotland Yard man said. He was pretty sharp, too, on the gardener, but very soon decided that he knew nothing of it. No stranger had been seen in the neighborhood, nor had passed the lodge gates. Besides, as the detective said, it scarcely seemed the work of a stranger. A stranger could scarcely have known enough to go straight to the room where a lady—only arrived the day before—had left a valuable jewel, and away again without being seen. So all the people about the house were suspected in turn. The servants offered, in a body, to have their boxes searched, and this was done; everything was turned over, from the butler's to the new kitchen-maid's. I don't know that I should have had this carried quite so far if I had been the loser myself, but it was my guest, and I was in such a horrible position. Well, there's little more to be said about that, unfortunately. Nothing came of it all, and the thing's as great a mystery now as ever. I believe the Scotland Yard man got as far as suspecting *me* before he gave it up altogether, but give it up he did in the end. I think that's all I know about the first robbery. Is it clear?"

"Oh, yes; I shall probably want to ask a few questions when I have seen the place, but they can wait. What next?"

"Well," Sir James pursued, "the next was a very trumpery affair, that I should have forgotten all about, probably, if it hadn't been for one circumstance. Even now I hardly think it could have been the work of the same hand. Four months or thereabout after Mrs. Heath's disaster—in February of this year, in fact—Mrs. Armitage, a young widow, who had been a school-fellow of my daughter's, stayed with us for a week or so. The girls don't trouble about the London season, you know, and I have no town house, so they were glad to have their old friend here for a little in the dull time. Mrs. Armitage is a very active young lady, and was scarcely in the house half-an-hour before she arranged a drive in a pony-cart with Eva—my daughter—to look up old people in the village that she used to know before she was married. So they set off in the afternoon, and made such a round of it that they were late for dinner. Mrs. Armitage had a small plain gold brooch—not at all valuable, you know; two or three pounds, I suppose—which she used to pin up a cloak or anything of that sort. Before she went out she stuck this in the pin-cushion on her dressing-table, and left a ring—rather a good one, I believe—lying close by."

"This," asked Hewitt, "was not in the room that Mrs. Heath had occupied, I take it?"

"No; this was in another part of the building. Well, the brooch went—taken, evidently, by some one in a deuce of a hurry, for, when Mrs. Armitage got back to her room, there was the pin-cushion with a little tear in it, where the brooch had been simply snatched off. But the curious thing was that the ring—worth a dozen of the brooch—was left where it had been put. Mrs. Armitage didn't remember whether or not she had locked the door herself, although she found it locked when she returned; but my niece, who was indoors all the time, went and tried it once—because she remembered that a gas-fitter was at work on the landing near by—and found it safely locked. The gas-fitter, whom we didn't know at the time, but who since seems to be quite an honest fellow, was ready to swear that nobody but my niece had been to the door while he was in sight of it—which was almost all the time. As to the window, the sash-line had broken that very morning, and Mrs. Armitage had propped open the bottom half about eight or ten inches with a brush; and, when she returned, that brush, sash, and all were exactly as she had left them. Now I scarcely need tell *you* what an awkward job it must have been for anybody to get noiselessly in at that unsupported window; and how unlikely he would have been to replace it, with the brush, exactly as he found it."

"Just so. I suppose the brooch, was really gone? I mean, there was no chance of Mrs. Armitage having mislaid it?"

"Oh, none at all! There was a most careful search."

"Then, as to getting in at the window, would it have been easy?"

"Well, yes," Sir James replied; "yes, perhaps it would. It was a first-floor window, and it looks over the roof and skylight of the billiard-room. I built the billiard-room myself—built it out from a smoking-room just at this corner. It would be easy enough to get at the window from the billiard-room roof. But, then," he added, "that couldn't have been the way. Somebody or other was in the billiard-room the whole time, and nobody could have got over the roof (which is nearly all skylight) without being seen and heard. I was there myself for an hour or two, taking a little practice."

"Well, was anything done?"

"Strict inquiry was made among the servants, of course, but nothing came of it. It was such a small matter that Mrs. Armitage wouldn't hear of my calling in the police or anything of that sort, although I felt pretty certain that there must be a dishonest servant about somewhere. A servant might take a plain brooch, you know, who would feel afraid of a valuable ring, the loss of which would be made a greater matter of."

"Well, yes, perhaps so, in the case of an inexperienced thief, who also would be likely to snatch up whatever she took in a hurry. But I'm doubtful. What made you connect these two robberies together?"

"Nothing whatever—for some months. They seemed quite of a different sort. But scarcely more than a month ago I met Mrs. Armitage at Brighton, and we talked, among other things, of the previous robbery—that of Mrs. Heath's bracelet. I described the circumstances pretty minutely, and, when I mentioned the match found on the table, she said: 'How strange! Why, *my* thief left a match on the dressing-table when he took my poor little brooch!'"

Hewitt nodded. "Yes," he said. "A spent match, of course?"

"Yes, of course, a spent match. She noticed it lying close by the pin-cushion, but threw it away without mentioning the circumstance. Still, it seemed rather curious to me that a match should be lit and dropped, in each case, on the dressing-cover an inch from where the article was taken. I mentioned it to Lloyd when I got back, and he agreed that it seemed significant."

"Scarcely," said Hewitt, shaking his head. "Scarcely, so far, to be called significant, although worth following up. Every-body uses matches in the dark, you know."

"Well, at any rate, the coincidence appealed to me so far that it struck me it might be worth while to describe the brooch to the police in order that they could trace it if it had been pawned. They had tried that, of course, over the bracelet without any result, but I fancied the shot might be worth making, and might possibly lead us on the track of the more serious robbery."

"Quite so. It was the right thing to do. Well?"

"Well, they found it. A woman had pawned it in London—at a shop in Chelsea. But that was some time before, and the pawnbroker had clean forgotten all about the woman's appearance. The name and address she gave were false. So that was the end of that business."

"Had any of the servants left you between the time the brooch was lost and the date of the pawn ticket?"

"No."

"Were all your servants at home on the day the brooch was pawned?"

"Oh, yes! I made that inquiry myself."

"Very good! What next?"

"Yesterday—and this is what made me send for you. My late wife's sister came here last Tuesday, and we gave her the room from which Mrs. Heath lost her bracelet. She had with her a very old-fashioned brooch, containing a miniature of her father, and set in front with three very fine brilliants and a few smaller stones. Here we are, though, at the Croft. I'll tell you the rest indoors."

Hewitt laid his hand on the baronet's arm. "Don't pull up, Sir James," he said. "Drive a little farther. I should like to have a general idea of the whole case before we go in."

"Very good!" Sir James Norris straightened the horse's head again and went on. "Late yesterday afternoon, as my sister-in-law was changing her dress, she left her room for a moment to speak to my daughter in her room, almost adjoining. She was gone no more than three minutes, or five at most, but on her return the brooch, which had been left on the table, had gone. Now the window was shut fast, and had not been tampered with. Of course the door was open, but so was my daughter's, and any body walking near must have been heard. But the strangest circumstance, and one that almost makes me wonder whether I have been awake to-day or not, was that there lay *a used match* on the very spot, as nearly as possible, where the brooch had been—and it was broad daylight!"

Hewitt rubbed his nose and looked thoughtfully before him. "Um—curious, certainly," he said, "Any thing else?"

"Nothing more than you shall see for yourself. I have had the room locked and watched till you could examine it. My sister-in-law had heard of your name, and suggested that you should be called in; so, of course, I did exactly as she wanted. That she should have lost that brooch, of all things, in my house is most unfortunate; you see, there was some small difference about the thing between my late wife and her sister when their mother died and left it. It's almost worse than the Heaths' bracelet business, and altogether I'm not pleased with things, I can assure you. See what a position it is for me! Here are three ladies, in the space of one year, robbed one after another in this mysterious fashion in my house, and I can't find the thief! It's horrible! People will be afraid to come near the place. And I can do nothing!"

"Ah, well, we'll see. Perhaps we had better turn back now. By-the-bye, were you thinking of having any alterations or additions made to your house?"

"No. What makes you ask?"

"I think you might at least consider the question of painting and decorating, Sir James—or, say, putting up another coach-house, or something. Because I should like to be (to the servants) the architect—or the builder, if you please—come to look around. You haven't told any of them about this business?"

"Not a word. Nobody knows but my relatives and Lloyd. I took every precaution myself, at once. As to your little disguise, be the architect by all means, and do as you please. If you can only find this thief and put an end to this horrible state of affairs, you'll do me the greatest service I've ever asked for—and as to your fee, I'll gladly make it whatever is usual, and three hundred in addition."

Martin Hewitt bowed. "You're very generous, Sir James, and you may be sure I'll do what I can. As a professional man, of course, a good fee always stimulates my interest, although this case of yours certainly seems interesting enough by itself."

"Most extraordinary! Don't you think so? Here are three persons, all ladies, all in my house, two even in the same room, each successively robbed of a piece of jewelry, each from a dressing-table, and a used match left behind in every case. All in the most difficult—one would say impossible—circumstances for a thief, and yet there is no clue!"

"Well, we won't say that just yet, Sir James; we must see. And we must guard against any undue predisposition to consider the robberies in a lump. Here we are at the lodge gate again. Is that your gardener—the man who left the ladder by the lawn on the first occasion you spoke of?" Mr. Hewitt nodded in the direction of a man who was clipping a box border.

"Yes; will you ask him any thing?"

"No, no; at any rate, not now. Remember the building alterations. I think, if there is no objection, I will look first at the room that the lady—Mrs.——" Hewitt looked up, inquiringly.

"My sister-in-law? Mrs. Cazenove. Oh, yes! you shall come to her room at once."

"Thank you. And I think Mrs. Cazenove had better be there."

They alighted, and a boy from the lodge led the horse and dog-cart away.

Mrs. Cazenove was a thin and faded, but quick and energetic, lady of middle age. She bent her head very slightly on learning Martin Hewitt's name, and said: "I must thank you, Mr. Hewitt, for your very prompt attention. I need scarcely say that any help you can afford in tracing the thief who has my property—whoever it may be—will make me most grateful. My room is quite ready for you to examine."

The room was on the second floor—the top floor at that part of the building. Some slight confusion of small articles of dress was observable in parts of the room.

"This, I take it," inquired Hewitt, "is exactly as it was at the time the brooch was missed?"

"Precisely," Mrs. Cazenove answered. "I have used another room, and put myself to some other inconveniences, to avoid any disturbance."

Hewitt stood before the dressing-table. "Then this is the used match," he observed, "exactly where it was found?"

"Yes."

"Where was the brooch?"

"I should say almost on the very same spot. Certainly no more than a very few inches away."

Hewitt examined the match closely. "It is burned very little," he remarked. "It would appear to have gone out at once. Could you hear it struck?"

"I heard nothing whatever; absolutely nothing."

"If you will step into Miss Norris' room now for a moment," Hewitt suggested, "we will try an experiment. Tell me if you hear matches struck, and how many. Where is the match-stand?"

The match-stand proved to be empty, but matches were found in Miss Norris' room, and the test was made. Each striking could be heard distinctly, even with one of the doors pushed to.

"Both your own door and Miss Norris' were open, I understand; the window shut and fastened inside as it is now, and nothing but the brooch was disturbed?"

"Yes, that was so."

"Thank you, Mrs. Cazenove. I don't think I need trouble you any further just at present. I think, Sir James," Hewitt added, turning to the baronet, who was standing by the door——"I think we will see the other room and take a walk outside the house, if you please. I suppose, by-the-bye, that there is no getting at the matches left behind on the first and second occasions?"

"No," Sir James answered. "Certainly not here. The Scotland Yard man may have kept his."

The room that Mrs. Armitage had occupied presented no peculiar feature. A few feet below the window the roof of the billiard-room was visible, consisting largely of skylight. Hewitt glanced casually about the walls, ascertained that the furniture and hangings had not been materially changed since the second robbery, and expressed his desire to see the windows from the outside. Before leaving the room, however, he wished to know the names of any persons who were known to have been about the house on the occasions of all three robberies.

"Just carry your mind back, Sir James," he said. "Begin with yourself, for instance. Where were you at these times?"

"When Mrs. Heath lost her bracelet, I was in Tagley Wood all the afternoon. When Mrs. Armitage was robbed, I believe I was somewhere about the place most of the time she was out. Yesterday I was down at the farm." Sir James' face broadened. "I don't know whether you call those suspicious movements," he added, and laughed.

"Not at all; I only asked you so that, remembering your own movements, you might the better recall those of the rest of the household. Was any body, to your knowledge—*any body*, mind—in the house on all three occasions?"

"Well, you know, it's quite impossible to answer for all the servants. You'll only get that by direct questioning—I can't possibly remember things of that sort. As to the family and visitors—why, you don't suspect any of them, do you?"

"I don't suspect a soul, Sir James," Hewitt answered, beaming genially, "not a soul. You see, I *can't* suspect people till I know something about where they were. It's quite possible there will be independent evidence enough as it is, but you must help me if you can. The visitors, now. Was there any visitor here each time—or even on the first and last occasions only?"

"No, not one. And my own sister, perhaps you will be pleased to know, was only there at the time of the first robbery."

"Just so! And your daughter, as I have gathered, was clearly absent from the spot each time—indeed, was in company with the party robbed. Your niece, now?"

"Why hang it all, Mr. Hewitt, I can't talk of my niece as a suspected criminal! The poor girl's under my protection, and I really can't allow——"

Hewitt raised his hand, and shook his head deprecatingly.

"My dear sir, haven't I said that I don't suspect a soul? *Do* let me know how the people were distributed, as nearly as possible. Let me see. It was your, niece, I think, who found that Mrs. Armitage's door was locked—this door, in fact—on the day she lost her brooch?"

"Yes, it was."

"Just so—at the time when Mrs. Armitage herself had forgotten whether she locked it or not. And yesterday—was she out then?"

"No, I think not. Indeed, she goes out very little—her health is usually bad. She was indoors, too, at the time of the Heath robbery, since you ask. But come, now, I don't like this. It's ridiculous to suppose that *she* knows any thing of it."

"I don't suppose it, as I have said. I am only asking for information. That is all your resident family, I take it, and you know nothing of anybody else's movements— except, perhaps, Mr. Lloyd's?"

"Lloyd? Well, you know yourself that he was out with the ladies when the first robbery took place. As to the others, I don't remember. Yesterday he was probably in his room, writing. I think that acquits *him*, eh?" Sir James looked quizzically into the broad face of the affable detective, who smiled and replied:

"Oh, of course nobody can be in two places at once, else what would become of the *alibi* as an institution? But, as I have said, I am only setting my facts in order. Now, you see, we get down to the servants—unless some stranger is the party wanted. Shall we go outside now?"

Lenton Croft was a large, desultory sort of house, nowhere more than three floors high, and mostly only two. It had been added to bit by bit, till it zigzagged about its site, as Sir James Norris expressed it, "like a game of dominoes." Hewitt scrutinized its external features carefully as they strolled around, and stopped some little while before the windows of the two bed-rooms he had just seen from the inside. Presently they approached the stables and coach-house, where a groom was washing the wheels of the dog-cart.

"Do you mind my smoking?" Hewitt asked Sir James. "Perhaps you will take a cigar yourself—they are not so bad, I think. I will ask your man for a light."

Sir James felt for his own match-box, but Hewitt had gone, and was lighting his cigar with a match from a box handed him by the groom. A smart little terrier was trotting about by the coach-house, and Hewitt stooped to rub its head. Then he made some observation about the dog, which enlisted the groom's interest, and was soon absorbed in a chat with the man. Sir James, waiting a little way off, tapped the stones rather impatiently with his foot, and presently moved away.

For full a quarter of an hour Hewitt chatted with the groom, and, when at last he came away and overtook Sir James, that gentleman was about re-entering the house.

"I beg your pardon, Sir James," Hewitt said, "for leaving you in that unceremonious fashion to talk to your groom, but a dog, Sir James—a good dog— will draw me anywhere."

"Oh!" replied Sir James, shortly.

"There is one other thing," Hewitt went on, disregarding the other's curtness, "that I should like to know: There are two windows directly below that of the room occupied yesterday by Mrs. Cazenove—one on each floor. What rooms do they light?"

"That on the ground floor is the morning-room; the other is Mr. Lloyd's—my secretary. A sort of study or sitting-room."

"Now you will see at once, Sir James," Hewitt pursued, with an affable determination to win the baronet back to good-humor—"you will see at once that, if a ladder had been used in Mrs. Heath's case, anybody looking from either of these rooms would have seen it."

"Of course! The Scotland Yard man questioned everybody as to that, but nobody seemed to have been in either of the rooms when the thing occurred; at any rate, nobody saw anything."

"Still, I think I should like to look out of those windows myself; it will, at least, give me an idea of what *was* in view and what was not, if anybody had been there."

Sir James Norris led the way to the morning-room. As they reached the door a young lady, carrying a book and walking very languidly, came out. Hewitt stepped aside to let her pass, and afterward said interrogatively: "Miss Norris, your daughter, Sir James?"

"No, my niece. Do you want to ask her anything? Dora, my dear," Sir James added, following her in the corridor, "this is Mr. Hewitt, who is investigating these wretched robberies for me. I think he would like to hear if you remember anything happening at any of the three times."

The lady bowed slightly, and said in a plaintive drawl: "I, uncle? Really, I don't remember anything; nothing at all."

"You found Mrs. Armitage's door locked, I believe," asked Hewitt, "when you tried it, on the afternoon when she lost her brooch?"

"Oh, yes; I believe it was locked. Yes, it was."

"Had the key been left in?"

"The key? Oh, no! I think not; no."

"Do you remember anything out of the common happening—anything whatever, no matter how trivial—on the day Mrs. Heath lost her bracelet?"

"No, really, I don't. I can't remember at all."

"Nor yesterday?"

"No, nothing. I don't remember anything."

"Thank you," said Hewitt, hastily; "thank you. Now the morning-room, Sir James."

In the morning-room Hewitt stayed but a few seconds, doing little more than casually glance out of the windows. In the room above he took a little longer time. It was a comfortable room, but with rather effeminate indications about its contents. Little pieces of draped silk-work hung about the furniture, and Japanese silk fans decorated the mantel-piece. Near the window was a cage containing a gray parrot, and the writing-table was decorated with two vases of flowers.

"Lloyd makes himself pretty comfortable, eh?" Sir James observed. "But it isn't likely anybody would be here while he was out, at the time that bracelet went."

"No," replied Hewitt, meditatively. "No, I suppose not."

He stared thoughtfully out of the window, and then, still deep in thought, rattled at the wires of the cage with a quill tooth-pick and played a moment with the parrot. Then, looking up at the window again, he said: "That is Mr. Lloyd, isn't it, coming back in a fly?"

"Yes, I think so. Is there anything else you would care to see here?"

"No, thank you," Hewitt replied; "I don't think there is."

They went down to the smoking-room, and Sir James went away to speak to his secretary. When he returned, Hewitt said quietly: "I think, Sir James—I *think* that I shall be able to give you your thief presently."

"What! Have you a clue? Who do you think? I began to believe you were hopelessly stumped."

"Well, yes. I have rather a good clue, although I can't tell you much about it just yet. But it is so good a clue that I should like to know now whether you are determined to prosecute when you have the criminal?"

"Why, bless me, of course," Sir James replied, with surprise. "It doesn't rest with me, you know—the property belongs to my friends. And even if *they* were disposed to let the thing slide, I shouldn't allow it—I couldn't, after they had been robbed in my house."

"Of course, of course! Then, if I can, I should like to send a message to Twyford by somebody perfectly trustworthy—not a servant. Could any body go?"

"Well, there's Lloyd, although he's only just back from his journey. But, if it's important, he'll go."

"It is important. The fact is we must have a policeman or two here this evening, and I'd like Mr. Lloyd to fetch them without telling any body else."

Sir James rang, and, in response to his message, Mr. Lloyd appeared. While Sir James gave his secretary his instructions, Hewitt strolled to the door of the smoking-room, and intercepted the latter as he came out.

"I'm sorry to give you this trouble, Mr. Lloyd," he said, "but I must stay here myself for a little, and somebody who can be trusted must go. Will you just bring back a police-constable with you? or rather two—two would be better. That is all that is wanted. You won't let the servants know, will you? Of course there will be a female searcher at the Twyford police-station? Ah—of course. Well, you needn't bring her, you know. That sort of thing is done at the station." And, chatting thus confidentially, Martin Hewitt saw him off.

When Hewitt returned to the smoking-room, Sir James said, suddenly: "Why, bless my soul, Mr. Hewitt, we haven't fed you! I'm awfully sorry. We came in rather late for lunch, you know, and this business has bothered me so I clean forgot everything else. There's no dinner till seven, so you'd better let me give you something now. I'm really sorry. Come along."

"Thank you, Sir James," Hewitt replied; "I won't take much. A few biscuits, perhaps, or something of that sort. And, by the by, if you don't mind, I rather think I should like to take it alone. The fact is I want to go over this case thoroughly by myself. Can you put me in a room?"

"Any room you like. Where will you go? The dining-room's rather large, but there's my study, that's pretty snug, or—"

"Perhaps I can go into Mr. Lloyd's room for half-an-hour or so; I don't think he'll mind, and it's pretty comfortable."

"Certainly, if you'd like. I'll tell them to send you whatever they've got."

"Thank you very much. Perhaps they'll also send me a lump of sugar and a walnut; it's—it's a little fad of mine."

"A—what? A lump of sugar and a walnut?" Sir James stopped for a moment, with his hand on the bell-rope. "Oh, certainly, if you'd like it; certainly," he added, and stared after this detective with curious tastes as he left the room.

When the vehicle, bringing back the secretary and the policeman, drew up on the drive, Martin Hewitt left the room on the first floor and proceeded down stairs. On the landing he met Sir James Norris and Mrs. Cazenove, who stared with astonishment on perceiving that the detective carried in his hand the parrot-cage.

"I think our business is about brought to a head now," Hewitt remarked, on the stairs. "Here are the police officers from Twyford." The men were standing in the hall with Mr. Lloyd, who, on catching sight of the cage in Hewitt's hand, paled suddenly.

"This is the person who will be charged, I think," Hewitt pursued, addressing the officers, and indicating Lloyd with his finger.

"What, Lloyd?" gasped Sir James, aghast. "No—not Lloyd—nonsense!"

"He doesn't seem to think it nonsense himself, does he?" Hewitt placidly observed. Lloyd had sank on a chair, and, gray of face, was staring blindly at the man he had run against at the office door that morning. His lips moved in spasms, but there was no sound. The wilted flower fell from his button-hole to the floor, but he did not move.

"This is his accomplice," Hewitt went on, placing the parrot and cage on the hall table, "though I doubt whether there will be any use in charging *him*. Eh, Polly?"

The parrot put his head aside and chuckled. "Hullo, Polly!" it quietly gurgled. "Come along!"

Sir James Norris was hopelessly bewildered. "Lloyd—Lloyd," he said, under his breath. "Lloyd—and that!"

"This was his little messenger, his useful Mercury," Hewitt explained, tapping the cage complacently; "in fact, the actual lifter. Hold him up!"

The last remark referred to the wretched Lloyd, who had fallen forward with something between a sob and a loud sigh. The policemen took him by the arms and propped him in his chair.

"System?" said Hewitt, with a shrug of the shoulders, an hour or two after in Sir James' study. "I can't say I have a system. I call it nothing but common-sense and a sharp pair of eyes. Nobody using these could help taking the right road in this case. I began at the match, just as the Scotland Yard man did, but I had the advantage of taking a line through three cases. To begin with, it was plain that that match, being left there in daylight, in Mrs. Cazenove's room, could not have been used to light the table-top, in the full glare of the window; therefore it had been used for some other purpose—*what* purpose I could not, at the moment, guess. Habitual thieves, you know, often have curious superstitions, and some will never take anything without leaving something behind—a pebble or a piece of coal, or something like that—in the premises they have been robbing. It seemed at first extremely likely that this was a case of that kind. The match had clearly been *brought in*—because, when I asked for matches, there were none in the stand, not even an empty box, and the room had not been disturbed. Also the match probably had not been struck there, nothing having been heard, although, of course, a mistake in this matter was just possible. This match, then, it was fair to assume, had been lit somewhere else and blown out immediately—I remarked at the time that it was very little burned. Plainly it could not have been treated thus for nothing, and the only possible object would have been to prevent it igniting accidentally. Following on this, it became obvious that the match was used, for whatever purpose, not *as* a match, but merely as a convenient splinter of wood.

"So far so good. But on examining the match very closely I observed, as you can see for yourself, certain rather sharp indentations in the wood. They are very small, you see, and scarcely visible, except upon narrow inspection; but there they are, and their positions are regular. See—there are two on each side, each opposite the corresponding mark of the other pair. The match, in fact, would seem to have been gripped in some fairly sharp instrument, holding it at two points above and two below—an instrument, as it may at once strike you, not unlike the beak of a bird.

"Now here was an idea. What living creature but a bird could possibly have entered Mrs. Heath's window without a ladder—supposing no ladder to have been used—or could have got into Mrs. Armitage's window without lifting the sash higher than the eight or ten inches it was already open? Plainly, nothing. Further, it is significant that only *one* article was stolen at a time, although others were about. A human being could have carried any reasonable number, but a bird could only take one at a time. But why should a bird carry a match in its beak? Certainly it must have been trained to do that for a purpose, and a little consideration made that purpose pretty clear. A noisy, chattering bird would probably betray itself at once. Therefore it must be trained to keep quiet both while going for and coming away with its plunder. What readier or more probably effectual way than, while teaching it to carry without dropping, to teach it also to keep quiet while carrying? The one thing would practically cover the other.

"I thought at once, of course, of a jackdaw or a magpie—these birds' thievish reputations made the guess natural. But the marks on the match were much too wide apart to have been made by the beak of either. I conjectured, therefore, that it must be a raven. So that, when we arrived near the coach-house, I seized the opportunity of a little chat with your groom on the subject of dogs and pets in general, and ascertained that there was no tame raven in the place. I also, incidentally, by getting a light from the coach-house box of matches, ascertained that the match found was of the sort generally used about the establishment—the large, thick, red-topped English match. But I further found that Mr. Lloyd had a parrot which was a most intelligent pet, and had been trained into comparative quietness—for a parrot. Also, I learned that more than once the groom had met Mr. Lloyd carrying his parrot under his coat, it having, as its owner explained, learned the trick of opening its cage-door and escaping.

"I said nothing, of course, to you of all this, because I had as yet nothing but a train of argument and no results. I got to Lloyd's room as soon as possible. My chief object in going there was achieved when I played with the parrot, and induced it to bite a quill tooth-pick.

"When you left me in the smoking-room, I compared the quill and the match very carefully, and found that the marks corresponded exactly. After this I felt very little doubt indeed. The fact of Lloyd having met the ladies walking before dark on the day of the first robbery proved nothing, because, since it was clear that the match had *not* been used to procure a light, the robbery might as easily have taken place in daylight as not—must have so taken place, in fact, if my conjectures were right. That they were right I felt no doubt. There could be no other explanation.

"When Mrs. Heath left her window open and her door shut, any body climbing upon the open sash of Lloyd's high window could have put the bird upon the sill above. The match placed in the bird's beak for the purpose I have indicated, and struck first, in case by accident it should ignite by rubbing against something and startle the bird—this match would, of course, be dropped just where the object to be removed was taken up; as you know, in every case the match was found almost upon the spot where the missing article had been left—scarcely a likely triple coincidence had the match been used by a human thief. This would have been done as soon after the ladies had left as possible, and there would then have been plenty of time for Lloyd to hurry out and meet them before dark—especially plenty of time to meet them *coming back*, as they must have been, since they were carrying their ferns. The match was an article well chosen for its purpose, as being a not altogether unlikely thing to find on a dressing-table, and, if noticed, likely to lead to the wrong conclusions adopted by the official detective.

"In Mrs. Armitage's case the taking of an inferior brooch and the leaving of a more valuable ring pointed clearly either to the operator being a fool or unable to distinguish values, and certainly, from other indications, the thief seemed no fool. The door was locked, and the gas-fitter, so to speak, on guard, and the window was only eight or ten inches open and propped with a brush. A human thief entering the window would have disturbed this arrangement, and would scarcely risk discovery by attempting to replace it, especially a thief in so great a hurry as to snatch the brooch up without unfastening the pin. The bird could pass through the opening as it was, and *would have* to tear the pin-cushion to pull the brooch off, probably holding the cushion down with its claw the while.

"Now in yesterday's case we had an alteration of conditions. The window was shut and fastened, but the door was open—but only left for a few minutes, during which time no sound was heard either of coming or going. Was it not possible, then, that the thief was *already* in the room, in hiding, while Mrs. Cazenove was there, and seized its first opportunity on her temporary absence? The room is full of draperies, hangings, and what not, allowing of plenty of concealment for a bird, and a bird could leave the place noiselessly and quickly. That the whole scheme was strange mattered not at all. Robberies presenting such unaccountable features must have been effected by strange means of one sort or another. There was no improbability. Consider how many hundreds of examples of infinitely higher degrees of bird-training are exhibited in the London streets every week for coppers.

"So that, on the whole, I felt pretty sure of my ground. But before taking any definite steps I resolved to see if Polly could not be persuaded to exhibit his accomplishments to an indulgent stranger. For that purpose I contrived to send Lloyd away again and have a quiet hour alone with his bird. A piece of sugar, as every-body knows, is a good parrot bribe; but a walnut, split in half, is a better—especially if the bird be used to it; so I got you to furnish me with both. Polly was shy at first, but I generally get along very well with pets, and a little perseverance soon led to a complete private performance for my benefit. Polly would take the match, mute as wax, jump on the table, pick up the brightest thing he could see, in a great hurry, leave the match behind, and scuttle away round the room; but at first wouldn't give up the plunder to *me*. It was enough. I also took the liberty, as you know, of a general look round, and discovered that little collection of Brummagem rings and trinkets that you have just seen—used in Polly's education, no doubt. When we sent Lloyd away, it struck me that he might as well be usefully employed as not, so I got him to fetch the police, deluding him a little, I fear, by talking about the servants and a female searcher. There will be no trouble about evidence; he'll confess. Of that I'm sure. I know the sort of man. But I doubt if you'll get Mrs. Cazenove's brooch back. You see, he has been to London to-day, and by this time the swag is probably broken up."

Sir James listened to Hewitt's explanation with many expressions of assent and some of surprise. When it was over, he smoked a few whiffs and then said: "But Mrs. Armitage's brooch was pawned, and by a woman."

"Exactly. I expect our friend Lloyd was rather disgusted at his small luck—probably gave the brooch to some female connection in London, and she realized on it. Such persons don't always trouble to give a correct address."

The two smoked in silence for a few minutes, and then Hewitt continued: "I don't expect our friend has had an easy job altogether with that bird. His successes at most have only been three, and I suspect he had many failures and not a few anxious moments that we know nothing of. I should judge as much merely from what the groom told me of frequently meeting Lloyd with his parrot. But the plan was not a bad one—not at all. Even if the bird had been caught in the act, it would only have been 'That mischievous parrot!' you see. And his master would only have been looking for him."

THE DUCHESS OF WILTSHIRE'S DIAMONDS

Guy Boothby

TO THE REFLECTIVE MIND THE RAPIDITY WITH WHICH THE INHABITANTS OF the world's greatest city seize upon a new name or idea, and familiarise themselves with it, can scarcely prove otherwise than astonishing. As an illustration of my meaning let me take the case of Klimo—the now famous private detective, who has won for himself the right to be considered as great as Lecocq, or even the late lamented Sherlock Holmes.

Up to a certain morning London had never even heard his name, nor had it the remotest notion as to who or what he might be. It was as sublimely ignorant and careless on the subject as the inhabitants of Kamtchatka or Peru. Within twenty-four hours, however, the whole aspect of the case was changed. The man, woman, or child who had not seen his posters, or heard his name, was counted an ignoramus unworthy of intercourse with human beings.

Princes became familiar with it as their trains bore them to Windsor to luncheon with the Queen; the nobility noticed and commented upon it as they drove about the town; merchants, and business men generally, read it as they made their ways by omnibus or underground, to their various shops and counting-houses; street boys called each other by it as a nickname; music hall artistes introduced it into their patter, while it was even rumoured that the Stock Exchange itself had paused in the full flood tide of business to manufacture a riddle on the subject.

That Klimo made his profession pay him well was certain, first from the fact that his advertisements must have cost a good round sum, and, second, because he had taken a mansion in Belverton Street, Park Lane, next door to Porchester House, where, to the dismay of that aristocratic neighbourhood, he advertised that he was prepared to receive and be consulted by his clients. The invitation was responded to with alacrity, and from that day forward, between the hours of twelve and two, the pavement upon the north side of the street was lined with carriages, every one containing some person desirous of testing the great man's skill.

I must here explain that I have narrated all this in order to show the state of affairs existing in Belverton Street and Park Lane when Simon Carne arrived, or was supposed to arrive, in England. If my memory serves me correctly, it was on

Wednesday, the 3rd of May, that the Earl of Amberley drove to Victoria to meet and welcome the man whose acquaintance he had made in India under such peculiar circumstances, and under the spell of whose fascination he and his family had fallen so completely.

Reaching the station, his lordship descended from his carriage, and made his way to the platform set apart for the reception of the Continental express. He walked with a jaunty air, and seemed to be on the best of terms with himself and the world in general. How little he suspected the existence of the noose into which he was so innocently running his head!

As if out of compliment to his arrival, the train put in an appearance within a few moments of his reaching the platform. He immediately placed himself in such a position that he could make sure of seeing the man he wanted, and waited patiently until he should come in sight. Carne, however, among the first batch; indeed, the majority of passengers had passed before his lordship caught sight of him.

One thing was very certain, however great the crush might have been, it would have been difficult to mistake Carne's figure. The man's infirmity and the peculiar beauty of his face rendered him easily recognisable. Possibly, after his long sojourn in India, he found the morning cold, for he wore a long fur coat, the collar of which he had turned up round his ears, thus making a fitting frame for his delicate face. On seeing Lord Amberley he hastened forward to greet him.

"This is most kind and friendly of you," he said, as he shook the other by the hand. "A fine day and Lord Amberley to meet me. One could scarcely imagine a better welcome."

As he spoke, one of his Indian servants approached and salaamed before him. He gave him an order, and received an answer in Hindustani, whereupon he turned again to Lord Amberley.

"You may imagine how anxious I am to see my new dwelling," he said. "My servant tells me that my carriage is here, so may I hope that you will drive back with me and see for yourself how I am likely to be lodged?"

"I shall be delighted," said Lord Amberley, who was longing for the opportunity, and they accordingly went out into the station yard together to discover a brougham, drawn by two magnificent horses, and with Nur Ali, in all the glory of white raiment and crested turban, on the box, waiting to receive them. His lordship dismissed his Victoria, and when Jowur Singh had taken his place beside his fellow servant upon the box, the carriage rolled out of the station yard in the direction of Hyde Park.

"I trust her ladyship is quite well," said Simon Carne politely, as they turned into Gloucester Place.

"Excellently well, thank you," replied his lordship. "She bade me welcome you to England in her name as well as my own, and I was to say that she is looking forward to seeing you."

"She is most kind, and I shall do myself the honour of calling upon her as soon as circumstances will permit," answered Carne. "I beg you will convey my best thanks to her for her thought of me."

While these polite speeches were passing between them they were rapidly approaching a large hoarding, on which was displayed a poster setting forth the name of the now famous detective, Klimo.

Simon Carne, leaning forward, studied it, and when they had passed, turned to his friend again.

"At Victoria and on all the hoardings we meet I see an enormous placard, bearing the word 'Klimo.' Pray, what does it mean?"

His lordship laughed.

"You are asking a question which, a month ago, was on the lips of nine out of every ten Londoners. It is only within the last fortnight that we have learned who and what 'Klimo' is."

"And pray what is he?"

"Well, the explanation is very simple. He is neither more nor less than a remarkably astute private detective, who has succeeded in attracting notice in such a way that half London has been induced to patronize him. I have had no dealings with the man myself. But a friend of mine, Lord Orpington, has been the victim of a most audacious burglary, and, the police having failed to solve the mystery, he has called Klimo in. We shall therefore see what he can do before many days are past. But, there, I expect you will soon know more about him than any of us."

"Indeed! And why?"

"For the simple reason that he has taken No. 1, Belverton Terrace, the house adjoining your own, and sees his clients there."

Simon Carne pursed up his lips, and appeared to be considering something.

"I trust he will not prove a nuisance," he said at last. "The agents who found me the house should have acquainted me with the fact. Private detectives, on however large a scale, scarcely strike one as the most desirable of neighbours—particularly for a man who is so fond of quiet as myself."

At this moment they were approaching their destination. As the carriage passed Belverton Street and pulled up, Lord Amberley pointed to a long line of vehicles standing before the detective's door.

"You can see for yourself something of the business he does," he said. "Those are the carriages of his clients, and it is probable that twice as many have arrived on foot."

"I shall certainly speak to the agent on the subject," said Carne, with a shadow of annoyance upon his face. "I consider the fact of this man's being so close to me a serious drawback to the house."

Jowur Singh here descended from the box and opened the door in order that his master and his guest might alight, while portly Ram Gafur, the butler, came down the steps and salaamed before them with Oriental obsequiousness. Carne greeted his domestics with kindly condescension, and then, accompanied by the ex-Viceroy, entered his new abode.

"I think you may congratulate yourself upon having secured one of the most desirable residences in London," said his lordship ten minutes or so later, when they had explored the principal rooms.

"I am very glad to hear you say so," said Carne. "I trust your lordship will remember that you will always be welcome in the house as long as I am its owner."

"It is very kind of you to say so," returned Lord Amberley warmly. "I shall look forward to some months of pleasant intercourse. And now I must be going. To-morrow, perhaps, if you have nothing better to do, you will give us the pleasure of your company at dinner. Your fame has already gone abroad, and we shall ask one or two nice people to meet you, including my brother and sister-in-law, Lord and Lady Gelpington, Lord and Lady Orpington, and my cousin, the Duchess of Wiltshire, whose interest in china and Indian art, as perhaps you know, is only second to your own."

"I shall be most glad to come."

"We may count on seeing you in Eaton Square, then, at eight o'clock?"

"If I am alive you may be sure I shall be there. Must you really go? Then good-bye, and many thanks for meeting me."

His lordship having left the house, Simon Carne went upstairs to his dressing-room, which it was to be noticed he found without inquiry, and rang the electric bell, beside the fireplace, three times. While he was waiting for it to be answered he stood looking out of the window at the long line of carriages in the street below.

"Everything is progressing admirably," he said to himself. "Amberley does not suspect any more than the world in general. As a proof he asks me to dinner to-morrow evening to meet his brother and sister-in-law, two of his particular friends, and above all Her Grace of Wiltshire. Of course I shall go, and when I bid Her Grace good-bye it will be strange if I am not one step nearer the interest on Liz's money."

At this moment the door opened, and his valet, the grave and respectable Belton, entered the room. Carne turned to greet him impatiently.

"Come, come, Belton," he said, "we must be quick. It is twenty minutes to twelve, and if we don't hurry, the folk next door will become impatient. Have you succeeded in doing what I spoke to you about last night?"

"I have done everything, sir."

"I am glad to hear it. Now lock that door and let us get to work. You can let me have your news while I am dressing."

Opening one side of a massive wardrobe, that completely filled one end of the room, Belton took from it a number of garments. They included a well-worn velvet coat, a baggy pair of trousers—so old that only a notorious pauper or a millionaire could have afforded to wear them—a flannel waistcoat, a Gladstone collar, a soft silk tie, and a pair of embroidered carpet slippers upon which no old clothes man in the most reckless way of business in Petticoat Lane would have advanced a single halfpenny. Into these he assisted his master to change.

"Now give me the wig, and unfasten the straps of this hump," said Carne, as the other placed the garments just referred to upon a neighbouring chair.

Belton did as he was ordered, and then there happened a thing the like of which no one would have believed. Having unbuckled a strap on either shoulder, and slipped his hand beneath the waistcoat, he withdrew a large *papier-maché* hump, which he carried away and carefully placed in a drawer of the bureau. Relieved of his burden, Simon Carne stood up as straight and well-made a man as any in Her Majesty's dominions. The malformation, for which so many, including the Earl and Countess of Amberley, had often pitied him, was nothing but a hoax intended to produce an effect which would permit him additional facilities of disguise.

The hump discarded, and the grey wig fitted carefully to his head in such a manner that not even a pinch of his own curly locks could be seen beneath it, he adorned his cheeks with a pair of *crépu*-hair whiskers, donned the flannel vest and the velvet coat previously mentioned, slipped his feet into the carpet slippers, placed a pair of smoked glasses upon his nose, and declared himself ready to proceed about his business. The man who would have known him for Simon Carne would have been as astute as, well, shall we say, as the private detective—Klimo himself.

"It's on the stroke of twelve," he said, as he gave a final glance at himself in the pier-glass above the dressing-table, and arranged his tie to his satisfaction. "Should any one call, instruct Ram Gafur to tell them that I have gone out on business, and shall not be back until three o'clock."

"Very good, sir."

"Now undo the door and let me go in."

Thus commanded, Belton went across to the large wardrobe which, as I have already said, covered the whole of one side of the room, and opened the middle door. Two or three garments were seen inside suspended on pegs, and these he removed, at the same time pushing towards the right the panel at the rear. When this was done a large aperture in the wall between the two houses was disclosed. Through this door Carne passed, drawing it behind him.

In No. 1, Belverton Terrace, the house occupied by the detective, whose presence in the street Carne seemed to find so objectionable, the entrance thus constructed was covered by the peculiar kind of confessional box in which Klimo invariably sat to receive his clients, the rearmost panels of which opened in the same fashion as those in the wardrobe in the dressing-room. These being pulled aside, he had but to draw them to again after him, take his seat, ring the electric bell to inform his housekeeper that he was ready, and then welcome his clients as quickly as they cared to come.

Punctually at two o'clock the interviews ceased, and Klimo, having reaped an excellent harvest of fees, returned to Porchester House to become Simon Carne once more.

Possibly it was due to the fact that the Earl and Countess of Amberley were brimming over with his praise, or it may have been the rumour that he was worth as many millions as you have fingers upon your hand that did it; one thing, however, was self evident, within twenty-four hours of the noble earl's meeting him at Victoria Station, Simon Carne was the talk, not only of fashionable, but also of unfashionable London.

That his household were, with one exception, natives of India, that he had paid a rental for Porchester House which ran into five figures, that he was the greatest living authority upon china and Indian art generally, and that he had come over to England in search of a wife, were among the smallest of the *canards* set afloat concerning him.

During dinner next evening Carne put forth every effort to please. He was placed on the right hand of his hostess and next to the Duchess of Wiltshire. To the latter he paid particular attention, and to such good purpose that when the ladies returned to the drawing-room afterwards, Her Grace was full of his praises. They had discussed china of all sorts, Carne had promised her a specimen which she had longed for all her life, but had never been able to obtain, and in return she had promised to show him the quaintly carved Indian casket in which the famous necklace, of which he had, of course, heard, spent most of its time. She would be wearing the jewels in question at her own ball in a week's time, she informed him, and if he would care to see the case when it came from her bankers on that day, she would be only too pleased to show it to him.

As Simon Carne drove home in his luxurious brougham afterwards, he smiled to himself as he thought of the success which was attending his first endeavour. Two of the guests, who were stewards of the Jockey Club, had heard with delight his idea of purchasing a horse, in order to have an interest in the Derby. While another, on hearing that he desired to become the possessor of a yacht, had offered to propose him for the R.C.Y.C. To crown it all, however, and much better than all, the Duchess of Wiltshire had promised to show him her famous diamonds.

"By this time next week," he said to himself, "Liz's interest should be considerably closer. But satisfactory as my progress has been hitherto, it is difficult to see how I am to get possession of the stones. From what I have been able to discover, they are only brought from the bank on the day the Duchess intends to wear them, and they are taken back by His Grace the morning following.

"While she has got them on her person it would be manifestly impossible to get them from her. And as, when she takes them off, they are returned to their box and placed in a safe, constructed in the wall of the bed-room adjoining, and which for the occasion is occupied by the butler and one of the under footmen, the only key being in the possession of the Duke himself, it would be equally foolish to hope to appropriate them. In what manner, therefore, I am to become their possessor passes my comprehension. However, one thing is certain, obtained they must be, and the attempt must be made on the night of the ball if possible. In the meantime I'll set my wits to work upon a plan."

Next day Simon Carne was the recipient of an invitation to the ball in question, and two days later he called upon the Duchess of Wiltshire, at her residence in Belgrave Square, with a plan prepared. He also took with him the small vase he had promised her four nights before. She received him most graciously, and their talk fell at once into the usual channel. Having examined her collection, and charmed her by means of one or two judicious criticisms, he asked permission to include photographs of certain of her treasures in his forthcoming book, then little by little he skilfully guided the conversation on to the subject of jewels.

"Since we are discussing gems, Mr. Carne," she said, "perhaps it would interest you to see my famous necklace. By good fortune I have it in the house now, for the reason that an alteration is being made to one of the clasps by my jewellers."

"I should like to see it immensely," answered Carne. "At one time and another I have had the good fortune to examine the jewels of the leading Indian princes, and I should like to be able to say that I had seen the famous Wiltshire necklace."

"Then you shall certainly have that honour," she answered with a smile. "If you will ring that bell I will send for it."

Carne rang the bell as requested, and when the butler entered he was given the key of the safe and ordered to bring the case to the drawing-room.

"We must not keep it very long," she observed while the man was absent. "It is to be returned to the bank in an hour's time."

"I am indeed fortunate," Carne replied, and turned to the description of some curious Indian wood carving, of which he was making a special feature in his book. As he explained, he had collected his illustrations from the doors of Indian temples, from the gateways of palaces, from old brass work, and even from carved chairs and boxes he had picked up in all sorts of odd corners. Her Grace was most interested.

"How strange that you should have mentioned it," she said. "If carved boxes have any interest for you, it is possible my jewel case itself may be of use to you. As I think I told you during Lady Amberley's dinner, it came from Benares, and has carved upon it the portraits of nearly every god in the Hindu Pantheon."

"You raise my curiosity to fever heat," said Carne.

A few moments later the servant returned, bringing with him a wooden box, about sixteen inches long, by twelve wide, and eight deep, which he placed upon a table beside his mistress, after which he retired.

"This is the case to which I have just been referring," said the Duchess, placing her hand on the article in question. "If you glance at it you will see how exquisitely it is carved."

Concealing his eagerness with an effort, Simon Carne drew his chair up to the table, and examined the box.

It was with justice she had described it as a work of art. What the wood was of which it was constructed Carne was unable to tell. It was dark and heavy, and, though it was not teak, closely resembled it. It was literally covered with quaint carving, and of its kind was an unique work of art.

"It is most curious and beautiful," said Carne when he had finished his examination. "In all my experience I can safely say I have never seen its equal. If you will permit me I should very much like to include a description and an illustration of it in my book."

"Of course you may do so; I shall be only too delighted," answered Her Grace. "If it will help you in your work I shall be glad to lend it to you for a few hours, in order that you may have the illustration made."

This was exactly what Carne had been waiting for, and he accepted the offer with alacrity.

"Very well, then," she said. "On the day of my ball, when it will be brought from the bank again, I will take the necklace out and send the case to you. I must make one proviso, however, and that is that you let me have it back the same day."

"I will certainly promise to do that," replied Carne.

"And now let us look inside," said his hostess.

Choosing a key from a bunch she carried in her pocket, she unlocked the casket, and lifted the lid. Accustomed as Carne had all his life been to the sight of gems, what he then saw before him almost took his breath away. The inside of the box, both sides and bottom, was quilted with the softest Russia leather, and on this luxurious couch reposed the famous necklace. The fire of the stones when the light caught them was sufficient to dazzle the eyes, so fierce was it.

As Carne could see, every gem was perfect of its kind, and there were no fewer than three hundred of them. The setting was a fine example of the jeweller's art, and last, but not least, the value of the whole affair was fifty thousand pounds, a mere fleabite to the man who had given it to his wife, but a fortune to any humbler person.

"And now that you have seen my property, what do you think of it?" asked the Duchess as she watched her visitor's face.

"It is very beautiful," he answered, "and I do not wonder that you are proud of it. Yes, the diamonds are very fine, but I think it is their abiding place that fascinates me more. Have you any objection to my measuring it?"

"Pray do so, if it is likely to be of any assistance to you," replied Her Grace.

Carne thereupon produced a small ivory rule, ran it over the box, and the figures he thus obtained he jotted down in his pocket-book.

Ten minutes later, when the case had been returned to the safe, he thanked the Duchess for her kindness and took his departure, promising to call in person for the empty case on the morning of the ball.

Reaching home he passed into his study, and, seating himself at his writing table, pulled a sheet of note paper towards him and began to sketch, as well as he could remember it, the box he had seen. Then he leant back in his chair and closed his eyes.

"I have cracked a good many hard nuts in my time," he said reflectively, "but never one that seemed so difficult at first sight as this. As far as I see at present, the case stands as follows: the box will be brought from the bank where it usually reposes to Wiltshire House on the morning of the dance. I shall be allowed to have possession of it, without the stones of course, for a period possibly extending from eleven o'clock in the morning to four or five, at any rate not later than seven, in the evening. After the ball the necklace will be returned to it, when it will be locked up in the safe, over which the butler and a footman will mount guard.

"To get into the room during the night is not only too risky, but physically out of the question; while to rob Her Grace of her treasure during the progress of the dance would be equally impossible. The Duke fetches the casket and takes it back to the bank himself, so that to all intents and purposes I am almost as far off the solution as ever."

Half an hour went by and found him still seated at his desk, staring at the drawing on the paper, then an hour. The traffic of the streets rolled past the house unheeded. Finally Jowur Singh announced his carriage, and, feeling that an idea might come to him with a change of scene, he set off for a drive in the park.

By this time his elegant mail phaeton, with its magnificent horses and Indian servant on the seat behind, was as well-known as Her Majesty's state equipage, and attracted almost as much attention. To-day, however, the fashionable world noticed that Simon Carne looked preoccupied. He was still working out his problem, but so far without much success. Suddenly something, no one will ever be able to say what, put an idea into his head. The notion was no sooner born in his brain than he left the park and drove quickly home. Ten minutes had scarcely elapsed before he was back in his study again, and had ordered that Wajib Baksh should be sent to him.

When the man he wanted put in an appearance, Carne handed him the paper upon which he had made the drawing of the jewel case.

"Look at that," he said, "and tell me what thou seest there."

"I see a box," answered the man, who by this time was well accustomed to his master's ways.

"As thou say'st, it is a box," said Carne. "The wood is heavy and thick, though what wood it is I do not know. The measurements are upon the paper below. Within, both the sides and bottom are quilted with soft leather, as I have also shown. Think now, Wajib Baksh, for in this case thou wilt need to have all thy wits about thee. Tell me is it in thy power, oh most cunning of all craftsmen, to insert such extra sides within this box that they, being held by a spring, shall lie so snug as not to be noticeable to the ordinary eye? Can it be so arranged that, when the box is locked, they shall fall flat upon the bottom, thus covering and holding fast what lies beneath them, and yet making the box appear to the eye as if it were empty. Is it possible for thee to do such a thing?"

Wajib Baksh did not reply for a few moments. His instinct told him what his master wanted, and he was not disposed to answer hastily, for he also saw that his reputation as the most cunning craftsman in India was at stake.

"If the Heaven-born will permit me the night for thought," he said at last, "I will come to him when he rises from his bed and tell him what I can do, and he can then give his orders as it pleases him."

"Very good," said Carne. "Then to-morrow morning I shall expect thy report. Let the work be good, and there will be many rupees for thee to touch in return. As to the lock and the way it shall act, let that be the concern of Hiram Singh."

Wajib Baksh salaamed and withdrew, and Simon Carne for the time being dismissed the matter from his mind.

Next morning, while he was dressing, Belton reported that the two artificers desired an interview with him. He ordered them to be admitted, and forthwith they entered the room. It was noticeable that Wajib Baksh carried in his hand a heavy box, which, upon Garne's motioning him to do so, he placed upon the table.

"Have ye thought over the matter?" he asked, seeing that the men waited for him to speak.

"We have thought of it," replied Hiram Singh, who always acted as spokesman for the pair. "If the Presence will deign to look, he will see that we have made a box of the size and shape such as he drew upon the paper."

"Yes, it is certainly a good copy," said Carne condescendingly, after he had examined it.

Wajib Baksh showed his white teeth in appreciation of the compliment, and Hiram Singh drew closer to the table.

"And now, if the Sahib will open it, he will in his wisdom be able to tell if it resembles the other that he has in his mind."

Carne opened the box as requested, and discovered that the interior was an exact counterfeit of the Duchess of Wiltshire's jewel case, even to the extent of the quilted leather lining which had been the other's principal feature. He admitted that the likeness was all that could be desired.

"As he is satisfied," said Hiram Singh, "it may be that the Protector of the Poor will deign to try an experiment with it. See, here is a comb. Let it be placed in the box, so—now he will see what he will see."

The broad, silver-backed comb, lying upon his dressing-table, was placed on the bottom of the box, the lid was closed, and the key turned in the lock. The case being securely fastened, Hiram Singh laid it before his master.

"I am to open it, I suppose?" said Carne, taking the key and replacing it in the lock.

"If my master pleases," replied the other.

Carne accordingly turned it in the lock, and, having done so, raised the lid and looked inside. His astonishment was complete. To all intents and purposes the box was empty. The comb was not to be seen, and yet the quilted sides and bottom were, to all appearances, just the same as when he had first looked inside.

"This is most wonderful," he said. And indeed it was as clever a conjuring trick as any he had ever seen.

"Nay, it is very simple," Wajib Baksh replied. "The Heaven-born told me that there must be no risk of detection."

He took the box in his own hands and, running his nails down the centre of the quilting, dividing the false bottom into two pieces; these he lifted out, revealing the comb lying upon the real bottom beneath.

"The sides, as my lord will see," said Hiram Singh, taking a step forward, "are held in their appointed places by these two springs. Thus, when the key is turned the springs relax, and the sides are driven by others into their places on the bottom, where the seams in the quilting mask the join. There is but one disadvantage. It is as follows: When the pieces which form the bottom are lifted out in order that my lord may get at whatever lies concealed beneath, the springs must of necessity stand revealed. However, to any one who knows sufficient of the working of the box to lift out the false bottom, it will be an easy matter to withdraw the springs and conceal them about his person."

"As you say that is an easy matter," said Carne, "and I shall not be likely to forget. Now one other question. Presuming I am in a position to put the real box into your hands for say eight hours, do you think that in that time you can fit it up so that detection will be impossible?"

"Assuredly, my lord," replied Hiram Singh with conviction. "There is but the lock and the fitting of the springs to be done. Three hours at most would suffice for that."

"I am pleased with you," said Carne. "As a proof of my satisfaction, when the work is finished you will each receive five hundred rupees. Now you can go."

According to his promise, ten o'clock on the Friday following found him in his hansom driving towards Belgrave Square. He was a little anxious, though the casual observer would scarcely have been able to tell it. The magnitude of the stake for which he was playing was enough to try the nerve of even such a past master in his profession as Simon Carne.

Arriving at the house he discovered some workmen erecting an awning across the footway in preparation for the ball that was to take place at night. It was not long, however, before he found himself in the boudoir, reminding Her Grace of her promise to permit him an opportunity of making a drawing of the famous jewel case. The Duchess was naturally busy, and within a quarter of an hour he was on his way home with the box placed on the seat of the carriage beside him.

"Now," he said, as he patted it good-humouredly, "if only the notion worked out by Hiram Singh and Wajib Baksh holds good, the famous Wiltshire diamonds will become my property before very many hours are passed. By this time to-morrow, I suppose, London will be all agog concerning the burglary."

On reaching his house he left his carriage, and himself carried the box into his study. Once there he rang his bell and ordered Hiram Singh and Wajib Baksh to be sent to him. When they arrived he showed them the box upon which they were to exercise their ingenuity.

"Bring your tools in here," he said, "and do the work under my own eyes. You have but nine hours before you, so you must make the most of them."

The men went for their implements, and as soon as they were ready set to work. All through the day they were kept hard at it, with the result that by five o'clock the alterations had been effected and the case stood ready. By the time Carne returned from his afternoon drive in the Park it was quite prepared for the part it was to play in his scheme. Having praised the men, he turned them out and locked the door, then went across the room and unlocked a drawer in his writing table. From it he took a flat leather jewel case, which he opened. It contained a necklace of counterfeit diamonds, if anything a little larger than the one he intended to try to obtain. He had purchased it that morning in the Burlington Arcade for the purpose of testing the apparatus his servants had made, and this he now proceeded to do.

Laying it carefully upon the bottom he closed the lid and turned the key. When he opened it again the necklace was gone, and even though he knew the secret he could not for the life of him see where the false bottom began and ended. After that he reset the trap and tossed the necklace carelessly in. To his delight it acted as well as on the previous occasion. He could scarcely contain his satisfaction. His conscience was sufficiently elastic to give him no trouble. To him it was scarcely a robbery he was planning, but an artistic trial of skill, in which he pitted his wits and cunning against the forces of society in general.

At half-past seven he dined, and afterwards smoked a meditative cigar over the evening paper in the billiard room. The invitations to the ball were for ten o'clock, and at nine-thirty he went to his dressing-room.

"Make me tidy as quickly as you can," he said to Belton when the latter appeared, "and while you are doing so listen to my final instructions.

"To-night, as you know, I am endeavouring to secure the Duchess of Wiltshire's necklace. To-morrow morning all London will resound with the hubbub, and I have been making my plans in such a way as to arrange that Klimo shall be the first person consulted. When the messenger calls, if call he does, see that the old woman next door bids him tell the Duke to come personally at twelve o'clock. Do you understand?"

"Perfectly, sir?"

"Very good. Now give me the jewel case, and let me be off. You need not sit up for me."

Precisely as the clocks in the neighbourhood were striking ten Simon Carne reached Belgrave Square, and, as he hoped, found himself the first guest.

His hostess and her husband received him in the ante-room of the drawing-room.

"I come laden with a thousand apologies," he said as he took Her Grace's hand, and bent over it with that ceremonious politeness which was one of the man's chief characteristics. "I am most unconscionably early, I know, but I hastened here in order that I might personally return the jewel case you so kindly lent me. I must trust to your generosity to forgive me. The drawings took longer than I expected."

"Please do not apologise," answered Her Grace. "It is very kind of you to have brought the case yourself. I hope the illustrations have proved successful. I shall look forward to seeing them as soon as they are ready. But I am keeping you holding the box. One of my servants will take it to my room."

She called a footman to her, and bade him take the box and place it upon her dressing-table.

"Before it goes I must let you see that I have not damaged it either externally or internally," said Carne with a laugh. "It is such a valuable case that I should never forgive myself if it had even received a scratch during the time it has been in my possession."

So saying he lifted the lid and allowed her to look inside. To all appearance it was exactly the same as when she had lent it to him earlier in the day.

"You have been most careful," she said. And then, with an air of banter, she continued: "If you desire it, I shall be pleased to give you a certificate to that effect."

They jested in this fashion for a few moments after the servant's departure, during which time Carne promised to call upon her the following morning at u o'clock, and to bring with him the illustrations he had made and a queer little piece of china he had had the good fortune to pick up in a dealer's shop the previous afternoon. By this time fashionable London was making its way up the grand staircase, and with its appearance further conversation became impossible.

Shortly after midnight Carne bade his hostess good-night and slipped away. He was perfectly satisfied with his evening's entertainment, and if the key of the jewel case were not turned before the jewels were placed in it, he was convinced they would become his property. It speaks well for his strength of nerve when I record the fact that on going to bed his slumbers were as peaceful and untroubled as those of a little child.

Breakfast was scarcely over next morning before a hansom drew up at his front door and Lord Amberley alighted. He was ushered into Carne's presence forthwith, and on seeing that the latter was surprised at his early visit, hastened to explain.

"My dear fellow," he said, as he took possession of the chair the other offered him, "I have come round to see you on most important business. As I told you last night at the dance, when you so kindly asked me to come and see the steam yacht you have purchased, I had an appointment with Wiltshire at half-past nine this morning. On reaching Belgrave Square, I found the whole house in confusion. Servants were running hither and thither with scared faces, the butler was on the borders of lunacy, the Duchess was well-nigh hysterical in her boudoir, while her husband was in his study vowing vengeance against all the world."

"You alarm me," said Carne, lighting a cigarette with a hand that was as steady as a rock. "What on earth has happened?"

"I think I might safely allow you fifty guesses and then wager a hundred pounds you'd not hit the mark; and yet in a certain measure it concerns you."

"Concerns me? Good gracious! What have I done to bring all this about?"

"Pray do not look so alarmed," said Amberley. "Personally you have done nothing. Indeed, on second thoughts, I don't know that I am right in saying that it concerns you at all. The fact of the matter is, Carne, a burglary took place last night at Wiltshire House, *and the famous necklace has disappeared.*"

"Good heavens! You don't say so?"

"But I *do*. The circumstances of the case are as follows: When my cousin retired to her room last night after the ball, she unclasped the necklace, and, in her husband's presence, placed it carefully in her jewel case, which she locked. That having been done, Wiltshire took the box to the room which contained the safe, and himself placed it there, locking the iron door with his own key. The room was occupied that night, according to custom, by the butler and one of the footmen, both of whom have been in the family since they were boys.

"Next morning, after breakfast, the Duke unlocked the safe and took out the box, intending to convey it to the Bank as usual. Before leaving, however, he placed it on his study-table and went upstairs to speak to his wife. He cannot remember exactly how long he was absent, but he feels convinced that he was not gone more than a quarter of an hour at the very utmost.

"Their conversation finished, she accompanied him downstairs, where she saw him take up the case to carry it to his carriage. Before he left the house, however, she said: 'I suppose you have looked to see that the necklace is all right?' 'How could I do so?' was his reply. 'You know you possess the only key that will fit it.'

"She felt in her pockets, but to her surprise the key was not there."

"If I were a detective I should say that that is a point to be remembered," said Carne with a smile. "Pray, where did she find her keys?"

"Upon her dressing-table," said Amberley. "Though she has not the slightest recollection of leaving them there."

"Well, when she had procured the keys, what happened?"

"Why, they opened the box, and, to their astonishment and dismay, *found it empty. The jewels were gone!*"

"Good gracious! What a terrible loss! It seems almost impossible that it can be true. And pray, what did they do?"

"At first they stood staring into the empty box, hardly believing the evidence of their own eyes. Stare how they would, however, they could not bring them back. The jewels had, without doubt, disappeared, but when and where the robbery had taken place it was impossible to say. After that they had up all the servants and questioned them, but the result was what they might have foreseen, no one from the butler to the kitchenmaid could throw any light upon the subject. To this minute it remains as great a mystery as when they first discovered it."

"I am more concerned than I can tell you," said Carne. "How thankful I ought to be that I returned the case to Her Grace last night. But in thinking of myself I am forgetting to ask what has brought you to me. If I can be of any assistance I hope you will command me."

"Well, I'll tell you why I have come," replied Lord Amberley. "Naturally, they are most anxious to have the mystery solved and the jewels recovered as soon as possible. Wiltshire wanted to send to Scotland Yard there and then, but his wife and I eventually persuaded him to consult Klimo. As you know, if the police authorities are called in first, he refuses the business altogether. Now, we thought, as you are his next door neighbour, you might possibly be able to assist us."

"You may be very sure, my lord, I will do everything that lies in my power. Let us go in and see him at once."

As he spoke he rose and threw what remained of his cigarette into the fireplace. His visitor having imitated his example, they procured their hats and walked round from Park Lane into Belverton Street to bring up at No. 1. After they had rung the bell the door was opened to them by the old woman who invariably received the detective's clients.

"Is Mr. Klimo at home?" asked Carne. "And if so, can we see him?"

The old lady was a little deaf, and the question had to be repeated before she could be made to understand what was wanted. As soon, however, as she realized their desire, she informed them that her master was absent from town, but would be back as usual at twelve o'clock to meet his clients.

"What on earth's to be done?" said the Earl, looking at his companion in dismay. "I am afraid I can't come back again, as I have a most important appointment at that hour."

"Do you think you could entrust the business to me?" asked Carne. "If so, I will make a point of seeing him at twelve o'clock, and could call at Wiltshire House afterwards and tell the Duke what I have done."

"That's very good of you," replied Amberley. "If you are sure it would not put you to too much trouble, that would be quite the best thing to be done."

"I will do it with pleasure," Carne replied. "I feel it my duty to help in whatever way I can."

"You are very kind," said the other. "Then, as I understand it, you are to call upon Klimo at twelve o'clock, and afterwards to let my cousins know what you have succeeded in doing. I only hope he will help us to secure the thief. We are having too many of these burglaries just now. I must catch this hansom and be off. Good-bye, and many thanks."

"Good-bye," said Carne, and shook him by the hand.

The hansom having rolled away, Carne retraced his steps to his own abode.

"It is really very strange," he muttered as he walked along, "how often chance condescends to lend her assistance to my little schemes. The mere fact that His Grace left the box unwatched in his study for a quarter of an hour may serve to throw the police off on quite another scent. I am also glad that they decided to open the case in the house, for if it had gone to the bankers' and had been placed in the strong room unexamined, I should never have been able to get possession of the jewels at all."

Three hours later he drove to Wiltshire House and saw the Duke. The Duchess was far too much upset by the catastrophe to see any one.

"This is really most kind of you, Mr. Carne," said His Grace when the other had supplied an elaborate account of his interview with Klimo. "We are extremely indebted to you. I am sorry he cannot come before ten o'clock to-night, and that he makes this stipulation of my seeing him alone, for I must confess I should like to have had some one else present to ask any questions that might escape me. But if that's his usual hour and custom, well, we must abide by it, that's all. I hope he will do some good, for this is the greatest calamity that has ever befallen me. As I told you just now, it has made my wife quite ill. She is confined to her bed-room and quite hysterical."

"You do not suspect any one, I suppose?" inquired Carne.

"Not a soul," the other answered. "The thing is such a mystery that we do not know what to think. I feel convinced, however, that my servants are as innocent as I am. Nothing will ever make me think them otherwise. I wish I could catch the fellow, that's all. I'd make him suffer for the trick he's played me."

Carne offered an appropriate reply, and after a little further conversation upon the subject, bade the irate nobleman good-bye and left the house. From Belgrave Square he drove to one of the clubs of which he had been elected a member, in search of Lord Orpington, with whom he had promised to lunch, and afterwards took him to a ship-builder's yard near Greenwich, in order to show him the steam yacht he had lately purchased.

It was close upon dinner time before he returned to his own residence. He brought Lord Orpington with him, and they dined in state together. At nine the latter bade him good-bye, and at ten Carne retired to his dressing-room and rang for Belton.

"What have you to report," he asked, "with regard to what I bade you do in Belgrave Square?"

"I followed your instructions to the letter," Belton replied. "Yesterday morning I wrote to Messrs. Horniblow and Jimson, the house agents in Piccadilly, in the name of Colonel Braithwaite, and asked for an order to view the residence to the right of Wiltshire House. I asked that the order might be sent direct to the house, where the Colonel would get it upon his arrival. This letter I posted myself in Basingstoke, as you desired me to do.

"At nine o'clock yesterday morning I dressed myself as much like an elderly army officer as possible, and took a cab to Belgrave Square. The caretaker, an old fellow of close upon seventy years of age, admitted me immediately upon hearing my name, and proposed that he should show me over the house. This, however, I told him was quite unnecessary, backing my speech with a present of half a crown, whereupon he returned to his breakfast perfectly satisfied, while I wandered about the house at my own leisure.

"Reaching the same floor as that upon which is situated the room in which the Duke's safe is kept, I discovered that your supposition was quite correct, and that it would be possible for a man, by opening the window, to make his way along the coping from one house to the other, without being seen. I made certain that there was no one in the bed-room in which the butler slept, and then arranged the long telescope walking-stick you gave me, and fixed one of my boots to it by means of the screw in the end. With this I was able to make a regular succession of footsteps in the dust along the ledge, between one window and the other.

"That done, I went downstairs again, bade the caretaker good-morning, and got into my cab. From Belgrave Square I drove to the shop of the pawnbroker whom you told me you had discovered was out of town. His assistant inquired my business, and was anxious to do what he could for me. I told him, however, that I must see his master personally, as it was about the sale of some diamonds I had had left me. I pretended to be annoyed that he was not at home, and muttered to myself, so that the man could hear, something about its meaning a journey to Amsterdam.

"Then I limped out of the shop, paid off my cab, and, walking down a by-street, removed my moustache, and altered my appearance by taking off my great coat and muffler. A few streets further on I purchased a bowler hat in place of the old-fashioned topper I had hitherto been wearing, and then took a cab from Piccadilly and came home."

"You have fulfilled my instructions admirably," said Carne. "And if the business comes off, as I expect it will, you shall receive your usual percentage. Now I must be turned into Klimo and be off to Belgrave Square to put His Grace of Wiltshire upon the track of this burglar."

Before he retired to rest that night Simon Carne took something, wrapped in a red silk handkerchief, from the capacious pocket of the coat Klimo had been wearing a few moments before. Having unrolled the covering, he held up to the light the magnificent necklace which for so many years had been the joy and pride of the ducal house of Wiltshire. The electric light played upon it, and touched it with a thousand different hues.

"Where so many have failed," he said to himself, as he wrapped it in the handkerchief again and locked it in his safe, "it is pleasant to be able to congratulate oneself on having succeeded. It is without its equal, and I don't think I shall be over-stepping the mark if I say that I think when she receives it Liz will be glad she lent me the money."

Next morning all London was astonished by the news that the famous Wiltshire diamonds had been stolen, and a few hours later Carne learnt from an evening paper that the detectives who had taken up the case, upon the supposed retirement from it of Klimo, were still completely at fault.

That evening he was to entertain several friends to dinner. They included Lord Amberley, Lord Orpington, and a prominent member of the Privy Council. Lord Amberley arrived late, but filled to overflowing with importance. His friends noticed his state, and questioned him.

"Well, gentlemen," he answered, as he took up a commanding position upon the drawing-room hearthrug, "I am in a position to inform you that Klimo has reported upon the case, and the upshot of it is that the Wiltshire Diamond Mystery is a mystery no longer."

"What do you mean?" asked the others in a chorus.

"I mean that he sent in his report to Wiltshire this afternoon, as arranged. From what he said the other night, after being alone in the room with the empty jewel case and a magnifying glass for two minutes or so, he was in a position to describe the *modus operandi*, and, what is more, to put the police on the scent of the burglar."

"And how *was* it worked?" asked Carne.

"From the empty house next door," replied the other. "On the morning of the burglary a man, purporting to be a retired army officer, called with an order to view, got the caretaker out of the way, clambered along to Wiltshire House by means of the parapet outside, reached the room during the time the servants were at breakfast, opened the safe, and abstracted the jewels."

"But how did Klimo find all this out?" asked Lord Orpington.

"By his own inimitable cleverness," replied Lord Amberley. "At any rate it has been proved that he was correct. The man *did* make his way from next door, and the police have since discovered that an individual, answering to the description given, visited a pawnbroker's shop in the city about an hour later, and stated that he had diamonds to sell."

"If that is so it turns out to be a very simple mystery after all," said Lord Orpington as they began their meal.

"Thanks to the ingenuity of the cleverest detective in the world," remarked Amberley.

"In that case here's a good health to Klimo," said the Privy Councillor, raising his glass.

"I will join you in that," said Simon Carne. "Here's a very good health to Klimo and his connection with the Duchess of Wiltshire's diamonds. May he always be equally successful!"

"Hear, hear to that," replied his guests.

THE MYSTERY OF THE FELWYN TUNNEL

L. T. Meade and Robert Eustace

I WAS MAKING EXPERIMENTS OF SOME INTEREST AT SOUTH KENSINGTON, AND hoped that I had perfected a small but not unimportant discovery, when, on returning home one evening in late October in the year 1893, I found a visiting card on my table. On it were inscribed the words, "Mr. Geoffrey Bainbridge." This name was quite unknown to me, so I rang the bell and inquired of my servant who the visitor had been. He described him as a gentleman who wished to see me on most urgent business, and said further that Mr. Bainbridge intended to call again later in the evening. It was with both curiosity and vexation that I awaited the return of the stranger. Urgent business with me generally meant a hurried rush to one part of the country or the other. I did not want to leave London just then; and when at half-past nine Mr. Geoffrey Bainbridge was ushered into my room, I received him with a certain coldness which he could not fail to perceive. He was a tall, well-dressed, elderly man. He immediately plunged into the object of his visit.

"I hope you do not consider my unexpected presence an intrusion, Mr. Bell," he said. "But I have heard of you from our mutual friends, the Greys of Uplands. You may remember once doing that family a great service."

"I remember perfectly well," I answered more cordially. "Pray tell me what you want; I shall listen with attention."

"I believe you are the one man in London who can help me," he continued. "I refer to a matter especially relating to your own particular study. I need hardly say that whatever you do will not be unrewarded."

"That is neither here nor there," I said; "but before you go any further, allow me to ask one question. Do you want me to leave London at present?"

He raised his eyebrows in dismay.

"I certainly do," he answered.

"Very well; pray proceed with your story."

He looked at me with anxiety.

"In the first place," he began, "I must tell you that I am chairman of the Lytton Vale Railway Company in Wales, and that it is on an important matter connected with our line that I have come to consult you. When I explain to you the nature of the mystery, you will not wonder, I think, at my soliciting your aid."

"I will give you my closest attention," I answered; and then I added, impelled to say the latter words by a certain expression on his face, "if I can see my way to assisting you I shall be ready to do so."

"Pray accept my cordial thanks," he replied. "I have come up from my place at Felwyn to-day on purpose to consult you. It is in that neighbourhood that the affair has occurred. As it is essential that you should be in possession of the facts of the whole matter, I will go over things just as they happened."

I bent forward and listened attentively.

"This day fortnight," continued Mr. Bainbridge, "our quiet little village was horrified by the news that the signalman on duty at the mouth of the Felwyn Tunnel had been found dead under the most mysterious circumstances. The tunnel is at the end of a long cutting between Llanlys and Felwyn stations. It is about a mile long, and the signal-box is on the Felwyn side. The place is extremely lonely, being six miles from the village across the mountains. The name of the poor fellow who met his death in this mysterious fashion was David Pritchard. I have known him from a boy, and he was quite one of the steadiest and most trustworthy men on the line. On Tuesday evening he went on duty at six o'clock; on Wednesday morning the day-man who had come to relieve him was surprised not to find him in the box. It was just getting daylight, and the 6:30 local was coming down, so he pulled the signals and let her through. Then he went out, and, looking up the line towards the tunnel, saw Pritchard lying beside the line close to the mouth of the tunnel. Roberts, the day-man, ran up to him and found, to his horror, that he was quite dead. At first Roberts naturally supposed that he had been cut down by a train, as there was a wound at the back of the head; but he was not lying on the metals. Roberts ran back to the box and telegraphed through to Felwyn Station. The message was sent on to the village, and at half-past seven o'clock the police inspector came up to my house with the news. He and I, with the local doctor, went off at once to the tunnel. We found the dead man lying beside the metals a few yards away from the mouth of the tunnel, and the doctor immediately gave him a careful examination. There was a depressed fracture at the back of the skull, which must have caused his death; but how he came by it was not so clear. On examining the whole place most carefully, we saw, further, that there were marks on the rocks at the steep side of the embankment as if some one had tried to scramble up them. Why the poor fellow had attempted such a climb, God only knows. In doing so he must have slipped and fallen back on to the line, thus causing the fracture of the skull. In no case could he have gone up more than eight or ten feet, as the banks of the cutting run sheer up, almost perpendicularly, beyond that point for more than a hundred and fifty feet. There are some sharp boulders beside the line, and it was possible that he might have fallen on one of these and so sustained the injury. The affair must have occurred some time between 11:45 p.m. and 6 a.m., as the engine-driver of the express at 11:45 p.m. states that the line was signalled clear, and he also caught sight of Pritchard in his box as he passed."

"This is deeply interesting," I said; "pray proceed."

Bainbridge looked at me earnestly; he then continued:—

"The whole thing is shrouded in mystery. Why should Pritchard have left his box and gone down to the tunnel? Why, having done so, should he have made a wild attempt to scale the side of the cutting, an impossible feat at any time? Had danger threatened, the ordinary course of things would have been to run up the line towards the signal-box. These points are quite unexplained. Another curious fact is that death appears to have taken place just before the day-man came on duty, as the light at the mouth of the tunnel had been put out, and it was one of the night signalman's duties to do this as soon as daylight appeared; it is possible, therefore, that Pritchard went down to the tunnel for that purpose. Against this theory, however, and an objection that seems to nullify it, is the evidence of Dr. Williams, who states that when he examined the body his opinion was that death had taken place some hours before. An inquest was held on the following day, but before it took place there was a new and most important development. I now come to what I consider the crucial point in the whole story.

"For a long time there had been a feud between Pritchard and another man of the name of Wynne, a platelayer on the line. The object of their quarrel was the blacksmith's daughter in the neighbouring village—a remarkably pretty girl and an arrant flirt. Both men were madly in love with her, and she played them off one against the other. The night but one before his death Pritchard and Wynne had met at the village inn, had quarrelled in the bar—Lucy, of course, being the subject of their difference. Wynne was heard to say (he was a man of powerful build and subject to fits of ungovernable rage) that he would have Pritchard's life. Pritchard swore a great oath that he would get Lucy on the following day to promise to marry him. This oath, it appears, he kept, and on his way to the signal-box on Tuesday evening met Wynne, and triumphantly told him that Lucy had promised to be his wife. The men had a hand-to-hand fight on the spot, several people from the village being witnesses of it. They were separated with difficulty, each vowing vengeance on the other. Pritchard went off to his duty at the signal-box and Wynne returned to the village to drown his sorrows at the public-house.

"Very late that same night Wynne was seen by a villager going in the direction of the tunnel. The man stopped him and questioned him. He explained that he had left some of his tools on the line, and was on his way to fetch them. The villager noticed that he looked queer and excited, but not wishing to pick a quarrel thought it best not to question him further. It has been proved that Wynne never returned home that night, but came back at an early hour on the following morning, looking dazed and stupid. He was arrested on suspicion, and at the inquest the verdict was against him."

"Has he given any explanation of his own movements?" I asked.

"Yes; but nothing that can clear him. As a matter of fact, his tools were nowhere to be seen on the line, nor did he bring them home with him. His own story is that being considerably the worse for drink, he had fallen down in one of the fields and slept there till morning."

"Things look black against him," I said.

"They do; but listen, I have something more to add. Here comes a very queer feature in the affair. Lucy Ray, the girl who had caused the feud between Pritchard and Wynne, after hearing the news of Pritchard's death, completely lost her head, and ran frantically about the village declaring that Wynne was the man she really loved, and that she had only accepted Pritchard in a fit of rage with Wynne for not himself bringing matters to the point. The case looks very bad against Wynne, and yesterday the magistrate committed him for trial at the coming assizes. The unhappy Lucy Ray and the young man's parents are in a state bordering on distraction."

"What is your own opinion with regard to Wynne's guilt?" I asked.

"Before God, Mr. Bell, I believe the poor fellow is innocent, but the evidence against him is very strong. One of the favourite theories is that he went down to the tunnel and extinguished the light, knowing that this would bring Pritchard out of his box to see what was the matter, and that he then attacked him, striking the blow which fractured the skull."

"Has any weapon been found about, with which he could have given such a blow?"

"No; nor has anything of the kind been discovered on Wynne's person; that fact is decidedly in his favour."

"But what about the marks on the rocks?" I asked.

"It is possible that Wynne may have made them in order to divert suspicion by making people think that Pritchard must have fallen, and so killed himself. The holders of this theory base their belief on the absolute want of cause for Pritchard's trying to scale the rock. The whole thing is the most absolute enigma. Some of the country folk have declared that the tunnel is haunted (and there certainly has been such a rumour current among them for years). That Pritchard saw some apparition, and in wild terror sought to escape from it by climbing the rocks, is another theory, but only the most imaginative hold it."

"Well, it is a most extraordinary case," I replied.

"Yes, Mr. Bell, and I should like to get your opinion of it. Do you see your way to elucidate the mystery?"

"Not at present; but I shall be happy to investigate the matter to my utmost ability."

"But you do not wish to leave London at present?"

"That is so; but a matter of such importance cannot be set aside. It appears, from what you say, that Wynne's life hangs more or less on my being able to clear away the mystery?"

"That is indeed the case. There ought not to be a single stone left unturned to get at the truth, for the sake of Wynne. Well, Mr. Bell, what do you propose to do?"

"To see the place without delay," I answered.

"That is right; when can you come?"

"Whenever you please."

"Will you come down to Felwyn with me to-morrow? I shall leave Paddington by the 7:10, and if you will be my guest I shall be only too pleased to put you up."

"That arrangement will suit me admirably," I replied. "I will meet you by the train you mention, and the affair shall have my best attention."

"Thank you," he said, rising. He shook hands with me and took his leave.

The next day I met Bainbridge at Paddington Station, and we were soon flying westward in the luxurious private compartment that had been reserved for him. I could see by his abstracted manner and his long lapses of silence that the mysterious affair at Felwyn Tunnel was occupying all his thoughts.

It was two o'clock in the afternoon when the train slowed down at the little station of Felwyn. The station-master was at the door in an instant to receive us.

"I have some terribly bad news for you, sir," he said, turning to Bainbridge as we alighted; "and yet in one sense it is a relief, for it seems to clear Wynne."

"What do you mean?" cried Bainbridge. "Bad news? Speak out at once!"

"Well, sir, it is this: there has been another death at Felwyn signal-box. John Davidson, who was on duty last night, was found dead at an early hour this morning in the very same place where we found poor Pritchard."

"Good God!" cried Bainbridge, starting back, "what an awful thing! What, in the name of Heaven, does it mean, Mr. Bell? This is too fearful. Thank goodness you have come down with us."

"It is as black a business as I ever heard of, sir," echoed the station-master; "and what we are to do I don't know. Poor Davidson was found dead this morning, and there was neither mark nor sign of what killed him—that is the extraordinary part of it. There's a perfect panic abroad, and not a signalman on the line will take duty to-night. I was quite in despair, and was afraid at one time that the line would have to be closed, but at last it occurred to me to wire to Lytton Vale, and they are sending down an inspector. I expect him by a special every moment. I believe this is he coming now," added the station-master, looking up the line.

There was the sound of a whistle down the valley, and in a few moments a single engine shot into the station, and an official in uniform stepped on to the platform.

"Good-evening, sir," he said, touching his cap to Bainbridge; "I have just been sent down to inquire into this affair at the Felwyn Tunnel, and though it seems more of a matter for a Scotland Yard detective than one of ourselves, there was nothing for it but to come. All the same, Mr. Bainbridge, I cannot say that I look forward to spending to-night alone at the place."

"You wish for the services of a detective, but you shall have some one better," said Bainbridge, turning towards me. "This gentleman, Mr. John Bell, is the man of all others for our business. I have just brought him down from London for the purpose."

An expression of relief flitted across the inspector's face.

"I am very glad to see you, sir," he said to me, "and I hope you will be able to spend the night with me in the signal-box. I must say I don't much relish the idea of tackling the thing single-handed; but with your help, sir, I think we ought to get to the bottom of it somehow. I am afraid there is not a man on the line who will take duty until we do. So it is most important that the thing should be cleared, and without delay."

I readily assented to the inspector's proposition, and Bainbridge and I arranged that we should call for him at four o'clock at the village inn and drive him to the tunnel.

We then stepped into the wagonette which was waiting for us, and drove to Bainbridge's house.

Mrs. Bainbridge came out to meet us, and was full of the tragedy. Two pretty girls also ran to greet their father, and to glance inquisitively at me. I could see that the entire family was in a state of much excitement.

"Lucy Ray has just left, father," said the elder of the girls. "We had much trouble to soothe her; she is in a frantic state."

"You have heard, Mr. Bell, all about this dreadful mystery?" said Mrs. Bainbridge as she led me towards the dining-room.

"Yes," I answered; "your husband has been good enough to give me every particular."

"And you have really come here to help us?"

"I hope I may be able to discover the cause," I answered.

"It certainly seems most extraordinary," continued Mrs. Bainbridge. "My dear," she continued, turning to her husband, "you can easily imagine the state we were all in this morning when the news of the second death was brought to us."

"For my part," said Ella Bainbridge, "I am sure that Felwyn Tunnel is haunted. The villagers have thought so for a long time, and this second death seems to prove it, does it not?" Here she looked anxiously at me.

"I can offer no opinion," I replied, "until I have sifted the matter thoroughly."

"Come, Ella, don't worry Mr. Bell," said her father; "if he is as hungry as I am, he must want his lunch."

We then seated ourselves at the table and commenced the meal. Bainbridge, although he professed to be hungry, was in such a state of excitement that he could scarcely eat. Immediately after lunch he left me to the care of his family and went into the village.

"It is just like him," said Mrs. Bainbridge; "he takes these sort of things to heart dreadfully. He is terribly upset about Lucy Ray, and also about the poor fellow Wynne. It is certainly a fearful tragedy from first to last."

"Well, at any rate," I said, "this fresh death will upset the evidence against Wynne."

"I hope so, and there is some satisfaction in the fact. Well, Mr. Bell, I see you have finished lunch; will you come into the drawing-room?"

I followed her into a pleasant room overlooking the valley of the Lytton.

By-and-by Bainbridge returned, and soon afterwards the dog-cart came to the door. My host and I mounted, Bainbridge took the reins, and we started off at a brisk pace.

"Matters get worse and worse," he said the moment we were alone. "If you don't clear things up to-night, Bell, I say frankly that I cannot imagine what will happen."

We entered the village, and as we rattled down the ill-paved streets I was greeted with curious glances on all sides. The people were standing about in groups, evidently talking about the tragedy and nothing else. Suddenly, as our trap bumped noisily over the paving-stones, a girl darted out of one of the houses and made frantic motions to Bainbridge to stop the horse. He pulled the mare nearly up on her haunches, and the girl came up to the side of the dog-cart.

"You have heard it?" she said, speaking eagerly and in a gasping voice. "The death which occurred this morning will clear Stephen Wynne, won't it, Mr. Bainbridge?—it will, you are sure, are you not?"

"It looks like it, Lucy, my poor girl," he answered. "But there, the whole thing is so terrible that I scarcely know what to think."

She was a pretty girl with dark eyes, and under ordinary circumstances must have had the vivacious expression of face and the brilliant complexion which so many of her countrywomen possess. But now her eyes were swollen with weeping and her complexion more or less disfigured by the agony she had gone through. She looked piteously at Bainbridge, her lips trembling. The next moment she burst into tears.

"Come away, Lucy," said a woman who had followed her out of the cottage; "Fie—for shame! don't trouble the gentlemen; come back and stay quiet."

"I can't, mother, I can't," said the unfortunate girl. "If they hang him, I'll go clean off my head. Oh, Mr. Bainbridge, do say that the second death has cleared him!"

"I have every hope that it will do so, Lucy," said Bainbridge, "but now don't keep us, there's a good girl; go back into the house. This gentleman has come down from London on purpose to look into the whole matter. I may have good news for you in the morning."

The girl raised her eyes to my face with a look of intense pleading. "Oh, I have been cruel and a fool, and I deserve everything," she gasped; "but, sir, for the love of Heaven, try to clear him."

I promised to do my best.

Bainbridge touched up the mare, she bounded forward, and Lucy disappeared into the cottage with her mother.

The next moment we drew up at the inn where the Inspector was waiting, and soon afterwards were bowling along between the high banks of the country lanes to the tunnel. It was a cold, still afternoon; the air was wonderfully keen, for a sharp frost had held the countryside in its grip for the last two days. The sun was just tipping the hills to westward when the trap pulled up at the top of the cutting. We hastily alighted, and the Inspector and I bade Bainbridge good-bye. He said that he only wished that he could stay with us for the night, assured us that little sleep would visit him, and that he would be back at the cutting at an early hour on the following morning; then the noise of his horse's feet was heard fainter and fainter as he drove back over the frost-bound roads. The Inspector and I ran along the little path to the wicket-gate in the fence, stamping our feet on the hard ground to restore circulation after our cold drive. The next moment we were looking down upon the scene of the mysterious deaths, and a weird and lonely place it looked. The tunnel was at one end of the rock cutting, the sides of which ran sheer down to the line for over a hundred and fifty feet. Above the tunnel's mouth the hills rose one upon the other. A more dreary place it would have been difficult to imagine. From a little clump of pines a delicate film of blue smoke rose straight up on the still air. This came from the chimney of the signal-box.

As we started to descend the precipitous path the Inspector sang out a cheery "Hullo!" The man on duty in the box immediately answered. His voice echoed and reverberated down the cutting, and the next moment he appeared at the door of the box. He told us that he would be with us immediately; but we called back to him to stay where he was, and the next instant the Inspector and I entered the box.

"The first thing to do," said Henderson the Inspector, "is to send a message down the line to announce our arrival."

This he did, and in a few moments a crawling goods train came panting up the cutting. After signalling her through we descended the wooden flight of steps which led from the box down to the line and walked along the metals towards the tunnel till we stood on the spot where poor Davidson had been found dead that morning. I examined the ground and all around it most carefully. Everything tallied exactly with the description I had received. There could be no possible way of approaching the spot except by going along the line, as the rocky sides of the cutting were inaccessible.

"It is a most extraordinary thing, sir," said the signalman whom we had come to relieve. "Davidson had neither mark nor sign on him—there he lay stone dead and cold, and not a bruise nowhere; but Pritchard had an awful wound at the back of the head. They said he got it by climbing the rocks—here, you can see the marks for yourself, sir. But now, is it likely that Pritchard would try to climb rocks like these, so steep as they are?"

"Certainly not," I replied.

"Then how do you account for the wound, sir?" asked the man with an anxious face.

"I cannot tell you at present," I answered.

"And you and Inspector Henderson are going to spend the night in the signal-box?"

"Yes."

A horrified expression crept over the signalman's face.

"God preserve you both," he said; "I wouldn't do it—not for fifty pounds. It's not the first time I have heard tell that Felwyn Tunnel is haunted. But, there, I won't say any more about that. It's a black business, and has given trouble enough. There's poor Wynne, the same thing as convicted of the murder of Pritchard; but now they say that Davidson's death will clear him. Davidson was as good a fellow as you would come across this side of the country; but for the matter of that, so was Pritchard. The whole thing is terrible—it upsets one, that it do, sir."

"I don't wonder at your feelings," I answered; "but now, see here, I want to make a most careful examination of everything. One of the theories is that Wynne crept down this rocky side and fractured Pritchard's skull. I believe such a feat to be impossible. On examining these rocks I see that a man might climb up the side of the tunnel as far as from eight to ten feet, utilising the sharp projections of rock for the purpose; but it would be out of the question for any man to come down the cutting. No; the only way Wynne could have approached Pritchard was by the line itself. But, after all, the real thing to discover is this," I continued: "what killed Davidson? Whatever caused his death is, beyond doubt, equally responsible for Pritchard's. I am now going into the tunnel."

Inspector Henderson went in with me. The place struck damp and chill. The walls were covered with green, evil-smelling fungi, and through the brickwork the moisture was oozing and had trickled down in long lines to the ground. Before us was nothing but dense darkness.

When we re-appeared the signalman was lighting the red lamp on the post, which stood about five feet from the ground just above the entrance to the tunnel.

"Is there plenty of oil?" asked the Inspector.

"Yes, sir, plenty," replied the man. "Is there anything more I can do for either of you gentlemen?" he asked, pausing, and evidently dying to be off.

"Nothing," answered Henderson; "I will wish you good-evening."

"Good-evening to you both," said the man. He made his way quickly up the path and was soon lost to sight.

Henderson and I then returned to the signal-box.

By this time it was nearly dark.

"How many trains pass in the night?" I asked of the Inspector.

"There's the 10:20 down express," he said, "it will pass here at about 10:40; then there's the 11:45 up, and then not another train till the 6:30 local to-morrow morning. We shan't have a very lively time," he added.

I approached the fire and bent over it, holding out my hands to try and get some warmth into them.

"It will take a good deal to persuade me to go down to the tunnel, whatever I may see there," said the man. "I don't think, Mr. Bell, I am a coward in any sense of the word, but there's something very uncanny about this place, right away from the rest of the world. I don't wonder one often hears of signalmen going mad in some of these lonely boxes. Have you any theory to account for these deaths, sir?"

"None at present," I replied.

"This second death puts the idea of Pritchard being murdered quite out of court," he continued.

"I am sure of it," I answered.

"And so am I, and that's one comfort," continued Henderson. "That poor girl, Lucy Ray, although she was to be blamed for her conduct, is much to be pitied now;

and as to poor Wynne himself, he protests his innocence through thick and thin. He was a wild fellow, but not the sort to take the life of a fellow-creature. I saw the doctor this afternoon while I was waiting for you at the inn, Mr. Bell, and also the police sergeant. They both say they do not know what Davidson died of. There was not the least sign of violence on the body."

"Well, I am as puzzled as the rest of you," I said. "I have one or two theories in my mind, but none of them will quite fit the situation."

The night was piercingly cold, and, although there was not a breath of wind, the keen and frosty air penetrated into the lonely signal-box. We spoke little, and both of us were doubtless absorbed by our own thoughts and speculations. As to Henderson, he looked distinctly uncomfortable, and I cannot say that my own feelings were too pleasant. Never had I been given a tougher problem to solve, and never had I been so utterly at my wits' end for a solution.

Now and then the Inspector got up and went to the telegraph instrument, which intermittently clicked away in its box. As he did so he made some casual remark and then sat down again. After the 10:40 had gone through, there followed a period of silence which seemed almost oppressive. All at once the stillness was broken by the whirr of the electric bell, which sounded so sharply in our ears that we both started. Henderson rose.

"That's the 11:45 coming," he said, and, going over to the three long levers, he pulled two of them down with a loud clang. The next moment, with a rush and a scream, the express tore down the cutting, the carriage lights streamed past in a rapid flash, the ground trembled, a few sparks from the engine whirled up into the darkness, and the train plunged into the tunnel.

"And now," said Henderson, as he pushed back the levers, "not another train till daylight. My word, it is cold!"

It was intensely so. I piled some more wood on the fire and, turning up the collar of my heavy ulster, sat down at one end of the bench and leant my back against the wall. Henderson did likewise; we were neither of us inclined to speak. As a rule, whenever I have any night work to do, I am never troubled with sleepiness, but on this occasion I felt unaccountably drowsy. I soon perceived that Henderson was in the same condition.

"Are you sleepy?" I asked of him.

"Dead with it, sir," was his answer; "but there's no fear, I won't drop off."

I got up and went to the window of the box. I felt certain that if I sat still any longer I should be in a sound sleep. This would never do. Already it was becoming a matter of torture to keep my eyes open. I began to pace up and down; I opened the door of the box and went out on the little platform.

"What's the matter, sir?" inquired Henderson, jumping up with a start.

"I cannot keep awake," I said.

"Nor can I," he answered, "and yet I have spent nights and nights of my life in signal-boxes and never was the least bit drowsy; perhaps it's the cold."

"Perhaps it is," I said; "but I have been out on as freezing nights before, and—"

The man did not reply; he had sat down again; his head was nodding.

I was just about to go up to him and shake him, when it suddenly occurred to me that I might as well let him have his sleep out. I soon heard him snoring, and he presently fell forward in a heap on the floor. By dint of walking up and down, I managed to keep from dropping off myself, and in torture which I shall never be able to describe, the night wore itself away. At last, towards morning, I awoke Henderson.

"You have had a good nap," I said; "but never mind, I have been on guard and nothing has occurred."

"Good God! have I been asleep?" cried the man.

"Sound," I answered.

"Well, I never felt anything like it," he replied. "Don't you find the air very close, sir?"

"No," I said; "it is as fresh as possible; it must be the cold."

"I'll just go and have a look at the light at the tunnel," said the man; "it will rouse me."

He went on to the little platform, whilst I bent over the fire and began to build it up. Presently he returned with a scared look on his face. I could see by the light of the oil lamp which hung on the wall that he was trembling.

"Mr. Bell," he said, "I believe there is somebody or something down at the mouth of the tunnel now." As he spoke he clutched me by the arm. "Go and look," he said; "whoever it is, it has put out the light."

"Put out the light?" I cried. "Why, what's the time?"

Henderson pulled out his watch.

"Thank goodness, most of the night is gone," he said; "I didn't know it was so late, it is half-past five."

"Then the local is not due for an hour yet?" I said.

"No; but who should put out the light?" cried Henderson.

I went to the door, flung it open, and looked out. The dim outline of the tunnel was just visible looming through the darkness, but the red light was out.

"What the dickens does it mean, sir?" gasped the Inspector. "I know the lamp had plenty of oil in it. Can there be any one standing in front of it, do you think?"

We waited and watched for a few moments, but nothing stirred.

"Come along," I said, "let us go down together and see what it is."

"I don't believe I can do it, sir; I really don't!"

"Nonsense," I cried. "I shall go down alone if you won't accompany me. Just hand me my stick, will you?"

"For God's sake, be careful, Mr. Bell. Don't go down, whatever you do. I expect this is what happened before, and the poor fellows went down to see what it was and died there. There's some devilry at work, that's my belief."

"That is as it may be," I answered shortly; "but we certainly shall not find out by stopping here. My business is to get to the bottom of this, and I am going to do it. That there is danger of some sort, I have very little doubt; but danger or not, I am going down."

"If you'll be warned by me, sir, you'll just stay quietly here."

"I must go down and see the matter out," was my answer. "Now listen to me, Henderson. I see that you are alarmed, and I don't wonder. Just stay quietly where you are and watch, but if I call come at once. Don't delay a single instant. Remember I am putting my life into your hands. If I call 'Come,' just come to me as quick as you can, for I may want help. Give me that lantern."

He unhitched it from the wall, and taking it from him, I walked cautiously down the steps on to the line. I still felt curiously, unaccountably drowsy and heavy. I wondered at this, for the moment was such a critical one as to make almost any man wide awake. Holding the lamp high above my head, I walked rapidly along the line. I hardly knew what I expected to find. Cautiously along the metals I made my way, peering right and left until I was close to the fatal spot where the bodies had been found. An uncontrollable shudder passed over me. The next moment, to my horror, without the slightest warning, the light I was carrying went out, leaving me in total darkness. I started back, and stumbling against one of the loose boulders reeled against the wall and nearly fell. What was the matter with me? I could hardly stand. I felt giddy and faint, and a horrible sensation of great tightness seized me across the chest. A loud ringing noise sounded in my ears. Struggling madly for breath, and with the fear of impending death upon me, I turned and tried to run from a danger I could neither understand nor grapple with. But before I had taken two steps my legs gave way from under me, and uttering a loud cry I fell insensible to the ground.

Out of an oblivion which, for all I knew, might have lasted for moments or centuries, a dawning consciousness came to me. I knew that I was lying on hard ground; that I was absolutely incapable of realising, nor had I the slightest inclination to discover, where I was. All I wanted was to lie quite still and undisturbed. Presently I opened my eyes.

Some one was bending over me and looking into my face.

"Thank God, he is not dead," I heard in whispered tones. Then, with a flash, memory returned to me.

"What has happened?" I asked.

"You may well ask that, sir," said the Inspector gravely. "It has been touch and go with you for the last quarter of an hour; and a near thing for me too."

I sat up and looked around me. Daylight was just beginning to break, and I saw that we were at the bottom of the steps that led up to the signal-box. My teeth were chattering with the cold and I was shivering like a man with ague.

"I am better now," I said; "just give me your hand."

I took his arm, and holding the rail with the other hand staggered up into the box and sat down on the bench.

"Yes, it has been a near shave," I said; "and a big price to pay for solving a mystery."

"Do you mean to say you know what it is?" asked Henderson eagerly.

"Yes," I answered, "I think I know now; but first tell me how long was I unconscious?"

"A good bit over half an hour, sir, I should think. As soon as I heard you call out I ran down as you told me, but before I got to you I nearly fainted. I never had such a horrible sensation in my life. I felt as weak as a baby, but I just managed to seize you by the arms and drag you along the line to the steps, and that was about all I could do."

"Well, I owe you my life," I said; "just hand me that brandy flask, I shall be the better for some of its contents."

I took a long pull. Just as I was laying the flask down Henderson started from my side.

"There," he cried, "the 6:30 is coming." The electric bell at the instrument suddenly began to ring. "Ought I to let her go through, sir?" he inquired.

"Certainly," I answered. "That is exactly what we want. Oh, she will be all right."

"No danger to her, sir?"

"None, none; let her go through."

He pulled the lever and the next moment the train tore through the cutting.

"Now I think it will be safe to go down again," I said. "I believe I shall be able to get to the bottom of this business."

Henderson stared at me aghast.

"Do you mean that you are going down again to the tunnel?" he gasped.

"Yes," I said; "give me those matches. You had better come too. I don't think there will be much danger now; and there is daylight, so we can see what we are about."

The man was very loth to obey me, but at last I managed to persuade him. We went down the line, walking slowly, and at this moment we both felt our courage revived by a broad and cheerful ray of sunshine.

"We must advance cautiously," I said, "and be ready to run back at a moment's notice."

"God knows, sir, I think we are running a great risk," panted poor Henderson; "and if that devil or whatever else it is should happen to be about—why, daylight or no daylight—"

"Nonsense! man," I interrupted; "if we are careful, no harm will happen to us now. Ah! and here we are!" We had reached the spot where I had fallen. "Just give me a match, Henderson."

He did so, and I immediately lit the lamp. Opening the glass of the lamp, I held it close to the ground and passed it to and fro. Suddenly the flame went out.

"Don't you understand now?" I said, looking up at the Inspector.

"No, I don't, sir," he replied with a bewildered expression.

Suddenly, before I could make an explanation, we both heard shouts from the top of the cutting, and looking up I saw Bainbridge hurrying down the path. He had come in the dog-cart to fetch us.

"Here's the mystery," I cried as he rushed up to us, "and a deadlier scheme of Dame Nature's to frighten and murder poor humanity I have never seen."

As I spoke I lit the lamp again and held it just above a tiny fissure in the rock. It was at once extinguished.

"What is it?" said Bainbridge, panting with excitement.

"Something that nearly finished *me*," I replied. "Why, this is a natural escape of choke damp. Carbonic acid gas—the deadliest gas imaginable, because it gives no warning of its presence, and it has no smell. It must have collected here during the hours of the night when no train was passing, and gradually rising put out the signal light. The constant rushing of the trains through the cutting all day would temporarily disperse it."

As I made this explanation Bainbridge stood like one electrified, while a curious expression of mingled relief and horror swept over Henderson's face.

"An escape of carbonic acid gas is not an uncommon phenomenon in volcanic districts," I continued, "as I take this to be; but it is odd what should have started it. It has sometimes been known to follow earthquake shocks, when there is a profound disturbance of the deep strata."

"It is strange that you should have said that," said Bainbridge, when he could find his voice.

"What do you mean?"

"Why, that about the earthquake. Don't you remember, Henderson," he added, turning to the Inspector, "we had felt a slight shock all over South Wales about three weeks back?"

"Then that, I think, explains it," I said. "It is evident that Pritchard really did climb the rocks in a frantic attempt to escape from the gas and fell back on to these boulders. The other man was cut down at once, before he had time to fly."

"But what is to happen now?" asked Bainbridge. "Will it go on for ever? How are we to stop it?"

"The fissure ought to be drenched with lime water, and then filled up; but all really depends on what is the size of the supply and also the depth. It is an extremely heavy gas, and would lie at the bottom of a cutting like water. I think there is more here just now than is good for us," I added.

"But how," continued Bainbridge, as we moved a few steps from the fatal spot, "do you account for the interval between the first death and the second?"

"The escape must have been intermittent. If wind blew down the cutting, as probably was the case before this frost set in, it would keep the gas so diluted that its effects would not be noticed. There was enough down here this morning, before that train came through, to poison an army. Indeed, if it had not been for Henderson's promptitude, there would have been another inquest—on myself."

I then related my own experience.

"Well, this clears Wynne, without doubt," said Bainbridge; "but alas! for the two poor fellows who were victims. Bell, the Lytton Vale Railway Company owe you unlimited thanks; you have doubtless saved many lives, and also the Company, for the line must have been closed if you had not made your valuable discovery. But now come home with me to breakfast. We can discuss all those matters later on."

THE CASE OF OSCAR BRODSKI

R. Austin Freeman

PART I: THE MECHANISM OF CRIME

A surprising amount of nonsense has been talked about conscience. On the one hand remorse (or the "again-bite," as certain scholars of ultra-Teutonic leanings would prefer to call it); on the other hand "an easy conscience": these have been accepted as the determining factors of happiness or the reverse.

Of course there is an element of truth in the "easy conscience" view, but it begs the whole question. A particularly hardy conscience may be quite easy under the most unfavourable conditions—conditions in which the more feeble conscience might be severely afflicted with the "again-bite." And, then, it seems to be the fact that some fortunate persons have no conscience at all; a negative gift that raises them above the mental vicissitudes of the common herd of humanity.

Now, Silas Hickler was a case in point. No one, looking into his cheerful, round face, beaming with benevolence and wreathed in perpetual smiles, would have imagined him to be a criminal. Least of all, his worthy, high-church housekeeper, who was a witness to his unvarying amiability, who constantly heard him carolling light-heartedly about the house and noted his appreciative zest at meal times.

Yet it is a fact that Silas earned his modest, though comfortable, income by the gentle art of burglary. A precarious trade and risky withal, yet not so very hazardous if pursued with judgment and moderation. And Silas was eminently a man of judgment. He worked invariably alone. He kept his own counsel. No confederate had he to turn King's Evidence at a pinch; no one he knew would bounce off in a fit of temper to Scotland Yard. Nor was he greedy and thriftless, as most criminals are. His "scoops" were few and far between, carefully planned, secretly executed, and the proceeds judiciously invested in "weekly property."

In early life Silas had been connected with the diamond industry, and he still did a little rather irregular dealing. In the trade he was suspected of transactions with I.D.B.s, and one or two indiscreet dealers had gone so far as to whisper the ominous word "fence." But Silas smiled a benevolent smile and went his way. He knew what he knew, and his clients in Amsterdam were not inquisitive.

Such was Silas Hickler. As he strolled round his garden in the dusk of an October evening, he seemed the very type of modest, middle-class prosperity. He was dressed in the travelling suit that he wore on his little continental trips; his bag was packed and stood in readiness on the sitting-room sofa. A parcel of diamonds (purchased honestly, though without impertinent questions, at Southampton) was in the inside pocket of his waistcoat, and another more valuable parcel was stowed in a cavity in the heel of his right boot. In an hour and a half it would be time for him to set out to catch the boat train at the junction; meanwhile there was nothing to do but stroll round the fading garden and consider how he should invest the proceeds of the impending deal. His housekeeper had gone over to Welham for the week's shopping, and would probably not be back until eleven o'clock. He was alone in the premises and just a trifle dull.

He was about to turn into the house when his ear caught the sound of footsteps on the unmade road that passed the end of the garden. He paused and listened. There was no other dwelling near, and the road led nowhere, fading away into the waste land beyond the house. Could this be a visitor? It seemed unlikely, for visitors were few at Silas Hickler's house. Meanwhile the footsteps continued to approach, ringing out with increasing loudness on the hard, stony path.

Silas strolled down to the gate, and, leaning on it, looked out with some curiosity. Presently a glow of light showed him the face of a man, apparently lighting his pipe; then a dim figure detached itself from the enveloping gloom, advanced towards him and halted opposite the garden. The stranger removed a cigarette from his mouth and, blowing out a cloud of smoke, asked—

"Can you tell me if this road will take me to Badsham Junction?"

"No," replied Hickler, "but there is a footpath farther on that leads to the station."

"Footpath!" growled the stranger. "I've had enough of footpaths. I came down from town to Catley intending to walk across to the junction. I started along the road, and then some fool directed me to a short cut, with the result that I have been blundering about in the dark for the last half-hour. My sight isn't very good, you know," he added.

"What train do you want to catch?" asked Hickler.

"Seven fifty-eight," was the reply.

"I am going to catch that train myself," said Silas, "but I shan't be starting for another hour. The station is only three-quarters of a mile from here. If you like to come in and take a rest, we can walk down together and then you'll be sure of not missing your way."

"It's very good of you," said the stranger, peering, with spectacled eyes, at the dark house, "but—I think—"

"Might as well wait here as at the station," said Silas in his genial way, holding the gate open, and the stranger, after a momentary hesitation, entered and, flinging away his cigarette, followed him to the door of the cottage.

The sitting-room was in darkness, save for the dull glow of the expiring fire, but, entering before his guest, Silas applied a match to the lamp that hung from the ceiling. As the flame leaped up, flooding the little interior with light, the two men regarded one another with mutual curiosity.

"Brodski, by Jingo!" was Hickler's silent commentary, as he looked at his guest. "Doesn't know me, evidently—wouldn't, of course, after all these years and with his bad eyesight. Take a seat, sir," he added aloud. "Will you join me in a little refreshment to while away the time?"

Brodski murmured an indistinct acceptance, and, as his host turned to open a cupboard, he deposited his hat (a hard, grey felt) on a chair in a corner, placed his bag on the edge of the table, resting his umbrella against it, and sat down in a small arm-chair.

"Have a biscuit?" said Hickler, as he placed a whisky-bottle on the table together with a couple of his best star-pattern tumblers and a siphon.

"Thanks, I think I will," said Brodski. "The railway journey and all this confounded tramping about, you know—"

"Yes," agreed Silas. "Doesn't do to start with an empty stomach. Hope you don't mind oat-cakes; I see they're the only biscuits I have."

Brodski hastened to assure him that oat-cakes were his special and peculiar fancy; and in confirmation, having mixed himself a stiff jorum, he fell to upon the biscuits with evident gusto.

Brodski was a deliberate feeder, and at present appeared to be somewhat sharp set. His measured munching being unfavourable to conversation, most of the talking fell to Silas; and, for once, that genial transgressor found the task embarrassing. The natural thing would have been to discuss his guest's destination and perhaps the object of his journey; but this was precisely what Hickler avoided doing. For he knew both, and instinct told him to keep his knowledge to himself.

Brodski was a diamond merchant of considerable reputation, and in a large way of business. He bought stones principally in the rough, and of these he was a most excellent judge. His fancy was for stones of somewhat unusual size and value, and it was well known to be his custom, when he had accumulated a sufficient stock, to carry them himself to Amsterdam and supervise the cutting of the rough stones. Of this Hickler was aware, and he had no doubt that Brodski was now starting on one of his periodical excursions; that somewhere in the recesses of his rather shabby clothing was concealed a paper packet possibly worth several thousand pounds.

Brodski sat by the table munching monotonously and talking little. Hickler sat opposite him, talking nervously and rather wildly at times, and watching his guest with a growing fascination. Precious stones, and especially diamonds, were Hickler's speciality. "Hard stuff"—silver plate—he avoided entirely; gold, excepting in the form of specie, he seldom touched; but stones, of which he could carry off a whole consignment in the heel of his boot and dispose of with absolute safety, formed the staple of his industry. And here was a man sitting opposite him with a parcel in his pocket containing the equivalent of a dozen of his most successful "scoops"; stones worth perhaps— Here he pulled himself up short and began to talk rapidly, though without much coherence. For, even as he talked, other words, formed subconsciously, seemed to insinuate themselves into the interstices of the sentences, and to carry on a parallel train of thought.

"Gets chilly in the evenings now, doesn't it?" said Hickler.

"It does indeed," Brodski agreed, and then resumed his slow munching, breathing audibly through his nose.

"Five thousand at least," the subconscious train of thought resumed; "probably six or seven, perhaps ten." Silas fidgeted in his chair and endeavoured to concentrate his ideas on some topic of interest. He was growing disagreeably conscious of a new and unfamiliar state of mind.

"Do you take any interest in gardening?" he asked. Next to diamonds and "weekly property," his besetting weakness was fuchsias.

Brodski chuckled sourly. "Hatton Garden is the nearest approach—" He broke off suddenly, and then added, "I am a Londoner, you know."

The abrupt break in the sentence was not unnoticed by Silas, nor had he any difficulty in interpreting it. A man who carries untold wealth upon his person must needs be wary in his speech.

"Yes," he answered absently, "it's hardly a Londoner's hobby." And then, half consciously, he began a rapid calculation. Put it at five thousand pounds. What would that represent in weekly property? His last set of houses had cost two hundred and fifty pounds apiece, and he had let them at ten shillings and sixpence a week. At that rate, five thousand pounds represented twenty houses at ten and sixpence a week—say ten pounds a week—one pound eight shillings a day—five hundred and twenty pounds a year—for life. It was a competency. Added to what he already had, it was wealth. With that income he could fling the tools of his trade into the river and live out the remainder of his life in comfort and security.

He glanced furtively at his guest across the table, and then looked away quickly as he felt stirring within him an impulse the nature of which he could not mistake. This must be put an end to. Crimes against the person he had always looked upon as sheer insanity. There was, it is true, that little affair of the Weybridge policeman, but that was unforeseen and unavoidable, and it was the constable's doing, after all. And there was the old housekeeper at Epsom, too, but, of course, if the old idiot would shriek in that insane fashion—well, it was an accident, very regrettable, to be sure, and no one could be more sorry for the mishap than himself. But deliberate homicide!—robbery from the person! It was the act of a stark lunatic.

Of course, if he had happened to be that sort of person, here was the opportunity of a lifetime. The immense booty, the empty house, the solitary neighbourhood, away from the main road and from other habitations; the time, the darkness—but, of course, there was the body to be thought of; that was always the difficulty. What to do with the body—Here he caught the shriek of the up express, rounding the curve in the line that ran past the waste land at the back of the house. The sound started a new train of thought, and, as he followed it out, his eyes fixed themselves on the unconscious and taciturn Brodski, as he sat thoughtfully sipping his whisky. At length, averting his gaze with an effort, he rose suddenly from his chair and turned to look at the clock on the mantelpiece, spreading out his hands before the dying fire. A tumult of strange sensations warned him to leave the house. He shivered slightly, though he was rather hot than chilly, and, turning his head, looked at the door.

"Seems to be a confounded draught," he said, with another slight shiver; "did I shut the door properly, I wonder? "He strode across the room, and, opening the door wide, looked out into the dark garden. A desire, sudden and urgent, had come over him to get out into the open air, to be on the road and have done with this madness that was knocking at the door of his brain.

"I wonder if it is worth while to start yet," he said, with a yearning glance at the murky, starless sky.

Brodski roused himself and looked round. "Is your clock right?" he asked.

Silas reluctantly admitted that it was.

"How long will it take us to walk to the station?" inquired Brodski.

"Oh, about twenty-five minutes to half-an-hour," replied Silas, unconsciously exaggerating the distance.

"Well," said Brodski, "we've got more than an hour yet, and it's more comfortable here than hanging about the station. I don't see the use of starting before we need."

"No; of course not," Silas agreed. A wave of strange emotion, half-regretful, half-triumphant, surged through his brain. For some moments he remained standing on the threshold, looking out dreamily into the night. Then he softly closed the door; and, seemingly without the exercise of his volition, the key turned noiselessly in the lock.

He returned to his chair and tried to open a conversation with the taciturn Brodski, but the words came faltering and disjointed. He felt his face growing hot, his brain full and tense, and there was a faint, high-pitched singing in his ears. He was conscious of watching his guest with a new and fearful interest, and, by sheer force of will, turned away his eyes; only to find them a moment later involuntarily returning to fix the unconscious man with yet more horrible intensity. And ever through his mind walked, like a dreadful procession, the thoughts of what that other man—the man of blood and violence—would do in these circumstances. Detail by detail the hideous synthesis fitted together the parts of the imagined crime, and arranged them in due sequence until they formed a succession of events, rational, connected and coherent.

He rose uneasily from his chair, with his eyes still riveted upon his guest. He could not sit any longer opposite that man with his hidden store of precious gems. The impulse that he recognized with fear and wonder was growing more ungovernable from moment to moment. If he stayed it would presently overpower him, and then— He shrank with horror from the dreadful thought, but his fingers itched to handle the diamonds. For Silas was, after all, a criminal by nature and habit. He was a beast of prey. His livelihood had never been earned; it had been taken by stealth or, if necessary, by force. His instincts were predacious, and the proximity of unguarded valuables suggested to him, as a logical consequence, their abstraction or seizure. His unwillingness to let these diamonds go away beyond his reach was fast becoming overwhelming.

But he would make one more effort to escape. He would keep out of Brodski's actual presence until the moment for starting came.

"If you'll excuse me," he said, "I will go and put on a thicker pair of boots. After all this dry weather we may get a change, and damp feet are very uncomfortable when you are travelling."

"Yes; dangerous too," agreed Brodski.

Silas walked through into the adjoining kitchen, where, by the light of the little lamp that was burning there, he had seen his stout, country boots placed, cleaned and in readiness, and sat down upon a chair to make the change. He did not, of course, intend to wear the country boots, for the diamonds were concealed in those he had on. But he would make the change and then alter his mind; it would all help to pass the time. He took a deep breath. It was a relief, at any rate, to be out of that room. Perhaps, if he stayed away, the temptation would pass. Brodski would go on his way— he wished that he was going alone—and the danger would be over—at least—and the opportunity would have gone—the diamonds—

He looked up as he slowly unlaced his boot. From where he sat he could see Brodski sitting by the table with his back towards the kitchen door. He had finished eating, now, and was composedly rolling a cigarette. Silas breathed heavily, and, slipping off his boot, sat for a while motionless, gazing steadily at the other man's back. Then he unlaced the other boot, still staring abstractedly at his unconscious guest, drew it off, and laid it very quietly on the floor.

Brodski calmly finished rolling his cigarette, licked the paper, put away his pouch, and, having dusted the crumbs of tobacco from his knees, began to search his pockets for a match. Suddenly, yielding to an uncontrollable impulse, Silas stood up and began stealthily to creep along the passage to the sitting-room. Not a sound came from his stockinged feet as they trod the stone floor of the passage. Silently as a cat he stole forward, breathing softly with parted lips, until he stood at the threshold of the room. His face flushed duskily, his eyes, wide and staring, glittered in the lamplight, and the racing blood hummed in his ears.

Brodski struck a match—Silas noted that it was a wooden vesta—lighted his cigarette, blew out the match and flung it into the fender. Then he replaced the box in his pocket and commenced to smoke.

Slowly and without a sound Silas crept forward into the room, step by step, with catlike stealthiness, until he stood close behind Brodski's chair—so close that he had to turn his head that his breath might not stir the hair upon the other man's head. So, for half-a-minute, he stood motionless, like a symbolical statue of Murder, glaring down with horrible, glittering eyes upon the unconscious diamond merchant, while his quick breath passed without a sound through his open mouth and his fingers writhed slowly like the tentacles of a giant hydra. And then, as noiselessly as ever, he backed away to the door, turned quickly and walked back into the kitchen.

He drew a deep breath. It had been a near thing. Brodski's life had hung upon a thread. For it had been so easy. Indeed, if he had happened, as he stood behind the man's chair, to have a weapon—a hammer, for instance, or even a stone—

He glanced round the kitchen and his eye lighted on a bar that had been left by the workmen who had put up the new greenhouse. It was an odd piece cut off from a square, wrought iron stanchion, and was about a foot long and perhaps three-quarters of an inch thick. Now, if he had had that in his hand a minute ago—

He picked the bar up, balanced it in his hand and swung it round his head. A formidable weapon this: silent, too. And it fitted the plan that had passed through his brain. Bah! He had better put the thing down.

But he did not. He stepped over to the door and looked again at Brodski, sitting, as before, meditatively smoking, with his back towards the kitchen.

Suddenly a change came over Silas. His face flushed, the veins of his neck stood out and a sullen scowl settled on his face. He drew out his watch, glanced at it earnestly and replaced it. Then he strode swiftly but silently along the passage into the sitting-room.

A pace away from his victim's chair he halted and took deliberate aim. The bar swung aloft, but not without some faint rustle of movement, for Brodski looked round quickly even as the iron whistled through the air. The movement disturbed the murderer's aim, and the bar glanced off his victim's head making only a trifling wound. Brodski sprang up with a tremulous, bleating cry, and clutched his assailant's arms with the tenacity of mortal terror.

Then began a terrible struggle, as the two men, locked in a deadly embrace, swayed to and fro and trampled backwards and forwards. The chair was overturned, an empty glass swept from the table and, with Brodski's spectacles, crushed beneath stamping feet. And thrice that dreadful, pitiful, bleating cry rang out into the night, filling Silas, despite his murderous frenzy, with terror lest some chance wayfarer should hear it. Gathering his great strength for a final effort, he forced his victim backwards on to the table and, snatching up a corner of the table-cloth, thrust it into his face and crammed it into his mouth, as it opened to utter another shriek. And thus they remained for a full two minutes, almost motionless, like some dreadful group of tragic allegory. Then, when the last faint twitchings had died away, Silas relaxed his grasp and let the limp body slip softly on to the floor.

It was over. For good or for evil, the thing was done. Silas stood up, breathing heavily, and, as he wiped the sweat from his face, he looked at the clock. The hands stood at one minute to seven. The whole thing had taken a little over three minutes. He had nearly an hour in which to finish his task. The goods train that entered into his scheme came by at twenty minutes past, and it was only three hundred yards to the line. Still, he must not waste time. He was now quite composed, and only disturbed by the thought that Brodski's cries might have been heard. If no one had heard them it was all plain sailing.

He stooped, and, gently disengaging the table-cloth from the dead man's teeth, began a careful search of his pockets. He was not long finding what he sought, and, as he pinched the paper packet and felt the little hard bodies grating on one another inside, his faint regrets for what had happened were swallowed up in self-congratulations.

He now set about his task with business-like briskness and an attentive eye on the clock. A few large drops of blood had fallen on the table-cloth, and there was a small bloody smear on the carpet by the dead man's head. Silas fetched from the kitchen some water, a nail-brush and a dry cloth, and, having washed out the stain from the table-cover—not forgetting the deal table-top underneath—and cleaned away the smear from the carpet and rubbed the damp places dry, he slipped a sheet of paper under the head of the corpse to prevent further contamination. Then he set the table-cloth straight, stood the chair upright, laid the broken spectacles on the table and picked up the cigarette, which had been trodden flat in the struggle, and flung it under the grate. Then there was the broken glass, which he swept up into a dust-pan. Part of it was the remains of the shattered tumbler, and the rest the fragments of the broken spectacles. He turned it out on to a sheet of paper and looked it over carefully, picking out the larger recognizable pieces of the spectacle-glasses and putting them aside on a separate slip of paper, together with a sprinkling of the minute fragments. The remainder he shot back into the dust-pan and, having hurriedly put on his boots, carried it out to the rubbish-heap at the back of the house.

It was now time to start. Hastily cutting off a length of string from his string-box—for Silas was an orderly man and despised the oddments of string with which many people make shift—he tied it to the dead man's bag and umbrella and slung them from his shoulder. Then he folded up the paper of broken glass, and, slipping it and the spectacles into his pocket, picked up the body and threw it over his shoulder. Brodski was a small, spare man, weighing not more than nine stone; not a very formidable burden for a big, athletic man like Silas.

The night was intensely dark, and, when Silas looked out of the back gate over the waste land that stretched from his house to the railway, he could hardly see twenty yards ahead. After listening cautiously and hearing no sound, he went out, shut the gate softly behind him and set forth at a good pace, though carefully, over the broken ground. His progress was not as silent as he could have wished, for, though the scanty turf that covered the gravelly land was thick enough to deaden his footfalls, the swinging bag and umbrella made an irritating noise; indeed, his movements were more hampered by them than by the weightier burden.

The distance to the line was about three hundred yards. Ordinarily he would have walked it in from three to four minutes, but now, going cautiously with his burden and stopping now and again to listen, it took him just six minutes to reach the three-bar fence that separated the waste land from the railway. Arrived here he halted for a moment and once more listened attentively, peering into the darkness on all sides. Not a living creature was to be seen or heard in this desolate spot, but, far away, the shriek of an engine's whistle warned him to hasten.

Lifting the corpse easily over the fence, he carried it a few yards farther to a point where the line curved sharply. Here he laid it face downwards, with the neck over the near rail. Drawing out his pocket-knife, he cut through the knot that fastened the umbrella to the string and also secured the bag; and when he had flung the bag and umbrella on the track beside the body, he carefully pocketed the string, excepting the little loop that had fallen to the ground when the knot was cut.

The quick snort and clanking rumble of an approaching goods train began now to be clearly audible. Rapidly, Silas drew from his pocket the battered spectacles and the packet of broken glass. The former he threw down by the dead man's head, and then, emptying the packet into his hand, sprinkled the fragments of glass around the spectacles.

He was none too soon. Already the quick, laboured puffing of the engine sounded close at hand. His impulse was to stay and watch; to witness the final catastrophe that should convert the murder into an accident or suicide. But it was hardly safe: it would be better that he should not be near lest he should not be able to get away without being seen. Hastily he climbed back over the fence and strode away across the rough fields, while the train came snorting and clattering towards the curve.

He had nearly reached his back gate when a sound from the line brought him to a sudden halt: it was a prolonged whistle accompanied by the groan of brakes and the loud clank of colliding trucks. The snorting of the engine had ceased and was replaced by the penetrating hiss of escaping steam.

The train had stopped!

For one brief moment Silas stood with bated breath and mouth agape like one petrified; then he strode forward quickly to the gate, and, letting himself in, silently slid the bolt. He was undeniably alarmed. What could have happened on the line? It was practically certain that the body had been seen; but what was happening now? and would they come to the house? He entered the kitchen, and having paused again to listen—for somebody might come and knock at the door at any moment—he walked through the sitting-room and looked round. All seemed in order there. There was the bar, though, lying where he had dropped it in the scuffle. He picked it up and held it under the lamp. There was no blood on it; only one or two hairs. Somewhat absently he wiped it with the table-cover, and then, running out through the kitchen into the back garden, dropped it over the wall into a bed of nettles. Not that there was anything incriminating in the bar, but, since he had used it as a weapon, it had somehow acquired a sinister aspect to his eye.

He now felt that it would be well to start for the station at once. It was not time yet, for it was barely twenty-five minutes past seven; but he did not wish to be found in the house if any one should come. His soft hat was on the sofa with his bag to which his umbrella was strapped. He put on the hat, caught up the bag and stepped over to the door; then he came back to turn down the lamp. And it was at this moment, when he stood with his hand raised to the burner, that his eye, travelling by chance into the dim corner of the room, lighted on Brodski's grey felt hat, reposing on the chair where the dead man had placed it when he entered the house.

Silas stood for a few moments as if petrified, with the chilly sweat of mortal fear standing in beads upon his forehead. Another instant and he would have turned the lamp down and gone on his way; and then—He strode over to the chair, snatched up the hat and looked inside it. Yes, there was the name, "Oscar Brodski," written plainly on the lining. If he had gone away, leaving it to be discovered, he would have been lost; indeed, even now, if a search-party should come to the house, it was enough to send him to the gallows.

His limbs shook with horror at the thought, but in spite of his panic he did not lose his self-possession. Darting through into the kitchen, he grabbed up a handful of the dry brush-wood that was kept for lighting fires and carried it to the sitting-room grate where he thrust it on the extinct, but still hot, embers, and crumpling up the paper that he had placed under Brodski's head—on which paper he now noticed, for the first time, a minute bloody smear—he poked it in under the wood, and, striking a wax match, set light to it. As the wood flared up, he hacked at the hat with his pocket-knife and threw the ragged strips into the blaze.

And all the while his heart was thumping and his hands a-tremble with the dread of discovery. The fragments of felt were far from inflammable, tending rather to fuse into cindery masses that smoked and smouldered, than to burn away into actual ash. Moreover, to his dismay, they emitted a powerful resinous stench mixed with the odour of burning hair, so that he had to open the kitchen window (since he dared not unlock the front door) to disperse the reek. And still, as he fed the fire with small cut fragments, he strained his ears to catch, above the crackling of the wood, the sound of the dreaded footsteps, the knock on the door that should be as the summons of Fate.

The time, too, was speeding on. Twenty-one minutes to eight! In a few minutes more he must set out or he would miss his train. He dropped the dismembered hat-brim on the blazing wood and ran up-stairs to open a window, since he must close that in the kitchen before he left. When he came back, the brim had already curled up into a black, clinkery mass that bubbled and hissed as the fat, pungent smoke rose from it sluggishly to the chimney.

Nineteen minutes to eight! It was time to start. He took up the poker and carefully beat the cinders into small particles, stirring them into the glowing embers of the wood and coal. There was now nothing unusual in the appearance of the grate. It was his constant custom to burn letters and other discarded articles in the sitting-room fire: his housekeeper would notice nothing out of the common. Indeed, the cinders would probably be reduced to ashes before she returned. He had been careful to notice that there were no metallic fittings of any kind in the hat, which might have escaped burning.

Once more he picked up his bag, took a last look round, turned down the lamp and, unlocking the door, held it open for a few moments. Then he went out, locked the door, pocketed the key (of which his housekeeper had a duplicate) and set off at a brisk pace for the station.

He arrived in good time after all, and, having taken his ticket, strolled through on to the platform. The train was not yet signalled, but there seemed to be an unusual stir in the place. The passengers were collected in a group at one end of the platform, and were all looking in one direction down the line; and, even as he walked towards them, with a certain tremulous, nauseating curiosity, two men emerged from the darkness and ascended the slope to the platform, carrying a stretcher covered with a tarpaulin. The passengers parted to let the bearers pass, turning fascinated eyes upon the shape that showed faintly through the rough pall; and, when the stretcher had been borne into the lamp-room, they fixed their attention upon a porter who followed carrying a hand-bag and an umbrella.

Suddenly one of the passengers started forward with an exclamation.

"Is that his umbrella?" he demanded.

"Yes, sir," answered the porter, stopping and holding it out for the speaker's inspection.

"My God!" ejaculated the passenger; then, turning sharply to a tall man who stood close by, he said excitedly: "That's Brodski's umbrella. I could swear to it. You remember Brodski?" The tall man nodded, and the passenger, turning once more to the porter, said: "I identify that umbrella. It belongs to a gentleman named Brodski. If you look in his hat you will see his name written in it. He always writes his name in his hat."

"We haven't found his hat yet," said the porter; "but here is the station-master coming up the line." He awaited the arrival of his superior and then announced: "This gentleman, sir, has identified the umbrella."

"Oh," said the station-master, "you recognize the umbrella, sir, do you? Then perhaps you would step into the lamp-room and see if you can identify the body."

The passenger recoiled with a look of alarm.

"Is it—is he—very much injured?" he asked tremulously.

"Well, yes," was the reply. "You see, the engine and six of the trucks went over him before they could stop the train. Took his head clean off, in fact."

"Shocking! shocking!" gasped the passenger. "I think, if you don't mind—I'd—I'd rather not. You don't think it's necessary, doctor, do you?"

"Yes, I do," replied the tall man. "Early identification may be of the first importance."

"Then I suppose I must," said the passenger.

Very reluctantly he allowed himself to be conducted by the station-master to the lamp-room, as the clang of the bell announced the approaching train. Silas Hickler followed and took his stand with the expectant crowd outside the closed door. In a few moments the passenger burst out, pale and awe-stricken, and rushed up to his tall friend. "It is!" he exclaimed breathlessly, "it's Brodski! Poor old Brodski! Horrible! horrible! He was to have met me here and come on with me to Amsterdam."

"Had he any—merchandize about him?" the tall man asked; and Silas strained his ears to catch the reply.

"He had some stones, no doubt, but I don't know what. His clerk will know, of course. By the way, doctor, could you watch the case for me? Just to be sure it was really an accident or—you know what. We were old friends, you know, fellow townsmen, too; we were both born in Warsaw. I'd like you to give an eye to the case."

"Very well," said the other. "I will satisfy myself that—there is nothing more than appears, and let you have a report. Will that do?"

"Thank you. It's excessively good of you, doctor. Ah! here comes the train. I hope it won't inconvenience you to stay and see to this matter."

"Not in the least," replied the doctor. "We are not due at Warmington until to-morrow afternoon, and I expect we can find out all that is necessary to know and still keep our appointment."

Silas looked long and curiously at the tall, imposing man who was, as it were, taking his seat at the chess-board, to play against him for his life. A formidable antagonist he looked, with his keen, thoughtful face, so resolute and calm. As Silas stepped into his carriage he looked back at his opponent, and thinking with deep discomfort of Brodski's hat, he hoped that he had made no other oversight.

PART II: THE MECHANISM OF DETECTION
(Related by Christopher Jervis, M.D.)

The singular circumstances that attended the death of Mr. Oscar Brodski, the well-known diamond merchant of Hatton Garden, illustrated very forcibly the importance of one or two points in medico-legal practice which Thorndyke was accustomed to insist were not sufficiently appreciated. What those points were, I shall leave my friend and teacher to state at the proper place; and meanwhile, as the case is in the highest degree instructive, I shall record the incidents in the order of their occurrence.

The dusk of an October evening was closing in as Thorndyke and I, the sole occupants of a smoking compartment, found ourselves approaching the little station of Ludham; and, as the train slowed down, we peered out at the knot of country people who were waiting on the platform. Suddenly Thorndyke exclaimed in a tone of surprise: "Why, that is surely Boscovitch!" and almost at the same moment a brisk, excitable little man darted at the door of our compartment and literally tumbled in.

"I hope I don't intrude on this learned conclave," he said, shaking hands genially and banging his Gladstone with impulsive violence into the rack; "but I saw your faces at the window, and naturally jumped at the chance of such pleasant companionship."

"You are very flattering," said Thorndyke; "so flattering that you leave us nothing to say. But what in the name of fortune are you doing at—what's the name of the place?—Ludham? "

"My brother has a little place a mile or so from here, and I have been spending a couple of days with him," Mr. Boscovitch explained. "I shall change at Badsham Junction and catch the boat train for Amsterdam. But whither are you two bound? I see you have your mysterious little green box up on the hat-rack, so I infer that you are on some romantic quest, eh? Going to unravel some dark and intricate crime?"

"No," replied Thorndyke. "We are bound for Warmington on a quite prosaic errand. I am instructed to watch the proceedings at an inquest there to-morrow on behalf of the Griffin Life Insurance Office, and we are travelling down to-night as it is rather a cross-country journey."

"But why the box of magic?" asked Boscovitch, glancing up at the hat-rack.

"I never go away from home without it," answered Thorndyke. "One never knows what may turn up; the trouble of carrying it is small when set off against the comfort of having one's appliances at hand in case of an emergency."

Boscovitch continued to stare up at the little square case covered with Willesden canvas. Presently he remarked: "I often used to wonder what you had in it when you were down at Chelmsford in connection with that bank murder—what an amazing case that was, by the way, and didn't your methods of research astonish the police!" As he still looked up wistfully at the case, Thorndyke good-naturedly lifted it down and unlocked it. As a matter of fact he was rather proud of his "portable laboratory," and certainly it was a triumph of condensation, for, small as it was—only a foot square by four inches deep—it contained a fairly complete outfit for a preliminary investigation.

"Wonderful!" exclaimed Boscovitch, when the case lay open before him, displaying its rows of little re-agent bottles, tiny test-tubes, diminutive spirit-lamp, dwarf microscope and assorted instruments on the same Lilliputian scale; "it's like a doll's house—everything looks as if it was seen through the wrong end of a telescope. But are these tiny things really efficient? That microscope now."

"Perfectly efficient at low and moderate magnifications," said Thorndyke. "It looks like a toy, but it isn't one; the lenses are the best that can be had. Of course, a full-sized instrument would be infinitely more convenient—but I shouldn't have it with me, and should have to make shift with a pocket-lens. And so with the rest of the undersized appliances; they are the alternative to no appliances."

Boscovitch pored over the case and its contents, fingering the instruments delicately and asking questions innumerable about their uses; indeed, his curiosity was but half appeased when, half-an-hour later, the train began to slow down.

"By Jove!" he exclaimed, starting up and seizing his bag, "here we are at the junction already. You change here too, don't you?"

"Yes," replied Thorndyke. "We take the branch train on to Warmington."

As we stepped out on to the platform, we became aware that something unusual was happening or had happened. All the passengers and most of the porters and supernumeraries were gathered at one end of the station, and all were looking intently into the darkness down the line.

"Anything wrong?" asked Mr. Boscovitch, addressing the station-inspector.

"Yes, sir," the official replied; "a man has been run over by the goods train about a mile down the line. The station-master has gone down with a stretcher to bring him in, and I expect that is his lantern that you see coming this way."

As we stood watching the dancing light grow momentarily brighter, flashing fitful reflections from the burnished rails, a man came out of the booking-office and joined the group of onlookers. He attracted my attention, as I afterwards remembered, for two reasons: in the first place his round, jolly face was excessively pale and bore a strained and wild expression, and, in the second, though he stared into the darkness with eager curiosity, he asked no questions.

The swinging lantern continued to approach, and then suddenly two men came into sight beaing a stretcher covered with a tarpaulin, through which the shape of a human figure was dimly discernible. They ascended the slope to the platform, and proceeded with their burden to the lamp-room, when the inquisitive gaze of the passengers was transferred to a porter who followed carrying a hand-bag and umbrella and to the station-master who brought up the rear with his lantern.

As the porter passed, Mr. Boscovitch started forward with sudden excitement.

"Is that his umbrella?" he asked.

"Yes, sir," answered the porter, stopping and holding it out for the speaker's inspection.

"My God!" ejaculated Boscovitch; then, turning sharply to Thorndyke, he exclaimed: "That's Brodski's umbrella. I could swear to it. You remember Brodski?"

Thorndyke nodded, and Boscovitch, turning once more to the porter, said: "I identify that umbrella. It belongs to a gentleman named Brodski. If you look in his hat, you will see his name written in it. He always writes his name in his hat."

"We haven't found his hat yet," said the porter; "but here is the station-master." He turned to his superior and announced: "This gentleman, sir, has identified the umbrella."

"Oh," said the station-master, "you recognize the umbrella, sir, do you? Then perhaps you would step into the lamp-room and see if you can identify the body."

Mr. Boscovitch recoiled with a look of alarm.

"Is it—is he—very much injured?" he asked nervously.

"Well, yes," was the reply. "You see, the engine and six of the trucks went over him before they could stop the train. Took his head clean off, in fact."

"Shocking! shocking!" gasped Boscovitch.

"I think—if you don't mind—I'd—I'd rather not. You don't think it necessary, doctor, do you?"

"Yes, I do," replied Thorndyke. "Early identification may be of the first importance."

"Then I suppose I must," said Boscovitch; and, with extreme reluctance, he followed the station-master to the lamp-room, as the loud ringing of the bell announced the approach of the boat train. His inspection must have been of the briefest, for, in a few moments, he burst out, pale and awe-stricken, and rushed up to Thorndyke.

"It is!" he exclaimed breathlessly, "it's Brodski! Poor old Brodski! Horrible! horrible! He was to have met me here and come on with me to Amsterdam."

"Had he any—merchandize about him?" Thorndyke asked; and, as he spoke, the stranger whom I had previously noticed, edged up closer as if to catch the reply.

"He had some stones, no doubt," answered Boscovitch, "but I don't know what they were. His clerk will know, of course. By the way, doctor, could you watch the case for me? Just to be sure it was really an accident or—you know what. We were old friends, you know, fellow townsmen, too; we were both born in Warsaw. I'd like you to give an eye to the case."

"Very well," said Thorndyke. "I will satisfy myself that there is nothing more than appears, and let you have a report. Will that do?"

"Thank you," said Boscovitch. "It's excessively good of you, doctor. Ah, here comes the train. I hope it won't inconvenience you to stay and see to this matter."

"Not in the least," replied Thorndyke. "We are not due at Warmington until to-morrow afternoon, and I expect we can find out all that is necessary to know and still keep our appointment."

As Thorndyke spoke, the stranger, who had kept close to us with the evident purpose of hearing what was said, bestowed on him a very curious and attentive look; and it was only when the train had actually come to rest by the platform that he hurried away to find a compartment.

No sooner had the train left the station than Thorndyke sought out the station-master and informed him of the instructions that he had received from Boscovitch. "Of course," he added, in conclusion, "we must not move in the matter until the police arrive. I suppose they have been informed?"

"Yes," replied the station-master; "I sent a message at once to the Chief Constable, and I expect him or an inspector at any moment. In fact, I think I will slip out to the approach and see if he is coming." He evidently wished to have a word in private with the police officer before committing himself to any statement.

As the official departed, Thorndyke and I began to pace the now empty platform, and my friend, as was his wont, when entering on a new inquiry, meditatively reviewed the features of the problem.

"In a case of this kind," he remarked, "we have to decide on one of three possible explanations: accident, suicide or homicide; and our decision will be determined by inferences from three sets of facts: first, the general facts of the case; second, the special data obtained by examination of the body, and, third, the special data obtained by examining the spot on which the body was found. Now the only general facts at present in our possession are that the deceased was a diamond merchant making a journey for a specific purpose and probably having on his person property of small bulk and great value. These facts are somewhat against the hypothesis of suicide and somewhat favourable to that of homicide. Facts relevant to the question of accident would be the existence or otherwise of a level crossing, a road or path leading to the line, an enclosing fence with or without a gate and any other facts rendering probable or otherwise the accidental presence of the deceased at the spot where the body was found. As we do not possess these facts, it is desirable that we extend our knowledge."

"Why not put a few discreet questions to the porter who brought in the bag and umbrella?" I suggested. "He is at this moment in earnest conversation with the ticket collector and would, no doubt, be glad of a new listener."

"An excellent suggestion, Jervis," answered Thorndyke. "Let us see what he has to tell us." We approached the porter and found him, as I had anticipated, bursting to unburden himself of the tragic story.

"The way the thing happened, sir, was this," he said, in answer to Thorndyke's question: "There's a sharpish bend in the road just at that place, and the goods train was just rounding the curve when the driver suddenly caught sight of something lying across the rails. As the engine turned, the head-lights shone on it and then he saw it was a man. He shut off steam at once, blew his whistle and put the brakes down hard, but, as you know, sir, a goods train takes some stopping; before they could bring her up, the engine and half-a-dozen trucks had gone over the poor beggar."

"Could the driver see how the man was lying?" Thorndyke asked.

"Yes, he could see him quite plain, because the head-lights were full on him. He was lying on his face with his neck over the near rail on the down side. His head was in the four-foot and his body by the side of the track. It looked as if he had laid himself out a-purpose."

"Is there a level crossing thereabouts? "asked Thorndyke.

"No, sir. No crossing, no road, no path, no nothing," said the porter, ruthlessly sacrificing grammar to emphasis. "He must have come across the fields and climbed over the fence to get on to the permanent way. Deliberate suicide is what it looks like."

"How did you learn all this?" Thorndyke inquired.

"Why, the driver, you see, sir, when him and his mate had lifted the body off the track, went on to the next signal-box and sent in his report by telegram. The station-master told me all about it as we walked down the line."

Thorndyke thanked the man for his information, and, as we strolled back towards the lamp-room, discussed the bearing of these new facts.

"Our friend is unquestionably right in one respect," he said; "this was not an accident. The man might, if he were near-sighted, deaf or stupid, have climbed over the fence and got knocked down by the train. But his position, lying across the rails, can only be explained by one of two hypotheses: either it was, as the porter says, deliberate suicide, or else the man was already dead or insensible. We must leave it at that until we have seen the body, that is, if the police will allow us to see it. But here comes the station-master and an officer with him. Let us hear what they have to say."

The two officials had evidently made up their minds to decline any outside assistance. The divisional surgeon would make the necessary examination, and information could be obtained through the usual channels. The production of Thorndyke's card, however, somewhat altered the situation. The police inspector hummed and hawed irresolutely, with the card in his hand, but finally agreed to allow us to view the body, and we entered the lamp-room together, the station-master leading the way to turn up the gas.

The stretcher stood on the floor by one wall, its grim burden still hidden by the tarpaulin, and the hand-bag and umbrella lay on a large box, together with the battered frame of a pair of spectacles from which the glasses had fallen out.

"Were these spectacles found by the body?" Thorndyke inquired.

"Yes," replied the station-master. "They were close to the head and the glass was scattered about on the ballast."

Thorndyke made a note in his pocket-book, and then, as the inspector removed the tarpaulin, he glanced down on the corpse, lying limply on the stretcher and looking grotesquely horrible with its displaced head and distorted limbs. For fully a minute he remained silently stooping over the uncanny object, on which the inspector was now throwing the light of a large lantern; then he stood up and said quietly to me: "I think we can eliminate two out of the three hypotheses."

The inspector looked at him quickly and was about to ask a question, when his attention was diverted by the travelling-case which Thorndyke had laid on a shelf and now opened to abstract a couple of pairs of dissecting forceps.

"We've no authority to make a *post mortem*, you know," said the inspector.

"No, of course not," said Thorndyke. "I am merely going to look into the mouth." With one pair of forceps he turned back the lip and, having scrutinized its inner surface, closely examined the teeth.

"May I trouble you for your lens, Jervis?" he said; and, as I handed him my doublet ready opened, the inspector brought the lantern close to the dead face and leaned forward eagerly. In his usual systematic fashion, Thorndyke slowly passed the lens along the whole range of sharp, uneven teeth, and then, bringing it back to the centre, examined with more minuteness the upper incisors. At length, very delicately, he picked out with his forceps some minute object from between two of the upper front teeth and held it in the focus of the lens. Anticipating his next move, I took a labelled microscope-slide from the case and handed it to him together with a dissecting needle, and, as he transferred the object to the slide and spread it out with the needle, I set up the little microscope on the shelf.

"A drop of Farrant and a cover-glass, please, Jervis," said Thorndyke.

I handed him the bottle, and, when he had let a drop of the mounting fluid fall gently on the object and put on the cover-slip, he placed the slide on the stage of the microscope and examined it attentively.

Happening to glance at the inspector, I observed on his countenance a faint grin, which he politely strove to suppress when he caught my eye.

"I was thinking, sir," he said apologetically, "that it's a bit off the track to be finding out what he had for dinner. He didn't die of unwholesome feeding."

Thorndyke looked up with a smile. "It doesn't do, inspector, to assume that anything is off the track in an inquiry of this kind. Every fact must have some significance, you know."

"I don't see any significance in the diet of a man who has had his head cut off," the inspector rejoined defiantly.

"Don't you? "said Thorndyke. "Is there no interest attaching to the last meal of a man who has met a violent death? These crumbs, for instance, that are scattered over the dead man's waistcoat. Can we learn nothing from them?"

"I don't see what you can learn," was the dogged rejoinder.

Thorndyke picked off the crumbs, one by one, with his forceps, and, having deposited them on a slide, inspected them, first with the lens and then through the microscope.

"I learn," said he, "that shortly before his death, the deceased partook of some kind of whole-meal biscuits, apparently composed partly of oatmeal."

"I call that nothing," said the inspector. "The question that we have got to settle is not what refreshments had the deceased been taking, but what was the cause of his death: did he commit suicide? was he killed by accident? or was there any foul play?"

"I beg your pardon," said Thorndyke, "the questions that remain to be settled are, who killed the deceased and with what motive? The others are already answered as far as I am concerned."

The inspector stared in sheer amazement not unmixed with incredulity.

"You haven't been long coming to a conclusion, sir," he said.

"No, it was a pretty obvious case of murder," said Thorndyke. "As to the motive, the deceased was a diamond merchant and is believed to have had a quantity of stones about his person. I should suggest that you search the body."

The inspector gave vent to an exclamation of disgust. "I see," he said. "It was just a guess on your part. The dead man was a diamond merchant and had valuable property about him; therefore he was murdered." He drew himself up, and, regarding Thorndyke with stern reproach, added: "But you must understand, sir, that this is a judicial inquiry, not a prize competition in a penny paper. And, as to searching the body, why, that is what I principally came for." He ostentatiously turned his back on us and proceeded systematically to turn out the dead man's pockets, laying the articles, as he removed them, on the box by the side of the hand-bag and umbrella.

While he was thus occupied, Thorndyke looked over the body generally, paying special attention to the soles of the boots, which, to the inspector's undissembled amusement, he very thoroughly examined with the lens.

"I should have thought, sir, that his feet were large enough to be seen with the naked eye," was his comment; "but perhaps," he added, with a sly glance at the station-master, "you're a little near-sighted."

Thorndyke chuckled good-humouredly, and, while the officer continued his search, he looked over the articles that had already been laid on the box. The purse and pocket-book he naturally left for the inspector to open, but the reading-glasses, pocket-knife and card-case and other small pocket articles were subjected to a searching scrutiny. The inspector watched him out of the corner of his eye with furtive amusement; saw him hold up the glasses to the light to estimate their refractive power, peer into the tobacco pouch, open the cigarette book and examine the watermark of the paper, and even inspect the contents of the silver match-box.

"What might you have expected to find in his tobacco pouch?" the officer asked, laying down a bunch of keys from the dead man's pocket.

"Tobacco," Thorndyke replied stolidly; "but I did not expect to find fine-cut Latakia. I don't remember ever having seen pure Latakia smoked in cigarettes."

"You do take an interest in things, sir," said the inspector, with a side glance at the stolid station-master.

"I do," Thorndyke agreed; "and I note that there are no diamonds among this collection."

"No, and we don't know that he had any about him; but there's a gold watch and chain, a diamond scarf-pin, and a purse containing"—he opened it and tipped out its contents into his hand—"twelve pounds in gold. That doesn't look much like robbery, does it? What do you say to the murder theory now?"

"My opinion is unchanged," said Thorndyke, "and I should like to examine the spot where the body was found. Has the engine been inspected?" he added, addressing the station-master.

"I telegraphed to Bradfield to have it examined," the official answered. "The report has probably come in by now. I'd better see before we start down the line."

We emerged from the lamp-room and, at the door, found the station-inspector waiting with a telegram. He handed it to the station-master, who read it aloud.

"The engine has been carefully examined by me. I find small smear of blood on near leading wheel and smaller one on next wheel following. No other marks." He glanced questioningly at Thorndyke, who nodded and remarked: "It will be interesting to see if the line tells the same tale."

The station-master looked puzzled and was apparently about to ask for an explanation; but the inspector, who had carefully pocketed the dead man's property, was impatient to start and, accordingly, when Thorndyke had repacked his case and, had, at his own request, been furnished with a lantern, we set off down the permanent way, Thorndyke carrying the light and I the indispensable green case.

"I am a little in the dark about this affair," I said, when we had allowed the two officials to draw ahead out of earshot; "you came to a conclusion remarkably quickly. What was it that so immediately determined the opinion of murder as against suicide?"

"It was a small matter but very conclusive," replied Thorndyke. "You noticed a small scalp-wound above the left temple? It was a glancing wound, and might easily have been made by the engine. But—the wound had bled; and it had bled for an appreciable time. There were two streams of blood from it, and in both the blood was firmly clotted and partially dried. But the man had been decapitated; and this wound if inflicted by the engine, must have been made after the decapitation, since it was on the side most distant from the engine as it approached. Now a decapitated head does not bleed. Therefore this wound was inflicted before the decapitation.

"But not only had the wound bled: the blood had trickled down in two streams at right angles to one another. First, in the order of time as shown by the appearance of the stream, it had trickled down the side of the face and dropped on the collar. The second stream ran from the wound to the back of the head. Now, you know, Jervis, there are no exceptions to the law of gravity. If the blood ran down the face towards the chin, the face must have been upright at the time; and if the blood trickled from the front to the back of the head, the head must have been horizontal and face upwards. But the man when he was seen by the engine driver, was lying *face downwards*. The only possible inference is that when the wound was inflicted, the man was in the upright position—standing or sitting; and that subsequently, and while he was still alive, he lay on his back for a sufficiently long time for the blood to have trickled to the back of his head."

"I see. I was a duffer not to have reasoned this out for myself," I remarked contritely.

"Quick observation and rapid inference come by practice," replied Thorndyke. "But, tell me, what did you notice about the face?"

"I thought there was a strong suggestion of asphyxia."

"Undoubtedly," said Thorndyke. "It was the face of a suffocated man. You must have noticed, too, that the tongue was very distinctly swollen and that on the inside of the upper lip were deep indentations made by the teeth, as well as one or two slight wounds, obviously caused by heavy pressure on the mouth. And now observe how completely these facts and inferences agree with those from the scalp wound. If we knew that the deceased had received a blow on the head, had struggled with his assailant and been finally borne down and suffocated, we should look for precisely those signs which we have found."

"By the way, what was it that you found wedged between the teeth? I did not get a chance to look through the microscope."

"Ah!" said Thorndyke, "there we not only get confirmation, but we carry our inferences a stage further. The object was a little tuft of some textile fabric. Under the microscope I found it to consist of several different fibres, differently dyed. The bulk of it consisted of wool fibres dyed crimson, but there were also cotton fibres dyed blue and a few which looked like jute, dyed yellow. It was obviously a parti-coloured fabric and might have been part of a woman's dress, though the presence of the jute is much more suggestive of a curtain or rug of inferior quality."

"And its importance?"

"Is that, if it is not part of an article of clothing, then it must have come from an article of furniture, and furniture suggests a habitation."

"That doesn't seem very conclusive," I objected.

"It is not; but it is valuable corroboration."

"Of what?"

"Of the suggestion offered by the soles of the dead man's boots. I examined them most minutely and could find no trace of sand, gravel or earth, in spite of the fact that he must have crossed fields and rough land to reach the place where he was found. What I did find was fine tobacco ash, a charred mark as if a cigar or cigarette had been trodden on, several crumbs of biscuit, and, on a projecting brad, some coloured fibres, apparently from a carpet. The manifest suggestion is that the man was killed in a house with a carpeted floor, and carried from thence to the railway."

I was silent for some moments. Well as I knew Thorndyke, I was completely taken by surprise; a sensation, indeed, that I experienced anew every time that I accompanied him on one of his investigations. His marvellous power of co-ordinating apparently insignificant facts, of arranging them into an ordered sequence and making them tell a coherent story, was a phenomenon that I never got used to; every exhibition of it astonished me afresh.

"If your inferences are correct," I said, "the problem is practically solved. There must be abundant traces inside the house. The only question is which house is it?"

"Quite so," replied Thorndyke; "that is the question, and a very difficult question it is. A glance at that interior would doubtless clear up the whole mystery. But how are we to get that glance? We cannot enter houses speculatively to see if they present traces of a murder. At present, our clue breaks off abruptly. The other end of it is in some unknown house, and, if we cannot join up the two ends, our problem remains unsolved. For the question is, you remember, Who killed Oscar Brodski?"

"Then what do you propose to do?" I asked.

"The next stage of the inquiry is to connect some particular house with this crime. To that end, I can only gather up all available facts and consider each in all its possible bearings. If I cannot establish any such connection, then the inquiry will have failed and we shall have to make a fresh start—say, at Amsterdam, if it turns out that Brodski really had diamonds on his person, as I have no doubt he had."

Here our conversation was interrupted by our arrival at the spot where the body had been found. The station-master had halted, and he and the inspector were now examining the near rail by the light of their lanterns.

"There's remarkably little blood about," said the former. "I've seen a good many accidents of this kind and there has always been a lot of blood, both on the engine and on the road. It's very curious."

Thorndyke glanced at the rail with but slight attention: that question had ceased to interest him. But the light of his lantern flashed on to the ground at the side of the track—a loose, gravelly soil mixed with fragments of chalk—and from thence to the soles of the inspector's boots, which were displayed as he knelt by the rail.

"You observe, Jervis?" he said in a low voice, and I nodded. The inspector's boot-soles were covered with adherent particles of gravel and conspicuously marked by the chalk on which he had trodden.

"You haven't found the hat, I suppose?" Thorndyke asked, stooping to pick up a short piece of string that lay on the ground at the side of the track.

"No," replied the inspector, "but it can't be far off. You seem to have found another clue, sir," he added, with a grin, glancing at the piece of string.

"Who knows," said Thorndyke. "A short end of white twine with a green strand in it. It may tell us something later. At any rate we'll keep it," and, taking from his pocket a small tin box containing, among other things, a number of seed envelopes, he slipped the string into one of the latter and scribbled a note in pencil on the outside. The inspector watched his proceedings with an indulgent smile, and then returned to his examination of the track, in which Thorndyke now joined.

"I suppose the poor chap was near-sighted," the officer remarked, indicating the remains of the shattered spectacles, "that might account for his having strayed on to the line."

"Possibly," said Thorndyke. He had already noticed the fragments scattered over a sleeper and the adjacent ballast, and now once more produced his "collecting-box," from which he took another seed envelope. "Would you hand me a pair of forceps, Jervis," he said; "and perhaps you wouldn't mind taking a pair yourself and helping me to gather up these fragments."

As I complied, the inspector looked up curiously.

"There isn't any doubt that these spectacles belonged to the deceased, is there?" he asked.

"He certainly wore spectacles, for I saw the mark on his nose."

"Still, there is no harm in verifying the fact," said Thorndyke, and he added to me in a lower tone, "Pick up every particle you can find, Jervis. It may be most important."

"I don't quite see how," I said, groping amongst the shingle by the light of the lantern in search of the tiny splinters of glass.

"Don't you?" returned Thorndyke. "Well, look at these fragments; some of them are a fair size, but many of these on the sleeper are mere grains. And consider their number. Obviously, the condition of the glass does not agree with the circumstances in which we find it. These are thick, concave spectacle-lenses broken into a great number of minute fragments. Now how were they broken? Not merely by falling, evidently: such a lens, when it is dropped, breaks into a small number of large pieces. Nor were they broken by the wheel passing over them, for they would then have been reduced to fine powder, and that powder would have been visible on the rail, which it is not. The spectacle-frames, you may remember, presented the same incongruity: they were battered and damaged more than they would have been by falling, but not nearly so much as they would have been if the wheel had passed over them."

"What do you suggest, then?" I asked.

"The appearances suggest that the spectacles had been trodden on. But, if the body was carried here, the probability is that the spectacles were carried here too, and that they were then already broken; for it is more likely that they were trodden on during the struggle than that the murderer trod on them after bringing them here. Hence the importance of picking up every fragment."

"But why?" I inquired, rather foolishly, I must admit.

"Because, if, when we have picked up every fragment that we can find, there still remains missing a larger portion of the lenses than we could reasonably expect, that would tend to support our hypothesis and we might find the missing remainder elsewhere. If, on the other hand, we find as much of the lenses as we could expect to find, we must conclude that they were broken on this spot."

While we were conducting our search, the two officials were circling around with their lanterns in quest of the missing hat; and, when we had at length picked up the last fragment, and a careful search, even aided by a lens, failed to reveal any other, we could see their lanterns moving, like will-o'-the-wisps, some distance down the line.

"We may as well see what we have got before our friends come back," said Thorndyke, glancing at the twinkling lights. "Lay the case down on the grass by the fence; it will serve for a table."

I did so, and Thorndyke, taking a letter from his pocket, opened it, spread it out flat on the case, securing it with a couple of heavy stones, although the night was quite calm. Then he tipped the contents of the seed envelope out on the paper, and, carefully spreading out the pieces of glass, looked at them for some moments in silence. And, as he looked, there stole over his face a very curious expression; with sudden eagerness he began picking out the larger fragments and laying them on two visiting-cards which he had taken from his card-case. Rapidly and with wonderful deftness he fitted the pieces together, and, as the reconstituted lenses began gradually to take shape on their cards, I looked on with growing excitement, for something in my colleague's manner told me that we were on the verge of a discovery.

At length the two ovals of glass lay on their respective cards, complete save for one or two small gaps; and the little heap that remained consisted of fragments so minute as to render further reconstruction impossible. Then Thorndyke leaned back and laughed softly.

"This is certainly an unlooked-for result," said he.

"What is?" I asked.

"Don't you see, my dear fellow? *There's too much glass.* We have almost completely built up the broken lenses, and the fragments that are left over are considerably more than are required to fill up the gaps."

I looked at the little heap of small fragments and saw at once that it was as he had said. There was a surplus of small pieces.

"This is very extraordinary," I said. "What do you think can be the explanation?"

"The fragments will probably tell us," he replied, "if we ask them intelligently."

He lifted the paper and the two cards carefully on to the ground, and, opening the case, took out the little microscope to which he fitted the lowest-power objective and eye-piece—having a combined magnification of only ten diameters. Then he transferred the minute fragments of glass to a slide, and, having arranged the lantern as a microscope-lamp, commenced his examination.

"Ha!" he exclaimed presently. "The plot thickens. There is too much glass and yet too little; that is to say, there are only one or two fragments here that belong to the spectacles; not nearly enough to complete the building up of the lenses. The remainder consists of a soft, uneven, moulded glass, easily distinguished from the clear, hard optical glass. These foreign fragments are all curved, as if they had formed part of a cylinder, and are, I should say, portions of a wine-glass or tumbler." He moved the slide once or twice, and then continued: "We are in luck, Jervis. Here is a fragment with two little diverging lines etched on it, evidently the points of an eight-rayed star—and here is another with three points—the ends of three rays. This enables us to reconstruct the vessel perfectly. It was a clear, thin glass—probably a tumbler— decorated with scattered stars; I dare say you know the pattern. Sometimes there is an ornamented band in addition, but generally the stars form the only decoration. Have a look at the specimen."

I had just applied my eye to the microscope when the station-master and the inspector came up. Our appearance, seated on the ground with the microscope between us, was too much for the police officer's gravity, and he laughed long and joyously.

"You must excuse me, gentlemen," he said apologetically, "but really, you know, to an old hand, like myself, it does look a little—well—you understand—I dare say a microscope is a very interesting and amusing thing, but it doesn't get you much forrader in a case like this, does it?"

"Perhaps not," replied Thorndyke. "By the way, where did you find the hat, after all?"

"We haven't found it," the inspector replied, a little sheepishly.

"Then we must help you to continue the search," said Thorndyke. "If you will wait a few moments, we will come with you." He poured a few drops of xylol balsam on the cards to fix the reconstituted lenses to their supports and then, packing them and the microscope in the case, announced that he was ready to start.

"Is there any village or hamlet near?" he asked the station-master.

"None nearer than Corfield. That is about half-a-mile from here."

"And where is the nearest road?"

"There is a half-made road that runs past a house about three hundred yards from here. It belonged to a building estate that was never built.

There is a footpath from it to the station."

"Are there any other houses near?"

"No. That is the only house for half-a-mile round, and there is no other road near here."

"Then the probability is that Brodski approached the railway from that direction, as he was found on that side of the permanent way."

The inspector agreeing with this view, we all set off slowly towards the house, piloted by the station-master and searching the ground as we went. The waste land over which we passed was covered with patches of docks and nettles, through each of which the inspector kicked his way, searching with feet and lantern for the missing hat. A walk of three hundred yards brought us to a low wall enclosing a garden, beyond which we could see a small house; and here we halted while the inspector waded into a large bed of nettles beside the wall and kicked vigorously. Suddenly there came a clinking sound mingled with objurgations, and the inspector hopped out holding one foot and soliloquizing profanely.

"I wonder what sort of a fool put a thing like that into a bed of nettles!" he exclaimed, stroking the injured foot. Thorndyke picked the object up and held it in the light of the lantern, displaying a piece of three-quarter inch rolled iron bar about a foot long. "It doesn't seem to have been there very long," he observed, examining it closely; "there is hardly any rust on it."

"It has been there long enough for me," growled the inspector, "and I'd like to bang it on the head of the blighter that put it there."

Callously indifferent to the inspector's sufferings, Thorndyke continued calmly to examine the bar. At length, resting his lantern on the wall, he produced his pocket-lens, with which he resumed his investigation, a proceeding that so exasperated the inspector that that afflicted official limped off in dudgeon, followed by the station-master, and we heard him, presently, rapping at the front door of the house.

"Give me a slide, Jervis, with a drop of Farrant on it," said Thorndyke. "There are some fibres sticking to this bar."

I prepared the slide, and, having handed it to him together with a cover-glass, a pair of forceps and a needle, set up the microscope on the wall.

"I'm sorry for the inspector," Thorndyke remarked, with his eye applied to the little instrument, "but that was a lucky kick for us. Just take a look at the specimen."

I did so, and, having moved the slide about until I had seen the whole of the object, I gave my opinion. "Red wool fibres, blue cotton fibres and some yellow, vegetable fibres that look like jute."

"Yes," said Thorndyke; "the same combination of fibres as that which we found on the dead man's teeth and probably from the same source. This bar has probably been wiped on that very curtain or rug with which poor Brodski was stifled. We will place it on the wall for future reference, and meanwhile, by hook or by crook, we must get into that house. This is much too plain a hint to be disregarded."

Hastily repacking the case, we hurried to the front of the house, where we found the two officials looking rather vaguely up the unmade road.

"There's a light in the house," said the inspector, "but there's no one at home. I have knocked a dozen times and got no answer. And I don't see what we are hanging about here for at all. The hat is probably close to where the body was found, and we shall find it in the morning."

Thorndyke made no reply, but, entering the garden, stepped up the path, and having knocked gently at the door, stooped and listened attentively at the key-hole.

"I tell you there's no one in the house, sir," said the inspector irritably; and, as Thorndyke continued to listen, he walked away, muttering angrily. As soon as he was gone, Thorndyke flashed his lantern over the door, the threshold, the path and the small flower-beds; and, from one of the latter, I presently saw him stoop and pick something up.

"Here is a highly instructive object, Jervis," he said, coming out to the gate, and displaying a cigarette of which only half-an-inch had been smoked.

"How instructive?" I asked. "What do you learn from it?"

"Many things," he replied. "It has been lit and thrown away unsmoked; that indicates a sudden change of purpose. It was thrown away at the entrance to the house, almost certainly by some one entering it. That person was probably a stranger, or he would have taken it in with him. But he had not expected to enter the house, or he would not have lit it. These are the general suggestions; now as to the particular ones. The paper of the cigarette is of the kind known as the 'Zig-Zag' brand; the very conspicuous water-mark is quite easy to see. Now Brodski's cigarette book was a 'Zig-Zag' book—so called from the way in which the papers pull out. But let us see what the tobacco is like." With a pin from his coat, he hooked out from the unburned end a wisp of dark, dirty brown tobacco, which he held out for my inspection.

"Fine-cut Latakia," I pronounced, without hesitation.

"Very well," said Thorndyke. "Here is a cigarette made of an unusual tobacco similar to that in Brodski's pouch and wrapped in an unusual paper similar to those in Brodski's cigarette-book. With due regard to the fourth rule of the syllogism, I suggest that this cigarette was made by Oscar Brodski. But, nevertheless, we will look for corroborative detail."

"What is that?" I asked.

"You may have noticed that Brodski's match-box contained round wooden vestas—which are also rather unusual. As he must have lighted the cigarette within a few steps of the gate, we ought to be able to find the match with which he lighted it. Let us try up the road in the direction from which he would probably have approached."

We walked very slowly up the road, searching the ground with the lantern, and we had hardly gone a dozen paces when I espied a match lying on the rough path and eagerly picked it up. It was a round wooden vesta.

Thorndyke examined it with interest and having deposited it, with the cigarette, in his "collecting-box," turned to retrace his steps. "There is now, Jervis, no reasonable doubt that Brodski was murdered in that house. We have succeeded in connecting that house with the crime, and now we have got to force an entrance and join up the other clues." We walked quickly back to the rear of the premises, where we found the inspector conversing disconsolately with the station-master.

"I think, sir," said the former, "we had better go back now; in fact, I don't see what we came here for, but—here! I say, sir, you mustn't do that!" For Thorndyke, without a word of warning, had sprung up lightly and thrown one of his long legs over the wall.

"I can't allow you to enter private premises, sir," continued the inspector; but Thorndyke quietly dropped down on the inside and turned to face the officer over the wall.

"Now, listen to me, inspector," said he. "I have good reasons for believing that the dead man, Brodski, has been in this house, in fact, I am prepared to swear an information to that effect. But time is precious; we must follow the scent while it is hot. And I am not proposing to break into the house off-hand. I merely wish to examine the dust-bin."

"The dust-bin!" gasped the inspector. "Well, you really are a most extraordinary gentleman! What do you expect to find in the dust-bin?"

"I am looking for a broken tumbler or wine-glass. It is a thin glass vessel decorated with a pattern of small, eight-pointed stars. It may be in the dust-bin or it may be inside the house."

The inspector hesitated, but Thorndyke's confident manner had evidently impressed him.

"We can soon see what is in the dust-bin," he said, "though what in creation a broken tumbler has to do with the case is more than I can understand. However, here goes." He sprang up on to the wall, and, as he dropped down into the garden, the station-master and I followed.

Thorndyke lingered a few moments by the gate examining the ground, while the two officials hurried up the path. Finding nothing of interest, however, he walked towards the house, looking keenly about him as he went; but we were hardly half-way up the path when we heard the voice of the inspector calling excitedly.

"Here you are, sir, this way," he sang out, and, as we hurried forward, we suddenly came on the two officials standing over a small rubbish-heap and looking the picture of astonishment. The glare of their lanterns illuminated the heap, and showed us the scattered fragments of a thin glass, star-pattern tumbler.

"I can't imagine how you guessed it was here, sir," said the inspector, with a new-born respect in his tone, "nor what you're going to do with it now you have found it."

"It is merely another link in the chain of evidence," said Thorndyke, taking a pair of forceps from the case and stooping over the heap. "Perhaps we shall find something else." He picked up several small fragments of glass, looked at them closely and dropped them again. Suddenly his eye caught a small splinter at the base of the heap. Seizing it with the forceps, he held it close to his eye in the strong lamplight, and, taking out his lens, examined it with minute attention. "Yes," he said at length, "this is what I was looking for. Let me have those two cards, Jervis."

I produced the two visiting-cards with the reconstructed lenses stuck to them, and, laying them on the lid of the case, threw the light of the lantern on them. Thorndyke looked at them intently for some time, and from them to the fragment that he held. Then, turning to the inspector, he said: "You saw me pick up this splinter of glass?"

"Yes, sir," replied the officer.

"And you saw where we found these spectacle-glasses and know whose they were?"

"Yes, sir. They are the dead man's spectacles, and you found them where the body had been."

"Very well," said Thorndyke; "now observe"; and, as the two officials craned forward with parted lips, he laid the little splinter in a gap in one of the lenses and then gave it a gentle push forward, when it occupied the gap perfectly, joining edge to edge with the adjacent fragments and rendering that portion of the lens complete.

"My God!" exclaimed the inspector. "How on earth did you know?"

"I must explain that later," said Thorndyke. "Meanwhile we had better have a look inside the house. I expect to find there a cigarette—or possibly a cigar—which has been trodden on, some whole-meal biscuits, possibly a wooden vesta, and perhaps even the missing hat."

At the mention of the hat, the inspector stepped eagerly to the back door, but, finding it bolted, he tried the window. This also was securely fastened and, on Thorndyke's advice, we went round to the front door.

"This door is locked too," said the inspector. "I'm afraid we shall have to break in. It's a nuisance, though."

"Have a look at the window," suggested Thorndyke.

The officer did so, struggling vainly to undo the patent catch with his pocket-knife.

"It's no go," he said, coming back to the door. "We shall have to——" He broke off with an astonished stare, for the door stood open and Thorndyke was putting something in his pocket.

"Your friend doesn't waste much time—even in picking a lock," he remarked to me, as we followed Thorndyke into the house; but his reflections were soon merged in a new surprise. Thorndyke had preceded us into a small sitting-room dimly lighted by a hanging lamp turned down low.

As we entered he turned up the light and glanced about the room. A whisky-bottle was on the table, with a siphon, a tumbler and a biscuit-box. Pointing to the latter, Thorndyke said to the inspector: "See what is in that box."

The inspector raised the lid and peeped in, the station-master peered over his shoulder, and then both stared at Thorndyke.

"How in the name of goodness did you know that there were whole-meal biscuits in the house, sir? "exclaimed the station-master.

"You'd be disappointed if I told you," replied Thorndyke. "But look at this." He pointed to the hearth, where lay a flattened, half-smoked cigarette and a round wooden vesta. The inspector gazed at these objects in silent wonder, while, as to the station-master, he continued to stare at Thorndyke with what I can only describe as superstitious awe.

"You have the dead man's property with you, I believe?" said my colleague.

"Yes," replied the inspector; "I put the things in my pocket for safety."

"Then," said Thorndyke, picking up the flattened cigarette, "let us have a look at his tobacco pouch."

As the officer produced and opened the pouch, Thorndyke neatly cut open the cigarette with his sharp pocket-knife. "Now," said he, "what kind of tobacco is in the pouch?"

The inspector took out a pinch, looked at it and smelt it distastefully. "It's one of those stinking tobaccos," he said, "that they put in mixtures—Latakia, I think."

"And what is this?" asked Thorndyke, pointing to the open cigarette.

"Same stuff, undoubtedly," replied the inspector.

"And now let us see his cigarette papers," said Thorndyke.

The little book, or rather packet—for it consisted of separated papers—was produced from the officer's pocket and a sample paper abstracted. Thorndyke laid the half-burnt paper beside it, and the inspector having examined the two, held them up to the light.

"There isn't much chance of mistaking that 'Zig-Zag' watermark," he said. "This cigarette was made by the deceased; there can't be the shadow of a doubt."

"One more point," said Thorndyke, laying the burnt wooden vesta on the table. "You have his match-box?"

The inspector brought forth the little silver casket, opened it and compared the wooden vestas that it contained with the burnt end. Then he shut the box with a snap.

"You've proved it up to the hilt," said he. "If we could only find the hat, we should have a complete case."

"I'm not sure that we haven't found the hat," said Thorndyke. "You notice that something besides coal has been burned in the grate."

The inspector ran eagerly to the fire-place and began, with feverish hands, to pick out the remains of the extinct fire. "The cinders are still warm," he said, "and they are certainly not all coal cinders. There has been wood burned here on top of the coal, and these little black lumps are neither coal nor wood. They may quite possibly be the remains of a burnt hat, but, lord! who can tell? You can put together the pieces of broken spectacle-glasses, but you can't build up a hat out of a few cinders." He held out a handful of little, black, spongy cinders and looked ruefully at Thorndyke, who took them from him and laid them out on a sheet of paper.

"We can't reconstitute the hat, certainly," my friend agreed, "but we may be able to ascertain the origin of these remains. They may not be cinders of a hat, after all." He lit a wax match and, taking up one of the charred fragments, applied the flame to it. The cindery mass fused at once with a crackling, seething sound, emitting a dense smoke, and instantly the air became charged with a pungent, resinous odour mingled with the smell of burning animal matter.

"Smells like varnish," the station-master remarked.

"Yes. Shellac," said Thorndyke; "so the first test gives a positive result. The next test will take more time."

He opened the green case and took from it a little flask, fitted for Marsh's arsenic test, with a safety funnel and escape tube, a small folding tripod, a spirit lamp and a disc of asbestos to serve as a sand-bath. Dropping into the flask several of the cindery masses, selected after careful inspection, he filled it up with alcohol and placed it on the disc, which he rested on the tripod. Then he lighted the spirit lamp underneath and sat down to wait for the alcohol to boil.

"There is one little point that we may as well settle," he said presently, as the bubbles began to rise in the flask. "Give me a slide with a drop of Farrant on it, Jervis."

I prepared the slide while Thorndyke, with a pair of forceps, picked out a tiny wisp from the table-cloth. "I fancy we have seen this fabric before," he remarked, as he laid the little pinch of fluff in the mounting fluid and slipped the slide on to the stage of the microscope. "Yes," he continued, looking into the eye-piece, "here are our old acquaintances, the red wool fibres, the blue cotton and the yellow jute. We must label this at once, or we may confuse it with the other specimens."

"Have you any idea how the deceased met his death?" the inspector asked.

"Yes," replied Thorndyke. "I take it that the murderer enticed him into this room and gave him some refreshments. The murderer sat in the chair in which you are sitting, Brodski sat in that small arm-chair. Then I imagine the murderer attacked him with that iron bar that you found among the nettles, failed to kill him at the first stroke, struggled with him and finally suffocated him with the table-cloth. By the way, there is just one more point. You recognize this piece of string?" He took from his "collecting-box" the little end of twine that had been picked up by the line. The inspector nodded. "If you look behind you, you will see where it came from."

The officer turned sharply and his eye lighted on a string-box on the mantelpiece. He lifted it down, and Thorndyke drew out from it a length of white twine with one green strand, which he compared with the piece in his hand. "The green strand in it makes the identification fairly certain," he said. "Of course the string was used to secure the umbrella and hand-bag. He could not have carried them in his hand, encumbered as he was with the corpse. But I expect our other specimen is ready now." He lifted the flask off the tripod, and, giving it a vigorous shake, examined the contents through his lens. The alcohol had now become dark-brown in colour, and was noticeably thicker and more syrupy in consistence.

"I think we have enough here for a rough test," said he, selecting a pipette and a slide from the case. He dipped the former into the flask and, having sucked up a few drops of the alcohol from the bottom, held the pipette over the slide on which he allowed the contained fluid to drop.

Laying a cover-glass on the little pool of alcohol, he put the slide on the microscope stage and examined it attentively, while we watched him in expectant silence.

At length he looked up, and, addressing the inspector, asked: "Do you know what felt hats are made of?"

"I can't say that I do, sir," replied the officer.

"Well, the better quality hats are made of rabbits' and hares' wool—the soft under-fur, you know—cemented together with shellac. Now there is very little doubt that these cinders contain shellac, and, with the microscope I find a number of small hairs of a rabbit. I have, therefore, little hesitation in saying that these cinders are the remains of a hard felt hat; and, as the hairs do not appear to be dyed, I should say it was a grey hat."

At this moment our conclave was interrupted by hurried footsteps on the garden path and, as we turned with one accord, an elderly woman burst into the room.

She stood for a moment in mute astonishment, and then, looking from one to the other, demanded: "Who are you? and what are you doing here?"

The inspector rose. "I am a police officer, madam," said he. "I can't give you any further information just now, but, if you will excuse me asking, who are you?"

"I am Mr. Hickler's housekeeper," she replied.

"And Mr. Hickler; are you expecting him home shortly?"

"No, I am not," was the curt reply. "Mr. Hickler is away from home just now. He left this evening by the boat train."

"For Amsterdam?" asked Thorndyke.

"I believe so, though I don't see what business it is of yours," the housekeeper answered.

"I thought he might, perhaps, be a diamond broker or merchant," said Thorndyke. "A good many of them travel by that train."

"So he is," said the woman, "at least, he has something to do with diamonds."

"Ah. Well, we must be going, Jervis," said Thorndyke, "we have finished here, and we have to find an hotel or inn. Can I have a word with you, inspector?"

The officer, now entirely humble and reverent, followed us out into the garden to receive Thorndyke's parting advice.

"You had better take possession of the house at once, and get rid of the housekeeper. Nothing must be removed. Preserve those cinders and see that the rubbish-heap is not disturbed, and, above all, don't have the room swept. The station-master or I will let them know at the police station, so that they can send an officer to relieve you."

With a friendly "good-night" we went on our way, guided by the station-master; and here our connection with the case came to an end. Hickler (whose Christian name turned out to be Silas) was, it is true, arrested as he stepped ashore from the steamer, and a packet of diamonds, subsequently identified as the property of Oscar Brodski, found upon his person. But he was never brought to trial, for on the return voyage he contrived to elude his guards for an instant as the ship was approaching the English coast, and it was not until three days later, when a handcuffed body was cast up on the lonely shore by Orfordness, that the authorities knew the fate of Silas Hickler.

"An appropriate and dramatic end to a singular and yet typical case," said Thorndyke, as he put down the newspaper. "I hope it has enlarged your knowledge, Jervis, and enabled you to form one or two useful corollaries."

"I prefer to hear you sing the medico-legal doxology," I answered, turning upon him like the proverbial worm and grinning derisively (which the worm does not).

"I know you do," he retorted, with mock gravity, "and I lament your lack of mental initiative. However, the points that this case illustrates are these: First, the danger of delay; the vital importance of instant action before that frail and fleeting thing that we call a clue has time to evaporate. A delay of a few hours would have left us with hardly a single datum. Second, the necessity of pursuing the most trivial clue to an absolute finish, as illustrated by the spectacles. Third, the urgent need of a trained scientist to aid the police; and, last," he concluded, with a smile, "we learn never to go abroad without the invaluable green case."

THE COIN OF DIONYSIUS

Ernest Bramah

I T WAS EIGHT O'CLOCK AT NIGHT AND RAINING, SCARCELY A TIME WHEN A BUSINESS so limited in its clientele as that of a coin dealer could hope to attract any customer, but a light was still showing in the small shop that bore over its window the name of Baxter, and in the even smaller office at the back the proprietor himself sat reading the latest *Pall Mall*. His enterprise seemed to be justified, for presently the door bell gave its announcement, and throwing down his paper Mr. Baxter went forward.

As a matter of fact the dealer had been expecting someone and his manner as he passed into the shop was unmistakably suggestive of a caller of importance. But at the first glance towards his visitor the excess of deference melted out of his bearing, leaving the urbane, self-possessed shopman in the presence of the casual customer.

"Mr. Baxter, I think?" said the latter. He had laid aside his dripping umbrella and was unbuttoning overcoat and coat to reach an inner pocket. "You hardly remember me, I suppose? Mr. Carlyle—two years ago I took up a case for you—"

"To be sure. Mr. Carlyle, the private detective—"

"Inquiry agent," corrected Mr. Carlyle precisely.

"Well," smiled Mr. Baxter, "for that matter I am a coin dealer and not an antiquarian or a numismatist. Is there anything in that way that I can do for you?"

"Yes," replied his visitor; "it is my turn to consult you." He had taken a small wash-leather bag from the inner pocket and now turned something carefully out upon the counter. "What can you tell me about that?"

The dealer gave the coin a moment's scrutiny.

"There is no question about this," he replied. "It is a Sicilian tetradrachm of Dionysius."

"Yes, I know that—I have it on the label out of the cabinet. I can tell you further that it's supposed to be one that Lord Seastoke gave two hundred and fifty pounds for at the Brice sale in '94."

"It seems to me that you can tell me more about it than I can tell you," remarked Mr. Baxter. "What is it that you really want to know?"

"I want to know," replied Mr. Carlyle, "whether it is genuine or not."

"Has any doubt been cast upon it?"

"Certain circumstances raised a suspicion—that is all."

The dealer took another look at the tetradrachm through his magnifying glass, holding it by the edge with the careful touch of an expert. Then he shook his head slowly in a confession of ignorance.

"Of course I could make a guess——"

"No, don't," interrupted Mr. Carlyle hastily. "An arrest hangs on it and nothing short of certainty is any good to me."

"Is that so, Mr. Carlyle?" said Mr. Baxter, with increased interest. "Well, to be quite candid, the thing is out of my line. Now if it was a rare Saxon penny or a doubtful noble I'd stake my reputation on my opinion, but I do very little in the classical series."

Mr. Carlyle did not attempt to conceal his disappointment as he returned the coin to the bag and replaced the bag in the inner pocket.

"I had been relying on you," he grumbled reproachfully. "Where on earth am I to go now?"

"There is always the British Museum."

"Ah, to be sure, thanks. But will anyone who can tell me be there now?"

"Now? No fear!" replied Mr. Baxter. "Go round in the morning——"

"But I must know to-night," explained the visitor, reduced to despair again. "To-morrow will be too late for the purpose."

Mr. Baxter did not hold out much encouragement in the circumstances.

"You can scarcely expect to find anyone at business now," he remarked. "I should have been gone these two hours myself only I happened to have an appointment with an American millionaire who fixed his own time." Something indistinguishable from a wink slid off Mr. Baxter's right eye. "Offmunson he's called, and a bright young pedigree-hunter has traced his descent from Offa, King of Mercia. So he—quite naturally—wants a set of Offas as a sort of collateral proof."

"Very interesting," murmured Mr. Carlyle, fidgeting with his watch. "I should love an hour's chat with you about your millionaire customers—some other time. Just now—look here, Baxter, can't you give me a line of introduction to some dealer in this sort of thing who happens to live in town? You must know dozens of experts."

"Why, bless my soul, Mr. Carlyle, I don't know a man of them away from his business," said Mr. Baxter, staring. "They may live in Park Lane or they may live in Petticoat Lane for all I know. Besides, there aren't so many experts as you seem to imagine. And the two best will very likely quarrel over it. You've had to do with 'expert witnesses,' I suppose?"

"I don't want a witness; there will be no need to give evidence. All I want is an absolutely authoritative pronouncement that I can act on. Is there no one who can really say whether the thing is genuine or not?"

Mr. Baxter's meaning silence became cynical in its implication as he continued to look at his visitor across the counter. Then he relaxed.

"Stay a bit; there is a man—an amateur—I remember hearing wonderful things about some time ago. They say he really does know."

"There you are," exclaimed Mr. Carlyle, much relieved. "There always is someone. Who is he?"

"Funny name," replied Baxter. "Something Wynn or Wynn something." He craned his neck to catch sight of an important motor car that was drawing to the kerb before his window. "Wynn Carrados! You'll excuse me now, Mr. Carlyle, won't you? This looks like Mr. Offmunson."

Mr. Carlyle hastily scribbled the name down on his cuff.

"Wynn Carrados, right. Where does he live?"

"Haven't the remotest idea," replied Baxter, referring the arrangement of his tie to the judgment of the wall mirror. "I have never seen the man myself. Now, Mr. Carlyle, I'm sorry I can't do any more for you. You won't mind, will you?"

Mr. Carlyle could not pretend to misunderstand. He enjoyed the distinction of holding open the door for the transatlantic representative of the line of Offa as he went out, and then made his way through the muddy streets back to his office. There was only one way of tracing a private individual at such short notice—through the pages of the directories, and the gentleman did not flatter himself by a very high estimate of his chances.

Fortune favoured him, however. He very soon discovered a Wynn Carrados living at Richmond, and, better still, further search failed to unearth another. There was, apparently, only one householder at all events of that name in the neighbourhood of London. He jotted down the address and set out for Richmond.

The house was some distance from the station, Mr. Carlyle learned. He took a taxicab and drove, dismissing the vehicle at the gate. He prided himself on his power of observation and the accuracy of the deductions which resulted from it—a detail of his business. "It's nothing more than using one's eyes and putting two and two together," he would modestly declare, when he wished to be deprecatory rather than impressive, and by the time he had reached the front door of "The Turrets" he had formed some opinion of the position and tastes of the man who lived there.

A man-servant admitted Mr. Carlyle and took in his card—his private card with the bare request for an interview that would not detain Mr. Carrados for ten minutes. Luck still favoured him; Mr. Carrados was at home and would see him at once. The servant, the hall through which they passed, and the room into which he was shown, all contributed something to the deductions which the quietly observant gentleman was half unconsciously recording.

"Mr. Carlyle," announced the servant.

The room was a library or study. The only occupant, a man of about Carlyle's own age, had been using a typewriter up to the moment of his visitor's entrance. He now turned and stood up with an expression of formal courtesy.

"It's very good of you to see me at this hour," apologized the caller.

The conventional expression of Mr. Carrados's face changed a little.

"Surely my man has got your name wrong?" he exclaimed. "Isn't it Louis Calling?"

The visitor stopped short and his agreeable smile gave place to a sudden flash of anger or annoyance.

"No, sir," he replied stiffly. "My name is on the card which you have before you."

"I beg your pardon," said Mr. Carrados, with perfect good-humour. "I hadn't seen it. But I used to know a Calling some years ago—at St. Michael's."

"St. Michael's!" Mr. Carlyle's features underwent another change, no less instant and sweeping than before. "St. Michael's! Wynn Carrados? Good heavens! it isn't Max Wynn—old 'Winning' Wynn?"

"A little older and a little fatter—yes," replied Carrados. "I *have* changed my name, you see."

"Extraordinary thing meeting like this," said his visitor, dropping into a chair and staring hard at Mr. Carrados. "I have changed more than my name. How did you recognize me?"

"The voice," replied Carrados. "It took me back to that little smoke-dried attic den of yours where we—"

"My God!" exclaimed Carlyle bitterly, "don't remind me of what we were going to do in those days." He looked round the well-furnished, handsome room and recalled the other signs of wealth that he had noticed. "At all events, you seem fairly comfortable, Wynn."

"I am alternately envied and pitied," replied Carrados, with a placid tolerance of circumstance that seemed characteristic of him. "Still, as you say, I am fairly comfortable."

"Envied, I can understand. But why are you pitied?"

"Because I am blind," was the tranquil reply.

"Blind!" exclaimed Mr. Carlyle, using his own eyes superlatively. "Do you mean—literally blind?"

"Literally. . . . I was riding along a bridle-path through a wood about a dozen years ago with a friend. He was in front. At one point a twig sprang back—you know how easily a thing like that happens. It just flicked my eye—nothing to think twice about."

"And that blinded you?"

"Yes, ultimately. It's called amaurosis."

"I can scarcely believe it. You seem so sure and self-reliant. Your eyes are full of expression—only a little quieter than they used to be. I believe you were typing when I came. . . . Aren't you having me?"

"You miss the dog and the stick?" smiled Carrados. "No; it's a fact."

"What an awful infliction for you, Max. You were always such an impulsive, reckless sort of fellow—never quiet. You must miss such a fearful lot."

"Has anyone else recognized you?" asked Carrados quietly.

"Ah, that was the voice, you said," replied Carlyle.

"Yes; but other people heard the voice as well. Only I had no blundering, self-confident eyes to be hoodwinked."

"That's a rum way of putting it," said Carlyle. "Are your ears never hoodwinked, may I ask?"

"Not now. Nor my fingers. Nor any of my other senses that have to look out for themselves."

"Well, well," murmured Mr. Carlyle, cut short in his sympathetic emotions. "I'm glad you take it so well. Of course, if you find it an advantage to be blind, old man—" He stopped and reddened. "I beg your pardon," he concluded stiffly.

"Not an advantage perhaps," replied the other thoughtfully. "Still it has compensations that one might not think of. A new world to explore, new experiences, new powers awakening; strange new perceptions; life in the fourth dimension. But why do you beg my pardon, Louis?"

"I am an ex-solicitor, struck off in connexion with the falsifying of a trust account, Mr. Carrados," replied Carlyle, rising.

"Sit down, Louis," said Carrados suavely. His face, even his incredibly living eyes, beamed placid good-nature. "The chair on which you will sit, the roof above you, all the comfortable surroundings to which you have so amiably alluded, are the direct result of falsifying a trust account. But do I call you 'Mr. Carlyle' in consequence? Certainly not, Louis."

"I did not falsify the account," cried Carlyle hotly. He sat down, however, and added more quietly: "But why do I tell you all this? I have never spoken of it before."

"Blindness invites confidence," replied Carrados. "We are out of the running—human rivalry ceases to exist. Besides, why shouldn't you? In my case the account *was* falsified."

"Of course that's all bunkum, Max," commented Carlyle. "Still, I appreciate your motive."

"Practically everything I possess was left to me by an American cousin, on the condition that I took the name of Carrados. He made his fortune by an ingenious conspiracy of doctoring the crop reports and unloading favourably in consequence. And I need hardly remind you that the receiver is equally guilty with the thief."

"But twice as safe. I know something of that, Max. . . . Have you any idea what my business is?"

"You shall tell me," replied Carrados.

"I run a private inquiry agency. When I lost my profession I had to do something for a living. This occurred. I dropped my name, changed my appearance and opened an office. I knew the legal side down to the ground and I got a retired Scotland Yard man to organize the outside work."

"Excellent!" cried Carrados. "Do you unearth many murders?"

"No," admitted Mr. Carlyle; "our business lies mostly on the conventional lines among divorce and defalcation."

"That's a pity," remarked Carrados. "Do you know, Louis, I always had a secret ambition to be a detective myself. I have even thought lately that I might still be able to do something at it if the chance came my way. That makes you smile?"

"Well, certainly, the idea—"

"Yes, the idea of a blind detective—the blind tracking the alert—"

"Of course, as you say, certain faculties are no doubt quickened," Mr. Carlyle hastened to add considerately, "but, seriously, with the exception of an artist, I don't suppose there is any man who is more utterly dependent on his eyes."

Whatever opinion Carrados might have held privately, his genial exterior did not betray a shadow of dissent. For a full minute he continued to smoke as though he derived an actual visual enjoyment from the blue sprays that travelled and dispersed across the room. He had already placed before his visitor a box containing cigars of a brand which that gentleman keenly appreciated but generally regarded as unattainable, and the matter-of-fact ease and certainty with which the blind man had brought the box and put it before him had sent a questioning flicker through Carlyle's mind.

"You used to be rather fond of art yourself, Louis," he remarked presently. "Give me your opinion of my latest purchase—the bronze lion on the cabinet there." Then, as Carlyle's gaze went about the room, he added quickly: "No, not that cabinet—the one on your left."

Carlyle shot a sharp glance at his host as he got up, but Carrados's expression was merely benignly complacent. Then he strolled across to the figure.

"Very nice," he admitted. "Late Flemish, isn't it?"

"No. It is a copy of Vidal's 'Roaring Lion.'"

"Vidal?"

"A French artist." The voice became indescribably flat. "He, also, had the misfortune to be blind, by the way."

"You old humbug, Max!" shrieked Carlyle, "you've been thinking that out for the last five minutes." Then the unfortunate man bit his lip and turned his back towards his host.

"Do you remember how we used to pile it up on that obtuse ass Sanders and then roast him?" asked Carrados, ignoring the half-smothered exclamation with which the other man had recalled himself.

"Yes," replied Carlyle quietly. "This is very good," he continued, addressing himself to the bronze again. "How ever did he do it?"

"With his hands."

"Naturally. But, I mean, how did he study his model?"

"Also with his hands. He called it 'seeing near.'"

"Even with a lion—handled it?"

"In such cases he required the services of a keeper, who brought the animal to bay while Vidal exercised his own particular gifts.... You don't feel inclined to put me on the track of a mystery, Louis?"

Unable to regard this request as anything but one of old Max's unquenchable pleasantries, Mr. Carlyle was on the point of making a suitable reply when a sudden thought caused him to smile knowingly. Up to that point he had, indeed, completely forgotten the object of his visit. Now that he remembered the doubtful Dionysius and Mr. Baxter's recommendation he immediately assumed that some mistake had been made. Either Max was not the Wynn Carrados he had been seeking or else the dealer had been misinformed; for although his host was wonderfully expert in the face of his misfortune, it was inconceivable that he could decide the genuineness of a coin without seeing it. The opportunity seemed a good one of getting even with Carrados by taking him at his word.

"Yes," he accordingly replied, with crisp deliberation, as he recrossed the room; "yes, I will, Max. Here is the clue to what seems to be a rather remarkable fraud." He put the tetradrachm into his host's hand. "What do you make of it?"

For a few seconds Carrados handled the piece with the delicate manipulation of his finger-tips while Carlyle looked on with a self-appreciative grin. Then with equal gravity the blind man weighed the coin in the balance of his hand. Finally he touched it with his tongue.

"Well?" demanded the other.

"Of course I have not much to go on, and if I was more fully in your confidence I might come to another conclusion——"

"Yes, yes," interposed Carlyle, with amused encouragement.

"Then I should advise you to arrest the parlourmaid, Nina Brun, communicate with the police authorities of Padua for particulars of the career of Helene Brunesi, and suggest to Lord Seastoke that he should return to London to see what further depredations have been made in his cabinet."

Mr. Carlyle's groping hand sought and found a chair, on to which he dropped blankly. His eyes were unable to detach themselves for a single moment from the very ordinary spectacle of Mr. Carrados's mildly benevolent face, while the sterilized ghost of his now forgotten amusement still lingered about his features.

"Good heavens!" he managed to articulate, "how do you know?"

"Isn't that what you wanted of me?" asked Carrados suavely.

"Don't humbug, Max," said Carlyle severely. "This is no joke." An undefined mistrust of his own powers suddenly possessed him in the presence of this mystery. "How do you come to know of Nina Brun and Lord Seastoke?"

"You are a detective, Louis," replied Carrados. "How does one know these things? By using one's eyes and putting two and two together."

Carlyle groaned and flung out an arm petulantly.

"Is it all bunkum, Max? Do you really see all the time—though that doesn't go very far towards explaining it."

"Like Vidal, I see very well—at close quarters," replied Carrados, lightly running a forefinger along the inscription on the tetradrachm. "For longer range I keep another pair of eyes. Would you like to test them?"

Mr. Carlyle's assent was not very gracious; it was, in fact, faintly sulky. He was suffering the annoyance of feeling distinctly unimpressive in his own department; but he was also curious.

"The bell is just behind you, if you don't mind," said his host. "Parkinson will appear. You might take note of him while he is in."

The man who had admitted Mr. Carlyle proved to be Parkinson.

"This gentleman is Mr. Carlyle, Parkinson," explained Carrados the moment the man entered. "You will remember him for the future?"

Parkinson's apologetic eye swept the visitor from head to foot, but so lightly and swiftly that it conveyed to that gentleman the comparison of being very deftly dusted.

"I will endeavour to do so, sir," replied Parkinson; turning again to his master.

"I shall be at home to Mr. Carlyle whenever he calls. That is all."

"Very well, sir."

"Now, Louis," remarked Mr. Carrados briskly, when the door had closed again, "you have had a good opportunity of studying Parkinson. What is he like?"

"In what way?"

"I mean as a matter of description. I am a blind man—I haven't seen my servant for twelve years—what idea can you give me of him? I asked you to notice."

"I know you did, but your Parkinson is the sort of man who has very little about him to describe. He is the embodiment of the ordinary. His height is about average—"

"Five feet nine," murmured Carrados. "Slightly above the mean."

"Scarcely noticeably so. Clean-shaven. Medium brown hair. No particularly marked features. Dark eyes. Good teeth."

"False," interposed Carrados. "The teeth—not the statement."

"Possibly," admitted Mr. Carlyle. "I am not a dental expert and I had no opportunity of examining Mr. Parkinson's mouth in detail. But what is the drift of all this?"

"His clothes?"

"Oh, just the ordinary evening dress of a valet. There is not much room for variety in that."

"You noticed, in fact, nothing special by which Parkinson could be identified?"

"Well, he wore an unusually broad gold ring on the little finger of the left hand."

"But that is removable. And yet Parkinson has an ineradicable mole—a small one, I admit—on his chin. And you a human sleuth-hound. Oh, Louis!"

"At all events," retorted Carlyle, writhing a little under this good-humoured satire, although it was easy enough to see in it Carrados's affectionate intention—"at all events, I dare say I can give as good a description of Parkinson as he can give of me."

"That is what we are going to test. Ring the bell again."

"Seriously?"

"Quite. I am trying my eyes against yours. If I can't give you fifty out of a hundred I'll renounce my private detectorial ambition for ever."

"It isn't quite the same," objected Carlyle, but he rang the bell.

"Come in and close the door, Parkinson," said Carrados when the man appeared. "Don't look at Mr. Carlyle again—in fact, you had better stand with your back towards him, he won't mind. Now describe to me his appearance as you observed it."

Parkinson tendered his respectful apologies to Mr. Carlyle for the liberty he was compelled to take, by the deferential quality of his voice.

"Mr. Carlyle, sir, wears patent leather boots of about size seven and very little used. There are five buttons, but on the left boot one button—the third up—is missing, leaving loose threads and not the more usual metal fastener. Mr. Carlyle's trousers, sir, are of a dark material, a dark grey line of about a quarter of an inch width on a darker ground. The bottoms are turned permanently up and are, just now, a little muddy, if I may say so."

"Very muddy," interposed Mr. Carlyle generously. "It is a wet night, Parkinson."

"Yes, sir; very unpleasant weather. If you will allow me, sir, I will brush you in the hall. The mud is dry now, I notice. Then, sir," continued Parkinson, reverting to the business in hand, "there are dark green cashmere hose. A curb-pattern key-chain passes into the left-hand trouser pocket."

From the visitor's nether garments the photographic-eyed Parkinson proceeded to higher ground, and with increasing wonder Mr. Carlyle listened to the faithful catalogue of his possessions. His fetter-and-link albert of gold and platinum was minutely described. His spotted blue ascot, with its gentlemanly pearl scarfpin, was set forth, and the fact that the buttonhole in the left lapel of his morning coat showed signs of use was duly noted. What Parkinson saw he recorded but he made no deductions. A handkerchief carried in the cuff of the right sleeve was simply that to him and not an indication that Mr. Carlyle was, indeed, left-handed.

But a more delicate part of Parkinson's undertaking remained. He approached it with a double cough.

"As regards Mr. Carlyle's personal appearance, sir—"

"No, enough!" cried the gentleman concerned hastily. "I am more than satisfied. You are a keen observer, Parkinson."

"I have trained myself to suit my master's requirements, sir," replied the man. He looked towards Mr. Carrados, received a nod and withdrew.

Mr. Carlyle was the first to speak.

"That man of yours would be worth five pounds a week to me, Max," he remarked thoughtfully. "But, of course—"

"I don't think that he would take it," replied Carrados, in a voice of equally detached speculation. "He suits me very well. But you have the chance of using his services—indirectly."

"You still mean that—seriously?"

"I notice in you a chronic disinclination to take me seriously, Louis. It is really—to an Englishman—almost painful. Is there something inherently comic about me or the atmosphere of The Turrets?"

"No, my friend," replied Mr. Carlyle, "but there is something essentially prosperous. That is what points to the improbable. Now what is it?"

"It might be merely a whim, but it is more than that," replied Carrados. "It is, well, partly vanity, partly *ennui*, partly"—certainly there was something more nearly tragic in his voice than comic now—"partly hope."

Mr. Carlyle was too tactful to pursue the subject.

"Those are three tolerable motives," he acquiesced. "I'll do anything you want, Max, on one condition."

"Agreed. And it is?"

"That you tell me how you knew so much of this affair." He tapped the silver coin which lay on the table near them. "I am not easily flabbergasted," he added.

"You won't believe that there is nothing to explain—that it was purely second-sight?"

"No," replied Carlyle tersely; "I won't."

"You are quite right. And yet the thing is very simple."

"They always are—when you know," soliloquized the other. "That's what makes them so confoundedly difficult when you don't."

"Here is this one then. In Padua, which seems to be regaining its old reputation as the birthplace of spurious antiques, by the way, there lives an ingenious craftsman named Pietro Stelli. This simple soul, who possesses a talent not inferior to that of Cavino at his best, has for many years turned his hand to the not unprofitable occupation of forging rare Greek and Roman coins. As a collector and student of certain Greek colonials and a specialist in forgeries I have been familiar with Stelli's workmanship for years. Latterly he seems to have come under the influence of an international crook called—at the moment—Dompierre, who soon saw a way of utilizing Stelli's genius on a royal scale. Helene Brunesi, who in private life is—and really is, I believe—Madame Dompierre, readily lent her services to the enterprise."

"Quite so," nodded Mr. Carlyle, as his host paused.

"You see the whole sequence, of course?"

"Not exactly—not in detail," confessed Mr. Carlyle.

"Dompierre's idea was to gain access to some of the most celebrated cabinets of Europe and substitute Stelli's fabrications for the genuine coins. The princely collection of rarities that he would thus amass might be difficult to dispose of safely but I have no doubt that he had matured his plans. Helene, in the person of Nina

Bran, an Anglicised French parlourmaid—a part which she fills to perfection—was to obtain wax impressions of the most valuable pieces and to make the exchange when the counterfeits reached her. In this way it was obviously hoped that the fraud would not come to light until long after the real coins had been sold, and I gather that she has already done her work successfully in several houses. Then, impressed by her excellent references and capable manner, my housekeeper engaged her, and for a few weeks she went about her duties here. It was fatal to this detail of the scheme, however, that I have the misfortune to be blind. I am told that Helene has so innocently angelic a face as to disarm suspicion, but I was incapable of being impressed and that good material was thrown away. But one morning my material fingers—which, of course, knew nothing of Helene's angelic face—discovered an unfamiliar touch about the surface of my favourite Euclideas, and, although there was doubtless nothing to be seen, my critical sense of smell reported that wax had been recently pressed against it. I began to make discreet inquiries and in the meantime my cabinets went to the local bank for safety. Helene countered by receiving a telegram from Angiers, calling her to the death-bed of her aged mother. The aged mother succumbed; duty compelled Helene to remain at the side of her stricken patriarchal father, and doubtless The Turrets was written off the syndicate's operations as a bad debt."

"Very interesting," admitted Mr. Carlyle; "but at the risk of seeming obtuse"—his manner had become delicately chastened—"I must say that I fail to trace the inevitable connexion between Nina Brun and this particular forgery—assuming that it is a forgery."

"Set your mind at rest about that, Louis," replied Carrados. "It is a forgery, and it is a forgery that none but Pietro Stelli could have achieved. That is the essential connexion. Of course, there are accessories. A private detective coming urgently to see me with a notable tetradrachm in his pocket, which he announces to be the clue to a remarkable fraud—well, really, Louis, one scarcely needs to be blind to see through that."

"And Lord Seastoke? I suppose you happened to discover that Nina Brun had gone there?"

"No, I cannot claim to have discovered that, or I should certainly have warned him at once when I found out—only recently—about the gang. As a matter of fact, the last information I had of Lord Seastoke was a line in yesterday's *Morning Post* to the effect that he was still at Cairo. But many of these pieces—" He brushed his finger almost lovingly across the vivid chariot race that embellished the reverse of the coin, and broke off to remark: "You really ought to take up the subject, Louis. You have no idea how useful it might prove to you some day."

"I really think I must," replied Carlyle grimly. "Two hundred and fifty pounds the original of this cost, I believe."

"Cheap, too; it would make five hundred pounds in New York to-day. As I was saying, many are literally unique. This gem by Kimon is—here is his signature, you see; Peter is particularly good at lettering—and as I handled the genuine tetradrachm about two years ago, when Lord Seastoke exhibited it at a meeting of our society in Albemarle Street, there is nothing at all wonderful in my being able to fix the locale of your mystery. Indeed, I feel that I ought to apologize for it all being so simple."

"I think," remarked Mr. Carlyle, critically examining the loose threads on his left boot, "that the apology on that head would be more appropriate from me."

A HUNT FOR A MURDERER

Dick Donovan

LONG YEARS AGO WHEN I WAS A YOUNG MAN, AND NEW TO THE PROFESSION, in which I have grown grey, I was stationed in London. I was full of zeal and energy, and particularly anxious to distinguish myself, but for some time I had to kick my heels in obscurity, as nothing occurred to give me the chance I panted for. Of course, I railed against fate, and thought that she had specially singled me out as a victim of her spite, and I began to think I would emigrate, try to discover the North Pole; find the Philosopher's Stone; fly through the air, or set to work upon some equally quixotic quest, when my old and respected chief, under whom I then served, called me into his room one morning and said—

"Here, youngster, I'm going to set you on a job that will test your mettle. A brutal murder was committed the night before last by a ferocious ruffian—a returned convict—who will stick at nothing. He has managed to get clear, and as he has baffled the police before, he is likely to do it again, for he is as cunning as a fox, as dangerous as a poison snake. We have reason to believe he is lurking somewhere in the East End. You will join the East End division of the staff, and use every individual effort to capture the brute."

As I heard these orders my heart beat violently, and I felt somehow as if my opportunity had come at last. Moreover, at the time, though I know now it was not so, I thought my chief spoke in rather a contemptuous tone to me, as though he was of opinion that I was a fool, and he would not have put me on this job if he had not been compelled, owing to there being an unusual pressure of business just then, which taxed the resources of our department very severely. This idea fired me, and I resolved to do or die.

With a respectful salute to the chief, and merely remarking quietly—

"I will do my best, sir."

I took my departure, feeling eager for the fray, and hoping and praying that the merit of capturing this human brute might fall to me.

It appeared that two evenings before, about eight o'clock, a policeman was called to quell a row in a public-house, not of the best repute, and situated in Ratcliff Highway, for ever rendered notorious by the diabolical crime of Williams, the murderer, who has been immortalised by the genius of De Quincey in that gem of English literature, "Murder Considered as one of the Fine Arts." The cause of the row was a well-known character named Peter Mogford, then a man of about fifty years of age, and quite thirty of those years he had served in prison. He was, in fact, one of those born criminals who, like the fierce and untameable hyænas, should either be caged or killed.

Mogford had commenced life as a soldier. Both his parents had passed a considerable portion of their lives in prison, and a brother had been transported for a terrible outrage on a woman. Peter's antecedents, therefore, were by no means calculated to create an impression in his favour, and he soon showed that he intended to beat the record. He proved to be the most troublesome man in the regiment. He drank, he stole from his comrades, he was mutinous; and though he was flogged, imprisoned, flogged and imprisoned again, he did not improve, and was at last drummed out of the army. Subsequently he became a sailor, but soon gave that up, and his career from that time was one of outrage of almost every conceivable kind, and he was no sooner out of prison than he was in again. His last term had been penal servitude for ten years, and at the time he committed the double murder which sent a shudder through the land he had only been released two months. On the night in question he had gone into a public-house in the "Highway," where a number of sailors and their sweethearts were carousing. Mogford had insulted one of the women, which had led to a fight between him and a sailor, during which he struck his opponent over the head with a quart pewter pot and had rendered him insensible. The row had then become general, and Mogford, who, although a little man, was possessed of a giant's strength, created great havoc, and the son of the landlord rushed out for a policeman. One happened to be close at hand, and with the aid of some of the sailors, Peter was secured, bound with a rope, and in a state bordering on frenzy with drink and baffled rage he was conveyed to the nearest "lock-up." It was a place never intended for desperate criminals, but was used principally for "drunk and incapables."

As Mogford complained that the rope hurt him, it was taken off, and he was then put into a cell and locked up for the night, and it was supposed that he had gone to sleep, as for three hours nothing was heard of him.

The station was then in charge of an old sergeant of police, whose duty it was to book any night cases, and a young constable was on duty with him. About midnight Mogford succeeded in noiselessly forcing the lock of his cell door, which was of the most flimsy kind. The old sergeant was nodding at his desk, and the constable was standing with his back to the fire, when Mogford suddenly appeared like an apparition. The constable sprang forward to try and stop his exit, but the ruffian seized a poker from the fire grate, and with one tremendous blow felled the constable like an ox. The old sergeant then tackled him, but Mogford beat him about the head with the poker until he too fell insensible. The criminal then rifled the desk of the small amount of money it contained, and made off. In a few minutes the sergeant had so far recovered consciousness as to be able to realise what had happened, and though he was terribly injured, part of his head being almost beaten to a jelly, lie managed to crawl to the street and raise an alarm.

When help came, a local doctor was immediately summoned, but he found the constable dead, and the sergeant in such a dangerous state that he had him removed immediately to the hospital. There he was able to make a full and detailed statement of the tragic affair, but he soon after lapsed into unconsciousness again, and never rallied, but expired at eight o'clock in the morning.

As Mogford was so well known it was considered that there would be no difficulty in effecting his arrest, but hour after hour went by and no tidings came of his capture. That night a house was broken into at Bow, and a considerable quantity of valuables carried off, including about ten pounds in cash, also a suit of clothes. A handkerchief that was found on the premises was recognised as one belonging to Mogford, and it was then felt that as he had succeeded in obtaining clothes and money, his capture might be difficult.

When the news spread the excitement was tremendous, and orders were given that every outlet from London was to be watched as far as possible and every haunt of criminals scoured. And so effectual did the cordon seem that it was deemed impossible he could long remain uncaptured. Nevertheless there was a prevailing opinion that the desperate ruffian would never be taken alive, and that any one attempting to take him would run the risk of losing his own life. Public excitement therefore was worked up to the fullest pitch, and from one end of the country to the other people were painfully anxious to hear of the capture of this savage human animal.

I have already indicated what my own feelings were when I heard that I was to be allowed to join in the hunt for the murderer. And though I was young and inexperienced at the time, I was bold enough, and as many would have said, egotistical enough, to think that the step sthen being taken to cut off the retreat of the fellow were not calculated to secure the object aimed at. When I got my orders the first thing I did was to make myself acquainted with the habits of the man, as well as learn every detail of his personal appearance. Although I kept my thoughts to myself, I came to the conclusion that he was possessed of the most extraordinary and ingenious cunning, and so daring that he might even succeed in altogether baffling his pursuers, even as a fox can sometimes baffle the best trained hounds.

Instead of joining in the full chase that was then going on, I ventured to think it might be as well first of all to try and find a track to follow up, and I quietly went to work to discover something about his relations. The most that I could learn was that he had an aunt living out at Ratcliff Highway; but as will presently be seen that "most" was to prove of great service. I was informed that one of the force had already visited this woman but could make nothing of her. That, however, did not deter me, and I was conceited enough to smile to myself as I thought the policeman must have bungled, for it wasn't likely that such a creature would give any information about her precious nephew, for she herself had been in prison and bore a very bad character. I therefore didn't visit her as one of the force, but in the character of a Jew crimp.[1] It was not an enviable character to assume, but the end justified the means, and the end was to try and bring to justice a cold-blooded murderer, and to prevent him if possible from shedding more blood.

The woman was known in the neighbourhood as "Mother Mogford," and she was then nearly eighty years of age, but looked much younger. She was a hideous specimen of womankind, in fact, about as repulsive a person as one could well picture. She occupied three small rooms and a kitchen in a very wretched house. As I entered she was sitting in a large chair smoking a short, dirty, cutty pipe.

"Well, what the devil do you want?" she growled. "You ain't one of those police blokes, are you?" she asked as she scrutinised me with her bleared eyes and grinned horribly.

"No, mother, I ain't," I answered. "I'm a pal of your nephew."

She broke into a screeching laugh as she exclaimed—

"I ain't going to be caught with that kind o' chaff, you know."

"What kind of chaff?"

"Look here, give it to us straight. What do you want?" she demanded, as she banged her bony fist on the table to emphasise her words.

"Why, mother, you don't know your friends," I answered with a laugh. "I want to do you a good turn. You know that the traps are after Pete."

"Yes," she growled. "A bloke came here and thought himself mighty clever, but he did not screw much out of this child."

She laughed cunningly, and I laughed in chorus, and drawing a little flat flask of gin from my pocket, I remarked, going to the door first of all and listening—

---

1. As is well known, *crimps* are the curse of sailors' lives, though, happily, modern legislation is gradually exterminating these human pests. For the benefit of the uninitiated it may not be out of place to explain that the crimps, which means here "to seize or grasp," are the wretches who lure and decoy sailors into dens of infamy. From the keepers of these dens the crimp receives a fee; and then when the unfortunate sailor has been robbed of his money and despoiled of everything that he possesses, the crimp is waiting for him, and undertakes to procure him a ship. This done, the seaman gets an advance note for a month's wages. The crimp takes the advance note, which may be for three or four pounds, according to the rate of wages being paid; he gives poor Jack a few articles of rubbish, which he calls a "rig-out," but often not worth half a dozen shillings; then he makes him drunk on the vilest of drink, and puts him on board his ship in a state of insensibility.—*The Author*.

"We'll have a drop o' the comfort together." I spoke in a mysterious sort of whisper, and taking up a handless cup that was on the table, I poured some gin into it and handed it to her. She poured the fiery stuff down her throat at one gulp, and wiping her thin lips with the back of her scraggy hand, she said—

"Ah, that's good for the stummick!"

I saw that I had gained a point, and being strongly impressed with the idea that she could give mo some valuable information—for I ought to have stated that Peter lived, when not in prison, in his aunt's house—I said, still in a mysterious and confidential whisper—

"I know what Pete's done, and that the cops are after him, but I want to put him right. You see he owes me three pounds, and I know there ain't much chance of my getting it unless I can ship him. Now, I've got to put some hands on board a New Yorker that's lying in the river, and leaves tomorrow for San Francisco. This is a chance for Pete to get away, and if you can tell me where I'm likely to find him I can ship him on the quiet, and will get his advance note, and pay myself the three pounds he owes me, and before anything can be known about it he'll be well out to sea."

As I told her this pardonable crammer I watched her narrowly, and I saw that her shrivelled face and beery eyes lighted up with an expression of delight and cunning, and my heart rejoiced as she asked, "Can you do this?" for the question assured me she knew of his whereabouts.

"Yes," I answered, "and I'll do it if I can find him, for I ain't a-going to lose my three quids if I can help it."

She struggled out of her chair with the aid of a stick, and hobbling to me seized my hand, and said—

"Are you straight?"[2]

"True as death," I answered.

"Well now, look here," she continued, "I've got some quids, and I'll give you ten of 'em if you'll get Peter clear."

"But where is he?" I asked, scarcely able to conceal the agitation I experienced as I began to dream of succeeding where the more practised men had failed.

She grinned hideously as she answered—

"He was here the day after he done the thing. He came 'cause he wanted some money. I saw something was up, and I asked him what it was, and he told me he had killed a bloke. But he said he'd never be tuk."

---

2. This is a common expression amongst the criminal classes, and means, Are you staunch? Are you to be depended upon?

"If I do what I have said there is no fear of his being taken," I answered.

"And you'll do it?" she asked with great eagerness.

"Yes, if I can make anything out of it."

"And you're straight?" she asked again.

"I've already told you," I returned, trying to keep down the excitement that was making my heart thump at my ribs.

She seemed to hesitate, and a fear came over me that after all she would refuse the information I was craving for. As it was, the old hag kept me on tenter hooks by saying with a hideous laugh, that almost seemed to have something fiendish about it—

"Aha! he's where all the cops in London won't find him." Then she once more seized my hand, and, putting her face so near to mine that her hot, gin-reeking breath caused me to turn away, she continued, "You put Pete on board a ship, so that he can get off, and I'll give you ten quid; but you needn't think you can bluff me.[3] You see Pete knows how to write. They learnt him in the prison, and before you get your ten quid you'll have to bring some writing from Pete to tell me that he is all right."

"Well, well," I exclaimed a little impatiently, and feeling disgusted with the cunning old wretch.

"Well, well," she echoed before I could say anything else, and startling me into a fear that she was after all going to withhold the information.

"But supposing I say it ain't well, well?" she continued; "I ain't agoing to take your word for it; and if you don't bring the writing, devil a halfpenny will you get from me."

"Look here, mother," I said, advancing to her and laying one of my hands on each of her shoulders in a familiar sort of way, "you've promised me ten pounds, and I am not such a fool as to miss the chance of getting a haul like that if it's possible to get it. Ten and the three sovereigns Pete owes me makes thirteen. That's a big lump. Now do you think I'm such an idiot as to miss that when it's in my way to pocket it? No, no, mother; I know how many beans make five, you bet. Now, tell me, where am I going to find Pete?"

She grinned diabolically, and then almost made me betray my exasperation by asking—

"Is there any more gin in the bottle?"

I drew out the flask from my pocket again, and emptied the contents of it into the cup, which I handed to her, and she drained it greedily. The fiery potion drew the tears from her red and raw-looking eyes, and for a moment she gasped for breath. She looked so horrible and repulsive that I fairly recoiled from her. Then, as I restored the flask to my pocket, I said—

---

3. "Bluff me"—to cheat.

"Well, I can't lose any more time; so if you don't tell me where I'm to find Pete, I'm off."

"Hold on, you fool," she cried. "I'm going to tell you. He's in the marshes."

My heart leapt into my mouth as I heard this, and I asked—

"What marshes?"

"Plumstead," she answered with a leer.

I did not wait to hear another word, but almost bounded out of the house, and with breathless speed went off to my chief, and requested him to place a dozen stalwart and tried men absolutely under my control. He looked at me incredulously, and smiled. There was irony in his smile, and it annoyed me, so I said warmly—

"If you do this, sir, I pledge myself to have the man, dead or alive."

This was a bold statement, because, after all, the old hag might have deceived me, or assuming that the murderer had gone to the marshes, he had perhaps left again. However, it was do or die with me, and I felt that I was either to distinguish myself, or for ever after remain unknown.

"Well, what do you want with the men?" the chief asked.

"I have got undoubtable information," I answered, "that the fellow is hiding in the marshes below Woolwich, and that means that he must be hunted down like a jungle tiger. A desperate man might baffle a regiment of soldiers in such a wilderness, but trust me, give me a chance; place me in charge of twelve good men, and I'll have him or perish myself."

The chief looked at me approvingly now, and said slowly—

"I admire your zeal and enthusiasm, and I'll give you the chance you ask for. The brute must be taken, dead or alive, but remember we prefer to have him alive. The dozen men are at your disposal. Lose no time, and report progress to me as soon as possible."

I could scarcely find words to thank him. My heart throbbed violently with suppressed excitement, and I felt that this hunt in the wilderness for a desperate human wretch, whose hands were reeking with the blood of his fellows, would put into the shade all the tiger hunts of which I had ever read.

The marshes below Woolwich, at the time I speak of, were as dreary a wilderness as any to be found in the British Islands. The wild wastes of sand stretched for seeming interminable miles, and were broken up into a bewildering maze by thousands of tidal streams, some mere tiny rivulets, others broad and deep. Great patches of swamp and dangerous quicksands added to the risks which any one venturing into this region of desolation had to face. The bittern boomed in the sedges, and the marsh herons, solitary and gaunt, looked spectral as they stood silently on the banks of the streams. Overhead the seamews, curlews, and gulls screeched in chorus with the wind, which piped weirdly as it blew coldly over the great expanse of grey sand dunes, which were unrelieved by a single tree or even a shrub. The only things that seemed to grow were sedges and a stunted wiry grass.

In this region of desolation a fugitive well provided with food, and at all acquainted with the intricacies of the streams and the lie of the swamps and quicksands, might long have defied capture; in fact, might even have escaped altogether if he could have reached the river or got on board of a ship or a barge. Or a bold swimmer could have dared the river, landing on the other side. Under any circumstances the hunt in such a place for a desperate criminal who knew that his life was forfeited to the law could not fail to be exciting, and attended with no inconsiderable risk to the pursuers.

Of course I had no means of knowing how Mogford was situated for provisions, or whether he had provided himself with firearms. But I divined that his intention was to get on board of a passing ship, or a barge that would take him down to Greenhithe, where, as he was well furnished with money, he might succeed in obtaining a passage in an outward-bound vessel. In planting my men, therefore, I did not lose sight of the necessity there was for cutting oft the fugitive's escape by the river.

In making my plans I could not shut my eyes to the possibility, and even probability, there was that Mother Mogford had after all deceived me, or it might even be that she herself had been put off the scent by her precious nephew; and if it so chanced that I was wrong, and while I was pursuing a phantom the desperado should be captured elsewhere, I was perfectly well aware that disgrace, if not absolute ruin, would fall upon me. But when I weighed all the *pros* and *cons* of the case it seemed to me that it was in the highest degree likely that the criminal had fled to the marshy wilderness, being well aware that no other place in that part of the kingdom could offer him so much security. This reflection consoled me, and I made a mental vow that if he had sought refuge there he should only leave the place as a prisoner or a corpse. Probably it would be the latter, for a savage and bloodthirsty tiger at bay is not usually taken alive.

The men who had been placed under my charge were discontented and lacking in zeal. This arose from jealousy and a contempt for me that they were at no pains to conceal. They thought I was an upstart, and that I had been guilty of arrogance in venturing to take any independent course in this hunt for the murderer.

"If you suppose, Donovan," said one fellow, "that you are going to find Mogford in this desert you must be a very simple young man. He ain't such a fool as to run into a trap like this."

There was a chorus of laughter, of course, at these words, but when it died away I remarked, without displaying a trace of irritation—

"I *am* a simple young man, but simple people have occasionally been known to do great deeds."

More laughter followed, and another man said—

"It seems to me this expedition is very like trying to put salt on a bird's tail. Mogford, you may depend upon it, will be safely caged before we even reach the marshes."

"Possibly," I answered, and then, after a pause, added, "and possibly not. Anyway, you have been placed under my orders, and all you have got to do is to obey my orders and do your duty. For any failure it is I who am responsible, not you."

To the general dead-set that was made against me there was an exception in the person of a shrewd, keen-witted, and determined little Irishman named Michael Owen.

"Howld yer wish, boys," he exclaimed, "for maybe the laugh will go agin ye before ye've taken the shine aff of yer brogues, and a foine figure ye'd cut, all of yess, if Donovan happens to pot the fellow we're arter, won't yer?"

"Yes, fine figures," retorted one in a tone that was meant to be sarcastic.

"Begorra, yes," cried Owen, "and you'll be the foinest of them all, and will get promotion backwards."

This caused a laugh at the expense of the man who had made the remark, and after that they did not venture upon any further criticism.

It was but natural that I should feel some partiality for the good-natured Irishman who had thus championed me, and in disposing of my little force I kept him near me. I instructed the others to form a cordon so far as practicable, but four of them were gradually to work towards the river, keeping within touch of each other, and exercising the utmost vigilance.

It will readily be understood that from the very nature of the ground it was impossible to follow any fixed route. As I have already said, the place was a maze, owing to the innumerable streams that bisected and intersected, and crossed and recrossed, running from and into each other, and twisting about at every conceivable angle. The high dunes and the long ridges prevented any extensive survey of the ground before me, while the many hollows afforded capital hiding for a fugitive.

Having given my instructions, we separated, and had soon lost sight of each other. Each man was provided with a shrill whistle, and two short sharp blasts were to be given by any man who might sight the fugitive. These blasts were to be taken up by the other members of the force, and so passed on.

Owen and I kept together as near as possible, but for many weary hours we tramped through the swamps and over the sand-hills, and waded through the shallow streams, but we saw nothing to relieve the melancholy monotony of sand and water.

Night began to fall, and with the fading of daylight my hopes went down to zero, and I could not help thinking then that the expedition would be a failure. I had previously arranged with my comrades that if night overtook us we were to pass the hours of darkness as best we could. This, of course, had caused a great deal of grumbling, but I was inflexible, being unwilling to give up the search until we had traversed the marshes in such a manner as to render it certain that no man was concealed within them.

Michael Owen and I scooped out a large hollow in a hillock and ensconced ourselves there, to try and get a few hours' sleep and await the coming dawn.

I managed to dose in fitful snatches only, for my mind was too disturbed, but Owen slept like the proverbial top, and snored like the traditional trooper.

As the steely light of the coming day began to spread itself over the wilderness, the effect was almost startlingly weird. Everything looked so cold, ghastly, and lifeless, while the silence, like the silence of a dead world, made itself felt. But as the light increased the sea-birds rose from their watery resting-places and began to wheel and scream overhead, and their shrill, harsh cries were a positive relief, for they, at least, broke tbe horrible stillness, which was not the stillness of repose, but of death and desolation.

I arose from my hole in the sand and shook myself, and then let my eyes wander all round the great expanse, and suddenly I started, for I saw, some distance away, a man on a sand-ridge. He might have been half a mile off, but his figure was clearly cut against the eastern sky. It was impossible to distinguish any of the details of his appearance, excepting that he was not one of our comrades. I had brought a pair of small but powerful binoculars with me, and whipping them out of my pocket I adjusted them to my eyes, and then with a cry I exclaimed—

"Owen, by Heaven, there's our man!"

The Irishman started to his feet, snatched the glasses from my hand, looked in the direction I had pointed, and then exclaimed—

"Be jabers, you are right!"

The binoculars revealed his features, showed that he was bareheaded, that his hair was unkempt, and that he was dressed in a nondescript way.

Without waiting to partake of a frugal meal of biscuit and cheese, with which we were provided, we started off at a quick pace. I was full of excitement, and the blood tingled in my veins. Our course was necessarily a devious one, owing to the streams, but as far as we could we kept our eyes on the spot where we had seen the man. We had lost sight of him for a time, but suddenly he appeared again, scanning the horizon, and shading his eyes with his hands. Then it became evident that he had seen us, for like a startled animal he bounded away.

There was now no longer room to doubt that we had traced the fugitive, and were on his heels. We blew our whistles, and the sounds were taken up and passed on, and echoed and re-echoed, and they must liave fallen upon the ears of the hunted man like a knell of doom.

We made out the figures of others of our comrades now, far off and scattered about, and we knew that the chase had been taken up. Then we saw the criminal double back, and for a while lost sight of him. Owen and I rushed along as well as the nature of the ground would permit, plunging through the streams, and sometimes sinking above the knees in marsh, ooze, and quicksand. For some time we had lost sight of our quarry, when suddenly we were startled by his springing up within two dozen yards of us. He had got on to a ridge to take a rapid survey, and seeing us he started off, and we went in full chase after him.

My companion and I were in a state of great excitement. In my own case every nerve and fibre in my body seemed stretched to its uttermost extent. Again we lost sight of the fugitive, as he was hidden in a hollow, but as we mounted we descried him again, and saw that we had gained upon him. A broad creek interposed itself in his course, but without hesitation lie plunged in and swam across, and as lie climbed out on the opposite bank he stood still for some minutes. We saw that when he came out of the water he had something between his teeth. It proved to be a double-barrelled pistol, and, taking deliberate aim, he fired twice. The first shot went away into space; at the second I saw my comrade fall and sprang to his aid. He had been hit on the very top of the left shoulder.

"Go you on," he said; "I'm not kilt yet."

I satisfied myself that the wound was not serious, and I told him to plant himself in a conspicuous spot, where he could be seen, and to try and staunch the bleeding with a wet handkerchief. Then I darted off once more, and I saw three or four of my little force converging towards me, so that it became evident we were hemming our man in. They had heard the pistol shot, and asked excitedly if either of us had been hit. I told them that Michael had, and sent one of them to look after him. Then we searched about for our man, but found him not. We had last seen him darting down into a hollow formed by two ridges of sand; but when we rushed for the spot he had gone.

The chase had become exciting now, and the scent hot; and the very men who a few hours ago had treated me with such contempt began to sing my praises; but I cut them short, and told them there was business to do. Then each seemed desirous of gaining the honour of having it said that he was the first to capture the villain. In different directions we saw others of our comrades, and we apprised them by our whistles that we had found the scent. Then I told my men to spread themselves out, but to keep within easy distance, for the hunted murderer, as we now knew, was armed, and would sell his worthless life dearly. I felt sure that he could not escape, and I confess to a burning desire to be able to capture him myself. But in the meantime where had he gone? He had for the time being given us the slip. I managed to gain a sand hillock, which enabled me to command a pretty wide area, and my heart leapt to my mouth as I caught sight of the fellow running along with his head bent low. I blew my whistle, and waved my hands in his direction, so as to convey an intimation to my comrades of the quarter he was in. Right ahead of him were two of my hunters, and I saw if I missed him he would run into their arms, so I made a wild plunge after him. But in a few minutes he evidently caught sight of those in front of him, and doubled back. He came within a dozen yards of me, and I could see that his eyes were starting from his head, while his face was ghastly and horrible in its greenish pallor. As he caught sight of me he uttered an oath, and, turning off sharply at an angle, plunged into a broad stream and swam across. I followed him, and when he landed on the other side he turned, and in his foaming rage he looked like some savage beast rather than a human being.

He covered me with his pistol and fired, but there was no discharge. He raised the hammer and fired again, with the same result, and it became evident that the weapon was soaked with water. With a fierce shriek of disappointment, he hurled the pistol at my head with all his might; but it fortunately fell short, and he turned and fled again.

I scrambled out of the water and followed. As luck would have it, the ground was pretty flat hereabouts, and I was enabled to keep him in sight, but he was fleeter than I, and I saw he was gaining in the race, so I sounded my whistle as I ran, and in a few moments I beheld one of my men ahead. The fugitive saw him too, and I heard a cry escape from his lips as he turned on a curve, which brought him to a river that was broad and deep, and running pretty strong. He plunged in and sank for a moment out of sight. When he rose it was obvious he was fagged, and I fancied he turned his eyes upon me with a look of despair and yet defiance.

I paused to blow a long, loud, warning blast on my whistle. I heard it answered and I blew again; then in I went after him. I was fresher than he, made more rapid strokes, and gained upon him until I could almost touch him, when, with a sudden movement, he faced round and grappled me. He had realised that his game was up— that he was at bay—but he was determined if possible to have more blood on his guilty soul, although he was within the shadow of death.

Amongst the few accomplishments that I really excelled in at school was that of swimming, and it was to serve me in good stead now, although at first I thought my last hour had come, for he seized me by the hair and held me under the water.

I managed, however, to get my head free; how I really don't know. Then I grappled him, and we struggled frantically together.

"You shall never get out alive!" he hissed in gasps.

But he was wrong. I had managed by some means, which I can scarcely describe, to drag him near enough to the edge to enable me to grasp the bank with one hand, while I held him by the other. I turned my eyes anxiously to see if help was coming, for I knew only too well that I could never hope to get him out of the water alone. We were both exhausted, and it was a question which would give in first. Although a maddening desperation lent him a certain strength, it would not hold out long, and I believe he would have succumbed before me, but that meant that he would be drowned, and I was particularly anxious to capture him alive.

It was a terrible and thrilling situation—one of those situations when a man's hopes, his future, his very life may be said to hang upon a hair, and it is impossible to predict if the hair will break or not.

I heard the gurgling of the water, and it mingled with the stertorous breathing of the wretch I was anxious to save, in order that the law might take its vengeance. I saw his fierce eyes glaring at me with something of fiendish hate in their expression.

Moments under such an awful strain seem minutes, and minutes hours. The whole terrible scene was enacted in a very brief space of time, and yet it seemed interminable. Then I heard a rush and a plunge, and saw a third man in the water. It was one of my comrades, who, as if to make up for the way he had treated me on the previous day, did not hesitate to jump to my rescue. Then a third man appeared on the scene, and by our united efforts we dragged the half-drowned wretch on to the bank, where he lay prostrated for some little time. Presently he recovered, and we helped him to his feet and handcuffed him. Never to my dying day shall I forget the look of utter despair that came into his pallid face as he felt the cold steel close on his wrists. His exhausted state had caused us to somewhat relax our watchfulness. He saw this, and with one mighty effort he threw himself backwards and fell with a great splash into the water again. We saw his feet appear above the surface for an instant or two, then he disappeared, and I have a notion that he must have literally dug his hands into the bottom of the river. In a few minutes his back showed on the surface; he was hanging limp then, with his head entirely covered. He was close to the bank, and we managed to grab him and land him.

But it was too late. Consciousness had fled, and though I could detect the beating of his heart for some minutes, it gradually ceased, and Peter Mogford, the most desperate ruffian of his time, was dead. He had at least succeeded in cheating man of his vengeance, and had robbed the public of a spectacle. We bore his worthless body back to London, and in due course it was consigned, to a dishonoured grave.

My companion Michael Owen speedily recovered from his wound, and he, in common with all of us who had taken part in that memorable man hunt, received a share of a considerable subscription that was raised by a grateful public; and in the process of time the authorities were pleased to recognise the service I had rendered by awarding me promotion. I thus gained something, but I do not think that anything could ever have tempted me to again engage in such an awful and sickening duty as was that hunt for a murderer in the Woolwich marshes.

THE TRAGEDY OF A THIRD SMOKER

C. J. Cutcliffe Hyne

I ABOMINATE DETECTIVE STORIES," SAID THE Q. C., LAYING DOWN HIS CUE ALONG the corner of the billiard-table and going across to the shelf where the cigar-boxes stood. "You see, when a man makes a detective story to write down on paper, he begins at the butt-end and works backwards. He notes his points and manufactures his clues to suit 'em, so it's all bound to work out right. In real life it's very different,"—he chose a Partaga, looking at it through his glasses thoughtfully—"and I ought to know; I've been studying the criminal mind for half my working life."

"But," said O'Malley, "a defending counsel is a different class of animal from the common detective."

"Oh, is he?" said the Q. C.; "that's all you know about it." He dragged one of the big chairs up into the deep chimney corner and settled himself in it, after many luxurious shruggings; then he spoke on, between whiffs at the Partaga.

"Now I'll just state you a case, and you'll see for yourself how we sometimes have to ravel out things. The solicitor who put the brief in my hands was, as solicitors go, a smart chap. He had built up a big business out of nothing, but criminal work was slightly out of his line. He had only taken up this case to oblige an old client, and I must say he made an uncommonly poor show of it. I never had such a thin brief given me in my life.

"The prisoner was to be tried on the capital charge; and if murder really had been committed, it was one of a most cold-blooded nature. Hanging would follow conviction as surely as night comes on the heels of day; and a client who gets the noose given him always damages his counsel's reputation, whether that counsel deserves it or not.

"As my brief put it, the case fined down to this:

"Two men got into an empty third-class smoking compartment at Addison Road. One of them, Guide, was a drain contractor; the other, Walker, was a foreman in Guide's employ. The train took them past the Shepherd's Bush and Grove Road Hammersmith stations without anything being reported; but at Shaftesbury Road Walker was found on the floor, stone dead, with a wound in the skull, and on the seat of the carriage was a small miner's pickaxe with one of its points smeared with blood.

"It was proved that Guide had been seen to leave the Shaftesbury Road station. He was dishevelled and agitated at the time, and this made the ticket collector notice him specially amongst the crowd of out-going passengers. After it was found out who he was, inquiries were made at his home. His wife stated that she had not seen him since Monday—the morning of Walker's death. She also let out that Walker had been causing him some annoyance of late, but she did not know about what. Subsequently—on the Friday, four days later—Guide was arrested at the West India Dock. He was trying to obtain employ as coal trimmer on an Australian steamer, obviously to escape from the country. On being charged he surrendered quietly, remarking that he supposed it was all up with him.

"That was the gist of my case, and the solicitor suggested that I should enter a plea of insanity.

Now, when I'd conned the evidence over—additional evidence to what I've told you, but all tending to the same end—I came to the conclusion that Guide was as sane as any of us are, and that, as a defence, insanity wouldn't have a leg to stand upon. 'The fellow,' I said, 'had much better enter a plea of guilty and let me pile up a long list of extenuating circumstances. A jury will always listen to those, and feeling grateful for being excused a long and wearisome trial, recommend to mercy out of sheer gratitude.' I wrote a note to this effect. On its receipt the solicitor came to see me—by the way, he was Barnes, a man of my own year at Cambridge.

"'My dear Grayson,' said he, 'I'm not altogether a fool. I know as well as you do that Guide would have the best chance if he pleaded guilty; but the difficult part of it is that he flatly refuses to do any such thing. He says he no more killed this fellow Walker than you or I did. I pointed out to him that the man couldn't very conveniently have slain himself, as the wound was well over at the top of his head, and had obviously been the result of a most terrific blow. At the P.M. it was shown that Walker's skull was of abnormal thickness, and the force required to drive through it even a heavy, sharp-pointed instrument like the pickaxe, must have been something tremendous.

"'I tell you, Grayson, I impressed upon the fellow that the case was as black as ink against him, and that he'd only irritate the jury by holding out; but I couldn't move him. He held doggedly to his tale—he had not killed Andrew Walker.'

"'He's not the first man who's stuck to an unlikely lie like that,' I remarked.

"'The curious part of it is,' said Barnes, 'I'm convinced that the man believes himself to be telling the absolute truth.'

"'Then what explanation has he to offer?'

"'None worth listening to. He owns that he and Walker had a fierce quarrel over money matters, which culminated in a personal struggle. He knows that he had one blow on the head which dazed him, and fancies that he must have had a second which reduced him to unconsciousness. When next he knew what was happening, he saw

Walker lying on the floor, stone dead, though he was still warm and supple. On the floor was the pickaxe, with one of its points slimy with blood. How it cane to be so he couldn't tell. He picked it up and laid it on a seat. Then in an instant the thought flashed across him how terribly black things looked against himself. He saw absolutely no chance of disproving them, and with the usual impulse of crude minds resolved at once to quit the country. With that idea he got out at the Shaftesbury Road Station, and being an ignorant man and without money, made his way down to the Ratcliff Highway—beg its pardon, St. George's High Street. Using that as a centre, he smelt about the docks at Limehouse and Millwall trying for a job in the stokehold; but as that neighbourhood is one of the best watched spots on earth, it is not a matter for surprise that he was very soon captured. That's about all I can tell you.'

" 'I'm afraid it doesn't lighten matters up very much.'

" 'I never said it would. The gist of this is down in your brief, Grayson. I only came round to chambers because of your letter.'

" 'Still,' I persisted, 'you threw out a hint that Guide had offered some explanation.'

" 'Oh, yes; but such a flimsy, improbable theory that no sane man could entertain it for a minute. In fact, he knew it to be absurd himself. After pressing him again and again to suggest how Walker could have been killed (with the view of extorting a confession), he said, in his slow, heavy way, "Why, I suppose, Mr. Barnes, someone else must ha' done it. Don't you think as a man could ha' got into the carriage whilst I was lying there stupid, and hit Walker with the pick and got out again afore I come to? Would that do, sir?"

" 'I didn't think,' added Barnes, drily, 'that it was worth following that theory any deeper. What do you say?'

"I thought for a minute and then spoke up. 'Look here, Barnes; if in the face of this cock-and-bull story Guide persists in his innocence, there may be something in it after all; and if by any thousand-to-one chance we could bring him clear, it would be a red feather in the caps of both of us. Do you object to my seeing the man personally?'

" 'It's a bit irregular,' said Barnes, doubtfully.

" 'I know it is bang in the teeth of etiquette. But suppose we compromise, and you come with me?'

" 'No, I won't do that. My time's busy just now; and besides, I don't want to run up the costs of this case higher than necessary. But if you choose to shove your other work aside and waste a couple of hours, just go and interview him by yourself, and we'll waive ceremony. I'll get the necessary prison order, and send it round to you to-morrow.'

"Next afternoon I went down to see Guide in the waiting-room at the Old Bailey. He was a middle-aged man, heavy-faced, and evidently knocked half stupid by the situation in which he found himself. He was perhaps as great a fool to his own interests as one might often meet with. There was no getting the simplest tale out of him except by regular question-and-answer cross-examination. What little he did tell seemed rather to confirm his guilt than otherwise; though, strange to say, I was beginning to believe him when he kept on assuring me between every other sentence that he did not commit the murder. Perhaps it was the stolid earnestness of the fellow in denying the crime which convinced me. One gets to read a good deal from facial expression when a man has watched what goes on in the criminal dock as long as I have done; and one can usually spot guilt under any mask.

"'But tell me,' I said, 'what did you quarrel about in the first instance?'

"'Money,' said Guide, moodily.'

"'That's vague. Tell me more. Did he owe you money?'

"'No, sir, it was t'other way on.'

"'Wages in arrear?'

"'No, it was money he had advanced me for the working of my business. You see Walker had always been a hard man, and he'd saved. He said he wanted his money back, he knowing that I was pinched a bit just then and couldn't pay. Then he tried to thrust himself into partnership with me in the business, which was a thing I didn't want. I'd good contracts on hand which I expected would bring me in a matter of nine thousand pounds, and I didn't want to share it with any man, least of all him. I told him so, and that's how the trouble began. But it was him that hit me first.'

"'Still, you returned the blow?'

"Guide passed a hand wearily over his forehead. 'I may have struck him back, sir—I was dazed, and I don't rightly remember. But before God I'll swear that I never lifted that pick to Andrew Walker —it was his pick.'

"'But,' I persisted, 'Walker couldn't very conveniently have murdered himself.'

"'No, sir, no no, he couldn't. I thought of that myself since I been in here, and I said to Mr. Barnes that perhaps somebody come into the carriage when I was knocked silly, and killed him; but Mr. Barnes he said that was absurd. Besides, who could have done it?'

"'Don't you know anybody, then, who would have wished for Walker's death?'

"'There was them that didn't like him,' said Guide, drearily.

"That was all I could get out of him, and I went away from the prison feeling very dissatisfied. I was stronger than ever in the belief that Guide was in no degree guilty, and yet for the life of me I did not see how to prove his innocence. He had not been a man of any strong character to begin with, and the shock of what he had gone through had utterly dazed him. It was hopeless to expect any reasonable explanation from him;

he had resigned himself to puzzlement. If he had gone melancholy mad before he came up to trial, I should not have been one whit surprised.

"I brooded over the matter for a couple of days, putting all the rest of my practice out of thought, but I didn't get any forwarder with it. I hate to give anything up as a bad job, and in this case I felt that there was on my shoulders a huge load of responsibility. Guide, I had thoroughly persuaded myself, had not murdered Andrew Walker; as sure as the case went into court, on its present grounding, the man would be hanged out of hand; and I persuaded myself that then I, and I alone, should be responsible for an innocent man's death.

"At the end of those two days only one course seemed open to me. It was foreign to the brief I held, but the only method left to bring in my client's innocence.

"I must find out who did really murder the man. I must try to implicate some third actor in the tragedy.

"To begin with, there was the railway carriage; but a little thought showed me that nothing was to be done there. The compartment would have been inspected by the police, and then swept and cleaned and garnished, and coupled on to its train once more, and used by unconscious passengers for weeks since the uproar occurred in it.

"All that I had got to go upon were the notes and relics held at Scotland Yard.

"The police authorities were very good. Of course, they were keen enough to bring off the prosecution with professional *éclat;* but they were not exactly anxious to hand over a poor wretch to the hangman if he was not thoroughly deserving of a dance on nothing. They placed at my disposal every scrap of their evidence, and said that they thought the reading of it all was plain beyond dispute. I thought so, too, at first. They sent an inspector to my chambers as their envoy.

"On one point, though, after a lot of thought, I did not quite agree with them. I held a grisly relic in my hand, gazing at it fixedly. It was a portion of Walker's skull—a disc of dry bone with a splintered aperture in the middle.

"'And so you think the pickaxe made that hole,' I said to the inspector.

"'I don't think there can be any doubt about it, Mr Grayson. Nothing else could have done it, and the point of the pick was smeared with blood.'

"'But would there be room to swing such a weapon in a third-class Metropolitan railway carriage?'

"'We thought of that, and at first it seemed a poser. The roof is low, and both Guide and Walker are tall men; but if Guide had gripped the shaft by the end, so, with his right hand pretty near against the head, so, he'd have had heaps of room to drive it with a sideways swing. I tried the thing for myself; it acted perfectly. Here's the pickaxe: you can see for yourself.'

"I did see, and I wasn't satisfied; but I didn't tell the inspector what I thought. It was clearer to me than ever that Guide had not committed the murder. What I asked the inspector was this: 'Had either of the men got any luggage in the carriage?'

"The inspector answered, with a laugh, 'Not quite, Mr. Grayson, or you would see it here.'

"Then I took on paper a rough outline of that fragment of bone, and an accurate sketch of exact size of the gash in it, and the inspector went away. One thing his visit had shown me. Andrew Walker was not slain by a blow from behind by the pickaxe.

"I met Barnes whilst I was nibbling lunch, and told him this. He heard me doubtfully. 'You may be right,' said he, 'but I'm bothered if I see what you have to go upon.'

"'You know what a pickaxe is like?' I said.

"'Certainly.'

"'A cross-section of one of the blades would be what?'

"'Square—or perhaps oblong.'

"'Quite so. Rectangular. What I want to get at is this: it wouldn't even be diamond shape, with the angles obtuse and acute alternately.'

"'Certainly not. The angles would be clean right-angles.'

"'Very good. Now look at this sketch of the hole in the skull, and tell me what you see.'

"Barnes put on his glasses, and gazed attentively for a minute or so, and then looked up. 'The pick point has crashed through without leaving any marks of its edges whatever.'

"'That is to say, there are none of your right-angles showing.'

"'None. But that does not go to prove anything.'

"'No. It's only about a tenth of my proof. It gives the vague initial idea. It made me look more carefully, and I saw this'—I pointed with my pencil to a corner of the sketch.

"Barnes whistled. 'A clean arc of a circle,' said he, 'cut in the bone as though a knife had done it. You saw that pickaxe. Was it much worn? Were the angles much rounded near the point?'

"'They were not. On the contrary, the pick, though an old one, had just been through the blacksmith's shop to be resharpened, and had not been used since. There was not a trace of wear upon it: of that I am certain.'

"Barnes whistled again in much perplexity. At length said he, 'It's an absolutely certain thing that Walker was not killed in the way they imagine. But I don't think this will get Guide off scot-free. There's too much other circumstantial evidence against him. Of course you'll do your best, but—'

"'It would be more than a toss up if I could avoid a conviction. Quite so. We must find out more. The question is, how was this wound made? Was there a third man in it?'

"'Guide may have jobbed him from behind with some other instrument, and afterwards thrown it out of window.'

"'Yes,' said I, 'but that is going on the assumption that Guide did the trick, which I don't for a moment think is the case. Besides, if he did throw anything out of window, it would most assuredly have been found. They keep the permanent way very thoroughly inspected upon the Metropolitan. No, Barnes. There is some other agent in this case, animate or inanimate, which so far we have overlooked completely; and an innocent man's life depends upon our ravelling it out.'

"Barnes lifted his shoulders helplessly, and took another sandwich. 'I don't see what we can do.'

"'Nor I, very clearly. But we must start from the commencement, and go over the ground inch by inch.'

"So wrapped up was I in the case by this time, that I could not fix my mind to anything else. Then and there I went out and set about my inquiries.

"With some trouble I found the compartment in which the tragedy had taken place, but learnt nothing new from it. The station and the railway people at Addison Road, Kensington, were similarly drawn blank. The ticket inspector at Shaftesbury Road, who distinctly remembered Guide's passage, at first seemed inclined to tell me nothing new, till I dragged it out of him by a regular emetic of questioning.

"Then he did remember that Guide had been carrying in his hand a carpenter's straw bass, as he passed through the wicket. He did not recollect whether he had mentioned this to the police: didn't see that it mattered.

"I thought differently, and with a new vague hope in my heart, posted back to the prison. I had heard no word of this hand-baggage from Guide. It remained to be seen what he had done with it.

"They remembered me from my previous visit, and let me in to the prisoner without much demur. Guide owned up to the basket at once. 'Yes,' he said, 'I had some few odd tools to carry from home, and as I couldn't find anything else handy to put them in I used the old carpenter's bass. I had an iron eye to splice on to the end of a windlass rope, a job that I like to do myself, to make sure it's done safe. I never thought about telling you of that bass before, sir. I didn't see as how it mattered.'

"'Where is the bass now?'"

"'In the Left Luggage Office at Shaftesbury Road Station. Name of Hopkins. I've lost the ticket.'

"'Where did you put your basket on entering the carriage at Addison Road?'

"'On the seat, sir, in the corner by the window.'

"And with that I left him.

"'Now,' thought I, 'I believe I can find out whether you murdered Walker or not,' and I drove back to Hammersmith.

"I inquired at the cloak-room. Yes, the carpenter's bass was there, beneath a dusty heap of other unclaimed luggage. There was demurrage to pay on it, which I offered promptly to hand over, but as I could produce no counterfoil bearing the name of Hopkins, the clerk, with a. smile, said that he could not let me have it. However, when he heard what I wanted, he made no objection to my having an overhaul.

"The two lugs of the bass were threaded together with a hammer. I took this away, and opened the sides. Within was a ball of marline, another of spun-yarn, a grease-pot, and several large iron eyes. Also a large marline-spike. It was this last that fixed my attention. It was brand new, with a bone handle and a bright brass ferrule. Most of the iron also was bright, but three inches of the point were stained with a faint dark brown. From a casual inspection I should have put this down to the marline-spike having been last used to make a splice on tarred rope; but now my suspicions made me think of something else.

"I raised the stained point to my nose. There was no smell of tar whatever. On the bright part there was the indefinable odour of iron; at the tip, that thin coat of dark brown varnish had blotted this scent completely away.

"I think my fingers trembled when I turned to the bass again.

"Yes, there, opposite to where the point of the marline-spike had been lying—it was tilted up over the ball of spun-yarn—was a closed-up gash in the side of the bass. The spike had passed through there, and then been withdrawn. Round the gash was a dim discoloration which I knew to be dried human blood.

"In my mind's eye I saw the whole ghastly accident clearly enough now. The two men had been standing up, struggling. Guide had gone down under a blow, knocked senseless, and Walker had stumbled over him. Pitching forward, face downwards, on to the seat before he could recover, his head had dashed violently against the carpenter's bass. The sharp marline-spike inside, with its heel resting against the solid wall of the carriage, had entered the top of his skull like a bayonet. No human hand had been raised against him, and yet he had been killed.

"I kept my own particular ramblings in this case remarkably quiet, and in court led up to my facts through ordinary cross-examination.

"At the proper psychological moment I called attention to the shape of the puncture in Walker's skull, and then dramatically sprang the bass and the marlinespike upon them unawares. After that, as the papers put it, 'there was applause in court, which was instantly suppressed.'"

"Oh, the conceit of the man," said O'Malley, laughing.

Grayson laughed too. "Well," he said, "I was younger then, and I suppose I was a trifle conceited. The Crown didn't throw up. But the jury chucked us a 'Not guilty' without leaving the box, and then leading counsel for the other side came across and congratulated me on having saved Guide from the gallows. 'Now I'd have bet anything on hanging that man,' said he."

THE GREEN-STONE GOD
AND THE STOCKBROKER

Fergus Hume

A S A RULE, THE AVERAGE DETECTIVE GETS TWICE THE CREDIT HE DESERVES. I am not talking of the novelist's miracle-monger, but of the flesh and blood reality who is liable to err, and who frequently proves such liability. You can take it as certain that a detective who sets down a clean run and no hitch as entirely due to his astucity, is young in years, and still younger in experience. Older men, who have been bamboozled a hundred times by the craft of criminality, recognize the influence of Chance to make or mar. There you have it! Nine times out of ten, Chance does more in clinching a case than all the dexterity and mother-wit of the man in charge. The exception must be engineered by an infallible apostle. Such a one is unknown to me—out of print.

This opinion, based rather on collective experience than on any one episode, can be substantiated by several incontrovertible facts. In this instance, one will suffice. Therefore, I take the Brixton case to illustrate Chance as a factor in human affairs. Had it not been for that Maori fetish—but such rather ends than begins the story, therefore it were wise to dismiss it for the moment. Yet that piece of green-stone hanged—a person mentioned hereafter.

When Mr. and Mrs. Paul Vincent set up housekeeping at Ulster Lodge they were regarded as decided acquisitions to Brixton society. She, pretty and musical; he, smart in looks, moderately well off, and an excellent tennis-player. Their progenitors, his father and her mother (both since deceased), had lived a life of undoubted middle-class respectability. The halo thereof still environed their children, who were, in consequence of such inherited grace and their own individualisms, much sought after by genteel Brixtonians. Moreover, this popular couple were devoted to each other, and even after three years of marriage they posed still as lovers. This was as it should be, and by admiring friends and relations the Vincents were regarded as paragons of matrimonial perfection. Vincent was a stockbroker; therefore he passed most of his time in the City.

Judge, then, of the commotion, when pretty Mrs. Vincent was discovered in the study, stabbed to the heart. So aimless a crime were scarce imaginable. She had many friends, no known enemies, yet she came to this tragic end. Closer examination revealed that the escritoire had been broken into, and Mr. Vincent declared himself the poorer by two hundred pounds. Primarily, therefore, robbery was the sole object, but, by reason of Mrs. Vincent's interference, the thief had been converted into a murderer.

So excellently had the assassin chosen his time, that such choice argued a close acquaintance with the domestic economy of Ulster Lodge. The husband was detained in town till midnight; the servants (cook and housemaid), on leave to attend wedding festivities, were absent till eleven o'clock. Mrs. Vincent therefore was absolutely alone in the house for six hours, during which period the crime had been committed. The servants discovered the body of their unfortunate mistress, and raised the alarm at once. Later on Vincent arrived, to find his wife dead, his house in possession of the police, and the two servants in hysterics. For that night nothing could be done, but at dawn a move was made towards elucidating the mystery. At this point I come into the story.

Instructed at nine o'clock to take charge of the case, by ten I was on the spot noting details and collecting evidence. Beyond removal of the body nothing had been disturbed, and the study was in precisely the same condition as when the crime was discovered. I examined carefully the apartment, and afterwards interrogated the cook, the housemaid, and, lastly, the master of the house. The result gave me slight hope of securing the assassin.

The room (a fair-sized one, looking out on to a lawn between house and road) was furnished in cheap bachelor fashion. An old-fashioned desk placed at right angles to the window, a round table reaching nigh the sill, two arm-chairs, three of the ordinary cane-seated kind, and on the mantelpiece an arrangement of pipes, pistols, boxing-gloves, and foils. One of these latter was missing.

A single glimpse showed how terrible a struggle had taken place before the murderer had overpowered his victim. The tablecloth lay disorderly on the floor, two of the lighter chairs were overturned, and the desk, with several drawers open, was hacked about considerably. No key was in the door-lock which faced the escritoire, and the window-snick was fastened securely.

Further search resulted in the following discoveries:—

1. A hatchet used for chopping wood (found near the desk).
2. A foil with the button broken off (lying under the table).
3. A green-stone idol (edged under the fender).

The cook (defiantly courageous by reason of brandy) declared that she had left the house at four o'clock on the previous day, and had returned close on eleven. The back door (to her surprise) was open. With the housemaid she went to inform her mistress of this fact, and found the body lying midway between door and fireplace. At once she called in the police. Her master and mistress were a most attached couple, and (so far as she knew) they had no enemies.

Similar evidence was obtained from the housemaid, with the additional information that the hatchet belonged to the wood-shed. The other rooms were undisturbed.

Poor young Vincent was so broken down by the tragedy that he could hardly answer my questions with calmness. Sympathizing with his natural grief, I interrogated him as delicately as was possible, and I am bound to admit that he replied with remarkable promptitude and clearness.

"What do you know of this unhappy affair?" I asked, when we were alone in the drawing-room. He refused to stay in the study, as was surely natural under the circumstances.

"Absolutely nothing," he replied. "I went to the City yesterday at ten in the morning, and, as I had business to do, I wired my wife I would not return till midnight. She was full of health and spirits when I last saw her, but now—" Incapable of further speech he made a gesture of despair. Then, after a pause, he added, "Have you any theory on the subject?"

"Judging from the wrecked condition of the desk I should say robbery—"

"Robbery?" he interrupted, changing colour. "Yes, that was the motive. I had two hundred pounds locked up in the desk."

"In gold or notes?"

"The latter. Four fifties. Bank of England."

"You are sure they are missing?"

"Yes. The drawer in which they were placed is smashed to pieces."

"Did any one know you had placed two hundred pounds therein?"

"No! Save my wife, and yet—ah!" he said, breaking off abruptly, "that is impossible."

"What is impossible?"

"I will tell you when I hear your theory."

"You got that notion out of novels of the shilling sort," I answered dryly; "every detective doesn't theorize on the instant. I haven't any particular theory that I know of. Whosoever committed this crime must have known your wife was alone in the house, and that there was two hundred pounds locked up in that desk. Did you mention these two facts to any one?"

Vincent pulled his moustache in some embarrassment. I guessed by the action that he had been indiscreet.

"I don't wish to get an innocent person into trouble," he said at length, "but I did mention it—to a man called Roy."

"For what reason?"

"It is a bit of a story. I lost two hundred to a friend at cards, and drew four fifties to pay him. He went out of town, so I locked up the money in my desk for safety. Last night Roy came to me at the club, much agitated, and asked me to loan him a hundred. Said it meant ruin else. I offered him a cheque, but he wanted cash. I then told him I had left two hundred at home, so, at the moment, I could not lay my hand on it. He asked if he could not go to Brixton for it, but I said the house was empty, and—"

"But it wasn't empty," I interrupted. "I believed it would be! I knew the servants were going to that wedding, and I thought my wife, instead of spending a lonely evening, would call on some friend."

"Well, and after you told Roy that the house was empty?"

"He went away, looking awfully cut up, and swore he must have the money at any price. But it is quite impossible he could have anything to do with this."

"I don't know. You told him where the money was, and that the house was unprotected, as you thought. What was more probable than that he should have come down with the intention of stealing the money? If so, what follows? Entering by the back door, he takes the hatchet from the wood-shed to open the desk. Your wife, hearing a noise, discovers him in the study. In a state of frenzy, he snatches a foil from the mantelpiece and kills her, then decamps with the money. There is your theory, and a mighty bad one—for Roy."

"You don't intend to arrest him?" asked Vincent quickly.

"Not on insufficient evidence! If he committed the crime and stole the money it is certain that, sooner or later, he will change the notes. Now, if I had the numbers—"

"Here are the numbers," said Vincent, producing his pocket-book. "I always take the numbers of such large notes. But surely," he added, as I copied them down— "surely you don't think Roy guilty?"

"I don't know. I should like to know his movements on that night."

"I cannot tell you. He saw me at the Chestnut Club about seven o'clock, and left immediately afterwards. I kept my business appointment, went to the Alhambra, and then returned home."

"Give me Roy's address, and describe his personal appearance."

"He is a medical student, and lodges at No. —, Gower Street. Tall, fair-haired—a good-looking young fellow."

"And his dress last night?"

"He wore evening dress, concealed by a fawn-coloured overcoat."

I duly noted these particulars, and I was about to take my leave, when I recollected the green-stone idol. It was so strange an object to find in prosaic Brixton that I could not help thinking it must have come there by accident.

"By the way, Mr. Vincent," said I, producing the monstrosity, "is this green-stone god your property?"

"I never saw it before," replied he, taking it in his hand. "Is it—ah!" he added, dropping the idol, "there is blood on it!"

"'Tis the blood of your wife, sir! If it does not belong to you, it does to the murderer. From the position in which this was found I fancy it slipped out of his breast-pocket as he stood over his victim. As you see, it is stained with blood. He must have lost his presence of mind, else he would not have left behind so damning a piece of evidence. This idol, sir, will hang the assassin of Mrs. Vincent!"

"I hope so; but, unless you are sure of Roy, do not mar his life by accusing him of this crime."

"I certainly should not arrest him without sufficient proof," I answered promptly, and so took my departure.

Vincent showed up very well in this preliminary conversation. Much as he desired to punish the criminal, yet he was unwilling to subject Roy to possibly unfounded suspicions. Had I not forced the club episode out of him I doubt whether he would have told it. As it was, the information gave me the necessary clue. Roy alone knew that the notes were in the escritoire, and imagined (owing to the mistake of Vincent) that the house was empty. Determined to have the money at any price (his own words), he intended but robbery, till the unexpected appearance of Mrs. Vincent merged the lesser in the greater crime.

My first step was to advise the Bank that four fifty-pound notes, numbered so and so, were stolen, and that the thief or his deputy would probably change them within a reasonable period. I did not say a word about the crime, and kept all special details out of the newspapers; for as the murderer would probably read up the reports, so as to shape his course by the action of the police, I judged it wiser that he should know as little as possible. Those minute press notices do more harm than good. They gratify the morbid appetite of the public, and put the criminal on his guard. Thereby the police work in the dark, but he—thanks to the posting up of special reporters—knows the doings of the law, and baffles it accordingly.

The green-stone idol worried me considerably. I wanted to know how it had got into the study of Ulster Lodge. When I knew that, I could nail my man. But there was considerable difficulty to overcome before such knowledge was available. Now a curiosity of this kind is not a common object in this country. A man who owns one must have come from New Zealand, or have obtained it from a New Zealand friend. He could not have picked it up in London. If he did, he would not carry it constantly about with him. It was therefore my idea that the murderer had received the idol from a friend on the day of the crime. That friend, to possess such an idol, must have been in communication with New Zealand. The chain of thought is somewhat complicated, but it began with curiosity about the idol, and ended in my looking up the list of steamers going to the Antipodes. Then I carried out a little design which need not be mentioned at this moment. In due time it will fit in with the hanging of Mrs. Vincent's assassin. Meanwhile, I followed up the clue of the bank-notes, and left the green-stone idol to evolve its own destiny. Thus I had two strings to my bow.

The crime was committed on the twentieth of June, and on the twenty-third two fifty-pound notes, with numbers corresponding to those stolen, were paid into the Bank of England. I was astonished at the little care exercised by the criminal in concealing his crime, but still more so when I learned that the money had been banked by a very respectable solicitor. Furnished with the address, I called on this gentleman. Mr. Maudsley received me politely, and he had no hesitation in telling me how the notes had come into his possession. I did not state my primary reason for the inquiry.

"I hope there is no trouble about these notes," said he, when I explained my errand. "I have had sufficient already."

"Indeed, Mr. Maudsley, and in what way?"

For answer he touched the bell, and when it was answered, "Ask Mr. Ford to step this way," he said. Then, turning to me, "I must reveal what I had hoped to keep secret, but I trust the revelation will remain with yourself."

"That is as I may decide after hearing it. I am a detective, Mr. Maudsley, and, you may be sure, I do not make these inquiries out of idle curiosity."

Before he could reply, a slender, weak-looking young man, nervously excited, entered the room. This was Mr. Ford, and he looked from me to Maudsley with some apprehension.

"This gentleman," said his employer, not unkindly, "comes from Scotland Yard about the money you paid me two days ago."

"It is all right, I hope?" stammered Ford, turning red and pale and red again.

"Where did you get the money?" I asked, parrying this question.

"From my sister."

I started when I heard this answer, and with good reason. My inquiries about Roy had revealed that he was in love with a hospital nurse whose name was Clara Ford. Without doubt she had obtained the notes from Roy, after he had stolen them from Ulster Lodge. But why the necessity of the robbery?

"Why did you get a hundred pounds from your sister?" I asked Ford.

He did not answer, but looked appealingly at Maudsley. That gentleman interposed.

"We must make a clean breast of it, Ford," he said, with a sigh; "if you have committed a second crime to conceal the first, I cannot help you. This time matters are not at my discretion."

"I have committed no crime," said Ford desperately, turning to me. "Sir, I may as well admit that I embezzled one hundred pounds from Mr. Maudsley to pay a gambling debt. He kindly and most generously consented to overlook the delinquency if I replaced the money. Not having it myself I asked my sister. She, a poor hospital nurse, had not the amount. Yet, as non-payment meant ruin to me, she asked a Mr. Julian Roy to help her. He at once agreed to do so, and gave her two fifty-pound notes. She handed them to me, and I gave them to Mr. Maudsley, who paid them into the bank."

This, then, was the reason of Roy's remark. He did not refer to his own ruin, but to that of Ford. To save this unhappy man, and for love of the sister, he had committed the crime. I did not need to see Clara Ford, but at once made up my mind to arrest Roy. The case was perfectly clear, and I was fully justified in taking this course. Meanwhile I made Maudsley and his clerk promise silence, as I did not wish Roy to be put on his guard by Miss Ford, through her brother.

"Gentlemen," I said, after a few moments' pause, "I cannot at present explain my reasons for asking these questions, as it would take too long, and I have no time to lose. Keep silent about this interview till to-morrow, and by that time you shall know all."

"Has Ford got into fresh trouble?" asked Maudsley anxiously.

"No, but some one else has."

"My sister," began Ford faintly, when I interrupted him at once.

"Your sister is all right, Mr. Ford. Pray trust in my discretion; no harm shall come to her or to you, if I can help it—but, above all, be silent."

This they readily promised, and I returned to Scotland Yard, quite satisfied that Roy would get no warning. The evidence was so clear that I could not doubt the guilt of Roy. Else how had he come in possession of the notes? Already there was sufficient proof to hang him, yet I hoped to clinch the certainty by proving his ownership of the green-stone idol. It did not belong to Vincent, or to his dead wife, yet some one must have brought it into the study. Why not Roy, who, to all appearances, had committed the crime, the more so as the image was splashed with the victim's blood? There was no difficulty in obtaining a warrant, and with this I went off to Gower Street.

Roy loudly protested his innocence. He denied all knowledge of the crime and of the idol. I expected the denial, but I was astonished at the defence he put forth. It was very ingenious, but so manifestly absurd that it did not shake my belief in his guilt. I let him talk himself out—which perhaps was wrong—but he would not be silent, and then I took him off in a cab.

"I swear I did not commit the crime," he said passionately; "no one was more astonished than I at the news of Mrs. Vincent's death."

"Yet you were at Ulster Lodge on the night in question?"

"I admit it," he replied frankly; "were I guilty I would not do so. But I was there at the request of Vincent."

"I must remind you that all you say now will be used in evidence against you."

"I don't care! I must defend myself. I asked Vincent for a hundred pounds, and—"

"Of course you did, to give to Miss Ford."

"How do you know that?" he asked sharply.

"From her brother, through Maudsley. He paid the notes supplied by you into the bank. If you wanted to conceal your crime you should not have been so reckless."

"I have committed no crime," retorted Roy fiercely. "I obtained the money from Vincent, at the request of Miss Ford, to save her brother from being convicted for embezzlement."

"Vincent denies that he gave you the money!"

"Then he lies. I asked him at the Chestnut Club for one hundred pounds. He had not that much on him, but said that two hundred were in his desk at home. As it was imperative that I should have the money on the night, I asked him to let me go down for it."

"And he refused!"

"He did not. He consented, and gave me a note to Mrs. Vincent, instructing her to hand me over a hundred pounds. I went to Brixton, got the money in two fifties, and gave them to Miss Ford. When I left Ulster Lodge, between eight and nine, Mrs. Vincent was in perfect health, and quite happy."

"An ingenious defence," said I doubtfully, "but Vincent absolutely denies that he gave you the money."

Roy stared hard at me to see if I were joking. Evidently the attitude of Vincent puzzled him greatly.

"That is ridiculous," said he quietly; "he wrote a note to his wife instructing her to hand me the money."

"Where is that note?"

"I gave it to Mrs. Vincent."

"It cannot be found," I answered; "if such a note were in her possession it would now be in mine."

"Don't you believe me?"

"How can I against the evidence of those notes and the denial of Vincent?"

"But he surely does not deny that he gave me the money?"

"He does."

"He must be mad," said Roy, in dismay; "one of my best friends, and to tell so great a falsehood. Why, if—"

"You had better be silent," I said, weary of this foolish talk; "if what you say is true, Vincent will exonerate you from complicity in the crime. If things occurred as you say, there is no sense in his denial."

This latter remark was made to stop the torrent of his speech. It was not my business to listen to incriminating declarations, or to ingenious defences. All that sort of thing is for judge and jury; therefore I ended the conversation as above, and marched off my prisoner. Whether the birds of the air carry news I do not know, but they must have been busy on this occasion, for next morning every newspaper in London was congratulating me on my clever capture of the supposed murderer. Some detectives would have been gratified by this public laudation—I was not. Roy's passionate protestations of innocence made me feel uneasy, and I doubted whether, after all, I had the right man under lock and key. Yet the evidence was strong against him. He admitted having been with Mrs. Vincent on the fatal night, he admitted possession of two fifty-pound notes. His only defence was the letter of the stockbroker, and this was missing—if, indeed, it had ever been written.

Vincent was terribly upset by the arrest of Roy. He liked the young man and he had believed in his innocence so far as was possible. But in the face of such strong evidence, he was forced to believe him guilty: yet he blamed himself severely that he had not lent the money, and so averted the catastrophe.

"I had no idea that the matter was of such moment," he said to me, "else I would have gone down to Brixton myself and have given him the money. Then his frenzy would have spared my wife, and himself a death on the scaffold."

"What do you think of his defence?"

"It is wholly untrue. I did not write a note, nor did I tell him to go to Brixton. Why should I, when I fully believed no one was in the house?"

"It was a pity you did not go home, Mr. Vincent, instead of to the Alhambra."

"It was a mistake," he assented, "but I had no idea Roy would attempt the robbery. Besides, I was under engagement to go to the theatre with my friend Dr. Monson."

"Do you think that idol belongs to Roy?"

"I can't say, I never saw it in his possession. Why?"

"Because I firmly believe that if Roy had not the idol in his pocket on that fatal night he is innocent. Oh, you look astonished, but the man who murdered your wife owns that idol."

The morning after this conversation a lady called at Scotland Yard, and asked to see me concerning the Brixton case. Fortunately, I was then in the neighbourhood, and, guessing who she was, I afforded her the interview she sought. When all left the room she raised her veil, and I saw before me a noble-looking woman, somewhat resembling Mr. Maudsley's clerk. Yet, by some contradiction of nature, her face was the more virile of the two.

"You are Miss Ford?" I said, guessing her identity.

"I am Clara Ford," she answered quietly. "I have come to see you about Mr. Roy."

"I am afraid nothing can be done to save him."

"Something must be done," she said passionately. "We are engaged to be married, and all a woman can do to save her lover I will do. Do you believe him to be guilty?"

"In the face of such evidence, Miss Ford——"

"I don't care what evidence is against him," she retorted; "he is as innocent of the crime as I am. Do you think that a man fresh from the committal of a crime would place the money won by that crime in the hands of the woman he professes to love? I tell you he is innocent."

"Mr. Vincent doesn't think so."

"Mr. Vincent!" said Miss Ford, with scornful emphasis. "Oh, yes! I quite believe *he* would think Julian guilty."

"Surely not if it were possible to think otherwise! He is, or rather was, a staunch friend to Mr. Roy."

"So staunch that he tried to break off the match between us. Listen to me, sir. I have told no one before, but I tell you now. Mr. Vincent is a villain. He pretended to be the friend of Julian, and yet he dared to make proposals to me—dishonourable proposals, for which I could have struck him. He, a married man, a pretended friend, wished me to leave Julian and fly with him."

"Surely you are mistaken, Miss Ford. Mr. Vincent was most devoted to his wife."

"He did not care at all for his wife," she replied steadily. "He was in love with me. To save Julian annoyance I did not tell him of the insults offered to me by Mr. Vincent. Now that Julian is in trouble by an unfortunate mistake, Mr. Vincent is delighted."

"It is impossible. I assure you Vincent is very sorry to——"

"You do not believe me," she said, interrupting. "Very well, I shall give you proof of the truth. Come to my brother's rooms in Bloomsbury. I shall send for Mr. Vincent, and if you are concealed you shall hear from his own lips how glad he is that my lover and his wife are removed from the path of his dishonourable passion."

"I will come, Miss Ford, but I think you are mistaken in Vincent."

"You shall see," she replied coldly. Then, with a sudden change of tone, "Is there no way of saving Julian? I am sure that he is innocent. Appearances are against him, but it was not he who committed the crime. Is there no way—no way?"

Moved by her earnest appeal, I produced the green-stone idol, and told her all I had done in connection with it. She listened eagerly, and readily grasped at the hope thus held out to her of saving Roy. When in possession of all the facts she considered in silence for some two minutes. At the end of that time she drew down her veil and prepared to take her departure.

"Come to my brother's rooms in Alfred Place, near Tottenham Court Road," said she, holding out her hand. "I promise you that there you shall see Mr. Vincent in his true character. Good-bye till Monday at three o'clock."

From the colour in her face and the bright light in her eye, I guessed that she had some scheme in her head for the saving of Roy. I think myself clever, but after that interview at Alfred Place I declare I am but a fool compared to this woman. She put two and two together, ferreted out unguessed-of evidence, and finally produced the most wonderful result. When she left me at this moment the green-stone idol was in her pocket. With that she hoped to prove the innocence of her lover and the guilt of another person. It was the cleverest thing I ever saw in my life.

The inquest on the body of Mrs. Vincent resulted in a verdict of wilful murder against some person or persons unknown. Then she was buried, and all London waited for the trial of Roy. He was brought up charged with the crime, reserved his defence, and in due course he was committed for trial. Meantime I called on Miss Ford at the appointed time, and found her alone.

"Mr. Vincent will be here shortly," she said calmly. "I see Julian is committed for trial."

"And he has reserved his defence."

"I shall defend him," said she, with a strange look in her face; "I am not afraid for him now. He saved my unhappy brother. I shall save him."

"Have you discovered anything?"

"I have discovered a good deal. Hush! That is Mr. Vincent," she added, as a cab drew up to the door. "Hide yourself behind this curtain, and do not appear until I give you the signal."

Wondering what she was about to do, I concealed myself as directed. The next moment Vincent was in the room, and then ensued one of the strangest of scenes. She received him coldly, and motioned him to a seat. Vincent was nervous, but she might have been of stone, so little emotion did she display.

"I have sent for you, Mr. Vincent," she said, "to ask for your help in releasing Julian."

"How can I help you?" he answered, in amazement—"willingly would I do so, but it is out of my power."

"I don't think it is!"

"I assure you, Clara," he began eagerly, when she cut him short.

"Yes, call me Clara! Say that you love me! Lie, like all men, and yet refuse to do what I wish."

"I am not going to help Julian to marry you," declared he sullenly. "You know that I love you—I love you dearly, I wish to marry you—"

"Is not that declaration rather soon after the death of your wife?"

"My wife is gone, poor soul, let her rest."

"Yet you loved her?"

"I never loved her," he said, rising to his feet. "I love you! From the first moment I saw you I loved you. My wife is dead! Julian Roy is in prison on a charge of murdering her. With these obstacles removed there is no reason why we should not marry."

"If I marry you," she said slowly, "will you help Julian to refute this charge?"

"I cannot! The evidence is too strong against him!"

"You know that he is innocent, Mr. Vincent."

"I do not! I believe that he murdered my wife."

"You believe that he murdered your wife," she reiterated, coming a step nearer and holding out the green-stone idol—"do you believe that he dropped this in the study when his hand struck the fatal blow?"

"I don't know!" he said, coolly glancing at the idol; "I never saw it before."

"Think again, Mr. Vincent—think again. Who was it that went to the Alhambra at eight o'clock with Dr. Monson, and met there the captain of a New Zealand steamer with whom he was acquainted?"

"It was I," said Vincent defiantly; "and what of that?"

"This!" she said in a loud voice. "This captain gave you the green-stone idol at the Alhambra, and you placed it in your breast-pocket. Shortly afterwards you followed to Brixton the man whose death you had plotted. You repaired to your house, killed your unhappy wife, who received you in all innocence, took the balance of the money, hacked the desk, and then dropped by accident this idol which convicts you of the crime."

During this speech she advanced step by step towards the wretched man, who, pale and anguished, retreated before her fury. He came right to my hiding-place, and almost fell into my arms. I had heard enough to convince me of his guilt, and the next moment I was struggling with him.

"It is a lie! a lie!" he said hoarsely, trying to escape.

"It is true!" said I, pinning him down. "From my soul I believe you to be guilty."

During the fight his pocket-book fell on the floor, and the papers therein were scattered. Miss Ford picked up one spotted with blood.

"The proof!" she said, holding it before us. The proof that Julian spoke the truth. There is the letter written by you which authorized your unhappy wife to give him one hundred pounds."

Vincent saw that all was against him, and gave in without further struggles, like the craven he was.

"Fate is too strong for me," he said, when I snapped handcuffs on his wrists. "I admit the crime. It was for love of you that I did it. I hated my wife, who was a drag on me, and I hated Roy, who loved you. In one sweep I thought to rid myself of both. His application for that money put the chance into my hand. I went to Brixton, I found that my wife had given the money as directed, and then I killed her with the foil snatched from the wall. I smashed the desk and overturned the chair, to favour the idea of the robbery, and then I left the house. Driving to a higher station than Brixton, I caught a train and was speedily back at the Alhambra. Monson never suspected my absence, thinking I was in a different corner of the house. I had thus an *alibi* ready. Had it not been for that letter, which I was fool enough to keep, and that infernal idol that dropped out of my pocket, I should have hanged Roy and married you. As it turns out, the idol has betrayed me. And now, sir," he added, turning to me, "you had better take me to gaol."

I did so there and then. After the legal formalities were gone through Julian Roy was released, and ultimately married Miss Ford. Vincent was hanged, as he well deserved to be, for so cowardly a crime. My reward was the green-stone god, which I keep as a memento of a very curious case. Some weeks later Miss Ford told me the way in which she had laid the trap.

"When you revealed your suspicions about the idol," she said, "I was convinced that Vincent had something to do with the crime. You mentioned Dr. Monson as having been with him at the Alhambra. He is one of the doctors at the hospital in which I am employed. I asked him about the idol, and showed it to him. He remembered it being given to Vincent by the captain of the *Kaitangata*. The curious look of the thing had impressed itself on his memory. On hearing this I went to the docks and I saw the captain. He recognized the idol, and remembered giving it to Vincent. From what you told me I guessed the way in which the plot had been carried out, so I spoke to Vincent as you heard. Most of it was guesswork, and only when I saw that letter was I absolutely sure of his guilt. It was due to the green-stone god."

So I think, but to chance also. But for the accident of the idol dropping out of Vincent's pocket, Roy would have been hanged for a crime of which he was innocent. Therefore do I say that in nine cases out of ten chance does more to clinch a case than all the dexterity of the man in charge.

THE CONTENTS OF THE COFFIN

J. S. Fletcher

Guilty!"

The foreman of the jury uttered the fatal word with the hesitation of a man who is loth to voice the decision which deprives a human being of his liberty. He and his fellow jurymen kept their eyes sedulously away from the man in the dock; Every one of them at some time or another had partaken of his good fare, drunk his vintage wines, smoked his cabinet cigars, and now . . .

"You find the prisoner guilty; and that is the verdict of you all?"

"We find the prisoner guilty, and that is the verdict of us all," repeated the foreman in dull tones. Something in his mien suggested that he was glad to have to say no more—he and his eleven companions in the cramped-in jury-box seemed to crave silence. They were wanting to get away, to breathe, to have done with an ugly passage in life of their little town. What need of more talking? It had been impossible not to find their old friend and neighbour guilty. Of course he was guilty—guilty as Cain or Judas. Get the thing over.

The man in the dock seemed to share the opinion of the jury. His face was absolutely emotionless as he heard the fatal word drop limply from the foreman's lips, and he shook his head with something of a contemptuous smile when asked if he had anything else to say as to why sentence should not be passed upon him. What was there to say?

"John Barr," said the stern-faced embodiment of justice whom he faced. "You have been convicted on the clearest evidence of the very serious crime of embezzlement. There were no less than nine counts in the indictment against you. It was only considered necessary to proceed with one—that relating to your embezzlement during the month of July, 1898, of a sum of three thousand seven hundred pounds, the moneys of your employers, the Mid-Yorkshire Banking Company—and upon that charge you have been found guilty. But it has been clearly established during the course of your trial that this sum forms almost an infinitesimal part of your depredations against your employers' funds. It seems almost incredible to me, who knew little of banking affairs, that it should have been possible for you to commit these depredations, but I note that the sums mentioned in the nine counts total up to the immense aggregate of one hundred and eighty-seven thousand pounds, and we have heard it stated by the prosecution that there are further sums to be accounted for, and that the probable total loss to the bank will exceed a quarter of a million sterling. Now there are several unfortunate features about the case, and not the least unfortunate lies in the fact that it is believed—and, from what I have gathered, justly believed—by the prosecution that a very considerable portion of the money which you have embezzled is at this moment, if not at your disposal, still within your cognizance. Appeals have been made to you from time to time, since you were first committed for trial, with respect to making restitution. All these appeals have been in vain. The last of these appeals was made to you here, in this court, this morning. You paid no regard to it. Now, if it be a fact that any part of the money of which you have robbed your employers is recoverable, let me beg of you to make proper restitution for the sake of your own conscience and the honour of your family, which, as I am informed, has long occupied a foremost position in this town. This has been a singularly painful case, and it is a painful thing for me, in the discharge of my duty, to feel obliged to pass upon you a sentence of ten years' penal servitude."

John Barr heard his sentence with as little show of emotion as he had heard the verdict of the jury. He looked round the court for a moment as if seeking some face. A man sitting in a retired seat caught his eye—a man who bore a distinct resemblance to himself, and who had listened to the whole of the proceedings with downcast head. This man was now regarding the convict with an intent look. John Barr, for the fraction of a second, returned it; then, with a quick glance round him—the glance of a man who looks at familiar objects and faces for the last time—he bowed to the seat of justice, turned, and was gone.

The people who had crowded the court since the doors first opened that morning, streamed out into the Market Place. There were several cases to come on yet, but the great case of the day was over, and all Normancaster wanted to get somewhere—home, inn-parlour, by-way, anywhere—to talk over the result. Ten years' penal servitude!—well, it was only what anyone could expect. And a quarter of a million of money—and had John Barr disposed of it in such a fashion that he could "handle it" when he "came out" of whatever penal settlement he would be sent to? Men were gabbling like geese over these questions, and particularly over the last, as they crossed the cobble stones of the Market Square, making for their favourite houses of resort.

Two men, leaving the court together drew aside from the throng and turned into a quiet street. One of them, a big, burly, bearded man was obviously excited; the other, an odd-looking little individual, dressed in an antique frock-coat and trousers much to short to reach the tops of his shoes, wore a rusty old-fashioned hat far back on his head, and carried a Gamp-like umbrella over his shoulder. You would have thought him an oddly-attired, respectable old party, who, after certain years of toil as operative, artisan, or the like, had retired on a competency. In that you would have been right—

but (as you might have gathered from his impassive face, his burning eyes, his rigid mouth) he was something more. Yet working in the dark as he did, mole-like, none of the people in the court that day had known him for Archer Dawe, the famous amateur detective, expert criminologist, a human ferret—none, at least, but the man at whose side he was now walking.

This man led Archer Dawe down a side street to the door of an office which formed part of the buildings of a big brewery. He unlocked the door; they entered; he locked the door behind them. Then, without a word, but pointing Archer Dawe to a seat, he went over to a cupboard, brought out whisky, soda, and glasses, and a box of cigars, and motioned the little man to help himself. They had both lighted cigars, both taken a hearty pull at their glasses before the big, bearded man spoke—vehemently.

"Dawe, it's a damned plant!"

Archer Dawe took another pull at his whisky-and-soda.

"What's your notion, Mr. Holland?" he inquired.

Mr. Holland stamped up and down his office for a few minutes. Then he fell to swinging his arms.

"It's a damned plant, Dawe!" he repeated. "And that chap Stephen Barr is in it as well as John. John's going to take the gruelling—being the younger and stronger. He'll be a model prisoner—he'll get out in some seven and a half years. Lord! What's that? And then . . ."

He fell to stamping the floor, to waving his arms again.

"You mean?" said Archer Dawe. "You mean . . ."

"I mean that they've got the money. It hasn't gone on the Stock Exchange. It's not gone on the Turf. It's not gone over the card table. They've got it. It's planted somewhere as safe as—as safe as I'm standing here, Dawe! Did you see John give Stephen that look before he left the dock? Eh?"

"I did," replied Archer Dawe.

"Now, I wonder what that meant? But—or, hang it," exclaimed Mr. Holland, "don't let's theorize—I want you to keep an eye on Stephen Barr. It's lucky that nobody knew you were in Normancaster—they would think this morning that you were some old fogey interested in the Castle and so on, who'd just dropped into the Court for an hour or so—you know, eh?"

"The matter stands thus," sad Archer Dawe, slowly. "John Barr, who for ten years has been manager of the Mid-Yorkshire Bank here in Normancaster, has been to-day convicted of the crime of embezzlement and sentenced to ten years' penal servitude. You, as a director of that bank, know that he has secured close upon a quarter million of your money; you, personally, believe that—eh?"

"I believe, as a private individual, that both of them have been in at this, that John's going to do his seven and a half years, and that in the meantime Stephen's going off to some other clime, there to prepare a comfortable place for his brother," said Mr. Holland. "Why bless me, John Barr will be only three and forty when he comes out, even if he serves his whole ten years—which he won't. And Stephen isn't anything like fifty yet. I've known them both since they were boys."

"Your plan of campaign, Mr. Holland?" said Archer Dawe.

"Well, I have one, I confess, Dawe," answered Mr. Holland. "I'm going to have it communicated to Stephen Barr by a secret channel this afternoon that applications for a warrant for his arrest is to be made to the borough magistrates first thing to-morrow morning. I want to see if that won't stir him. Now, I happen to live exactly opposite his house, and I shall have a watch kept on his movements. I want you to stay here in my private office—there, you see, is a bed-room attached to it, with all the conveniences, so that you'll be comfortable if you have to stay the night, and of course, I'll see that you have everything in the shape of food and so on. If I telephone you that Stephen Barr makes a sudden move from his house, you'll be ready to follow him—you've plenty of disguises, I suppose?"

"Oh, yes," answered Archer Dawe, with a glance at his old portmanteau. "But, Mr. Holland, do you think that Stephen Barr would set off from here like that? Wouldn't it look like—giving himself away?"

"No," replied Mr. Holland. "And for this reason—Stephen Barr always goes up to town once a week—has done so for the last two years—why, nobody knows. He has no particular day; sometimes it's Monday, sometimes Thursday, sometimes Friday. My notion is that if he's startled by the rumour about the warrant he'll go to-night. If he does I want you to go with him, and to keep an eye on him."

"Then in that case I shall hold myself in readiness an hour before the night train starts," said Archer Dawe.

"And in the meantime," said Mr. Holland, "I shall put you in charge of a confidential clerk of mine who will see that you are properly taken care of, and will be at your disposal. At half-past four tea shall be sent in, and at half-past six dinner—after that, Dawe, make your toilet, and be on the *qui vive* for the telephone. The clerk will be with you to the end—here, I'll have him in and introduce him."

If anybody had been able to look through the carefully-closed blind of Mr. Holland's office at a quarter-past seven o'clock that evening they would have seen a dapper little gentleman who from his attire might have been a judge, a doctor, or a barrister, leisurely finishing a bottle of claret in company with a younger man who was obviously lost in admiration of his elderly friend's cleverness in the art of making up.

"Well, you're a perfect marvel in that line, Mr. Dawe," said the confidential clerk. "I go in a good deal myself for amateur theatricals, but I couldn't make up as you do, sir. Now that you've got into these clothes and done your hair in a different fashion, you look another man. And it's your attention to small details, sir—that bank-stock with the old-fashioned gold pin, and the gold-rimmed spectacles instead of your ordinary ones—my word, those little touches do make a difference!"

"It's the details that do make a difference, young man," said Archer Dawe. "And no detail is too small or undignifi . . ."

A sharp tinkle of the telephone bell interrupted him. He nodded to the clerk.

"Take a message," he said. "If it's from Holland, tell me word for word what he says."

In another minute the clerk turned to him. "Mr. Holland says: 'Barr has just left his house, obviously for the station. Tell Dawe to follow him wherever he goes.'"

"Answer, 'All right,'" said Archer Dawe.

He drank off his claret as the clerk hung up the receiver again, and began to button his smartly-cut morning coat. His glanced wandered to an overcoat, a rug, a Gladstone bag, and a glossy hat which lay out in orderly fashion on a side-table.

"There's a lot of time, Mr. Dawe," said the clerk, interpreting the glance. "You see, Barr lives opposite to Mr. Holland, a good three-quarters of a mile from here. He'll walk to the station and he'll have to pass down this street—the station's just at the bottom. We can watch him pass this window—there, you can see out."

Archer Dawe nodded. With a tacit understanding he and the clerk posted themselves at the window, arranging one of the slats of the Venetian blinds so that they could see into the street beneath. There was a yellowish autumn fog there, and everything was very cold and still. No one came or went, up or down, until at last a man, cloaked to the eyes, carrying a bag in one hand, a rug in the other, hurried into the light of opposite gas-lamp, crossed it, and disappeared into the gloom again. "That's Barr!" whispered the clerk.

Archer Dawe looked at his watch.

"Eight minutes yet," he said. "Plenty of time."

The clerk helped the amateur detective on with his fashionable fur-lined overcoat, and handed him his fashionable broad-brimmed silk hat and gold-mounted umbrella.

"By George, you do look a real old swell!" he said, with an admiring chuckle. "Wish I could get myself up like that for our theatricals—it's fine."

"Good-bye," said Archer Dawe.

He slipped quietly out into the fog, and made his way, rug over arm, bag in hand, to the station, where he took a first-class ticket for King's Cross. There was no one on the platform but Stephen Barr and two or three porters moving ghostlike in the fog. The mail came steaming in and pulled up, seeming to fret at even a moment's delay; a door was opened, Stephen Barr stepped in. Archer Dawe followed; the train was off again. He was alone with his quarry.

During the four hours' run to London these two scarcely spoke, except to remark on the coldness of night. But as they were at last running into King's Cross and were putting away their travelling caps and arranging their rugs, Archer Dawe remarked pleasantly:

"It's a great convenience to have an hotel attached to these London termini—one doesn't feel inclined to drive far after a four hours' journey at this time of night and this season of the year. It's something to be able to step straight from the train into the Great Northern Hotel."

Stephen Barr nodded.

"Yes," he said, "and a very comfortable hotel it is, too. I always stay there when I come to town—it is very convenient, as you say."

"And to those of us who happen to be passing through town," said Archer Dawe, with a marked emphasis on the penultimate word, "it is much more pleasant to break the journey here than to be driven across London at midnight to another station. Old men like me, sir, begin to appreciate their little comforts."

The same porter carried Stephen Barr's bag and Archer Dawe's bag into the hotel; the clerk in the office gave Stephen Barr number 45, and Archer Dawe number 46. Stephen Barr and Archer Dawe took a little hot whisky and water together in the smoking-room before retiring, and enjoyed a little friendly conversation. Archer Dawe was perhaps a little garrulous about himself—he gave Stephen Barr to understand that he, Archer, was a famous consulting physician of Brighton, that he had been north to an important consultation, and that he had spent a few hours at Normancaster on his way back in order to look over the castle. He also mentioned incidentally that he might stay in town for a day or two, as he was anxious to see one or two experiments which were just then being carried on in some of the medical schools. Stephen Barr thought his travelling companion a very pleasant old gentleman.

In the privacy of number 46, Archer Dawe sized up Stephen Barr as a man who at that moment was brooding over some big scheme and would probably lie awake all night thinking about it. As for himself, he meant to sleep, but he had first of all some work to do, and he set to work to do it as soon as the corridor was quiet.

Had any of the hotel officials seen what it was that Archer Dawe did they would have jumped to the conclusion that a burglar was in the house. For he produced from his bag a curiously ingenious instrument with which he swiftly and noiselessly cut out of the door of his room a solid plug of wood about one-third of an inch in diameter—

cut it out cleanly, so that it could be fitted in an withdrawn at will. Withdrawn, the orifice which lit left commanded a full view of the door of 45 opposite: fitted in again, nobody could have told that it had even been cut out.

This done, Archer Dawe went to bed. But early in the morning he was up at his peep-hole, waiting there patiently until Stephen Barr emerged and made his way towards the bathroom. This was a chance on which Archer Dawe had gambled. He seized it at once. He darted across the corridor, secured the key of 45, and in a moment had secured an excellent impression of it in wax.

The specialist from Brighton, more talkative and urbane than ever, begged permission to seat himself at Stephen Barr's table when he entered the coffee-room and found that gentleman breakfasting alone. They got on very well, but Archer Dawe decided that his travelling companion of the previous evening was still deep in thought, and had spent most of the night awake. He noticed also that Stephen Barr had a poor appetite.

Going into the smoking-room an hour later, Archer Dawe found Stephen Barr in conversation with a man of apparently thirty years of age—a man who seemed to have a strong family likeness to him. They were in the quietest corner of the room, and their conversation was being carried on in whispers. Presently they left the room, and Arthur Dawe saw them go upstairs together.

After a time Archer Dawe walked out of the hotel, went across to the station, and wrote out two telegrams. The first was addressed to Robert Holland, Esq., Normancaster, and ran as follows:

I have seen him here and under observation. He is in conversation with a man of apparently thirty, medium height, light complexion, sandy hair and moustache, blue eyes, wears eye glasses, has strong resemblance to Stephen and John. Say if you know anything of this man.

The other was addressed to a certain personage at Scotland Yard:

Send Mason here in character of clergyman, to lunch with me at half-past one. Tell him to ask for Dr. Archer, and to meet me in the smoking-room.

This done, Archer Dawe, carrying his wax impression with great care, took a hansom and set off to a certain establishment which he knew of, where, before noon, a quick workman turned him out a brand-new key. Getting back to the hotel a little before one he found a telegram awaiting him. He carried it into the smoking-room and opened the envelope.

The man you describe is undoubtedly their nephew, James. He was at one time a solicitor, but was struck off the rolls three years ago, after conviction for misappropriation. Watch them both and spare no expense. Holland.

Under the very eyes of Stephen Barr and his nephew, who were again conversing in a quiet corner, Archer Dawe tore this communication into minute shreds. He affected to take no notice of the Barrs, but he saw that they had a companion with them—a man who, from his general appearance, he set down as a medical practitioner. Glancing at this person from time to time, Archer Dawe formed the conclusion that he was much of a muchness with the younger Barr—there was something furtive, and shifty, if not absolutely sinister in his face. And Archer Dawe was a past-master in the art of reading character in faces.

Whatever the conference was about between these three it broke up just before Archer Dawe was expecting Mason. The two Barrs rose, shook hands with the third man, and walked with him toward the door.

"Then I'll expect you and Dr. Hislop at seven o'clock to-night, doctor?" said Stephen, in a loud voice. "We'll dine and go to the theatre afterwards. And, by the bye, I wish you'd bring me another bottle of that medicine you gave me last time; I've had a touch again of the old complaint this morning."

"I will," replied the third man. "But if you've felt any symptom of that sort, let me advise you to keep quiet this afternoon. You'd better lie down for a while after lunch."

Stephen Barr nodded and smiled, and the stranger left, as Mason, in the correct attire of a prosperous-looking clergyman, entered the room. He and Archer Dawe greeted each other in a manner befitting their respective parts, and were soon in apparently genial and friendly conversation. The two Barrs had retired to their corner again; in the centre of the room three young gentlemen in very loud clothes were discussing in equally loud voices the merits of certain sporting guns which they had come up to town to purchase. Otherwise the room was empty.

Archer Dawe gave Mason a brief outline of the case as it had so far been revealed to him. His notion, he said, was that some plot was afoot by which Stephen Barr was to get clear away without exciting suspicion, and that that plot was to be worked there, in the hotel:

"And that's why I sent for you," he concluded. "I can't work the thing alone. I want you to find men who can keep a steady watch on every exit from this place and can be trusted to follow Stephen Barr wherever he goes, whether it's day or night. I've a strong notion that some coup is in brewing for to-night."

"That's done easily enough," answered Mason, "if we can keep a watch on him for the next two hours I'll engage that he won't move a yard without being followed. Here, I'll go round to the nearest station and telephone at once, and then come back to lunch with you."

Two hours later the pseudo-clergyman and the pseudo-doctor having lunched together and afterwards taken their ease over coffee and cigars, the former again absented himself for a while, and came back smiling.

"That's all right, Mr. Dawe," he said. "He can't move a foot out of this place without being shadowed—night or day. Make yourself easy. And now I must be off—let me know at the Yard if you want anything further, and lets hear how it goes on."

Then the two separated and Archer Dawe, knowing that his man was under the strictest surveillance, went out for a constitutional. Returning to the hotel just after six o'clock, he was met on turning out of Euston Road by a plainly-dressed man who first smiled, then winked, and as he passed him, whispered his name.

"One of Mr. Mason's men, sir," he said, as Archer Dawe came to a standstill. "The man has been out this afternoon. He and the younger man drove first to an office in Bedford Row, stayed there a quarter of an hour, and then drove to the Bank of Argentina. They were there half an hour; then came back here. They're safe inside, sir. We're keeping a strict watch—there's plenty of us on the job."

Archer Dawe had a table all to himself that night at dinner. Mr. Stephen Barr's party occupied one close by. There were five of them—Stephen himself, his nephew, the man Archer Dawe had seen them with that morning, another man whom he conjectured to be the Dr. Hislop he had heard mentioned, and a lady of apparently thirty, whom he soon put down as the nephew's wife. There was a good deal of laughing and talking amongst the party, and Stephen Barr himself seemed to be its life and soul.

Dinner was nearly over, and Archer Dawe, straining his ears for all they were worth, and using his eyes when he dared, had neither seen nor heard anything that gave him assistance. But there was suddenly a slight commotion at the next table. Looking round, he saw that Stephen Barr had fallen back in his chair, and was pressing one hand over the region of his heart—the other was crushing his eyes and forehead, whereon a frown of deep pain had gathered. A groan was slowly forced from his lips.

The men at Stephen Barr's table sprang to their feet. One of them beckoned to a waiter. Ere the rest of the people in the room had grasped the situation, the three men and the waiter were carrying Stephen Barr away. The lady, obviously much distressed, followed in their wake.

Archer Dawe beckoned to the head-waiter, who was standing near.

"I'm afraid that gentleman's very ill," he said.

"Yes, sir. I've him like that before, sir. It's his heart, sir. Well-known customer here, sir. Those two medical gentlemen have attended him here before, sir, often— Dr. Hislop and Dr. Brownson. Very weak heart, I should say, sir. Carry him off some day—sudden."

Archer Dawe finished his supper hurriedly and slipped upstairs to his own room, slipped into it unobserved by anyone. And once inside, he drew out the plug from the hole in the door, and settled himself for what might be a long and wearying vigil.

During the next hour Archer Dawe saw many strange things. A few minutes after he had posted himself with his eye to the peep-hole which his foresight had devised, the man whom he now knew as Dr. Brownson came hurriedly out of 45, and sped away along the corridor. Archer Dawe heard the key turned upon him as he left the room. This was exactly at 8:20.

At 8:40, this man came just as hurriedly back. He was accompanied by a tall, middle-aged woman in the garb of a district nurse, and he carried a small black bag in his hand. He tapped twice at the door of 45, and he and the woman were instantly admitted. Once more Archer Dawe heard the key turned in the lock.

At 8:48 the door was opened again. Three people came out. One of them was the man who, from what the waiter had said, was Dr. Hislop; the other was James Barr; the third was the lady who had made the fifth at Stephen Barr's dinner-table. She leaned on James Barr's arm and held a handkerchief to her eyes. And again the door was locked as soon as those leaving the room had crossed the threshold.

Archer Dawe slipped out of his room as soon as he thought these people would be clear of the corridor and the stairs. He reached the hall in time to see the two men assisting the lady into a four-wheeled cab. She still held the handkerchief to her eyes and seemed to be in great grief. When the cab had driven away the two men stepped back into the hotel and went to the manager's office. There they remained for some minutes. Coming out at length, they went upstairs again.

Archer Dawe strolled out of the door, making pretence of examining the weather. Turning in again he was met by the under-manager, who smiled in an apologetic manner.

"I believe sir," he said, in a low voice, "you are the gentleman in 46."

"I am," replied Archer Dawe.

"Well, sir, of course it is necessary to keep these sad affairs very quiet in an hotel, as you are aware. The poor gentleman in 45, the room opposite yours, is dead."

"Dead?"

"Yes, sir—he died twenty minutes ago. Heart failure. You are, I believe, a medical man, sir. Yes, then you will understand. He had his own two doctors with him at the time—nothing could be done. He has had these attacks here before. I was wondering if you would like to be transferred to another room, sir."

"No, I don't know that I should—I am not squeamish about these things," replied Archer Dawe.

"Well, sir, I thought it best to mention it to you. Certainly the—the body will not be in the house all night. As the doctors were well acquainted with the deceased gentelman's complaint they will be able to certify, so there will be no need for an inquest. A—a coffin is coming at half-past ten, sir, and they are going to remove the body to Normancaster, where the dead gentleman lived, by the night mail. These two gentlemen are going to make arrangements now, sir, I believe."

Archer Dawe turned and saw James Barr and Dr. Hislop descending the staircase. They passed him and the under-manager, went down the steps of the front entrance, and separated, Barr crossing over to the Station, and Hislop entering a hansom cab.

"No, you need not change my room, thank you," said Archer Dawe to the under-manager, and left him. "I do not mind at all."

He dawdled about the smoking-room for a while, then went upstairs again. And once more he applied himself to the hole in the door. At 9:10 the nurse came out, followed by the man whom he knew as Dr. Brownson. Brownson locked the door and put the key in his pocket. He and the nurse went along the corridor whispering. Archer Dawe cautiously opened his door and tip-toed after them until he saw them descend the stairs. Then he turned back. Now was his chance! The two women were gone; the three men were gone. There could be nothing in 45 but—what?

In another instant he had whipped out the key which he had caused to be made that morning, had slipped it into the lock of the door behind which so much mystery seemed to be concealed, and had entered the room. His hand sought and found the electric light, and as it flashed out he took one swift glance around him.

The room was empty. Empty! There was neither dead man nor living man in it. Everything was in order. Two large travelling trunks stood side by side against the wall; a large Gladstone bag, strapped, stood near them; a smaller one, which Arthur Dawe recognized as that which Stephen Barr had taken with him the night before, stood, similarly strapped, on the stand at the foot of the bed. But on the bed itself there was no stark figure. The room was empty of dead man or living man.

Archer Dawe saw all these things in a moment. He turned out the light, re-locked the door, and went downstairs into the smoking-room, where he lighted a cigar and sipped a whiskey-and-soda. On the other side of the room Dr. Brownson was similarly employed. As Archer Dawe looked at him, he thought of Holland's words of the previous afternoon. "Dawe, it's a damned plant!"

But where could Stephen Barr be? How had he slipped out of the hotel unobserved? Well, anyway, unless he had very skilfully disguised himself, Mason's men would follow him. He must wait for news. At ten minutes past ten James Barr came back and joined Brownson; at twenty minutes past Archer Dawe, having somewhat ostentatiously betrayed symptoms of sleepiness and weariness, betook himself upstairs. And once more he glued his eye to the little peep-hole which his ingenious centre-bit had made the night before.

A few minutes later James Barr and Brownson came upstairs and entered 45. Five more minutes went by, and then the watcher heard the tread of several men's feet sounding on the corridor in the opposite direction. Then Hislop came into view—followed by four men carrying an oak coffin. Two other men came behind.

And now Archer Dawe noted a significant circumstance. When Hislop tapped at the door and James Barr opened it, these two and Brownson took the coffin from the men and carried it within the room. Then the door was locked. Five, ten, fifteen, twenty, twenty-five minutes went by—the door was opened. The six men entered the room—came out again, carrying the coffin. They went away with it by the way they had come, Hislop following them. Then James Barr and Brownson came out of the room, locked the door, and went downstairs. When Archer Dawe, following them, reached the hall, they were crossing from the hotel to the station.

At that moment a hansom, the horse of which had obviously been urged to its full extent, dashed up to the entrance. Mason sprang out and ran up the steps. He saw Archer Dawe—seized him.

"Dawe!" he exclaimed. "We got him—got him at Victoria! He was off for the Continent, and then for the Argentine. We got him to the Yard, and by George! he's given us the slip after all—for ever! He must have had something concealed in hollow tooth—he's poisoned himself!"

"Dead!" exclaimed Archer Dawe.

"As a door-nail!" said Mason. "But—we found two hundred thousand pounds worth of securities on him. And . . ."

Archer Dawe dragged him out of the hotel and across to the station.

"Quick, man, quick!" he cried. "The coffin—the coffin—and the other three men. We must have them. Get half-a-dozen police—quick!"

When they had dispatched James Barr, Dr. Brownson and Dr. Hislop, to the nearest police-station in charge of certain stalwart constables, Archer Dawe, Mason and some inquisitive and wondering railway officials broke open the coffin in which, according to the plate upon it, the remains of Stephen Barr were supposed to rest. There was a moment of suspense when the lid was removed . . .

Lead ingots, carefully and skilfully packed tight in cotton-wool.

SIR GILBERT MURRELL'S PICTURE

Victor L. Whitechurch

THE AFFAIR OF THE GOODS TRUCK ON THE DIDCOT AND NEWBURY BRANCH of the Great Western Railway was of singular interest, and found a prominent place in Thorpe Hazell's notebook. It was owing partly to chance, and partly to Hazell's sagacity, that the main incidents in the story were discovered, but he always declared that the chief interest to his mind was the unique method by which a very daring plan was carried out.

He was staying with a friend at Newbury at the time, and had taken his camera down with him, for he was a bit of an amateur photographer as well as book-lover, though his photos generally consisted of trains and engines. He had just come in from a morning's ramble with his camera slung over his shoulder, and was preparing to partake of two plasmon biscuits, when his friend met him in the hail.

"I say, Hazell," he began, "you're just the fellow they want here."

"What's up?" asked Hazell, taking off his camera and commencing some "exercises."

"I've just been down to the station. I know the station-master very well, and he tells me an awfully queer thing happened on the line last night."

"Where?"

"On the Didcot branch. It's a single line, you know, running through the Berkshire Downs to Didcot."

Hazell smiled, and went on whirling his arms round his head.

"Kind of you to give me the information," he said, "but I happen to know the line. But what's occurred?"

"Well, it appears a goods train left Didcot last night bound through to Winchester, and that one of the waggons never arrived here at Newbury."

"Not very much in that," replied Hazell, still at his "exercises," "unless the waggon in question was behind the brake and the couplings snapped, in which case the next train along might have run into it."

"Oh, no. The waggon was in the middle of the train."

"Probably left in a siding by mistake," replied Hazell.

"But the station-master says that all the stations along the line have been wired to, and that it isn't at any of them."

"Very likely it never left Didcot."

"He declares there is no doubt about that."

"Well, you begin to interest me," replied Hazell, stopping his whirligigs and beginning to eat his plasmon. "There may be something in it, though very often a waggon is mislaid. But I'll go down to the station."

"I'll go with you, Hazell, and introduce you to the stationmaster. He has heard of your reputation."

Ten minutes later they were in the station-master's office, Hazell having re-slung his camera.

"Very glad to meet you," said that functionary, "for this affair promises to be mysterious. *I* can't make it out at all."

"Do you know what the truck contained?"

"That's just where the bother comes in, sir. It was valuable property. There's a loan exhibition of pictures at Winchester next week, and this waggon was bringing down some of them from Leamington. They belong to Sir Gilbert Murrell—three of them, I believe—large pictures, and each in a separate packing-case."

"H'm—this sounds very funny. Are you sure the truck was on the train?"

"Simpson, the brakesman, is here now, and I'll send for him. Then you can hear the story in his own words."

So the goods guard appeared on the scene. Hazell looked at him narrowly, but there was nothing suspicious in his honest face.

"I know the waggon was on the train when we left Didcot," he said in answer to inquiries, "and I noticed it at Upton, the next station, where we took a couple off. It was the fifth or sixth in front of my brake. I'm quite certain of that. We stopped at Compton to take up a cattle truck, but I didn't get out there. Then we ran right through to Newbury, without stopping at the other stations, and then I discovered that the waggon was not on the train. I thought very likely it might have been left at Upton or Compton by mistake, but I was wrong, for they say it isn't there. That's all I know about it, sir. A rum go, ain't it?"

"Extraordinary!" exclaimed Hazell. "You must have made a mistake."

"No, sir, I'm sure I haven't."

"Did the driver of the train notice anything?"

"No, sir."

"Well, but the thing's impossible," said Hazell. "A loaded waggon couldn't have been spirited away. What time was it when you left Didcot?"

"About eight o'clock, sir."

"Ah—quite dark. You noticed nothing along the line?"

"Nothing, sir."

"You were in your brake all the time, I suppose?"

"Yes, sir—while we were running."

At this moment there came a knock at the station-master's door and a porter entered.

"There's a passenger train just in from the Didcot branch," said the man, "and the driver reports that he saw a truck loaded with packing-cases in Churn siding."

"Well, I'm blowed!" exclaimed the brakesman. "Why, we ran through Churn without a stop—trains never do stop there except in camp time."

"Where is Churn?" asked Hazell, for once at a loss.

"It's merely a platform and a siding close to the camping ground between Upton and Compton," replied the station-master, "for the convenience of troops only, and very rarely used except in the summer, when soldiers are encamped there."[1]

"I should very much like to see the place, and as soon as possible," said Hazell.

"So you shall," replied the station-master. "A train will soon start on the branch. Inspector Hill shall go with you, and instruction shall be given to the driver to stop there, while a return train can pick you both up."

In less than an hour Hazell and Inspector Hill alighted at Churn. It is a lonely enough place, situated in a vast flat basin of the Downs, scarcely relieved by a single tree, and far from all human habitation with the exception of a lonely shepherd's cottage some half a mile away.

The "station" itself is only a single platform, with a shelter and a solitary siding, terminating in what is known in railway language as a "dead end"—that is, in this case, wooden buffers to stop any trucks. This siding runs off from the single line of rail at points from the Didcot direction of the line.

And in this siding was the lost truck, right against the "dead end," filled with three packing-cases, and labeled "Leamington to Winchester, via Newbury." There could be no doubt about it at all. But how it had got there from the middle of a train running through without a stop was a mystery even to the acute mind of Thorpe Hazell.

"Well," said the inspector when they had gazed long enough at the truck; "we'd better have a look at the points. Come along."

There is not even a signal-box at this primitive station. The points are actuated by two levers in a ground frame, standing close by the side of the line, one lever unlocking and the other shifting the same points.

"How about these points?" said Hazell as they drew near. "You only use them so occasionally, that I suppose they are kept out of action?"

---

1. The incident here recorded occurred before June, 1905, in which month Churn was dignified with a place in Bradshaw as a "station" at which trains stop by signal.—V. L. W.

"Certainly," replied the inspector, "a block of wood is bolted down between the end of the point rail and the main rail, fixed as a wedge—ah! there it is, you see, quite untouched; and the levers themselves are locked—here's the keyhole in the ground frame. This is the strangest thing I've ever come across, Mr. Hazell."

Thorpe Hazell stood looking at the points and levers sorely puzzled. They must have been worked to get that truck in the siding, he knew well. But how?

Suddenly his face lit up. Oil evidently had been used to loosen the nut of the bolt that fixed the wedge of wood. Then his eyes fell on the handle of one of the two levers, and a slight exclamation of joy escaped him.

"Look," said the inspector at that moment, "it's impossible to pull them off," and he stretched out his hand towards a lever. To his astonishment Hazell seized him by the collar and dragged him back before he could touch it.

"I beg your pardon," he exclaimed, "hope I've not hurt you, but I want to photograph those levers first, if you don't mind."

The inspector watched him rather sullenly as he fixed his camera on a folding tripod stand he had with him, only a few inches from the handle of one of the levers, and took two very careful photographs of it.

"Can't see the use of that, sir," growled the inspector. But Hazell vouchsafed no reply.

"Let him find it out for himself," he thought.

Then he said aloud:

"I fancy they must have had that block out, inspector—and it's evident the points must have been set to get the truck where it is. How it was done is a problem, but if the doer of it was anything of a regular criminal, I think we might find *him*."

"How?" asked the puzzled inspector.

"Ah," was the response, "I'd rather not say at present. Now, I should very much like to know whether those pictures are intact?"

"We shall soon find that out," replied the inspector, "for we'll take the truck back with us." And he commenced undoing the bolt with a spanner, after which he unlocked the levers.

"H'm—they work pretty freely," he remarked as he pulled one.

"Quite so," said Hazell, "they've been oiled recently."

There was an hour or so before the return train would pass, and Hazell occupied it by walking to the shepherd's cottage.

"I am hungry," he explained to the woman there, "and hunger is Nature's dictate for food. Can you oblige me with a couple of onions and a broomstick?"

And she talks to-day of the strange man who "kept a swingin' o' that there broomstick round 'is 'ead and then eat them onions as solemn as a judge."

The first thing Hazell did on returning to Newbury was to develop his photographs. The plates were dry enough by the evening for him to print one or two photos on gaslight-paper and to enclose the clearest of them with a letter to a Scotland Yard official whom he knew, stating that he would call for an answer, as he intended returning to town in a couple of days. The following evening he received a note from the station-master, which read—

DEAR SIR,

I promised to let you know if the pictures in the cases on that truck were in any way tampered with. I have just received a report from Winchester by which I understand that they have been unpacked and carefully examined by the Committee of the Loan Exhibition. The Committee are perfectly satisfied that they have not been damaged or interfered with in any way, and that they have been received just as they left the owner's hands.

We are still at a loss to account for the running of the waggon on to Churn siding or for the object in doing so. An official has been down from Paddington, and, at his request, we are not making the affair public—the goods having arrived in safety. I am sure you will observe confidence in this matter.

"More mysterious than ever," said Hazell to himself. "I can't understand it at all." The next day he called at Scotland Yard and saw the official.

"I've had no difficulty with your little matter, you'll be glad to hear," he said. "We looked up our records and very soon spotted your man."

"Who is he?"

"His real name is Edgar Jeffreys, but we know him under several aliases. He's served four sentences for burglary and robbery—the latter, a daring theft from a train, so he's in your line, Mr. Hazell. What's he been up to, and how did you get that print?"

"Well," replied Hazell, "I don't quite know yet what he's been doing. But I should like to be able to find him if anything turns up. Never mind how I got the print—the affair is quite a private one at present, and nothing may come of it."

The official wrote an address on a bit of paper and handed it to Hazell.

"He's living there just now, under the name of Allen. We keep such men in sight, and I'll let you know if he moves."

When Hazell opened his paper the following morning he gave a cry of joy. And no wonder, for this is what he saw:

MYSTERY OF A PICTURE.

SIR GILBERT MURRELL AND THE WINCHESTER LOAN EXHIBITION.

AN EXTRAORDINARY CHARGE.

The Committee of the Loan Exhibition of Pictures to be opened next week at Winchester are in a state of very natural excitement brought about by a strange charge that has been made against them by Sir Gilbert Murrell.

Sir Gilbert, who lives at Leamington, is the owner of several very valuable pictures, among them being the celebrated "Holy Family," by Velasquez. This picture, with two others, was dispatched by him from Leamington to be exhibited at Winchester, and yesterday he journeyed to that city in order to make himself satisfied with the hanging arrangements, as he had particularly stipulated that "The Holy Family" was to be placed in a prominent position.

The picture in question was standing on the floor of the gallery, leaning against a pillar, when Sir Gilbert arrived with some representatives of the Committee.

Nothing occurred till he happened to walk behind the canvas, when he astounded those present by saying that the picture was not his at all, declaring that a copy had been substituted, and stating that he was absolutely certain on account of certain private marks of his at the back of the canvas which were quite indecipherable, and which were now missing. He admitted that the painting itself in every way resembled his picture, and that it was the cleverest forgery he had ever seen; but a very painful scene took place, the hanging committee stating that the picture had been received by them from the railway company just as it stood.

At present the whole affair is a mystery, but Sir Gilbert insisted most emphatically to our correspondent, who was able to see him, that the picture was certainly not his, and said that as the original is extremely valuable he intends holding the Committee responsible for the substitution which, he declares, has taken place.

It was evident to Hazell that the papers had not, as yet, got hold of the mysterious incident at Churn. As a matter of fact, the railway company had kept that affair strictly to themselves, and the loan committee knew nothing of what had happened on the line.

But Hazell saw that inquiries would be made, and determined to probe the mystery without delay. He saw at once that if there was any truth in Sir Gilbert's story the substitution had taken place in that lonely siding at Churn. He was staying at his London flat, and five minutes after he had read the paragraph had called a hansom and was being hurried off to a friend of his who was well known in art circles as a critic and art historian.

"I can tell you exactly what you want to know," said he, "for I've only just been looking it up, so as to have an article in the evening papers on it. There was a famous copy of the picture of Velasquez, said to have been painted by a pupil of his, and for some years there was quite a controversy among the respective owners as to which was the genuine one—just as there is to-day about a Madonna belonging to a gentleman at St. Moritz, but which a Vienna gallery also claims to possess.

"However, in the case of 'The Holy Family,' the dispute was ultimately settled once and for all years ago, and undoubtedly Sir Gilbert Murrell held the genuine picture. What became of the copy no one knows. For twenty years all trace of it has been lost. There—that's all I can tell you. I shall pad it out a bit in my article, and I must get to work on it at once. Good-bye!"

"One moment—where was the copy last seen?"

"Oh! the old Earl of Ringmere had it last, but when he knew it to be a forgery he is said to have sold it for a mere song, all interest in it being lost, you see."

"Let me see, he's a very old man, isn't he?"

"Yes—nearly eighty—a perfect enthusiast on pictures still, though."

"Only *said* to have sold it," muttered Hazell to himself, as he left the house; "that's very vague—and there's no knowing what these enthusiasts will do when they're really bent on a thing. Sometimes they lose all sense of honesty. I've known fellows actually rob a friend's collection of stamps or butterflies. What if there's something in it? By George, what an awful scandal there would be! It seems to me that if such a scandal were prevented I'd be thanked all round. Anyhow, I'll have a shot at it on spec. And I must find out how that truck was run off the line."

When once Hazell was on the track of a railway mystery he never let a moment slip by. In an hour's time, he was at the address given him at Scotland Yard. On his way there he took a card from his case, a blank one, and wrote on it, "From the Earl of Ringmere." This he put into an envelope.

"It's a bold stroke," he said to himself, "but, if there's anything in it, it's worth trying."

So he asked for Allen. The woman who opened the door looked at him suspiciously, and said she didn't think Mr. Allen was in.

"Give him this envelope," replied Hazell. In a couple of minutes she returned, and asked him to follow her.

A short, wiry-looking man, with sharp, evil-looking eyes, stood in the room waiting for him and looking at him suspiciously.

"Well," he snapped, "what is it—what do you want?"

"I come on behalf of the Earl of Ringmere. You will know that when I mention Churn," replied Hazell, playing his trump card boldly.

"Well," went on the man, "what about that?"

Hazell wheeled round, locked the door suddenly, put the key in his pocket, and then faced his man. The latter darted forward, but Hazell had a revolver pointing at him in a twinkling.

"You—detective!"

"No, I'm not—I told you I came on behalf of the Earl—that looks like hunting up matters for his sake, doesn't it?"

"What does the old fool mean?" asked Jeffreys.

"Oh! I see you know all about it. Now listen to me quietly, and you may come to a little reason. You changed that picture at Churn the other night."

"You seem to know a lot about it," sneered the other, but less defiantly.

"Well, I do—but not quite all. You were foolish to leave your traces on that lever, eh?"

"How did I do that?" exclaimed the man, giving himself away.

"You'd been dabbling about with oil, you see, and you left your thumb-print on the handle. I photographed it, and they recognised it at Scotland Yard. Quite simple."

Jeffreys swore beneath his breath.

"I wish you'd tell me what you mean," he said.

"Certainly. I expect you've been well paid for this little job."

"If I have, I'm not going to take any risks. I told the old man so. He's worse than I am—he put me up to getting the picture. Let him take his chance when it comes out—I suppose he wants to keep his name out of it, that's why you're here."

"You're not quite right. Now just listen to me. You're a villain, and you deserve to suffer; but I'm acting in a purely private capacity, and I fancy if I can get the original picture back to its owner that it will be better for all parties to hush this affair up. Has the old Earl got it?"

"No, not yet," admitted the other, "he was too artful. But he knows where it is, and so do I."

"Ah—now you're talking sense! Look here! You make a clean breast of it, and I'll take it down on paper. You shall swear to the truth of your statement before a commissioner for oaths—he need not see the actual confession. I shall hold this in case it is necessary; but if you help me to get the picture back to Sir Gilbert, I don't think it will be."

After a little more conversation, Jeffreys explained. Before he did so, however, Hazell had taken a bottle of milk and a hunch of wholemeal bread from his pocket, and calmly proceeded to perform "exercises" and then to eat his "lunch," while Jeffreys told the following story:

"It was the old Earl who did it. How he got hold of me doesn't matter—perhaps I got hold of him—maybe I put him up to it—but that's not the question. He'd kept that forged picture of his in a lumber room for years, but he always had his eye on the genuine one. He paid a long price for the forgery, and he got to think that he ought to have the original. But there, he's mad on pictures.

"Well, as I say, he kept the forgery out of sight and let folks think he'd sold it, but all the time he was in hopes of getting it changed somehow for the original.

"Then I came along and undertook the job for him. There were three of us in it, for it was a ticklish business. We found out by what train the picture was to travel—that was easy enough. I got hold of a key to unlock that ground frame, and the screwing off of the bolt was a mere nothing. I oiled the points well, so that the thing should work as I wanted it to.

"One pal was with me—in the siding, ready to clap on the side brake when the truck was running in. I was to work the points, and my other pal, who had the most awkward job of all, was on the goods train—under a tarpaulin in a truck. He had two lengths of very stout rope with a hook at each end of them.

"When the train left Upton, he started his job. Goods trains travel very slowly, and there was plenty of time. Counting from the back brake van, the truck we wanted to run off was No. 5. First he hooked No. 4 truck to No. 6—fixing the hook at the side of the end of both trucks, and having the slack in his hand, coiled up.

"Then when the train ran down a bit of a decline he uncoupled No. 5 from No. 4—standing on No. 5 to do it. That was easy enough, for he'd taken a coupling staff with him; then he paid out the slack till it was tight. Next he hooked his second rope from No. 5 to No. 6, uncoupled No. 5 from No. 6, and paid out the slack of the second rope.

"Now you can see what happened. The last few trucks of the train were being drawn by a long rope reaching from No. 4 to No. 6, and leaving a space in between. In the middle of this space No. 5 ran, drawn by a short rope from No. 6. My pal stood on No. 6, with a sharp knife in his hand.

"The rest was easy. I held the lever, close by the side of the line—coming forward to it as soon as the engine passed. The instant the space appeared after No. 6 I pulled it over, and No. 5 took the siding points, while my pal cut the rope at the same moment.

"Directly the truck had run by and off I reversed the lever so that the rest of the train following took the main line. There is a decline before Compton, and the last four trucks came running down to the main body of the train, while my pal hauled in the slack and finally coupled No. 4 to No. 6 when they came together. He jumped from the train as it ran very slowly into Compton. That's how it was done."

Hazell's eyes sparkled.

"It's the cleverest thing I've heard of on the line," he said.

"Think so? Well, it wanted some handling. The next thing was to unscrew the packing-case, take the picture out of the frame, and put the forgery we'd brought with us in its place. That took us some time, but there was no fear of interruption in that lonely part. Then I took the picture off, rolling it up first, and hid it. The old Earl insisted on this. I was to tell him where it was, and he was going to wait for a few weeks and then get it himself."

"Where did you hide it?"

"You're sure you're going to hush this up?"

"You'd have been in charge long ago if I were not."

"Well, there's a path from Churn to East Ilsley across the downs, and on the right-hand of that path is an old sheep well—quite dry. It's down there. You can easily find the string if you look for it—fixed near the top."

Hazell took down the man's confession, which was duly attested. His conscience told him that perhaps he ought to have taken stronger measures.

"I told you I was merely a private individual," said Hazell to Sir Gilbert Murrell. "I have acted in a purely private capacity in bringing you your picture."

Sir Gilbert looked from the canvas to the calm face of Hazell.

"Who are you, sir?" he asked.

"Well, I rather aspire to be a book-collector; you may have read my little monogram on 'Jacobean Bindings?' "

"No," said Sir Gilbert, "I have not had that pleasure. But I must inquire further into this. How did you get this picture? Where was it—who—"

"Sir Gilbert," broke in Hazell, "I could tell you the whole truth, of course. I am not in any way to blame myself. By chance, as much as anything else, I discovered how your picture had been stolen, and where it was."

"But I want to know all about it. I shall prosecute—I—"

"I think not. Now, do you remember where the forged picture was seen last?"

"Yes; the Earl of Ringmere had it—he sold it."

"Did he?"

"Eh?"

"What if he kept it all this time?" said Hazell, with a peculiar look.

There was a long silence.

"Good heavens!" exclaimed Sir Gilbert at length. "You don't mean *that*. Why, he has one foot in the grave—a very old man—I was dining with him only a fortnight ago."

"Ah! Well, I think you are content now, Sir Gilbert?"

"It is terrible—terrible! I have the picture back, but I wouldn't have the scandal known for worlds."

"It never need be," replied Hazell. "You will make it all right with the Winchester people?"

"Yes—yes—even if I have to admit I was mistaken, and let the forgery stay through the exhibition."

"I think that would be the best way," replied Hazell, who never regretted his action.

"Of course, Jeffreys ought to have been punished," he said to himself; "but it was a clever idea—a clever idea!"

"May I offer you some lunch?" asked Sir Gilbert.

"Thank you; but I am a vegetarian, and—"

"I think my cook could arrange something—let me ring."

"It is very good of you, but I ordered a dish of lentils and a salad at the station restaurant. But if you will allow me just to go through my physical training ante luncheon exercises here, it would save me the trouble of a more or less public display at the station."

"Certainly," replied the rather bewildered Baronet; whereupon Hazell threw off his coat and commenced whirling his arms like a windmill.

"Digestion should be considered *before* a meal," he explained.

THE HUNDRED THOUSAND DOLLAR ROBBERY

Hesketh Prichard

I WANT THE WHOLE AFFAIR KEPT UNOFFICIAL AND SECRET," SAID HARRIS, THE bank manager.

November Joe nodded. He was seated on the extreme edge of a chair in the manager's private office, looking curiously out of place in that prim, richly furnished room.

"The truth is," continued Harris, "we bankers cannot afford to have our customers' minds unsettled. There are, as you know, Joe, numbers of small depositors, especially in the rural districts, who would be scared out of their seven senses if they knew that this infernal Cecil James Atterson had made off with a hundred thousand dollars. They'd never trust us again."

"A hundred thousand dollars is a wonderful lot of money," agreed Joe.

"Our reserve is over twenty millions, two hundred times a hundred thousand," replied Harris grandiloquently.

Joe smiled in his pensive manner. "That so? Then I guess the bank won't be hurt if Atterson escapes," said he.

"I shall be bitterly disappointed if you permit him to do so," returned Harris. "But here, let's get down to business."

On the previous night, Harris, the manager of the Quebec Branch of the Grand Banks of Canada, had rung me up to borrow November Joe, who was at the time building a log camp for me on one of my properties. I sent Joe a telegram, with the result that within five hours of its receipt he had walked the twenty miles into Quebec, and was now with me at the bank ready to hear Harris's account of the robbery.

The manager cleared his throat and began with a question:—

"Have you ever seen Atterson?"

"No."

"I thought you might have. He always spends his vacations in the woods— fishing, usually. The last two years he has fished Red River. This is what happened. On Saturday I told him to go down to the strong-room to fetch up a fresh batch of dollar and five-dollar bills, as we were short. It happened that in the same safe there was a number of bearer securities. Atterson soon brought me the notes I had sent him for with the keys. That was about noon on Saturday. We closed at one o'clock. Yesterday,

Monday, Atterson did not turn up. At first I thought nothing of it, but when it came to afternoon, and he had neither appeared nor sent any reason for his absence, I began to smell a rat. I went down to the strong-room and found that over one hundred thousand dollars in notes and bearer securities were missing.

"I communicated at once with the police and they started to make inquiries. I must tell you that Atterson lived in a boarding-house behind the Frontenac. No one had seen him on Sunday, but on Saturday night a fellow-boarder, called Collings, reports Atterson as going to his room about 10:30. He was the last person who saw him. Atterson spoke to him and said he was off to spend Sunday on the south shore. From that moment Atterson has vanished."

"Didn't the police find out anything further?" inquired Joe.

"Well, we couldn't trace him at any of the railway stations."

"I s'pose they wired to every other police-station within a hundred miles?"

"They did, and that is what brought you into it."

"Why?"

"The constable at Roberville replied that a man answering to the description of Atterson was seen by a farmer walking along the Stoneham road, and heading north, on Sunday morning, early."

"No more facts?"

"No."

"Then let's get back to the robbery. Why are you so plumb sure Atterson done it?"

"The notes and securities were there on Saturday morning."

"How do you know?"

"It's my business to know. I saw them myself."

"Huh! . . . And no one else went down to the strong-room?"

"Only Atterson. The second clerk—it is a rule that no employee may visit the strong-room alone—remained at the head of the stairs, while Atterson descended."

"Who keeps the key?"

"I do."

"And it was never out of your possession?"

"Never."

November was silent for a few moments. "How long has Atterson been with the bank?

"Two years odd."

"Anything ag'in' him before?"

"Nothing."

At this point a clerk knocked at the door and, entering, brought in some letters. Harris stiffened as he noticed the writing on one of them. He cut it open and, when the clerk was gone out, he read aloud:—

DEAR HARRIS,—

   I hereby resign my splendid and lucrative position in the Grand Banks of Canada. It is a dog's dirty life; anyway it is so for a man of spirit. You can give the week's screw that's owing to me to buy milk and bath buns for the next meeting of directors.

Yours truly,
C. J. ATTERSON

"What's the postmark?" asked Joe.

"Rimouski. Sunday, 9:30 a.m."

"It looks like Atterson's the thief," remarked Joe.

"I've always been sure of it!" cried Harris.

"I wasn't," said Joe.

"Are you sure of it now?"

"I'm inclined that way because Atterson had that letter posted by a con—con—what's the word?"

"Confederate?"

"You've got it. He was seen here in town on Saturday at 10:30, and he couldn't have posted no letter in Rimouski in time for the 9:30 a.m. on Sunday unless he'd gone there on the 7 o'clock express on Saturday evening. Yes, Atterson's the thief, all right. And if that really was he they saw Stoneham ways, he's had time to get thirty miles of bush between us and him, and he can go right on till he's on the Labrador. I doubt you'll see your hundred thousand dollars again, Mr. Harris."

"Bah! You can trail him easily enough?"

Joe shook his head. "If you was to put me on his tracks I could," said he, "but up there in the Laurentides he'll sure pinch a canoe and make along a waterway."

"H'm!" coughed Harris. "My directors won't want to pay you two dollars a day for nothing."

"Two dollars a day?" said Joe in his gentle voice. "I shouldn't 'a' thought the two hundred times a hundred thousand dollars could stand a *strain* like that!"

I laughed. "Look here, November, I think I'd like to make this bargain for you."

"Yes, sure," said the young woodsman.

"Then I'll sell your services to Mr. Harris here for five dollars a day if you fail, and ten per cent of the sum you recover if you succeed."

Joe looked at me with wide eyes, but he said nothing.

"Well, Harris, is it on or off?" I asked.

"Oh, on, I suppose, confound you!" said Harris.

November looked at both of us with a broad smile.

Twenty hours later, Joe, a police trooper named Hobson, and I were deep in the woods. We had hardly paused to interview the farmer at Roberville, and then had passed on down the old deserted roads until at last we entered the forest, or, as it is locally called, the "bush."

"Where are you heading for?" Hobson had asked Joe.

"Red River, because if it really was Atterson the farmer saw, I guess he'll have gone up there."

"Why do you think that?"

"Red River's the overflow of Snow Lake, and there is several trappers has canoes on Snow Lake. There's none of them trappers there now in July month, so he can steal a canoe easy. Besides, a man who fears pursuit always likes to get into a country he knows, and you heard Mr. Harris say how Atterson had fished Red River two vacations. Besides"—here Joe stopped and pointed to the ground—"them's Atterson's tracks," he said. "Leastways, it's a black fox to a lynx pelt they are his."

"But you've never seen him. What reason have you . . . ?" demanded Hobson.

"When first we happened on them about four hours back, while you was lightin' your pipe," replied Joe, "they come out of the bush, and when we reached near Carrier's place they went back into the bush again. Then a mile beyond Carrier's out of the bush they come on to the road again. What can that circumventin' mean? Feller who made the tracks don't want to be seen. Number 8 boots, city-made, nails in 'em, rubber heels. Come on."

I will not attempt to describe our journey hour by hour, nor tell how November held to the trail, following it over areas of hard ground and rock, noticing a scratch here and a broken twig there. The trooper, Hobson, proved to be a good track-reader, but he thought himself a better, and, it seemed to me, was a little jealous of Joe's obvious superiority.

We slept that night beside the trail. According to November, the thief was now not many hours ahead of us. Everything depended upon whether he could reach Red River and a canoe before we caught up with him. Still it was not possible to follow a trail in the darkness, so perforce we camped. The next morning November wakened us at daylight and once more we hastened forward.

For some time we followed Atterson's footsteps and then found that they left the road. The police officer went crashing along till Joe stopped him with a gesture.

"Listen!" he whispered.

We moved on quietly and saw that, not fifty yards ahead of us, a man was walking excitedly up and down. His face was quite clear in the slanting sunlight, a resolute face with a small, dark mustache, and a two-days' growth of beard. His head was sunk upon his chest in an attitude of the utmost despair, he waved his hands, and on the still air there came to us the sound of his monotonous muttering.

We crept upon him. As we did so, Hobson leapt forward and, snapping his handcuffs on the man's wrists, cried:—

"Cecil Atterson, I've got you!"

Atterson sprang like a man on a wire, his face went dead white. He stood quite still for a moment as if dazed, then he said in a strangled voice:—

"Got me, have you? Much good may it do you!"

"Hand over that packet you're carrying," answered Hobson.

There was another pause.

"By the way, I'd like to hear exactly what I'm charged with," said Atterson.

"Like to hear!" said Hobson. "You know! Theft of one hundred thousand dollars from the Grand Banks. May as well hand them over and put me to no more trouble!"

"You can take all the trouble you like," said the prisoner.

Hobson plunged his hand into Atterson's pockets, and searched him thoroughly, but found nothing.

"They are not on him," he cried. "Try his pack."

From the pack November produced a square bottle of whiskey, some bread, salt, a slab of mutton—that was all.

"Where have you hidden the stuff?" demanded Hobson.

Suddenly Atterson laughed.

"So you think I robbed the bank?" he said. "I've my own down on them, and I'm glad they've been hit by some one, though I'm not the man. Anyway, I'll have you and them for wrongful arrest with violence." Then he turned to us. "You two are witnesses."

"Do you deny you're Cecil Atterson?" said Hobson.

"No, I'm Atterson right enough."

"Then look here, Atterson, your best chance is to show us where you've hid the stuff. Your counsel can put that in your favour at your trial."

"I'm not taking any advice just now, thank you. I have said I know nothing of the robbery.'"

Hobson looked him up and down. "You'll sing another song by and by," he said ironically. "We may as well start in now, Joe, and find where he's cached that packet."

November was fingering over the pack which lay open on the ground, examining it and its contents with concentrated attention. Atterson had sunk down under a tree like a man wearied out.

Hobson and Joe made a rapid examination of the vicinity. A few yards brought them to the end of Atterson's tracks.

"Here's where he slept," said Hobson. "It's all pretty clear. He was dog-tired and just collapsed. I guess that was last night. It's an old camping-place, this." The policeman pointed to weathered beds of balsam and the scars of several camp-fires.

"Yes," he continued, "that's what it is. But the trouble is where has he cached the bank's property?"

For upwards of an hour Hobson searched every conceivable spot, but not so November Joe, who, after a couple of quick casts down to the river, made a fire, put on the kettle, and lit his pipe. Atterson, from under his tree, watched the proceedings with a drowsy lack of interest that struck me as being particularly well simulated.

At length Hobson ceased his exertions, and accepted a cup of the tea Joe had brewed.

"There's nothing cached round here," he said in a voice low enough to escape the prisoner's ear, "and his"—he indicated Atterson's recumbent form with his hand—"trail stops right where he slept. He never moved a foot beyond that nor went down to the river, one hundred yards away. I guess what he's done is clear enough."

"Huh!" said Joe. "Think so?"

"Yep! The chap's either cached them or handed them to an accomplice on the back trail."

"That's so? And what are you going to do next?"

"I'm thinking he'll confess all right when I get him alone." He stood up as November moved to take a cup of tea over to Atterson.

"No, you don't," he cried. "Prisoner Atterson neither eats nor drinks between here and Quebec unless he confesses where he has the stuff hid."

"We'd best be going now," he continued as November, shrugging, came back to the fireside. "You two walk on and let me get a word quiet with the prisoner."

"I'm staying here," said Joe.

"What for?" cried Hobson.

"I'm employed by Bank Manager Harris to recover stolen property," replied Joe.

"But," expostulated Hobson, "Atterson's trail stops right here where he slept. There are no other tracks, so no one could have visited him. Do you think he's got the bills and papers hid about here after all?"

"No," said Joe.

Hobson stared at the answer, then turned to go.

"Well," said he, "you take your way and I'll take mine. I reckon I'll get a confession out of him before we reach Quebec. He's a pretty tired man, and he don't rest nor sleep, no, nor sit down, till he's put me wise as to where he hid the stuff he stole."

"He won't ever put you wise," said Joe definitely.

"Why do you say that?"

"'Cause he can't. He don't know himself."

"Bah!" was all Hobson's answer as he turned on his heel.

November Joe did not move as Hobson, his wrist strapped to Atterson's, disappeared down the trail by which we had come.

"Well," I said, "what next?"

"I'll take another look around." Joe leapt to his feet and went quickly over the ground. I accompanied him.

"What do you make of it?" he said at last.

"Nothing," I answered. "There are no tracks nor other signs at all, except these two or three places where old logs have been lying—I expect Atterson picked them up for his fire. I don't understand what you are getting at any more than Hobson does."

"Huh!" said Joe, and led the way down to the river, which, though not more than fifty yards away, was hidden from us by the thick trees.

It was a slow-flowing river, and in the soft mud of the margin I saw, to my surprise, the quite recent traces of a canoe having been beached. Beside the canoe, there was also on the mud the faint mark of a paddle having lain at full length.

Joe pointed to it. The paddle had evidently, I thought, fallen from the canoe, for the impression it had left on the soft surface was very slight.

"How long ago was the canoe here?"

"At first light—maybe between three and four o'clock," replied Joe.

"Then I don't see how it helps you at all. Its coming can't have anything to do with the Atterson robbery, for the distance from here to the camp is too far to throw a packet, and the absence of tracks makes it clear that Atterson cannot have handed the loot over to a confederate in the canoe. Isn't that right?"

"Looks that way," admitted Joe.

"Then the canoe can be only a coincidence."

November shook his head. "I wouldn't go quite so far as to say that, Mr. Quaritch."

Once again he rapidly went over the ground near the river, then returned to the spot where Atterson had slept, following a slightly different track to that by which we had come. Then taking the hatchet from his belt, he split a dead log or two for a fire and hung up the kettle once more. I guessed from this that he had seen at least some daylight in a matter that was still obscure and inexplicable to me.

"I wonder if Atterson has confessed to Hobson yet," I said, meaning to draw Joe.

"He may confess about the robbery, but he can't tell any one where the bank property is."

"You said that before, Joe. You seem very sure of it."

"I am sure. Atterson doesn't know, because *he's* been robbed in his turn."

"Robbed!" I exclaimed.

Joe nodded.

"And the robber?"

"'Bout five foot six; light-weight; very handsome; has black hair; is, I think, under twenty-five years old; and lives in Lendeville, or near it."

"Joe, you've nothing to go on!" I cried. "Are you sure of this? How can you know?"

"I'll tell you when I've got those bank bills back. One thing's sure—Atterson'll be better off doing five years' hard than if he'd— But here, Mr. Quaritch, I'm going too fast. Drink your tea, and then let us make Lendeville. It's all of eight miles upstream."

It was still early afternoon when we arrived in Lendeville, which could hardly be called a village, except in the Canadian acceptance of that term. It was composed of a few scattered farms and a single general store. Outside one of the farmhouses Joe paused.

"I know the chap that lives in here," he said. "He's a pretty mean kind of a man, Mr. Quaritch. I may find a way to make him talk, though if he thought I wanted information he'd not part with it."

We found the farmer at home, a dour fellow, whose father had emigrated from the north of Scotland half a century earlier.

"Say, McAndrew," began Joe, "there's a chance I'll be bringing a party up on to Red River month after next for the moose-calling. What's your price for hiring two strong horses and a good buckboard to take us and our outfit on from here to the Burnt Lands by Sandy Pond?"

"Twenty dollars."

"Huh!" said Joe, "we don't want to buy the old horses!"

The Scotchman's shaven lips (he wore a chin-beard and whiskers) opened. "It would na' pay to do it for less."

"Then there's others as will."

"And what might their names be?" inquired McAndrew ironically.

"Them as took up Bank-Clerk Atterson when he was here six weeks back."

"Weel, you're wrang!" cried McAndrew, "for Bank-Clerk Atterson juist walked in with young Simon Pointarré and lived with the family at their new mill. So the price is twenty, or I'll nae harness a horse for ye!"

"Then I'll have to go on to Simon Pointarré. I've heard him well spoken of."

"Have ye now? That's queer, for he . . ."

"Maybe, then, it was his brother," said Joe quickly.

"Which?"

"The other one that was with Atterson at Red River."

"There was nae one, only the old man, Simon, and the two girrls."

"Well, anyway, I've got my sportsmen's interests to mind," said November, "and I'll ask the Pointarré's price before I close with yours."

"I'll make a reduce to seventeen dollars if ye agree here and now."

November said something further of Atterson's high regard for Simon Pointarré, which goaded old McAndrew to fury.

"And I'll suppose it was love of Simon that made him employ that family," he snarled. "Oh, yes, that's comic. 'Twas Simon and no that grinning lassie they call Phèdre! . . . Atterson? Tush! I tell ye, if ever a man made a fule o' himself . . ."

But here, despite McAndrew's protests, Joe left the farm.

At the store which was next visited, we learned the position of the Pointarré steading and the fact that old Pointarré, the daughters, Phèdre and Claire, and one son, Simon, were at home, while the other sons were on duty at the mill.

Joe and I walked together along various trails until from a hillside we were able to look down upon the farm, and in a few minutes we were knocking at the door.

It was opened by a girl of about twenty years of age; her bright brown eyes and hair made her very good-looking. Joe gave her a quick glance.

"I came to see your sister," said he.

"Simon," called the girl, "here's a man to see Phèdre."

"What's his business?" growled a man's voice from the inner room.

"I've a message for Miss Pointarré," said Joe.

"Let him leave it with you, Claire," again growled the voice.

"I was to give it to her and no one else," persisted Joe.

This brought Simon to the door. He was a powerful young French-Canadian with up-brushed hair and a dark mustache. He stared at us.

"I've never seen you before," he said at last. "No, I'm going south and I promised I'd leave a message passing through," replied Joe. "Who sent you?"

"Can't tell that, but I guess Miss Pointarré will know when I give her the message."

"Well, I suppose you'd best see her. She's down bringing in the cows. You'll find her below there in the meadow"; he waved his arm to where we could see a small stream that ran under wooded hills at a distance of about half a mile. "Yes, you'll find her there below."

Joe thanked him and we set off.

It did not take us long to locate the cows, but there was no sign of the girl. Then, taking up a well-marked trail which led away into the bush, we advanced upon it in silence till, round a clump of pines, it debouched upon a large open shed or byre. Two or three cows stood at the farther end of it, and near them with her back to us was a girl with the sun shining on the burnished coils of her black hair.

A twig broke under my foot and she swung round at the noise.

"What do you want?" she asked.

She was tall and really gloriously handsome.

"I've come from Atterson. I've just seen him," said November.

I fancied her breath caught for the fraction of a second, but only a haughty surprise showed in her face.

"There are many people who see him every day. What of that?" she retorted.

"Not many have seen him to-day, or even yesterday."

Her dark blue eyes were fixed on November. "Is he ill? What do you mean?"

"Huh! Don't they read the newspaper in Lendeville? There's something about him going round. I came thinking you'd sure want to hear," said November.

The colour rose in Phèdre's beautiful face.

"They're saying," went on Joe, "that he robbed the bank where he is employed of a hundred thousand dollars, and instead of trying to get away on the train or by one of the steamers, he made for the woods. That was all right if a Roberville farmer hadn't seen him. So they put the police on his track and I went with the police."

Phèdre turned away as if bored. "What interest have I in this? It *ennuies* me to listen."

"Wait!" replied November. "With the police I went, and soon struck Atterson's trail on the old Colonial Post Road, and in time come up with Atterson himself nigh Red River. The police takes Atterson prisoner and searches him."

"And got the money back!" she said scornfully. "Well, it sounds silly enough. I don't want to hear more."

"The best is coming, Miss Pointarré. They took him but they found nothing. Though they searched him and all roundabout the camp, they found nothing."

"He had hidden it, I suppose."

"So the police thought. And I thought the same, till . . ." (November's gaze never left her face) "till I see his eyes. The pupils were like pin-points in his head." He paused and added, "I got the bottle of whiskey that was in his pack. It'll go in as evidence."

"Of what?" she cried impatiently.

"That Atterson was drugged and the bank property stole from him. You see," continued Joe, "this robbery wasn't altogether Atterson's own idea."

"Ah!"

"No, I guess he had the first notion of it when he was on his vacation six weeks back. . . . He was in love with a wonderful handsome girl. Blue eyes she had and black hair, and her teeth was as good as yours. She pretended to be in love with him, but all along she was in love with—well, I can't say who she was in love with—herself likely. Anyway, I expect she used all her influence to make Atterson rob the bank and then light out for the woods with the stuff. He does all she wants. On his way to the woods she meets him with a pack of food and necessaries. In that pack was a bottle of drugged whiskey. She asks him where he's going to camp that night, he suspects nothing and tells her, and off she goes in a canoe up Red River till she comes to opposite where he's lying drugged. She lands and robs him, but she don't want him to know who done that, so she plays an old game to conceal her tracks. She's a rare active young woman, so she carries out her plan, gets back to her canoe and home to Lendeville . . . . Need I tell any more about her?"

During Joe's story Phèdre's colour had slowly died away.

"You are very clever!" she said bitterly. "But why should you tell *me* all this?"

"Because I'm going to advise you to hand over the hundred thousand dollars you took from Atterson. I'm in this case for the bank."

"I?" she exclaimed violently. "Do you dare to say that I had anything whatever to do with this robbery, that I have the hundred thousand dollars? . . . Bah! I know nothing about it. How should I?"

Joe shrugged his shoulders. "Then I beg your pardon, Miss Pointarré, and I say good-bye. I must go and make my report to the police and let them act their own way." He turned, but before he had gone more than a step or two, she called to him.

"There is one point you have missed for all your cleverness," she said. "Suppose what you have said is true, may it not be that the girl who robbed Atterson took the money just to return it to the bank?"

"Don't seem to be that way, for she has just denied all knowledge of the property, and denied she had it before two witnesses. Besides, when Atterson comes to know that he's been made a cat's-paw of, he'll be liable to turn King's evidence. No, miss, your only chance is to hand over the stuff—here and now."

"To you!" she scoffed. "And who are you? What right have you . . ."

"I'm in this case for the bank. Old McAndrew knows me well and can tell you my name."

"What is it?"

"People mostly call me November Joe."

She threw back her head—every attitude, every movement of hers was wonderful. "Now, supposing that the money could be found . . . what would you do?"

"I'd go to the bank and tell them I'd make shift to get every cent back safe for them if they'd agree not to prosecute . . . anybody."

"So you are man enough not to wish to see me in trouble?"

November looked at her. "I was sure not thinking of you at all," he said simply, "but of Bank-Clerk Atterson, who's lost the girl he robbed for and ruined himself for. I'd hate to see that chap over-punished with a dose of gaol too. . . . But the bank people only wants their money, and I guess if they get that they'll be apt to think the less said about the robbery the better. So if you take my advice—why, now's the time to see old McAndrew. You see, Miss Pointarré, I've got the cinch on you."

She stood still for a while. "I'll see old man McAndrew," she cried suddenly. "I'll lead. It's near enough this way."

Joe turned after her, and I followed. Without arousing McAndrew's suspicions, Joe satisfied the girl as to his identity.

Before dark she met us again. "There!" she said, thrusting a packet into Joe's hand. "But look out for yourself! Atterson isn't the only man who'd break the law for love of me. Think of that at night in the lonely bush!"

I saw her sharp white teeth grind together as the words came from between them.

"My!" ejaculated November looking after her receding figure, "she's a bad loser, ain't she, Mr. Quaritch?"

We went back into Quebec, and Joe made over to the bank the amount of their loss as soon as Harris, the manager, agreed (rather against his will) that no questions should be asked nor action taken.

The same evening I, not being under the same embargo regarding questions, inquired from Joe how in the world the fair Phèdre covered her tracks from the canoe to where Atterson was lying.

"That was simple for an active girl. She walked ashore along the paddle, and after her return to the canoe threw water upon the mark it made in the mud. Didn't you notice how faint it was?"

"But when she got on shore—how did she hide her trail then?"

"It's not a new trick. She took a couple of short logs with her in the canoe. First she'd put one down and step onto it, then she'd put the other one farther and step onto that. Next she'd lift the one behind, and so on. Why did she do that? Well, I reckon she thought the trick good enough to blind Atterson. If he'd found a woman's tracks after being robbed, he'd have suspected."

"But you said before we left Atterson's camp that whoever robbed him was middle height, a light weight, and had black hair."

"Well, hadn't she? Light weight because the logs wasn't much drove into the ground, not tall since the marks of them was so close together."

"But the black hair?"

Joe laughed. "That was the surest thing of the lot, and put me wise to it and Phèdre at the start. Twisted up in the buckle of the pack she gave Atterson I found several strands of splendid black hair. She must 'a' caught her hair in the buckles while carrying it."

"But, Joe, you also said at Red River that the person who robbed Atterson was not more than twenty-five years old?"

"Well, the hair proved it was a woman, and what but being in love with her face would make a slap-up bank-clerk like Atterson have any truck with a settler's girl? And them kind are early ripe and go off their looks at twenty-five. I guess, Mr. Quaritch, her age was a pretty safe shot."

THE HAMMER OF GOD

G. K. Chesterton

THE LITTLE VILLAGE OF BOHUN BEACON WAS PERCHED ON A HILL SO STEEP that the tall spire of its church seemed only like the peak of a small mountain. At the foot of the church stood a smithy, generally red with fires and always littered with hammers and scraps of iron; opposite to this, over a rude cross of cobbled paths, was "The Blue Boar," the only inn of the place. It was upon this crossway, in the lifting of a leaden and silver daybreak, that two brothers met in the street and spoke; though one was beginning the day and the other finishing it. The Rev. and Hon. Wilfred Bohun was very devout, and was making his way to some austere exercises of prayer or contemplation at dawn. Colonel the Hon. Norman Bohun, his elder brother, was by no means devout, and was sitting in evening dress on the bench outside "The Blue Boar," drinking what the philosophic observer was free to regard either as his last glass on Tuesday or his first on Wednesday. The colonel was not particular.

The Bohuns were one of the very few aristocratic families really dating from the Middle Ages, and their pennon had actually seen Palestine. But it is a great mistake to suppose that such houses stand high in chivalric tradition. Few except the poor preserve traditions. Aristocrats live not in traditions but in fashions. The Bohuns had been Mohocks under Queen Anne and Mashers under Queen Victoria. But like more than one of the really ancient houses, they had rotted in the last two centuries into mere drunkards and dandy degenerates, till there had even come a whisper of insanity. Certainly there was something hardly human about the colonel's wolfish pursuit of pleasure, and his chronic resolution not to go home till morning had a touch of the hideous clarity of insomnia. He was a tall, fine animal, elderly, but with hair still startlingly yellow. He would have looked merely blonde and leonine, but his blue eyes were sunk so deep in his face that they looked black. They were a little too close together. He had very long yellow moustaches; on each side of them a fold or furrow from nostril to jaw, so that a sneer seemed cut into his face. Over his evening clothes he wore a curious pale yellow coat that looked more like a very light dressing gown than an overcoat, and on the back of his head was stuck an extraordinary broad-brimmed hat of a bright green colour, evidently some oriental curiosity caught up at random. He was proud of appearing in such incongruous attires—proud of the fact that he always made them look congruous.

His brother the curate had also the yellow hair and the elegance, but he was buttoned up to the chin in black, and his face was clean-shaven, cultivated, and a little nervous. He seemed to live for nothing but his religion; but there were some who said (notably the blacksmith, who was a Presbyterian) that it was a love of Gothic architecture rather than of God, and that his haunting of the church like a ghost was only another and purer turn of the almost morbid thirst for beauty which sent his brother raging after women and wine. This charge was doubtful, while the man's practical piety was indubitable. Indeed, the charge was mostly an ignorant misunderstanding of the love of solitude and secret prayer, and was founded on his being often found kneeling, not before the altar, but in peculiar places, in the crypts or gallery, or even in the belfry. He was at the moment about to enter the church through the yard of the smithy, but stopped and frowned a little as he saw his brother's cavernous eyes staring in the same direction. On the hypothesis that the colonel was interested in the church he did not waste any speculations. There only remained the blacksmith's shop, and though the blacksmith was a Puritan and none of his people, Wilfred Bohun had heard some scandals about a beautiful and rather celebrated wife. He flung a suspicious look across the shed, and the colonel stood up laughing to speak to him.

"Good morning, Wilfred," he said. "Like a good landlord I am watching sleeplessly over my people. I am going to call on the blacksmith."

Wilfred looked at the ground, and said: "The blacksmith is out. He is over at Greenford."

"I know," answered the other with silent laughter; "that is why I am calling on him."

"Norman," said the cleric, with his eye on a pebble in the road, "are you ever afraid of thunderbolts?"

"What do you mean?" asked the colonel. "Is your hobby meteorology?"

"I mean," said Wilfred, without looking up, "do you ever think that God might strike you in the street?"

"I beg your pardon," said the colonel; "I see your hobby is folk-lore."

"I know your hobby is blasphemy," retorted the religious man, stung in the one live place of his nature. "But if you do not fear God, you have good reason to fear man."

The elder raised his eyebrows politely. "Fear man?" he said.

"Barnes the blacksmith is the biggest and strongest man for forty miles round," said the clergyman sternly. "I know you are no coward or weakling, but he could throw you over the wall."

This struck home, being true, and the lowering line by mouth and nostril darkened and deepened. For a moment he stood with the heavy sneer on his face. But in an instant Colonel Bohun had recovered his own cruel good humour and laughed, showing two dog-like front teeth under his yellow moustache. "In that case, my dear Wilfred," he said quite carelessly, "it was wise for the last of the Bohuns to come out partially in armour."

And he took off the queer round hat covered with green, showing that it was lined within with steel. Wilfred recognised it indeed as a light Japanese or Chinese helmet torn down from a trophy that hung in the old family hall.

"It was the first hat to hand," explained his brother airily; "always the nearest hat—and the nearest woman."

"The blacksmith is away at Greenford," said Wilfred quietly; "the time of his return is unsettled."

And with that he turned and went into the church with bowed head, crossing himself like one who wishes to be quit of an unclean spirit. He was anxious to forget such grossness in the cool twilight of his tall Gothic cloisters; but on that morning it was fated that his still round of religious exercises should be everywhere arrested by small shocks. As he entered the church, hitherto always empty at that hour, a kneeling figure rose hastily to its feet and came towards the full daylight of the doorway. When the curate saw it he stood still with surprise. For the early worshipper was none other than the village idiot, a nephew of the blacksmith, one who neither would nor could care for the church or for anything else. He was always called "Mad Joe," and seemed to have no other name; he was a dark, strong, slouching lad, with a heavy white face, dark straight hair, and a mouth always open. As he passed the priest, his moon-calf countenance gave no hint of what he had been doing or thinking of. He had never been known to pray before. What sort of prayers was he saying now? Extraordinary prayers surely.

Wilfred Bohun stood rooted to the spot long enough to see the idiot go out into the sunshine, and even to see his dissolute brother hail him with a sort of avuncular jocularity. The last thing he saw was the colonel throwing pennies at the open mouth of Joe, with the serious appearance of trying to hit it.

This ugly sunlight picture of the stupidity and cruelty of the earth sent the ascetic finally to his prayers for purification and new thoughts. He went up to a pew in the gallery, which brought him under a coloured window which he loved and always quieted his spirit; a blue window with an angel carrying lilies. There he began to think less about the half-wit, with his livid face and mouth like a fish. He began to think less of his evil brother, pacing like a lean lion in his horrible hunger. He sank deeper and deeper into those cold and sweet colours of silver blossoms and sapphire sky.

In this place half an hour afterwards he was found by Gibbs, the village cobbler, who had been sent for him in some haste. He got to his feet with promptitude, for he knew that no small matter would have brought Gibbs into such a place at all. The cobbler was, as in many villages, an atheist, and his appearance in church was a shade more extraordinary than Mad Joe's. It was a morning of theological enigmas.

"What is it?" asked Wilfred Bohun rather stiffly, but putting out a trembling hand for his hat.

The atheist spoke in a tone that, coming from him, was quite startlingly respectful, and even, as it were, huskily sympathetic.

"You must excuse me, sir," he said in a hoarse whisper, "but we didn't think it right not to let you know at once. I'm afraid a rather dreadful thing has happened, sir. I'm afraid your brother—"

Wilfred clenched his frail hands. "What devilry has he done now?" he cried in involuntary passion.

"Why, sir," said the cobbler, coughing, "I'm afraid he's done nothing, and won't do anything. I'm afraid he's done for. You had really better come down, sir."

The curate followed the cobbler down a short winding stair which brought them out at an entrance rather higher than the street. Bohun saw the tragedy in one glance, flat underneath him like a plan. In the yard of the smithy were standing five or six men mostly in black, one in an inspector's uniform. They included the doctor, the Presbyterian minister, and the priest from the Roman Catholic chapel, to which the blacksmith's wife belonged. The latter was speaking to her, indeed, very rapidly, in an undertone, as she, a magnificent woman with red-gold hair, was sobbing blindly on a bench. Between these two groups, and just clear of the main heap of hammers, lay a man in evening dress, spread-eagled and flat on his face. From the height above Wilfred could have sworn to every item of his costume and appearance, down to the Bohun rings upon his fingers; but the skull was only a hideous splash, like a star of blackness and blood.

Wilfred Bohun gave but one glance, and ran down the steps into the yard. The doctor, who was the family physician, saluted him, but he scarcely took any notice. He could only stammer out: "My brother is dead. What does it mean? What is this horrible mystery?" There was an unhappy silence; and then the cobbler, the most outspoken man present, answered: "Plenty of horror, sir," he said; "but not much mystery."

"What do you mean?" asked Wilfred, with a white face.

"It's plain enough," answered Gibbs. "There is only one man for forty miles round that could have struck such a blow as that, and he's the man that had most reason to."

"We must not prejudge anything," put in the doctor, a tall, black-bearded man, rather nervously; "but it is competent for me to corroborate what Mr. Gibbs says about the nature of the blow, sir; it is an incredible blow. Mr. Gibbs says that only one man in this district could have done it. I should have said myself that nobody could have done it."

A shudder of superstition went through the slight figure of the curate. "I can hardly understand," he said.

"Mr. Bohun," said the doctor in a low voice, "metaphors literally fail me. It is inadequate to say that the skull was smashed to bits like an eggshell. Fragments of bone were driven into the body and the ground like bullets into a mud wall. It was the hand of a giant."

He was silent a moment, looking grimly through his glasses; then he added: "The thing has one advantage—that it clears most people of suspicion at one stroke. If you or I or any normally made man in the country were accused of this crime, we should be acquitted as an infant would be acquitted of stealing the Nelson column."

"That's what I say," repeated the cobbler obstinately; "there's only one man that could have done it, and he's the man that would have done it. Where's Simeon Barnes, the blacksmith?"

"He's over at Greenford," faltered the curate.

"More likely over in France," muttered the cobbler.

"No; he is in neither of those places," said a small and colourless voice, which came from the little Roman priest who had joined the group. "As a matter of fact, he is coming up the road at this moment."

The little priest was not an interesting man to look at, having stubbly brown hair and a round and stolid face. But if he had been as splendid as Apollo no one would have looked at him at that moment. Everyone turned round and peered at the pathway which wound across the plain below, along which was indeed walking, at his own huge stride and with a hammer on his shoulder, Simeon the smith. He was a bony and gigantic man, with deep, dark, sinister eyes and a dark chin beard. He was walking and talking quietly with two other men; and though he was never specially cheerful, he seemed quite at his ease.

"My God!" cried the atheistic cobbler, "and there's the hammer he did it with."

"No," said the inspector, a sensible-looking man with a sandy moustache, speaking for the first time. "There's the hammer he did it with over there by the church wall. We have left it and the body exactly as they are."

All glanced round and the short priest went across and looked down in silence at the tool where it lay. It was one of the smallest and the lightest of the hammers, and would not have caught the eye among the rest; but on the iron edge of it were blood and yellow hair.

After a silence the short priest spoke without looking up, and there was a new note in his dull voice. "Mr. Gibbs was hardly right," he said, "in saying that there is no mystery. There is at least the mystery of why so big a man should attempt so big a blow with so little a hammer."

"Oh, never mind that," cried Gibbs, in a fever. "What are we to do with Simeon Barnes?"

"Leave him alone," said the priest quietly. "He is coming here of himself. I know those two men with him. They are very good fellows from Greenford, and they have come over about the Presbyterian chapel."

Even as he spoke the tall smith swung round the corner of the church, and strode into his own yard. Then he stood there quite still, and the hammer fell from his hand. The inspector, who had preserved impenetrable propriety, immediately went up to him.

"I won't ask you, Mr. Barnes," he said, "whether you know anything about what has happened here. You are not bound to say. I hope you don't know, and that you will be able to prove it. But I must go through the form of arresting you in the King's name for the murder of Colonel Norman Bohun."

"You are not bound to say anything," said the cobbler in officious excitement. "They've got to prove everything. They haven't proved yet that it is Colonel Bohun, with the head all smashed up like that."

"That won't wash," said the doctor aside to the priest. "That's out of the detective stories. I was the colonel's medical man, and I knew his body better than he did. He had very fine hands, but quite peculiar ones. The second and third fingers were the same length. Oh, that's the colonel right enough."

As he glanced at the brained corpse upon the ground the iron eyes of the motionless blacksmith followed them and rested there also.

"Is Colonel Bohun dead?" said the smith quite calmly. "Then he's damned."

"Don't say anything! Oh, don't say anything," cried the atheist cobbler, dancing about in an ecstasy of admiration of the English legal system. For no man is such a legalist as the good Secularist.

The blacksmith turned on him over his shoulder the august face of a fanatic.

"It's well for you infidels to dodge like foxes because the world's law favours you," he said; "but God guards His own in His pocket, as you shall see this day."

Then he pointed to the colonel and said: "When did this dog die in his sins?"

"Moderate your language," said the doctor.

"Moderate the Bible's language, and I'll moderate mine. When did he die?"

"I saw him alive at six o'clock this morning," stammered Wilfred Bohun.

"God is good," said the smith. "Mr. Inspector, I have not the slightest objection to being arrested. It is you who may object to arresting me. I don't mind leaving the court without a stain on my character. You do mind perhaps leaving the court with a bad set-back in your career."

The solid inspector for the first time looked at the blacksmith with a lively eye; as did everybody else, except the short, strange priest, who was still looking down at the little hammer that had dealt the dreadful blow.

"There are two men standing outside this shop," went on the blacksmith with ponderous lucidity, "good tradesmen in Greenford whom you all know, who will swear that they saw me from before midnight till daybreak and long after in the committee-room of our Revival Mission, which sits all night, we save souls so fast. In Greenford itself twenty people could swear to me for all that time. If I were a heathen, Mr. Inspector, I would let you walk on to your downfall. But as a Christian man I feel bound to give you your chance, and ask you whether you will hear my alibi now or in court."

The inspector seemed for the first time disturbed, and said, "Of course I should be glad to clear you altogether now."

The smith walked out of his yard with the same long and easy stride, and returned to his two friends from Greenford, who were indeed friends of nearly everyone present. Each of them said a few words which no one ever thought of disbelieving. When they had spoken, the innocence of Simeon stood up as solid as the great church above them.

One of those silences struck the group which are more strange and insufferable than any speech. Madly, in order to make conversation, the curate said to the Catholic priest:

"You seem very much interested in that hammer, Father Brown."

"Yes, I am," said Father Brown; "why is it such a small hammer?"

The doctor swung round on him.

"By George, that's true," he cried; "who would use a little hammer with ten larger hammers lying about?"

Then he lowered his voice in the curate's ear and said: "Only the kind of person that can't lift a large hammer. It is not a question of force or courage between the sexes. It's a question of lifting power in the shoulders. A bold woman could commit ten murders with a light hammer and never turn a hair. She could not kill a beetle with a heavy one."

Wilfred Bohun was staring at him with a sort of hypnotised horror, while Father Brown listened with his head a little on one side, really interested and attentive. The doctor went on with more hissing emphasis:

"Why do these idiots always assume that the only person who hates the wife's lover is the wife's husband? Nine times out of ten the person who most hates the wife's lover is the wife. Who knows what insolence or treachery he had shown her—look there?"

He made a momentary gesture towards the red-haired woman on the bench. She had lifted her head at last and the tears were drying on her splendid face. But the eyes were fixed on the corpse with an electric glare that had in it something of idiocy.

The Rev. Wilfred Bohun made a limp gesture as if waving away all desire to know; but Father Brown, dusting off his sleeve some ashes blown from the furnace, spoke in his indifferent way.

"You are like so many doctors," he said; "your mental science is really suggestive. It is your physical science that is utterly impossible. I agree that the woman wants to kill the co-respondent much more than the petitioner does. And I agree that a woman will always pick up a small hammer instead of a big one. But the difficulty is one of physical impossibility. No woman ever born could have smashed a man's skull out flat like that." Then he added reflectively, after a pause: "These people haven't grasped the whole of it. The man was actually wearing an iron helmet, and the blow scattered it like broken glass. Look at that woman. Look at her arms."

Silence held them all up again, and then the doctor said rather sulkily: "Well, I may be wrong; there are objections to everything. But I stick to the main point. No man but an idiot would pick up that little hammer if he could use a big hammer."

With that the lean and quivering hands of Wilfred Bohun went up to his head and seemed to clutch his scanty yellow hair. After an instant they dropped, and he cried: "That was the word I wanted; you have said the word."

Then he continued, mastering his discomposure: "The words you said were, 'No man but an idiot would pick up the small hammer.' "

"Yes," said the doctor. "Well?"

"Well," said the curate, "no man but an idiot did." The rest stared at him with eyes arrested and riveted, and he went on in a febrile and feminine agitation.

"I am a priest," he cried unsteadily, "and a priest should be no shedder of blood. I—I mean that he should bring no one to the gallows. And I thank God that I see the criminal clearly now—because he is a criminal who cannot be brought to the gallows."

"You will not denounce him?" inquired the doctor.

"He would not be hanged if I did denounce him," answered Wilfred with a wild but curiously happy smile. "When I went into the church this morning I found a madman praying there—that poor Joe, who has been wrong all his life. God knows what he prayed; but with such strange folk it is not incredible to suppose that their prayers are all upside down. Very likely a lunatic would pray before killing a man. When I last saw poor Joe he was with my brother. My brother was mocking him."

"By Jove!" cried the doctor, "this is talking at last. But how do you explain—"

The Rev. Wilfred was almost trembling with the excitement of his own glimpse of the truth. "Don't you see; don't you see," he cried feverishly; "that is the only theory that covers both the queer things, that answers both the riddles. The two riddles are the little hammer and the big blow. The smith might have struck the big blow, but would not have chosen the little hammer. His wife would have chosen the little hammer, but she could not have struck the big blow. But the madman might have done both. As for the little hammer—why, he was mad and might have picked up anything. And for the big blow, have you never heard, doctor, that a maniac in his paroxysm may have the strength of ten men?"

The doctor drew a deep breath and then said, "By golly, I believe you've got it."

Father Brown had fixed his eyes on the speaker so long and steadily as to prove that his large grey, ox-like eyes were not quite so insignificant as the rest of his face. When silence had fallen he said with marked respect: "Mr. Bohun, yours is the only theory yet propounded which holds water every way and is essentially unassailable. I think, therefore, that you deserve to be told, on my positive knowledge, that it is not the true one." And with that the old little man walked away and stared again at the hammer.

"That fellow seems to know more than he ought to," whispered the doctor peevishly to Wilfred. "Those popish priests are deucedly sly."

"No, no," said Bohun, with a sort of wild fatigue. "It was the lunatic. It was the lunatic."

The group of the two clerics and the doctor had fallen away from the more official group containing the inspector and the man he had arrested. Now, however, that their own party had broken up, they heard voices from the others. The priest looked up quietly and then looked down again as he heard the blacksmith say in a loud voice:

"I hope I've convinced you, Mr. Inspector. I'm a strong man, as you say, but I couldn't have flung my hammer bang here from Greenford. My hammer hasn't got wings that it should come flying half a mile over hedges and fields."

The inspector laughed amicably and said: "No, I think you can be considered out of it, though it's one of the rummiest coincidences I ever saw. I can only ask you to give us all the assistance you can in finding a man as big and strong as yourself. By George! you might be useful, if only to hold him! I suppose you yourself have no guess at the man?"

"I may have a guess," said the pale smith, "but it is not at a man." Then, seeing the scared eyes turn towards his wife on the bench, he put his huge hand on her shoulder and said: "Nor a woman either."

"What do you mean?" asked the inspector jocularly. "You don't think cows use hammers, do you?"

"I think no thing of flesh held that hammer," said the blacksmith in a stifled voice; "mortally speaking, I think the man died alone."

Wilfred made a sudden forward movement and peered at him with burning eyes.

"Do you mean to say, Barnes," came the sharp voice of the cobbler, "that the hammer jumped up of itself and knocked the man down?"

"Oh, you gentlemen may stare and snigger," cried Simeon; "you clergymen who tell us on Sunday in what a stillness the Lord smote Sennacherib. I believe that One who walks invisible in every house defended the honour of mine, and laid the defiler dead before the door of it. I believe the force in that blow was just the force there is in earthquakes, and no force less."

Wilfred said, with a voice utterly undescribable: "I told Norman myself to beware of the thunderbolt."

"That agent is outside my jurisdiction," said the inspector with a slight smile.

"You are not outside His," answered the smith; "see you to it," and, turning his broad back, he went into the house.

The shaken Wilfred was led away by Father Brown, who had an easy and friendly way with him. "Let us get out of this horrid place, Mr. Bohun," he said. "May I look inside your church? I hear it's one of the oldest in England. We take some interest, you know," he added with a comical grimace, "in old English churches."

Wilfred Bohun did not smile, for humour was never his strong point. But he nodded rather eagerly, being only too ready to explain the Gothic splendours to someone more likely to be sympathetic than the Presbyterian blacksmith or the atheist cobbler.

"By all means," he said; "let us go in at this side." And he led the way into the high side entrance at the top of the flight of steps. Father Brown was mounting the first step to follow him when he felt a hand on his shoulder, and turned to behold the dark, thin figure of the doctor, his face darker yet with suspicion.

"Sir," said the physician harshly, "you appear to know some secrets in this black business. May I ask if you are going to keep them to yourself?"

"Why, doctor," answered the priest, smiling quite pleasantly, "there is one very good reason why a man of my trade should keep things to himself when he is not sure of them, and that is that it is so constantly his duty to keep them to himself when he is sure of them. But if you think I have been discourteously reticent with you or anyone, I will go to the extreme limit of my custom. I will give you two very large hints."

"Well, sir?" said the doctor gloomily.

"First," said Father Brown quietly, "the thing is quite in your own province. It is a matter of physical science. The blacksmith is mistaken, not perhaps in saying that the blow was divine, but certainly in saying that it came by a miracle. It was no miracle, doctor, except in so far as man is himself a miracle, with his strange and wicked and yet half-heroic heart. The force that smashed that skull was a force well known to scientists—one of the most frequently debated of the laws of nature."

The doctor, who was looking at him with frowning intentness, only said: "And the other hint?"

"The other hint is this," said the priest. "Do you remember the blacksmith, though he believes in miracles, talking scornfully of the impossible fairy tale that his hammer had wings and flew half a mile across country?"

"Yes," said the doctor, "I remember that."

"Well," added Father Brown, with a broad smile, "that fairy tale was the nearest thing to the real truth that has been said to-day." And with that he turned his back and stumped up the steps after the curate.

The Reverend Wilfred, who had been waiting for him, pale and impatient, as if this little delay were the last straw for his nerves, led him immediately to his favourite corner of the church, that part of the gallery closest to the carved roof and lit by the wonderful window with the angel. The little Latin priest explored and admired everything exhaustively, talking cheerfully but in a low voice all the time. When in the course of his investigation he found the side exit and the winding stair down which Wilfred had rushed to find his brother dead, Father Brown ran not down but up, with the agility of a monkey, and his clear voice came from an outer platform above.

"Come up here, Mr. Bohun," he called. "The air will do you good."

Bohun followed him, and came out on a kind of stone gallery or balcony outside the building, from which one could see the illimitable plain in which their small hill stood, wooded away to the purple horizon and dotted with villages and farms. Clear and square, but quite small beneath them, was the blacksmith's yard, where the inspector still stood taking notes and the corpse still lay like a smashed fly.

"Might be the map of the world, mightn't it?" said Father Brown.

"Yes," said Bohun very gravely, and nodded his head.

Immediately beneath and about them the lines of the Gothic building plunged outwards into the void with a sickening swiftness akin to suicide. There is that element of Titan energy in the architecture of the Middle Ages that, from whatever aspect it be seen, it always seems to be rushing away, like the strong back of some maddened horse. This church was hewn out of ancient and silent stone, bearded with old fungoids and stained with the nests of birds. And yet, when they saw it from below, it sprang like a fountain at the stars; and when they saw it, as now, from above, it poured like a cataract into a voiceless pit. For these two men on the tower were left alone with the most terrible aspect of the Gothic; the monstrous foreshortening and disproportion, the dizzy perspectives, the glimpses of great things small and small things great; a topsy-turvydom of stone in the mid-air. Details of stone, enormous by their proximity, were relieved against a pattern of fields and farms, pygmy in their distance. A carved bird or beast at a corner seemed like some vast walking or flying dragon wasting the pastures and villages below. The whole atmosphere was dizzy and dangerous, as if men were upheld in air amid the gyrating wings of colossal genii; and the whole of that old church, as tall and rich as a cathedral, seemed to sit upon the sunlit country like a cloud-burst.

"I think there is something rather dangerous about standing on these high places even to pray," said Father Brown. "Heights were made to be looked at, not to be looked from."

"Do you mean that one may fall over," asked Wilfred.

"I mean that one's soul may fall if one's body doesn't," said the other priest.

"I scarcely understand you," remarked Bohun indistinctly.

"Look at that blacksmith, for instance," went on Father Brown calmly; "a good man, but not a Christian—hard, imperious, unforgiving. Well, his Scotch religion was made up by men who prayed on hills and high crags, and learnt to look down on the world more than to look up at heaven. Humility is the mother of giants. One sees great things from the valley; only small things from the peak."

"But he—he didn't do it," said Bohun tremulously.

"No," said the other in an odd voice; "we know he didn't do it."

After a moment he resumed, looking tranquilly out over the plain with his pale grey eyes. "I knew a man," he said, "who began by worshipping with others before the altar, but who grew fond of high and lonely places to pray from, corners or niches in the belfry or the spire. And once in one of those dizzy places, where the whole world seemed to turn under him like a wheel, his brain turned also, and he fancied he was God. So that though he was a good man, he committed a great crime."

Wilfred's face was turned away, but his bony hands turned blue and white as they tightened on the parapet of stone.

"He thought it was given to *him* to judge the world and strike down the sinner. He would never have had such a thought if he had been kneeling with other men upon a floor. But he saw all men walking about like insects. He saw one especially strutting just below him, insolent and evident by a bright green hat—a poisonous insect."

Rooks cawed round the corners of the belfry; but there was no other sound till Father Brown went on.

"This also tempted him, that he had in his hand one of the most awful engines of nature; I mean gravitation, that mad and quickening rush by which all earth's creatures fly back to her heart when released. See, the inspector is strutting just below us in the smithy. If I were to toss a pebble over this parapet it would be something like a bullet by the time it struck him. If I were to drop a hammer—even a small hammer—"

Wilfred Bohun threw one leg over the parapet, and Father Brown had him in a minute by the collar.

"Not by that door," he said quite gently; "that door leads to hell."

Bohun staggered back against the wall, and stared at him with frightful eyes.

"How do you know all this?" he cried. "Are you a devil?"

"I am a man," answered Father Brown gravely; "and therefore have all devils in my heart. Listen to me," he said after a short pause. "I know what you did—at least, I can guess the great part of it. When you left your brother you were racked with no unrighteous rage, to the extent even that you snatched up a small hammer, half inclined to kill him with his foulness on his mouth. Recoiling, you thrust it under your buttoned coat instead, and rushed into the church. You pray wildly in many places, under the angel window, upon the platform above, and a higher platform still, from which you could see the colonel's Eastern hat like the back of a green beetle crawling about. Then something snapped in your soul, and you let God's thunderbolt fall."

Wilfred put a weak hand to his head, and asked in a low voice: "How did you know that his hat looked like a green beetle?"

"Oh, that," said the other with the shadow of a smile, "that was common sense. But hear me further. I say I know all this; but no one else shall know it. The next step is for you; I shall take no more steps; I will seal this with the seal of confession. If you ask me why, there are many reasons, and only one that concerns you. I leave things to you because you have not yet gone very far wrong, as assassins go. You did not help to fix the crime on the smith when it was easy; or on his wife, when that was easy. You tried to fix it on the imbecile because you knew that he could not suffer. That was one of the gleams that it is my business to find in assassins. And now come down into the village, and go your own way as free as the wind; for I have said my last word."

They went down the winding stairs in utter silence, and came out into the sunlight by the smithy. Wilfred Bohun carefully unlatched the wooden gate of the yard, and going up to the inspector, said: "I wish to give myself up; I have killed my brother."

THE RIDDLE OF THE 5:28

T. W. Hanshew

I

It was exactly thirty-two minutes past five o'clock on the evening of Friday, December 9th, when the station-master at Anerley received the following communication by wire from the signal box at Forest Hill:

> 5:28 down from London Bridge just passed. One first-class compartment in total darkness. Investigate.

As two stations, Sydenham and Penge, lie between Forest Hill and Anerley, in the ordinary course of events this signal-box message would have been despatched to one or the other of these; but it so happens that the 5:28 from London Bridge to Croydon is a special train, which makes no stop short of Anerley station on the way down, consequently the signalman had no choice but to act as he did.

"Wire fused, I reckon, or filament burnt out. That's the worst of electric light," commented the station-master when he received the communication. "Get a light of some sort from the lamp-room, Webb. They'll have to put up with that as far as Croydon. Move sharp. She'll be along presently." Then he took up a lantern (for, in addition to fog, a slight, sifting snow had come on about an hour previously, rendering the evening one of darkness and extreme discomfort) and crossed by way of the tunnel over to the down platform to be ready for the train's arrival, having some little difficulty in progressing easily, for it so happened that a local celebrity had been entertaining the newly elected Lord Mayor that day, and in consequence both the up and the down platforms were unusually crowded for the season and the hour.

Promptly at 5:42, the scheduled time for its arrival, the train came pelting up the snow-covered metals from Penge, and made its first stop since starting. It was packed to the point of suffocation, as it always is, and in an instant the station was in a state of congestion. Far down the uncovered portion of the platform Webb, the porter, who had now joined the station-master, spied a gap in the long line of brightly lighted windows, and the pair bore down upon it forthwith, each with a glowing lantern in his hand.

"Here she is. Now, then, let's see what's the difficulty," said the station-master, as they came abreast of the light-less compartment, where, much to his surprise, he found nobody leaning out and making a "to-do" over the matter. "Looks as if the blessed thing was empty, though that's by no means likely in a packed train like the 5:28. Hallo! Door's locked. And here's an 'Engaged' label on the window. What the dickens did I do with my key? Oh, here it is. Now, then, let's see what's amiss."

A great deal was amiss, as he saw the instant he unlocked the door and pulled it open, for the first lifting of the lantern made the cause of the darkness startlingly plain. The shallow glass globe which should have been in the centre of the ceiling had been smashed, ragged fragments of it still clinging to their fastenings, and the three electric bulbs had been removed bodily. A downward glance showed him that both these and the fragments of the broken globe lay on one seat, partly wrapped in a wet cloth, and on the other— He gave a jump and a howl, and retreated a step or two in a state of absolute panic. For there in a corner, with his face toward the engine, half sat, half leaned, the figure of a dead man, with a bullet-hole between his eyes, and a small, nickel-plated revolver loosely clasped in the bent fingers of one limp and lifeless hand.

The body was that of a man whose age could not, at the most, have exceeded eight-and-thirty, a man who must, in life, have been more than ordinarily handsome. His hair and moustache were fair, his clothing was of extreme elegance in both material and fashioning, he wore no jewellery of any description, unless one excepts a plain gold ring on the fourth finger of the left hand, his feet were shod in patent-leather boots, in the rack overhead rested a shining silk hat of the newest fashion, an orange-wood walking-stick, and a pair of gray suede gloves. An evening paper lay between his feet, open, as though it had been read, and in his buttonhole there was a single mauve orchid of exquisite beauty and delicacy. The body was quite alone in the compartment, and there was not a scrap of luggage of any description.

"Suicide," gulped the startled station-master as soon as he could find strength to say anything; then he hastily slammed and relocked the door, set Webb on guard before it, and flew to notify the engine driver and to send word to the local police.

The news of the tragedy spread like wildfire, but the station-master, who had his wits about him, would allow nobody to leave the station until the authorities had arrived, and suffered no man or woman to come within a yard of the compartment where the dead man lay.

Some one has said that "nothing comes by chance," but whether that is true or not, it happened that Mr. Maverick Narkom was among those who had attended the lunch in honour of the Lord Mayor that day, and that, at the very moment when this ghastly discovery was made on the down platform at Anerley station, he was standing with the crowd on the up one, waiting for the train to Victoria. This train was to convey Cleek, whom he had promised to join at Anerley, returning from a day spent with Captain Morrison and his daughter in the beautiful home they had bought when the law decided that the captain was the legitimate heir of George Carboys and lawful successor to Abdul ben Meerza's money.

As soon as the news of the tragedy reached him Mr. Narkom crossed to the scene of action and made known his identity, and by the time the local police reached the theatre of events he was in full possession of the case, and had already taken certain steps with regard to the matter.

It was he who first thought of looking to see if any name was attached, as is often the case, to the "Engaged" label secured to the window of the compartment occupied by the dead man. There was. Written in pencil under the blue-printed "Engaged" were the three words, "For Lord Stavornell."

"By George!" he exclaimed, as he read the name which was one that half England had heard of at one time or another, and knew to belong to a man whose wild, dissipated life and violent temper had passed into proverb. "Come to the end at last, has he! Give me your lantern, porter, and open the door. Let's have a look and see if there's any mistake or—" The whistle of the arriving train for Victoria cut in upon his words, and, putting the local police in charge he ran for the tunnel, made for the up platform, and caught Cleek. He remained in conversation with him for two or three minutes after the Victoria train had gone on its way, and was still talking with him in undertones when, a brief tune later, they appeared from the tunnel and bore down on the spot where the local police were on guard over the dark compartment.

"Mr. George Headland, one of my best men," he explained to the local inspector, who had just arrived. "Let us have all the light you can, please. Mr. Headland wishes to view the body. Crowd round, the rest of you, and keep the passengers back. Pull down the blinds of the compartment before you turn on your bull's-eyes. All right, porter. Tell the engine driver he'll get his orders in a minute. Now then, Cl—Headland, decide; it rests with you."

Cleek opened the door of the compartment, stepped in, gave one glance at the dead man, and then spoke.

"Murder!" he said. "Look how the pistol lies in his hand. Wait a moment, however, and let me make sure." Then he took the revolver from the yielding fingers, smelt it, smiled, then "broke" it, and looked at the cylinder. "Just as I supposed," he added, turning to Narkom. "One chamber has been fouled by a shot and one cartridge has been exploded. But not to-day, not even yesterday. That sour smell tells its own story, Mr. Narkom. This revolver was discharged two or three days ago. The assassin had everything prepared for this little event; but he was a fool, for all his cleverness, for you will observe that in his haste, when he put the revolver in the dead hand to make it appear a case of suicide, he laid it down just as he himself took it from his pocket, with the butt toward the victim's body and the muzzle pointing outward between the thumb and forefinger, and with the bottom of the cylinder, instead of the top of the trigger, touching the ball of the thumb! It is a clear case of murder, Mr. Narkom."

"But, sir," interposed the station-master, overhearing this assertion, and looking at Cleek with eyes of blank bewilderment, "if somebody killed him, where has that 'somebody' gone? This train has made no stop until now since it started from London Bridge; so, even if the party was in it at the start, how in the world could he get out?"

"Maybe he chucked hisself out of the window, guv'ner," suggested Webb; "or maybe he slipped out and hung on to the footboard until the train slowed down, and then dropped off just before it come into the station here."

"Don't talk rubbish, Webb. Both doors were locked and both windows closed when we discovered the body. You saw that as plainly as I."

"Lummy, sir, so I did. Then where could he a-went to—and how?"

"Station-master," struck in Cleek, turning from examining the body, "get your men to examine all tickets, both in the train and out of it, and if there's one that's not clipped as it passed the barrier at London Bridge, look out for it, and detain the holder. I'll take the gate here, and examine all local tickets. Meantime, wire all up the road to every station from here to London Bridge, and find out if any other signalman than the one at Forest Hill noticed this dark compartment when the train went past."

Both suggestions were acted upon immediately. But every ticket, save, of course, the season ones—and the holders of these were in every case identified—was found to be properly clipped; and, in the end, every signal-box from New Cross on wired back: "All compartments lighted when train passed here."

"That narrows the search, Mr. Narkom," said Cleek, when he heard this. "The lights were put out somewhere between Honor Oak Park and Forest Hill, and it was between Honor Oak Park and Anerley the murderer made his escape. Inspector"—he turned to the officer in command of the local police—"do me a favour. Put your men in charge of this carriage, and let the train proceed. Norwood Junction is the next station, I believe, and there's a side track there. Have the carriage shunted, and keep close guard over it until Mr. Narkom and I arrive."

"Right you are, sir. Anything else?"

"Yes. Have the station-master at the junction equip a hand-car with a searchlight, and send it here as expeditiously as possible. If anybody or anything has left this train between this point and Honor Oak Park, Mr. Narkom, this thin coating of snow will betray the fact beyond the question of a doubt."

Twenty minutes later the hand-car put in an appearance, manned by a couple of linemen from the junction, and, word having been wired up the line to hold back all trains for a period of half an hour in the interests of Scotland Yard, Cleek and Narkom boarded the vehicle, and went whizzing up the metals in the direction of Honor Oak Park, the shifting searchlight sweeping the path from left to right and glaring brilliantly on the surface of the fallen snow.

Four lines of tracks gleamed steel-bright against its spotless level—the two outer ones being those employed by the local trains going to and fro between London and the suburbs, the two inner ones belonging to the main line—but not one footstep indented the thin surface of that broad expanse of snow from one end of the journey to the other.

"The murderer, whoever he is or wherever he went, never set foot upon so much as one inch of this ground, that's certain," said Narkom, as he gave the order to reverse the car and return. "You feel satisfied of that, do you not, my dear fellow?"

"Thoroughly, Mr. Narkom; there can't be two opinions upon that point. But, at the same time, he *did* leave the train, otherwise we should have found him in it."

"Granted. But the question is, *when* did he get in and *how* did he get out? We know from the evidence of the passengers that the tram never stopped for one instant between London Bridge station and Anerley; that all compartments were alight up to the time it passed Honor Oak Park; that nobody abroad of it heard a sound of a pistol-shot; that the assassin could not have crept along the footboard and got into some other compartment, for *all* were so densely crowded that half a dozen people were standing in each, so he could not have entered without somebody making room for him to open the door and get in. No such thing happened, no such thing could happen, without a dozen or more people being aware of it; so the idea of a confederate may be dismissed without a thought. The unmarked surface of the snow shows that nobody alighted, was thrown out, or fell out between the two points where the tragedy must have occurred; both windows were shut and both doors of the compartment locked when the train made its first stop; yet the fellow was gone. My dear chap, are you sure, are you really *sure*, that it isn't a case of suicide after all?"

Cleek gave his shoulders a lurch and smiled indulgently.

"My dear Mr. Narkom," he said, "the position of the revolver in the dead man's hand ought, as I pointed out to you, to settle that question, even if there were no other discrepancies. In the natural order of things, a man who had just put a bullet into his own brain would, if he were sitting erect, as Lord Stavornell was, drop the revolver in the spasmodic opening and shutting of the hands in the final convulsion; but, if he retained any sort of a hold upon it, be sure his forefinger would be in the loop of the trigger. He wouldn't be holding the weapon backward, so to speak, with the cylinder against the ball of his thumb and the hammer against the base of the middle finger. If he had held it that way he simply couldn't have shot himself if he had tried. Then, if you didn't remark it, there was no scorch of powder upon the face, for another thing; and, for a third, the bullet-hole was between the eyes, a most unlikely target for a man bent upon blowing out his own brains; the temple or the roof of the mouth are the points to which natural impulse—" He stopped and laid a sharp, quick-shutting hand on the shoulder of one of the two men who were operating the car. "Turn back!" he exclaimed. "Reverse the action, and go back a dozen yards or so."

The impetus of the car would not permit of this at once, but after running on for a little time longer it answered to the brake, slowed down, stopped, and then began to back, scudding along the rail until Cleek again called it to a halt. They were within gunshot of the station at Sydenham when this occurred; the glaring searchlight was still playing on the metals and the thin layer of snow between, and Cleek's face seemed all eyes as he bent over and studied the ground over which they were gliding. Of a sudden, however, he gave a little satisfied grunt, jumped down, and picked up a shining metal object, about two and a half inches long, which lay in the space between the tracks of the main and the local lines. It was a guard's key for the locking and unlocking of compartment doors, one of the small T-shaped kind that you can buy of almost any iron-monger for sixpence or a shilling any day. It was wet from contact with the snow, but quite unrusted, showing that it had not been lying there long, and it needed but a glance to reveal the fact that it was brand new and of recent purchase.

Cleek held it out on his palm as he climbed back upon the car and rejoined Narkom.

"Wherever he got on, Mr. Narkom, here is where the murderer got off, you see, and either dropped or flung away this key when he had relocked the compartment after him," he said. "And yet, as you see, there is not a footstep, beyond those I have myself just made, to be discovered anywhere. From the position in which this key was lying, one thing is certain, however: our man got out on the opposite side from the platform toward which the train was hastening and in the middle of the right of way."

"What a mad idea! If there had been a main line express passing at the time the fellow ran the risk of being cut to pieces. None of them slow down before they prepare to make their first stop at East Croydon, and about this spot they would be going like the wind."

"Yes," said Cleek, looking fixedly at the shining bit of metal on his palm; "going like the wind. And the suction would be enormous between two speeding trains. A step outside, and he'd have been under the wheels in a wink. Yes, it would have been certain death, instant death, if there had been a main line train passing at the time; and that he was not sucked down and ground under the wheels proves that there *wasn't*." Then he puckered up his brows in that manner which Narkom had come to understand meant a thoughtfulness it was impolitic to disturb, and stood silent for a long, long time.

"Mr. Narkom," he said suddenly, "I think we have discovered all that there is to be discovered in this direction. Let us get on to Norwood Junction as speedily as possible. I want to examine that compartment and that dead body a little more closely. Besides, our half hour is about up, and the trains will be running again shortly, so we'd better get out of the way."

"Any ideas, old chap?"

"Yes, bushels of them. But they all may be exploded in another half hour. Still, these are the days of scientific marvels. Water does run uphill and men do fly, and both are in defiance of the laws of gravitation."

"Which means?"

"That I shall leave the hand-car at Sydenham, Mr. Narkom, and 'phone up to London Bridge station; there are one or two points I wish to ask some questions about. Afterward I'll hire a motor from some local garage and join you at Norwood Junction in an hour's time. Let no one see the body or enter the compartment where it lies until I come. One question, however: is my memory at fault, or was it not Lord Stavornell who was mixed up in that little affair with the French dancer, Mademoiselle Fifi de Lesparre, who was such a rage in town about a year ago?"

"Yes; that's the chap," said Narkom in reply. "And a rare bad lot he has been all his life, I can tell you. I dare say that Fifi herself was no better than she ought to have been, chucking over her country-bred husband as soon as she came into popularity, and having men of the Stavornell class tagging after her; but whether she was or was not, Stavornell broke up that home. And if that French husband had done the right thing, he would have thrashed him within an inch of his life instead of acting like a fool in a play and challenging him. Stavornell laughed at the challenge, of course; and if all that is said of him is true, he was at the bottom of the shabby trick which finally forced the poor devil to get out of the country. When his wife, Fifi, left him, the poor wretch nearly went off his head; and, as he hadn't fifty shillings in the world, he was in a dickens of a pickle when *somebody* induced a lot of milliners, dressmakers, and the like, to whom it was said that Fifi owed bills, to put their accounts into the hands of a collecting agency and to proceed against him for settlement of his wife's accounts. That was why he got out of the country post-haste. The case made a great stir at the tune, and the scandal of it was so great that, although the fact never got into the papers, Stavornell's wife left him, refusing to live another hour with such a man."

"Oh, he had a wife, then?"

"Yes; one of the most beautiful women in the kingdom. They had been married only a year when the scandal of the Fifi affair arose. That was another of his dirty tricks forcing that poor creature to marry him."

"She did so against her will?"

"Yes. She was engaged to another fellow at the time, an army chap who was out in India. Her father, too, was an army man, a Colonel Something-or-other, poor as the proverbial church mouse, addicted to hard drinking, cardplaying, horse-racing, and about as selfish an old brute as they make 'em. The girl took a deep dislike to Lord Stavornell the minute she saw him; knew his reputation, and refused to receive him. That's the very reason he determined to marry her, humble her pride, as it were, and repay her for her scorn of him.

"He got her father into his clutches, deliberately, of course, lent him money, took his IOU's for card debts and all that sort of thing, until the old brute was up to his ears in debt and with no prospect of paying it off. Of course, when he'd got him to that point, Stavornell demanded the money, but finally agreed to wipe the debt out entirely if the daughter married him. They went at her, poor creature, those two, with all the mercilessness of a couple of wolves. Her father would be disgraced, kicked out of the army, barred from all the clubs, reduced to beggary, and all that, if she did not yield; and in the end they so played upon her feelings, that to save him she gave in; Stavornell took out a special license, and they were married. Of course, the man never cared for her; he only wanted his revenge on her, and they say he led her a dog's life from the hour they came back to England from their honeymoon."

"Poor creature!" said Cleek sympathetically. "And what became of the other chap, the lover she wanted to marry and who was out in India at the time all this happened?"

"Oh, they say he went on like a madman when he heard it. Swore he'd kill Stavornell, and all that, but quieted down after a time, and accepted the inevitable with the best grace possible. Crawford is his name. He was a lieutenant at the time, but he's got his captaincy since, and I believe is on leave and in England at present—as madly and as hopelessly in love with the girl of his heart as ever."

"Why 'hopelessly,' Mr. Narkom? Such a man as Stavornell must have given his wife grounds for divorce a dozen times over."

"Not a doubt of it. There isn't a judge in England who wouldn't have set her free from the scoundrel long ago if she had cared to bring the case into the courts. But Lady Stavornell is a strong Church-woman, my dear fellow; she doesn't believe in divorce, and nothing on earth could persuade her to marry Captain Crawford so long as her first husband still remained alive."

"Oho!" said Cleek. "Then Fifi's husband isn't the only man with a grievance and a cause? There's another, eh?"

"Another? I expect there must be a dozen, if the truth were known. There's only one creature in the world I ever heard of as having a good word to say for the man."

"And who might that be?"

"The Hon. Mrs. Brinkworth, widow of his younger brother. You'd think the man was an angel to hear her sing his praises. Her husband, too, was a wild sort. Left her up to her ears in debt, without a penny to bless herself, and with a boy of five to rear and educate. Stavornell seems always to have liked her. At any rate, he came to the rescue, paid off the debts, settled an annuity upon her, and arranged to have the boy sent to Eton as soon as he was old enough. I expect the boy is at the bottom of this good streak in him if all is told; for, having no children of his own— I say! By George, old chap! Why, that nipper, being the heir in the direct line, is Lord Stavornell now that the uncle is dead! A lucky stroke for him, by Jupiter!"

"Yes," agreed Cleek. "Lucky for him; lucky for Lady Stavornell; lucky for Captain Crawford; and *unlucky* for the Hon. Mrs. Brinkworth and Mademoiselle Fifi de Lesparre. So, of course—Sydenham at last. Good-bye for a little time, Mr. Narkom. Join you at Norwood Junction as soon as possible, and—I say!"

"Yes, old chap?"

"Wire through to the Low Level station at Crystal Palace, will you? and inquire if anybody has mislaid an ironing-board or lost an Indian canoe. See you later. So long."

Then he stepped up on to the station platform, and went in quest of a telephone booth.

II

It was after nine o'clock when he turned up at Norwood Junction, as calm, serene, and imperturbable as ever, and found Narkom awaiting him in a small private room which the station clerk had placed at his disposal.

"My dear fellow, I never was so glad!" exclaimed the superintendent, jumping up excitedly as Cleek entered. "What kept you so long? I've been on thorns. Got bushels to tell you. First off, as Stavornell's identity is established beyond doubt, and no time has been lost in wiring the news of the murder to his relatives, both Lady Stavornell and Mrs. Brinkworth have wired back that they are coming on. I expect them at any minute now. And here's a piece of news for you. Fifi's husband is in England. The Hon. Mrs. Brinkworth has wired me to that effect. Says she has means of knowing that he came over from France the other day; and that she herself saw him in London this morning when she was up there shopping."

"Oho!" commented Cleek. "Got her wits about her, that lady, evidently. Find anything at the Crystal Palace Low Level, Mr. Narkom?"

"Yes. My dear Cleek, I don't know whether you are a wizard or what, and I can't conceive what reason you can have for making such an inquiry, but—"

"Which was it? Canoe or ironing-board?"

"Neither, as it happens. But they've got a lady's folding cutting table; you know the sort, one of those that women use for dressmaking operations; and possible to be folded up flat, so they can be tucked away. Nobody knows who left it; but it's there awaiting an owner; and it was found—"

"Oh, I can guess that," interposed Cleek nonchalantly. "It was in a first-class compartment of the 5:18 from London Bridge, which reached the Low Level at 5:43. No, never mind questions for a few minutes, please. Let's go and have a look at the body. I want to satisfy myself regarding the point of what in the world Stavornell was doing on a suburban train at a time when he ought, properly, to be on his way home to his rooms at the Ritz, preparing to dress for dinner; and I want to find out, if possible, what means that chap with the little dark moustache used to get him to go out of town in his ordinary afternoon dress and by that particular train."

"Chap with the small dark moustache? Who do you mean by that?"

"Party that killed him. My 'phone to London Bridge station has cleared the way a bit. It seems that Lord Stavornell engaged that compartment in that particular train by telephone at three o'clock this afternoon. He arrived all alone, and was in no end of a temper because the carriage was dirty; had it swept out, and stood waiting while it was being done. After that the porter says he found him laughing and talking with a dark-moustached little man, apparently of continental origin, dressed in a Norfolk suit and carrying a brown leather portmanteau. Of course, as the platform was crowded, nobody seems to have taken any notice of the dark-moustached little man; and the porter doesn't know where he went nor when—only that he never saw him again. But I know where he went, Mr. Narkom, and I know, too, what was in that portmanteau. An air pistol, for one thing; also a mallet or hammer and that wet cloth we found, both of which were for the purpose of smashing the electric light globe without sound. And he went into that compartment with his victim!"

"Yes; but, man alive, how did he get out? Where did he go after that, and what became of the brown leather portmanteau?"

"I hope to be able to answer both questions before this night is over, Mr. Narkom. Meantime, let us go and have a look at the body, and settle one of the little points that bother me."

The superintendent led the way to the siding where the shunted carriage stood, closely guarded by the police; and, lanterns having been procured from the lamp-room, Cleek was soon deep in the business of examining the compartment and its silent occupant.

Aided by the better light, he now perceived something which, in the first hurried examination, had escaped him, or, if it had not—which is, perhaps, open to question— he had made no comment upon. It was a spot about the size of an ordinary dinner plate on the crimson carpet which covered the floor of the compartment. It was slightly darker than the rest of the surface, and was at the foot of the corner seat directly facing the dead man.

"I think we can fairly decide, Mr. Narkom, on the evidence of that," said Cleek, pointing to it, "that Lord Stavornell did have a companion in this compartment, and that it was the little dark man with the small moustache. Put your hand on the spot. Damp, you see; the effect of some one who had walked through the snow sitting down with his feet on this particular seat. Now look here." He passed his handkerchief over the stain, and held it out for Narkom's inspection. It was slightly browned by the operation. "Just the amount of dirt the soles of one's boots would be likely to collect if one came with wet feet along the muddy platform of the station."

"Yes; but, my dear chap, that might easily have happened—particularly on such a day as this has been— before Lord Stavornell's arrival. He can't have been the only person to enter this compartment since morning."

"Granted. But he is supposed to have been the only person who entered it after it was swept, Mr. Narkom; and that, as I told you, was done by his orders immediately before the train started. We've got past the point of 'guesswork' now. We've estab-lished the presence of the second party beyond all question. We also know that he was a person with whom Stavornell felt at ease, and was intimate enough with to feel no necessity for putting himself out by entertaining with those little courtesies one is naturally obliged to show a guest."

"How do you make that out?"

"This newspaper. He was reading at the time he was shot. You can see for yourself where the bullet went through—this hole here close to the top of the paper. When a man invites another man to occupy with him a compartment which he has engaged for his own exclusive use—and this Stavornell must have done, otherwise the man couldn't have been travelling with him—and then proceeds to read the news instead of troubling himself to treat his companion as a guest, it is pretty safe to say that they are acquaintances of long standing, and upon such terms of intimacy that the social amenities may be dispensed with inoffensively. Now look at the position of this newspaper lying between the dead man's feet. Curved round the ankle and the lower part of the calf of the left leg. If we hadn't found the key we still should have known that the murderer got out on that side of the carriage."

"How should we have known?"

"Because a paper which has simply been dropped could not have assumed that position without the aid of a strong current of air. The opening of that door on the right-hand side of the body supplied that current, and supplied it with such strength and violence that the paper was, as one might say, absolutely sucked round the man's leg. That is a positive proof that the train was moving at the time it happened, for the day, as you know, has been windless.

"Now look! No powder on the face, no smell of it in the compartment; and yet the pistol found in his hand is an ordinary American-made thirty-eight calibre revolver. We have an amateur assassin to deal with, Mr. Narkom, not a hardened criminal; and the witlessness of the fellow is enough to bring the case to an end before this night is over. Why didn't he discharge that revolver to-day, and have enough sense to bring a thimbleful of powder to burn in this compartment after the work was done? One knows in an instant that the weapon used was an air-pistol, and that the fellow's only thought was how to do the thing without sound, not how to do it with sense. I don't suppose that there are three places in all London that stock air-pistols, and I don't suppose that they sell so many as two in a whole year's time. But if one has been sold or repaired at any of the shops in the past six months—well, Dollops will know that in less than no time. I 'phoned him to make inquiries. His task's an easy one, and I've no doubt he will bring back the word I want in short order. And now, Mr. Narkom, as our friend the assassin is such a blundering, short-sighted individual, it's just possible that, forgetting so many other important things, he may have neglected to search the body of his victim. Let us do it for him."

As he spoke he bent over the dead man and commenced to search the clothing. He slid his hand into the inner pocket of the creaseless morning coat and drew out a notebook and two or three letters. All were addressed in the handwriting of women, but only one seemed to possess any interest for Cleek. It was written on pink notepaper, enclosed in a pink envelope, and was postmarked "Croydon, December 9, 2:30 p.m.," and bore those outward marks which betokened its delivery, not in course of post, but by express messenger. One instant after Cleek had looked at it he knew he need seek no further for the inforformation he desired. It read:

Piggy! Stupid boy! The ball of the dress fancy is not for to-morrow, but to-night. I have make sudden discoverment. Come quick, by the train that shall leave London Bridge at the time of twenty-eight minute after the hour of five. You shall not fail of this, or it shall make much difficulties for me, as I come to meet it on arrival. Do not bother of the costume; I will have one ready for you. I have one large joke of the somebody else that is coming, which will make you scream of the laughter. Burn this—FIFI.

And at the bottom of the sheet:

Do burn this. I have hurt the hand, and must use the writing of my maid; and I do not want you to treasure that.

"There's the explanation, Mr. Narkom," said Cleek as he held the letter out. "That's why he came by this particular train. There's the snare. That's how he was lured."

"By Fifi!" said Narkom. "By Jove! I rather fancied from the first that we should find that she or her husband had something to do with it."

"Did you?" said Cleek with a smile. "I didn't, then; and I don't even yet!"

Narkom opened his lips to make some comment upon this, but closed them suddenly and said nothing. For at that moment one of the constables put in an appearance with news that, "Two ladies and two gentlemen have arrived, sir, and are asking permission to view the body for purposes of identification. Here are the names, sir, on this slip of paper."

"Lady Stavornell; Colonel Murchison; Hon. Mrs, Brinkworth; Captain James Crawford," Narkom read aloud; then looked up inquiringly at Cleek.

"Yes," he said. "Let them come. And—Mr. Narkom?"

"Yes?"

"Do you happen to know where they come from?"

"Yes. I learned that when I sent word of Stavornell's death to them this evening. Lady Stavornell and her father have for the past week been stopping at Cleethorp Hydro, to which they went for the purpose of remaining over the Christmas holidays; and, oddly enough, both Mrs. Brinkworth and Captain Crawford turned up at the same place for the same purpose the day before yesterday. It can't be very pleasant for them, I should imagine, for I believe the two ladies are not very friendly."

"Naturally not," said Cleek, half abstractedly. "The one loathing the man, the other loving him. I want to see those two ladies; and I particularly want to see those two men. After that—" Here his voice dropped off. Then he stood looking up at the shattered globe, and rubbing his chin between his thumb and forefinger and wrinkling up his brows after the manner of a man who is trying to solve a problem in mental arithmetic. And Narkom, unwise in that direction for once, chose to interrupt his thoughts, for no greater reason than that he had thrice heard him mutter, "Suction—displacement—resistance."

"Working out a problem, old chap?" he ventured. "Can I help you? I used to be rather good at that sort of thing."

"Were you?" said Cleek, a trifle testily. "Then tell me something. Combating a suction power of about two pounds to the square inch, how much wind does it take to make a cutting-table fly, with an unknown weight upon it, from the Sydenham switch to the Low Level station? When you've worked that out, you've got the murderer. And when you do get him he won't be any man you ever saw or ever heard of in all the days of your life! But he will be light enough to hop like a bird, heavy enough to pull up a wire rope with about three hundred pounds on the end of it, and there will be two holes of about an inch in diameter and a foot apart in one end of the table that flew."

"My dear chap!" began Narkom in tones of blank bewilderment, then stopped suddenly and screwed round on his heel. For a familiar voice had sung out suddenly a yard or two distant: "Ah! keep yer 'air on! Don't get to thinkin' you're Niagara Falls jist because yer got water on the brain!" And there, struggling in the grip of a constable, who had laid strong hands upon him, stood Dollops with a kit-bag in one hand and a half-devoured bath bun in the other.

"All right there, constable; let the boy pass. He's one of us!" rapped out Cleek; and in an instant the detaining hand fell, and Dollops' chest went out like a pouter pigeon's.

"Catch on to that, Suburbs?" said he, giving the constable a look of blighting scorn; and, swaggering by like a mighty conqueror, joined Cleek at the compartment door. "Nailed it at the second rap, guv'ner," he said in an undertone. "Fell down on Carnage's, picked myself up on Loader, Tottenham Court Road; 14127 A, manufactured Stockholm. Valve tightened—old customer—day before yesterday in the afternoon."

"Good boy! good boy!" said Cleek, patting him approvingly. "Keep your tongue between your teeth. Scuttle off, and find out where there's a garage, and then wait outside the station till I come."

"Right you are, sir," responded Dollops, bolting the remainder of the bun. Then he ducked down and slipped away. And Cleek, stepping back into the shadow, where his features might not be too clearly seen until he was ready that they should be, stood and narrowly watched the small procession which was being piloted to the scene of the tragedy. A moment later the four persons already announced passed under Cleek's watchful eye, and stood in the dead man's presence. Lady Stavornell, tall, graceful, beautiful, looking as one might look whose lifelong martyrdom had come at last to a glorious end; Captain Crawford, bronzed, agitated, a trifle nervous, short of stature, slight of build, with a rather cynical mouth and a small dark moustache; the Hon. Mrs. Brinkworth, a timid, dove-eyed, little wisp of a woman, with a clinging, pathetic, almost childish manner, her soft eyes red with grief, her mobile mouth a-quiver with pain, the marks of tears on her lovely little face; and, last of all, Colonel Murchison, heavy, bull-necked, ponderous of body, and purple of visage a living, breathing monument of Self.

"Hum-m-m!" muttered Cleek to himself, as this unattractive person passed by. "Not he—not by his hand. He never struck the blow—too cowardly, too careful. And yet—Poor little woman!" And his sympathetic eyes went past the others—past Mrs. Brinkworth, sobbing and wringing her hands and calling piteously on the dead to speak—and dwelt long and tenderly upon Lady Stavornell.

A moment he stood there silent, watching, listening, making neither movement nor sound; then of a sudden he put forth his hand and tapped Narkom's arm.

"Detain this party, every member of it, by any means, on any pretext, for another forty-five minutes," he whispered. "I said the assassin was a fool; I said the blunders made it possible for the case to be concluded to-night, did I not? Wait for me. In three-quarters of an hour the murderer will be here on this spot with me!" Then he screwed round on his heel, and before Narkom could speak was gone, soundlessly and completely gone, just as he used to go in his Vanishing Cracksman's days, leaving just that promise behind him.

III

It wanted but thirteen minutes of being midnight when the gathering about the siding where the shunted carriage containing the body of the murdered man still stood received something in the nature of a shock when, on glancing round as a sharp whistle shrilled a warning note, they saw an engine, attached to one solitary carriage, backing along the metals and bearing down upon them.

"I say, Mr. Knockem, or Narkhim, or whatever your name is," blurted out Colonel Murchison, as he hastily caught the Hon. Mrs. Brinkworth by the arm and whisked her back from the metals, leaving his daughter to be looked after by Captain Crawford, "look out for your blessed bobbies. Somebody's shunting another coach in on top of us; and if the ass doesn't look what he's doing— There! I told you!" as the coach in question settled with a slight jar against that containing the body of Lord Stavornell. "Of all the blundering, pig-headed fools! Might have killed some of us. What next, I wonder?"

What next, as a matter of fact, gave him cause for even greater wonder; for as the two carriages met, the door of the last compartment in the one which had just arrived opened briskly, and out of it stepped first a couple of uniformed policemen, next a ginger-haired youth with a kit-bag in one hand and a saveloy in the other, then the trim figure of the lady who had so long and popularly been known in the music-hall world as Mademoiselle Fifi de Lesparre, and last of all—"Cleek!" blurted out Narkom, overcome with amazement, as he saw the serenely alighting figure. And "Cleek!" went in a little rippling murmur throughout the entire gathering, civilians and local police alike.

"All right, Mr. Narkom," said Cleek himself, with a slight shrug of the shoulders. "Even the best of us slip up sometimes; and since everybody knows now, we'll have to make the best of it. Gentlemen, ladies, you, too, my colleagues, my best respects. Now to business." Then he stepped out of the shadow in which he had alighted into the full glow of the lanterns and the flare which had been lit close to the door of the dead man's carriage, conscious that every eye was fixed upon his face and that the members of the local force were silently and breathlessly "spotting" him. But in that moment the weird birth-gift had been put into practice, and Narkom fetched a sort of sigh of relief as he saw that a sagging eyelid, a twisted lip, a queer, blurred *something* about all the features, had set upon that face a living mask that hid effectually the face he knew so well.

"To business?" he repeated. "Ah, yes, quite so, my dear Cleek. Shall I tell the ladies and gentlemen of your promise? Well, listen. Mr. Cleek is more than a quarter of an hour beyond the time he set, but he gave me his word that this riddle would be solved to-night, to-night, ladies and gentlemen, and that when I saw him here the murderer would be with him."

"Oh, bless him! bless him!" burst forth Mrs. Brinkworth impulsively. "And he brings her! That wicked woman! Oh, I knew that she had something to do with it."

"Your pardon, Mrs. Brinkworth, but for once your woman's intuition is at fault," said Cleek quietly. "Mademoiselle Fifi is not here as a prisoner, but as a witness for the Crown. She has had nothing even in the remotest to do with the crime. Her name was used to trap Lord Stavornell to his death. But the lady is here to prove that she never heard of the note which was found on Lord Stavornell's body; to prove also that, although it is true she did expect to go to a fancy-dress ball with his lordship, that fancy-dress ball does not occur until next Friday, the sixteenth inst., not the ninth, and that she never even heard of any alteration in the date."

"Ah, non! non! non! nevaire! I do swear!" chimed in Fifi herself, almost hysterical with fright. "I know nossing—nossing!"

"That is true," said Cleek quietly. "There is not any question of Mademoiselle Fifi's complete innocence of any connection with this murder."

"Then her husband?" ventured Captain Crawford agitatedly. "Surely you have heard what Mrs. Brinkworth has said about seeing him in town to-day?"

"Yes, I have heard, Captain. But it so happens that I know for a certainty M. Philippe de Lesparre had no more to do with it than had his wife."

"But, my dear sir," interposed the colonel; "the—er —foreign person at the station, the little slim man in the Norfolk suit, the fellow with the little dark moustache? What of him?"

"A great deal of him. But there are other men who are slight, other men who have little dark moustaches, Colonel. That description would answer for Captain Crawford here; and if he, too, were in town to-day—"

"I was in town!" blurted out the captain, a sudden tremor in his voice, a sudden pallor showing through his tan. "But, good God, man! you—you can't possibly insinuate—"

"No, I do not," interposed Cleek. "Set your mind at rest upon that point, Captain; for the simple reason that the little dark man is a little dark fiction; in other words, he does not and never did exist!"

"What's that?" fairly gasped Narkom. "Never existed? But, my dear Cleek, you told me that the porter at London Bridge saw him and—"

"I told you what the porter told me; what the porter thought he saw, and what we shall, no doubt, find out in time at least fifty other people thought they saw, and what was, doubtless, the 'good joke' alluded to in the forged note. The only man against whom we need direct our attention, the only man who had any hand in this murder, is a big, burly, strong-armed one like Colonel Murchison here."

"What's that?" roared out the colonel furiously. "By the Lord Harry, do you dare to assert that I—I sir—killed the man?"

"No, I do not. And for the best of reasons. The assassin was shut up in that compartment with Lord Stavornell from the moment he left London Bridge; and I happen to know, Colonel, that although you were in town to-day, you never put foot aboard the 5:28 from the moment it started to the one in which it stopped. And at that final moment, Colonel," he reached round, took something from his pocket, and then held it out on the palm of his hand, "at that final moment, Colonel, you were passing the barrier at the Crystal Palace Low Level with a lady, whose ticket from London Bridge had never been clipped, and with this air-pistol, which she had restored to you, in your coat pocket!"

"W-w-what crazy nonsense is this, sir? I never saw the blessed thing in all my life."

"Oh, yes, Colonel. Loader, of Tottenham Court Road, repaired the valve for you the day before yesterday, and I found it in your room just—Quick! nab him, Petrie! Well played! After the king, the trump; after the confederate, the assassin! And so—" He sprang suddenly, like a jumping cat, and there was a click of steel, a shrill, despairing cry, then the rustle of something falling. When Captain Crawford and Lady Stavornell turned and looked, he was standing with both hands on his hips, looking frowningly down on the spot where the Hon. Mrs. Brinkworth lay, curled up in a limp, unconscious heap, with a pair of handcuffs locked on her folded wrists.

"I said that when the murderer was found, Mr. Narkom," he said as the superintendent moved toward him, "it would be no man you ever saw or ever heard of in all your life. I knew it was a woman from the bungling, unmanlike way that pistol was laid in the dead hand; the only question I had to answer was *which* woman—Fifi, Lady Stavornell, or this wretched little hypocrite. Here's your 'little dark man," here's the assassin. The Norfolk suit and the false moustache are in her room at the hydro. She made Stavornell think that she, too, was going to the fancy ball, and that the surprise Fifi had planned was for her to meet him as she did and travel with him. When the train was under way she shot him. Why? Easily explained, my dear chap. His death made her little son heir to the estates. During his minority she would have the handling of the funds; with them she and her precious husband would have a gay life of it in their own selfish little way!"

"Her what? Lord, man, do you mean to say that she and the colonel—"

"Were privately married seven weeks ago, Mr. Narkom. The certificate of their union was tucked away in Colonel Murchison's private effects, where it was found this evening."

"How was the escape from the compartment managed after the murder was accomplished?" said Cleek, answering Narkom's query, as they whizzed home through the darkness together by the last up train that night. "Simplest thing in the world. As you know, the 5:28 from London Bridge runs without stop to Anerley. Well, the 5:18 from the same starting-point runs to the Crystal Palace Low Level, taking the main line tracks as far as Sydenham, where it branches off at the switch and curves away in an opposite direction. That is to day, for a considerable distance they run parallel, but eventually diverge.

"Now, as the 5:18 is a train with several stops, the 5:28, being a through one, overtakes her, and several times between Brockley and Sydenham they run side by side, at so steady a pace and on such narrow gauge that the footboard running along the side of the one train is not more than two and a half feet separated from the other. Their pace is so regular, their progress so even, that one could with ease step from the footboard of the one to the footboard of the other but for the horrible suction which would inevitably draw the person attempting it down under the wheels.

"Well, something had to be devised to overcome the danger of that suction. But what? I asked myself, for I guessed from the first how the escape had occurred, and I knew that such a thing absolutely required the assistance of a confederate. That meant that the confederate would have to do, on the 5:18, exactly what they had trapped Stavornell into doing on the other train: that is, secure a private compartment, so that when the time came for the escape to be accomplished he could remove the electric bulbs from the roof of his compartment, open the door, and, when the two came abreast, the assassin could do the same on the other train, and presto! the dead man would be alone. But what to use to overcome the danger of that horrible suction?"

"Ah, I see now what you were driving at when you inquired about the ironing-board or the Indian canoe. The necessary sections to construct a sort of bridge could be packed in either?"

"Yes. But they chose a simple plan, the cutting-table. A good move that. Its breadth minimised the peril of the suction; only, of course, it would have to be pulled up afterward, to leave no clue, and the added space would call for enormous strength to overcome the power of that suction; and enormous strength meant a powerful man. The rest you can put together without being told, Mr. Narkom. When that little vixen finished her man, she put out the lights, opened the door (deliberately locking it after her to make the thing more baffling), crossed over on that table, was helped into the other compartment by Murchison, and then as expeditiously as possible slipped on the loose feminine outer garments she carried with her in the brown portmanteau, the table was hauled up and taken in—nothing but wire rope for that, sir—and the thing was done.

"Murchison, of course, purchased two tickets, so that they might pass the barrier at the Low Level unquestioned when they left, but he wasn't able to get the extra ticket clipped at London Bridge because there was no passenger for it. That's how I got on to the little game! For the rest, they planned well. Those two trains being always packed, nobody could see the escape from the one to the other, because people would be standing up in every compartment, and the windows completely blocked. But if— Hullo! Victoria at last, thank goodness, 'and so to bed,' as Pepys says. The riddle's solved, Mr. Narkom. Good-night!"

AMERICAN RIVALS

THE AFFAIR OF THE DOUBLE THUMB PRINT

Charles Felton Pidgin

W ITH THE DEATH ABROAD OF THE HONOURABLE QUINCY ADAMS SAWYER, United States Ambassador to Vienna, his son, also named Quincy Adams, came into possession of the remnants of what had once been a large fortune. The fortune, however, had been greatly impaired, as the tastes of the senior Quincy Adams Sawyer had developed more in the direction of adventure and travel than in that of sober business, a fact which led eventually to bad investments and disastrous results. Therefore, when the elder Sawyer, cool and debonair to the end, shook his son's hand for the last time and calmly bade him farewell, he left behind an amount sufficient to provide a small income for that son, but by no means sufficient to make him entirely independent.

To the younger Quincy Adams Sawyer, however, the loss of his father's fortune, which had always been his to command, was a matter of minor importance. As the father had lived with the main idea of seeing strange sights and meeting new people, so, likewise, did the son find that strange adventures and unexpected experiences were to him as the breath of life. Nor did this fact force itself on him at the time of his father's death, it having been well founded long previous to that event, for the younger Quincy had led a constantly changing existence since his earliest youth.

When he entered the high school in his younger days, after a decidedly tempestuous course through the lower grades, it was with an already established reputation for deviltry. But, once in that school, and to the surprise of his new instructors, who, it must be confessed, acknowledged his introduction to them with a decided feeling of regret, he devoted himself to his studies with a mild docility that was astounding. The reason for this apparent change was a peculiar one. Quincy, purely in the pursuit of his own inclinations, had made friends with the police inspectors and had entered upon an exhaustive study of police matters, a study to which many subjects in his school curriculum, as he early discovered, lent a wealth of information that was invaluable. For instance, he early made the discovery that, if one were able to deal out, in grudgingly small amount, scientific information concerning chemical analysis and kindred subjects, it was easy to secure in return information concerning the more ordinary points of police work. Thus Quincy's four years in the high school passed with mutual profit to himself and to the police inspectors.

At the end of his course he entered the great university located in the back-yard of his home city, carrying with him resources that were invaluable in the particular style of course he had selected. He was personally acquainted with every police captain on the force, could call every inspector by his first name, and had shown at various times marked talent in the actual work of the detection of criminals. As Quincy's education progressed, so, in like ratio, did that of the police inspectors, particularly along the lines of chemistry and psychology. This fact was perhaps due not so much to the desire for increased learning on the part of the inspectors, or the hunger for knowledge on Quincy's side, as to the spirited arguments with which Quincy's visits to the police stations were enlivened, for it has long been established that men cannot continuously argue along given lines without gaining more and more information with which to strengthen their arguments. By the time Quincy had completed the first half of his freshman year so great had his friendship with the police become that it was a generally acknowledged fact throughout the college that Sawyer could easily murder the mayor and escape without so much as a reprimand!

By the time he had finished his sophomore year he knew police work and methods from Alpha to Omega. Also, he had exhausted the resources of his university so far as sociology was concerned and had browsed about casually through what few other courses chanced to appeal to him. He had joined every club and secret society to which he was eligible, had been in countless altercations with the faculty, and had generally blazed a path that was startling in its numerous ramifications. Then, as a grand climax, the influence of the police not extending to the dean and the faculty, he was unconditionally expelled. Expelled with a thoroughness and expedition that left a rankling suspicion that the faculty, as a whole, was delighted with the opportunity of dispensing with his presence, and sincerely trusted that he might never stray their way again.

Nothing daunted by his summary removal, Quincy packed his trunk, shook hands all around with the police inspectors, who watched his leave-taking with sincere regret, and blithely departed for Vienna, where his father received him with solemn words and twinkling eyes, for Quincy's progress had been regularly reported. The quiet life of a foreign embassy, however, had no attraction for Quincy, and it was but a short time before he once more packed up his belongings and again set forth into the world at large. During the five ensuing years he travelled ceaselessly, visiting every civilized nation on the globe's face, to say nothing of many nations which were far from being civilized. Being a rolling stone, he, of course, gathered no moss, but in place of that rather questionable commodity he gathered what in later years was to be of inestimable value to him; namely, information and experience.

Therefore, at the time of his father's death, the fact that his expected fortune had vanished in thin air lowered Quincy's spirits not a jot. He had already decided on the profession which he intended to follow, and, in order to establish himself in that profession, his little remnant of money would be as useful as would have been his father's vast fortune. Consequently, he took up his residence in Boston, his early home. He said nothing of his purpose for a time, but quietly set to work to establish a reputation for himself in private detective work. He kept in the background as much as was possible, not wishing to launch himself until at least one important case had come his way and been successfully dealt with. At last, after a year of work and waiting, it came. His name flashed into the limelight like a comet across a dark sky, and, within a week, the city in general, and his old friends in particular, knew that Quincy Adams Sawyer had returned to his former haunts and had established himself as a private detective.

His project at last auspiciously launched, Quincy abandoned his previous mode of living and turned the suite of rooms, which had served him as living-rooms and office combined, into a suite for living purposes only. He then removed his professional quarters to a small office in the centre of the city, hung out a brass plate on which appeared the single word "Sawyer," and plunged into the work which his sudden fame had brought him with all the zest and power of which he was capable. His standing as a detective was now firmly established and grew day by day as his old friends, the police inspectors, judiciously turned many private cases his way. That he had a marked ability in their particular line they had all along known, and, now that he had chosen, in a way, to cast his lot among them, they welcomed him with a heartiness which left nothing to be desired. And, in return, Quincy's regard for his old friends increased. The staff had changed somewhat since his earlier acquaintance with it, many of the old faces were gone and many new ones had appeared in their places, but the sum total made up the same old staff and to its members he was kin.

His friendly relations with the local police thus renewed, it was consequently no surprise to Quincy when Inspector Gates, of the department, appeared one morning in the doorway of his office and glanced questioningly within. The inspector was one of the newer men of the staff, and had gained his promotion from the ranks during Quincy's absence from the country. He was a young man of decidedly pleasing appearance, whose frank face and honest eyes invited both trust and friendship, while his age, being about equal in years to Quincy's, proved that he had intelligence of a marked degree, since he had so early in life been chosen for the staff of inspectors. He had, furthermore, the face of a statesman coupled with the build of a prize-fighter, and Quincy surveyed his mighty bulk with admiration as he paused in the doorway.

"Are you busy this morning, Mr. Sawyer?" Gates inquired in a voice of drawing-room politeness.

"Not particularly so," Quincy replied smilingly. "Take a chair and, here, have a cigar."

Gates deposited his weight on a protesting chair, accepted the proffered cigar, and stared at Quincy speculatively.

"Mr. Sawyer," he said finally, "I want your help in a case. You see it's this way. I'm a comparatively new man on the staff and this is my first big case. If I'm successful in it, my future is assured; but, if I fail, it may be years before I get another chance. The case is a peculiar one and one offering every chance of failure. That is the selfish end of it, but there is also another side. There is an old lady involved, and also she's such a bully old lady and she takes everything so cool that I'm blamed if I'm not sorry for her, and I want to succeed in this case for her sake as well as mine. I don't mean that she's suspected of anything, but she seems to be on the receiving end of the crime, so to speak, and she certainly is in danger from some source or other. That's why I came here, hoping that if you did not chance to be very busy you might give me a lift."

"Of course," Quincy replied as Gates paused uncertainly. "My business is very quiet at present, and if you have an interesting case I shall be overjoyed to help you out with it. You fellows have done me a good many neighbourly turns of late, and I'd be a poor stick indeed if I were not ready to reciprocate. Now let me hear the details, please."

"The story is this," Gates stated slowly. "Mrs. Marion Patterson and her grandson, Fred Hemenway, live in one of the old-time houses in the Back Bay. Mrs. Patterson is reputed to be comfortably well off, although I do not believe that she is considered wealthy in the broad sense of the word. She lives very quietly, keeps no carriage or automobile and only one servant, a woman who has been with her since she first commenced housekeeping as a young bride, years ago. Hemenway, her grandson, is a young man engaged in the real estate business, although his business is centred largely, I imagine, on property owned by his grandmother, as she holds numerous houses and buildings in this city and the neighbouring towns. He is, so far as I have been able to discover, an excellent fellow in every way. That for the introduction.

"The story proper commences at a time a week ago, last Tuesday evening, to be exact. Hemenway, on that evening, had remained down town in his office, after hours, to work on some papers that are connected with a land jumble he is mixed up in. According to his story he had worked until about ten o'clock without interruption, and had almost succeeded in tracing out the various points which he desired to settle. Then, without any warning whatever, without his even becoming aware that any person had entered his office, he was struck on the head and rendered unconscious. He did not regain consciousness until after midnight, and, even when his senses returned, they were in such befogged shape that he could fix his mind on no subject save his desire to return home. Consequently it was not until the next morning that the police were notified and I was detailed on the case. I went to his office with him and found things much as he had described them. The papers he had been working over were still on the desk, somewhat damaged by ink, as the ink bottle had been overturned during the assault and its contents had flowed freely over the desk and everything upon it.

"The most curious part of the whole affair, however, was the fact that, so far as we could discover, not a single article in the room had been taken or disturbed. Whether Hemenway's assailant became frightened after striking the blow, and fancied that he had done more damage than he had originally intended, or whether he intended to kill Hemenway outright, and had no other purpose in view, I have been unable to decide. But, whatever his purpose may have been, the fact remains that nothing was disturbed. He did, however, leave behind him a clue. The clue was a thumb print firmly printed and clearly defined on the door just above the knob. He had, you see, carelessly smeared his thumb with the ink from Hemenway's desk, and, on making his exit, had tranferred the ink to the door, leaving a perfect impression of his thumb. I photographed the impression and have made a careful search of the records at headquarters, but I can find no print there which corresponds to the one on Hemenway's door. Therefore the conclusion must be that the assailant is not an old-timer or we would have his finger prints.

"I worked on the case unceasingly, as I wished to solve it, not only for the ends of justice, but for my own credit as well, and you, knowing police departments as you do, will realize that such a desire was not so completely selfish as it sounds. But work as I would, I was unable to make any headway whatever. Then came the next step in the case, and one which was even more surprising than the first. Last night the old lady was assaulted, and I assure you, Sawyer, that, had she been one of my own relatives, I could not have felt more savage toward her assailant than I do, for if there was ever an old lady who was white clear through, she is the one.

"The assault happened in a manner somewhat similar to that on her grandson. She was in her sitting-room, reading, while she waited for her grandson, who was again detained in his office by night work. She is somewhat deaf, so it is not surprising that she heard no sounds such as would have been made by a man forcibly entering the house. The assailant entered through one of the windows, which he forced open. Then he must have crossed directly to where she was sitting and repeated the assault he had made on Hemenway, namely, he struck her on the head and knocked her unconscious. She did not recover until Hemenway returned at a late hour and found her. He immediately sent for a doctor, who cared for her, and then, when she had regained consciousness, he telephoned for me.

"I rushed at once to the house, but she was unable to tell me anything other than the bits of information which I have given you. I searched the room for clues and found one, a repetition of that in Hemenway's office. The difference in this case, however, was in the fact that the thumb print was clearly defined on the face of a small mirror which lay on the table, and the print was identical with that on the door of Hemenway's office. Therefore we can be certain that these assaults were committed by the same person, but aside from that there is no other clue. We cannot even discover a motive, as in neither case was anything taken, which plainly indicates that robbery was not the intention. Neither have they, so far as either knows, an enemy who would wish to put them out of the way. Furthermore, it does not seem that the assailant intended to kill them, for on both occasions he was careful to strike only a stunning blow, and one that would not result in death. That takes away the possibility of murder as the reason for the assaults, besides which is the apparent absence of any motive for a murder. There you have the case, Sawyer, and the stories of the two assaults which are connected with it. Will you take hold of it with me?" He stared at Quincy anxiously as he finished.

"I certainly shall take hold of it," Quincy replied heartily. "It strikes me that you have unearthed a case of unusual interest."

"You'll think it has interest when you undertake to unravel it," Gates responded grimly.

"All right; but we shall try," Quincy laughed. "Now let us go up to the Back Bay residence and make our start there before the trail gets too old. We can take in Hemenway's office later, if it becomes necessary."

The Back Bay residence of Mrs. Patterson differed only in minor details from the residences which surround it on every hand. It was a plain, brick house with a disguised areaway at one side and with the usual flight of stone steps leading up to the front door. Ascending these steps, Quincy and Gates were admitted by the elderly serving woman and were shown at once to the little sitting-room where the assault of the preceding evening had occurred. Nobody was in the room at the time, and, while Gates pointed out the several points of interest, and indicated the spot occupied by Mrs. Patterson when she was struck down, Quincy examined the room and its contents. After searching the room, Quincy walked across to the large window and peered down into the areaway just beneath him, raising the window and examining the woodwork at the end of his scrutiny.

"Humph!" he muttered. "An old-fashioned window-catch of no value whatever as a lock. Slid back when a knife blade was pressed against it. You can see, Gates, where the knife scarred the wood."

Apparently deciding that nothing of value was to be gained at the window, he next crossed to the table, where he stood for a long time looking down at the thumb print still plainly visible on the glass of the small mirror.

"Has this mirror been moved, Gates?" he inquired.

"Yes, I was obliged to move it when I photographed the thumb print, but I marked the spot where it lay and replaced it exactly."

For a moment Quincy was silent, but at last he remarked in a voice that seemed half speculative and half questioning: "I wonder, Gates, what logical reason a man could have had for touching that mirror in the first place. It lies so far in on the table that he wouldn't be likely to have leaned on it by accident, but yet he must have touched it in some way. What do you suppose he wished to see?"

Gates shook his head silently. "I am sure I don't understand," he replied. "It seems all a piece with the other points of the affair. What logical reason could he have had for knocking the old lady on the head, so far as logic is concerned?"

Quincy remained thoughtful for a few moments. "Will Mrs. Patterson be able to see us this morning?" he then inquired.

"I think so. She's pretty plucky and she'll be ready to give us every point of information she has if she can talk at all. She was too dazed to talk much last night, but I don't think that she is seriously injured. I'll call the servant and inquire."

He pressed the button and they waited in silence; but, when the door was finally pushed open, it was not the servant who appeared before them. Quincy saw framed in the doorway a young man whose cool eyes flashed sharply over them, and whose appearance gave every indication of ready resourcefulness and unhesitating action. Gates greeted the man in friendly fashion and turned toward Quincy.

"Mr. Hemenway, Sawyer," he said. "It is probable that he will be able to answer our questions."

"No," Hemenway replied briefly. "My grandmother wishes to talk to you herself. She is sitting up and has nearly recovered from her blow. She wishes me to conduct you up-stairs."

Without further words he faced about and ascended the gracefully curving stairway, Quincy and Gates following at his heels. At the head of the stairs he turned and conducted them along the corridor to an open door, where he stood aside and signed them to precede him. Within the room Quincy found himself facing a smiling old lady who sat propped up in an easy chair, amid pillows and cushions, staring at him with sharp, twinkling eyes. Aside from a small bandage which encircled her head, she gave no sign of the adventure she had so recently experienced and seemed, in all, but little the worse for the attack.

"Isn't she plucky?" Gates whispered admiringly. "Do you wonder I'm so anxious to catch the man who struck her?"

Quincy nodded briefly, and glanced up at the sound of the woman's voice.

"Have you gentlemen been able to formulate any reason for the unpleasant attentions which have been shown to my grandson and myself?" she inquired in a voice which Quincy noted to be as clear as her eyes.

"Not yet," he replied with gentle respect; "but we hope to do so soon. If you and Mr. Hemenway will tell us everything you can about the affair it may help us to solve the problem more readily."

"I can tell you little," Mrs. Patterson replied with an emphasizing nod of her head. "I heard nothing and saw nothing. All I know is that I was struck from behind and was unconscious until I opened my eyes and found Fred bending over me."

"You were struck from behind!" Quincy ejaculated. "You are sure of that?"

"Positive, sir." Another nod of the head accompanied the statement.

"And how were you sitting? Were you facing the table or turned sideways to it?"

"I was facing the table. I always sit that way when I read because the drop lamp is so high it reflects better on my book than when I am turned from it. Fred says I should turn my back to it as he does, but you will notice that he wears glasses while I don't," she concluded with a merry little laugh.

Quincy smiled silently, but seemed satisfied with the result of his questioning, for he turned at once to Hemenway.

"Are you able to recall the facts preceding the blow which rendered you unconscious?" he inquired.

"Nothing of value," was the immediate reply. "Like my grandmother I neither heard nor saw anything, for I was too much occupied with my work to think of aught else."

"May I inquire what you were working on?"

The man hesitated for a moment, but at last responded: "Certainly, although I hardly see how it can have any bearing on the case. I am involved in a most important law case which has been in litigation for more than a year and which is now coming up for settlement within a week. The case involves some real estate which is at present my property, and which is claimed by a corporation which has been formed for the purpose of booming certain land of which mine is the keystone. Without it their company is worthless. I am frank to say that there is some foundation for their claims, although I think that by every degree of right the land belongs to me. I was at work over titles and maps in connection with it at the time when I was assaulted. So deeply was I interested in the work that I hardly think I would have noted an earthquake."

"There is nothing about those papers that would tempt the other side of this case to steal them, is there?" Quincy inquired sharply.

"No, not a thing. They possess duplicates of the very papers I was working over and would not have been in the least interested in the possession of mine. Furthermore, even had the company desired to secure my papers, of what advantage would it have been to them to assault my grandmother in the manner you have noted? She had no papers, nor information, concerning the matter. And, above all, had it been the agent of that company who committed these attacks, he would have had a definite purpose in view, such as the stealing of the papers, and I am certain that not a single thing is missing, either here or at my office. No, gentlemen, we must look in some other direction for the assailant. That, to me, is very evident."

"What is the name of that real estate company, Mr. Hemenway?" Quincy asked.

"The Lorillard Realty Corporation," Hemenway replied. "Peter Lorillard is its president and principal stockholder. But, as I said, you may rest assured that they had nothing to gain by such methods as these."

"Yes, yes, I understand," Quincy remarked impatiently. "I wish, however, to get hold of every possible clue in connection with this affair. You have no enemies who would be likely to use such methods as have been employed?"

"None, so far as I know. Had the affair ended with the assault on me at the office I should undoubtedly have set it down to an attack by possible enemies, or to an assault with robbery for a motive, thinking that the man might in some way have been frightened away before having time in which to complete the robbery. This second assault, however, seems to do away with that possibility. These things cannot be the result of a coincidence, gentlemen. They must be in some way connected, although in what way I am free to confess I do not know."

"You are still at work on your law case?"

"Oh, yes. It is very important, and I cannot neglect it, even with such occurrences as these taking place."

Quincy had nothing to say for a few moments; but was evidently thinking deeply. "I believe," he remarked at last, "that I must once more examine the sitting-room. Will you accompany me, Mr. Hemenway?"

Hemenway readily assented, and was half-way to the door before the voice of his grandmother arrested him. "Wait a moment, Fred," she called. "I want to go, too. I want to watch all that is going on," she added with a smile.

Hemenway instantly stopped and, returning, put his grandmother's arm through his and conducted her toward the stairway, the others following behind. When the old lady had been comfortably seated, the investigation of the room was renewed.

Quincy walked at once to the window, which he again examined with great care. "Gates," he said at last, "come here a moment. I want a snapshot of the thumb print on this window."

Gates strode across the room with interest written large on his face. "That isn't the same thumb print!" he exclaimed, after a momentary glance.

"That's why I want a photograph of it," Quincy blandly answered him.

Gates seemed unsatisfied with the remark and the lack of information it contained, but he readily recognized the importance of Quincy's discovery, and at once busied himself with his camera. He carefully dusted the pane about the print and made two exposures, turning questioningly to Quincy when he had finished.

"Now," Quincy said, "I want your camera for a few minutes."

The camera was at once handed to him, and with it he retraced his steps to the table, where he minutely studied the small mirror.

"When you photographed that thumb print, Gates, by what part did you hold the mirror?" he asked.

"By the very tip end of the handle." Gates was plainly on pins and needles through curiosity at the turn events were taking, but he asked no questions.

Quincy rested the mirror against a pile of books and busied himself in front of it for several minutes. He first tried the light from one direction, and then from another, all the time whistling softly under his breath. At the end of fifteen minutes the fruit of his efforts consisted of three exposures with the camera and several badly puzzled companions, but the companions were destined to remain in their puzzled state.

"Now, Gates," he remarked, with a satisfied smile as he carefully replaced the mirror and returned the camera, "I think we have discovered very nearly all that is to be found here. We must now go where we may be able to run across other clues. Perhaps, Mr. Hemenway, we shall call at your office later in the day, but that is a decided uncertainty."

He courteously took leave of Mrs. Patterson, jerked his head imperatively at Gates, and quietly followed Hemenway toward the front door. His first step, when once outside the house, was to push open the gate of the areaway and to stare speculatively up at the window of the room from which they had just come.

"The man who forced that lock and climbed through the window must have been decidedly active, Gates," he remarked, still measuring the distance with his eye. "It would require considerable skill to climb up that waterspout and then to crawl out along the ledge; and yet that, I think, must have been the mode of entrance employed. Well, come on, we have work elsewhere," and he faced sharply about, leaving the question of the mode of entrance for future consideration.

"Now, Gates," Quincy continued, after a protracted spell of silence, "I don't think that we shall be able to do much actual work before evening. I have a few minor matters which I wish to consider, but that portion of the work I can best do alone. Do you know Tim McMahon's saloon over in the West End?"

"Sure," Gates responded, fresh interest showing in his face. "I was on that beat a year, and got my first experience as a cop over there. But what about Tim?"

"Oh, there is nothing in particular that I wish to say about Tim, it is his saloon that I am interested in. Would they know you over there if you should show up?"

"Tim would, but he's pretty straight himself, no matter what his patrons may be. He'd keep quiet if I tipped him the wink."

"Good. I want you to meet me there at eight o'clock tonight. Go into Tim's back room and, if I am not there, wait for me."

Gates grinned. "Say," he remarked, "you seem to be tolerably familiar with that place."

"It was one of my sociology laboratories," Quincy assured him. "Tim and I are old cronies."

"I suppose," Gates continued, after a short pause, "that you know what you are doing, but I'll swear that it gets past me. Are you on a particular trail, or are you trusting to luck?"

"I am following a definite path," Quincy assured him. "Meet me at Tim's according to instructions and you may see something interesting. Oh, before we separate for the day, I want one more thing from you. Lend me your thumb a minute."

As Gates wonderingly complied, Quincy carefully inked the thumb with a fountain pen and made an impression of the print on the back of an old envelope. He then made an impression of his own thumb, carefully examined both to make certain that they were perfect, and placed the envelope in an inner pocket. Next, with Gates' permission, he removed the film from the inspector's camera and, pocketing it, together with photographic copies of the two thumb prints appearing in the case, he bade the inspector a smiling farewell and disappeared in the direction of his own office.

He did not at once return to his office, however, but made his way to a small sporting goods shop which made a specialty of developing plates and films for amateur photographers. There he perched on a counter for a long time, while his own films were being developed and printed. With the prints at last in his possession, he retired into his office and there spent several hours studying and comparing the various thumb prints in the small collection.

At times he scowled fiercely, as though the matter were not untangling to his complete satisfaction; but again and again a silent smile broke through the scowl, and when at last he rose from his hours of study it was with the air of one who had at least partially solved a knotty problem. He stretched himself with many grunts and strainings of his muscles, yawned wearily and stared out of his window at the buildings in the vicinity. He finally reached for his hat, but even as his fingers touched its brim, he was halted by the ringing of the telephone bell. Picking up the 'phone he called lazily into it.

"Hello. This you, Sawyer?" came an exerted voice from the other end of the wire. "Say, this is Gates talking. The fat's kicked over for fair and the deuce is to pay. Hemenway has been kidnapped or spirited away somewhere!"

"Kidnapped! Nonsense!" Quincy exclaimed. "It isn't possible to kidnap a grown man right in broad daylight in a city the size of this."

"But it's been done, I tell you," Gates persisted. "The old lady just called me up to tell me about it. It seems the door bell rang a short time ago and he answered the bell. When he didn't come back for a long time she sent the servant to find out what was keeping him, as she's naturally a little nervous. The servant found the front door open, but there was no sign of Hemenway anywhere. He had disappeared completely."

"He stepped out somewhere with whoever wanted to see him," Quincy suggested.

"Stepped out nothing! His hat hangs where he left it last night, and he didn't even have a coat on. He wouldn't be stepping out in his shirt-sleeves if he intended to be gone long. The old lady waited half an hour more for him to show up and then, when he didn't come, she had the servant make inquiries. A fellow in the next house said that he had seen a closed carriage drive up to Hemenway's door and saw two men get out of it. He didn't pay any particular attention to them, and didn't notice the carriage again, until just as it was driving away. Then, he says, he caught a glimpse of a fellow without a coat in the carriage and that one of the others seemed to be holding his hand over that man's mouth. That don't look as though he went away of his own accord, does it?"

Quincy gave a low whistle at the news and stood for several seconds uncertainly tapping on the 'phone. Then his air of assurance returned and he replied sharply: "Never mind about this, Gates; you carry out our former program and meet me at Tim McMahon's tonight. I'm going out to look for Hemenway, but the chances are against my finding him this afternoon, even though I think I know what has become of him. You can safely tell the old lady that no harm will come to him, but beyond that I can't say anything yet. Be sure and meet me at Tim's."

The receiver clicked back on the hook, and Quincy whirled quickly toward a spacious closet at one side of his office.

Late in the afternoon a disreputable-appearing tatterdemalion slouched into one of the most notorious dives in the West End. The man, after a quick glance about the room, timidly approached the bar; but the forbidding frown of the bartender seemed to alter his purpose, for he turned abruptly and sank into a chair near one of the billiard tables. A game was in progress, and for many minutes his heavy-lidded eyes disinterestedly followed the success of one after another of the players. Nobody paid particular notice to him and he returned the courtesy, his eyes being fixed on the balls rather than on the players. At last, however, the clerk in charge of the tables approached in a leisurely fashion and the eyes of the loafer gleamed momentarily with sudden interest.

"Rabbit," he whispered softly, as the young clerk stood before him.

At the sound of the name the man turned sharply and stared with open suspicion. "Well, what do youse want?" he demanded, approaching slowly.

The man indicated a chair at his side. "Sit down a minute," he invited.

Rabbit somewhat reluctantly complied, still keeping his eyes fixed suspiciously on his companion. "Say, look a-here," he growled, "I ain't settin' up no drinks today. Get that into your bean."

A shade of amusement crossed the ragged man's face and, with a look of silent warning, he pushed back his hat, revealing his whole face for a moment before returning the hat to its original position.

"Mr. Sawyer!" Rabbit gasped in amazement. "I ain't seen youse since you was in college and I was a pin boy down to O'Neil's. Say, are youse down and out?" he asked with ready sympathy, correcting himself almost immediately. "Oh, I know. They tells me youse is a fly one now." He asked no questions, apparently divining the fact that his part was to answer and not to interrogate.

"Seen Long Tom lately?" Qnincy inquired in a low voice, after an interval of silence.

"So it's him, is it?" Rabbit muttered in a voice equally low. "Say, this won't be gettin' me into trouble, will it?"

"No, you're safe enough," Quincy assured him. "You won't be snitching because Tom isn't hiding out yet."

"That's so, too," Rabbit remarked thoughtfully. "Well, him and Ike McKechnie was in here this mornin'. I ain't seen 'em since. What's their job?"

"So Ike's in it, is he?" Quincy soliloquized. "I suspected as much. I'm not dead sure of their job, Rabbit, but I have a very good idea. But, remember this. If I don't tell you that they're wanted, nor why, they can't blame you for what may happen to them. Have they been around here often of late?"

"I ain't seen 'em before for two weeks. I guess they've been hangin' out down to O'Neil's or over to Tim McMahon's. They've both been havin' lots of the ready lately, and I guess this joint got too cheap for 'em."

"What did they do in here this morning? Drink or talk business?"

"Talked business, I guess. They was over at one of the tables a long time punishin' a pint or two of booze. I didn't go near 'em because I never had no use for Long Tom, and Ike never had no use for me. They didn't look like they wanted company, anyhow."

Quincy's hand disappeared into the breast of his ragged coat. When it once more became visible a bill peeped from between two of his fingers, and on the corner of the bill was plainly to be seen a figure five. Rabbit's eyes shone hungrily as they rested on the bill, and his face took on an added look of interest.

"That's yours," Quincy informed him, "if you will find out for certain whether or not Ike and Tom have hired any rooms up-stairs, and, if so, for how long."

Rabbit's long limbs were endowed with all the speed of the animal which had lent him its name, but he was too wise to exhibit his speed at the present moment and, in that way, arouse suspicion by too great haste. He arose in leisurely fashion and sauntered carelessly about the room, gradually drawing nearer to the bar. At length, he reached his goal and, leaning lazily across it, carelessly addressed a short sentence to the bartender. He talked in low tones with that worthy individual for some time before again taking up his circuitous route among the tables. At length he again sank into the chair at Quincy's side.

"They've got one room," he whispered through the corner of his mouth, his head all the while turned in the opposite direction. "It's hired for a week. They've got a friend in it now, but the bartender wouldn't tell me when he came, and says he don't know who the guy is."

"Good," Quincy whispered, as the money surreptitiously changed hands. "Keep your eyes open and there may be another fiver coming to you later on."

Rabbit again drifted out among the tables, while Quincy resumed his attitude of bleary somnolence. Finally he, too, arose unsteadily and approached the bar. With many sage shakes of his head, and numerous low-voiced comments to the forbidding bartender, he searched through all his pockets until, with almost superhuman endeavour, he had accumulated the sum of ten cents. He laid the money on the bar, poured out a glass of the vile whisky and then, when the bartender turned to replace the bottle, dumped the contents of the glass on the floor. That accomplished, he made his way out of the place ostentatiously wiping his lips and giving every indication of satisfied thirst.

Once outside, he turned sharply from the back street on which the saloon was located and hastily made his way to the nearest corner. There he boarded a car and was whirled away to the centre of the city, where, once again in his office, he removed his ragged clothes and resumed his normal appearance.

"Let me see," he muttered thoughtfully, as he dropped into a chair. "I wonder what Ike has been up to of late years. I've somewhat lost track of him since I've been away." He picked up a city directory and hastily scanned its pages. "Yes, here we find him. Jeremiah McKechnie, attorney-at-law. So he hasn't been debarred at any rate and, judging from the location of his office, he must be doing very well financially. He has brains, certainly, or he would never have emerged from his existence as a keeper of a pawn-shop, during which previous period, I suppose, he accumulated the name 'Ike.'" He paused thoughtfully for a time, and then turned to a business gazetteer of the city, a page of which seemed to hold his attention for a long period. At last he arose and shook his shoulders impatiently, glancing at his watch and then out into the deepening twilight. "Well," he muttered, "everything is now ready and the stage is set. It is only necessary to await the raising of the curtain."

He walked at a leisurely pace out of his office and to the nearest restaurant where he seated himself for a comfortable meal. The waiter bowed cordially, for Quincy, both during and since his college days, had made friends with men in all walks of life, a fact which was of ever increasing value to him in his present profession.

"Saw an old friend of yours in here today, Mr. Sawyer," the waiter informed him while busily laying the table. "Leastwise he was an old acquaintance, but perhaps you wouldn't call him a friend."

"Who was it?" Quincy inquirecj with an interested smile.

"Ike McKechnie. He was in here for lunch. Ike seems to be getting quite up in the world of late," the waiter concluded, as he hurried away with Quincy's order.

At the information Quincy smiled broadly. Unconsciously he seemed to have been trailing Ike McKechnie all day and very closely, a fact which was of much interest to him.

"Was Ike alone?" he inquired, when the waiter had returned.

"No," was the reply. "He had some stout old gent with him and they seemed to be on extra good terms from the way they talked and laughed. The old gent looked like ready money and heaps of it, too."

Quincy made no further inquiries nor comments on the subject, devoting himself soberly to his meal. This piece of information added nothing to the structure of evidence he had erected, but it served to a marked degree to substantiate his theories and to make him more certain than ever that he was on the right track. He then dismissed the entire matter from his mind while he finished his dinner and, when at last he arose and sauntered out, carelessly puffing a cigar, an observer would have thought him the last person to be intimately connected with a deep and complicated problem.

Tim McMahon's saloon blazed with light as Quincy strolled nonchalantly in at the appointed hour. The saloon was of a somewhat better class than its neighbours and catered to a trade with greater resources than might be discovered in the ordinary West End saloon patron. Ward politicians, small grafters and the general run of municipal hangers-on made the place their headquarters, and to it, for that reason, practically every member of the ward's political representation made his way at one time or another during the year. Minor plots against the city's treasury were laid there almost nightly, and it was a poor week indeed when a small portion of that same treasury did not, by means of some subtle pretext, find its way into Tim's coffers. Gambling was allowed "on the quiet," but rows of any sort were strictly prohibited, for Tim was exceedingly jealous of his saloon's reputation and, as the result, the man who "started anything" was in grave danger of being immediately propelled to the middle of the sidewalk with forceful energy.

As Quincy picked his way through the small crowd, the genial face of Tim himself appeared from around the lower corner of the bar. Seeing Quincy he advanced with outstretched hand and ready smile, in memory of Quincy's "laboratory days," many of which had been spent within those walls while the young man absorbed, from his surroundings, lore of political forays and gained a speaking acquaintance with every notorious character in the district. Tim jerked his head in the direction of the back room as his hand met Quincy's in friendly clasp.

"Gates is in there," he growled in his thick, rumbling voice. "Say, what's up, any-how?" he continued anxiously. "You fellows ain't going to start trouble in my place, are you?"

"Not unless the trouble starts on the other side and you refuse to back us, Tim," Quincy assured him with a meaning glance. "We're after two of your best customers, but they are to blame, because they've used your back room as a meeting-place where they've planned crooked work that's outside the regular." To Tim and his confreres any plot against the city as a whole was "the regular" and was allowed, but plots against individuals were firmly tabooed.

Tim's eyes gleamed angrily. "They're trying to put my place in bad with the bulls, are they?" he growled in a voice indicative of rising wrath.

"They are in a fair way to do so," Quincy assured him; "but, if you will give us your backing when we need it, the bulls will have nothing to do with this case, with the exception of Gates, and he's a friend of yours. They'll yell blue murder, Tim, when we land on them; but we have the goods and we can prove it to you before we're through."

"I'll take your word for it, Sawyer," Tim answered, "especially if you'll show me the goods afterward. Now, who are the men and what do you want me to do?"

"The men," Quincy answered slowly, "are Ike McKechnie and Long Tom." Tim whistled, but said nothing. "When they come in I want you to tip us off. We'll get them into one of the private rooms and then we'll ring for drinks. When we do that you are to answer the bell yourself and then we'll tell you what else to do. Has anyone spoken for Room Eight? No? All right, then. We'll take them to Room Eight, and, if you do your part, you'll have no trouble over this, and you'll get your place free of a pretty pair of crooks."

Tim nodded emphatic agreement with the plan and Quincy left him, making his way into the back room where Gates was impatiently waiting. Gates glanced up questioningly as Quincy approached. "Everything going well?" he inquired.

"Excellently," Quincy assured him, dropping into a chair on the opposite side of the table. "Our men will undoubtedly put in an appearance here later on in the evening."

Gates raised his eyebrows. "Our men?" he repeated.

Quincy nodded. "Gates, do you know Ike McKechnie and Long Tom?"

Gates shook his head negatively after several moments of careful reflection. "I don't remember ever having heard of either of them," he said.

"So much the better. They know me, which is bad; but I think that we shall have little trouble in overcoming that difficulty. Tim will tip us off when they appear outside and I can point them out to you when they come in here, as they are certain to do. Now, the idea is this. I am drunk, hopelessly drunk, and we want to play poker. The chances are strong that they'll remember me as easy money, and they'll be ready enough to play, provided their suspicions are not aroused. If their suspicions do become aroused, they'll agree to play anyway because they won't dare do anything else. Your job is to round them up and get them interested. Then we will all go to Room Eight,—don't forget that number,—and, when we are once there, I imagine that developments will follow each other very rapidly. You have the plan correctly?"

Gates nodded quietly and Quincy sank back in an excellent assumption of a drunken stupor.

For perhaps half an hour they remained in their positions, silent save for the occasional maudlin remarks from Quincy, thrown out from time to time for the benefit of the various patrons of the saloon with which the place was filling. At last Tim's face appeared in the doorway, and his glance flashed quickly over the assemblage until it rested on Gates. He nodded meaningly and then stared in anxious astonishment at Quincy, but a cautious wink from Gates reassured him and his head disappeared. Hardly had the door closed after him before it reopened to admit the eagerly awaited pair, Long Tom and Lawyer Ike McKechnie.

Gates sized them up as they advanced, and mentally classified each before they had reached the middle of the room. In McKechnie he saw a man whom nature had evidently intended to be slim, but who had so far improved on nature's designs as to become remarkably fat and florid as to features, although his body still maintained its original gangling formation. His face was filled with egotistical pomposity and the condescending manner with which he addressed his companion from time to time showed beyond doubt that, in his own mind, at least, Lawyer McKechnie was a figure to be reckoned with. Long Tom, on the other hand, outwardly possessed neither egotism nor self-assertion. An exceptionally tall man, and one whose extreme, slimness made his height seem even greater, he carried with him an air of furtiveness and foxlike cunning that would be sufficient at first glance to, arouse the suspicions of even the most trusting of men. He appeared to rely on McKechnie as on a guide or commander, and implicitly obeyed every suggestion emanating from that worthy source.

As the men cast about them for a vacant table, Gates arose and nonchalantly approached them, both men halting, with eyes fixed questioningly and expectantly upon him as he came up with them.

"My friend and I," he said with a backward jerk of his thumb in Quincy's direction, "want a little game. We've engaged a room and have been waiting for someone to come in who looked as if he could play a gentleman's game. Are you in on it?"

McKechnie grinned uncertainly and shifted his position slightly so as to obtain a better view of Quincy. "For the love of Mike!" he exclaimed, as his eye fell on the silent figure at the table. "It's young Sawyer and as full as a goat." He fixed his eyes speculatively on Gates. "Sawyer used to carry a fair roll," he stated meditatively.

Gates caught the implied interrogation. "Believe me," he stated emphatically, "Sawyer's roll hasn't diminished any."

McKechnie grinned in secret anticipation. "We're on," he announced. "Where's your room?"

After much shaking and many protesting groans and growls Quincy was at last imbued with sufficient interest in his surroundings to climb to his feet and be led, leaning heavily on Gates, in the direction of Room Eight. Once there, Gates dropped him unceremoniously into the chair nearest the door and busied himself with preparations for the game. As he moved and talked, however, his watchful eyes were continuously roving in Quincy's direction, where they were at last rewarded by the sight of a sharp wink.

"Guess we'd better start right by having some drinks brought up, hadn't we?" he questioned, the invitation being met by fervent expressions of assent. In accordance with the evident desire of the company, therefore, he leaned over and pressed long on the button.

To the surprise of Long Tom and McKechnie it was Tim McMahon, himself, who answered the summons, and he further added to their surprise by carefully closing the door as he entered and placing his broad back against it.

"What'll you have?" was his husky greeting.

Surprises appeared to abound in that particular room, as Long Tom and McKechnie were about to discover, for, hardly had Tim's inquiry been made, before Quincy abruptly emerged from his lethargy and sat up, fixing his eyes on McKechnie's face. Suspicion immediately appeared in that individual's eyes and his hands convulsively grasped the edge of the table.

"What kind of a plant is this?" he demanded savagely. "You fellows spring your game quick, whatever it is."

Quincy laughed softly and meaningly. "Our game, Ike?" he inquired. "You surprise me. Indeed you do." He half rose, and leaned across the table, as he continued, but the smile had disappeared from his face, leaving in its place a look of cold accusation. "We're playing no game, Ike McKechnie, as you are about to discover. I am superseding my friend, Inspector Gates, a trifle, but it will amount to the same thing in the end. Ike McKechnie, I arrest you in the name of the Commonwealth of Massachusetts on the charge of abduction and as being an accessory before the fact on a charge of murderous assault. Long Tom, I arrest you under the same authority on the charge of abduction and of assault with intent to kill, the latter charge containing two counts."

"And I," Gates broke in, "must warn you that whatever you say from this time forth may be used against you at your trial."

For a moment the pair stared dumbly in Quincy's direction, too stupefied to move or speak; but their state of paralysis lasted only momentarily. With a vicious snarl McKechnie sprang from his chair straight on Gates, who, taken off his guard, fell heavily to the floor. Long Tom was no whit behind his pal in readiness and, as Quincy grappled with McKechnie, Tom plunged in behind, getting a strangle hold about Quincy's neck and bearing him to the floor. As Quincy fell McKechnie leaped back, drew a revolver and turned with a savage grunt of triumph toward McMahon. If he had thoughts of over-awing the saloon keeper by show of arms, however, he was doomed to bitter disappointment, for Tim, though slow of movement, could move like a cyclone when once he got under way.

As McKechnie's revolver whipped into view, Tim, moving with the irresistible force of a runaway express train, struck him, head-on, and the two rolled to the floor amid a chaos of splintered chairs and overturned furniture. As the crash of the fall sounded, and mingled with it came the grunts of McKechnie, groaning beneath Tim's massive bulk, Long Tom suddenly loosened his hold on Quincy and turned to flee. But he was too late. Gates, having regained his scattered wits during the few moments occupied by the short conflict, had taken up his position in the doorway, and Tom found himself staring into the barrel of a business-like revolver.

"Better quit it, Tom," Gates advised him quietly. "It's all over now."

Before Long Tom could make up his own mind as to his step, Gates' muscular arm had seized him and hurled him across the room into a chair, where he sank down cowed and silent. McKechnie followed, propelled by a vigorous thrust from Tim, and the fight for freedom ended almost as abruptly as it had begun.

"Look here, Tim," McKechnie snarled, at last regaining some of his self-control. "Are you going to stand for this? Are you going to let us be pinched on any such fool charge, and in your own place?"

"Ah, cheese!" was Tim's disgusted retort. "A healthy bunch of regard you're showin' for my place all of a sudden, ain't you? Do you think I'm goin' to butt in on the bulls and put my place to the everlastin' bad just for the likes of you? Not by a heap. This administration ain't none too friendly toward me as things is, and you can bet your bottom dollar that I ain't takin' chances. What'd you go to work and get my place mixed up in this for, anyway? That's what I want to know," he continued savagely.

McKechnie subsided, seemingly too overcome to speak, but not so with Long Tom. While the discussion had been in progress he had hitched himself about until he had secured an open passage between his chair and the window. With a leap he cleared the chair and covered half the distance to his desired goal, and another bound took him to the window itself. But he had not been sufficiently cautious in his original movements, for every furtive hitch of the chair had been noted by Quincy and, as Long Tom threw himself at the window ledge, he was sharply upset and hurled struggling to the floor, with Quincy astride him. Twist and squirm as he would, his arms were relentlessly borne back until two sharp metallic clicks informed him as plainly as words that further resistance would be useless. As he struggled to his feet his eyes fell on a small object which Quincy held in his hand, and, in spite of himself, he paled visibly at the sight. Quincy stood silently regarding the object, an expression of disgust on his face. Then, with a nauseated shrug, he dropped the object into his own pocket. As he looked up into Long Tom's shifting eyes, however, that individual shuddered violently and the light of hope appeared to have utterly vanished from his face.

"Handcuff Ike, Gates," came Quincy's curt command, and in a few moments McKechnie's wrists were adorned with rings of gleaming steel.

"Now," Quincy continued, "we have work elsewhere for the time being. I want to leave these men here, Tim, until we come back." Tim nodded assent to the proposition and glared balefully at the prisoners. "You'll make certain they don't escape while we are gone?" Quincy continued.

"Oh, they won't escape," Tim affirmed grimly. "I'll sit right here myself, and keep 'em company until you get back. I want to know the rest of this tale."

"Say, Sawyer," Gates protested in an undertone, as they made their way out of the building. "Aren't we taking a long chance in arresting these men? Are you sure of your ground?"

"Absolutely," Quincy replied soberly. "I was sure of it from the first, but I caught Long Tom with the goods just now and there isn't a bit of doubt left. I lifted a little object from his pocket that will give you a start when you see it."

"Where are we headed for, anyhow?" Gates next asked as they dropped from a surface car at a dark corner in the West End.

"We are going after Hemenway," Quincy informed him. "And, by the way, Gates, you have not the least show in the world of passing muster where we are going. You look altogether too trim."

"But I can't work up any kind of a disguise now," Gates protested.

"Oh, yes, you can. A scientific disguise has nothing to do with false whiskers and changed clothes, in spite of what the popular version of the subject may be. Here, let me show you how to go about it. First push that hat toward the back of your head; no, a little farther and a bit to one side. That's right. Next roll the right hand lapel of your coat over a little, so that the lapel and about half your collar will remain out of place. Correct. Then stick this in your other lapel." He put in place a cheap button bearing a pointless phrase printed on it, a button of the type sold with cigarettes. "Lastly, put this jewel in your tie." He extended a tie pin set with a large flashy gem.

"Gee," Gates muttered. "Is that sparkler the real thing?"

"The real thing in paste, yes. It will flash like fire when the light strikes it from the proper angle. Now take your face between those big paws of yours and rub it heartily so as to give you a flushed appearance, and if you don't pass anywhere as a low class tout I'm mistaken."

Quincy surveyed his handiwork as a makeup artist with a grin, and then made a few hasty changes in his own appearance, achieving a result which Gates greeted with a snort of derision.

"If I look like you do I'm ashamed of myself," Gates grinned as they moved off.

The saloon which Quincy had visited in the afternoon maintained its same general appearance as they entered. The crowd of loungers and hangers-on was a little larger, perhaps; but the same sullen bartender stood at his place, Rabbit still circulated among the billiard tables, and the same furtive type of men slunk about the room, grunting at one another in subdued tones.

"Got a table vacant, Sport?" Quincy demanded in a loud tone of Rabbit, sinking his voice to a whisper as he fired a second question. "What room is Long Tom's friend in?"

"Naw, there ain't none vacant," Rabbit responded with a gleam of recognition in his eyes. "Up-stairs, first room to the right," he concluded in a whisper.

"Well," Quincy continued, "my friend and I want to play off a bet. Call us when there's a table vacant and there'll be something in it for you." A meaning glance accompanied the words, and as Quincy moved off Rabbit found another bill in his hand.

Going directly to the bar they called for drinks, and, the crowd about being too large to allow for their dispensing of the vile liquid by way of the floor, they were forced to drink it. "Rat poison," Quincy heard Gates disgustedly mutter as he set his glass on the bar. Quincy then addressed the bartender:

"My friend and I," he said, "want a room. Got one for us?"

The bartender eyed him critically and, appearing to detect nothing suspicious about either of the prospective guests, replied: "Yes. A dollar a night in advance."

Quincy produced the money, peeling it from a very slender roll, and the pair were conducted to the floor above by a seedy-looking bell boy. As the door of their room closed Quincy listened intently while the footfalls of the bell boy slowly receded down the corridor. When the sounds had died away he jerked open the door and was in the corridor, Gates striding briskly after him. They rushed silently to the door Rabbit had described, and Quincy turned the knob, finding, as he had expected, that the door was locked.

"Open it," he commanded tersely, and Gates was instantly at work with his skeleton keys. The lock was old fashioned and yielded quickly, allowing the pair to gain entrance after merely a momentary delay. The room was in darkness, but Quincy's flashlight quickly revealed the electric switch, and the lights immediately flashed forth.

There on the bed lay Hemenway, securely bound and gagged.

Working rapidly, it was but a few moments before they had untied the various knots and Hemenway sat slowly up, gingerly stretching his arms to allow for the returning circulation.

"They kidnapped me," he sputtered, as soon as he was able to speak. "They enticed me into a cab and brought me here. I've been tied up ever since."

"Why didn't you yell or raise a rough house to attract attention?" Gates demanded.

"Yell!" Hemenway snorted. "I couldn't yell. One of them had a grip on my neck, and I had my hands full trying to keep him from choking me to death. I thought at first that killing me was their intention, and I fought like a cat to get away from them. I bit, clawed, struck, kicked and did everything a man could do, but I couldn't break that hold on my throat and, fighting against two of them as I was, it didn't take a great while before I was too exhausted to keep up the struggle. When I stopped fighting they loosened up on me a little and I had a chance to get my breath while they were driving to this place. I couldn't attract any outside attention, though, because they pulled the curtains down and one of them had his hand on me ready to grab me by the throat again if I made the least movement.

"When we got to this place they drove in by means of some back alley, and there was another blackguard waiting for them at the door. He was a bartender, I should think, and the three of them dragged me out of the hack. I broke away from them somewhat, and got down in the street on my back, and, believe me, there were some sore shins in that crowd before they could get me up again. I kicked and howled and raised all kinds of a ruction, but it was no use. I couldn't seem to attract any attention at all and, as soon as I tired myself out again, they dragged me up here and tied me up. I've been tied up just as you found me ever since. That bartender has been up every once in a while, since, to make sure that I wasn't getting the ropes loose, but I haven't seen anything of the other pair."

"Would you know the other men?" Quincy questioned.

"You bet I would," Hemenway replied with savage conviction. "I'd know them anywhere. And, if I ever do meet them again——" The pause which followed the remark was filled with significant promise.

"Come," Quincy stated. "We can't waste time here. It would be dangerous."

Even as he spoke, footsteps sounded at the foot of the stairs, followed almost immediately by Rabbit's bawling summons: "Say, you gents. There's a table vacant now."

For a moment silence reigned, and then the three in the doorway heard a fierce sibilant whisper from half way up the stairs. "You fool, what did you do that for?"

"They told me to," Rabbit whined in protest. "They told me to holler when there was a table."

"Come," said Gates in a low growl. "The longer we wait the harder our job will be."

He leaped through the door, with the others close at his heels. Down the flight of stairs they charged and, before the bartender, for it was he, had time in which to recover himself, a blow from Gates' mighty fist sent him flying out of the way, reeling and staggering against the wall. From the direction of the saloon came the alarmed cry of "cops," followed by the scurrying of many feet. In their path stood the Rabbit, cleverly simulating silent terror; but, as the trio bounded his way, one eye closed slowly and a quick jerk of his thumb indicated a doorway.

The slight delay in getting their bearings was sufficient to complicate their escape. The bartender had regained his feet and, thirsting for vengeance, came at them with a yell, calling all the while for the aid of his friends in the saloon. Gates leaped forward to meet him, but found quickly that he had his hands full, for the bartender showed himself to be a skilled boxer, undoubtedly a product of the prize ring. His first blow sent Gates back, dazed and half falling, and, without pausing an instant, he followed up his advantage to such good purpose that Gates became fully occupied in trying to parry the blows, without being given an opportunity to strike in his own behalf.

To make matters worse there came a rush of feet from the direction of the saloon and it was evident to the detectives and Hemenway that it would be but a matter of a few seconds before they were set upon by overwhelming numbers. Again, however, it was the Rabbit who came to their rescue. With a shrill squeal of assumed terror he turned about and dived headlong through the door, striking among the advancing legs and so entangling them that in an instant the doorway was choked with a heap of struggling human beings, all striving to regain their feet and advance to the attack.

But, the slight delay caused by Rabbit's manœuvre had been sufficient to once more turn the tide, for the bartender, suddenly beset on either side by Quincy and Hemenway, while Gates occupied him from in front, found himself to be greatly at a disadvantage. His arms were simultaneously pinioned to his sides and then, with a sudden heave by the three men in unison, he was propelled headlong into the struggling mass that choked the doorway. Their way once more free from obstruction, the trio sprang toward the door which the Rabbit had indicated and plunged through it, finding themselves in a narrow alley, at one end of which gleamed the lights of a street, and from which end came the dull clanging of street car gongs. A short run carried them the length of the alley and, having gained the street, it was but a few moments before they were aboard a surface car and bound in the direction of Tim McMahon's saloon.

The status of affairs in Room Eight appeared to have changed not at all during their absence. McKechnie and Long Tom still sat where they had been left, staring gloomily at each other, while Tim slouched back in a chair and puffed at his stubby clay pipe in grim silence. Such was the sight which met Hemenway's gaze as he entered, but the silent inactivity of the place was of short duration following his entrance. As his eyes fell on the prisoners he grasped sharply at Quincy's arm.

"Those are the men," he exclaimed excitedly. "They are the ones who were in that cab."

"I know it," Quincy assured him quietly. "We are now about to call their game and the result will be interesting."

While the brief colloquy was going on Gates had been sharply scanning Long Tom's face, noting the various shades of pallor that were intermittently appearing on it, and watching the expression of fear grow ever stronger as the man's imagination became active.

"Look at Long Tom," he whispered to Quincy. "It will need only the mildest of examinations to twist a confession from him."

"We don't need it," Quincy replied. "We have the goods on them both, and they can't shake away under any consideration. Now, Mr. Hemenway," he continued, turning half about, "I am able to introduce you to the man who assaulted you in your office, and then followed it up by an assault on your grandmother in her own home. You are proud of your work, aren't you, Tom? It takes a man of unusual courage to sneak up behind an old lady and hit her over the head."

"But, why?" Hemenway gasped, looking from Quincy to Long Tom, and evidently struggling in a fog of mystification. "Why should he have done it? I am sure I never saw the man before, and, for the life of me, I cannot see what enmity he could have toward my grandmother and myself."

"He had none, Hemenway. I assure you that he had none whatever. This little game was a stroke in a certain class of high finance. Our collection," indicating the prisoners, "is still short one curio, but that need make no difference at present. You will best be able to understand the affair if I give you a more detailed account of it, and the reasons causing it, as I have figured them out.

"My starting point, Mr. Hemenway, was here. It was perfectly evident, from the mode employed in the assaults on yourself and on your grandmother, that whoever committed the deeds had no intention of doing either of you a lasting injury. The blows dealt in each case were too light to cause death, being merely what are called in police parlance 'sleepers," or stunning blows. They were struck, I judged, with a sandbag, and by the hand of a man well versed in the art of sandbagging. If the blows were not intended to cause death, or serious injury, their motive could not, therefore, have been revenge. The robbery theory passed out of the case hand-in-hand with the theory of enmity, or revenge, because in each case you testified that nothing whatever had been taken. Consequently, I was obliged to seek elsewhere for a motive, and it was not until you told me of the pending law settlement of your contested property rights that I commenced to see a glimmer of light in the case.

"I seized on that theory and worked at it, finding that it quickly unfolded a most plausible motive for the assaults; namely, that the man who was contesting your rights was preparing to spring some sort of a trap, and that he wished to keep your attention engaged elsewhere while he was working out his little game. Nothing will focus a man's attention more readily, as a rule, than an assault on him, and you were therefore attacked. But, even then, you did not relax your efforts in the preparation of your property case, and it became necessary for your opponent to take another step, the result being the attack on your grandmother. But, even then, your opponent evidently was not fully satisfied, for we have seen that you were kidnapped and carried to the place where we found you,—your room, let me add, having been hired for a week, which argues that you were doomed to confinement until after the case had come to trial. There, I think, we have the motive of this affair."

"But," Hemenway protested; "would they have dared to kidnap me for any such reason as that? I saw the two men and would have been able to identify them at any time."

"Yes," Quincy replied with a smile. "You could have identified them to your own satisfaction; but you have no idea what beautiful alibis they would have been provided with, had you brought your charge against them. The chances are strong that, instead of having your case against them upheld, the only result of your charge would have been that you would have found yourself ordered out of court and have been reprimanded for bringing in charges so evidently the result of your own drunken imagination. Yes, that is what your charge would have been called, so don't look shocked. These men would have been supplied with an endless chain of witnesses who would have corroborated whatever alibi the defence happened to choose. You can see how little risk they ran in abducting you. Remember, also, that they are backed by Peter Lorillard, of the Lorillard Realty Corporation, and that Mr. McKechnie is that corporation's chief counsel. There you have the whole affair in a nutshell."

"But, Sawyer," Gates broke in. "All that is interesting and necessary, but how did you settle on Long Tom? That is what I want to find out."

"Well," Quincy continued, "that part was the result of deduction. I have shown how I traced the affair to Lorillard's company and how McKechnie is the company's counsel. I have also shown that I believed both victims to have been sandbagged. Now, a sandbag is a weapon that requires great skill in its use. It leaves no mark when a blow is struck with it, it is silent, and above all it is deadly. In the hands of an inexperienced man a sandbag is one of the most dangerous of weapons; but an expert can so judge the force of his blow as to make it as wicked or as harmless as he pleases. You must observe that nobody other than an expert could have struck the blows in this particular case, for you will readily see that it required a far different blow to strike down a young man than was required to incapacitate an aged woman. Had the same blows been used the inevitable result would have been death for Mrs. Patterson. Therefore I discovered that I must search for a sandbag expert.

"Strange as it may seem, sandbag experts are very few and far between in this city, for the sandbag, as Inspector Gates will tell you, is rarely used here. In fact, as I ran back over the list of my variously accomplished acquaintances, I could think of only one man whom I absolutely knew to be a sandbag expert. That man was Long Tom, who learned the art in Chicago, I believe, several years ago. Long Tom, also, was a close pal of Ike McKechnie, which fact formed a second link connecting him with the case. From time to time, as I followed out the thread of evidence, I found other connections which strengthened my belief. Now, Gates, before I continue my story, will you please take Tom's thumb print and compare it with the photographs of the prints figuring in this case. Compare it carefully with the one in Mr. Hemen way's office, but above all compare it very carefully with the one which appeared on the mirror in Mrs. Patterson's room."

As Gates stepped forward to comply with Quincy's instructions a sneering grin of triumph flashed for a moment over McKechnie's face, but no answering grin came back from Long Tom, who was sullenly extending his thumb for the impression. Gates went rapidly about his work and in a few moments had the impression of Long Tom's thumb laid beside the photographs on the card table. As he bent over the table to make the comparison, however, an expression of astonishment appeared on his face, and he strained sharply forward.

"Sawyer," he exclaimed excitedly. "These prints are not the same!"

"Of course they aren't the same," McKechnie sneered. "You fellows are in bad, and you'd better take these irons off Tom and me, or you'll sweat proper for this job." He glared threateningly as he concluded.

"Don't grow overheated, Ike," Quincy cautioned him coolly. "Remember that I didn't say they were the same. In fact, I knew they were not."

With the exception of Long Tom all regarded him incredulously; but the sandbagger still sat with head bowed hopelessly, and with an air of complete dejection.

"Now, listen," Quincy continued, "because right here we have the keystone of the whole affair, and one of diabolical cunning it is. You will remember, Gates, that I carefully questioned Mrs. Patterson in order to discover whether her assailant approached her from one side or from behind. Now, Gates, approaching as he did from behind, how in the world could he have so manœuvred as to accidentally touch a mirror which lay on the table some distance in front of her? Furthermore, why should a man, in leaving an office which was well lighted, carefully impress his thumb on the door some distance above the knob? Were those actions accidental? Most assuredly they were not.

"Those thumb prints were placed purposely, and with the desire that they should be discovered. Why? Because they were not the prints of the assailant's thumb, but were artificial prints intended to throw investigators off the track. He well knew that no court in the world would convict him on such circumstantial evidence as might be offered against him, provided it could be shown that his thumb print was different from those found on the scenes of his crimes.

"Study that photograph of the thumb print on the mirror, Gates. Don't you see the peculiarity it possesses? Look at it. It is a double thumb print. You can see the tip of another thumb at the side of the main print and farther over on the mirror you can see where two knuckles lightly touched the glass. Do you follow me? Good. Now, look here."

As he concluded he drew from his pocket the object he had taken from Long Tom and laid it on the table, still keeping it covered with his hand. Slowly he removed his hand, and left lying on the table a mummified human thumb, at which his companions stared aghast.

"That," he stated triumphantly, "is the key to the thumb-print riddle. That thumb, treated by some process which preserved it, has been used for the purpose of hiding the tracks of the real criminal in this case. It was a simple matter for the man to rub the thumb on the palm of his hand until it gathered sufficient moisture and oil to make an impression on the glass, or to dip it in ink, as was the method in the office. When making the imprint on the mirror, however, he made the fatal error of touching the tip of his own thumb to the glass while holding the dummy, and thus he supplied us with the suspicious phenomenon of a double thumb print. That thumb," he regarded it with disgust, "is so far gone that it could never have been used again, but it did its work in this case and, but for the slightest of slips on the part of Long Tom, it would have defeated us."

For some time after he had concluded his remarks no word was spoken, the only sounds in the room being the nervously excited breathing of the men or the creaking of a chair as one shifted his position. Then McKechnie moodily raised his eyes.

"You can't take it all out on us," he growled. "Lorillard has got to come in for his share. He planned it."

"Lorillard," Quincy stated, "has already been arrested. He was taken on my complaint early in the evening and is now awaiting you at police headquarters. Will you go to the station in a cab without making any trouble or shall I have Inspector Gates call a patrol wagon?"

McKechnie glared sullenly at the handcuffs which pinioned his wrists. "We'll go in a cab," he growled. "I guess the game's up."

THE ART OF FORGERY

Rodrigues Ottolengui

O NE WET AFTERNOON, WHEN ALL NEW YORK WAS HURRYING HOMEWARD under dripping umbrellas, or crowding into already overcrowded trolley cars, newsboys were screaming "Extra! Extra," and selling their papers like hot cakes. The scarehead, in glaring red letters, read: "FORGERY IN HIGH LIFE."

Mr. Mitchel tossed a nickel to a boy in exchange for a paper, as he ascended the steps of an elevated station. He read the story on his way home. His interest grew as he recognized familiar names. The prisoner, for an arrest had been made, was Matthew Martin, the son of Montgomery Martin, an old acquaintance. The young man was known to Mr. Mitchel only by sight. The other name was Anthony P. Dunn, a Wall Street broker, and an employer of young Martin. Mr. Dunn was known to Mr. Mitchel only as a member of one of his clubs.

This was the newspaper's account:

An important arrest was made this afternoon at the Importer's National Bank, when a scion of an old Knickerbocker family was given into custody for attempting to pass a forged check for five thousand dollars. The prisoner is Matthew Martin, only son of the late Montgomery Martin, who was for forty years a prominent and highly honored member of the best social circles of this city. It will be recalled that the sad death of the elder Mr. Martin was caused by the failure of the business house of which he was a retired member. With remarkable honesty, Mr. Martin gave up all of his property to help pay the losses for which he was legally, but not through his own acts, responsible.

After the death of his father, about a year ago, Mr. Matthew Martin, the son, with commendable industry, sought and obtained a position where he might at least support himself, it being, of course, no longer possible for him to live the fashionable life of a wealthy man's son. Young Martin entered the employment of an old friend of his father, Mr. Anthony P. Dunn, a well-known and wealthy Wall Street broker. It appears that from the first Mr. Dunn placed implicit confidence in his old friend's son, so that he soon rose to a confidential position in this important house. In the exigencies of business on the Street actual cash is often a necessity, and latterly it has been Mr. Dunn's habit to send young Martin to the bank with checks of considerable magnitude. In this way he was known to the cashier and tellers, and until to-day checks presented by him have been cashed promptly without question. Something in the young man's manner this afternoon, when he came into the bank just before closing time and handed in a check for five thousand dollars, seems to have attracted the notice of the paying-teller and to have aroused his suspicions. At any rate, he scrutinized the check more closely than usual, and then asked young Martin to wait a moment, as he would have to go into the vault for the money. Passing out of sight of the man at the window, the teller went to the telephone and called up Mr. Dunn, asking him whether he had sent the check which had been presented. Mr. Dunn promptly declared that he had not done so, and was asked to visit the bank. The hour for closing having come, the outer doors were shut, and thus young Martin was virtually a prisoner. Nothing was said to him, however, and the paying-teller did not return to the window. Nevertheless, the young man apparently was either unsuspicious or else oblivious. Indeed, the latter word seems the more exact, as the detective of the bank declares that he seemed abstracted, as he patiently stood waiting at the window during the fifteen minutes that passed before Mr. Dunn reached the bank and was admitted. On his arrival, Mr. Dunn was taken to the cashier's private room, and the check was shown to him. He unhesitatingly pronounced it to be a forgery, and asked by whom it had been presented. He appeared to be terribly shocked when told that it had been brought to the bank by his clerk, young Martin. The old man broke down, seemed greatly overcome as he vainly tried to suppress his sobs, crying, "This is terrible! terrible! Thank God his parents have not lived to see this day."

Mr. Dunn pleaded that the matter should be hushed up, but banks have no sentiment to waste on forgers. Martin was therefore called into the presence of his employer and the bank officials, and told that his crime had been detected. At first he seemed dazed, as though slowly emerging from a trance. Asked for an explanation, he finally said:

"Do I understand that Mr. Dunn says the check is a forgery?"

"He does," replied the cashier.

"Will you say as much to me?" asked young Martin, turning to Mr. Dunn.

"It is a terrible thing to be compelled to say so," replied that gentleman, after some hesitation, "but what else can I say?"

"You did not sign that check?" asked Martin.

"I certainly did not," was Mr. Dunn's reply.

This was followed by a silence which was painfully felt by all the men present. Martin apparently relapsed into his abstraction. It almost seemed as though he were under the influence of some narcotic. At length the cashier again spoke.

"Well, young man," said he, "you are in a very serious predicament. What have you to say?"

"Nothing," answered he. "Absolutely nothing, I make neither defense nor explanation. Nor will I ever do so."

This rather unusual stand for a few moments nonplussed the officials, but at last, shrugging his shoulders, the cashier turned to the detective and said:

"Take him to police headquarters and make a charge against him."

Martin made no resistance, but calmly followed the detective out of the bank and soon was locked in a cell at the police station.

On the day following his arrest, he was taken before a magistrate, where be waived examination, and was held for the grand jury. That body indicted him, and within two weeks he was called to trial. Some persons remarked upon the swiftness with which the usually slow machinery of justice was moving, but this was scarcely strange in view of the evidence, and the persistence of the prisoner that he had no explanation to offer. Counsel was assigned to him, but in spite of the young lawyer's really clever management of the case, handicapped as he was by his client's silence and seeming indifference, the result was a foregone conclusion. The jury found a verdict of "guilty" without leaving their seats.

The evidence offered by the prosecution was not voluminous, but it was most convincing. First there was the paying-teller, who declared that he had doubted the signature when presented. Next was called Mr. Dunn, a reluctant witness, and, consequently, doubly effective. He denied the signature on the stand, as he had done in the bank. He was overcome by emotion, and all in the court-room sympathized with this man, who was compelled to testify against the son of an old friend. In corroboration of these two witnesses, three handwriting experts were introduced, all of whom declared that the entire check was a tracing. The prosecution then placed in evidence a check for the same amount of money, which had been previously presented at the bank by Martin and which had been cashed without question. The experts declared that this check had been used as a model, and that the spurious check had been placed over it, probably against a windowpane, and the tracings made first with a pencil, and afterwards with pen and ink. To remove the least shadow of doubt, one of the experts applied a chemical to a part of the writing on the forged check, removed the ink, and disclosed the pencil tracing beneath. The verdict having been pronounced, the prisoner was remanded for sentence, and with bowed head, but still without uttering a word in his own behalf, this last representative of an honorable family was led away to prison.

Mr. Mitchel read the various newspaper accounts of the case, as he had read the first one, with an interest slightly intensified by the fact that the names of the principals were known to him. Yet he had allowed the matter to pass from his mind almost entirely, when one morning he was surprised to receive a call from Mr. Barnes, who was accompanied by a young and rather attractive woman.

"I desire to enlist your services," began the detective, "in behalf of this young lady, Miss Dunn."

"Not the daughter of Anthony Dunn?" asked Mr. Mitchel.

"The same," said Mr. Barnes.

"And how may I assist the young lady?"

"I hardly know myself," said Mr. Barnes. "I hesitated to come to you, but she applied to me for assistance, and I must confess that I do not see that anything can be done, unless, indeed, you can see a way. It is that forgery case, young Martin, you know."

"Do you think that he is innocent, Miss Dunn?" asked Mr. Mitchel, turning to the girl.

"I know it," said she, confidently, looking straight at Mr. Mitchel. "I know it, but I cannot prove it. That is what I wish you to do."

"Tell me why you think this man innocent?"

"A woman's reason," said she. "I feel it. You see, I love him." She made the admission with delightful artlessness and sincerity.

"I surmised as much," said Mr. Mitchel, "else you would not have moved in his behalf. But we must have something more tangible."

"Suppose I could tell you why he has made no defense?"

"Ah! That would be important!"

"Very well, then. He has kept silent because he loves me."

Mr. Mitchel started, and thought deeply for a moment.

"I see, I see," said he, at last. "Now, a few questions, if you please, Miss Dunn, and remember that I also now believe in Mr. Martin, and if you will be candid with me, I will save him. First tell me why you have waited until after his conviction before taking this step?"

"I did not wait a moment. But I was in Europe. I started back by the first steamer, after I read a brief account of Mr. Martin's arrest in a newspaper."

"Tell me exactly when you went to Europe, and, if there is no objection, why?"

"From the newspaper accounts I figure that I sailed on the day before Mr. Martin's arrest. I went by a slow ship, as I wished the benefit of a long sea voyage for my health. But the weather retarded our progress so that we were really two weeks in crossing, instead of the usual ten days. It was a week after my arrival in London that I read of Mr. Martin's trouble. I had called on a friend and while waiting for her, I picked up a New York paper from her reading table. Almost the first thing that attracted my attention was the report of the arrest. I have come back on the fastest ship sailing, but I find the trial over and the verdict against him. It almost seems as though there has been an attempt to 'railroad him.' I think that is the newspaper expression. Oh, you asked me why I went to Europe. I could tell you that I went for my health, but that is only partly true. I had planned such a trip, but hastened my departure because of a scene which I had with Mr. Martin."

"A scene? A quarrel, do you mean?"

"Hardly that. Rather, let us say a misunderstanding. Mr. Martin is impulsive, impetuous, impatient. That makes three adjectives, but they describe him. I am more phlegmatic, more patient, and, besides, I have ideals, ambitions. Mr. Martin on the evening in question told me of his love, and with perfect candor I expressed my pleasure at his avowal, and admitted that I loved him in return. He was delighted and at once exhibited that impulsiveness to which I have alluded. He wanted me to marry him within three months."

"You declined?"

"I laughed at him. I was really amused by his impetuosity, though flattered, too, in a way. But I reminded him of his lack of means to support a wife in the style to which I have been accustomed. I pointed out that though I might say I would live on love in a cottage, I hoped I was sensible enough to know that with my tastes, that sort of thing would bring happiness to neither of us. I therefore told him that we would wait till his fortunes were bettered. I pointed out that his father had risen to wealth by his own efforts, and said I would honor him and respect him all the more if he should do likewise."

"You seem to have quite modern views on matrimony," said Mr. Mitchel, smiling.

"I don't know. I simply wish to be happy when I do marry, and I thought I was giving Mr. Martin good advice."

"I think you were."

"He did not. He declared that in these times the only short road to fortune would be by speculation. Then he laughed in a curious way, and said something which some women would not repeat to you. But I think you should know the exact facts."

"By all means. What was the remark?"

"He said, 'Some men in my place would borrow from your father, with or without his consent, and make a Wall Street plunge to win the daughter. If caught, perhaps you might take pity on me and prevent a prosecution, by marrying me. How does the scheme strike you?' "

"I should not advise Miss Dunn to repeat that near the District Attorney's office," said Mr. Barnes. "She would be lending still greater color to their theory of the affair."

"I know," said Miss Dunn, "but that was simply a stupid remark made on the impulse of the moment by a man impatient of the delay exacted by his sweetheart. You can understand that, can you not, Mr. Mitchel?"

"Your construction is perfectly possible," said Mr. Mitchel, "but Mr. Barnes is right. I should not tell that to a newspaper reporter. It is so ingenious. The lover borrows, that is, takes, his employer's money and speculates. If successful, he paves the way to fortune, returns the cash, and, in time, marries the girl. If caught, he looks to the girl's love to save him, and he gets his wife even more quickly. But we must go at once to see Mr. Martin. It is quite important to do something before sentence is passed, and I believe to-morrow has been set for the final disposition of the case."

An hour later Mr. Mitchel and Miss Dunn were admitted to see young Martin. At first he declined the interview, though Mr. Mitchel had obtained a letter of introduction from his attorney. As a final resource, Miss Dunn wrote on her visiting card:

"I have crossed the Atlantic to see you because I love you. You must see us."

Thus he was persuaded, but though at first sight of the girl, Mr. Martin impulsively started forward, arms outstretched as though desirous of embracing her, almost instantly he controlled himself, and when he spoke his tone betokened no unwonted interest in her.

"Of course, Miss Dunn, after your long voyage and generous interest in me at such a time, I could not refuse to see you, as I have all others. But why distress yourself about me, a convicted felon?"

"Convicted but not sentenced," said the girl.

"Now, Mr. Martin," said Mr. Mitchel, "you must no longer interfere with the course of justice."

"How have I done so?"

"By making no defense. Your reason may be a chivalrous one, but it is foolish nevertheless."

"You seem to know it. May I ask how?"

"Miss Dunn told me in part, and the rest I have guessed. She says that you do not defend yourself because you love her."

"A curious evidence of love, is it not?" said Mr. Martin. "One would imagine that Sing Sing were a short cut to a girl's heart."

"Of course, you are not acting as you have with any idea of winning Miss Dunn. You are sacrificing yourself for her, or so you imagine."

"Perhaps you can explain the nature of this sacrifice?"

"If I tell you the true reason of your conduct, will you admit it, and be guided by us as to the future?"

"I cannot promise. Your knowledge of my reason would not militate against its potency. It would still exist."

"Perhaps not," said Miss Dunn. "Tell him your idea of his reason, Mr. Mitchel. I am curious to know whether you have guessed the truth, as I have."

"It is really very clear," said Mr. Mitchel, "so clear that I was astonished that a clever man like Mr. Barnes should have admitted that he did not understand. Let us recall that when accused of this crime Mr. Martin's only reply was to ask whether Mr. Dunn himself would deny that he had made the check. Mr. Dunn did so, and from that moment Mr. Martin adopted the policy of silence. Next you, Miss Dunn, appear on the scene and declare that Mr. Martin is acting through love of you. What could be more obvious? Mr. Dunn himself forged that check and sent Mr. Martin with it to the bank. He knew that when he denied having made it. No one would believe Mr. Martin's assertion that he had received it properly, especially after the experts had discovered that it had been traced, as it was intended that they should. Had he meant you to get the money he would simply have written a new check, declaring it a forgery when it came back to him through the regular channels. He wanted the arrest to occur at once."

"How does this fairy tale strike you, Miss Dunn?" asked Mr. Martin.

"Mr. Mitchel has echoed my own suspicions. You believed that the evidence against you would convict you in any event, while to tell your story would be to disgrace my name. But you have acted wrongly, Matthew, even though I respect you and love you for it all the more."

"Then you believe in me?" asked Mr. Martin, much agitated.

"As I believe in my Heavenly Father!"

"Thank God! Thank God!" cried Mr. Martin, falling to his knees and seizing Miss Dunn's hand, which he covered with kisses.

"Now, then," said Mr. Mitchel, as soon as the young man had recovered his composure, "do you persist in your course, or will you tell us that you are innocent?"

"I am innocent!" said Mr. Martin. "You have guessed the situation. I know nothing whatever about the making of the check. Mr. Dunn gave it to me and I was astounded when he repudiated it. But how does this avail? We cannot prove it."

"You do not know. If it is the truth, it should be provable."

"But even so, how can I consent to have my sweetheart's name dragged in the mire?"

"If you will not agree on any other terms," said Miss Dunn, demurely, "we might change my name—to yours, for example. But suppose I tell you that Dunn is not really my name?"

"What?" cried both men at once.

"The facts are very simple and explain Mr. Dunn's conduct," said the girl. "I am legally his daughter, but only by adoption. My father years ago was Mr. Dunn's partner and best friend. He died leaving me an orphan, and leaving, also, a comfortable fortune, which should be mine at the age of twenty-one, or when I should marry. You see, my father never meant any one to control me in that respect. Mr. Dunn was the executor and my guardian. I was only a little tot, and after two years, adoption papers were legally drawn up. Now, don't you see—"

"Of course we do." interrupted Mr. Mitchel. "Dunn has your fortune tangled up, if he has it at all. He was not anxious to have you marry soon, and ask for an accounting. Therefore, he took advantage of your trip to Europe, and during your absence tried, as you have said, to 'railroad' your sweetheart. The next step will be to prove this young man's innocence."

"I fear you are too late, good friends," said Mr. Martin. "I am to be sentenced tomorrow."

"We shall see," said Mr. Mitchel. "We will be present in court. And, now, good-by, I have no time to lose. You may remain a little longer, if you wish, Miss Dunn. I will leave the cab at the door for you and take another." Without giving her a chance to object, he hurried away.

Mr. Mitchel in his own mind already had an idea of how it might be possible to save young Martin, and he spent the rest of the day working in his behalf, conjointly with Mr. Merivale, the attorney. First they called upon the judge, explained the situation to him and obtained from him an order which would enable them to see the checks which had figured in the case; they also made an appointment for an interview with him during the evening. Next, they sought the District Attorney, and having told their story, that gentleman readily consented to be present at the meeting in the evening and to bring with him the same handwriting experts who had testified at the trial.

Thus it happened that this party of gentlemen assembled at the home of Judge Chisholm, on the evening before the day appointed for the sentencing of young Martin.

"Well, gentlemen," said the judge, "we are all here, so let us get to work. I must admit I am intensely curious to know how this gentleman expects to prove Martin's innocence, and as I am informed, through the very handwriting experts whose testimony so convincingly satisfied us all of his guilt. The situation is most extraordinary."

"And yet I consider it quite simple," said Mr. Mitchel. "May I have your close attention? I have separately related to all of you the rather tardy explanation given by young Martin. But considering that his case appeared hopeless, his story being sufficiently unusual to be incredible, we can all see how he felt it best to keep silent to save the name of his sweetheart. Now, the question is, can we corroborate his story? In brief, it is that the check was given to him by Mr. Dunn. Dunn, of course, denies this, and declares the check to have been a forgery. The interesting development then comes out, through these gentlemen, the handwriting experts, that the check is indeed a forgery, being, moreover, a tracing from a similar genuine check, which had passed through Mr. Martin's hands. One of the experts applied chemicals with which he removed the ink and revealed the lead pencil tracings beneath. I have asked him to come to-night prepared to repeat this experiment."

"I am ready to do so," said one of the experts.

"In a few moments. This brings out a peculiar situation. The experts proved unquestionably that the repudiated check was traced from one previously in existence. This has been made to serve as evidence not only of forgery, but of forgery by Mr. Martin."

"Of course," interrupted the judge, "the evidence of the experts only acted corroboratively of the theory of the prosecution. On their testimony that the check was a tracing no particular person could have been found guilty of making the forged check. But, in connection with the proved presentation of the check by Martin, together with the repudiation of it by Dunn, and all this added to the lack of defense on the part of the accused, the expert testimony unquestionably and rightfully regulated the verdict against the prisoner."

"Exactly. But now that a defense is offered, let us sift our evidence once more. We find then that the only actual proof present is that offered by these gentlemen, that the disputed check is a tracing from a genuine one. And it is this which will save Mr. Martin. Every other point made by the prosecution is now in dispute, and the final judgment must depend on whether Martin or Dunn traced that check."

"I fail to see how you can solve that knotty point," interposed the District Attorney.

"Please follow my argument and we shall see," said Mr. Mitchel. "First, let us inquire as to the opportunity which each man had to accomplish this. We learn that the original, the undisputed check was made a month before the other. The time will be important. It was sent to the bank by Martin, and was accepted and cashed. The genuine check then was in Martin's possession for less than an hour, on a day a month prior to his arrest. If he made the false check he must have done it on that day and during that hour."

"He may have had access to it since then," said the District Attorney.

"Impossible. The genuine check was in the possession of the bank from the time it was cashed until the very morning of the day on which the alleged forgery was presented, when it was returned to Mr. Dunn personally, shortly after the opening of the bank. Martin during that morning was attending to a commission out of town, and as soon as he reached the office, at two-thirty, to be exact, he was sent to the bank with the forged check, reaching there as they were closing. Thus at best he had but about ten minutes in which to discover a check, which had been only that morning returned from the bank, make a tracing from it and present it at the bank. That is to say, this must have occurred between two-thirty when he reached the office and the time when he arrived at the bank. Moreover, he must have been able to return the genuine check, since it was furnished to the prosecution by Mr. Dunn."

"Very well argued," said the judge. "I think it is clear that if Martin forged the check he must have done so when the genuine check was legitimately in his possession. How does that help you?"

"I think it will clear our man," said Mr. Mitchel. "Examine the genuine check, if you please. You observe that the bank has stamped the word 'Paid' on the check. This has been done with a punch which has cut out round holes that serve to make up the letters. If the experts will look closely on the face of the check they will observe that in a number of places these holes cut the writing. Am I correct?"

"Quite correct."

"Very good. Now, if Mr. Dunn made the false check, using this as his model, he made the tracing after it was returned to him from the bank, and, consequently, when these holes existed. Now, the experiment which I suggest is this: Apply the chemicals necessary and remove the ink entirely from the words 'Five thousand dollars.' Leave the signature for the present. It may prove useful at the next trial, when our experiment may be repeated before another jury."

"You seem certain of success," said the judge, smiling.

"We are dealing with an upright judge, sir," said Mr. Mitchel, and both men bowed.

Meanwhile the expert was at work, and in a few minutes declared that the ink had been removed.

"Do you find that the pencil tracing is continuous?" asked Mr. Mitchel. "That is, are the words written uninterruptedly."

"No. There are five places where breaks occur."

"Now, please, will you superimpose one check over the other, and tell me whether or not the breaks in the pencil writing do not exactly agree with holes in the genuine check?"

"They do exactly," both experts.

"That proves, your honor," said Mr. Mitchel, "that the spurious check was traced from the genuine one after it had been cashed by the bank. After it had left Mr. Martin's possession. Since that time, you previously admitted that Martin could not have done it."

The District Attorney closely scrutinized the checks, and then handed them to the judge, who also made a thorough examination.

"You have made your point, Mr. Mitchel," said the judge, finally. "Your man is innocent."

"Then you will grant an application tomorrow for a new trial?"

"Certainly. Will you object?" said the judge, turning to the District Attorney.

"Not at all," said that gentleman. "On the contrary, I would suggest that Dunn be arrested to-night."

"By all means have that done," assented the judge.

But when the officers visited Dunn's house and attempted to arrest him, be deliberately shot himself through the head. Later, it was found, as Mr. Mitchel had suggested, that most of Miss Dunn's fortune had disappeared.

THE CASE OF HELEN BOND

Arthur B. Reeve

I T HAS ALWAYS SEEMED STRANGE TO ME THAT NO ONE HAS EVER ENDOWED A professorship in criminal science in any of our large universities."

Craig Kennedy laid down his evening paper and filled his pipe with my tobacco. He and I were ensconced in a neat bachelor apartment on the Heights, not far from the university. Craig was an assistant professor of chemistry, and I was on the staff of the *Star*.

Settling back in my chair, I remarked: "Well, why should there be a chair in criminal science? I've done my turn at police headquarters reporting, and I can tell you, Craig, it's no place for a college professor. Crime is just crime, and as for dealing with it, the good detective is born and bred to it. College professors for the sociology of the thing, yes; for the detection of it, give me a Byrnes or a Devery."

"On the contrary," replied Craig, "there is a distinct place for science in the detection of crime. On the Continent they are far in advance of us in that respect. We are mere children beside a dozen crime-specialists I could name in Paris. You must remember also, Walter," he continued, warming to his subject, "that it's only within the past ten years or so that we have had the really practical college professor who could do it. The silk-stockinged variety is out of date. To-day it is the college professor who is the third arbitrator in labor disputes, who reforms the currency in the Far East, who heads our tariff commissions and conserves our farms and forests. We have professors of everything else. Why not professors of crime?

"Colleges have gone a long way from the old ideal of pure culture, and they have got down to solving the hard facts of life—all except one. They still treat crime in the old way, study its statistics, and pore over its causes and the theories by which it can be prevented. But as for running the criminal down scientifically, relentlessly—bah! we haven't made an inch of progress since your Byrnes and Devery."

"Doubtless you will write a thesis on this most interesting subject," I suggested, "and let it go at that."

"No, I am serious. I mean exactly what I say. I am going to apply science to the detection of crime, the same sort of methods by which you trace out the presence of a chemical or run an unknown germ to earth. And before I have gone far I am going to enlist Walter Jameson as an aide. I think I shall need you in my business."

"How do I come in?"

"Well, for one thing, you will get a scoop, a beat—whatever you call it in that newspaper jargon of yours."

I smiled in a skeptical way, such as newspapermen are wont to affect toward a thing until it is done—after which we make a wild scramble to exploit it.

"I'm willing to bet you our next box of cigars," resumed Craig, "that you don't know the most fascinating story in your own paper to-night."

"I'll bet I do," I said, "for I was one of about a dozen who worked it up. It's the Shaw murder trial. There isn't another that's even a bad second."

"I am afraid the cigars will be on you, Walter. Crowded over on the second page by a lot of rot that everyone has read for the fiftieth time now, you will find about half a column on the sudden death of John G. Fletcher."

I laughed. "Craig," I said, "that demonstrates what I just said—this is no place for a professor. Believe me, when you put up a simple death from apoplexy against a murder trial, and such a murder trial—well, you demonstrate what I have said."

Nevertheless Craig picked up the paper and read the account slowly aloud.

JOHN G. FLETCHER, STEEL-MAGNATE, DIES SUDDENLY

John Graham Fletcher, the aged philanthropist and steel-maker, was found dead in his library this mornng at his home at Fletcherwood, Great Neck, Long Island.

It had always been Mr. Fletcher's custom to rise at seven o'clock. This morning his housekeeper became alarmed when he had not appeared by nine o'clock. Listening at the door, she heard no sound. It was not locked, and on entering she found the former steel-magnate lying lifeless on the floor between his bed-room and the library adjoining. His personal physician, Dr. W. C. Bryant, was immediately notified.

Close examination of the body revealed that his face was slightly discolored, and the cause of death was given by the physician as apoplexy. He had evidently been dead about eight or nine hours when discovered. Curiously the safe in the library in which he kept his papers and a large sum of cash was found opened, but as far as is known nothing is missing.

Mr. Fletcher is survived by a nephew, John G. Fletcher II, who is the Blake professor of bacteriology at ——— University, and by a grandniece, Miss Helen Bond. Professor Fletcher was informed of the sad occurrence shortly after leaving a class this morning and hurried out to Fletcherwood. He would make no statement other than that he was inexpressibly shocked.

Miss Bond, who has for several years resided with the family of Mrs. Frances Greene, of Little Neck, is prostrated by the shock.

Then followed an account of the life of the great steel-maker and a list of his philanthropies.

"Now," continued Craig, determined to make a convert of me, "just before you came in, Jack Fletcher called me up from Great Neck. You probably don't know it, but it has been privately reported in the inner circle of the university that old Fletcher was to leave the bulk of his fortune for founding a great school of preventive medicine, and that the only proviso was that his nephew should head the school. The professor told me that the will was missing from the safe, and that it was the only thing missing. From his excitement I judge that there is more to the story than he cared to tell over the 'phone. He said his car was on the way to the city, and he asked if I wouldn't come out and help him—he wouldn't say how. Now I know him pretty well, and I'm going to ask you to come along, Walter, for the express purpose of keeping this thing out of the newspapers—understand?—until we get to the bottom of it."

A few minutes later the telephone rang, and the hall-boy announced that a "cyar is waitin' fer Perfessor Kennedy, sah." We hustled down into it, the chauffeur lounged down carelessly into his seat, and we were off across the city, and out on the road to Great Neck with amazing speed.

We found Fletcherwood a splendid estate directly on the bay, with a long driveway leading up to the door. Professor Fletcher met us at the porte-cochère, and I was glad to note that, far from taking me as an intruder, he seemed rather relieved that some one who understood the ways of the newspapers could stand between him and any possible reporters who might drop in.

He ushered us directly into the library and closed the door. It seemed as if he could scarcely wait to tell his story to some one.

"Kennedy," he began, "look at that safe door."

We looked. It had been drilled through in such a way as to break the combination. It was a heavy door, closely fitting, the best kind for a small safe that the state of the art had produced. Yet clearly it had been tampered with, and successfully.

Fletcher swung the door wide and pointed to a little compartment inside whose steel door had been jimmied open. Then out of it he carefully lifted a steel box and deposited it on the library table.

"I suppose everybody has been handling that box?" asked Craig quickly.

A smile flitted across Fletcher's features. "I thought of that, Kennedy," he said. "I remembered what you once told me about finger-prints. Only myself has about touched it, and I was careful to take hold of it only on the sides. The will was placed in this box, and the key to the box was usually in the lock. Well, the will is gone. That's all; nothing else was touched. But for the life of me I can't find a mark on the box, not a finger-mark. Now on a hot and humid summer night like last night I should say it was pretty likely that anyone touching this metal box would have left finger-marks. Shouldn't you think so, Kennedy?"

Kennedy nodded and continued to examine the place where the compartment had been jimmied. A low whistle aroused us. Coming over to the table, Craig tore a white sheet of paper off a pad lying there and deposited a couple of small particles on it.

"I found them sticking on the jagged edges of the steel where it had been forced," he said. Then he whipped out a pocket magnifying-glass. "Not from a rubber glove," he commented, half to himself. "By Jove, one side of them shows lines that look as if they were the lines on a person's fingers, and the other side is perfectly smooth. There's not a chance of using them as a clue, except—well, I didn't know criminals in America knew that stunt."

"What stunt?"

"Why, you know how keen the new-fangled detectives are on the finger-print system? Well, the first thing some of the up-to-date criminals in Europe did was to wear rubber gloves so that they would leave no prints. But you can't work very well with rubber gloves. Last fall in Paris I heard of a fellow who had given the police a lot of trouble. He never left a mark, or at least it was no good if he did. He painted his hands lightly with a liquid rubber which he had invented himself. It did all that rubber gloves would do and yet left him the free use of his fingers with practically the same keenness of touch. Fletcher, whatever is at the bottom of this affair, I feel sure right now that you have to deal with no ordinary criminal."

"Do you suppose there are any relatives besides those we know of?" I asked Kennedy when Fletcher had left the room to summon the servants.

"No," he replied, "I think not. Fletcher and Helen Bond, his second cousin, to whom he is engaged, are the only two."

Kennedy continued to study the library. He walked in and out of the doors and examined the windows and viewed the safe from all angles. "The old gentleman's bed-room is here," he said, indicating a door. "Now a good smart noise or perhaps even a light shining through the transom from the library might arouse him. Suppose he woke up suddenly and entered by this door. He would see the thief at work on the safe. He would become violently excited—it wouldn't be necessary for the intruder to commit a murder to get rid of the old gentleman then. Nature and passion would take care of that. Yes, that part of reconstructing the story is simple. But who was the intruder?"

Just then Fletcher returned with the servants. The questioning was long and tedious, and developed nothing except that the butler admitted that he was uncertain whether the windows in the library were locked. The gardener was very obtuse, but finally contributed one possibly important fact. He had noted in the morning that the back gate, leading into a disused road closer to the bay than the main highway in front of the house, was open. It was rarely used, and was kept closed only by an ordinary hook. Whoever had opened it had evidently forgotten to hook it. He had thought it strange that it was unhooked, and in closing it he had noticed in the mud of the roadway marks that seemed to indicate that an automobile had stood there.

After the servants had gone, Fletcher asked us to excuse him for a while, as he wished to run over to the Greenes', who lived across the bay. Miss Bond was completely prostrated by the death of her uncle, he said, and was in an extremely nervous condition. Meanwhile if we found any need of a machine we might use his uncle's, or in fact anything around the place, if we wanted it.

"Walter," said Craig, when Fletcher had gone, "I want to run back to town tonight, and I have something I'd like to have you do, too."

We were soon speeding back along the splendid road to Long Island City, while he laid out our program.

"You go down to the *Star* office," he said, "and look through all the clippings on the whole Fletcher family. Get a complete story of the life of Helen Bond, too—what she has done in society, with whom she has been seen mostly, whether she has made any trips abroad, and whether she has ever been engaged—you know, anything likely to be significant. I'm going up to the apartment to get my camera and then to the laboratory to get some rather bulky paraphernalia I want to take out to Fletcherwood. Meet me at the Columbus Circle station at, say half-past ten."

So we separated. My search revealed the fact that Miss Bond had always been intimate with the ultra-fashionable set, had spent last summer in Europe, a good part of the time in Switzerland and Paris with the Greenes. As far as I could find out she had never been reported engaged, but plenty of fortunes as well as foreign titles had been buzzing about the ward of the steel-magnate.

Craig and I met at the appointed time. He had a lot of paraphernalia with him, and it did not add to our comfort as we sped back, but it wasn't much over half an hour before we again found ourselves nearing Great Neck.

Instead of going directly back to Fletcherwood, however, Craig had told the chauffeur to stop at the plant of the local electric light and power company, where he asked if he might see the record of the amount of current used the night before.

The curve sprawled across the ruled surface of the sheet by the automatic registering-needle was irregular, showing the ups and downs of the current used, rising sharply from sundown and gradually declining after nine o'clock, as the lights went out. Somewhere between eleven and twelve o'clock, however, the irregular fall of the curve was broken by a quite noticeable upward twist.

Craig asked the men if that usually happened. They were quite sure that the curve as a rule went gradually down until twelve o'clock, when the power was shut off. But they did not see anything remarkable in it. "Oh, I suppose some of the big houses had guests," volunteered the foreman, "and just to show off the place perhaps they turned on all the lights. I don't know, sir, what it was, but it couldn't have been a heavy drain, or we would have noticed it at the time, and the lights would all have been dim."

"Well," said Craig, "just watch and see if it occurs again to-night about the same time."

"All right, sir."

"And when you close down the plant for the night, will you bring the record card up to Fletcherwood?" asked Craig, slipping a bill into the pocket of the foreman's shirt.

"I will, and thank you, sir."

It was nearly half-past eleven when Craig had got his apparatus set up in the library at Fletcherwood. Then he unscrewed all the bulbs from the chandelier in the library and attached in their places connections with the usual green silk-covered flexible wire rope. These were then joined up to a little instrument which to me looked like a drill. Next he muffled the drill with a wad of felt and applied it to the safe door.

I could hear the dull tat-tat of the drill. Going into the bed-room and closing the door, I found that it was still audible to me, but an old man, inclined to deafness and asleep, would scarcely have been awakened by it. In about ten minutes Craig displayed a neat little hole in the safe door opposite the one made by the cracksman in the combination.

"I'm glad you're honest," I said, "or else we might be afraid of you—perhaps even make you prove an alibi for last night's job!"

He ignored my bantering and said in a tone such as he might have used before a class of students in the gentle art of scientific safe-cracking: "Now if the power company's curve is just the same to-night as last night that will show how the thing was done. I wanted to be sure of it, so I thought I'd try this apparatus which I smuggled in from Paris last year. I believe the old man happened to be wakeful and heard it."

Then he pried off the door of the interior compartment which had been jimmied open. "Perhaps we may learn something by looking at this door and studying the marks left by the jimmy, by means of this new instrument of mine," he said.

On the library table he fastened an arrangement with two upright posts supporting a dial which he called a "dynamometer." The uprights were braced in the back, and the whole thing reminded me of a miniature guillotine.

"This is my mechanical detective," said Craig proudly. "It was devised by Bertillon himself, and he personally gave me permission to copy his own machine. You see, it is devised to measure pressure. Now let's take an ordinary jimmy and see just how much pressure it takes to duplicate those marks on this door."

Craig laid the piece of steel on the dynamometer in the position it had occupied in the safe, and braced it tightly. Then he took a jimmy and pressed on it with all his strength. The steel door was connected with the indicator, and the needle spun around until it indicated a pressure such as only a strong man could have exerted. Comparing the marks made in the steel by the experiment and by the safe-cracker, it was evident that no such pressure had been necessary. Apparently the lock on the door was only a trifling affair, and the steel itself was not very tough. The safe-makers had relied on the first line of defense to repel attack.

Craig tried again and again, each time using less force. At last he got a mark just about similar to the original marks on the steel.

"Well, well, what do you think of that?" he exclaimed reflectively. "A child could have done that part of the job."

Just then the lights went off for the night. Craig lighted the oil-lamp, and sat in silence until the electric light plant foreman appeared with the card-record, which showed a curve practically identical with that of the night before.

A few moments later Professor Fletcher's machine came up the driveway, and he joined us with a worried and preoccupied look on his face that he could not conceal. "She's terribly broken up by the suddenness of it all," he murmured as he sank into an armchair. "The shock has been too much for her. In fact I hadn't the heart to tell her anything about the robbery, poor girl." Then in a moment he asked, "Any more clues yet, Kennedy?"

"Well, nothing of first importance. I have only been trying to reconstruct the story of the robbery so that I can reason out a motive and a few details; then when the real clues come along we won't have so much ground to cover. The cracksman was certainly clever. He used an electric drill to break the combination and ran it by the electric light current."

"Whew!" exclaimed the professor, "is that so? He must have been above the average. That's interesting."

"By the way, Fletcher," said Kennedy, "I wish you would introduce me to your fiancée to-morrow. I would like to know her."

"Gladly," Fletcher replied, "only you must be careful what you talk about. Remember, the death of uncle has been quite a shock to her—he was her only relative besides myself."

"I will," promised Kennedy, "and by the way, she may think it strange that I'm out here at a time like this. Perhaps you had better tell her I'm a nerve specialist or something of that sort—anything not to connect me with the robbery, which you say you haven't told her about."

The next morning found Kennedy out bright and early, for he had not had a very good chance to do anything during the night except reconstruct the details. He was now down by the back gate with his camera, where I found him turning it end-down and photographing the road. Together we made a thorough search of the woods and the road about the gate, but could discover absolutely nothing.

After breakfast I improvised a dark room and developed the films, while Craig went down the back lane along the shore "looking for clues," as he said briefly. Toward noon he returned, and I could see "Ask me no questions" enameled all over his countenance. So I said nothing, but handed him the photographs of the road. He took them and laid them down in a long line on the library floor. They seemed to consist of little ridges of dirt on either side of a series of regular round spots, some of the spots very clear and distinct on the sides, others quite obscure in the center. Now and then where you would expect to one of the spots, just for the symmetry of the thing, it was missing. As I looked at the line of photographs on the floor I saw that they were a photograph of the track made by the tire of an automobile, and I suddenly recalled what the gardener had said.

Next Craig produced the results of his morning's work, which consisted of several dozen sheets of white paper, carefully separated into three bundles. These he also laid down in long lines on the floor, each package in a separate line. Then I began to realize what he was doing, and became fascinated in watching him on his hands and knees eagerly scanning the papers and comparing them with the photographs. At last he gathered up two of the sets of papers very decisively and threw them away. Then he shifted the third set a bit, and laid it closely parallel to the photographs.

"Look at these, Walter," he said. "Now take this deep and sharp indentation. Well, there's a corresponding one in the photograph. So you can pick them out one for another. Now here's one missing altogether on the paper. So it is in the photograph."

Almost like a schoolboy in his glee, he was comparing the little round circles made by the metal insertions in an automobile tire. Time and again I had seen imprints like that left in the dust and grease of an asphalted street or the mud of a road. It had never occurred to me that they might be used in any way. Yet here Craig was, calmly tracing out the similarity before my very eyes, identifying the marks made in the photograph with the prints left on the bits of paper.

As I followed him, I felt a most curious feeling of admiration for his genius. "Craig," I cried, "that's the thumb-print of an automobile."

"There speaks the yellow journalist," he answered merrily. "'Thumb Print System Applied to Motor Cars'—I can see the Sunday feature story you have in your mind with that headline already. Yes, Walter, that's precisely what this is. The Berlin police have used it a number of times with the most startling results."

"But, Craig," I exclaimed suddenly, "the paper prints, where did you get them? What machine is it?"

"It's one not very far from here," he answered sententiously, and I saw he would say nothing more that might fix a false suspicion on anyone. Still, my curiosity was so great that if there had been an opportunity I certainly should have tried out his plan on all the cars in the Fletcher garage.

Kennedy would say nothing more, and we ate our luncheon in silence. Fletcher, who had decided to lunch with the Greenes, called Kennedy up on the telephone to tell him it would be all right for him to call on Miss Bond later in the afternoon.

"And I may bring over the apparatus I described to you to determine just what her nervous condition is?" he asked. Apparently the answer was yes, for Kennedy hung up the receiver with a satisfied, "Good-by."

"Walter, I want you to come along with me this afternoon as my assistant. Remember I'm now Dr. Kennedy, the nerve specialist, and you are Dr. Jameson, my colleague, and we are to be in consultation on a most important case."

"Do you think that's fair?" I asked hotly—"to take that girl off her guard, to insinuate yourself into her confidence as a medical adviser, and worm out of her some kind of fact incriminating some one? I suppose that's your plan, and I don't like the ethics, or rather the lack of ethics, of the thing."

"Now think a minute, Walter. Perhaps I am a Jesuit, I don't know. Certainly I feel that the end will justify the means. I have an idea that I can get from Miss Bond the only clue that I need, one that will lead straight to the criminal. Who knows? I have a suspicion that the thing I'm going to do is the highest form of your so-called ethics. If what Fletcher tells us is true that girl is going insane over this thing. Why should she be so shocked over the death of an uncle she did not live with? I tell you she knows something about this case that it is necessary for us to know, too. If she doesn't tell some one, it will eat her mind out. I'll add a dinner to the box of cigars we have already bet on case that what I'm going to do is for the best—for her best."

Again I yielded, for I was coming to have more and more faith in the old Kennedy I had seen made over into a first-class detective, and together We started for the Greenes', Craig carrying something in one of those long black hand-bags which physicians affect.

Fletcher met us on the driveway. He seemed to be very much affected, for his face was drawn, and he shifted from one position to another nervously, from which we inferred that Miss Bond was feeling worse. It was late afternoon, almost verging on twilight, as he led us through the reception-hall and thence out onto a long porch overlooking the bay and redolent with honeysuckle.

Miss Bond was half reclining in a wicker chair as we entered. She started to rise to greet us, but Fletcher gently restrained her, saying, as he introduced us, that he guessed the doctors would pardon any informality from an invalid.

Fletcher is a pretty fine fellow, and I had come to like him; but I soon found myself wondering what he had ever done to deserve winning such a girl as Helen Bond. She was what I had described in my stories as the new type of woman, tall and athletic, yet without any affectation of mannishness. The very first thought that struck me was the incongruousness of a girl of her type suffering from an attack of "nerves," and I felt sure it must be as Craig had said, that she was concealing a secret that was having a terrible effect on her. A casual glance might not have betrayed the true state of her feelings, for her dark hair and large brown eyes and the tan of many suns on her face and arms betokened anything but the neurasthenic. One felt instinctively that she was, with all her athletic grace, primarily a womanly woman.

The sun sinking toward the hills across the bay softened the brown of her skin and, as I observed by watching her closely, served partially to conceal the nervousness which was wholly unnatural in a girl of such poise. When she smiled there was a false note in it; it was forced. The fact that that false note, whatever it meant, was so ill concealed impressed me. Had she been other than the natural, whole-souled Helen Bond whom people knew so well, she no doubt could have concealed her nervousness better. It was sufficiently evident to me that she was going through a mental hell of conflicting emotions that would have killed a woman of less self-control. I felt that I would like to be in Fletcher's shoes—doubly so when, at Kennedy's request, he withdrew, leaving me to witness the torture of a woman of such fine sensibilities, already hunted remorselessly by her own thoughts.

Still, I will give Kennedy credit for a tactfulness that I didn't know the old fellow possessed. He carried through the preliminary questions very well for a pseudo-doctor, appealing to me as his assistant on inconsequential things that enabled me to "save my face" perfectly. When he came to the critical moment of opening the black bag, he made a very appropriate and easy remark about not having brought any sharp shiny instruments or nasty black drugs.

"All I wish to do, Miss Bond, is to make a few simple little tests of your nervous condition. One of them we specialists call reaction time, and another is a test of heart action. Neither is of any seriousness at all, so I beg of you not to become excited, for the chief value consists in having the patient perfectly quiet and normal. After they are over I think I'll know whether to prescribe absolute rest or a visit to Newport."

She smiled languidly as he adjusted a long, tightly fitting rubber glove on her shapely forearm and then encased it in a larger, absolutely inflexible covering of leather. Between the rubber glove and the leather covering was a liquid communicating by a glass tube with a sort of dial. Craig had often explained to me how the pressure of the blood was registered most minutely on the dial, showing the varied emotions as keenly as if you had taken a peep into the very mind of the subject. I think he said the experimental psychologists called the thing a "plethysmograph."

Then he had an apparatus which measured "association time." The essential part of this instrument was the operation of a very delicate stop-watch, and this duty was given to me. It was nothing more nor less than measuring the time that elapsed between his questions to her and her answers, while he recorded the actual questions and answers and noted the results which I worked out. Neither of us was unfamiliar with the process; in fact, Craig carried it off as if he did that sort of thing as an every-day employment, although I think it was the first time he had ever tried both these instruments together.

"Now, Miss Bond," he said, and his voice was so reassuring and persuasive that I could see she was not made even a shade more nervous by our simple preparations, "the game—it is just like a children's parlor game—is just this: I will say a word—take 'dog,' for instance. You are to answer back immediately the first word that comes into your mind suggested by it—say 'cat.' I will say 'chain,' for example, and probably you will answer 'collar,' and so on. Do you catch my meaning? It may seem ridiculous, no doubt, but before we are through I feel sure you'll see how valuable such a test is, particularly in a simple case of nervousness such as yours."

I don't think she found any sinister interpretation in his words, but I did, and if ever I wanted to call Craig down it was then, but my voice seemed to stick in my throat. He was beginning. It was clearly up to me to give in and not interfere. As closely as I was able I kept my eyes riveted on the watch and other apparatus, while my ears and heart followed with mingled emotions the low, musical voice of the girl.

I will not give all the test, for there was much of it, particularly at the start, that was in reality valueless, since it was merely leading up to the "surprise tests." From the colorless questions Kennedy suddenly changed. It was done in an instant, when Miss Bond had been completely disarmed and put off her guard.

"Night," said Kennedy. "Day," came back the reply from Miss Bond.

"Automobile." "Horse."

"Bay." "Beach."

"Road." "Forest."

"Gate." "Fence."

"Path." "Shrubs."

"Porch." "House."

Did I detect or imagine a faint hesitation?

"Window." "Curtain."

Yes, it was plain that time. But the words followed one another in quick succession. There was no rest. She had no chance to collect herself. I noted the marked difference in the reaction time and, in my sympathy, damned this cold, scientific third degree.

"Paris." "France."

"Quartier Latin" "Students."

"Apaches." "Really, Dr. Kennedy, there is nothing I can associate with them." "Very well, let us try again," he replied with a forced unconcern. No lawyer out of court could have reveled in an opportunity for putting leading questions more ruthlessly than did Kennedy. He snapped out his words sharply and unexpectedly.

"Chandelier." "Light."

"Electric light," he emphasized. "Broadway," she answered, endeavoring to force a new association of ideas to replace one which she strove to conceal.

"Safe." "Vaults." Out of the comer of my eye I could see that the indicator showed a tremendously increased heart action. As for the reaction time, I noted that it was growing longer and more significant. Remorselessly he pressed his words home. Mentally I cursed him.

"Rubber." "Tire."

"Steel." "Pittsburg," she cried at random.

"Strong-box," No answer.

"Lock." Again no answer. He hurried his words. I was leaning forward, tense with excitement and sympathy.

"Key." Silence and a fluttering of the blood-pressure indicator.

"Will."

As the last word was uttered her air of frightened defiance was swept away. With a cry of anguish, she swayed to her feet. "No, no, Doctor, you must not, you must not," she cried with outstretched arms. "Why do you pick out those words of all others? Can it be——" If I had not caught her I believe she would have fainted.

The indicator showed a heart alternately throbbing with feverish excitement and almost stopping with fear. What would Kennedy do next, I wondered, determined to shut him off as soon as I possibly could. From the moment I had seen her I had been under her spell. Mine should have been Fletcher's place, I knew, though I cannot but say that I felt a certain grim pleasure in supporting even momentarily such a woman in her time of need.

"Can it be that you have guessed what no one in the world, no, not even dear old Jack, dreams? Oh, I shall go mad, mad, mad!"

Kennedy was on his feet in an instant, advancing toward her. The look in his eyes was answer enough for her. She knew that he knew, and she paled and shuddered, shrinking away from him toward me.

"Miss Bond," he said in a voice that forced attention—it was low and vibrating with feeling—"Miss Bond, have you ever told a lie to shield a friend?"

"Yes," she said, her eyes meeting his.

"So can I," came back the same tense voice, "when I know the truth about that friend."

Then for the first time tears came in a storm. Her breath was quick and feverish. "No one will ever believe, no one will understand. They will say that I killed him, that I murdered him."

Through it all I stood almost speechless, puzzled. What did it all mean?

"No," said Kennedy, "no, for they will never know of it."

"Never know?"

"Never—if in the end justice is done. Have you the will? Or did you destroy it?" It was a bold stroke.

"Yes. No. Here it is. How could I destroy it, even though it was burning the very soul out of me?"

She literally tore the paper from the bosom of her dress and cast it from her in horror and terror.

Kennedy picked it up, opened it, and glanced hurriedly through it. "Miss Bond," he said, "Jack shall never know a word of this. I shall tell him that the will has been found unexpectedly in John Fletcher's desk among some other papers. Walter, swear on your honor as a gentleman that this will was found in old Fletcher's desk."

"Dr. Kennedy, how can I ever thank you?"

"By telling me just how you came by this will, so that when you and Fletcher are married I may be as good a friend, without suspicion, to you as I am to him. I think a full confession would do you good, Miss Bond. Would you prefer to have Dr. Jameson not hear it?"

"No, he may stay."

"This much I know, Miss Bond. Last summer in Paris with the Greenes you must have chanced to hear of Pillard, the apache, one of the most noted cracksmen the world has ever produced. You sought him out. He taught you how to paint your fingers with a rubber composition, how to use an electric drill, how to use the old-fashioned jimmy. You went down to Fletcherwood by the back road about a quarter after eleven the night of the robbery in the Greenes' little electric runabout. You entered the library by an unlocked window, you coupled your drill to the electric light connections of the chandelier. You had to work quickly, for the power would go off at midnight, yet you could not do the job later, when they were sleeping more soundly, for the very same reason. John Fletcher was wakeful that night. Somehow or other he heard you at work. He entered the library and, by the light streaming from his bed-room, he saw who it was. In anger he must have addressed you, and his passion got the better of his age—he fell suddenly on the floor with a stroke of apoplexy. As you bent over him he died. But why did you ever attempt so foolish an undertaking? Didn't you know that other people knew of the will and its terms, that you were sure to be traced out in the end, if not by friends, by foes? How did you suppose you could profit by destroying the will, of which others knew the provisions?"

"Let me tell my story, what of it you have not already learned. It is uncanny that you should have learned so much. I can't imagine how it was possible to do it. I will make a clean breast of it—I did it because I loved Jack. Yes, strange as it sounds, it was not love of self that made me do it. I was, I am madly in love with Jack. No other man has ever inspired such respect and love as he has. His work in the university I have fairly gloated over. And yet—and yet, Dr. Kennedy, can you not see that I am different from Jack? What would I do with the income of the wife of even the dean of the new school? The annuity provided for me in that will is paltry. I need millions. From the tiniest baby I have been reared that way. I have always expected this fortune. I have been given everything I wanted. But it is different when one is married—you must have your own money. I need a fortune, for then I could have the town house, the country house, the yacht, the motors, the clothes, the servants that I need—they are as much a part of my life as your profession is of yours.

"And now it was all to slip from my hands. True, it was to go in such a way by this last will as to make Jack happy in his new school. I could have let that go, if that was all. There are other fortunes that have been laid at my feet. But I wanted Jack, and I knew Jack wanted me. Dear boy, he never could realize how utterly unhappy intellectual poverty would have made me and how my unhappiness would have reacted on him in the end. In reality this great and beneficent philanthropy was finally to blight both our love and our lives.

"What was I to do? Stand by and see my life and my love mined or refuse Jack for the fortune of a man I did not love? Helen Bond is not that kind of a woman, I said to myself. I consulted the greatest lawyer I knew. I put a hypothetical case to him, and asked his opinion in such a way as to make him believe he was advising me how to make an unbreakable will. He told me of provisions and clauses to avoid, particularly in making benefactions. That was what I wanted to know. I would put one of those clauses in my uncle's will. I practised uncle's writing till I was as good a forger of that clause as anyone could have become. I had the very words in his own handwriting to practise from.

"Then I went to Paris and, as you have guessed, learned how to get things out of a safe like that of uncle's. Before God, all I planned to do was to get that will, change it, replace it, and trust that uncle would never notice the change. Then when he was gone, I would have contested the will. I would have got my full share either by court proceedings or by settlement out of court. You see, I had planned it all out. The school would have been founded—I, we would have founded it. What difference, I said, did thirty millions or fifty millions make to an impersonal school, a school not yet even in existence? The twenty million dollars or so difference, or even half of it, meant life and love to me.

"I had planned to steal the cash in the safe, anything to divert attention from the will and make it look like a plain robbery. I would have done the altering of the will that night and have returned it to the safe before morning. But it was not to be. I had almost opened the safe when my uncle entered the room. His anger completely unnerved me, and from the moment I saw him on the floor to this I haven't had a sane thought. I forgot to take the cash, I forgot everything but that will. My only thought was that I must get it and destroy it. I doubt if I could have altered it with my nerves so upset. There, now you have my whole story. I am at your mercy."

"No," said Kennedy, "believe me, there is a mental statute of limitations that as far as Jameson and myself are concerned has already erased this affair. Walter, will you find Fletcher?"

I found the professor pacing up and down the gravel walk impatiently.

"Fletcher," said Kennedy, "a night's rest is all Miss Bond really needs. It is simply a case of overwrought nerves, and it will pass of itself. Still, I would advise a change of scene as soon as possible. Good afternoon, Miss Bond, and my best wishes for your health."

"Good afternoon, Dr. Kennedy. Good afternoon, Dr. Jameson.

I for one was glad to make my escape.

A half-hour later, Kennedy, with well-simulated excitement, was racing me in the car up to the Greenes' again. We literally burst unannounced into the tête-à-tête on the porch.

"Fletcher, Fletcher," cried Kennedy, "look what Walter and I have just discovered in a tin strong-box poked off in the back of your uncle's desk!"

Fletcher seized the will and by the dim light that shone through from the hall read it hastily. "Thank God," he cried; "the school is provided for as I thought."

"Isn't it glorious!" murmured Helen.

True to my instinct I muttered, "Another good newspaper yarn killed."

THE AMATEUR

Richard Harding Davis

I

It was February off the Banks, and so thick was the weather that, on the upper decks, one could have driven a sleigh. Inside the smoking-room Austin Ford, as securely sheltered from the blizzard as though he had been sitting in front of a wood fire at his club, ordered hot gin for himself and the ship's doctor. The ship's doctor had gone below on another "hurry call" from the widow. At the first luncheon on board the widow had sat on the right of Doctor Sparrow, with Austin Ford facing her. But since then, except to the doctor, she had been invisible. So, at frequent intervals, the ill health of the widow had deprived Ford of the society of the doctor. That it deprived him, also, of the society of the widow did not concern him. *Her* life had not been spent upon ocean liners; she could not remember when state-rooms were named after the States of the Union. She could not tell him of shipwrecks and salvage, of smugglers and of the modern pirates who found their victims in the smoking-room.

Ford was on his way to England to act as the London correspondent of the New York *Republic*. For three years on that most sensational of the New York dailies he had been the star man, the chief muckraker, the chief sleuth. His interest was in crime. Not in crimes committed in passion or inspired by drink, but in such offences against law and society as are perpetrated with nice intelligence. The murderer, the burglar, the strong-arm men who, in side streets, waylay respectable citizens did not appeal to him. The man he studied, pursued, and exposed was the cashier who evolved a new method of covering up his peculations, the dishonest president of an insurance company, the confidence man who used no concealed weapon other than his wit. Toward the criminals he pursued young Ford felt no personal animosity. He harassed them as he would have shot a hawk killing chickens. Not because he disliked the hawk, but because the battle was unequal, and because he felt sorry for the chickens.

Had you called Austin Ford an amateur detective he would have been greatly annoyed. He argued that his position was similar to that of the dramatic critic. The dramatic critic warned the public against bad plays; Ford warned it against bad men. Having done that, he left it to the public to determine whether the bad man should thrive or perish.

When the managing editor told him of his appointment to London, Ford had protested that his work lay in New York; that of London and the English, except as a tourist and sight-seer, he knew nothing.

"That's just why we are sending you," explained the managing editor. "Our readers are ignorant. To make them read about London you've got to tell them about themselves in London. They like to know who's been presented at court, about the American girls who have married dukes; and which ones opened a bazaar, and which one opened a hat shop, and which is getting a divorce. Don't send us anything concerning suffragettes and Dreadnaughts. Just send us stuff about Americans. If you take your meals in the Carlton grill-room and drink at the Cecil you can pick up more good stories than we can print. You will find lots of your friends over there. Some of those girls who married dukes," he suggested, "know you, don't they?"

"Not since they married dukes," said Ford.

"Well, anyway, all your other friends will be there," continued the managing editor encouragingly. "Now that they have shut up the tracks here all the con men have gone to London. They say an American can't take a drink at the Salisbury without his fellow-countrymen having a fight as to which one will sell him a gold brick."

Ford's eyes lightened in pleasurable anticipation.

"Look them over," urged the managing editor, "and send us a special. Call it 'The American Invasion.' Don't you see a story in it?"

"It will be the first one I send you," said Ford. The ship's doctor returned from his visit below decks and sank into the leather cushion close to Ford's elbow. For a few moments the older man sipped doubtfully at his gin and water, and, as though perplexed, rubbed his hand over his bald and shining head. "I told her to talk to you," he said fretfully.

"Her? Who?" inquired Ford. "Oh, the widow?"

"You were right about that," said Doctor Sparrow; "she is not a widow."

The reporter smiled complacently.

"Do you know why I thought not?" he demanded. "Because all the time she was at luncheon she kept turning over her wedding-ring as though she was not used to it. It was a new ring, too. I told you then she was not a widow."

"Do you always notice things like that?" asked the doctor.

"Not on purpose," said the amateur detective; "I can't help it. I see ten things where other people see only one; just as some men run ten times as fast as other men. We have tried it out often at the office; put all sorts of junk under a newspaper, lifted the newspaper for five seconds, and then each man wrote down what he had seen.

Out of twenty things I would remember seventeen. The next best guess would be about nine. Once I saw a man lift his coat collar to hide his face. It was in the Grand Central Station. I stopped him, and told him he was wanted. Turned out he *was* wanted. It was Goldberg, making his getaway to Canada."

"It is a gift," said the doctor.

"No, it's a nuisance," laughed the reporter. "I see so many things I don't want to see. I see that people are wearing clothes that are not made for them. I see when women are lying to me. I can see when men are on the verge of a nervous breakdown, and whether it is drink or debt or morphine—"

The doctor snorted triumphantly.

"You did not see that the widow was on the verge of a breakdown!"

"No," returned the reporter. "Is she? I'm sorry."

"If you're sorry," urged the doctor eagerly, "you'll help her. She is going to London alone to find her husband. He has disappeared. She thinks that he has been murdered, or that he is lying ill in some hospital. I told her if any one could help her to find him you could. I had to say something. She's very ill."

"To find her husband in London?" repeated Ford. "London is a large town."

"She has photographs of him and she knows where he spends his time," pleaded the doctor. "He is a company promoter. It should be easy for you."

"Maybe he doesn't want her to find him," said Ford. "Then it wouldn't be so easy for me."

The old doctor sighed heavily. "I know," he murmured. "I thought of that, too. And she is so very pretty."

"That was another thing I noticed," said Ford.

The doctor gave no heed.

"She must stop worrying," he exclaimed, "or she will have a mental collapse. I have tried sedatives, but they don't touch her. I want to give her courage. She is frightened. She's left a baby boy at home, and she's fearful that something will happen to him, and she's frightened at being at sea, frightened at being alone in London; it's pitiful." The old man shook his head. "Pitiful! Will you talk to her now?" he asked.

"Nonsense!" exclaimed Ford. "She doesn't want to tell the story of her life to strange young men."

"But it was she suggested it," cried the doctor. "She asked me if you were Austin Ford, the great detective."

Ford snorted scornfully. "She did not!" he protested. His tone was that of a man who hopes to be contradicted.

"But she did," insisted the doctor, "and I told her your specialty was tracing persons. Her face lightened at once; it gave her hope. She will listen to you. Speak very gently and kindly and confidently. Say you are sure you can find him."

"Where is the lady now?" asked Ford.

Doctor Sparrow scrambled eagerly to his feet. "She cannot leave her cabin," he answered.

The widow, as Ford and Doctor Sparrow still thought of her, was lying on the sofa that ran the length of the stateroom, parallel with the lower berth. She was fully dressed, except that instead of her bodice she wore a kimono that left her throat and arms bare. She had been sleeping, and when their entrance awoke her, her blue eyes regarded them uncomprehendingly. Ford, hidden from her by the doctor, observed that not only was she very pretty, but that she was absurdly young, and that the drowsy smile she turned upon the old man before she noted the presence of Ford was as innocent as that of a baby. Her cheeks were flushed, her eyes brilliant, her yellow curls had become loosened and were spread upon the pillow. When she saw Ford she caught the kimono so closely around her throat that she choked. Had the doctor not pushed her down she would have stood.

"I thought," she stammered, "he was an *old* man."

The doctor, misunderstanding, hastened to reassure her. "Mr. Ford is old in experience," he said soothingly. "He has had remarkable success. Why, he found a criminal once just because the man wore a collar. And he found Walsh, the burglar, and Phillips, the forger, and a gang of counterfeiters—"

Mrs. Ashton turned upon him, her eyes wide with wonder. "But *my* husband," she protested, "is not a criminal!"

"My dear lady!" the doctor cried. "I did not mean that, of course not. I meant, if Mr. Ford can find men who don't wish to be found, how easy for him to find a man who—" He turned helplessly to Ford. "You tell her," he begged.

Ford sat down on a steamer-trunk that protruded from beneath the berth, and, turning to the widow, gave her the full benefit of his working smile. It was confiding, helpless, appealing. It showed a trustfulness in the person to whom it was addressed that caused that individual to believe Ford needed protection from a wicked world.

"Doctor Sparrow tells me," began Ford timidly, "you have lost your husband's address; that you will let me try to find him. If I can help in any way I should be glad."

The young girl regarded him, apparently, with disappointment. It was as though Doctor Sparrow had led her to expect a man full of years and authority, a man upon whom she could lean; not a youth whose smile seemed to beg one not to scold him. She gave Ford three photographs, bound together with a string.

"When Doctor Sparrow told me you could help me I got out these," she said.

Ford jotted down a mental note to the effect that she "got them out." That is, she did not keep them where she could always look at them. That she was not used to look at them was evident by the fact that they were bound together.

The first photograph showed three men standing in an open place and leaning on a railing. One of them was smiling toward the photographer. He was a good-looking young man of about thirty years of age, well fed, well dressed, and apparently well satisfied with the world and himself. Ford's own smile had disappeared. His eyes were alert and interested.

"The one with the Panama hat pulled down over his eyes is your husband?" he asked.

"Yes," assented the widow. Her tone showed slight surprise.

"This was taken about a year ago?" inquired Ford. "Must have been," he answered himself; "they haven't raced at the Bay since then. This was taken in front of the club stand—probably for the *Telegraph*?" He lifted his eyes inquiringly.

Rising on her elbow the young wife bent forward toward the photograph. "Does it say that there," she asked doubtfully. "How did you guess that?"

In his role as chorus the ship's doctor exclaimed with enthusiasm: "Didn't I tell you? He's wonderful."

Ford cut him off impatiently. "You never saw a rail as high as that except around a racetrack," he muttered. "And the badge in his buttonhole and the angle of the stand all show—"

He interrupted himself to address the widow. "This is an owner's badge. What was the name of his stable?"

"I don't know," she answered. She regarded the young man with sudden uneasiness. "They only owned one horse, but I believe that gave them the privilege of—"

"I see," exclaimed Ford. "Your husband is a bookmaker. But in London he is a promoter of companies."

"So my friend tells me," said Mrs. Ashton. "She's just got back from London. Her husband told her that Harry, my husband, was always at the American bar in the Cecil or at the Salisbury or the Savoy." The girl shook her head. "But a woman can't go looking for a man there," she protested. "That's why I thought you—"

"That'll be all right," Ford assured her hurriedly. "It's a coincidence, but it happens that my own work takes me to these hotels, and if your husband is there I will find him." He returned the photographs.

"Hadn't you better keep one?" she asked.

"I won't forget him," said the reporter. "Besides"—he turned his eyes toward the doctor and, as though thinking aloud, said—"he may have grown a beard."

There was a pause.

The eyes of the woman grew troubled. Her lips pressed together as though in a sudden access of pain.

"And he may," Ford continued, "have changed his name."

As though fearful, if she spoke, the tears would fall, the girl nodded her head stiffly.

Having learned what he wanted to know Ford applied to the wound a soothing ointment of promises and encouragement.

"He's as good as found," he protested. "You will see him in a day, two days after you land."

The girl's eyes opened happily. She clasped her hands together and raised them.

"You will try?" she begged. "You will find him for me"—she corrected herself eagerly—"for me and the baby?"

The loose sleeves of the kimono fell back to her shoulders showing the white arms; the eyes raised to Ford were glistening with tears.

"Of course I will find him," growled the reporter.

He freed himself from the appeal in the eyes of the young mother and left the cabin. The doctor followed. He was bubbling over with enthusiasm.

"That was fine!" he cried. "You said just the right thing. There will be no collapse now."

His satisfaction was swept away in a burst of disgust.

"The blackguard!" he protested. "To desert a wife as young as that and as pretty as that."

"So I have been thinking," said the reporter. "I guess," he added gravely, "what is going to happen is that before I find her husband I will have got to know him pretty well."

Apparently, young Mrs. Ashton believed everything would come to pass just as Ford promised it would and as he chose to order it; for the next day, with a color not born of fever in her cheeks and courage in her eyes, she joined Ford and the doctor at the luncheon-table. Her attention was concentrated on the younger man. In him she saw the one person who could bring her husband to her.

"She acts," growled the doctor later in the smoking-room, "as though she was afraid you were going to back out of your promise and jump overboard."

"Don't think," he protested violently, "it's you she's interested in. All she sees in you is what you can do for her. Can you see that?"

"Any one as clever at seeing things as I am," returned the reporter, "cannot help but see that."

Later, as Ford was walking on the upper deck, Mrs. Ashton came toward him, beating her way against the wind. Without a trace of coquetry or self-consciousness, and with a sigh of content, she laid her hand on his arm.

"When I don't see you," she exclaimed as simply as a child, "I feel so frightened. When I see you I know all will come right. Do you mind if I walk with you?" she asked. "And do you mind if every now and then I ask you to tell me again it will all come right?"

For the three days following Mrs. Ashton and Ford were constantly together. Or, at least, Mrs. Ashton was constantly with Ford. She told him that when she sat in her cabin the old fears returned to her, and in these moments of panic she searched the ship for him.

The doctor protested that he was growing jealous.

"I'm not so greatly to be envied," suggested Ford. "'Harry' at meals three times a day and on deck all the rest of the day becomes monotonous. On a closer acquaintance with Harry he seems to be a decent sort of a young man; at least he seems to have been at one time very much in love with her."

"Well," sighed the doctor sentimentally, "she is certainly very much in love with Harry."

Ford shook his head non-committingly. "I don't know her story," he said. "Don't want to know it."

The ship was in the Channel, on her way to Cherbourg, and running as smoothly as a clock. From the shore friendly lights told them they were nearing their journey's end; that the land was on every side. Seated on a steamer-chair next to his in the semi-darkness of the deck, Mrs. Ashton began to talk nervously and eagerly.

"Now that we are so near," she murmured, "I have got to tell you something. If you did not know I would feel I had not been fair. You might think that when you were doing so much for me I should have been more honest."

She drew a long breath. "It's so hard," she said.

"Wait," commanded Ford. "Is it going to help me to find him?"

"No."

"Then don't tell me."

His tone caused the girl to start. She leaned toward him and peered into his face. His eyes, as he looked back to her, were kind and comprehending.

"You mean," said the amateur detective, "that your husband has deserted you. That if it were not for the baby you would not try to find him. Is that it?"

Mrs. Ashton breathed quickly and turned her face away.

"Yes," she whispered. "That is it."

There was a long pause. When she faced him again the fact that there was no longer a secret between them seemed to give her courage.

"Maybe," she said, "you can understand. Maybe you can tell me what it means. I have thought and thought. I have gone over it and over it until when I go back to it my head aches. I have done nothing else but think, and I can't make it seem better. I can't find any excuse. I have had no one to talk to, no one I could tell. I have thought maybe a man could understand." She raised her eyes appealingly.

"If you can only make it seem less cruel. Don't you see," she cried miserably, "I want to believe; I want to forgive him. I want to think he loves me. Oh! I want so to be able to love him; but how can I? I can't! I can't!"

In the week in which they had been thrown together the girl unconsciously had told Ford much about herself and her husband. What she now told him was but an amplification of what he had guessed.

She had met Ashton a year and a half before, when she had just left school at the convent and had returned to live with her family. Her home was at Far Rockaway. Her father was a cashier in a bank at Long Island City. One night, with a party of friends, she had been taken to a dance at one of the beach hotels, and there met Ashton. At that time he was one of a firm that was making book at the Aqueduct race-track. The girl had met very few men and with them was shy and frightened, but with Ashton she found herself at once at ease. That night he drove her and her friends home in his touring-car and the next day they teased her about her conquest. It made her very happy. After that she went to hops at the hotel, and as the bookmaker did not dance, the two young people sat upon the piazza. Then Ashton came to see her at her own house, but when her father learned that the young man who had been calling upon her was a bookmaker he told him he could not associate with his daughter.

But the girl was now deeply in love with Ashton, and apparently he with her. He begged her to marry him. They knew that to this, partly from prejudice and partly owing to his position in the bank, her father would object. Accordingly they agreed that in August, when the racing moved to Saratoga, they would run away and get married at that place. Their plan was that Ashton would leave for Saratoga with the other racing men, and that she would join him the next day.

They had arranged to be married by a magistrate, and Ashton had shown her a letter from one at Saratoga who consented to perform the ceremony. He had given her an engagement ring and two thousand dollars, which he asked her to keep for him, lest tempted at the track he should lose it.

But she assured Ford it was not such material things as a letter, a ring, or gift of money that had led her to trust Ashton. His fear of losing her, his complete subjection to her wishes, his happiness in her presence, all seemed to prove that to make her happy was his one wish, and that he could do anything to make her unhappy appeared impossible.

They were married the morning she arrived at Saratoga; and the same day departed for Niagara Falls and Quebec. The honeymoon lasted ten days. They were ten days of complete happiness. No one, so the girl declared, could have been more kind, more unselfishly considerate than her husband. They returned to Saratoga and engaged a suite of rooms at one of the big hotels. Ashton was not satisfied with the rooms shown him, and leaving her upstairs returned to the office floor to ask for others.

Since that moment his wife had never seen him nor heard from him.

On the day of her marriage young Mrs. Ashton had written to her father, asking him to give her his good wishes and pardon. He refused both. As she had feared, he did not consider that for a bank clerk a gambler made a desirable son-in-law; and the letters he wrote his daughter were so bitter that in reply she informed him he had forced her to choose between her family and her husband, and that she chose her husband. In consequence, when she found herself deserted she felt she could not return to her people. She remained in Saratoga. There she moved into cheap lodgings, and in order that the two thousand dollars Ashton had left with her might be saved for his child, she had learned to typewrite, and after four months had been able to support herself. Within the last month a girl friend, who had known both Ashton and herself before they were married, had written her that her husband was living in London. For the sake of her son she had at once determined to make an effort to seek him out.

"The son, nonsense!" exclaimed the doctor, when Ford retold the story. "She is not crossing the ocean because she is worried about the future of her son. She seeks her own happiness. The woman is in love with her husband."

Ford shook his head.

"I don't know!" he objected. "She's so extravagant in her praise of Harry that it seems unreal. It sounds insincere. Then, again, when I swear I will find him she shows a delight that you might describe as savage, almost vindictive. As though, if I did find Harry, the first thing she would do would be to stick a knife in him."

"Maybe," volunteered the doctor sadly, "she has heard there is a woman in the case. Maybe she is the one she's thinking of sticking the knife into?"

"Well," declared the reporter, "if she doesn't stop looking savage every time I promise to find Harry I won't find Harry. Why should I act the part of Fate, anyway? How do I know that Harry hasn't got a wife in London and several in the States? How do we know he didn't leave his country for his country's good? That's what it looks like to me. How can we tell what confronted him the day he went down to the hotel desk to change his rooms and, instead, got into his touring-car and beat the speed limit to Canada. Whom did he meet in the hotel corridor? A woman with a perfectly good marriage certificate, or a detective with a perfectly good warrant? Or did Harry find out that his bride had a devil of a temper of her own, and that for him marriage was a failure? The widow is certainly a very charming young woman, but there may be two sides to this."

"You are a cynic, sir," protested the doctor.

"That may be," growled the reporter, "but I am not a private detective agency, or a matrimonial bureau, and before I hear myself saying, 'Bless you, my children!' both of these young people will have to show me why they should not be kept asunder."

II

On the afternoon of their arrival in London Ford convoyed Mrs. Ashton to an old-established private hotel in Craven Street.

"Here," he explained, "you will be within a few hundred yards of the place in which your husband is said to spend his time. I will be living in the same hotel. If I find him you will know it in ten minutes."

The widow gave a little gasp, whether of excitement or of happiness Ford could not determine.

"Whatever happens," she begged, "will you let me hear from you sometimes? You are the only person I know in London—and—it's so big it frightens me. I don't want to be a burden," she went on eagerly, "but if I can feel you are within call—"

"What you need," said Ford heartily, "is less of the doctor's nerve tonic and sleeping draughts, and a little innocent diversion. To-night I am going to take you to the Savoy to supper."

Mrs. Ashton exclaimed delightedly, and then was filled with misgivings.

"I have nothing to wear," she protested, "and over here, in the evening, the women dress so well. I have a dinner gown," she exclaimed, "but it's black. Would that do?"

Ford assured her nothing could be better. He had a man's vanity in liking a woman with whom he was seen in public to be pretty and smartly dressed, and he felt sure that in black the blond beauty of Mrs. Ashton would appear to advantage. They arranged to meet at eleven on the promenade leading to the Savoy supper-room, and parted with mutual satisfaction at the prospect.

The finding of Harry Ashton was so simple that in its very simplicity it appeared spectacular.

On leaving Mrs. Ashton, Ford engaged rooms at the Hotel Cecil. Before visiting his rooms he made his way to the American bar. He did not go there seeking Harry Ashton. His object was entirely self-centred. His purpose was to drink to himself and to the lights of London. But as though by appointment, the man he had promised to find was waiting for him. As Ford entered the room, at a table facing the door sat Ashton. There was no mistaking him. He wore a mustache, but it was no disguise. He was the same good-natured, good-looking youth who, in the photograph from under a Panama hat, had smiled upon the world. With a glad cry Ford rushed toward him.

"Fancy meeting *you*!" he exclaimed.

Mr. Ashton's good-natured smile did not relax. He merely shook his head.

"Afraid you have made a mistake," he said. The reporter regarded him blankly. His face showed his disappointment.

"Aren't you Charles W. Garrett, of New York?" he demanded.

"Not me," said Mr. Ashton.

"But," Ford insisted in hurt tones, as though he were being trifled with, "you have been told you look like him, haven't you?"

Mr. Ashton's good nature was unassailable.

"Sorry," he declared, "never heard of him."

Ford became garrulous, he could not believe two men could look so much alike. It was a remarkable coincidence. The stranger must certainly have a drink, the drink intended for his twin. Ashton was bored, but accepted. He was well acquainted with the easy good-fellowship of his countrymen. The room in which he sat was a meeting-place for them. He considered that they were always giving each other drinks, and not only were they always introducing themselves, but saying, "Shake hands with my friend, Mr. So-and-So." After five minutes they showed each other photographs of the children. This one, though as loquacious as the others, seemed better dressed, more "wise"; he brought to the exile the atmosphere of his beloved Broadway, so Ashton drank to him pleasantly.

"My name is Sydney Carter," he volunteered.

As a poker-player skims over the cards in his hand, Ford, in his mind's eye, ran over the value of giving or not giving his right name. He decided that Ashton would not have heard it and that, if he gave a false one, there was a chance that later Ashton might find out that he had done so. Accordingly he said, "Mine is Austin Ford," and seated himself at Ashton's table. Within ten minutes the man he had promised to pluck from among the eight million inhabitants of London was smiling sympathetically at his jests and buying a drink.

On the steamer Ford had rehearsed the story with which, should he meet Ashton, he would introduce himself. It was one arranged to fit with his theory that Ashton was a crook. If Ashton were a crook Ford argued that to at once ingratiate himself in his good graces he also must be a crook. His plan was to invite Ashton to co-operate with him in some scheme that was openly dishonest. By so doing he hoped apparently to place himself at Ashton's mercy. He believed if he could persuade Ashton he was more of a rascal than Ashton himself, and an exceedingly stupid rascal, any distrust the bookmaker might feel toward him would disappear. He made his advances so openly, and apparently showed his hand so carelessly, that, from being bored, Ashton became puzzled, then interested; and when Ford insisted he should dine with him, he considered it so necessary to find out who the youth might be who was forcing himself upon him that he accepted the invitation.

They adjourned to dress and an hour later, at Ford's suggestion, they met at the Carlton. There Ford ordered a dinner calculated to lull his newly made friend into a mood suited to confidence, but which had on Ashton exactly the opposite effect. Merely for the pleasure of his company, utter strangers were not in the habit of treating him to strawberries in February, and vintage champagne; and, in consequence, in Ford's hospitality he saw only cause for suspicion. If, as he had first feared, Ford was a New York detective, it was most important he should know that. No one better than Ashton understood that, at that moment, his presence in New York meant, for the police, unalloyed satisfaction, and for himself undisturbed solitude. But Ford was unlike any detective of his acquaintance; and his acquaintance had been extensive. It was true Ford was familiar with all the habits of Broadway and the Tenderloin. Of places with which Ashton was intimate, and of men with whom Ashton had formerly been well acquainted, he talked glibly. But, if he were a detective, Ashton considered, they certainly had improved the class.

The restaurant into which for the first time Ashton had penetrated, and in which he felt ill at ease, was to Ford, he observed, a matter of course. Evidently for Ford it held no terrors. He criticised the service, patronized the head waiters, and grumbled at the food; and when, on leaving the restaurant, an Englishman and his wife stopped at their table to greet him, he accepted their welcome to London without embarrassment.

Ashton, rolling his cigar between his lips, observed the incident with increasing bewilderment.

"You've got some swell friends," he growled. "I'll bet you never met *them* at Healey's!"

"I meet all kinds of people in my business," said Ford. "I once sold that man some mining stock, and the joke of it was," he added, smiling knowingly, "it turned out to be good."

Ashton decided that the psychological moment had arrived.

"What *is* your business?" he asked.

"I'm a company promoter," said Ford easily. "I thought I told you."

"I did not tell you that I was a company promoter, too, did I?" demanded Ashton.

"No," answered Ford, with apparent surprise. "Are you? That's funny."

Ashton watched for the next move, but the subject seemed in no way to interest Ford. Instead of following it up he began afresh.

"Have you any money lying idle?" he asked abruptly. "About a thousand pounds."

Ashton recognized that the mysterious stranger was about to disclose both himself and whatever object he had in seeking him out. He cast a quick glance about him.

"I can always find money," he said guardedly. "What's the proposition?"

With pretended nervousness Ford leaned forward and began the story he had rehearsed. It was a new version of an old swindle and to every self-respecting confidence man was well known as the "sick engineer" game. The plot is very simple. The sick engineer is supposed to be a mining engineer who, as an expert, has examined a gold mine and reported against it. For his services the company paid him partly in stock. He falls ill and is at the point of death. While he has been ill much gold has been found in the mine he examined, and the stock which he considers worthless is now valuable. Of this, owing to his illness, he is ignorant. One confidence man acts the part of the sick engineer, and the other that of a broker who knows the engineer possesses the stock but has no money with which to purchase it from him. For a share of the stock he offers to tell the dupe where it and the engineer can be found. They visit the man, apparently at the point of death, and the dupe gives him money for his stock. Later the dupe finds the stock is worthless, and the supposed engineer and the supposed broker divide the money he paid for it. In telling the story Ford pretended he was the broker and that he thought in Ashton he had found a dupe who would buy the stock from the sick engineer.

As the story unfolded and Ashton appreciated the part Ford expected him to play in it, his emotions were so varied that he was in danger of apoplexy. Amusement, joy, chagrin, and indignation illuminated his countenance. His cigar ceased to burn, and with his eyes opened wide he regarded Ford in pitying wonder.

"Wait!" he commanded. He shook his head uncomprehendingly. "Tell me," he asked, "do I look as easy as that, or are you just naturally foolish?"

Ford pretended to fall into a state of great alarm.

"I don't understand," he stammered.

"Why, son," exclaimed Ashton kindly, "I was taught that story in the public schools. I invented it. I stopped using it before you cut your teeth. Gee!" he exclaimed delightedly. "I knew I had grown respectable-looking, but I didn't think I was so damned respectable-looking as that!" He began to laugh silently; so greatly was he amused that the tears shone in his eyes and his shoulders shook.

"I'm sorry for you, son," he protested, "but that's the funniest thing that's come my way in two years. And you buying me hot-house grapes, too, and fancy water! I wish you could see your face," he taunted.

Ford pretended to be greatly chagrined.

"All right," he declared roughly. "The laugh's on me this time, but just because I lost one trick, don't think I don't know my business. Now that I'm wise to what *you* are we can work together and—"

The face of young Mr. Ashton became instantly grave. His jaws snapped like a trap. When he spoke his tone was assured and slightly contemptuous.

"Not with *me* you can't work!" he said.

"Don't think because I fell down on this," Ford began hotly.

"I'm not thinking of you at all," said Ashton. "You're a nice little fellow all right, but you have sized me up wrong. I am on the 'straight and narrow' that leads back to little old New York and God's country, and I am warranted not to run off my trolley."

The words were in the vernacular, but the tone in which the young man spoke rang so confidently that it brought to Ford a pleasant thrill of satisfaction. From the first he had found in the personality of the young man something winning and likable; a shrewd manliness and tolerant good-humor. His eyes may have shown his sympathy, for, in sudden confidence, Ashton leaned nearer.

"It's like this," he said. "Several years ago I made a bad break and, about a year later, they got on to me and I had to cut and run. In a month the law of limitation lets me loose and I can go back. And you can bet I'm *going* back. I will be on the bowsprit of the first boat. I've had all I want of the 'fugitive-from-justice' game, thank you, and I have taken good care to keep a clean bill of health so that I won't have to play it again. They've been trying to get me for several years—especially the Pinkertons. They have chased me all over Europe. Chased me with all kinds of men; sometimes with women; they've tried everything except blood-hounds. At first I thought *you* were a 'Pink,' that's why—"

"I!" interrupted Ford, exploding derisively. "That's *good*! That's one on *you*." He ceased laughing and regarded Ashton kindly. "How do you know I'm not?" he asked.

For an instant the face of the bookmaker grew a shade less red and his eyes searched those of Ford in a quick agony of suspicion. Ford continued to smile steadily at him, and Ashton breathed with relief.

"I'll take a chance with you," he said, "and if you are as bad a detective as you are a sport I needn't worry."

They both laughed, and, with sudden mutual liking, each raised his glass and nodded.

"But they haven't got me yet," continued Ashton, "and unless they get me in the next thirty days I'm free. So you needn't think that I'll help you. It's 'never again' for me. The first time, that was the fault of the crowd I ran with; the second time, that would be *my* fault. And there ain't going to be any second time."

He shook his head doggedly, and with squared shoulders leaned back in his chair.

"If it only breaks right for me," he declared, "I'll settle down in one of those 'Own-your own-homes,' forty-five minutes from Broadway, and never leave the wife and the baby."

The words almost brought Ford to his feet. He had forgotten the wife and the baby. He endeavored to explain his surprise by a sudden assumption of incredulity.

"Fancy you married!" he exclaimed.

"Married!" protested Ashton. "I'm married to the finest little lady that ever wore skirts, and in thirty-seven days I'll see her again. Thirty-seven days," he repeated impatiently. "Gee! That's a hell of a long time!"

Ford studied the young man with increased interest. That he was speaking sincerely, from the heart, there seemed no possible doubt.

Ashton frowned and his face clouded. "I've not been able to treat her just right," he volunteered. "If she wrote me, the letters might give them a clew, and I don't write *her* because I don't want her to know all my troubles until they're over. But I know," he added, "that five minutes' talk will set it all right. That is, if she still feels about me the way I feel about her."

The man crushed his cigar in his fingers and threw the pieces on the floor. "That's what's been the worst!" he exclaimed bitterly. "Not hearing, not knowing. It's been hell!"

His eyes as he raised them were filled with suffering, deep and genuine.

Ford rose suddenly. "Let's go down to the Savoy for supper," he said.

"Supper!" growled Ashton. "What's the use of supper? Do you suppose cold chicken and a sardine can keep me from *thinking*?"

Ford placed his hand on the other's shoulder.

"You come with me," he said kindly. "I'm going to do you a favor. I'm going to bring you a piece of luck. Don't ask me any questions," he commanded hurriedly. "Just take my word for it."

They had sat so late over their cigars that when they reached the restaurant on the Embankment the supper-room was already partly filled, and the corridors and lounge were brilliantly lit and gay with well-dressed women. Ashton regarded the scene with gloomy eyes. Since he had spoken of his wife he had remained silent, chewing savagely on a fresh cigar. But Ford was grandly excited. He did not know exactly what he intended to do. He was prepared to let events direct themselves, but of two things he was assured: Mrs. Ashton loved her husband, and her husband loved her. As the god in the car who was to bring them together, he felt a delightful responsibility.

The young men left the coat-room and came down the short flight of steps that leads to the wide lounge of the restaurant. Ford slightly in advance, searching with his eyes for Mrs. Ashton, found her seated alone in the lounge, evidently waiting for him. At the first glance she was hardly be recognized. Her low-cut dinner gown of black satin that clung to her like a wet bath robe was the last word of the new fashion; and since Ford had seen her her blond hair had been arranged by an artist. Her appearance was smart, elegant, daring. She was easily the prettiest and most striking-looking woman in the room, and for an instant Ford stood gazing at her, trying to find in the self-possessed young woman the deserted wife of the steamer. She did not see Ford. Her eyes were following the progress down the hall of a woman, and her profile was toward him.

The thought of the happiness he was about to bring to two young people gave Ford the sense of a genuine triumph, and when he turned to Ashton to point out his wife to him he was thrilling with pride and satisfaction. His triumph received a bewildering shock. Already Ashton had discovered the presence of Mrs. Ashton. He was standing transfixed, lost to his surroundings, devouring her with his eyes. And then, to the amazement of Ford, his eyes filled with fear, doubt, and anger. Swiftly, with the movement of a man ducking a blow, he turned and sprang up the stairs and into the coat-room. Ford, bewildered and more conscious of his surroundings, followed him less quickly, and was in consequence only in time to see Ashton, dragging his overcoat behind him, disappear into the court-yard. He seized his own coat and raced in pursuit. As he ran into the court-yard Ashton, in the Strand, was just closing the door of a taxicab, but before the chauffeur could free it from the surrounding traffic, Ford had dragged the door open, and leaped inside. Ashton was huddled in the corner, panting, his face pale with alarm.

"What the devil ails you?" roared Ford. "Are you trying to shake me? You've got to come back. You must speak to her."

"Speak to her!" repeated Ashton. His voice was sunk to a whisper. The look of alarm in his face was confused with one grim and menacing. "Did you know she was there?" he demanded softly. "Did you take me there, knowing——?"

"Of course I knew," protested Ford. "She's been looking for you—"

His voice subsided in a squeak of amazement and pain. Ashton's left hand had shot out and swiftly seized his throat. With the other he pressed an automatic revolver against Ford's shirt front.

"I know she's been looking for me," the man whispered thickly. "For two years she's been looking for me. I know all about *her*! But, *who in hell are you?*"

Ford, gasping and gurgling, protested loyally.

"You are wrong!" he cried. "She's been at home waiting for you. She thinks you have deserted her and your baby. I tell you she loves you, you fool, she *loves* you!"

The fingers on his throat suddenly relaxed; the flaming eyes of Ashton, glaring into his, wavered and grew wide with amazement.

"Loves me," he whispered. "*Who* loves me?"

"Your wife," protested Ford; "the girl at the Savoy, your wife."

Again the fingers of Ashton pressed deep around his neck.

"That is not my wife," he whispered. His voice was unpleasantly cold and grim. "That's 'Baby Belle,' with her hair dyed, a detective lady of the Pinkertons, hired to find me. And *you* know it. Now, who are *you?*"

To permit him to reply Ashton released his hand, but at the same moment, in a sudden access of fear, dug the revolver deeper into the pit of Ford's stomach.

"Quick!" he commanded. "Never mind the girl. *Who are you?*"

Ford collapsed against the cushioned corner of the cab. "And she begged me to find you," he roared, "because she *loved* you, because she wanted to *believe* in you!" He held his arms above his head. "Go ahead and shoot!" he cried. "You want to know who I am?" he demanded. His voice rang with rage. "I'm an amateur. Just a natural born fool-amateur! Go on and shoot!"

The gun in Ashton's hand sank to his knee. Between doubt and laughter his face was twisted in strange lines. The cab was whirling through a narrow, unlit street leading to Covent Garden. Opening the door Ashton called to the chauffeur, and then turned to Ford.

"You get off here!" he commanded. "Maybe you're a 'Pink,' maybe you're a good fellow. I think you're a good fellow, but I'm not taking any chances. Get out!"

Ford scrambled to the street, and as the taxicab again butted itself forward, Ashton leaned far through the window. "Good-by, son," he called. "Send me a picture-postal card to Paris. For I am off to Maxim's," he cried, "and you can go to—"

"Not at all!" shouted the amateur detective indignantly. "I'm going back to take supper with 'Baby Belle'!"

THE PROBLEM OF CELL 13

Jacques Futrelle

I

Practically all those letters remaining in the alphabet after Augustus S.F.X. Van Dusen was named were afterward acquired by that gentleman in the course of a brilliant scientific career, and, being honorably acquired, were tacked on to the other end. His name, therefore, taken with all that belonged to it, was a wonderfully imposing structure. He was a Ph.D., an LL.D., an F.R.S., an M.D., and an M.D.S. He was also some other things—just what he himself couldn't say—through recognition of his ability by various foreign educational and scientific institutions.

In appearance he was no less striking than in nomenclature. He was slender with the droop of the student in his thin shoulders and the pallor of a close, sedentary life on his clean-shaven face. His eyes wore a perpetual, forbidding squint—the squint of a man who studies little things—and when they could be seen at all through his thick spectacles, were mere slits of watery blue. But above his eyes was his most striking feature. This was a tall, broad brow, almost abnormal in height and width, crowned by a heavy shock of bushy, yellow hair. All these things conspired to give him a peculiar, almost grotesque, personality.

Professor Van Dusen was remotely German. For generations his ancestors had been noted in the sciences; he was the logical result, the master mind. First and above all he was a logician. At least thirty-five years of the half-century or so of his existence had been devoted exclusively to proving that two and two always equal four, except in unusual cases, where they equal three or five, as the case may be. He stood broadly on the general proposition that all things that start must go somewhere, and was able to bring the concentrated mental force of his forefathers to bear on a given problem. Incidentally it may be remarked that Professor Van Dusen wore a No. 8 hat.

The world at large had heard vaguely of Professor Van Dusen as The Thinking Machine. It was a newspaper catch-phrase applied to him at the time of a remarkable exhibition at chess; he had demonstrated then that a stranger to the game might, by the force of inevitable logic, defeat a champion who had devoted a lifetime to its study. The Thinking Machine! Perhaps that more nearly described him than all his honorary initials, for he spent week after week, month after month, in the seclusion of his small laboratory from which had gone forth thoughts that staggered scientific associates and deeply stirred the world at large.

It was only occasionally that The Thinking Machine had visitors, and these were usually men who, themselves high in the sciences, dropped in to argue a point and perhaps convince themselves. Two of these men, Dr. Charles Ransome and Alfred Fielding, called one evening to discuss some theory which is not of consequence here.

"Such a thing is impossible," declared Dr. Ransome emphatically, in the course of the conversation.

"Nothing is impossible," declared The Thinking Machine with equal emphasis. He always spoke petulantly. "The mind is master of all things. When science fully recognizes that fact a great advance will have been made."

"How about the airship?" asked Dr. Ransome.

"That's not impossible at all," asserted The Thinking Machine. "It will be invented some time. I'd do it myself, but I'm busy."

Dr. Ransome laughed tolerantly.

"I've heard you say such things before," he said. "But they mean nothing. Mind may be master of matter, but it hasn't yet found a way to apply itself. There are some things that can't be *thought* out of existence, or rather which would not yield to any amount of thinking."

"What, for instance?" demanded The Thinking Machine.

Dr. Ransome was thoughtful for a moment as he smoked.

"Well, say prison walls," he replied. "No man can think himself out of a cell. If he could, there would be no prisoners."

"A man can so apply his brain and ingenuity that he can leave a cell, which is the same thing," snapped The Thinking Machine.

Dr. Ransome was slightly amused.

"Let's suppose a case," he said, after a moment. "Take a cell where prisoners under sentence of death are confined—men who are desperate and, maddened by fear, would take any chance to escape—suppose you were locked in such a cell. Could you escape?"

"Certainly," declared The Thinking Machine.

"Of course," said Mr. Fielding, who entered the conversation for the first time, "you might wreck the cell with an explosive—but inside, a prisoner, you couldn't have that."

"There would be nothing of that kind," said The Thinking Machine. "You might treat me precisely as you treated prisoners under sentence of death, and I would leave the cell."

"Not unless you entered it with tools prepared to get out," said Dr. Ransome.

The Thinking Machine was visibly annoyed and his blue eyes snapped.

"Lock me in any cell in any prison anywhere at any time, wearing only what is necessary, and I'll escape in a week," he declared, sharply.

Dr. Ransome sat up straight in the chair, interested. Mr. Fielding lighted a new cigar.

"You mean you could actually *think* yourself out? "asked Dr. Ransome.

"I would get out," was the response.

"Are you serious?"

"Certainly I am serious."

Dr. Ransome and Mr. Fielding were silent for a long time.

"Would you be willing to try it?" asked Mr. Fielding, finally.

"Certainly," said Professor Van Dusen, and there was a trace of irony in his voice. "I have done more asinine things than that to convince other men of less important truths."

The tone was offensive and there was an undercurrent strongly resembling anger on both sides. Of course it was an absurd thing, but Professor Van Dusen reiterated his willingness to undertake the escape and it was decided upon.

"To begin now," added Dr. Ransome.

"I'd prefer that it begin to-morrow," said The Thinking Machine, "because—"

"No, now," said Mr. Fielding, flatly. "You are arrested, figuratively, of course, without any warning locked in a cell with no chance to communicate with friends, and left there with identically the same care and attention that would be given to a man under sentence of death. Are you willing?"

"All right, now, then," said The Thinking Machine, and he arose.

"Say, the death-cell in Chisholm Prison."

"The death-cell in Chisholm Prison."

"And what will you wear? "

"As little as possible," said The Thinking Machine. "Shoes, stockings, trousers and a shirt."

"You will permit yourself to be searched, of course?"

"I am to be treated precisely as all prisoners are treated," said The Thinking Machine. "No more attention and no less."

There were some preliminaries to be arranged in the matter of obtaining permission for the test, but all three were influential men and everything was done satisfactorily by telephone, albeit the prison commissioners, to whom the experiment was explained on purely scientific grounds, were sadly bewildered. Professor Van Dusen would be the most distinguished prisoner they had ever entertained.

When The Thinking Machine had donned those things which he was to wear during his incarceration he called the little old woman who was his housekeeper, cook and maid servant all in one.

"Martha," he said, "it is now twenty-seven minutes past nine o'clock. I am going away. One week from to-night, at half-past nine, these gentlemen and one, possibly two, others will take supper with me here. Remember Dr. Ransome is very fond of artichokes."

The three men were driven to Chisholm Prison, where the Warden was awaiting them, having been informed of the matter by telephone. He understood merely that the eminent Professor Van Dusen was to be his prisoner, if he could keep him, for one week; that he had committed no crime, but that he was to be treated as all other prisoners were treated.

"Search him," instructed Dr. Ransome.

The Thinking Machine was searched. Nothing was found on him; the pockets of the trousers were empty; the white, still-bosomed shirt had no pocket. The shoes and stockings were removed, examined, then replaced. As he watched all these preliminaries—the rigid search and noted the pitiful, childlike physical weakness of the man, the colorless face, and the thin, white hands—Dr. Ransome almost regretted his part in the affair.

"Are you sure you want to do this?" he asked.

"Would you be convinced if I did not?" inquired The Thinking Machine in turn.

"No."

"All right. I'll do it."

What sympathy Dr. Ransome had was dissipated by the tone. It nettled him, and he resolved to see the experiment to the end; it would be a stinging reproof to egotism.

"It will be impossible for him to communicate with anyone outside?" he asked.

"Absolutely impossible," replied the warden. "He will not be permitted writing materials of any sort."

"And your jailers, would they deliver a message from him?"

"Not one word, directly or indirectly," said the warden. "You may rest assured of that. They will report anything he might say or turn over to me anything he might give them."

"That seems entirely satisfactory," said Mr. Fielding, who was frankly interested in the problem.

"Of course, in the event he fails," said Dr. Ransome, "and asks for his liberty, you understand you are to set him free?"

"I understand," replied the warden.

The Thinking Machine stood listening, but had nothing to say until this was all ended, then:

"I should like to make three small requests. You may grant them or not, as you wish."

"No special favors, now," warned Mr. Fielding.

"I am asking none," was the stiff response. "I would like to have some tooth powder—buy it yourself to see that it is tooth powder—and I should like to have one five-dollar and two ten-dollar bills."

Dr. Ransome, Mr. Fielding and the warden exchanged astonished glances. They were not surprised at the request for tooth powder, but were at the request for money.

"Is there any man with whom our friend would come in contact that he could bribe with twenty-five dollars?" asked Dr. Ransome of the warden.

"Not for twenty-five hundred dollars," was the positive reply.

"Well, let him have them," said Mr. Fielding. "I think they are harmless enough."

"And what is the third request?" asked Dr. Ransome.

"I should like to have my shoes polished."

Again the astonished glances were exchanged. This last request was the height of absurdity, so they agreed to it. These things all being attended to, The Thinking Machine was led back into the prison from which he had undertaken to escape.

"Here is Cell 13," said the warden, stopping three doors down the steel corridor. "This is where we keep condemned murderers. No one can leave it without my permission; and no one in it can communicate with the outside. I'll stake my reputation on that. It's only three doors back of my office and I can readily hear any unusual noise."

"Will this cell do, gentlemen?" asked The Thinking Machine. I here was a touch of irony in his voice.

"Admirably," was the reply.

The heavy steel door was thrown open, there was a great scurrying and scampering of tiny feet, and The Thinking Machine passed into the gloom of the cell. Then the door was closed and double locked by the warden.

"What is that noise in there?" asked Dr. Ransome, through the bars.

"Rats—dozens of them," replied The Thinking Machine, tersely.

The three men, with final good-nights, were turning away when The Thinking Machine called:

"What time is it exactly, warden?"

"Eleven seventeen," replied the warden.

"Thanks. I will join you gentlemen in your office at half-past eight o'clock one week from to-night," said The Thinking Machine.

"And if you do not?"

"There is no 'if' about it."

II

Chisholm Prison was a great, spreading structure of granite, four stories in all, which stood in the center of acres of open space. It was surrounded by a wall of solid masonry eighteen feet high, and so smoothly finished inside and out as to offer no foothold to a climber, no matter how expert. Atop of this fence, as a further precaution, was a five-foot fence of steel rods, each terminating in a keen point. This fence in itself marked an absolute deadline between freedom and imprisonment, for, even if a man escaped from his cell, it would seem impossible for him to pass the wall.

The yard, which on all sides of the prison building was twenty-five feet wide, that being the distance from the building to the wall, was by day an exercise ground for those prisoners to whom was granted the boon of occasional semi-liberty. But that was not for those in Cell 13. At all times of the day there were armed guards in the yard, four of them, one patrolling each side of the prison building.

By night the yard was almost as brilliantly lighted as by day. On each of the four sides was a great arc light which rose above the prison wall and gave to the guards a clear sight. The lights, too, brightly illuminated the spiked top of the wall. The wires which fed the arc lights ran up the side of the prison building on insulators and from the top story led out to the poles supporting the arc lights.

All these things were seen and comprehended by The Thinking Machine, who was only enabled to see out his closely barred cell window by standing on his bed. This was on the morning following his incarceration. He gathered, too, that the river lay over there beyond the wall somewhere, because he heard faintly the pulsation of a motor boat and high up in the air saw a river bird. From that same direction came the shouts of boys at play and the occasional crack of a batted ball. He knew then that between the prison wall and the river was an open space, a playground.

Chisholm Prison was regarded as absolutely safe. No man had ever escaped from it. The Thinking Machine, from his perch on the bed, seeing what he saw, could readily understand why. The walls of the cell, though built he judged twenty years before, were perfectly solid, and the window bars of new iron had not a shadow of rust on them. The window itself, even with the bars out, would be a difficult mode of egress because it was small.

Yet, seeing these things, The Thinking Machine was not discouraged. Instead, he thoughtfully squinted at the great arc light—there was bright sunlight now—and traced with his eyes the wire which led from it to the building. That electric wire, he reasoned, must come down the side of the building not a great distance from his cell. That might be worth knowing.

Cell 13 was on the same floor with the offices of the prison—that is, not in the basement, nor yet upstairs. There were only four steps up to the office floor, therefore the level of the floor must be only three or four feet above the ground. He couldn't see the ground directly beneath his window, but he could see it further out toward the wall. It would be an easy drop from the window. Well and good.

Then The Thinking Machine fell to remembering how he had come to the cell. First, there was the outside guard's booth, a part of the wall. There were two heavily barred gates there, both of steel. At this gate was one man always on guard. He admitted persons to the prison after much clanking of keys and locks, and let them out when ordered to do so. The warden's office was in the prison building, and in order to reach that official from the prison yard one had to pass a gate of solid steel with only a peep-hole in it. Then coming from that inner office to Cell 13, where he was now, one must pass a heavy wooden door and two steel doors into the corridors of the prison; and always there was the double-locked door of Cell 13 to reckon with.

There were then, The Thinking Machine recalled, seven doors to be overcome before one could pass from Cell 13 into the outer world, a free man. But against this was the fact that he was rarely interrupted. A jailer appeared at his cell door at six in the morning with a breakfast of prison fare; he would come again at noon, and again at six in the afternoon. At nine o'clock at night would come the inspection tour. That would be all.

"It's admirably arranged, this prison system," was the mental tribute paid by The Thinking Machine. "I'll have to study it a little when I get out. I had no idea there was such great care exercised in the prisons."

There was nothing, positively nothing, in his cell, except his iron bed, so firmly put together that no man could tear it to pieces save with sledges or a file. He had neither of these. There was not even a chair, or a small table, or a bit of tin or crockery. Nothing! The jailer stood by when he ate, then took away the wooden spoon and bowl which he had used.

One by one these things sank into the brain of The Thinking Machine. When the last possibility had been considered he began an examination of his cell. From the roof, down the walls on all sides, he examined the stones and the cement between them. He stamped over the floor carefully time after time, but it was cement, perfectly solid. After the examination he sat on the edge of the iron bed and was lost in thought for a long time. For Professor Augustus S.F.X. Van Dusen, The Thinking Machine, had something to think about.

He was disturbed by a rat, which ran across his foot, then scampered away into a dark corner of the cell, frightened at its own daring. After awhile The

Thinking Machine, squinting steadily into the darkness of the corner where the rat had gone, was able to make out in the gloom many little beady eyes staring at him. He counted six pair, and there were perhaps others; he didn't see very well.

Then The Thinking Machine, from his seat on the bed, noticed for the first time the bottom of his cell door. There was an opening there of two inches between the steel bar and the floor. Still looking steadily at this opening, The Thinking Machine backed suddenly into the corner where he had seen the heady eyes. There was a great scampering of tiny feet, several squeaks of frightened rodents, and then silence.

None of the rats had gone out the door, yet there were none in the cell. Therefore there must be another way out of the cell, however small. The Thinking Machine, on hands and knees, started a search for this spot, feeling in the darkness with his long, slender fingers.

At last his search was rewarded. He came upon a small opening in the floor, level with the cement. It was perfectly round and somewhat larger than a silver dollar. This was the way the rats had gone. He put his fingers deep into the opening; it seemed to be a disused drainage pipe and was dry and dusty.

Having satisfied himself on this point, he sat on the bed again for an hour, then made another inspection of his surroundings through the small cell window. One of the outside guards stood directly opposite, beside the wall, and happened to be looking at the window of Cell 13 when the head of The Thinking Machine appeared. But the scientist didn't notice the guard.

Noon came and the jailer appeared with the prison dinner of repulsively plain food. At home The Thinking Machine merely ate to live; here he took what was offered without comment. Occasionally he spoke to the jailer who stood outside the door watching him.

"Any improvements made here in the last few years?" he asked.

"Nothing particularly," replied the jailer. "New wall was built four years ago."

"Anything done to the prison proper?"

"Painted the woodwork outside, and I believe about seven years ago a new system of plumbing was put in."

"Ah!" said the prisoner. "How far is the river over there?"

"About three hundred feet. The boys have a baseball ground between the wall and the river."

The Thinking Machine had nothing further to say just then, but when the jailer was ready to go he asked for some water.

"I get very thirsty here," he explained. "Would it be possible for you to leave a little water in a bowl for me? "

"I'll ask the warden," replied the jailer, and he went away.

Half an hour later he returned with water in a small earthen bowl.

"The warden says you may keep this bowl," he informed the prisoner. "But you must show it to me when I ask for it. If it is broken, it will be the last."

"Thank you," said The Thinking Machine. "I shan't break it."

The jailer went on about his duties. For just the fraction of a second it seemed that The Thinking Machine wanted to ask a question, but he didn't.

Two hours later this same jailer, in passing the door of Cell No. 13, heard a noise inside and stopped. The Thinking Machine was down on his hands and knees in a corner of the cell, and from that same corner came several frightened squeaks. The jailer looked on interestedly.

"Ah, I've got you," he heard the prisoner say.

"Got what? "he asked, sharply.

"One of these rats," was the reply. "See?" And between the scientist's long fingers the jailer saw a small gray rat struggling. The prisoner brought it over to the light and looked at it closely. "It's a water rat," he said.

"Ain't you got anything better to do than to catch rats?" asked the jailer.

"It's disgraceful that they should be here at all," was the irritated reply. "Take this one away and kill it. There are dozens more where it came from."

The jailer took the wriggling, squirmy rodent and flung it down on the floor violently. It gave one squeak and lay still. Later he reported the incident to the warden, who only smiled.

Still later that afternoon the outside armed guard on Cell 13 side of the prison looked up again at the window and saw the prisoner looking out. He saw a hand raised to the barred window and then something white fluttered to the ground, directly under the window of Cell 13. It was a little roll of linen, evidently of white shirting material, and tied around it was a five-dollar bill. The guard looked up at the window again, but the face had disappeared.

With a grim smile he took the little linen roll and the five-dollar bill to the warden's office. There together they deciphered something which was written on it with a queer sort of ink, frequently blurred. On the outside was this:

"Finder of this please deliver to Dr. Charles Ransome."

"Ah," said the warden, with a chuckle. "Plan of escape number one has gone wrong." Then, as an afterthought: "But why did he address it to Dr. Ransome?"

"And where did he get the pen and ink to write with?" asked the guard.

The warden looked at the guard and the guard looked at the warden. There was no apparent solution of that mystery. The warden studied the writing carefully, then shook his head.

"Well, let's see what he was going to say to Dr. Ransome," he said at length, still puzzled, and he unrolled the inner piece of linen.

"Well, if that—what—what do you think of that?" he asked, dazed.

The guard took the bit of linen and read this:

Epa cseot d'net niiy awe htto n'si sih.
T.

III

The warden spent an hour wondering what sort of a cipher it was, and half an hour wondering why his prisoner should attempt to communicate with Dr. Ransome, who was the cause of him being there. After this the warden devoted some thought to the question of where the prisoner got writing materials, and what sort of writing materials he had. With the idea of illuminating this point, he examined the linen again. It was a torn part of a white shirt and had ragged edges.

Now it was possible to account for the linen, but what the prisoner had used to write with was another matter. The warden knew it would have been impossible for him to have either pen or pencil, and, besides, neither pen nor pencil had been used in this writing. What, then? The warden decided to personally investigate. The Thinking Machine was his prisoner; he had orders to hold his prisoners; if this one sought to escape by sending cipher messages to persons outside, he would stop it, as he would have stopped it in the case of any other prisoner.

The warden went back to Cell 13 and found The Thinking Machine on his hands and knees on the floor, engaged in nothing more alarming than catching rats. The prisoner heard the warden's step and turned to him quickly.

"It's disgraceful," he snapped, "these rats. There are scores of them."

"Other men have been able to stand them," said the warden. "Here is another shirt for you—let me have the one you have on."

"Why?" demanded The Thinking Machine, quickly. His tone was hardly natural, his manner suggested actual perturbation.

"You have attempted to communicate with Dr. Ransome," said the warden severely. "As my prisoner, it is my duty to put a stop to it."

The Thinking Machine was silent for a moment. "All right," he said, finally. "Do your duty."

The warden smiled grimly. The prisoner arose from the floor and removed the white shirt, putting on instead a striped convict shirt the warden had brought. The warden took the white shirt eagerly, and then and there compared the pieces of linen on which was written the cipher with certain torn places in the shirt. The Thinking Machine looked on curiously.

"The guard brought *you* those, then?" he asked.

"He certainly did," replied the warden triumphantly. "And that ends your first attempt to escape."

The Thinking Machine watched the warden as he, by comparison, established to his own satisfaction that only two pieces of linen had been torn from the white shirt.

"What did you write this with?" demanded the warden.

"I should think it a part of your duty to find out," said The Thinking Machine, irritably.

The warden started to say some harsh things, then restrained himself and made a minute search of the cell and of the prisoner instead. He found absolutely nothing; not even a match or toothpick which might have been used for a pen. The same mystery surrounded the fluid with which the cipher had been written. Although the warden left Cell 13 visibly annoyed, he took the torn shirt in triumph.

"Well, writing notes on a shirt won't get him out, that's certain," he told himself with some complacency. He put the linen scraps into his desk to await developments. "If that man escapes from that cell I'll—hang it—I'll resign."

On the third day of his incarceration The Thinking Machine openly attempted to bribe his way out. The jailer had brought his dinner and was leaning against the barred door, waiting, when The Thinking Machine began the conversation.

"The drainage pipes of the prison lead to the river, don't they?" he asked.

"Yes," said the jailer.

"I suppose they are very small?"

"Too small to crawl through, if that's what you're thinking about," was the grinning response.

There was silence until The Thinking Machine finished his meal. Then:

"You know I'm not a criminal, don't you?"

"Yes."

"And that I've a perfect right to be freed if I demand it?"

"Yes."

"Well, I came here believing that I could make my escape," said the prisoner, and his squint eyes studied the face of the jailer. "Would you consider a financial reward for aiding me to escape?"

The jailer, who happened to be an honest man, looked at the slender, weak figure of the prisoner, at the large head with its mass of yellow hair, and was almost sorry.

"I guess prisons like these were not built for the likes of you to get out of," he said, at last.

"But would you consider a proposition to help me get out?" the prisoner insisted, almost beseechingly.

"No," said the jailer, shortly.

"Five hundred dollars," urged The Thinking Machine. "I am not a criminal."

"No," said the jailer.

"A thousand?"

"No," again said the jailer, and he started away hurriedly to escape further temptation. Then he turned back. "If you should give me ten thousand dollars I couldn't get you out. You'd have to pass through seven doors, and I only have the keys to two."

Then he told the warden all about it.

"Plan number two fails," said the warden, smiling grimly. "First a cipher, then bribery."

When the jailer was on his way to Cell 13 at six o'clock, again bearing food to The Thinking Machine, he paused, startled by the unmistakable scrape, scrape of steel against steel. It stopped at the sound of his steps, then craftily the jailer, who was beyond the prisoner's range of vision, resumed his tramping, the sound being apparently that of a man going away from Cell 13. As a matter of fact he was in the same spot.

After a moment there came again the steady scrape, scrape, and the jailer crept cautiously on tiptoes to the door and peered between the bars. The Thinking Machine was standing on the iron bed working at the bars of the little window. He was using a file, judging from the backward and forward swing of his arms.

Cautiously the jailer crept back to the office, summoned the warden in person, and they returned to Cell 13 on tiptoes. The steady scrape was still audible. The warden listened to satisfy himself and then suddenly appeared at the door.

"Well ?" he demanded, and there was a smile on his face.

The Thinking Machine glanced back from his perch on the bed and leaped suddenly to the floor, making frantic efforts to hide something. The warden went in, with hand extended.

"Give it up," he said.

"No," said the prisoner, sharply.

"Come, give it up," urged the warden. "I don't want to have to search you again."

"No," repeated the prisoner.

"What was it, a file?" asked the warden.

The Thinking Machine was silent and stood squinting at the warden with something very nearly approaching disappointment on his face—nearly, but not quite. The warden was almost sympathetic.

"Plan number three fails, eh?" he asked, good-naturedly. "Too bad, isn't it?"

The prisoner didn't say.

"Search him," instructed the warden.

The jailer searched the prisoner carefully. At last, artfully concealed in the waist band of the trousers, he found a piece of steel about two inches long, with one side curved like a half moon.

"Ah," said the warden, as he received it from the jailer. "From your shoe heel," and he smiled pleasantly.

The jailer continued his search and on the other side of the trousers waist band found another piece of steel identical with the first. The edges showed where they had been worn against the bars of the window.

"You couldn't saw a way through those bars with these," said the warden.

"I could have," said The Thinking Machine firmly.

"In six months, perhaps," said the warden, goodnaturedly.

The warden shook his head slowly as he gazed into the slightly flushed face of his prisoner.

"Ready to give it up?" he asked.

"I haven't started yet," was the prompt reply.

Then came another exhaustive search of the cell. Carefully the two men went over it, finally turning out the bed and searching that. Nothing. The warden in person climbed upon the bed and examined the bars of the window where the prisoner had been sawing. When he looked he was amused.

"Just made it a little bright by hard rubbing," he said to the prisoner, who stood looking on with a somewhat crestfallen air. The warden grasped the iron bars in his strong hands and tried to shake them. They were immovable, set firmly in the solid granite. He examined each in turn and found them all satisfactory. Finally he climbed down from the bed.

"Give it up, professor," he advised.

The Thinking Machine shook his head and the warden and jailer passed on again. As they disappeared down the corridor The Thinking Machine sat on the edge of the bed with his head in his hands.

"He's crazy to try to get out of that cell," commented the jailer.

"Of course he can't get out," said the warden. "But he's clever. I would like to know what he wrote that cipher with."

It was four o'clock next morning when an awful, heart-racking shriek of terror resounded through the great prison. It came from a cell, somewhere about the center, and its tone told a tale of horror, agony, terrible fear. The warden heard and with three of his men rushed into the long corridor leading to Cell 13.

IV

As they ran there came again that awful cry. It died away in a sort of wail. The white faces of prisoners appeared at cell doors upstairs and down, staring out wonderingly, frightened.

"It's that fool in Cell 13," grumbled the warden.

He stopped and stared in as one of the jailers flashed a lantern. "That fool in Cell 13" lay comfortably on his cot, flat on his back with his mouth open, snoring. Even as they looked there came again the piercing cry, from somewhere above. The warden's face blanched a little as he started up the stairs. There on the top floor he found a man in Cell 43, directly above Cell 13, but two floors higher, cowering in a corner of his cell.

"What's the matter?" demanded the warden.

"Thank God you've come," exclaimed the prisoner, and he cast himself against the bars of his cell.

"What is it?" demanded the warden again.

He threw open the door and went in. The prisoner dropped on his knees and clasped the warden about the body. His face was white with terror, his eyes were widely distended, and he was shuddering. His hands, icy cold, clutched at the warden's.

"Take me out of this cell, please take me out," he pleaded.

"What's the matter with you, anyhow?" insisted the warden, impatiently.

"I heard something—something," said the prisoner, and his eyes roved nervously around the cell.

"What did you hear?"

"I—I can't tell you," stammered the prisoner. Then, in a sudden burst of terror: "Take me out of this cell—put me anywhere—but take me out of here."

The warden and the three jailers exchanged glances.

"Who is this fellow? What's he accused of?" asked the warden.

"Joseph Ballard," said one of the jailers. "He's accused of throwing acid in a woman's face. She died from it."

"But they can't prove it," gasped the prisoner. "They can't prove it. Please put me in some other cell."

He was still clinging to the warden, and that official threw his arms off roughly. Then for a time he stood looking at the cowering wretch, who seemed possessed of all the wild, unreasoning terror of a child.

"Look here, Ballard," said the warden, finally, "if you heard anything, I want to know what it was. Now tell me."

"I can't, I can't," was the reply. He was sobbing.

"Where did it come from?"

"I don't know. Everywhere—nowhere. I just heard it."

"What was it—a voice?"

"Please don't make me answer," pleaded the prisoner.

"You must answer," said the warden, sharply.

"It was a voice—but—but it wasn't human," was the sobbing reply.

"Voice, but not human?" repeated the warden, puzzled.

"It sounded muffled and—and far away—and ghostly," explained the man.

"Did it come from inside or outside the prison?"

"It didn't seem to come from anywhere—it was just here, here, everywhere. I heard it. I heard it."

For an hour the warden tried to get the story, but Ballard had become suddenly obstinate and would say nothing—only pleaded to be placed in another cell, or to have one of the jailers remain near him until daylight. These requests were gruffly refused.

"And see here," said the warden, in conclusion, "if there's any more of this screaming I'll put you in the padded cell."

Then the warden went his way, a sadly puzzled man. Ballard sat at his cell door until daylight, his face, drawn and white with terror, pressed against the bars, and looked out into the prison with wide, staring eyes.

That day, the fourth since the incarceration of The Thinking Machine, was enlivened considerably by the volunteer prisoner, who spent most of his time at the little window of his cell. He began proceedings by throwing another piece of linen down to the guard, who picked it up dutifully and took it to the warden. On it was written:

"Only three days more."

The warden was in no way surprised at what he read; he understood that The Thinking Machine meant only three days more of his imprisonment, and he regarded the note as a boast. But how was the thing written? Where had The Thinking Machine found this new piece of linen? Where? How? He carefully examined the linen. It was white, of fine texture, shirting material. He took the shirt which he had taken and carefully fitted the two original pieces of the linen to the torn places. This third piece was entirely superfluous; it didn't fit anywhere, and yet it was unmistakably the same goods.

"And where—where does he get anything to write with?" demanded the warden of the world at large.

Still later on the fourth day The Thinking Machine, through the window of his cell, spoke to the armed guard outside.

"What day of the month is it?" he asked.

"The fifteenth," was the answer.

The Thinking Machine made a mental astronomical calculation and satisfied himself that the moon would not rise until after nine o'clock that night. Then he asked another question:

"Who attends to those arc lights?"

"Man from the company."

"You have no electricians in the building?"

"No."

"I should think you could save money if you had your own man."

"None of my business," replied the guard.

The guard noticed The Thinking Machine at the cell window frequently during that day, but always the face seemed listless and there was a certain wistfulness in the squint eyes behind the glasses. After a while he accepted the presence of the leonine head as a matter of course. He had seen other prisoners do the same thing; it was the longing for the outside world.

That afternoon, just before the day guard was relieved, the head appeared at the window again, and The Thinking Machine's hand held something out between the bars. It fluttered to the ground and the guard picked it up. It was a five-dollar bill.

"That's for you," called the prisoner.

As usual, the guard took it to the warden. That gentleman looked at it suspiciously; he looked at everything that came from Cell 13 with suspicion.

"He said it was for me," explained the guard.

"It's a sort of a tip, I suppose," said the warden. "I see no particular reason why you shouldn't accept—"

Suddenly he stopped. He had remembered that The Thinking Machine had gone into Cell 13 with one five-dollar bill and two ten-dollar bills; twenty-five dollars in all. Now a five-dollar bill had been tied around the first pieces of linen that came from the cell.

The warden still had it, and to convince himself he took it out and looked at it. It was five dollars; yet here was another five dollars, and The Thinking Machine had only had ten-dollar bills.

"Perhaps somebody changed one of the bills for him," he thought at last, with a sigh of relief.

But then and there he made up his mind. He would search Cell 13 as a cell was never before searched in this world. When a man could write at will, and change money, and do other wholly inexplicable things, there was something radically wrong with his prison. He planned to enter the cell at night—three o'clock would be an excellent time. The Thinking Machine must do all the weird things he did sometime. Night seemed the most reasonable.

Thus it happened that the warden stealthily descended upon Cell 13 that night at three o'clock. He paused at the door and listened. There was no sound save the steady, regular breathing of the prisoner. The keys unfastened the double locks with scarcely a clank, and the warden entered, locking the door behind him. Suddenly he flashed his dark-lantern in the face of the recumbent figure.

If the warden had planned to startle The Thinking Machine he was mistaken, for that individual merely opened his eyes quietly, reached for his glasses and inquired, in a most matter-of-fact tone:

"Who is it?"

It would be useless to describe the search that the warden made. It was minute. Not one inch of the cell or the bed was overlooked. He found the round hole in the floor, and with a flash of inspiration thrust his thick fingers into it. After a moment of fumbling there he drew up something and looked at it in the light of his lantern.

"Ugh!" he exclaimed.

The thing he had taken out was a rat—a dead rat. His inspiration fled as a mist before the sun. But he continued the search. The Thinking Machine, without a word, arose and kicked the rat out of the cell into the corridor.

The warden climbed on the bed and tried the steel bars in the tiny window. They were perfectly rigid; every bar of the door was the same.

Then the warden searched the prisoner's clothing, beginning at the shoes. Nothing hidden in them! Then the trousers waist band. Still nothing! Then the pockets of the trousers. From one side he drew out some paper money and examined it.

"Five one-dollar bills," he gasped.

"That's right," said the prisoner.

"But the—you had two tens and a five—what the—how do you do it?"

"That's my business," said The Thinking Machine.

"Did any of my men change this money for you—on your word of honor?"

The Thinking Machine paused just a fraction of a second.

"No," he said.

"Well, do you make it?" asked the warden. He was prepared to believe anything.

"That's my business," again said the prisoner.

The warden glared at the eminent scientist fiercely. He felt—he knew—that this man was making a fool of him, yet he didn't know how. If he were a real prisoner he would get the truth—but, then, perhaps, those inexplicable things which had happened would not have been brought before him so sharply. Neither of the men spoke for a long time, then suddenly the warden turned fiercely and left the cell, slamming the door behind him. He didn't dare to speak, then.

He glanced at the clock. It was ten minutes to four. He had hardly settled himself in bed when again came that heart-breaking shriek through the prison. With a few muttered words, which, while not elegant, were highly expressive, he relighted his lantern and rushed through the prison again to the cell on the upper floor.

Again Ballard was crushing himself against the steel door, shrieking, shrieking at the top of his voice. He stopped only when the warden flashed his lamp in the cell.

"Take me out, take me out," he screamed. "I did it, I did it, I killed her. Take it away."

"Take what away?" asked the warden.

"I threw the acid in her face—I did it—I confess. Take me out of here."

Ballard's condition was pitiable; it was only an act of mercy to let him out into the corridor. There he crouched in a corner, like an animal at bay, and clasped his hands to his ears. It took half an hour to calm him sufficiently for him to speak. Then he told incoherently what had happened. On the night before at four o'clock he had heard a voice—a sepulchral voice, muffled and wailing in tone.

"What did it say?" asked the warden, curiously.

"Acid—acid—acid!" gasped the prisoner. "It accused me. Acid! I threw the acid, and the woman died. Oh!" It was a long, shuddering wail of terror.

"Acid?" echoed the warden, puzzled. The case was beyond him.

"Acid. That's all I heard—that one word, repeated several times. There were other things, too, but I didn't hear them."

"That was last night, eh?" asked the warden. "What happened to-night—what frightened you just now? "

"It was the same thing," gasped the prisoner. "Acid—acid—acid!" He covered his face with his hands and sat shivering. "It was acid I used on her, but I didn't mean to kill her. I just heard the words. It was something accusing me—accusing me." He mumbled, and was silent.

"Did you hear anything else?"

"Yes—but I couldn't understand—only a little bit—just a word or two."

"Well, what was it?"

"I heard 'acid' three times, then I heard a long, moaning sound, then—then—I heard 'No. 8 hat.' I heard that twice."

"No. 8 hat," repeated the warden. "What the devil—No. 8 hat? Accusing voices of conscience have never talked about No. 8 hats, so far as I ever heard."

"He's insane," said one of the jailers, with an air of finality.

"I believe you," said the warden. "He must be. He probably heard something and got frightened. He's trembling now. No. 8 hat! What the—"

V

When the fifth day of The Thinking Machine's imprisonment rolled around the warden was wearing a hunted look. He was anxious for the end of the thing. He could not help but feel that his distinguished prisoner had been amusing himself. And if this were so, The Thinking Machine had lost none of his sense of humor. For on this fifth day he flung down another linen note to the outside guard, bearing the words: "Only two days more." Also he flung down half a dollar.

Now the warden knew—he *knew*—that the man in Cell 13 didn't have any half dollars—he *couldn't* have any half dollars, no more than he could have pen and ink and linen, and yet he did have them. It was a condition, not a theory; that is one reason why the warden was wearing a hunted look.

That ghastly, uncanny thing, too, about "Acid" and "No. 8 hat" clung to him tenaciously. They didn't mean anything, of course, merely the ravings of an insane murderer who had been driven by fear to confess his crime, still there were so many things that "didn't mean anything" happening in the prison now since The Thinking Machine was there.

On the sixth day the warden received a postal stating that Dr. Ransome and Mr. Fielding would be at Chisholm Prison on the following evening, Thursday, and in the event Professor Van Dusen had not yet escaped—and they presumed he had not because they had not heard from him—they would meet him there.

"In the event he had not yet escaped!" The warden smiled grimly. Escaped!

The Thinking Machine enlivened this day for the warden with three notes. They were on the usual linen and bore generally on the appointment at half-past eight o'clock Thursday night, which appointment the scientist had made at the time of his imprisonment.

On the afternoon of the seventh day the warden passed Cell 13 and glanced in. The Thinking Machine was lying on the iron bed, apparently sleeping lightly. The cell appeared precisely as it always did from a casual glance. The warden would swear that no man was going to leave it between that hour—it was then four o'clock—and half-past eight o'clock that evening.

On his way back past the cell the warden heard the steady breathing again, and coming close to the door looked in. He wouldn't have done so if The Thinking Machine had been looking, but now—well, it was different.

A ray of light came through the high window and fell on the face of the sleeping man. It occurred to the warden for the first time that his prisoner appeared haggard and weary. Just then The Thinking Machine stirred slightly and the warden hurried on up the corridor guiltily. That evening after six o'clock he saw the jailer.

"Everything all right in Cell 13?" he asked.

"Yes, sir," replied the jailer. "He didn't eat much, though."

It was with a feeling of having done his duty that the warden received Dr. Ransome and Mr. Fielding shortly after seven o'clock. He intended to show them the linen notes and lay before them the full story of his woes, which was a long one. But before this came to pass the guard from the river side of the prison yard entered the office.

"The arc light in my side of the yard won't light," he informed the warden.

"Confound it, that man's a hoodoo," thundered the official. "Everything has happened since he's been here."

The guard went back to his post in the darkness, and the warden 'phoned to the electric light company.

"This is Chisholm Prison," he said through the 'phone. "Send three or four men down here quick, to fix an arc light."

The reply was evidently satisfactory, for the warden hung up the receiver and passed out into the yard. While Dr. Ransome and Mr. Fielding sat waiting the guard at the outer gate came in with a special delivery letter. Dr. Ransome happened to notice the address, and, when the guard went out, looked at the letter more closely.

"By George!" he exclaimed.

"What is it?" asked Mr. Fielding.

Silently the doctor offered the letter. Mr. Fielding examined it closely.

"Coincidence," he said. "It must be."

It was nearly eight o'clock when the warden returned to his office. The electricians had arrived in a wagon, and were now at work. The warden pressed the buzz-button communicating with the man at the outer gate in the wall.

"How many electricians came in?" he asked, over the short 'phone. "Four? Three workmen in jumpers and overalls and the manager? Frock coat and silk hat? All right. Be certain that only four go out. That's all."

He turned to Dr. Ransome and Mr. Fielding. "We have to be careful here—particularly," and there was broad sarcasm in his tone, "since we have scientists locked up."

The warden picked up the special delivery letter carelessly, and then began to open it.

"When I read this I want to tell you gentlemen something about how—Great Caesar!" he ended, suddenly, as he glanced at the letter. He sat with mouth open, motionless, from astonishment.

"What is it?" asked Mr. Fielding.

"A special delivery letter from Cell 13," gasped the warden. "An invitation to supper."

"What?" and the two others arose, unanimously.

The warden sat dazed, staring at the letter for a moment, then called sharply to a guard outside in the corridor.

"Run down to Cell 13 and see if that man's in there."

The guard went as directed, while Dr. Ransome and Mr. Fielding examined the letter.

"It's Van Dusen's handwriting; there's no question of that," said Dr. Ransome. "I've seen too much of it."

Just then the buzz on the telephone from the outer gate sounded, and the warden, in a semi-trance, picked up the receiver.

"Hello! Two reporters, eh? Let 'em come in." He turned suddenly to the doctor and Mr. Fielding. "Why, the man *can't* be out. He must be in his cell."

Just at that moment the guard returned.

"He's still in his cell, sir," he reported. "I saw him. He's lying down."

"There, I told you so," said the warden, and he breathed freely again. "But how did he mail that letter?"

There was a rap on the steel door which led from the jail yard into the warden's office.

"It's the reporters," said the warden. "Let them in," he instructed the guard; then to the two other gentlemen: "Don't say anything about this before them, because I'd never hear the last of it."

The door opened, and the two men from the front gate entered.

"Good-evening, gentlemen," said one. That was Hutchinson Hatch; the warden knew him well.

"Well?" demanded the other, irritably. "I'm here."

That was The Thinking Machine.

He squinted belligerently at the warden, who sat with mouth agape. For the moment that official had nothing to say. Dr. Ransome and Mr. Fielding were amazed, but they didn't know what the warden knew. They were only amazed; he was paralyzed. Hutchinson Hatch, the reporter, took in the scene with greedy eyes.

"How—how—how did you do it?" gasped the warden, finally.

"Come back to the cell," said The Thinking Machine, in the irritated voice which his scientific associates knew so well.

The warden, still in a condition bordering on trance, led the way.

"Flash your light in there," directed The Thinking Machine.

The warden did so. There was nothing unusual in the appearance of the cell, and there—there on the bed lay the figure of The Thinking Machine. Certainly! There was the yellow hair! Again the Warden looked at the man beside him and wondered at the strangeness of his own dreams.

With trembling hands he unlocked the cell door and The Thinking Machine passed inside. "See here," he said.

He kicked at the steel bars in the bottom of the cell door and three of them were pushed out of place. A fourth broke off and rolled away in the corridor.

"And here, too," directed the erstwhile prisoner as he stood on the bed to reach the small window. He swept his hand across the opening and every bar came out.

"What's this in the bed?" demanded the warden, who was slowly recovering.

"A wig," was the reply. "Turn down the cover."

The warden did so. Beneath it lay a large coil of strong rope, thirty feet or more, a dagger, three files, ten feet of electric wire, a thin, powerful pair of steel pliers, a small tack hammer with its handle, and—and a Derringer pistol.

"How did you do it?" demanded the warden.

"You gentlemen have an engagement to supper with me at half-past nine o'clock," said The Thinking Machine. "Come on, or we shall be late."

"But how did you do it?" insisted the warden.

"Don't ever think you can hold any man who can use his brain," said The Thinking Machine. "Come on; we shall be late."

VI

It was an impatient supper party in the rooms of Professor Van Dusen and a somewhat silent one. The guests were Dr. Ransome, Albert Fielding, the warden, and Hutchinson Hatch, reporter. The meal was served to the minute, in accordance with Professor Van Dusen's instructions of one week before; Dr.

Ransome found the artichokes delicious. At last the supper was finished and The Thinking Machine turned full on Dr. Ransome and squinted at him fiercely.

"Do you believe it now?" he demanded.

"I do," replied Dr. Ransome.

"Do you admit that it was a fair test?"

"I do."

With the others, particularly the warden, he was waiting anxiously for the explanation.

"Suppose you tell us how——" began Mr. Fielding.

"Yes, tell us how," said the warden.

The Thinking Machine readjusted his glasses, took a couple of preparatory squints at his audience, and began the story. He told it from the beginning logically; and no man ever talked to more interested listeners.

"My agreement was," he began, "to go into a cell, carrying nothing except what was necessary to wear, and to leave that cell within a week. I had never seen Chisholm Prison. When I went into the cell I asked for tooth powder, two ten and one five-dollar bills, and also to have my shoes blacked. Even if these requests had been refused it would not have mattered seriously. But you agreed to them.

"I knew there would be nothing in the cell which you thought I might use to advantage. So when the warden locked the door on me I was apparently helpless, unless I could turn three seemingly innocent things to use. They were things which would have been permitted any prisoner under sentence of death, were they not, warden?"

"Tooth powder and polished shoes, yes, but not money," replied the warden.

"Anything is dangerous in the hands of a man who knows how to use it," went on The Thinking Machine. "I did nothing that first night but sleep and chase rats." He glared at the warden. "When the matter was broached I knew I could do nothing that night, so suggested next day. You gentlemen thought I wanted time to arrange an escape with outside assistance, but this was not true. I knew I could communicate with whom I pleased, when I pleased."

The warden stared at him a moment, then went on smoking solemnly.

"I was aroused next morning at six o'clock by the jailer with my breakfast," continued the scientist. "He told me dinner was at twelve and supper at six. Between these times, I gathered, I would be pretty much to myself. So immediately after breakfast I examined my outside surroundings from my cell window. One look told me it would be useless to try to scale the wall, even should I decide to leave my cell by the window, for my purpose was to leave not only the cell, but the prison. Of course, I could have gone over the wall, but it would have taken me longer to lay my plans that way. Therefore, for the moment, I dismissed all idea of that.

"From this first observation I knew the river was on that side of the prison, and that there was also a playground there. Subsequently these surmises were verified by a keeper. I knew then one important thing—that anyone might approach the prison wall from that side if necessary without attracting any particular attention. That was well to remember. I remembered it.

"But the outside thing which most attracted my attention was the feed wire to the are light which ran within a few feet—probably three or four—of my cell window. I knew that would be valuable in the event I found it necessary to cut off that arc light."

"Oh, you shut it off to-night, then?" asked the warden.

"Having learned all I could from that window," resumed The Thinking Machine, without heeding the interruption, "I considered the idea of escaping through the prison proper. I recalled just how I had come into the cell, which I knew would be the only way. Seven doors lay between me and the outside. So, also for the time being, I gave up the idea of escaping that way. And I couldn't go through the solid granite walls of the cell."

The Thinking Machine paused for a moment and Dr. Ransome lighted a new cigar. For several minutes there was silence, then the scientific jail-breaker went on:

"While I was thinking about these things a rat ran across my foot. It suggested a new line of thought. There were at least half a dozen rats in the cell—I could see their beady eyes. Yet I had noticed none come under the cell door. I frightened them purposely and watched the cell door to see if they went out that way. They did not, but they were gone. Obviously they went another way. Another way meant another opening.

"I searched for this opening and found it. It was an old drain pipe, long unused and partly choked with dirt and dust. But this was the way the rats had come. They came from somewhere. Where? Drain pipes usually lead outside prison grounds. This one probably led to the river, or near it. The rats must therefore come from that direction. If they came a part of the way, I reasoned that they came all the way, because it was extremely unlikely that a solid iron or lead pipe would have any hole in it except at the exit.

"When the jailer came with my luncheon he told me two important things, although he didn't know it. One was that a new system of plumbing had been put in the prison seven years before; another that the river was only three hundred feet away. Then I knew positively that the pipe was a part of an old system; I knew, too, that it slanted generally toward the river. But did the pipe end in the water or on land?

"This was the next question to be decided. I decided it by catching several of the rats in the cell. My jailer was surprised to see me engaged in this work. I examined at least a dozen of them. They were perfectly dry; they had come through the pipe, and, most important of all, they were *not house rats, but field rats*. The other end of the pipe was on land, then, outside the prison walls. So far, so good.

"Then, I knew that if I worked freely from this point I must attract the warden's attention in another direction. You see, by telling the warden that I had come there to escape you made the test more severe, because I had to trick him by false scents."

The warden looked up with a sad expression in his eyes.

"The first thing was to make him think I was trying to communicate with you, Dr. Ransome. So I wrote a note on a piece of linen I tore from my shirt, addressed it to Dr. Ransome, tied a five-dollar bill around it and threw it out the window. I knew the guard would take it to the warden, but I rather hoped the warden would send it as addressed. Have you that first linen note, warden?"

The warden produced the cipher.

"What the deuce does it mean, anyhow?" he asked.

"Read it backward, beginning with the 'T' signature and disregard the division into words," instructed The Thinking Machine.

The warden did so.

"T-h-i-s, this," he spelled, studied it a moment, then read it off, grinning:

"This is not the way I intend to escape."

"Well, now what do you think o' that?" he demanded, still grinning.

"I knew that would attract your attention, just as it did," said The Thinking Machine, "and if you really found out what it was it would be a sort of gentle rebuke."

"What did you write it with?" asked Dr. Ransome, after he had examined the linen and passed it to Mr. Fielding.

"This," said the erstwhile prisoner, and he extended his foot. On it was the shoe he had worn in prison, though the polish was gone-scraped off clean. "The shoe blacking, moistened with water, was my ink; the metal tip of the shoe lace made a fairly good pen."

The warden looked up and suddenly burst into a laugh, half of relief, half of amusement.

"You're a wonder," he said, admiringly. "Go on.'"

"That precipitated a search of my cell by the warden, as I had intended," continued The Thinking Machine. "I was anxious to get the warden into the habit of searching my cell, so that finally, constantly finding nothing, he would get disgusted and quit. This at last happened, practically."

The warden blushed.

"He then took my white shirt away and gave me a prison shirt. He was satisfied that those two pieces of the shirt were all that was missing. But while he was searching my cell I had another piece of that same shirt, about nine inches square, rolled into a small ball in my mouth."

"Nine inches of that shirt?" demanded the warden. "Where did it come from?"

"The bosoms of all stiff white shirts are of triple thickness," was the explanation. "I tore out the inside thickness, leaving the bosom only two thicknesses. I knew you wouldn't see it. So much for that."

There was a little pause, and the warden looked from one to another of the men with a sheepish grin.

"Having disposed of the warden for the time being by giving him something else to think about, I took my first serious step toward freedom," said Professor Van Dusen. "I knew, within reason, that the pipe led somewhere to the playground outside; I knew a great many boys played there; I knew that rats came into my cell from out there. Could I communicate with some one outside with these things at hand?

"First was necessary, I saw, a long and fairly reliable thread, so—but here," he pulled up his trousers legs and showed that the tops of both stockings, of fine, strong lisle, were gone. "I unraveled those—after I got them started it wasn't difficult—and I had easily a quarter of a mile of thread that I could depend on.

"Then on half of my remaining linen I wrote, laboriously enough I assure you, a letter explaining my situation to this gentleman here," and he indicated Hutchinson Hatch. "I knew he would assist me—for the value of the newspaper story. I tied firmly to this linen letter a ten-dollar bill—there is no surer way of attracting the eye of anyone—and wrote on the linen: 'Finder of this deliver to Hutchinson Hatch, *Daily American*, who will give another ten dollars for the information.'

"The next thing was to get this note outside on that playground where a boy might find it. There were two ways, but I chose the best. I took one of the rats—I became adept in catching them—tied the linen and money firmly to one leg, fastened my lisle thread to another, and turned him loose in the drain pipe. I reasoned that the natural fright of the rodent would make him run until he was outside the pipe and then out on earth he would probably stop to gnaw off the linen and money.

"From the moment the rat disappeared into that dusty pipe I became anxious. I was taking so many chances. The rat might gnaw the string, of which I held one end; other rats might gnaw it; the rat might run out of the pipe and leave the linen and money where they would never be found; a thousand other things might have happened. So began some nervous hours, but the fact that the rat ran on until only a few feet of the string remained in my cell made me think he was outside the pipe. I had carefully instructed Mr. Hatch what to do in case the note reached him. The question was: Would it reach him?

"This done, I could only wait and make other plans in case this one failed. I openly attempted to bribe my jailer, and learned from him that he held the keys to only two of seven doors between me and freedom. Then I did something else to make the warden nervous. I took the steel supports out of the heels of my shoes and made a pretense of sawing the bars of my cell window. The warden raised a pretty row about that. He developed, too, the habit of shaking the bars of my cell window to see if they were solid. They were—then."

Again the warden grinned. He had ceased being astonished.

"With this one plan I had done all I could and could only wait to see what happened," the scientist went on. "I couldn't know whether my note had been delivered or even found, or whether the mouse had gnawed it up. And I didn't dare to draw back through the pipe that one slender thread which connected me with the outside.

"When I went to bed that night I didn't sleep, for fear there would come the slight signal twitch at the thread which was to tell me that Mr. Hatch had received the note. At half-past three o'clock, I judge, I felt this twitch, and no prisoner actually under sentence of death ever welcomed a thing more heartily."

The Thinking Machine stopped and turned to the reporter.

"You'd better explain just what you did," he said.

"The linen note was brought to me by a small boy who had been playing baseball," said Mr. Hatch. "I immediately saw a big story in it, so I gave the boy another ten dollars, and got several spools of silk, some twine, and a roll of light, pliable wire. The professor's note suggested that I have the finder of the note show me just where it was picked up, and told me to make my search from there, beginning at two o'clock in the morning. If I found the other end of the thread I was to twitch it gently three times, then a fourth.

"I began the search with a small bulb electric light. It was an hour and twenty minutes before I found the end of the drain pipe, half hidden in weeds. The pipe was very large there, say twelve inches across. Then I found the end of the lisle thread, twitched it as directed and immediately I got an answering twitch.

"Then I fastened the silk to this and Professor Van Dusen began to pull it into his cell. I nearly had heart disease for fear the string would break. To the end of the silk I fastened the twine, and when that had been pulled in I tied on the wire. Then that was drawn into the pipe and we had a substantial line, which rats couldn't gnaw, from the mouth of the drain into the cell."

The Thinking Machine raised his hand and Hatch stopped.

"All this was done in absolute silence," said the scientist. "But when the wire reached my hand I could have shouted. Then we tried another experiment, which Mr. Hatch was prepared for. I tested the pipe as a speaking tube. Neither of us could hear very clearly, but I dared not speak loud for fear of attracting attention in the prison. At last I made him understand what I wanted immediately. He seemed to have great difficulty in understanding when I asked for nitric acid, and I repeated the word 'acid' several times.

"Then I heard a shriek from a cell above me. I knew instantly that some one had overheard, and when I heard you coming, Mr. Warden, I feigned sleep. If you had entered my cell at that moment that whole plan of escape would have ended there. But you passed on. That was the nearest I ever came to being caught.

"Having established this improvised trolley it is easy to see how I got things in the cell and made them disappear at will. I merely dropped them back into the pipe. You, Mr. Warden, could not have reached the connecting wire with your fingers; they are too large. My fingers, you see, are longer and more slender. In addition I guarded the top of that pipe with a rat—you remember how."

"I remember," said the warden, with a grimace.

"I thought that if any one were tempted to investigate that hole the rat would dampen his ardor. Mr. Hatch could not send me anything useful through the pipe until next night, although he did send me change for ten dollars as a test, so I proceeded with other parts of my plan. Then I evolved the method of escape, which I finally employed.

"In order to carry this out successfully it was necessary for the guard in the yard to get accustomed to seeing me at the cell window. I arranged this by dropping linen notes to him, boastful in tone, to make the warden believe, if possible, one of his assistants was communicating with the outside for me. I would stand at my window for hours gazing out, so the guard could see, and occasionally I spoke to him. In that way I learned that the prison had no electricians of its own, but was dependent upon the lighting company if anything should go wrong.

"That cleared the way to freedom perfectly. Early in the evening of the last day of my imprisonment, when it was dark, I planned to cut the feed wire which was only a few feet from my window, reaching it with an acid-tipped wire I had. That would make that side of the prison perfectly dark while the electricians were searching for the break. That would also bring Mr. Hatch into the prison yard.

"There was only one more thing to do before I actually began the work of setting myself free. This was to arrange final details with Mr. Hatch through our speaking tube. I did this within half an hour after the warden left my cell on the fourth night of my imprisonment. Mr. Hatch again had serious difficulty in understanding me, and I repeated the word 'acid' to him several times, and later the words: 'Number eight hat'—that's my size—and these were the things which made a prisoner upstairs confess to murder, so one of the jailers told me next day. This prisoner heard our voices, confused of course, through the pipe, which also went to his cell. The cell directly over me was not occupied, hence no one else heard.

"Of course the actual work of cutting the steel bars out of the window and door was comparatively easy with nitric acid, which I got through the pipe in thin bottles, but it took time. Hour after hour on the fifth and sixth and seven days the guard below was looking at me as I worked on the bars of the window with the acid on a piece of wire. I used the tooth powder to prevent the acid spreading. I looked away abstractedly as I worked and each minute the acid cut deeper into the metal. I noticed that the jailers always tried the door by shaking the upper part, never the lower bars, therefore I cut the lower bars, leaving them hanging in place by thin strips of metal. But that was a bit of dare-deviltry. I could not have gone that way so easily."

The Thinking Machine sat silent for several minutes.

"I think that makes everything clear," he went on. "Whatever points I have not explained were merely to confuse the warden and jailers. These things in my bed I brought in to please Mr. Hatch, who wanted to improve the story. Of course, the wig was necessary in my plan. The special delivery letter I wrote and directed in my cell with Mr. Hatch's fountain pen, then sent it out to him and he mailed it. That's all, I think."

"But your actually leaving the prison grounds and then coming in through the outer gate to my office?" asked the warden.

"Perfectly simple," said the scientist. "I cut the electric light wire with acid, as I said, when the current was off. Therefore when the current was turned on the arc didn't light. I knew it would take some time to find out what was the matter and make repairs. When the guard went to report to you the yard was dark. I crept out the window—it was a tight fit, too—replaced the bars by standing on a narrow ledge and remained in a shadow until the force of electricians arrived. Mr. Hatch was one of them.

"When I saw him I spoke and he handed me a cap, a jumper and overalls, which I put on within ten feet of you, Mr. Warden, while you were in the yard. Later Mr. Hatch called me, presumably as a workman, and together we went out the gate to get something out of the wagon. The gate guard let us pass out readily as two workmen who had just passed in. We changed our clothing and reappeared, asking to see you. We saw you. That's all."

There was silence for several minutes. Dr. Ransome was first to speak.

"Wonderful!" he exclaimed. "Perfectly amazing."

"How did Mr. Hatch happen to come with the electricians?" asked Mr. Fielding.

"His father is manager of the company," replied The Thinking Machine.

"But what if there had been no Mr. Hatch outside to help? "

"Every prisoner has one friend outside who would help him escape if he could."

"Suppose—just suppose—there had been no old plumbing system there?" asked the warden, curiously.

"There were two other ways out," said The Thinking Machine, enigmatically.

Ten minutes later the telephone bell rang. It was a request for the warden.

"Light all right, eh?" the warden asked, through the 'phone. "Good. Wire cut beside Cell 13? Yes, I know. One electrician too many? What's that? Two came out?"

The warden turned to the others with a puzzled expression.

"He only let in four electricians, he has let out two and says there are three left."

"I was the odd one," said The Thinking Machine.

"Oh," said the warden. "I see." Then through the 'phone: "Let the fifth man go. He's all right."

THE ANGEL OF THE LORD

Melville Davisson Post

I ALWAYS THOUGHT MY FATHER TOOK A LONG CHANCE, BUT SOMEBODY HAD TO take it and certainly I was the one least likely to be suspected. It was a wild country. There were no banks. We had to pay for the cattle, and somebody had to carry the money. My father and my uncle were always being watched. My father was right, I think.

"Abner," he said, "I'm going to send Martin. No one will ever suppose that we would trust this money to a child."

My uncle drummed on the table and rapped his heels on the floor. He was a bachelor, stern and silent. But he could talk . . . and when he did, he began at the beginning and you heard him through; and what he said—well, he stood behind it.

"To stop Martin," my father went on, "would be only to lose the money; but to stop you would be to get somebody killed."

I knew what my father meant. He meant that no one would undertake to rob Abner until after he had shot him to death.

I ought to say a word about my Uncle Abner. He was one of those austere, deeply religious men who were the product of the Reformation. He always carried a Bible in his pocket and he read it where he pleased. Once the crowd at Roy's Tavern tried to make sport of him when he got his book out by the fire; but they never tried it again. When the fight was over Abner paid Roy eighteen silver dollars for the broken chairs and the table—and he was the only man in the tavern who could ride a horse. Abner belonged to the church militant, and his God was a war lord.

So that is how they came to send me. The money was in greenbacks in packages. They wrapped it up in newspaper and put it into a pair of saddle-bags, and I set out. I was about nine years old. No, it was not as bad as you think. I could ride a horse all day when I was nine years old—most any kind of a horse. I was tough as whit'-leather, and I knew the country I was going into. You must not picture a little boy rolling a hoop in the park.

It was an afternoon in early autumn. The clay roads froze in the night; they thawed out in the day and they were a bit sticky. I was to stop at Roy's Tavern, south of the river, and go on in the morning. Now and then I passed some cattle driver, but no one overtook me on the road until almost sundown; then I heard a horse behind me and a man came up. I knew him. He was a cattleman named Dix. He had once been a shipper, but he had come in for a good deal of bad luck. His partner, Alkire, had absconded with a big sum of money due the grazers. This had ruined Dix; he had given up his land, which wasn't very much, to the grazers. After that he had gone over the mountain to his people, got together a pretty big sum of money and bought a large tract of grazing land. Foreign claimants had sued him in the courts on some old title and he had lost the whole tract and the money that he had paid for it. He had married a remote cousin of ours and he had always lived on her lands, adjoining those of my Uncle Abner.

Dix seemed surprised to see me on the road.

"So it's you, Martin," he said; "I thought Abner would be going into the upcountry."

One gets to be a pretty cunning youngster, even at this age, and I told no one what I was about.

"Father wants the cattle over the river to run a month," I returned easily, "and I'm going up there to give his orders to the grazers."

He looked me over, then he rapped the saddlebags with his knuckles. "You carry a good deal of baggage, my lad."

I laughed. "Horse feed," I said. "You know my father! A horse must be fed at dinner time, but a man can go till he gets it."

One was always glad of any company on the road, and we fell into an idle talk. Dix said he was going out into the Ten Mile country; and I have always thought that was, in fact, his intention. The road turned south about a mile our side of the tavern. I never liked Dix; he was of an apologetic manner, with a cunning, irresolute face.

A little later a man passed us at a gallop. He was a drover named Marks, who lived beyond my Uncle Abner, and he was riding hard to get in before night. He hailed us, but he did not stop; we got a shower of mud and Dix cursed him. I have never seen a more evil face. I suppose it was because Dix usually had a grin about his mouth, and when that sort of face gets twisted there's nothing like it.

After that he was silent. He rode with his head down and his fingers plucking at his jaw, like a man in some perplexity. At the crossroads he stopped and sat for some time in the saddle, looking before him. I left him there, but at the bridge he overtook me. He said he had concluded to get some supper and go on after that.

Roy's Tavern consisted of a single big room, with a loft above it for sleeping quarters. A narrow covered way connected this room with the house in which Roy and his family lived. We used to hang our saddles on wooden pegs in this covered way. I have seen that wall so hung with saddles that you could not find a place for another stirrup. But to-night Dix and I were alone in the tavern. He looked cunningly at me when I took the saddle-bags with me into the big room and when I went with them up the ladder into the loft. But he said nothing—in fact, he had scarcely spoken. It was cold; the road had begun to freeze when we got in. Roy had lighted a big fire. I left Dix before it. I did not take off my clothes, because Roy's beds were mattresses of wheat straw covered with heifer skins—good enough for summer but pretty cold on such a night, even with the heavy, hand-woven coverlet in big white and black checks.

I put the saddle-bags under my head and lay down. I went at once to sleep, but I suddenly awaked. I thought there was a candle in the loft, but it was a gleam of light from the fire below, shining through a crack in the floor. I lay and watched it, the coverlet pulled up to my chin. Then I began to wonder why the fire burned so brightly. Dix ought to be on his way some time and it was a custom for the last man to rake out the fire. There was not a sound. The light streamed steadily through the crack.

Presently it occurred to me that Dix had forgotten the fire and that I ought to go down and rake it out. Roy always warned us about the fire when he went to bed. I got up, wrapped the great coverlet around me, went over to the gleam of light and looked down through the crack in the floor. I had to lie out at full length to get my eye against the board. The hickory logs had turned to great embers and glowed like a furnace of red coals.

Before this fire stood Dix. He was holding out his hands and turning himself about as though he were cold to the marrow; but with all that chill upon him, when the man's face came into the light I saw it covered with a sprinkling of sweat.

I shall carry the memory of that face. The grin was there at the mouth, but it was pulled about; the eyelids were drawn in; the teeth were clamped together. I have seen a dog poisoned with strychnine look like that.

I lay there and watched the thing. It was as though something potent and evil dwelling within the man were in travail to re-form his face upon its image. You cannot realize how that devilish labor held me—the face worked as though it were some plastic stuff, and the sweat oozed through. And all the time the man was cold; and he was crowding into the fire and turning himself about and putting out his hands. And it was as though the heat would no more enter in and warm him than it will enter in and warm the ice.

It seemed to scorch him and leave him cold—and he was fearfully and desperately cold! I could smell the singe of the fire on him, but it had no power against this diabolic chill. I began myself to shiver, although I had the heavy coverlet wrapped around me.

The thing was a fascinating horror; I seemed to be looking down into the chamber of some abominable maternity. The room was filled with the steady red light of the fire. Not a shadow moved in it. And there was silence. The man had taken off his boots and he twisted before the fire without a sound. It was like the shuddering tales of possession or transformation by a drug. I thought the man would burn himself to death. His clothes smoked. How could he be so cold?

Then, finally, the thing was over! I did not see it for his face was in the fire. But suddenly he grew composed and stepped back into the room. I tell you I was afraid to look! I do not know what thing I expected to see there, but I did not think it would be Dix.

Well, it was Dix; but not the Dix that any of us knew. There was a certain apology, a certain indecision, a certain servility in that other Dix, and these things showed about his face. But there was none of these weaknesses in this man.

His face had been pulled into planes of firmness and decision; the slack in his features had been taken up; the furtive moving of the eye was gone. He stood now squarely on his feet and he was full of courage. But I was afraid of him as I have never been afraid of any human creature in this world! Something that had been servile in him, that had skulked behind disguises, that had worn the habiliments of subterfuge, had now come forth; and it had molded the features of the man to its abominable courage.

Presently he began to move swiftly about the room. He looked out at the window and he listened at the door; then he went softly into the covered way. I thought he was going on his journey; but then he could not be going with his boots there beside the fire. In a moment he returned with a saddle blanket in his hand and came softly across the room to the ladder.

Then I understood the thing that he intended, and I was motionless with fear. I tried to get up, but I could not. I could only lie there with my eye strained to the crack in the floor. His foot was on the ladder, and I could already feel his hand on my throat and that blanket on my face, and the suffocation of death in me, when far away on the hard road I heard a horse!

He heard it, too, for he stopped on the ladder and turned his evil face about toward the door. The horse was on the long hill beyond the bridge, and he was coming as though the devil rode in his saddle. It was a hard, dark night. The frozen road was like flint; I could hear the iron of the shoes ring. Whoever rode that horse rode for his life, or for something more than his life, or he was mad. I heard the horse strike the bridge and thunder across it. And all the while Dix hung there on the ladder by his hands and listened. Now he sprang softly down, pulled on his boots and stood up before the fire, his face—this new face—gleaming with its evil courage. The next moment the horse stopped.

I could hear him plunge under the bit, his iron shoes ripping the frozen road; then the door leaped back and my Uncle Abner was in the room. I was so glad that my heart almost choked me and for a moment I could hardly see—everything was in a sort of mist.

Abner swept the room in a glance, then he stopped.

"Thank God!" he said; "I'm in time." And he drew his hand down over his face with the fingers hard and close as though he pulled something away.

"In time for what?" said Dix.

Abner looked him over. And I could see the muscles of his big shoulders stiffen as he looked. And again he looked him over. Then he spoke and his voice was strange.

"Dix," he said, "is it you?"

"Who would it be but me?" said Dix.

"It might be the devil," said Abner. "Do you know what your face looks like?"

"No matter what it looks like!" said Dix.

"And so," said Abner, "we have got courage with this new face."

Dix threw up his head.

"Now, look here, Abner," he said, "I've had about enough of your big manner. You ride a horse to death and you come plunging in here; what the devil's wrong with you?"

"There's nothing wrong with me," replied Abner, and his voice was low. "But there's something damnably wrong with you, Dix."

"The devil take you," said Dix, and I saw him measure Abner with his eye. It was not fear that held him back; fear was gone out of the creature; I think it was a kind of prudence.

Abner's eyes kindled, but his voice remained low and steady.

"Those are big words," he said.

"Well," cried Dix, "get out of the door then and let me pass!"

"Not just yet," said Abner; "I have something to say to you."

"Say it then," cried Dix, "and get out of the door."

"Why hurry?" said Abner. "It's a long time until daylight, and I have a good deal to say."

"You'll not say it to me," said Dix. "I've got a trip to make tonight; get out of the door."

Abner did not move. "You've got a longer trip to make tonight than you think, Dix," he said; "but you're going to hear what I have to say before you set out on it."

I saw Dix rise on his toes and I knew what he wished for. He wished for a weapon; and he wished for the bulk of bone and muscle that would have a chance against Abner. But he had neither the one nor the other. And he stood there on his toes and began to curse—low, vicious, withering oaths, that were like the swish of a knife.

Abner was looking at the man with a curious interest.

"It is strange," he said, as though speaking to himself, "but it explains the thing. While one is the servant of neither, one has the courage of neither; but when he finally makes his choice he gets what his master has to give him."

Then he spoke to Dix.

"Sit down!" he said; and it was in that deep, level voice that Abner used when he was standing close behind his words. Every man in the hills knew that voice; one had only a moment to decide after he heard it. Dix knew that, and yet for one instant he hung there on his toes, his eyes shimmering like a weasel's, his mouth twisting. He was not afraid! If he had had the ghost of a chance against Abner he would have taken it. But he knew he had not, and with an oath he threw the saddle blanket into a corner and sat down by the fire.

Abner came away from the door then. He took off his great coat. He put a log on the fire and he sat down across the hearth from Dix. The new hickory sprang crackling into flames. For a good while there was silence; the two men sat at either end of the hearth without a word. Abner seemed to have fallen into a study of the man before him. Finally he spoke:

"Dix," he said, "do you believe in the providence of God?"

Dix flung up his head.

"Abner," he cried, "if you are going to talk nonsense I promise you upon my oath that I will not stay to listen."

Abner did not at once reply. He seemed to begin now at another point.

"Dix," he said, "you've had a good deal of bad luck. . . . Perhaps you wish it put that way."

"Now, Abner," he cried, "you speak the truth; I have had hell's luck."

"Hell's luck you have had," replied Abner. "It is a good word. I accept it. Your partner disappeared with all the money of the grazers on the other side of the river; you lost the land in your lawsuit; and you are to-night without a dollar. That was a big tract of land to lose. Where did you get so great a sum of money?"

"I have told you a hundred times," replied Dix. "I got it from my people over the mountains. You know where I got it."

"Yes," said Abner. "I know where you got it, Dix. And I know another thing. But first I want to show you this," and he took a little penknife out of his pocket. "And I want to tell you that I believe in the providence of God, Dix."

"I don't care a fiddler's damn what you believe in," said Dix.

"But you do care what I know," replied Abner.

"What do you know?" said Dix.

"I know where your partner is," replied Abner.

I was uncertain about what Dix was going to do, but finally he answered with a sneer.

"Then you know something that nobody else knows."

"Yes," replied Abner, "there is another man who knows."

"Who?" said Dix.

"You," said Abner.

Dix leaned over in his chair and looked at Abner closely.

"Abner," he cried, "you are talking nonsense. Nobody knows where Alkire is. If I knew I'd go after him."

"Dix," Abner answered, and it was again in that deep, level voice, "if I had got here five minutes later you would have gone after him. I can promise you that, Dix.

"Now, listen! I was in the upcountry when I got your word about the partnership; and I was on my way back when at Big Run I broke a stirrup-leather. I had no knife and I went into the store and bought this one; then the storekeeper told me that Alkire had gone to see you. I didn't want to interfere with him and I turned back. . . . So I did not become your partner. And so I did not disappear. . . . What was it that prevented? The broken stirrup-leather? The knife? In old times, Dix, men were so blind that God had to open their eyes before they could see His angel in the way before them. . . . They are still blind, but they ought not to be that blind. . . . Well, on the night that Alkire disappeared I met him on his way to your house. It was out there at the bridge. He had broken a stirrup-leather and he was trying to fasten it with a nail. He asked me if I had a knife, and I gave him this one. It was beginning to rain and I went on, leaving him there in the road with the knife in his hand."

Abner paused; the muscles of his great iron jaw contracted.

"God forgive me," he said; "it was His angel again! I never saw Alkire after that."

"Nobody ever saw him after that," said Dix. "He got out of the hills that night."

"No," replied Abner; "it was not in the night when Alkire started on his journey; it was in the day."

"Abner," said Dix, "you talk like a fool. If Alkire had traveled the road in the day somebody would have seen him."

"Nobody could see him on the road he traveled," replied Abner.

"What road?" said Dix.

"Dix," replied Abner, "you will learn that soon enough."

Abner looked hard at the man.

"You saw Alkire when he started on his journey," he continued; "but did you see who it was that went with him?"

"Nobody went with him," replied Dix; "Alkire rode alone."

"Not alone," said Abner; "there was another."

"I didn't see him," said Dix.

"And yet," continued Abner, "you made Alkire go with him."

I saw cunning enter Dix's face. He was puzzled, but he thought Abner off the scent.

"And I made Alkire go with somebody, did I? Well, who was it? Did you see him?"

"Nobody ever saw him."

"He must be a stranger."

"No," replied Abner, "he rode the hills before we came into them."

"Indeed!" said Dix. "And what kind of a horse did he ride?"

"White!" said Abner.

Dix got some inkling of what Abner meant now, and his face grew livid.

"What are you driving at?" he cried. "You sit here beating around the bush. If you know anything, say it out; let's hear it. What is it?"

Abner put out his big sinewy hand as though to thrust Dix back into his chair.

"Listen!" he said. "Two days after that I wanted to get out into the Ten Mile country and I went through your lands; I rode a path through the narrow valley west of your house. At a point on the path where there is an apple tree something caught my eye and I stopped. Five minutes later I knew exactly what had happened under that apple tree. . . . Someone had ridden there; he had stopped under that tree; then something happened and the horse had run away—I knew that by the tracks of a horse on this path. I knew that the horse had a rider and that it had stopped under this tree, because there was a limb cut from the tree at a certain height. I knew the horse had remained there, because the small twigs of the apple limb had been pared off, and they lay in a heap on the path. I knew that something had frightened the horse and that it had run away, because the sod was torn up where it had jumped. . . . Ten minutes later I knew that the rider had not been in the saddle when the horse jumped; I knew what it was that had frightened the horse; and I knew that the thing had occurred the day before. Now, how did I know that?

"Listen! I put my horse into the tracks of that other horse under the tree and studied the ground. Immediately I saw where the weeds beside the path had been crushed, as though some animal had been lying down there, and in the very center of that bed I saw a little heap of fresh earth. That was strange, Dix, that fresh earth where the animal had been lying down! It had come there after the animal had got up, or else it would have been pressed flat. But where had it come from?

"I got off and walked around the apple tree, moving out from it in an ever-widening circle. Finally I found an ant heap, the top of which had been scraped away as though one had taken up the loose earth in his hands. Then I went back and plucked up some of the earth. The under clods of it were colored as with red paint. . . . No, it wasn't paint.

"There was a brush fence some fifty yards away. I went over to it and followed it down.

"Opposite the apple tree the weeds were again crushed as though some animal had lain there. I sat down in that place and drew a line with my eye across a log of the fence to a limb of the apple tree. Then I got on my horse and again put him in the tracks of that other horse under the tree; the imaginary line passed through the pit of my stomach! . . . I am four inches taller than Alkire."

It was then that Dix began to curse. I had seen his face work while Abner was speaking and that spray of sweat had reappeared. But he kept the courage he had got.

"Lord Almighty, man!" he cried. "How prettily you sum it up! We shall presently have Lawyer Abner with his brief. Because my renters have killed a calf; because one of their horses frightened at the blood has bolted, and because they cover the blood with earth so the other horses traveling the path may not do the like; straightway I have shot Alkire out of his saddle. . . . Man! What a mare's nest! And now, Lawyer Abner, with your neat little conclusions, what did I do with Alkire after I had killed him? Did I cause him to vanish into the air with a smell of sulphur or did I cause the earth to yawn and Alkire to descend into its bowels?"

"Dix," replied Abner, "your words move somewhat near the truth."

"Upon my soul," cried Dix, "you compliment me. If I had that trick of magic, believe me, you would be already some distance down."

Abner remained a moment silent.

"Dix," he said, "what does it mean when one finds a plot of earth resodded?"

"Is that a riddle?" cried Dix. "Well, confound me, if I don't answer it! You charge me with murder and then you fling in this neat conundrum. Now, what could be the answer to that riddle, Abner? If one had done a murder this sod would overlie a grave and Alkire would be in it in his bloody shirt. Do I give the answer?"

"You do not," replied Abner.

"No!" cried Dix. "Your sodded plot no grave, and Alkire not within it waiting for the trump of Gabriel! Why, man, where are your little damned conclusions?"

"Dix," said Abner, "you do not deceive me in the least; Alkire is not sleeping in a grave."

"Then in the air," sneered Dix, "with a smell of sulphur?"

"Nor in the air," said Abner.

"Then consumed with fire, like the priests of Baal?"

"Nor with fire," said Abner.

Dix had got back the quiet of his face; this banter had put him where he was when Abner entered. "This is all fools' talk," he said; "if I had killed Alkire, what could I have done with the body? And the horse! What could I have done with the horse? Remember, no man has ever seen Alkire's horse any more than he has seen Alkire—and for the reason that Alkire rode him out of the hills that night. Now, look here, Abner, you have asked me a good many questions. I will ask you one. Among your little conclusions do you find that I did this thing alone or with the aid of others?"

"Dix," replied Abner, "I will answer that upon my own belief you had no accomplice."

"Then," said Dix, "how could I have carried off the horse? Alkire I might carry; but his horse weighed thirteen hundred pounds!"

"Dix," said Abner, "no man helped you do this thing; but there were men who helped you to conceal it."

"And now," cried Dix, "the man is going mad! Who could I trust with such work, I ask you? Have I a renter that would not tell it when he moved on to another's land, or when he got a quart of cider in him? Where are the men who helped me?"

"Dix," said Abner, "they have been dead these fifty years."

I heard Dix laugh then, and his evil face lighted as though a candle were behind it. And, in truth, I thought he had got Abner silenced.

"In the name of Heaven!" he cried. "With such proofs it is a wonder that you did not have me hanged."

"And hanged you should have been," said Abner.

"Well," cried Dix, "go and tell the sheriff, and mind you lay before him those little, neat conclusions: How from a horse track and the place where a calf was butchered you have reasoned on Alkire's murder, and to conceal the body and the horse you have reasoned on the aid of men who were rotting in their graves when I was born; and see how he will receive you!"

Abner gave no attention to the man's flippant speech. He got his great silver watch out of his pocket, pressed the stem and looked. Then he spoke in his deep, even voice.

"Dix," he said, "it is nearly midnight; in an hour you must be on your journey, and I have something more to say. Listen! I knew this thing had been done the previous day because it had rained on the night that I met Alkire, and the earth of this ant heap had been disturbed after that. Moreover, this earth had been frozen, and that showed a night had passed since it had been placed there. And I knew the rider of that horse was Alkire because, beside the path near the severed twigs lay my knife, where it had fallen from his hand. This much I learned in some fifteen minutes; the rest took somewhat longer.

"I followed the track of the horse until it stopped in the little valley below. It was easy to follow while the horse ran, because the sod was torn; but when it ceased to run there was no track that I could follow. There was a little stream threading the valley, and I began at the wood and came slowly up to see if I could find where the horse had crossed. Finally I found a horse track and there was also a man's track, which meant that you had caught the horse and were leading it away. But where?

"On the rising ground above there was an old orchard where there had once been a house. The work about that house had been done a hundred years. It was rotted down now. You had opened this orchard into the pasture. I rode all over the face of this hill and finally I entered this orchard. There was a great, flat, moss-covered stone lying a few steps from where the house had stood. As I looked I noticed that the moss growing from it into the earth had been broken along the edges of the stone, and then I noticed that for a few feet about the stone the ground had been resodded. I got down and lifted up some of this new sod. Under it the earth had been soaked with that . . . red paint.

"It was clever of you, Dix, to resod the ground; that took only a little time and it effectually concealed the place where you had killed the horse; but it was foolish of you to forget that the broken moss around the edges of the great flat stone could not be mended."

"Abner!" cried Dix. "Stop!" And I saw that spray of sweat, and his face working like kneaded bread, and the shiver of that abominable chill on him.

Abner was silent for a moment and then he went on, but from another quarter.

"Twice," said Abner, "the Angel of the Lord stood before me and I did not know it; but the third time I knew it. It is not in the cry of the wind, nor in the voice of many waters that His presence is made known to us. That man in Israel had only the sign that the beast under him would not go on. Twice I had as good a sign, and tonight, when Marks broke a stirrup-leather before my house and called me to the door and asked me for a knife to mend it, I saw and I came!"

The log that Abner had thrown on was burned down, and the fire was again a mass of embers; the room was filled with that dull red light. Dix had got on to his feet, and he stood now twisting before the fire, his hands reaching out to it, and that cold creeping in his bones, and the smell of the fire on him.

Abner rose. And when he spoke his voice was like a thing that has dimensions and weight.

"Dix," he said, "you robbed the grazers; you shot Alkire out of his saddle; and a child you would have murdered!"

And I saw the sleeve of Abner's coat begin to move, then it stopped. He stood staring at something against the wall. I looked to see what the thing was, but I did not see it. Abner was looking beyond the wall, as though it had been moved away.

And all the time Dix had been shaking with that hellish cold, and twisting on the hearth and crowding into the fire. Then he fell back, and he was the Dix I knew—his face was slack; his eye was furtive; and he was full of terror.

It was his weak whine that awakened Abner. He put up his hand and brought the fingers hard down over his face, and then he looked at this new creature, cringing and beset with fears.

"Dix," he said, "Alkire was a just man; he sleeps as peacefully in that abandoned well under his horse as he would sleep in the churchyard. My hand has been held back; you may go. Vengeance is mine, I will repay, saith the Lord."

"But where shall I go, Abner?" the creature wailed; "I have no money and I am cold."

Abner took out his leather wallet and flung it toward the door.

"There is money," he said—"a hundred dollars—and there is my coat. Go! But if I find you in the hills to-morrow, or if I ever find you, I warn you in the name of the living God that I will stamp you out of life!"

I saw the loathsome thing writhe into Abner's coat and seize the wallet and slip out through the door; and a moment later I heard a horse. And I crept back on to Roy's heifer skin.

When I came down at daylight my Uncle Abner was reading by the fire.

THE WIRE-DEVIL

Francis Lynde

CONNOLLY, OFF-TRICK DIVISION DESPATCHER DOUBLING ON THE EARLY NIGHT trick for Jenner, whose baby was sick, snapped his key-switch at the close of a rapid fire of orders sent to straighten out a freight-train tangle on the Magdalene district, sat back in his chair, and reached for his corn-cob pipe with a fat man's sigh of relief.

Over in the corner of the bare, dingy office, Bolton, night man on the car-record wire, was rattling away at his type-writer; and on the wall opposite the despatcher's table the electrically timed standard clock was ticking off the minutes between eight-fifty-five and nine. While Connolly was striking a match to light his pipe, Bolton tore the type-written sheet out of his machine and twisted himself in his chair to ask a question.

"What's the good word from the Apache Limited?" he inquired, his evil little eyes blinking indecently. And then, before Connolly could reply: "It's up to me to 'buy' for the boys to-night. My little girl-doll is comin' on the Apache. Whadda you know about that: chasin' me all the way from little old New York."

The fat despatcher knew precisely where the Limited was, but he glanced at his train-sheet from sheer force of habit.

"On time at Angels, double-heading with the Nine-thirteen, and the Six-five," he said. Then he shifted over to the car-record man's cause for jubilation. "I didn't know you were a married man, Bolton. If I ever get out of the woods and make good on the job, I'm going to do it myself."

Bolton's mouth widened like a split in a parchment mask, and his laugh was a dry cackle.

"Married—that's a bully good joke. I'll have to tell it to the little doll-girl, when she comes."

Connolly was Irish chiefly by virtue of his name. He entirely missed the pointing of the car-record man's remark, but the apparent gibe touched his vanity and his round and naturally ruddy face grew a shade darker.

"Meaning that no girl with half a chance at other fellows would look twice at a fat slouch like me? That's where you're off your trolley. There is one, Barry, and she's pretty enough to make a wooden-Indian cigar-sign get down from his block and chase her up the street for another look-in. But I've got to make good and pull down a wad, first."

The car-record man's laugh this time was an unchaste sneer.

"Aw, chuck it!" he derided. "Whadda you want to tie yourself up for when there's plenty of—"

"Say, that'll do," Connolly broke in, with a frown of cleanly disgust, taking Bolton's meaning at last. Then he changed the subject abruptly. "Mr. Maxwell's got him a new chum: seen him?"

Bolton nodded.

"Sure, I have; couldn't help seein' him if you happened to look his way. What is he?—champion All-America heavy-weight?"

The despatcher shook his head. "College professor, somebody said; one of Mr. Maxwell's classmates. Specializes in something or other; I didn't hear what."

Again the tag-wire operator's laugh crackled like a snapping of dry twigs. He had risen from his chair and was half-sitting, half-leaning, upon his table-desk, his hands resting palms down, with the fingers curled under the table edge—his characteristic loafing attitude.

"He might specialize in any old thing," he jeered, with a small man's bickering hostility for a big one in his tone. "All he's got to do is to reach out and take it; nobody but a fellow in the Joe Gans class'd have the nerve to tell him not to. I saw him sittin' on the Topaz porch with the super as I came over. He's so big it made me sick at my stomach to look at him."

Connolly's pipe had gone out, burned out, and he was feeling in his pockets for the tobacco sack. While he was doing it the corridor door opened and Calmaine, the superintendent's chief clerk, came in, let himself briskly through the gate in the counter railing, and leaned over Connolly's shoulder to glance at the train-sheet.

"Everything moving along all right, Dan?" he asked.

"Is now," said the despatcher, still feeling absently for the missing tobacco sack. "Twenty-one and Twenty-eight got balled up on their orders over on the other side of the range, but I guess I've got 'em straightened out, after so long a time. . . . Now what the dickens did I do with that tobacco of mine, I wonder?"

"Have a cigar," said the chief clerk, laying one on the glass-topped wire-table. Calmaine, eastern trunk-line bred, had been inclined to cockiness when he came West, but a year with Maxwell, whose standing was that of the Short Line's best-beloved tyrant, had taken a good deal of it out of him.

"Thanks," returned Connolly, with a fat man's grin, "not for me when I'm despatching trains. The corn-cob goes with the job. Sit in here on the wire for a minute while I go up to the bunk-room and look in my other coat."

Calmaine took the vacated chair and ran his eye along the latest additions to the many columns of figures on the train-sheet. Bolton in his far corner was still loafing, though his night's work of taking and typing the wire car reports from the various stations on the double division was scarcely begun. "You think you're a little tin god on wheels, don't you?" he muttered under his breath, blinking and scowling across at the well-groomed young man sitting in Connolly's chair. "You can let down with Dan Connolly all right, but when it comes to throwin' a bone to the other new dog, you ain't it. One o' these times I'm goin' to jump up and bite you."

The object of this splenetic outburst was still bending over the train-sheet, abstractedly unconscious of Bolton's presence. From the conductors' room beyond the wire office three or four trainmen drifted in to look over the bulletin-board notices; and still Connolly did not return.

Suddenly the sounder in front of the substitute set up a furious chatter, clicking out a monotonous repetition of the "G.S." call, breaking at intervals with the signature "Ag," the code letters for Angels, the desert-edge town from which the Apache Limited had been last reported. Calmaine flicked his key-switch and cut in quickly with the answering signal. Then, reaching for pad and pen, he wrote out the message that came boiling over the wire.

G.S.

     Apache Limited in ditch at Lobo Cut four miles west. Both engines crumpled up. Two engine-men, one route agent, under wreck. Everything off but rear Pullman. Train on fire and lot of passengers pinned down. Hurry help quick.

                                               AG.

Calmaine was an alert young man, well abreast of his job and altogether capable. But before he could yelp twice Connolly had come in, and it was the fat despatcher who gave the alarm.

"My Lord, Bolton—see here!" he shouted, pushing Calmaine aside as an incumbrance. And then, when the car-record man came over to stare vacantly at the fateful message: "Get a move! Send somebody after Mr. Maxwell, quick! Then get busy on that yard wire and turn out the wrecking crew. Get Dawson on the 'phone and tell him I'll have a clear track for him by the time his wreck-wagons are ready! Jump at it, man! Your wife isn't the only one that's needing help! *Wake up!*"

Over on the sidewalk loggia porch of the Hotel Topaz fronting the electric-lighted railroad plaza, Maxwell, the division superintendent, was sitting out the evening with a broad-shouldered, solidly built young man whose big frame, clear gray eyes, and fighting jaw were the outward presentments of a foot-ball "back" rather than those of the traditional college professor.

"I don't mind piping myself off to you, Dick, though the full size of my job isn't generally known," the athletic-looking stop-over guest was saying. "You got the first part of it right; I'm down on the Department of Agriculture pay-rolls as a chemistry sharp. But outside of that I've half a dozen little hobbies which they let me ride now and then. You'll guess what one of them is when I tell you that I was the man who fried out the evidence in the post-office cases last winter."

"What!" exclaimed Maxwell. "But your name didn't appear."

The big man with the smooth-shaven, boyish face smiled contentedly.

"My name never appears. That is the high card in the game. So far as that goes, I never mess or meddle in the police details. My part of the job is always and only the theoretical stunt. They come to me and I tell 'em what to do. And just about half the time they haven't the least idea why they are doing it."

"Say, Calvin; that interests me a lot more than you know," was the young super-intendent's eager comment. "I wish you didn't have to go on to the coast to-morrow morning. We've developed an original little Chinese puzzle of our own here in the Timanyoni that is pretty nearly driving the last one of us wild-eyed. If you could stop over—"

The interruption came in the shape of a one-armed man with a lantern, sprinting like a base-runner across from the railroad building to the hotel. It was the night watchman summoned by the despatcher, and ten seconds later he had delivered his message.

"The Lord have mercy!" gasped the superintendent, bounding out of his chair, "the Limited?—in the ditch and on fire, you say? For Heaven's sake, where?"

"'Tis at Lobo Cut; 'tis Angels reporting it, sorr, so Misther Connolly did be saying. He's clearing f'r the wreck-train now, and he axed would you be coming over."

"Tell him I'll be over in a minute or two: as soon as I've called up the hospital and turned out the doctors."

"Yis, sorr; but Misther Bolton's doing that same now. They do be saying his wife's on the train, and he's *that* near crazy."

Maxwell turned to his guest.

"You see how it is with us poor railroad devils, Calvin. It's a bad case of 'have to,' and I know you'll excuse me. Just the same, it's an infernal outrage—when we haven't been able to get together for a dog's age."

The chemistry sharp, as he had called himself, was standing up and stretching his arms over his head like a pole-vaulter hardening his muscles for the jump.

"I'll trot over to your shop with you, Dick, if you don't object," he said good-naturedly. "I want to see what happens when you get a hurry call like this."

In the despatcher's office Connolly was hammering at his key like a madman, with the sweat running down his full-moon face and the hand which was not in use shaking as if the left half of him had been ague-smitten. Trainmen were coming and going, and the alarm whistle at the shops was bellowing the wreck call at ten-second intervals. Everybody made way for Maxwell when he pushed through the counter gate with his big guest at his heels.

"Any more news, Dan?"

The despatcher flicked his closing switch, and immediately the ague spread to the hand which was no longer steadied on the key.

"Nothing. I've been clearing, and everything is getting out of the way. I've tried twice to get Angels, but I can't raise anybody. I guess Garner, the operator, has set his signals at block and gone to gather up what help he can find."

Just then more men came crowding in from the corridor, and one of them, a small man with hot eyes and a harsh voice, barked at Connolly.

"Orders for the wreck-wagons, Dan; we're ready to go."

Out of the throng behind the counter barrier Bolton, yellow-faced and ghastly, fought his way to the gate and besought the superintendent.

"Let me go, too, Mr. Maxwell!" he panted. "My God! I've got to go!"

"Of course, you shall go, Barry," said the superintendent with quick kindliness, remembering what the watchman had said about Bolton's wife being on the ditched train. "Dan, send the caller after Catherton and let him take Bolton's wire." Then he turned to his guest, who had been standing aside and looking on with a level-eyed gaze that lost no detail. "It's hello and good-by for us, Sprague, old man; that is, unless you'd care to go along?"

The guest decided instantly. "I was just about to ask you if you couldn't count me in," he returned; and together they followed the rough-tongued little conductor in a hurried dash for the platform.

The wrecking-train had been backed down to the station spur to take on the hospital car, and it was standing ready for the eastward flight; two flatcars loaded with blocking and tackle, a desert tank-car filled with water, two work-train boxes crowded to the doors with men, and, next to the engine, which was one of the big "Pacific types" used on the fast-mail runs, a heavy steam crane powerful enough to lift a locomotive and swing it clear at a single hitch.

"Who's pulling us, Blacklock?" Maxwell asked, overtaking the little man with the hot eyes.

"Young Cargill."

Maxwell turned to Sprague.

"I'm going on the engine, Calvin. There's room for you if you care to try it. If you don't, I'll turn you over to Dawson, our master mechanic, and he'll make you at home in the doctors' car."

"I guess I'm in for all of it," was the even-toned reply, and they ran forward to climb to the cab of the big mail flyer.

"My friend, Mr. Sprague, Cargill," snapped Maxwell, introducing the stranger to the handsome young fellow in overalls and jumper perched upon the high right-hand seat, and Cargill pulled off his glove to shake hands.

"You'll find the Ten-sixteen a pretty hard rider," he began; but Maxwell cut him short.

"You have a clear track, and Blacklock's got your orders. Open her up and see what you can do. It's a plain case of 'get there' to-night, Billy. The minutes may mean just so many lives saved or lost."

"*Right!*" yelled the fireman, leaning from the gangway to get Blacklock's signal; and at the word the engineer's hand shot to the lever, the great engine shook itself free, and the rescue race was begun.

For the first few miles of the race the track was measurably straight. Maxwell stood on the raised step at Sprague's elbow, steadying himself with a grip on the sill of the opened side window. When he saw that the ex-fullback was making hard work of it he shouted in the big man's ear.

"Loosen up a bit and take the roll with her," he advised, and Sprague nodded and tried it.

"That's much better," he called back. "What are we making now?"

"Forty, or a little more. She's good for sixty, and so is Cargill, but the tangents are too short to let us hit the limit."

"And the wreck—how far away is it?"

"An hour and forty-five minutes from Brewster, on a passenger schedule. We'll better that by ten or fifteen minutes, though."

Evidently young Cargill meant to better it if he could. At Tabor Mine, ten miles out, the big engine's exhaust had become a continuous roaring blast, and the tiny station at the mine siding flashed through the beam of the electric headlight like some living thing in full flight to the rear. At Kensett, where the line skirts the reservoir lake of the Timanyoni High Line Irrigation Company, they passed a long freight on the siding; the caboose was only a few yards inside of the clear post, and Sprague winced involuntarily when the engine cab shot past the freight's rear end with what seemed only an inch or two to spare.

Corona was the next night telegraph station, and here the wrecking special met the two following sections of the freight drawn out upon the sidings to right and left.

Cargill's grip closed upon the throttle when the switch and station lights swept into view; but the station semaphore was wigwagging the "clear" signal, and once more the big man on the fireman's box sat tight while the flying special roared through the narrow main-line alley left by the two side-tracked freights.

Maxwell was holding his watch in his hand when the special cleared the switches at Corona and the great beam of the headlight began to flick to right and left in the dodging race among the foot-hills.

"We'll make Timanyoni, at the mouth of the canyon, in ten minutes' better time than our fast mail makes it," he said to Sprague; and the Government man nodded grimly.

"It's all right, Dick," he shouted back. "Just the same, I'd like to know how a man ever acquires the nerve to send a train around the hill corners this way when he hasn't the slightest notion of what may be waiting for him five hundred yards in the future."

Apparently the stalwart young fellow on the opposite side of the cab owned the necessary nerve. Easing the huge flyer skilfully around the sharpest of the turnings, he drove it to the limit on the tangents in spurts that seemed to promise certain destruction at the next crooking of the track. But the wheels of the train were still shrilling safely on the steel when the headlight beam, playing steadily for the moment, brought the lonely station at the canyon's mouth into its field.

Cargill was whistling peremptorily for the signal before the short train had fully straightened itself on the tangent below the station. But for some reason the red light on the station semaphore remained inert. Instantly the sweating fireman jerked his fire-door open, and the four pairs of eyes in the flyer's cab were all fixed upon the motionless red dot over the track when Cargill sounded his second call.

While the whistle echoes were still yelling in the surrounding hills the climax came. Out of the station door darted a man with a red lantern. Cargill pounced upon the throttle, and in the same second the brakes went into the emergency notch with a jerk that flung the superintendent and the fireman against the boiler-head and slammed the guest unceremoniously into the cab corner.

At the shriek of the brakes, the man with the red lantern turned and ran in the opposite direction, waving his signal light frantically; and the wrecking special was still only shrilling and skidding to its stop when a long passenger-train drawn by two engines slid smoothly out of the canyon portal and came grinding down the grade with lire spurting from every suddenly clipped wheel-rim.

Thanks to the man with the red lantern, there were half a dozen car-lengths to spare between the two trains when the double stop was made. But Maxwell was swearing hotly when, with Sprague for a close second, he dropped from the step of the panting 1016 and ran to meet the conductor of the passenger-train in the middle of the scant safety distance. Like the superintendent, the conductor was also boiling over with profanity, but he swallowed the cursing portion of his wrath hastily when he recognized the "big boss."

"Oh, it's you, is it, Mr. Maxwell?" he blurted out. "By hen! I was getting ready to cuss somebody out, red-hot! What's the trouble?"

"There doesn't seem to be any," snapped Maxwell shortly. "Is this the Limited?"

"Sure it is," replied the conductor. "Hadn't it ought to be?"

"And you haven't been in the ditch?"

The big red-faced train captain grinned.

"Not that anybody's heard of. Is that what's the matter? Was you coming to pick us up?"

Maxwell's answer was a barked-out string of orders.

"Let these wreck-wagons in on the siding. Find Blacklock and tell him to get orders to follow you to Brewster as second section. Pull out as quick as you can. You're ten minutes off time, right now!"

In the drawing-room of the rear sleeper of the limited, Maxwell closed the door on his guest and himself, passed his cigar-case, lighted a fresh cigar in his own behalf, and said nothing until after the short shifting stunt had been worked out and the Apache Limited was once more racing on its way westward. Then he opened up.

"You've got it now, Calvin; the thing that has been smashing more nerves for us than we can afford to lose. Of course, you understand what has happened. That blood-curdling report of an accident was a fake wire; God only knows where it came from, or who sent it."

"And there have been others?" queried Sprague.

"A dozen of them, first and last. It began about a month ago. Sometimes it's merely foolish; at other times it's like this—a thing to bring your heart into your mouth."

"And you mean to say you haven't been able to run it down?"

"Run it down? If there is anything we haven't done it's some little item that has been merely overlooked. We've had about all of the company detectives here, first and last, and the best of them have had to give it up. There is nothing to work on; absolutely nothing. This wire to-night purported to come from Angels; as a matter of fact, it may have come from anywhere east of Brewster and this side of Copah. When we come to examine the Angels operator, we'll probably find that he doesn't know a thing about it—not a thing in the wide world."

"Yet it was a real wire?"

"Calmaine, my own chief clerk, took it from the sounder and wrote it down. It seems that Connolly, the night despatcher, had gone out for a moment and Calmaine was holding down the wires for him. I saw the message before we left. The call and signature were all right, and the exact time, nine-thirteen, was given."

"Wire-tappers?" suggested the listener, who had grown shrewdly sympathetic.

"That is what we've all thought. But to tap a wire, you have to cut in on it somewhere. Of course, it could be done in any one of a thousand isolated places, but hardly without leaving some trace. Wickert, our wire-chief, has been over the lines east and west with a magnifying-glass, you might say."

For the measuring of a few other miles of the westward flight of the train the big man in the opposite seat said nothing. Then he began again.

"Have you tried to figure out a motive, Dick?"

"That is precisely what is driving every one of us stark, staring mad, Calvin," was the sober confession. "There isn't any motive—there can't be!"

"No trouble with the labor unions?"

"Not a bit in the world. More than that, the men have spent good money of their own trying to help us find out—as a measure of self-protection. You can see what they're afraid of; what we are all afraid of. Everybody is losing nerve, and if the scare keeps up, we'll have real trouble—plenty of it."

"And you say the source of the thing can't be localized?"

"No. We have a double division, with Brewster as the common head-quarters. Sometimes the yelp comes from the east, and sometimes from the west."

Again the big-bodied chemistry expert sank back in his seat and fell into the thoughtful trance. When he came out of it, it was to say:

"You've probably settled it for yourself that it isn't a plant for a train robbery— the kind of robbery which would be made easier by a wreck."

Maxwell shook his head.

"A pile of cross-ties would be much simpler."

"Doubtless. We'll cancel that and come to the next hypothesis. Could it be the work of some crazy telegraph operator?"

"We've threshed out the crazy guess. It doesn't prove up. A madman would slip up now and then—trip himself. I have a file of the fake messages. They were not sent by a lunatic."

"Call it another cancellation," said the guest. "You are convinced that some sane person is doing it. Very good. What is the object? You say you can't find out; which merely means that you've been attacking it from the wrong angle. Or, rather, you've let the professional detectives give you their angle. What you need is a bit of first-class amateur work."

The superintendent laughed mirthlessly. "If I could only find the amateur I'd hire him, Calvin,—if it took a year's salary. I don't know what the wire-devil's object is, but I can catalogue the results. These periodical scares are demoralizing the entire Short Line. The service is on the ragged edge of a chaotic blow-up. Half the men in the train crews are running on their bare nerves, and the operators who have to handle train-orders are not much better."

"Yes," said the guest quietly. "I've been noticing. I saw only one man in your office who wasn't scared stiff; and the conductor of this train we're riding on had a pretty bad attack of the tremolos when you told him what the wrecking-train was out for."

"Who, Garrighan? No, you're mistaken there. He's one of the cold-blooded ones," said the superintendent confidently.

"Excuse me, Dick; I'm never mistaken on that side of the fence. There were signs, plenty of them. Ninety-eight men in every hundred will duck and put up one or both arms if you strike at them suddenly. Garrighan did neither, you'll say; but if you had been watching him as closely as I was, you would have seen that he started to do both."

Maxwell was regarding his former classmate curiously.

"Is that how you do it? Is that the way you caught the post-office thieves, Calvin?"

The chemistry expert laughed.

"It's only a little pointer on methods," he averred. "When my attention was first called to such things—it was on a case in the Department of Justice in which I was required to give expert testimony—I was very strongly impressed with the crudities of the ordinary detective methods. I said to myself that what was needed was some one who could apply good, careful laboratory practice; a habit of observation which counts nothing too small to be weighed and measured."

"Go on," said Maxwell.

"The idea came to me that I'd like to try it on, and I did. My theory is correct. Human beings react under certain given conditions just as readily, and just as inevitably, as the inorganic substances react in a laboratory experiment."

Maxwell reached for the box of safety matches and passed it to Sprague, whose cigar had gone out.

"I wish you could stay and put this railroad of ours into your test-tube, Calvin. We're teetering along on the edge of an earthquake—oh, yes—I know you'll say it's only a scare; but the worst panic that has ever gone into history was only a scare in the beginning. One of these fine nights some engineer or some operator with the bare nerves will lose his grip. You know about what that will mean. We've escaped alive, so far; but the first real wreck that hits us will be just about the same as dropping a lighted match into a barrel of gunpowder; I thought it had come tonight; I'm glad it hasn't, but I know it's only postponed."

The chemistry man nodded.

"Somebody is reaching for you with a big stick; that is very evident, Maxwell. And there are brains behind it, too, when you come to think of it. If you wanted to kill a man without getting hanged for murder, one way to do it would be to persuade him to commit suicide. Has it ever occurred to you that somebody may be trying the same experiment on your railroad?"

"Good Lord, no!"

"Stranger things have happened. But that is beside the mark. You say you are needing help. I've half a mind to stop off and give you a bit of a lift."

"By Jove, Calvin!—if you would—"

"Call it a go," interrupted the guest. "I'll take a chance and say that my business in San Francisco can wait a few days. The fellow I'm after out there won't run away; it's the one thing he doesn't dare to do."

"Say, old man! but that's bully of you!" exclaimed the host, reaching across to grip the hand of helping. "You shall have everything in sight; I'll put every man on the two divisions under your orders, and you can have a special train and my private car. If you don't see what you want, just ask—"

The chemistry sharp was holding up his hand and laughing.

"No, no; hold on, Dick. You'll have to let me tackle the thing in my own way, and there won't be any grand-stand plays in it—in fact, I don't mean to appear personally in it at all. Let's see where we stand. You have a division detective of some sort, haven't you?—a fellow who does the gun-play act when it becomes necessary?"

"We have; a young fellow named Archer Tarbell, who got his experience chasing cattle thieves in Montana. He's a fine fellow, and it's breaking his heart because he can't get the nippers on our wire-devil."

"All right. I may want to use him. Now another matter. You have a live newspaper in Brewster; I bought a copy of it on the train this morning. If I remember right, it's called *The Tribune*. Is it friendly to your railroad?"

"Ordinarily, yes; though Treadwell, the owner, is independent enough to print anything that he thinks is news."

"Know him pretty well?"

"Very well, indeed."

"Good. When we get in, make it your first care to see the newspaper people and to persuade them not to make any mention of this little miss-go of to-night. That's the first move and it's an important one. Can you work it?"

"Sure. But I don't see the point."

"Never mind about that; I probably sha'n't do anything that you think I ought to do. Now about this man Tarbell; is he known as a company detective?"

"No, not generally known; he's on the pay-roll as a spare operator—relief man, you know."

"That's better. When I meet him I'll see if I can't get him interested in chemistry. That's how you're going to account for me, you know. I'm an old friend of yours, a Government man out of the Department of Agriculture off on a vacation. Incidentally, I might be wanting to buy a mine, or something of that sort—anything to start the town gossip on a harmless chase and to keep it as far as possible from the real reason for my stopover."

"Everything goes," said Maxwell. "I'll start the gossip. What else?"

"Nothing out of the ordinary. I shall ask you to give me the run of your railroad office, and I'd like to meet anybody and everybody, when it falls in naturally—but always as the chemistry sharp; get that well ground into your cosmos. But here—what's this? Are we already back in Brewster?"

"We are," said the superintendent, with a glance out of the window. Then he became the regretful host again. "I hate to have you go back to the hotel, Calvin. It's just my crooked luck to have you come along when the house is shut up and Mrs. Maxwell and the babies are out of town. They're due to come home in a day or two, and I'm selfish enough to hope that we can keep you over. Let's drop off here at the crossing. It's nearer to the hotel, and it'll give me a chance to reach *The Tribune* office before Treadwell's young men come in with their scare stuff."

It was a half-hour after the arrival of the unwrecked Limited, and the story of the curious false alarm was just getting itself passed from lip to ear among the loungers in the Hotel Topaz lobby, when the Government man came down from his room to file a rather lengthy New York message with the hotel telegraph operator.

"Cipher?—holy smoke!" exclaimed the young man at the lobby wire desk; but a liberal tip made it look easier, and he added: "All right, I'm good for it, I guess, and I'll get it through as quick as I can. Answer to your room?"

"If you please," said the guest; and, as it was by this time well on toward midnight, he went to bed.

By noon of the day following the false-alarm run of the wrecking-train to Timanyoni Canyon, all Brewster, or at least the railroad part of it, knew that Superintendent

Maxwell was entertaining an old college classmate at the Hotel Topaz. For the town portion of the gossip there was some little disagreement as to Mr. Calvin Sprague's state and standing. Some had it that the big, handsome athlete was a foot-ball coach taking his vacation between seasons. Others said that he was a capitalist in disguise, looking for a ground-floor investment in Timanyoni mines.

These were Mr. Sprague's placings for the man in the street. But to the rank and file in the railroad head-quarters building Sprague figured in his proper character as a Government drug-mixer on a holiday; a royal good fellow who fraternized instantly with everybody, whose naïve ignorance about railroading was a joke, and whose vast unknowledge was nicely balanced by a keen and comradely curiosity to learn all that anybody could tell him about the complex workings of a railroad headquarters in action.

Naturally, and possibly because Davis, the chief despatcher, was willing to be hospitable, he spent an hour of the forenoon in the wire office, ingenuously absorbing detail and evincing an interest in the day's work that made Davis, ordinarily a rather reticent man, transform himself into a lecturer on the theory and practice of railway telegraphy.

It was in Davis's office that he met Tarbell; and the keen-eyed, sober-faced young fellow who was carried on the division pay-rolls as a relief operator became his guide on a walking tour of the shops and the yards. Tarbell saw in Mr. Maxwell's guest nothing more than an exceedingly affable gentleman with an immense capacity for interesting himself in the workaday details of a railroad outfit; but at one o'clock, when Maxwell joined Sprague at a quiet corner table for two in the hotel café, there were several surprises awaiting the superintendent.

"Getting it shaken down a little so that you'll know where to begin?" was Maxwell's opening question; and the ex-fullback laughed.

"You must take me for a sleuth of the common or garden variety," he retorted. "Did you suppose I had thrown away an entire forenoon scoring for a start? Not so, Richard; not even remotely so. I've been finding out a lot of things. I am even able to suggest an improvement or two in your telegraph installation."

"For example?" said Maxwell.

"Both of your yard offices are cut in on the working wire. If this were my railroad I'd put them on a pony circuit and cut them out of the main line."

"Why would you?"

"We'll have to go back a little for the specific answer in the present case; back to last night, and to the young man who chased out with a red lantern to keep us from running into the passenger train which wasn't wrecked. Why do you suppose he did that?"

"That's easy; he heard the passenger coming down the canyon."

"That was the inference, of course. But when you have taken the thirty-third degree in the exact science of observation, Dick, you'll learn to distrust inferences and to accept only conclusions. He didn't hear the passenger; he didn't know it was coming. If you had been observing him as closely as I was, you would have seen him write this down in his actions as plain as print. He had a much better reason for stopping us—and the passenger. It was a wire order from somebody. If you don't believe it, have Davis call him up and ask him, when you go back to your office."

Notwithstanding the criticism just passed upon him by his table-mate, Maxwell again caught at an inference.

"You've found the wire-devil, Calvin? You've got to the bottom of the thing in a single forenoon?"

"No; not quite to the bottom. But some few things I have learned, beyond any question of doubt. In the first place, this trouble of yours is pretty serious; far more serious than you suspect. In fact, it is designed to remove your railroad from the map, not by murder outright, but by what you might call incited suicide. The condition which you described last night is painfully apparent, even to an outsider like myself. Half of your men are potential powder-mines, ready to blow up if the spark is applied."

"Go on," said Maxwell eagerly. "What else did you find out?"

"I learned that a stop-all-trains order was sent to your young man at the canyon station last night, and that, in all probability, it was sent from Brewster. The ultimate question fines itself down to this: did your night despatcher, Connolly, send that order through his own instrument in his own office? or did he, or some other, send it from the upper yard office?—which, as I have remarked, is rather injudiciously cut in on the regular working wire. I'll venture to make the answer positive; the order was sent from the yard office."

"Connolly!" said the superintendent under his breath. "I can't believe it, Calvin. Who ever heard of a fat villain?"

"Go a little easy on the inferences," laughed the chemistry expert. "I didn't say it was Connolly, though it looks rather bad for him at the present stage of the game. He is in debt, and he wants to get married."

"But, good Lord! what has that got to do with—"

"Hold on," interposed the expert calmly. "We haven't come to that part of it yet. As I say, this stop-order was sent from the yard office. How do I know? Because the sender left his trail behind him in the shape of a wire recently cut and recoupled—the cut-out being made to keep the message from repeating itself in the head-quarters office where it might be heard by anybody who happened to be standing around."

"But Connolly couldn't leave his wire to go to the yard office."

"Unfortunately for him, he did leave it. About half an hour after the wrecking-train left he called Davis, who was sleeping in one of the bunk-rooms in your wickiup attic. His excuse was that he was so rattled that he couldn't hold himself down at the train-desk. Davis relieved him for an hour or so, and then he came back."

"Still I can't believe it of Connolly," Maxwell persisted. "If he sent that message to Timanyoni last night, that makes him responsible for all the others—the devil-messages, as the men are calling them. Some of these have come in the night, while he was on duty. How could he have worked it in that case?"

Again the chemistry expert laughed. "A suspicious person might draw a bunch of inferences," he said, "throwing out a dark hint or so about a concealed cut-in on the wires after they enter the attic of the railroad building and a hidden set of instruments. Also, the same person would probably point to the fact that Connolly wasn't at his desk when the fake wreck notice came last night. It was your chief clerk, Calmaine, who took it from the wire, and he tells me he was subbing for Connolly for a few minutes while Connolly went upstairs for his smoking-tobacco."

"My Lord!" said Maxwell; "you've put it upon Connolly, fair and square, Calvin; it's all over but the hanging!"

"There you go again," joked the Government man, with his good-natured grin. "I haven't said it is Connolly. But I will say this: with another half-day at it, I'll probably be able to turn the case over to Tarbell—and the newspapers."

"The newspapers?"

"Yes. That will be a part of the cure for the crazy sickness among your men. Sit tight and say nothing, and by this evening I'll be ready to put you next."

It was late in the afternoon, and the man from Washington had spent much of the intervening time loafing in the different offices sheltered by the head-quarters roof, when young Tarbell got a telephone summons from the hotel. In the writing-room, which was otherwise deserted, he found the superintendent's guest waiting for him. Sprague waved him to a chair and began at once.

"What did you find out, Mr. Tarbell?"

"Nothing to hurt. The fellow you was askin' about went out on the wreck-train and came back on it."

"You're sure of that?"

"Sure of the first part, and not so sure of the last. I've found half a dozen o' the men who saw him get on the train here, and saw him after he was on. They're a little hazy about the back trip, but he must've come back that way, because he didn't come on the Limited."

"And his wife?"

Tarbell's lip curled in honest cleanliness.

"He ain't got any wife. It was his girl he was expectin', and she didn't come."

"And afterward?" suggested the questioner.

"After he got back he showed up in the office and took his job again, lettin' Catherton go home."

The Government man's eyes narrowed and after a moment he began again.

"How near can you come to keeping your own counsel, Mr. Tarbell?" he demanded abruptly.

"I reckon I can talk a few without sayin' much," said the ex-cowboy. And then, after a pause: "You mean that you don't want to be mixed up in this thing by name, Mr. Sprague?"

"You've hit it exactly. You've got your start and I want you to work it out yourself. You have the line. Somebody—somebody who is not a thousand miles from your head-quarters building over yonder—is working this scare, working it for a purpose which he wishes to accomplish without making himself actually and legally responsible. Had you got that far in your own reasoning, Mr. Tarbell?"

"No, indeed," was the prompt reply. "I reckon I'm only a plug when it comes down to the sure-enough, fine-haired part of it."

"You'll learn, after a bit," said the chemistry expert shortly. "But let that go. You have the facts now, and they are driven pretty well into a corner. Can you go and get your man?"

Tarbell got up and shoved his hands into his pockets.

"I reckon I can," he admitted slowly, and started to move away. But at the door the big man at the writing-desk recalled him.

"Don't go on supposition, Tarbell. Ask yourself, when you get outside, if you've got the evidence that the court will demand. Ask yourself, also, if you know of your own knowledge, or if you've only allowed yourself to be hypnotized into your belief. If you can get satisfactory answers to these questions, go to it and bring back the money, as they say up in Seattle."

For what remained of the afternoon after Tarbell went away, Sprague sat in the writing-room and wrote letters, sealing and addressing the last one just as Maxwell came over to go to dinner with him. At table there were plenty of uncut back-numbers in the way of college reminiscences to be threshed over, and Sprague carefully kept the talk in this innocuous field until after they had left the dining-room to go for a smoke on the loggia porch. When the cigars were alight, Maxwell would no longer be choked off.

"Anything new in the wire-devil business, Calvin?" he asked.

"I've turned the case over to Tarbell, as I promised. I'm through with my part of it."

"What's that!" ejaculated the superintendent. "You've got your man?"

"Tarbell will get him—most probably before we go to bed to-night. He's a fine young fellow, that reformed cowboy of yours, Dick. I like him."

Maxwell was still gasping. "You're a wonder, Calvin—a latter-day wizard! Good Heavens! Do you realize that we've been working on this thing for a month? And you've cleaned it up in a day!"

The chemistry expert was smiling good-naturedly.

"Perhaps I came at a fortuitous moment, and had exceptional advantages," he demurred.

"But are you sure?" demanded Maxwell soberly.

"So sure that if your 'devil' had caused any loss of life in his monkeyings, I could go into court and hang him."

"Thank God!" said the superintendent; and then again, as if an enormous weight had been lifted from his shoulders, "Thank God!"

Sprague looked up quickly.

"You've been taking it pretty hard, haven't you, Dick? Any special reason?"

"Yes. You know Ford, our president: he has made the Pacific Southwestern System—made it out of whole cloth; and, incidentally, he has made a good few of us fellows who have fought with him shoulder to shoulder from the first. When I was last in New York, a couple of months ago, he rode from the club to the station in the taxi with me. He was in trouble of some sort—he didn't tell me what it was; but the last thing he said as I was boarding the train gave me some notion of it. 'Run that jerk-water Short Line of yours, Dick, as if you were carrying all your eggs to market and had them all in one basket,' he said, and then he added: 'No wrecks, Dick, if you have to sit up nights to head them off.' "

Sprague was smoking peacefully. It was perhaps too much to expect that a man whose problems were chiefly in the field of laboratory science should be very deeply interested in one in which the elements were merely human. When he spoke again it was to recur to his favorable impression of Tarbell. "I like that young fellow," he said in conclusion. "He'll pull you out of the hole—with a little timely help from the newspapers. When he gets the ball into his hands and starts down the field with it, you'd best be prepared for some pretty sensational developments. They're due."

For a little while Maxwell said nothing, and the fine lines between his eyes deepened slowly into a frown of anxiety. Finally he said: "I've got 'em, too, Calvin—

the 'jimmies," I mean. My wife and the two kiddies are coming home on the 'Apache' to-night, and don't you know, I had half a mind to wire her to stop over in Copah until I could go after her? That's a pretty pass for things to come to, isn't it?—when a man's afraid to have the members of his family ride over his own particular piece of railroad?"

Sprague flipped the ash from his cigar.

"That's one of the bridges you don't have to cross until you come to it."

Maxwell got out of his chair and refused Sprague's offer of a fresh cigar.

"No," he said; "this has been one of the days when I've smoked too much. I'm going over to the office to keep my finger on the pulse of things. When it gets too dull for you over here, come across and break in. If I'm not in my own office, you'll find me in room eleven—the despatcher's—keeping tab on the movements of the Apache Limited."

Fully two hours beyond the time when the superintendent had crossed the railroad plaza to climb the stair of the head-quarters building, Tarbell, strolling along the plaza-fronting street, swung himself over the railing of the loggia porch and took the chair next to the man from Washington, who was still sitting as Maxwell had left him and still smoking.

"I've been waiting for you," said the patient smoker, without taking his eyes from the row of lighted windows in the railroad building opposite.

"I allowed you would be," rejoined Tarbell in his gentle Tennessee-mountain drawl. And then, quite as calmly: "I reckon I've found the answers to all them questions you 'lotted to me. I reckon I've got him."

"I've been betting on you, Tarbell," was the word of approval. Then: "It comes pretty near home, doesn't it?"

"It sure does. It's goin' to hurt Mr. Maxwell good and plenty. He counts all the men in the home office as his fam'ly, and there's never been one o' them to go back on him till now."

"What is your evidence?" queried Sprague.

"I reckon you'd call it circumstantial—and so will the judge. But it hobbles him all right. There's a cut-in on the despatcher's wires over yonder, 'way up under the roof where nobody'd find it, with four little fine lead wires goin' down in the wall. I couldn't find where they come out at, but I reckon that don't make any difference: they're *there*."

"Anything else?"

"Yes. I've got a letter that I hooked out of his coat pocket not ten minutes ago; a letter from some gang boss o' his'n in New York, givin' him goss for not showin' up results, and allowin' to pull some sort of a gun on him if the papers don't begin to print scare heads about a certain railroad management, *pronto.*"

The chemistry expert smiled shrewdly.

"You are not the young man I took you for, Tarbell, if you are not wringing your brain like a wet towel to make it tell you why anybody in New York should wish to see Nevada Short Line wreck bulletins in the newspapers."

"That ain't no joke, neither," Tarbell admitted gravely, adding, "I been hopin' maybe it would come out in the round-up."

"Yes," said Sprague, half-absently. "It will come out in the round-up." And then, after a thoughtful pause, "Perhaps we'd better go over and relieve Mr. Maxwell's mind. But first it wouldn't be a bad idea to telephone the editor of *The Tribune* and ask him to send his railroad reporter down to Mr. Maxwell's office. If you say that Mr. Maxwell will probably have a bit of first-page stuff for him, it won't be necessary to go into details."

Tarbell went into the hotel lobby to telephone, and afterward they crossed the plaza to the working head-quarters of the double division. Finding the superintendent's office open and lighted but unoccupied, they went on to the despatcher's room. In the public space outside of the counter railing three or four trainmen were grouped in front of the bulletin-board looking for their assignments on the night trains and thumbing the file of posted "General Orders."

Behind the railing Connolly was sitting at his glass-topped wire-table with the train-sheet under his hand and the superintendent at his elbow. Over in the corner under his green-shaded electric bulb, Bolton, the sallow-faced car-record man, was fingering the keys of his type-writer.

Tarbell opened the gate in the railing to admit Sprague and himself. Maxwell looked up and nodded a welcome to his guest.

"Got tired of sitting it out alone, did you?" he said; and then, "I'll be with you in a minute and we'll go over to my office. I'm waiting to get Timanyoni's report of the Limited."

"Mrs. Maxwell is on the train?"

Maxwell nodded, and a moment later Connolly's sounder clicked out Timanyoni's report of the passing train. The fat despatcher was nervous. It showed in his rattling of the key as he OK'd the canyon station's report, and again in a small disaster when, in reaching for his pen to make the train-sheet entry, he overset his ink-well.

"Well, I'm damned!" he grunted, snatching at the train-sheet and pushing the ink flood back with his free hand. Maxwell came to the rescue, and so did Tarbell; and a liberal application of blotters stopped the flood. But at the close of the incident Connolly's hands were well blackened.

It was at this conjuncture that Davis, the chief despatcher, came in on the way up to his room in the attic half-story above. Connolly appealed to him at once.

"If you'll sit in here, just for a minute, Davis, while I go wash my hands?" he said, adding: "I'd ought to be kicked all the way downstairs!"

When Davis had taken the chair and Connolly had gone out, Tarbell whispered to the superintendent. Maxwell nodded, and made a sign to Sprague. When he had closed the door of the despatcher's room behind himself and his guest, he explained:

"Tarbell says he is ready, and we may as well have it over with. Do you want to be present?"

"As a spectator, yes," said the expert.

"All right; we'll go to my office and wait for Archer."

The waiting interval proved to be short. Maxwell had just thrown his roll-top desk open, and the Government man had planted his big bulk solidly in the half-shadowed window-seat, when the door opened and Connolly came in, his full-moon face a frightened blank and his hands still ink-blackened. Tarbell was only a step behind the despatcher, and the reporter from *The Tribune* office was at Tarbell's heels. When the three were inside, Tarbell shut the door and put his back against it.

"Here's your man, Mr. Maxwell," he said briefly; and Sprague, who had started to his feet at the door opening, sat down again in the shadow and said nothing.

Maxwell pointed brusquely to a chair at the desk end. "Sit down, Dan," he snapped. And then: "I suppose you know what you're here for?"

Connolly fell into the chair as if the sharp command had been a blow.

"Know what I'm here for?" he stammered.

"Yes. Nothing will be gained by dodging. You may as well make a clean breast of it. You've been faking these scare wreck reports—don't lie about it; we've got the evidence. I want to know who is behind you. Who bribed you to do this thing?"

"Before God, Mr. Maxwell!" the culprit began, with the sweat rolling down his face; but Maxwell stopped him with a quick gesture.

"I've told you it was no use to try to lie out of it. I have here on my desk a letter which was taken from your coat pocket to-night, since you came on duty; a letter from which you were careful enough to tear the signature, but on which you were not careful enough to destroy the date line. In that letter the writer threatens to give you away to the New York police if you don't get busy and give the newspapers a string of Nevada Short Line wrecks to write about. That is enough to send you over the road, but there's more. The working wires east and west have been cut under the roof of this building, and leads taken off. The leads disappear in the wall back of your bunk-room.

I don't ask you what you have to say for yourself; I want you to tell us, right here and now, who planned the thing, and what it was intended to accomplish."

Connolly had been slowly collapsing in his chair under the merciless fire of accusation, and a pasty pallor was driving the pink out of his round face.

"My God!" he gasped thickly; and then he repeated, "My God!" A silence crammed with threatenings settled down upon the small office-room. Suddenly it was broken by the sound of hurried footfalls in the corridor, and Tarbell was hurled half-way across the room when the door was flung open from without.

It was young Cargill, the engineer, who burst into the private office, and his lips were white.

"The Limited!" he broke out. "She's overrun her orders at Corona and she's due to meet Second Eighteen on the single track!"

It was the Government man who led the rush to the despatcher's room, a rush in which even the fat culprit joined. In the wire office Davis had the key; his jaw was set and the perspiration was standing thickly on his forehead, but he had not lost his nerve. Calmaine, the chief clerk, was hanging over his shoulder, and outside of the railing the group of trainmen had grown to a breathless crowd, pressing to hear the latest word.

When Maxwell's party pushed through the gate, Sprague was still in the lead, and his quick glance took in every detail of the scene. Like a flash he turned upon Tarbell, who was fumbling a pair of handcuffs in his pocket, and pinioned him in a grip that was like the nip of a vice.

"Not yet!", he whispered in Tarbell's ear; and then Davis snapped his switch and spoke.

"It's no use," he said, and his harsh tone was only a thin mask for the break in his voice. "It's the real thing this time. First Eighteen was ready to pull out of Corona when the Limited went by. Corringer left his wire and chased the freight, hoping to get its engine to cut loose and run after the passenger. He couldn't catch it."

A low murmur ran through the crowd packed against the counter railing and somebody whispered, "It's got the boss; his wife and babies are on that train. Look at him!"

Maxwell had gripped the back of a chair and he was staring hot-eyed at the despatcher.

"Do something, Davis," he pleaded. "Don't sit there and let those trains come together! For Christ's sake, think of something!"

The chief despatcher ducked his head as if he were dodging a blow and swallowed hard.

"There isn't anything to do, Mr. Maxwell—you know there isn't anything," he began in low tones. "If there was—"

It was Connolly who made the break. Twisting away from Tarbell's grip on his arm he flung himself upon Davis.

"Get out o' that chair and let me have the key," he wheezed; and when Davis did not move quickly enough he pounced upon the key standing. Davis got up and quietly slid the chair under the night man who sank heavily into it without missing a letter in the call he was insistently clicking out, over and over again in endless repetition.

"What is it?" whispered the newspaper man, who was standing aside with Tarbell and Sprague; and Tarbell answered:

"It's the Corcoran coal mine—about half-way between Corona and the first station this side, and a half-mile up the gulch. They've got a private wire, but they ain't got any night operator."

Davis overheard the whisper and shook his head.

"Dan's got his wits with him," he said, in open admiration. "There's a young time-keeper that sleeps in the coal company's office shack, and he's learning to plug in on the wire a little. If Dan can only wake him—" And then, in sudden sharp self-accusation: "God forgive me! why didn't I think of it and save all the time that's been wasted?" Then, as Connolly closed the circuit and a halting reply clicked through the receiving instrument: "He's got him! Thank the Lord, he's got him! If he can only make him understand what's wanted, there's a chance—just one chance in a thousand!"

With the very seconds now freighted with disaster, and with only the crudest of amateur telegraphers at the other end of the wire, nine men out of ten would have blown up and lost the thousandth part of a chance remaining. But Connolly was the tenth man. With his left hand shaking until it was beating a tattoo on the glass table top he hitched his chair closer and began to spell out, letter by letter, the brief call for help upon which so much depended. Tarbell translated for Sprague, word by word. "Hurry—down—to—main-line—and—throw—your—switch—to—red. Then— run—west—and—flag—passenger."

The key-switch clicked on the final word, and for five long, dragging seconds the silence was a keen agony. Then the sounder began hesitantly: dot—pause—dot; dash—dot—dash, it spelled; and Tarbell translated under his breath, "He says 'OK'. Now, if he can only chase his feet fast enough—"

How Maxwell managed to live and not die through the interminable twenty minutes that followed; how Davis and Tarbell and Connolly hung breathless over the wire-table, while the throng outside of the railing, augmented now to a jammed crowd of sympathetic watchers, rustled and moved and whispered in awed undertones—are themes upon which the rank and file of the Nevada Short Line still enlarge in the roundhouse tool-rooms and in the switch shanties when the crews are waiting for a delayed train.

The dreadful interval seemed as if it would never be outworn, but the end came at last when the hesitant clicking of the sounder was resumed.

"Call it out, Dan," shouted somebody among the waiting trainmen, and Connolly pronounced the words slowly as the amateur at the end of the private wire ticked them off.

"Both—trains—safe—freight—backing—to—blind—siding—at—Quentin—switch—passenger—following—under—flag."

A shout went up that drowned the feeble patter of the telegraph instruments and made the windows rattle. "Bully for the kid at the coal mine!"

"Bully for Danny Connolly!" "Come out here, Danny, till we get a chanst at you!"

Maxwell fought his way stubbornly through the crowd, with the newspaper man, Sprague, Tarbell, and Connolly following in his wake. When the five were once more behind the closed door of the private office across the hall, the superintendent turned morosely upon the night despatcher, and he was so full of the thing he was about to do that he did not notice that his guest had taken Tarbell aside for a whispered conference.

"You've drawn the teeth of the law, this time, Connolly," he said sharply. "After what you've just done I'm not going to send you to jail. But the least you can do is to tell me who hired you and sent you out here to make trouble for us. If you'll do that—"

It was Sprague's hand on his shoulder that stopped him, and then he noticed that Tarbell had disappeared. "Just a minute—until Tarbell gets back," said the guest, in low tones; and while he was saying it, the door opened suddenly and the ex-cowboy returned, thrusting a sallow-faced young fellow, shirt-sleeved and livid with fear, into the office ahead of him. Then the Government man went on in the same low tone, "You can say to this young man all the things you were going to say to Mr. Connolly. There was a little miscue on Tarbell's part, and I was just going to tell you about it when the train trouble butted in." Then to the fat despatcher, "Mr. Connolly, sit down. You've jolly well earned the right to look on and listen."

Connolly sat down heavily, and so did the superintendent. Thereupon the man from Washington slipped easily into the breach, turning briskly upon the yellow-faced car-record operator.

"Step up here, Bolton, and make a clean sweep of it to Mr. Maxwell. Tell him how a certain firm of New York brokers—you needn't give the names now—sent you, a convicted bucket-shop wire-tapper, out here to disarrange things on this railroad for stock-jobbing purposes. Then tell him how you tapped the despatcher's wires and put a set of concealed keys under your car-record table in the other room. Tell him how, after you'd faked that wreck message last night, you ran a bluff for sympathy, and how, when it had worked, your nerve flickered and you dropped from the wrecking train in the yard and sent a stop-order from the yard office. Come to the front and loosen up!"

Bolton was shuffling forward and was beginning a tremulous confession when Maxwell stopped him harshly.

"You can keep all that to tell in court!" he snapped. And then to Tarbell: "Take him away, Archer. And you go back to your job, Dan, and let Davis go to bed. What I've got to say to you will keep." Then to the young man from the *Tribune*, who had his note-book out and was scribbling down his story at breakneck speed: "Write out what you please, Scanlan, but tell Mr. Kendall that I'll be up to the office presently, and that I'd like to see the story before it goes to the linotypes."

When the room was cleared, the snappy little superintendent spun his chair around to face his guest.

"Calvin," he said solemnly, "you'll never know how near you came to making me break my heart to-night. If I'd had to send Dan Connolly to jail after what he did in the other room a little while ago—"

The chemistry expert was grinning joyously.

"It was a curious little slip," he commented. "I thought Tarbell was on; never suspected for a moment that he wasn't until he butted Connolly in here and shot him at you."

"But you knew Connolly wasn't the man? How on top of earth did you run it down, in a single day? I can't surround it, even yet."

"It wasn't much of a nut to crack," laughed the expert easily. "I hope you'll have a harder one for me the next time I happen along. I got my pointer last night—before I knew anything at all about the nature of your trouble. You see, Bolton was the only man in the outfit who wasn't sincerely jarred and horrified by that fake message. I saw it the minute I'd had a look into his eyes. From that on it was easy enough."

"I don't see it," objected Maxwell.

"Don't you? I merely argued backward from the results your wire-devil was trying to obtain and sent a cipher message to a friend of mine in New York. He put me next to a nice little plot in the Street to hamper Ford and break down your company credit. Then I loafed around your shack here until I found Bolton's wire machinery. Bolton didn't catch on, but he was suspicious enough of a stranger like me to take a little measure of precaution by slipping that incriminating letter into Connolly's coat pocket. I supposed Tarbell knew that, or I'd have told him."

Maxwell had been listening in appreciative admiration, but gratitude came quickly to the fore when Sprague paused.

"Calvin, there's no telling how many lives you've saved by this little stop-over of yours here in Timanyoni Park!" he broke out. "You've done it. When that story, properly trimmed down, comes out in the *Tribune* to-morrow morning, the bare-nerves strain will go off like that"—snapping his fingers. "I wish I could show you. . . . By George! there's the Limited pulling in. I've got to go down and meet the wife and kiddies!"

The big-bodied man who called himself a chemistry sharp and confessed to the riding of many hobbies rose up with a laugh.

"You want to show me? All right: take me downstairs with you and show me Mrs. Maxwell and the babies. As for the other, you know as well as I do that it's all in the day's work. Pitch out or we'll miss the folks—and that would be worse than getting another message from the wire-devil."

PHILO GUBB'S GREATEST CASE

Ellis Parker Butler

P HILO GUBB, WRAPPED IN HIS BATHROBE, WENT TO THE DOOR OF THE ROOM that was the headquarters of his business of paper-hanging and decorating as well as the office of his detective business, and opened the door a crack. It was still early in the morning, but Mr. Gubb was a modest man, and, lest any one should see him in his scanty attire, he peered through the crack of the door before he stepped hastily into the hall and captured his copy of the *Riverbank Daily Eagle*. When he had secured the still damp newspaper, he returned to his cot bed and spread himself out to read comfortably.

It was a hot Iowa morning. Business was so slack that if Mr. Gubb had not taken out his set of eight varieties of false whiskers daily and brushed them carefully, the moths would have been able to devour them at leisure.

P. Gubb opened the *Eagle*. The first words that met his eye caused him to sit upright on his cot. At the top of the first column of the first page were the headlines.

MYSTERIOUS DEATH OF HENRY SMITZ
Body Found In Mississippi River By Boatman Early This A.M.
Foul Play Suspected

Mr. Gubb unfolded the paper and read the item under the headlines with the most intense interest. Foul play meant the possibility of an opportunity to put to use once more the precepts of the Course of Twelve Lessons, and with them fresh in his mind Detective Gubb was eager to undertake the solution of any mystery that Riverbank could furnish. This was the article:—

Just as we go to press we receive word through Policeman Michael O'Toole that the well-known mussel-dredger and boatman, Samuel Fliggis (Long Sam), while dredging for mussels last night just below the bridge, recovered the body of Henry Smitz, late of this place.

Mr. Smitz had been missing for three days and his wife had been greatly worried. Mr. Brownson, of the Brownson Packing Company, by whom he was employed, admitted that Mr. Smitz had been missing for several days.

The body was found sewed in a sack. Foul play is suspected.

"I should think foul play would be suspected," exclaimed Philo Gubb, "if a man was sewed into a bag and deposited into the Mississippi River until dead."

He propped the paper against the foot of the cot bed and was still reading when some one knocked on his door. He wrapped his bathrobe carefully about him and opened the door. A young woman with tear-dimmed eyes stood in the doorway.

"Mr. P. Gubb?" she asked. "I'm sorry to disturb you so early in the morning, Mr. Gubb, but I couldn't sleep all night. I came on a matter of business, as you might say. There's a couple of things I want you to do."

"Paper-hanging or deteckating?" asked P. Gubb.

"Both," said the young woman. "My name is Smitz—Emily Smitz. My husband—"

"I'm aware of the knowledge of your loss, ma'am," said the paper-hanger detective gently.

"Lots of people know of it," said Mrs. Smitz. "I guess everybody knows of it— I told the police to try to find Henry, so it is no secret. And I want you to come up as soon as you get dressed, and paper my bed-room."

Mr. Gubb looked at the young woman as if he thought she had gone insane under the burden of her woe.

"And then I want you to find Henry," she said, "because I've heard you can do so well in the detecting line."

Mr. Gubb suddenly realized that the poor creature did not yet know the full extent of her loss. He gazed down upon her with pity in his bird-like eyes.

"I know you'll think it strange," the young woman went on, "that I should ask you to paper a bed-room first, when my husband is lost; but if he is gone it is because I was a mean, stubborn thing. We never quarreled in our lives, Mr. Gubb, until I picked out the wall-paper for our bed-room, and Henry said parrots and birds-of-paradise and tropical flowers that were as big as umbrellas would look awful on our bed-room wall. So I said he hadn't anything but Low Dutch taste, and he got mad. 'All right, have it your own way,' he said, and I went and had Mr. Skaggs put the paper on the wall, and the next day Henry didn't come home at all.

"If I'd thought Henry would take it that way, I'd rather had the wall bare, Mr. Gubb. I've cried and cried, and last night I made up my mind it was all my fault and that when Henry came home he'd find a decent paper on the wall. I don't mind telling you, Mr. Gubb, that when the paper was on the wall it looked worse than it looked in the roll. It looked crazy."

"Yes'm," said Mr. Gubb, "it often does. But, however, there's something you'd ought to know right away about Henry."

The young woman stared wide-eyed at Mr. Gubb for a moment; she turned as white as her shirt-waist.

"Henry is dead!" she cried, and collapsed into Mr. Gubb's long, thin arms.

Mr. Gubb, the inert form of the young woman in his arms, glanced around with a startled gaze. He stood miserably, not knowing what to do, when suddenly he saw Policeman O'Toole coming toward him down the hall. Policeman O'Toole was leading by the arm a man whose wrists bore clanking handcuffs.

"What's this now?" asked the policeman none too gently, as he saw the bathrobed Mr. Gubb holding the fainting woman in his arms.

"I am exceedingly glad you have come," said Mr. Gubb. "The only meaning into it, is that this is Mrs. H. Smitz, widow-lady, fainted onto me against my will and wishes."

"I was only askin'," said Policeman O'Toole politely enough.

"You shouldn't ask such things until you're asked to ask," said Mr. Gubb.

After looking into Mr. Gubb's room to see that there was no easy means of escape, O'Toole pushed his prisoner into the room and took the limp form of Mrs. Smitz from Mr. Gubb, who entered the room and closed the door.

"I may as well say what I want to say right now," said the handcuffed man as soon as he was alone with Mr. Gubb. "I've heard of Detective Gubb, off and on, many a time, and as soon as I got into this trouble I said, 'Gubb's the man that can get me out if any one can.' My name is Herman Wiggins."

"Glad to meet you," said Mr. Gubb, slipping his long legs into his trousers.

"And I give you my word for what it is worth," continued Mr. Wiggins, "that I'm as innocent of this crime as the babe unborn."

"What crime?" asked Mr. Gubb.

"Why, killing Hen Smitz—what crime did you think?" said Mr. Wiggins. "Do I look like a man that would go and murder a man just because—"

He hesitated and Mr. Gubb, who was slipping his suspenders over his bony shoulders, looked at Mr. Wiggins with keen eyes.

"Well, just because him and me had words in fun," said Mr. Wiggins, "I leave it to you, can't a man say words in fun once in a while?"

"Certainly sure," said Mr. Gubb.

"I guess so," said Mr. Wiggins. "Anybody'd know a man don't mean all he says. When I went and told Hen Smitz I'd murder him as sure as green apples grow on a tree, I was just fooling. But this fool policeman—"

"Mr. O'Toole?"

"Yes. They gave him this Hen Smitz case to look into, and the first thing he did was to arrest me for murder. Nervy, I call it."

Policeman O'Toole opened the door a crack and peeked in. Seeing Mr. Gubb well along in his dressing operations, he opened the door wider and assisted Mrs. Smitz to a chair. She was still limp, but she was a brave little woman and was trying to control her sobs.

"Through?" O'Toole asked Wiggins. "If you are, come along back to jail."

"Now, don't talk to me in that tone of voice," said Mr. Wiggins angrily. "No, I'm not through. You don't know how to treat a gentleman like a gentleman, and never did."

He turned to Mr. Gubb.

"The long and short of it is this: I'm arrested for the murder of Hen Smitz, and I didn't murder him and I want you to take my case and get me out of jail."

"Ah, stuff!" exclaimed O'Toole. "You murdered him and you know you did. What's the use talkin'?"

Mrs. Smitz leaned forward in her chair.

"Murdered Henry?" she cried. "He never murdered Henry. I murdered him."

"Now, ma'am," said O'Toole politely, "I hate to contradict a lady, but you never murdered him at all. This man here murdered him, and I've got the proof on him."

"I murdered him!" cried Mrs. Smitz again. "I drove him out of his right mind and made him kill himself."

"Nothing of the sort," declared O'Toole. "This man Wiggins murdered him."

"I did not!" exclaimed Mr. Wiggins indignantly. "Some other man did it."

It seemed a deadlock, for each was quite positive. Mr. Gubb looked from one to the other doubtfully.

"All right, take me back to jail," said Mr. Wiggins. "You look up the case, Mr. Gubb; that's all I came here for. Will you do it? Dig into it, hey?"

"I most certainly shall be glad to so do," said Mr. Gubb, "at the regular terms."

O'Toole led his prisoner away.

For a few minutes Mrs. Smitz sat silent, her hands clasped, staring at the floor. Then she looked up into Mr. Gubb's eyes.

"You will work on this case, Mr. Gubb, won't you?" she begged. "I have a little money—I'll give it all to have you do your best. It is cruel—cruel to have that poor man suffer under the charge of murder when I know so well Henry killed himself because I was cross with him. You can prove he killed himself—that it was my fault. You will?"

"The way the deteckative profession operates onto a case," said Mr. Gubb, "isn't to go to work to prove anything particularly especial. It finds a clue or clues and follows them to where they lead to. That I shall be willing to do."

"That is all I could ask," said Mrs. Smitz gratefully.

Arising from her seat with difficulty, she walked tremblingly to the door. Mr. Gubb assisted her down the stairs, and it was not until she was gone that he remembered that she did not know the body of her husband had been found—sewed in a sack and at the bottom of the river. Young husbands have been known to quarrel with their wives over matters as trivial as bed-room wall-paper; they have even been known to leave home for several days at a time when angry; in extreme cases they have even been known to seek death at their own hands; but it is not at all usual for a young husband to leave home for several days and then in cold blood sew himself in a sack and jump into the river. In the first place there are easier ways of terminating one's life; in the second place a man can jump into the river with perfect ease without going to the trouble of sewing himself in a sack; and in the third place it is exceedingly difficult for a man to sew himself into a sack. It is almost impossible.

To sew himself into a sack a man must have no little skill, and he must have a large, roomy sack. He takes, let us say, a sack-needle, threaded with a good length of twine; he steps into the sack and pulls it up over his head; he then reaches above his head, holding the mouth of the sack together with one hand while he sews with the other hand. In hot anger this would be quite impossible.

Philo Gubb thought of all this as he looked through his disguises, selecting one suitable for the work he had in hand. He had just decided that the most appropriate disguise would be "Number 13, Undertaker," and had picked up the close black wig, and long, drooping mustache, when he had another thought. Given a bag sufficiently loose to permit free motion of the hands and arms, and a man, even in hot anger, might sew himself in. A man, intent on suicidally bagging himself, would sew the mouth of the bag shut and would then cut a slit in the front of the bag large enough to crawl into. He would then crawl into the bag and sew up the slit, which would be immediately in front of his hands. It could be done! Philo Gubb chose from his wardrobe a black frock coat and a silk hat with a wide band of crape. He carefully locked his door and went down to the street.

On a day as hot as this day promised to be, a frock coat and a silk hat could be nothing but distressingly uncomfortable. Between his door and the corner, eight various citizens spoke to Philo Gubb, calling him by name. In fact, Riverbank was as accustomed to seeing P. Gubb in disguise as out of disguise, and while a few children might be interested by the sight of Detective Gubb in disguise, the older citizens thought no more of it, as a rule, than of seeing Banker Jennings appear in a pink shirt one day and a blue striped one the next. No one ever accused Banker Jennings of trying to hide his identity by a change of shirts, and no one imagined that

P. Gubb was trying to disguise himself when he put on a disguise. They considered it a mere business custom, just as a butcher tied on a white apron before he went behind his counter.

This was why, instead of wondering who the tall, dark-garbed stranger might be, Banker Jennings greeted Philo Gubb cheerfully.

"Ah, Gubb!" he said. "So you are going to work on this Smitz case, are you? Glad of it, and wish you luck. Hope you place the crime on the right man and get him the full penalty. Let me tell you there's nothing in this rumor of Smitz being short of money. We did lend him money, but we never pressed him for it. We never even asked him for interest. I told him a dozen times he could have as much more from us as he wanted, within reason, whenever he wanted it, and that he could pay me when his invention was on the market."

"No report of news of any such rumor has as yet come to my hearing," said P. Gubb, "but since you mention it, I'll take it for less than it is worth."

"And that's less than nothing," said the banker. "Have you any clue?"

"I'm on my way to find one at the present moment of time," said Mr. Gubb.

"Well, let me give you a pointer," said the banker. "Get a line on Herman Wiggins or some of his crew, understand? Don't say I said a word,—I don't want to be brought into this,—but Smitz was afraid of Wiggins and his crew. He told me so. He said Wiggins had threatened to murder him."

"Mr. Wiggins is at present in the custody of the county jail for killing H. Smitz with intent to murder him," said Mr. Gubb.

"Oh, then—then it's all settled," said the banker. "They've proved it on him. I thought they would. Well, I suppose you've got to do your little bit of detecting just the same. Got to air the camphor out of the false hair, eh?"

The banker waved a cheerful hand at P. Gubb and passed into his banking institution.

Detective Gubb, cordially greeted by his many friends and admirers, passed on down the main street, and by the time he reached the street that led to the river he was followed by a large and growing group intent on the pleasant occupation of watching a detective detect.

As Mr. Gubb walked toward the river, other citizens joined the group, but all kept a respectful distance behind him. When Mr. Gubb reached River Street and his false mustache fell off, the interest of the audience stopped short three paces behind him and stood until he had rescued the mustache and once more placed its wires in his nostrils. Then, when he moved forward again, they too moved forward. Never, perhaps, in the history of crime was a detective favored with a more respectful gallery.

On the edge of the river, Mr. Gubb found Long Sam Fliggis, the mussel dredger, seated on an empty tar-barrel with his own audience ranged before him listening while he told, for the fortieth time, the story of his finding of the body of H. Smitz. As Philo Gubb approached, Long Sam ceased speaking, and his audience and Mr. Gubb's gallery merged into one great circle which respectfully looked and listened while Mr. Gubb questioned the mussel dredger.

"Suicide?" said Long Sam scoffingly. "Why, he wan't no more a suicide than I am right now. He was murdered or wan't nothin'! I've dredged up some suicides in my day, and some of 'em had stones tied to 'em, to make sure they'd sink, and some thought they'd sink without no ballast, but nary one of 'em ever sewed himself into a bag, and I give my word," he said positively, "that Hen Smitz couldn't have sewed himself into that burlap bag unless some one done the sewing. Then the feller that did it was an assistant-suicide, and the way I look at it is that an assistant-suicide is jest the same as a murderer."

The crowd murmured approval, but Mr. Gubb held up his hand for silence.

"In certain kinds of burlap bags it is possibly probable a man could sew himself into it," said Mr. Gubb, and the crowd, seeing the logic of the remark applauded gently but feelingly.

"You ain't seen the way he was sewed up," said Long Sam, "or you wouldn't talk like that."

"I haven't yet took a look," admitted Mr. Gubb, "but I aim so to do immediately after I find a clue onto which to work up my case. An A-1 deteckative can't set forth to work until he has a clue, that being a rule of the game."

"What kind of a clue was you lookin' for?" asked Long Sam. "What's a clue, anyway?"

"A clue," said P. Gubb, "is almost anything connected with the late lamented, but generally something that nobody but a deteckative would think had anything to do with anything whatsoever. Not infrequently often it is a button."

"Well, I've got no button except them that is sewed onto me," said Long Sam, "but if this here sack-needle will do any good——"

He brought from his pocket the point of a heavy sack-needle and laid it in Philo Gubb's palm. Mr. Gubb looked at it carefully. In the eye of the needle still remained a few inches of twine.

"I cut that off 'n the burlap he was sewed up in," volunteered Long Sam, "I thought I'd keep it as a sort of nice little souvenir. I'd like it back again when you don't need it for a clue no more."

"Certainly sure," agreed Mr. Gubb, and he examined the needle carefully.

There are two kinds of sack-needles in general use. In both, the point of the needle is curved to facilitate pushing it into and out of a closely filled sack; in both, the curved portion is somewhat flattened so that the thumb and finger may secure a firm grasp to pull the needle through; but in one style the eye is at the end of the shaft while in the other it is near the point. This needle was like neither; the eye was midway of the shaft; the needle was pointed at each end and the curved portions were not flattened. Mr. Gubb noticed another thing—the twine was not the ordinary loosely twisted hemp twine, but a hard, smooth cotton cord, like carpet warp.

"Thank you," said Mr. Gubb, "and now I will go elsewhere to investigate to a further extent, and it is not necessarily imperative that everybody should accompany along with me if they don't want to."

But everybody did want to, it seemed. Long Sam and his audience joined Mr. Gubb's gallery and, with a dozen or so newcomers, they followed Mr. Gubb at a decent distance as he walked toward the plant of the Brownson Packing Company, which stood on the riverbank some two blocks away.

It was here Henry Smitz had worked. Six or eight buildings of various sizes, the largest of which stood immediately on the river's edge, together with the "yards" or pens, all enclosed by a high board fence, constituted the plant of the packing company, and as Mr. Gubb appeared at the gate the watchman there stood aside to let him enter.

"Good-morning, Mr. Gubb," he said pleasantly. "I been sort of expecting you. Always right on the job when there's crime being done, ain't you? You'll find Merkel and Brill and Jokosky and the rest of Wiggins's crew in the main building, and I guess they'll tell you just what they told the police. They hate it, but what else can they say? It's the truth."

"What is the truth?" asked Mr. Gubb.

"That Wiggins was dead sore at Hen Smitz," said the watchman. "That Wiggins told Hen he'd do for him if he lost them their jobs like he said he would. That's the truth."

Mr. Gubb—his admiring followers were halted at the gate by the watchman— entered the large building and inquired his way to Mr. Wiggins's department. He found it on the side of the building toward the river and on the ground floor. On one side the vast room led into the refrigerating room of the company; on the other it opened upon a long but narrow dock that ran the width of the building.

Along the outer edge of the dock were tied two barges, and into these barges some of Wiggins's crew were dumping mutton—not legs of mutton but entire sheep, neatly sewed in burlap. The large room was the packing and shipping room, and the work of Wiggins's crew was that of sewing the slaughtered and refrigerated sheep carcasses in burlap for shipment. Bales of burlap stood against one wall; strands of hemp twine ready for the needle hung from pegs in the wall and the posts that supported the floor above. The contiguity of the refrigerating room gave the room a pleasantly cool atmosphere.

Mr. Gubb glanced sharply around. Here was the burlap, here were needles, here was twine. Yonder was the river into which Hen Smitz had been thrown. He glanced across the narrow dock at the blue river. As his eye returned he noticed one of the men carefully sweeping the dock with a broom—sweeping fragments of glass into the river. As the men in the room watched him curiously, Mr. Gubb picked up a piece of burlap and put it in his pocket, wrapped a strand of twine around his finger and pocketed the twine, examined the needles stuck in improvised needle-holders made by boring gimlet holes in the wall, and then walked to the dock and picked up one of the pieces of glass.

"Clues," he remarked, and gave his attention to the work of questioning the men.

Although manifestly reluctant, they honestly admitted that Wiggins had more than once threatened Hen Smitz—that he hated Hen Smitz with the hatred of a man who has been threatened with the loss of his job. Mr. Gubb learned that Hen Smitz had been the foreman for the entire building—a sort of autocrat with, as Wiggins's crew informed him, an easy job. He had only to see that the crews in the building turned out more work this year than they did last year. "'Ficiency" had been his motto, they said, and they hated "'Ficiency."

Mr. Gubb's gallery was awaiting him at the gate, and its members were in a heated discussion as to what Mr. Gubb had been doing. They ceased at once when he appeared and fell in behind him as he walked away from the packing house and toward the undertaking establishment of Mr. Holworthy Bartman, on the main street. Here, joining the curious group already assembled, the gallery was forced to wait while Mr. Gubb entered. His task was an unpleasant but necessary one. He must visit the little "morgue" at the back of Mr. Bartman's establishment.

The body of poor Hen Smitz had not yet been removed from the bag in which it had been found, and it was to the bag Mr. Gubb gave his closest attention. The bag—in order that the body might be identified—had not been ripped, but had been cut, and not a stitch had been severed. It did not take Mr. Gubb a moment to see that Hen Smitz had not been sewed in a bag at all. He had been sewed in burlap— burlap "yard goods," to use a shopkeeper's term—and it was burlap identical with that used by Mr. Wiggins and his crew. It was no loose bag of burlap—but a close-fitting wrapping of burlap; a cocoon of burlap that had been drawn tight around the body, as burlap is drawn tight around the carcass of sheep for shipment, like a mummy's wrappings.

It would have been utterly impossible for Hen Smitz to have sewed himself into the casing, not only because it bound his arms tight to his sides, but because the burlap was lapped over and sewed from the outside. This, once and for all, ended the suicide theory. The question was: Who was the murderer?

As Philo Gubb turned away from the bier, Undertaker Bartman entered the morgue.

"The crowd outside is getting impatient, Mr. Gubb," he said in his soft, undertakery voice. "It is getting on toward their lunch hour, and they want to crowd into my front office to find out what you've learned. I'm afraid they'll break my plate-glass windows, they're pushing so hard against them. I don't want to hurry you, but if you would go out and tell them Wiggins is the murderer they'll go away. Of course there's no doubt about Wiggins being the murderer, since he has admitted he asked the stock-keeper for the electric-light bulb."

"What bulb?" asked Philo Gubb.

"The electric-light bulb we found sewed inside this burlap when we sliced it open," said Bartman. "Matter of fact, we found it in Hen's hand. O'Toole took it for a clue and I guess it fixes the murder on Wiggins beyond all doubt. The stock-keeper says Wiggins got it from him."

"And what does Wiggins remark on that subject?" asked Mr. Gubb.

"Not a word," said Bartman. "His lawyer told him not to open his mouth, and he won't. Listen to that crowd out there!"

"I will attend to that crowd right presently," said P. Gubb, sternly. "What I should wish to know now is why Mister Wiggins went and sewed an electric-light bulb in with the corpse for."

"In the first place," said Mr. Bartman, "he didn't sew it in with any corpse, because Hen Smitz wasn't a corpse when he was sewed in that burlap, unless Wiggins drowned him first, for Dr. Mortimer says Hen Smitz died of drowning; and in the second place, if you had a live man to sew in burlap, and had to hold him while you sewed him, you'd be liable to sew anything in with him.

"My idea is that Wiggins and some of his crew jumped on Hen Smitz and threw him down, and some of them held him while the others sewed him in. My idea is that Wiggins got that electric-light bulb to replace one that had burned out, and that he met Hen Smitz and had words with him, and they clinched, and Hen Smitz grabbed the bulb, and then the others came, and they sewed him into the burlap and dumped him into the river.

"So all you've got to do is to go out and tell that crowd that Wiggins did it and that you 'll let them know who helped him as soon as you find out. And you better do it before they break my windows."

Detective Gubb turned and went out of the morgue. As he left the undertaker's establishment the crowd gave a slight cheer, but Mr. Gubb walked hurriedly toward the jail. He found Policeman O'Toole there and questioned him about the bulb; and O'Toole, proud to be the center of so large and interested a gathering of his fellow citizens, pulled the bulb from his pocket and handed it to Mr. Gubb, while he repeated in more detail the facts given by Mr. Bartman. Mr. Gubb looked at the bulb.

"I presume to suppose," he said, "that Mr. Wiggins asked the stock-keeper for a new bulb to replace one that was burned out?"

"You're right," said O'Toole. "Why?"

"For the reason that this bulb is a burned-out bulb," said Mr. Gubb.

And so it was. The inner surface of the bulb was darkened slightly, and the filament of carbon was severed. O'Toole took the bulb and examined it curiously.

"That's odd, ain't it?" he said.

"It might so seem to the non-deteckative mind," said Mr. Gubb, "but to the deteckative mind, nothing is odd."

"No, no, this ain't so odd, either," said O'Toole, "for whether Hen Smitz grabbed the bulb before Wiggins changed the new one for the old one, or after he changed it, don't make so much difference, when you come to think of it."

"To the deteckative mind," said Mr. Gubb, "it makes the difference that this ain't the bulb you thought it was, and hence consequently it ain't the bulb Mister Wiggins got from the stock-keeper."

Mr. Gubb started away. The crowd followed him. He did not go in search of the original bulb at once. He returned first to his room, where he changed his undertaker disguise for Number Six, that of a blue woolen-shirted laboring-man with a long brown beard. Then he led the way back to the packing house.

Again the crowd was halted at the gate, but again P. Gubb passed inside, and he found the stockkeeper eating his luncheon out of a tin pail. The stock-keeper was perfectly willing to talk.

"It was like this," said the stock-keeper. "We've been working overtime in some departments down here, and Wiggins and his crew had to work overtime the night Hen Smitz was murdered. Hen and Wiggins was at outs, or anyway I heard Hen tell Wiggins he'd better be hunting another job because he wouldn't have this one long, and Wiggins told Hen that if he lost his job he'd murder him—Wiggins would murder Hen, that is. I didn't think it was much of anything but loose talk at the time. But Hen was working overtime too. He'd been working nights up in that little room of his on the second floor for quite some time, and this night Wiggins come to me and he says Hen had asked him for a fresh thirty-two-candle-power bulb. So I give it to Wiggins, and then I went home. And, come to find out, Wiggins sewed that bulb up with Hen."

"Perhaps maybe you have sack-needles like this into your stock-room," said P. Gubb, producing the needle Long Sam had given him. The stockkeeper took the needle and examined it carefully.

"Never had any like that," he said.

"Now, if," said Philo Gubb,—"if the bulb that was sewed up into the burlap with Henry Smitz wasn't a new bulb, and if Mr. Wiggins had given the new bulb to Henry, and if Henry had changed the new bulb for an old one, where would he have changed it at?"

"Up in his room, where he was always tinkering at that machine of his," said the stock-keeper.

"Could I have the pleasure of taking a look into that there room for a moment of time?" asked Mr. Gubb.

The stock-keeper arose, returned the remnants of his luncheon to his dinner-pail and led the way up the stairs. He opened the door of the room Henry Smitz had used as a work-room, and P. Gubb walked in. The room was in some confusion, but, except in one or two particulars, no more than a workroom is apt to be. A rather cumbrous machine—the invention on which Henry Smitz had been working—stood as the murdered man had left it, all its levers, wheels, arms, and cogs intact. A chair, tipped over, lay on the floor. A roll of burlap stood on a roller by the machine. Looking up, Mr. Gubb saw, on the ceiling, the lighting fixture of the room, and in it was a clean, shining thirty-two-candle-power bulb. Where another similar bulb might have been in the other socket was a plug from which an insulated wire, evidently to furnish power, ran to the small motor connected with the machine on which Henry Smitz had been working.

The stock-keeper was the first to speak.

"Hello!" he said. "Somebody broke that window!" And it was true. Somebody had not only broken the window, but had broken every pane and the sash itself. But Mr. Gubb was not interested in this. He was gazing at the electric bulb and thinking of Part Two, Lesson Six of the Course of Twelve Lessons—"How to Identify by Fingerprints, with General Remarks on the Bertillon System." He looked about for some means of reaching the bulb above his head. His eye lit on the fallen chair. By placing the chair upright and placing one foot on the frame of Henry Smitz's machine and the other on the chair-back, he could reach the bulb. He righted the chair and stepped onto its seat. He put one foot on the frame of Henry Smitz's machine; very carefully he put the other foot on the top of the chair-back. He reached upward and unscrewed the bulb.

The stock-keeper saw the chair totter. He sprang forward to steady it, but he was too late. Philo Gubb, grasping the air, fell on the broad, level board that formed the middle part of Henry Smitz's machine.

The effect was instantaneous. The cogs and wheels of the machine began to revolve rapidly. Two strong, steel arms flopped down and held Detective Gubb to the table, clamping his arms to his side. The roll of burlap unrolled, and as it unrolled, the loose end was seized and slipped under Mr. Gubb and wrapped around him and drawn taut, bundling him as a sheep's carcass is bundled. An arm reached down and back and forth, with a sewing motion, and passed from Mr. Gubb's head to his feet. As it reached his feet a knife sliced the burlap in which he was wrapped from the burlap on the roll.

And then a most surprising thing happened. As if the board on which he lay had been a catapult, it suddenly and unexpectedly raised Philo Gubb and tossed him through the open window. The stock-keeper heard a muffled scream and then a great splash, but when he ran to the window, the great paper-hanger detective had disappeared in the bosom of the Mississippi.

Like Henry Smitz he had tried to reach the ceiling by standing on the chair-back; like Henry Smitz he had fallen upon the newly invented burlaping and loading machine; like Henry Smitz he had been wrapped and thrown through the window into the river; but, unlike Henry Smitz, he had not been sewn into the burlap, because Philo Gubb had the double-pointed shuttle-action needle in his pocket.

Page Seventeen of Lesson Eleven of the Rising Sun Detective Agency's Correspondence School of Detecting Course of Twelve Lessons, says:—

In cases of extreme difficulty of solution it is well for the detective to reenact as nearly as possible the probable action of the crime.

Mr. Philo Gubb had done so. He had also proved that a man may be sewn in a sack and drowned in a river without committing willful suicide or being the victim of foul play.

The Female
of the Species

THE LOST DIAMONDS

W. S. Hayward

I. THE DUKE OF RUSTENBURGH

Every one knew the Duke of Rustenburgh. He was a celebrity in all the European capitals, not on account of his position, or anything that he had ever done to make himself conspicuous, but because he had in his possession the most famous precious stones in the world. They were extremely rare and valuable; the duke had been a collector of these glittering pebbles from his boyhood, and at the death of his father, the thirteenth Duke of Rustenburgh, he inherited all the heirlooms of the family, among which were several tiaras and bracelets formed of stones of great price. He had no territorial possessions; what land he had acquired a title to at the death of his father he had long ago sold to provide money for the furtherance of his favourite hobby, and so he carried his fortune about with him wherever he went; and a splendid fortune it was. With it he could have bought up many petty German states and principalities; but he preferred dwelling in seclusion, except when he sallied forth into society to display his wonderful diamonds. He always wore as many as decency and propriety would allow him; but he had found out at a very early age that only a woman can display jewellery as it ought to be exhibited. So he married the first woman he met, not because he loved her, but because he wanted a sort of barber's-block upon which he could show his jewels. She was the daughter of a Paris banker, and brought him a large sum as her dowry, which he spent before a week was over in buying the wonderful Blo-y-nor diamond, which had for centuries been in the possession of the kings of Delhi, but which, owing to those vicissitudes which affect monarchs as well as plebeians, was now in the Parisian market. This acquisition made him inexpressibly happy for many weeks, and he undertook a trip to Russia in order to parade his new purchase before the *virtuosi* of St. Petersburg. Whenever anybody met him, they always used to say, "Well, duke, have you bought any more diamonds?" And the ladies would beg as an especial favour that they might come to his hotel and have a peep at the famous Blo-y-nor, which was turning the heads of half the diamond merchants in Europe. Some people can tell you the pedigrees of illustrious families, some are great at the pedigrees of horses, but the duke's favourite study was the genealogy of precious stones; he knew the names of all the wonderful stones in existence, where they came from, and in whose possession they were; how many hands they had passed through, and whether they were of the first and purest water. He had compiled an essay, which he called the

"History of Precious Stones," more for his own edification and pleasure than anything else; but the public had taken it up, and the Duke of Rustenburgh was favourably known for his little and unambitious treatise, which, in spite of its faults of style and grammatical errors, was entertaining. Its blemishes were to be corrected in the second edition by a gentleman who was a member of the *Société des Gena de Lettres*, and his name, widely known in connexion with the Paris press, was a sufficient guarantee for the accuracy of the contemplated corrections.

It cannot be said that the duchess was happy. She was a woman of extravagant tastes and habits, which the parsimony of the illustrious husband would not allow her to gratify. If a relation died and left her some money he spent it all immediately in buying diamonds—such was his almost insane passion for these glittering baubles. He loved a scintillation from one of these glittering bits of glass more than he did his wife's whole body, and she, poor thing, knew it. When she went out, she literally blazed with diamonds; but that was not what she wished for. She did not care about so much empty show, and so her heart was driven back upon its own resources; she pined for an affection which was denied to her ardent longing, and to avoid distraction, she plunged recklessly into a search for excitement. Where was the wished-for stimulation to be found so well or so effectually as at the gambling table? So the Duchess of Rustenburgh, through her husband's folly, became a confirmed gambler. Wherever the fashionable vice obtained in London, Paris, or Vienna, there was she a constant visitor. All the money she could scrape together was devoted to the gratification of her hobby, which the duke had himself created. Sometimes she won, and at other times she was unsuccessful. Fortune was fickle, and like Janus, exhibited two faces alternately, showing them now to the delight of the beholder, afterwards to his unutterable confusion and dismay. At Hamburgh there is a private entrance to the gaming-house, and a private staircase leading to a private box in which the gamester is concealed from view. Many times has a small exquisitely gloved hand obtruded itself through the narrow aperture in the box, and laid on the surface of the table a rouleau of bank-notes. This was the Duchess of Rustenburgh. The duke took little or no notice of this proclivity of his wife's. If any one spoke to him about it, he would reply, "Poor child, *Elle s'amuse*," and this answer he considered a good and sufficient reason for the terrible plunge she had taken headlong into the dangerous ocean which sooner or later engulfs all its rack and ruin-bent votaries. The duke adhered to the old style of dress because he could wear shoes with diamond buckles, and he took snuff because it gave him an excuse for having the box set most profusely with jewels, and he offered a pinch to all his friends, so that they might admire the splendour of the receptacle for the pulverizing mixture. And so the world wagged and laughed at the foolish old Duke of Rustenburgh, but behind the smile lurked a secret admiration of his incomparable diamonds.

II. A FALSE SCENT

H ave you heard the news?"

"I can't say I have. What is it?"

"The Duke of Rustenburgh's lost his diamonds."

"Has he, indeed?"

"It will break his heart, I should think."

"So I should imagine. Lost his diamonds, has he? Poor fellow!"

I happened to be posting a letter at the General Post-office when this information fell upon my ears. The speakers were two friends who had come with the same object in view as myself, and having accomplished it they walked away. I pondered their words over carefully as I went home, because any loss or robbery was in my way. It was my business to discover the perpetrators of theft, and so I immediately began to think how I could turn the information to account. I never did things in a hurry. I always deliberated; so that by reflection I should be able to hit upon the right path, which would lead me eventually to success, if such a consummation were to be achieved by mortal means. After dinner the same day I sallied forth; I went to head-quarters, where I obtained all the necessary information. The robbery, for such it was, had been committed in London, where the duke and duchess happened to be staying, as usual. They were staying at an hotel. The duke was beside himself with mortification and rage. His vexatious passion knew no bounds, and he frantically offered prodigious sums for the recovery of his stolen treasures. The priceless Blo-y-nor was among the missing stones, and that alone was worth a king's ransom. On the day upon which the loss was discovered, it appeared that one Karl Fulchöck had decamped. This man was the duke's valet, the only son of the man who had held the same position of trust for very many years. On the death of the elder Fulchöck, his widow entreated his grace to take her son into his employment. Thinking he might safely do so, he consented to her urgent wishes, and the young Karl, not quite twenty-three years of age, entered the duke's service as *valet de chambre*. A photograph of the man had been sent to the police-office, and faithfully copied. I secured one of the imitations, as did most of the detective police, who embarked upon the chase on speculation. Many detectives have more than one piece of employment on their hands at one time, because they are tempted by the rewards; and this cupidity and grasping after money is very often the cause of their failure. I never in my life attempted more than one thing at a time, because know very well that if my hands were overloaded I should get confused, and fail in my endeavours, which, however strenuous, could not possibly be complete. I was aware that in engaging in this matter I was undertaking a contest with the keenest wits and most fertile brains in the force; but I was rejoiced at this, for if I proved myself cleverer than they turned out to be, it would redound to my credit and give me a higher position than the one I now occupied. The Rustenburgh diamond robbery was a *cause célèbre*, and I applied myself to it with all diligence. Whenever I happened to be in company with birds of my own feather I found that they were unanimously of opinion that Karl Fulchöck, the absconding valet, was the actual culprit; so they one and all devoted themselves to his capture. If he was not the guilty person, or in some way connected with the robber or robbers, why should he run away? At first sight this seemed to be an unanswerable argument, and I remarked that the oldest officers in the force shared the general opinion. I, however, thought differently. I was as positive as one can be, about anything uncertain, that they were all on a false scent. I had fortified myself with all the information I could glean respecting the Duke and Duchess of Rustenburgh; and I did not join in the hue and cry of Karl Fulchöck, who up to the seventh day after the commission of the robbery remained undiscovered.

This led me to believe that he had powerful protectors, and was in safe keeping. I paid a visit one day to the room in which he had slept when at the hotel. Casting my eyes carefully round, I perceived all the evidences of a hasty flight. I deduced an important inference from this fact. If Karl Fulchöck really planned such a dignified robbery of such magnitude, he must have been a man of some calculation—he would not have left letters, clothes, and papers scattered about in the way he had done. I was an indifferent German scholar, so I brought a lady with me who faithfully translated some letters in a woman's handwriting. They were from a German girl, with whom Karl had been in love before he left his fatherland. A half-written reply to one of her epistles was found in a desk, and a locket lay beside it. I did not hear that he was a young man of immoral habits or loose character; on the contrary, every one with whom he had come in contact gave him an excellent character for sobriety, honesty, and chastity. He was not extravagant in his habits. He was in the receipt of a liberal salary from the duke, his master, and he had placed away a small sum every month which he faithfully transmitted to his father. Certainly, if he had been a cool, calculating man of mature age, he might have left all his traps and effects in rude disorder, so as to baffle and confuse his pursuers; but nothing transpired to give one the idea that he was cool or calculating. The opinion I formed of Karl Fulchöck was that he was a plain, honest, straightforward, hardworking young man; that he loved his mother and loved his German sweetheart, that he was proud of being in the duke's service, and had always striven to do his duty in the state of life in which he had been placed. The conclusion I came to after leaving his bed-chamber was that he had been *suddenly and unexpectedly abducted*, and that he was at the present time in the hands of the real perpetrators of the audacious outrage upon the duke's property. But who were these perpetrators? I made a shrewd guess as to the identity of one of them, and that was no less a personage than the Duchess of Rustenburgh herself. Whether she was the instigator of the robbery or not I did not pretend to say, but that she had a hand in it I would have sworn in any court of justice in Great Britain. It behoved me to go very carefully to work, because to denounce so powerful a lady as her Grace without full and adequate proof would be to make oneself ridiculous, and to cause the important accusation to recoil against its originator. Of course I did not say a word about my suspicions to any soul living. If I ever achieved a triumph, which I sometimes did, I did not like my laurels shared by any one else. Such as they were I approved of wearing them myself without any partnership in the wreath. The propensity of the Duchess of Rustenburgh for gambling was almost as well known as the duke's passion for diamonds. She was reported to have been a heavy loser on more than one occasion lately, and I, in conjunction with others, wondered, where she obtained the money from to satisfy her debts of honour, who so likely to accommodate her as a money-lender? Her security was good; in point of fact, it could not have been better. Now, my theory was that her Grace had lost large sums of money over the fatal and unpropitious green-baize, upon whose alluring surface she so often played her favourite game of Baccarat—the most fashionable of all gambling games in polite circles. Having lost the money, it was absolutely necessary, for the sake of her credit, that she should pay it. But she had not the money to satisfy her creditors. The duke would not trust her with a single halfpenny. She was then, perforce, driven to the Jews, who would, according to my own experience of the amiable and accommodating Israelites, be only too glad to do her paper to any amount. A time, however, must come when even a money-lending Jew requires payment of sums advanced, for although sixty per cent. is very fair (or unfair) interest, it is gratifying to handle one's principal occasionally. Not having the money to satisfy the Jews, her Grace had, I surmised, listened too readily to their pernicious counsels, and had lent herself to the plundering of the unsuspecting husband. Karl Fulchöck had been hastily removed and kept in durance so that suspicion might be diverted from the actual channel, and turned into another and fallacious current, which was sure in the end to lead to nothing. These were not random thoughts. I had made minute observations, and deduced, as I have before said, the inferences I have stated. I was convinced that the duchess was the culprit, and it was towards her that I now turned my attention. It was clear that she had not done what amounted to a felony of a serious nature without having an able accomplice at her elbow—a man of tact and of experience, who knew how to conduct matters in a scientific manner. So I began to watch her movements to see if I could trace her to any particular house. This once discovered would be equivalent to gaining half the battle. I set to work in a very cautious manner, so as not to rouse the faintest shadow of suspicion in the mind of her Grace, and I did not allow a syllable to fall from my lips which might indicate to those engaged in the same enterprise as myself that they were on a false scent. All the efforts of the police were ineffectual to discover the remotest trace of Karl Fulchöck. This strengthened my opinion, which was further encouraged owing to no signs of the missing diamonds having been seen. The man who had supplied the Duchess of Rustenburgh with money must, I felt assured, be a capitalist of extensive means. Having once got the diamonds in his possession he could afford to wait a year or two before he realized them. He wasn't a vulgar thief who was pushed for immediate supplies of petty cash. He was the man to lock up the precious stones in his strong box and keep them there until the excitement had cooled down and the vigour of the search was somewhat abated. The unfortunate Karl was, I apprehended, a thorn in his side, for he must have been at a loss to know what to do with him. I hoped sincerely that I should be able to prevent any violence being used which would tend to shorten his life, for I was persuaded that the poor fellow was a victim and not the rascal it was the intent of them to make him appear.

III. CHAINED TO THE WALL

I invariably employed a boy to discover minute and petty details which it was inconvenient for me to investigate myself. It was imperative that I should be apprised of the movements of the Duchess of Rustenburgh. I could not stand outside her hotel and watch her go out, and then rush round the corner, spring on the back of a horse ready saddled and bridled, and follow in pursuit, but I could send my factotum and let him make his observations; no one would take any notice of him, and even a policeman would, out of pity for his ragged attire, refrain from moving him on. I picked up Jack Doyle one day with his hand in a gentleman's pocket; in another instant the handkerchief would have been gone, and the boy with it, but I seized him by the arm, and led him whining and sobbing into a quiet bye-street, where I could talk to him more at my case than I could in a crowded thoroughfare. I did not begin my harangue by telling him that he had been guilty of a serious offence against the law of the land, for which any sitting magistrate at the nearest police-court would send him to a reformatory—a mild term for rigorous imprisonment and hard work.

He was already perfectly well aware of the fact, but the following dialogue ensued between us.

"You were picking that gentleman's pocket."

"Yes, mum," he replied, with his knuckles in his eyes.

"What did you do it for?"

"Cos I was hungry, mum."

This declaration was followed by a remarkably fine whine and a puerile sniff.

"You did not expect to find anything eatable in a pocket, did you?"

"Didn't know, mum."

"Oh yes, you did. How long have you been a thief? Tell me the truth, and it will be better for you."

"Going on three year, mum; ever since father was killed falling from a scaffold, and mother was took and died with the fever."

"To whom do you take what you steal, and what does he give you for them?"

"Don't like to say," he replied, doggedly.

"Well, I wont press you. Of course you don't care to betray your employer. Do you like the life you are leading?"

"Can't do nothing else."

"Have you ever tried?"

"Not as I know on."

"How can you tell then?"

Dead silence for a brief space, followed by whines, grunts, groans, and sniffs.

"Would you like to lead an honest life?"

The boy's face brightened, and he replied, "I should indeed, mum."

"Would you like to be my servant?"

"You wouldn't take me," he said, sceptically.

"I will, if you'll promise to behave well."

"I'll promise, mum, if you'll try me."

"What's your name?"

"Jack Doyle."

I put Mr. Jack into a cab, took him home and had him washed and dressed. I treated him kindly, gave him a certain weekly sum for wages, so that he might not be tempted to return to his own way of living from absolute want of pocket-money, and I found that my investment was not such a bad one after all. The boy served me well and faithfully, and I could rely upon him. If I gave him a commission to execute, he would do it, notwithstanding it might cost him an infinity of trouble. He always avoided his old haunts, and when I had the time to spare I taught him to read and write, and inculcated high moral precepts in his fertile mind. He improved under my tuition, and I looked upon him as a brand snatched from the burning.

It was Jack that I employed to watch the Duchess of Rustenburgh. I took lodgings in a mews close by, so that he could run and tell me directly he saw her going out. He could not mistake her, for I had pointed her out to him on a previous occasion. We remained on the alert for three days, during which time she never so much as stirred out of the house. I supposed that the duke was so excessively annoyed and put out by the loss of his diamonds, that he required her dutiful allegiance, and would not let her leave him. When she contrived to escape this despotism, she did not order her carriage, but walked down the street. As soon as Jack saw her issue from the hotel, he came and told me. I had a cab in readiness, and I jumped into it. Jack got on the box, and away we went, overtaking her just as she was getting into a hack vehicle; we followed it, and tracked it to a house in Bloomsbury. The duchess stayed there for at least two hours, and then went straight home, dismissing her cab at the bottom of the street, close to the spot where she had first entered it. Her not driving to her hotel was a suspicious circumstance in my eyes. I went to the neighbourhood of her friend's house to make inquiries respecting the inmates. It was as I had imagined: a notorious money-lender lived there. Armed with this information, I at once called upon Colonel Warner, and asked for a select body of police. He wished to know why I wanted them.

"Have you found the Duke's diamonds?" he said, in a bantering way, never supposing for one moment that I had obtained, as I thought, a clue to them.

"I believe I have," I replied.

"What! are you in earnest?"

"Perfectly so. Can I have the men?"

"As many as you like; choose them yourself."

I wrote down on a piece of paper the names of several officers with whose worth I was well acquainted, and desired that they might be told to hold themselves in readiness for me at six o'clock that evening.

"Upon my word, Mrs. Paschal, we shall have you at the top of the tree soon," remarked the Colonel; "I was just beginning to think that you were not so clever as people think. All our fellows have been at fault, and I shall think more than ever of the Lady Detectives if you accomplish what you lead me to suppose you can."

"You may depend upon my doing my best."

"That I don't doubt for a moment. Well, don't let me keep you; you shall have these men at six o'clock."

I did not tell the police that I wanted them to help me to capture the state diamonds of the Duke of Rustenburgh, nor did they ask any questions; they only knew that they were ordered on special duty, and it was no business of theirs to inquire its nature. I left some outside the house; two I took with me for personal protection and to assist me when I had effected an entry, knocked boldly at the door, and asked for Mr. Lupus, which was the name of the money-lender whom I suspected to be in league with the duchess, who liked gambling better than diamonds.

The servant said he had just finished dinner, but she had no doubt he would see us if we would wait a short time.

I replied that we should be glad to do so, as we came on important business connected with a loan and was desirous of seeing her master that evening.

With my attendant satellites, who were attired in undress, and resembled well-to-do tradesmen, I was ushered into a waiting-room.

The minutes that elapsed before the appearance of Mr. Lupus were passed by me in great anxiety and suspense. If I were right in my conjectures, I should in a small way make my fortune. I should gain a large access of reputation, and a considerable sum of money, which the duke, in the first agony of his loss, had offered. But if I were wrong, I should be overwhelmed with ridicule and confusion.

When the servant came back, she desired me to follow her, as her master would receive me in his study. That was what I wished for. I had instructed the three policemen to take advantage of the first opportunity that offered, and search the house to see if they could find a young man whom I imagined was confined upon the premises. I could keep the money-lender engaged in conversation, whilst I had the satisfaction of knowing that my work was being effectually done in my absence. I left my coadjutors sitting in an unconcerned attitude, with a stolid and indifferent look upon their faces. They never allowed their faces to betray what was passing within them, and it was for their wonderful self-possession and their carriage that I had chosen them from amongst their "confrères." Mr. Lupus was a tall, thin man, with a profusion of hair upon his face. He looked steadily at me, and certainly showed no indication of being the guilty man I took him for.

"Sit down, my dear madam," he exclaimed politely. "Take this chair. Do you come on your own account, or are you the emissary of another?"

"I come for another," I replied.

"And those gentlemen my servant told me were waiting with you—"

"Are no friends of mine. I know nothing about them. I suppose they are waiting to see you on business."

"Possibly; but allow me to ask from whom you come?"

I lowered my voice, and replied, "From the duchess."

"Rustenburgh?" be queried.

"Yes," I replied.

"Are you her servant?"

"I am one of them—not the one she usually sends on confidential missions, but in the absence of that one she has selected me."

"Imprudent; but I think I begin to understand you. What do you want?"

"As usual, money," I replied.

"Money! always money," he cried, holding up his hands, "why, she would drain the bullion vaults of the Bank of England in a year."

"She is sadly extravagant, but you must remember she is unlucky."

"She should not play so high."

"I agree with you; but what can you do for her?"

"To-night?"'

"Yes, at once."

"Absolutely nothing."

"Her Grace anticipated this, and told me to say that if you would send her a diamond she could dispose of it."

"What do you mean?" he replied, eyeing me with great acuteness.

I assumed an air of innocence, and replied—"I mean nothing in particular. I am only delivering a message with which I was charged."

"I know nothing of any diamonds. Tell her Grace she must be mistaken."

"Certainly. I was instructed to say that her Grace was very hard pressed; in fact, it was almost a matter of life and death with her."

"If she sends me such messages, and is so pertinacious in her demands, I may as well shut up my house and run away, for I cannot stand such a perpetual drain upon my resources."

"What shall I say when I return?"

"Say I refused."

"In that case, sir, I have only three words more to utter, and then I can go back, having fulfilled the commands of the duchess to the letter."

"What are they?"

I went close to him, and said in a distinct voice—"Blo-y-nor!"

He started, and exclaimed—"Her Grace must indeed be in a dilemma since she sends me that signal. Stay, I will see what I can do for you."

He went to a safe which stood in a corner of the room, opened it with one of those patent keys belonging to locks that defy picking, and opening a drawer, took out a roll of notes. As he did so, I fancied I saw the glitter of diamonds. Going to a table, he carefully took down the number of each note, and then gave them to me, saying, "Excuse the remark, but I know the numbers of these notes, and if they do not in their entirety find their way to the duchess, they will be stopped at the Bank."

"If her Grace trusts me, I do not see why you should object to do so," I replied, with dignity.

"I trust nobody," he said, with a cynical smile. "I meant no offence, however. I was merely taking a precautionary measure, which every business man is justified in doing."

As I was folding up the notes, a servant rushed precipitately into the room, exclaiming—

"Oh! sir, I do think there's thieves in the house."

"What?" vociferated Mr. Lupus.

"Thieves, sir. They're going on anyhow!"

"Who—when—can't you speak?"

"Downstairs, sir—the cellar, sir, and—oh! the young man, sir."

Uttering a wild exclamation, Mr. Lupus ran to the safe, closed it, and put the key in his pocket, then he hastily followed his servant; I left the room with him. We descended to the lower regions, where I saw my men. They had forced open the door of a cellar, and were gazing with a puzzled expression upon what they saw. The cellar was of limited dimensions, probably eight feet by three. The wine-bins had been removed, and nothing remained but its plain whitewashed walls. On the ground, upon a heap of straw, a young man was lying. The sickly glare of the candle fell upon his upturned countenance which was ghastly pale.

In an instant I recognised Karl Fulchöck. The poor fellow seemed beside himself with terror. He did not know what new torture or what fresh imprisonment awaited him.

Mr. Lupus glared at the men who had invaded the privacy of his house in a demoniac manner.

"Shut the door," he cried; "what right have you here?"

I gave them a rapid sign, and they seized him. He struggled desperately, but although a strong man, what was he in the arms of three men equally as powerful as himself? In less than three minutes from the commencement of the struggle, the result of which was not for one moment doubtful, Mr. Lupus was a prisoner. The handcuffs were around his wrists, and he was subdued and helpless.

It was now time to turn my attention to Karl Fulchöck. He had risen to his feet during the contest, and now that he was standing up I noticed what I had not remarked before. He was chained to the wall. A chain constructed of formidable links surrounded his waist, and was fastened to a staple driven into a brick. A loaf of bread lay upon the straw, together with a pannikin of water.

I thought it was now time to assume my authority.

"Liberate that man," I said to one of the officers. He drew a chisel and a hammer from his pocket, and sinking down on his knees upon the straw, began his task; half a brick sufficed him for an anvil, and in a short time one link of the chain was severed, and Karl was free. He ran forward and sank on his knees before me, saying in very good English—

"What do I not owe you?"

"Nothing, Karl Fulchöck," I replied. "Your sufferings are over now."

Overcome by his emotions, he fell forward on his face and swooned away. Leaving one of the policemen in charge of him, I told the other two to conduct Mr. Lupus upstairs.

This gentleman had been a silent spectator of these exciting events up to the present time, but he now exclaimed in a bitter voice,—"Done, by Heavens!"

I smiled sardonically, and we went upstairs.

Once more in the study, I felt in Mr. Lupus's waistcoat-pocket for the key of the safe. I found it. When the safe was opened I ransacked it, and to my great satisfaction found a quantity of the missing diamonds. Amongst them was the Blo-y-nor.

"I seize them in the name of the Queen," I exclaimed, triumphantly.

As I was securing them about my person, Mr. Lupus recovered his equable demeanour, and throwing himself into a chair, said, with an unconcerned laugh—

"When you have finished your apparently interesting occupation, listen to me."

"I am ready to do so now."

"What do you intend to do with me?"

"I shall take you to the nearest police-station."

"You will do nothing of the sort."

"Indeed! Why not?"

"Because if you do, you expose the Duchess of Rustenburgh, as well as me."

This was a difficulty I had not thought of.

I hesitated before I replied.

"Shall I tell you what you had better do?" continued Mr. Lupus.

"If you like."

"Very well. There is nothing like judgment in times like these. Take me to the duke's hotel; confront me with himself and his duchess, and let them deal with me."

"Why so?"

"Is not the reason apparent? The Duke of Rustenburgh will never allow me to be prosecuted, because he knows that such a course would only disgrace his wife."

"There is something in that."

"Of course there is."

"Are all the jewels here?" I demanded.

"All but a few trifling ones that I have disposed of."

After considering for a time, I concluded that it would be better to do as Mr. Lupus suggested, so I ordered Karl Fulchöck to be brought upstairs. He had recovered his temporary weakness, and could walk without any assistance. I sent for two cabs, and having embarked in them, we travelled to the duke's hotel. When we arrived there, and I sent in word that I brought news of his precious diamonds, we were at once admitted. On seeing Karl, the duke ran forward, crying—

"That's the wretch; that's the one. Send him to prison! *Scélérat*, where are my diamonds?"

"They are here, your Grace," I exclaimed, handing those I had rescued to him.

He caught hold of them. Scanned them eagerly, and then pressing them to his bosom, burst into tears. The reaction was too painful to be borne without this natural vent.

The duchess was in the room engaged in eating some olives when we arrived. Directly she cast her eyes upon the man Lupus, she turned pale as death, and would have flown from the apartment but I detained her, forcing her mildly into a chair.

The whole circumstances were at length explained to the duke, and he hurled his ducal anathema at Lupus, who did not seem to be much affected by the demonstration. Having regained his diamonds, Rustenhurg did not care particularly to revenge himself when he knew that if he did so he would cover his wife with confusion and disgrace. So he consented to the affair being hushed up, and Mr. Lupus escaped with a whole skin, although he did not deserve the clemency he met with. He was however out of pocket through his dealing with her Grace. He had advanced her large sums of money, and, as I had supposed, which she had never paid him. He had not had time to sell the diamonds, although had I been two days later, they would have all been sent to Australia.

Turning to me, after all had been explained, the duke said, "I cannot express my gratitude to you, madam."

Karl Fulchöck next engrossed his attention. He spoke to him in German, and said, as well as I could understand, "that he would endeavour to make him all the reparation which lay in his power."

To Mr. Lupus he exclaimed, "Go, sir; you escape the life-long imprisonment you have earned; but you will, like Cain, carry with you a heavy weight arising from a consciousness of crime."

"Oh dear no," replied Mr. Lupus calmly. "I am rather proud of the whole transaction. I certainly have failed in the end, and that failure I shall regret. Another time when I essay a similar affair I shall be more on my guard against female detectives."

This last part of his speech was accompanied by a vicious glance out in my direction.

I never knew what became of Mr. Lupus; but I have been informed that the countess left off gambling from that day. Nothing would induce her to touch cards or dice; while the duke treated her, as he ought to have done at first, with greater consideration and kindness, and thought less of his diamonds. I received the reward, and was much complimented by all who knew me and who were acquainted with the affair upon the sagacity I had displayed in recovering the lost diamonds.

THE UNKNOWN WEAPON

Andrew Forrester

I AM ABOUT TO SET OUT HERE ONE OF THE MOST REMARKABLE CASES WHICH have come under my actual observation.

I will give the particulars, as far as I can, in the form of a narrative.

The scene of the affair lay in a midland county, and on the outskirts of a very rustic and retired village, which has at no time come before the attention of the world.

Here are the exact preliminary facts of the case. Of course I alter names, for as this case is now to become public, and as the inquiries which took place at the time not only ended in disappointment, but by some inexplicable means did not arrest the public curiosity, there can be no wisdom in covering the names and places with such a thin veil of fiction as will allow of the truth being seen below that literary gauze. The names and places here used are wholly fictitious, and in no degree represent or shadow out the actual personages or localities.

The mansion at which the mystery which I am about to analyse took place was the manor-house while its occupant, the squire of the district, was also the lord of the manor. I will call him Petleigh.

I may at once state here, though the fact did not come to my knowledge till after the catastrophe, that the squire was a thoroughly mean man, with but one other passion than the love of money, and that was a greed for plate.

Every man who has lived with his eyes open has come across human beings who concentrate within themselves the most wonderful contradictions. Here is a man who lives so scampishly that it is a question if ever he earnt an honest shilling, and yet he would firmly believe his moral character would be lost did he enter a theatre; there is an individual who never sent away a creditor or took more than a just commercial discount, while any day in the week he may be arrested upon a charge which would make him a scandal to his family.

So with Squire Petleigh. That he was extremely avaricious there can be no doubt, while his desire for the possession and display of plate was almost a mania.

His silver was quite a tradition in the county. At every meal—and I have heard the meals at Petleighcote were neither abundant nor succulent—enough plate stood upon the table to pay for the feeding of the poor of the whole county for a month. He would eat a mutton chop off silver.

Mr. Petleigh was in parliament, and in the season came up to town, where he had the smallest and most miserable house ever rented by a wealthy county member.

Avaricious, and therefore illiberal, Petleigh would not keep up two establishments; and so, when he came to town for the parliamentary season, he brought with him his country establishment, all the servants composing which were paid but third-class fares up to town.

The domestics I am quite sure, from what I learnt, were far from satisfactory people; a condition of things which was quite natural, seeing that they were not treated well, and were taken on at the lowest possible rate of wages.

The only servitor who remained permanently on the establishment was the housekeeper at the manor-house, Mrs. Quinion.

It was whispered in the neighbourhood that she had been the foster-sister ("and perhaps more") of the late Mrs. Petleigh; and it was stated with sufiicient openness, and I am afraid also with some general amount of chuckling satisfaction, that the squire had been bitten with his lady.

The truth stood that Petleigh had married the daughter of a Liverpool merchant in the great hope of an alliance with her fortune, which at the date of her marriage promised to be large. But cotton commerce, even twenty-five years ago, was a risky business, and to curtail here particulars which are only remotely essential to the absolute comprehension of this narrative, he never had a penny with her, and his wife's father, who had led a deplorably irregular life, started for America and died there.

Mrs. Petleigh had but one child, Graham Petleigh, and she died when he was about twelve years of age.

During Mrs. Petleigh's life, the housekeeper at Petleighcote was the foster-sister to whom reference has been made. I myself believe that it would have been more truthful to call Mrs. Quinion the natural sister of the squire's wife.

Be that as it may, after the lady's death Mrs. Quinion, in a half-conceded, and after an uncomfortable fashion, became in a measure the actual mistress of Petleighcote.

Possibly the squire was aware of a relationship to his wife at which I have hinted, and was therefore not unready in recognising that it was better she should be in the house than any other woman. For, apart from his avariciousness and his mania for the display of plate, I found beyond all dispute that he was a man of very estimable judgment.

Again, Mrs. Quinion fell in with his avaricious humour. She shaved down his household expenses, and was herself contented with a very moderate remuneration.

From all I learnt, I came to the conclusion that Petleighcote had long been the most uncomfortable house in the county, the display of plate only tending to intensify the general barrenness.

Very few visitors came to the house, and hospitality was unknown; yet, notwithstanding these drawbacks, Petleigh stood very well in the county, and indeed, on the occasion of one or two charitable collections, he had appeared in print with sufficient success.

Those of my readers who live in the country will comprehend the style of the squire's household when I say that he grudged permission to shoot rabbits on his ground. Whenever possible, all the year round, specimens of that rather tiring food were to be found in Squire Petleigh's larder. In fact, I learnt that a young curate who remained a short time at Tram (the village), in gentle satire of this cheap system of rations, called Petleighcote the "Warren."

The son, Graham Petleigh, was brought up in a deplorable style, the father being willing to persuade himself, perhaps, that as he had been disappointed in his hopes of a fortune with the mother, the son did not call for that consideration to which he would have been entitled had the mother brought her husband increased riches. It is certain that the boy roughed life. All the schooling he got was that which could be afforded by a foundation grammar school, which happened fortunately to exist at Tram.

To this establishment he went sometimes, while at others he was off with lads miserably below him in station, upon some expedition which was not perhaps, as a rule, so respectable an employment as studying the humanities.

Evidently the boy was shamefully ill-used; for he was neglected.

By the time he was nineteen or twenty (all these particulars I learnt readily after the catastrophe, for the townsfolk were only too eager to talk of the unfortunate young man)—by the time he was nineteen or twenty, a score of years of neglect bore their fruit. He was ready, beyond any question, for any mad performance. Poaching especially was his delight, perhaps in a great measure because he found it profitable; because, to state the truth, he was kept totally without money, and to this disadvantage he added a second, that of being unable to spread what money he did obtain over any expanse of time.

I have no doubt myself that the depredations on his father's estate might have with justice been put to his account, and, from the inquiries I made, I am equally free to believe that when any small article of the mass of plate about the premises was missing, that the son knew a good deal more than was satisfactory of the lost valuables.

That Mrs. Quinion, the housekeeper, was extremely devoted to the young man is certain; but the money she received as wages, and whatever private or other means she had, could not cover the demands made upon them by young Graham Petleigh, who certainly spent money, though where it came from was a matter of very great uncertainty.

From the portrait I saw of him, he must have been of a daring, roving, jovial disposition—a youngster not inclined to let duty come between him and his inclinations; one, in short, who would get more out of the world than he would give it.

The plate was carried up to town each year with the establishment, the boxes being under the special guardianship of the butler, who never let them out of his sight between the country and town houses. The man, I have heard, looked forward to those journeys with absolute fear.

From what I learnt, I suppose the convoy of plate boxes numbered well on towards a score.

Graham Petleigh sometimes accompanied his father to town, and at other times was sent to a relative in Cornwall. I believe it suited father and son better that the latter should be packed off to Cornwall in the parliamentary season, for in town the lad necessarily became comparatively expensive—an objection in the eyes of the father, while the son found himself in a world to which, thanks to the education he had received, he was totally unfitted.

Young Petleigh's passion was horses, and there was not a farmer on the father's estate, or in the neighbourhood of Tram, who was not plagued for the loan of this or that horse—for the young man had none of his own.

On my part, I believe if the youth had no self-respect, the want was in a great measure owing to the father having had not any for his son.

I know I need scarcely add, that when a man is passionately fond of horses generally be bets on those quadrupeds.

It did not call for many inquiries to ascertain that young Petleigh had "put" a good deal of money upon horses, and that, as a rule, he had been lucky with them. The young man wanted some excitement, some occupation, and he found it in betting. Have I said that after the young heir was taken from the school he was allowed to run loose? This was the case. I presume the father could not bring his mind to incurring the expense of entering his son at some profession.

Things then at Petleighcote were in this condition; the father neglectful and avaricious; the son careless, neglected, and daily slipping down the ladder of life; and the houekeeper, Mrs. Quinion, saying nothing, doing nothing, but existing, and perhaps showing that she was attached to her foster-sister's son. She was a woman of much sound and discriminating sense, and it is certain that she expressed herself to the effect that she foresaw the young man was being silently, steadfastly, unceasingly ruined.

All these preliminaries comprehended, I may proceed to the action of this narrative.

It was the 19th of May (the year is unimportant), and early in the morning when the discovery was made, by the gardener to Squire Petleigh—one Tom Brown.

Outside the great hall-door, and huddled together in an extraordinary fashion, the gardener, at half-past five in the morning (a Tuesday), found lying a human form. And when he came to make an examination, he discovered that it was the dead body of the young squire.

Seizing the handle of the great bell, he quickly sounded an alarm, and within a minute the housekeeper herself and the one servant, who together numbered the household which slept at Petleighcote when the squire was in town, stood on the threshold of the open door.

The housekeeper was half-dressed, the servant wench was huddled up in a petticoat and a blanket.

The news spread very rapidly, by means of the gardener's boy, who, wondering where his master was stopping, came loafing about the house, quickly to find the use of his legs.

"He must have had a fit," said the housekeeper; and it was a flying message to that effect carried by the boy into the village, which brought the village doctor to the spot in the quickest possible time.

It was then found that the catastrophe was due to no *fit*.

A very slight examination showed that the young squire had died from a stab caused by a rough iron barb, the metal shaft of which was six inches long, and which still remained in the body.

At the inquest, the medical man deposed that very great force must have been used in thrusting the barb into the body, for one of the ribs had been half severed by the act. The stab given, the barb had evidently been drawn back with the view of extracting it—a purpose which had failed, the flanges of the barb having fixed themselves firmly in the cartilage and tissue about it. It was impossible the deceased could have turned the barb against himself in the manner in which it had been used.

Asked what this barb appeared like, the surgeon was unable to reply. He had never seen such a weapon before. He supposed it had been fixed in a shaft of wood, from which it had been wrenched by the strength with which the barb, after the thrust, had been held by the parts surrounding the wound.

The barb was handed round to the jury, and every man cordially agreed with his neighbour that he had never seen anything of the kind before; it was equally strange to all of them.

The squire, who took the catastrophe with great coolness, gave evidence to the effect that he had seen his son on the morning previous to the discovery of the murder, and about noon—seventeen and a half hours before the catastrophe was discovered. He did not know his son was about to leave town, where he had been staying. He added that he had not missed the young man; his son was in the habit of being his own master, and going where he liked. He could offer no explanation as to why his son had returned to the country, or why the materials found upon him were there. He could offer no explanation in any way about anything connected with the matter.

It was said, as a scandal in Tram, that the squire exhibited no emotion upon giving his evidence, and that when he sat down after his examination be appeared relieved.

Furthermore, it was intimated that upon being called upon to submit to a kind of cross-examination, he appeared to be anxious, and answered the few questions guardedly.

These questions were put by one of the jurymen—a solicitor's clerk (of some acuteness it was evident), who was the Tram oracle.

It is perhaps necessary for the right understanding of this case, that these questions should be here reported, and their answers also.

They ran as follows:—

"Do you think your son died where he was found?"

"I have formed no opinion."

"Do you think he had been in your house?"

"Certainly not."

"Why are you so certain?"

"Because had he entered the house, my housekeeper would have known of his coming."

"Is your housekeeper here?"

"Yes."

"Has it been intended that she should be called as a witness?"

"Yes."

"Do you think your son attempted to break into your house?"

[The reason for this question I will make apparent shortly. By the way, I should, perhaps, here at once explain that I obtained all these particulars of the evidence from the county paper.]

"Do you think your son attempted to break into your house?"

"Why should he?"

"That is not my question. Do you think he attempted to break into your house?"

"No, I do not."

"You swear that, Mr. Petleigh?"

[By the way, there was no love lost between the squire and the Tram oracle, for the simple reason that not any existed that could be spilt.]

"I do swear it."

"Do you think there was anybody in the house he wished to visit clandestinely?"

"No."

"Who were in the house?"

"Mrs. Quinion, my housekeeper, and one servant woman."

"Is the servant here?"

"Yes."

"What kind of a woman is she?"

"Really Mr. Mortoun you can see her and judge for yourself."

"So we can. I am only going to ask one question more."

"I reserve to myself the decision whether I shall or shall not answer it."

"I think you will answer it, Mr. Petleigh."

"It remains, sir, to be seen. Put your question."

"It is very simple—do you intend to offer a reward for the discovery of the murderer of your son?"

The squire made no reply.

"You have heard my question, Mr. Petleigh."

"I have."

"And what is your answer?"

The squire paused for some moments. I should state that I am adding the particulars of the inquest I picked up, or detected if you like better, to the information afforded by the county paper to which I have already referred.

"I refuse to reply," said the squire.

Mortoun thereupon applied to the coroner for his ruling.

Now it appears evident to me that this juryman had some hidden motive in thus questioning the squire, If this were so, I am free to confess I never discovered it beyond any question of doubt. I may or I may not have hit on his motive. I believe I did.

It is clear that the question Mr. Mortoun urged was badly put, for how could the father decide whether he would offer a reward for the discovery of a murderer who did not legally exist till after the finding of the jury? And indeed it may furthermore be added that this question had no bearing upon the elucidation of the mystery, or at all events it had no apparent bearing upon the facts of the catastrophe.

It is evident that Mr. Mortoun was actuated in all probability by one of two motives, both of which were obscure. One might have been an attempt really to obtain a clue to the murder, the other might have been the endeavour to bring the squire, with whom it has been said he lived had friends, into disrespect with the county.

The oracle-juryman immediately applied to the coroner, who at once admitted that the question was not pertinent, but nevertheless urged the squire as the question had been put to answer it.

It is evident that the coroner saw the awkward position in which the squire was placed, and spoke as he did in order to enable the squire to come out of the difficulty in the least objectionable manner.

But as I have said, Mr. Petleigh, all his incongruities and faults apart, was a clear-seeing man of a good and clear mind. As I saw the want of consistency in the question, as I read it, so he must have remarked the same failure when it was addressed to him.

For after patiently hearing the coroner to the end of his remarks, Petleigh said, quietly,—

"How can I say I will offer a reward for the discovery of certain murderers when the jury have not yet returned a verdict of murder?"

"But supposing the jury do return such a verdict?" asked Mortoun.

"Why then it will be time for you to ask your question."

I learnt that the juryman smiled as he bowed and said he was satisfied.

It appears to me that at that point Mr. Mortoun must have either gained that information which fitted in with his theory, or, accepting the lower motive for his question, that he felt he had now sufficiently damaged the squire in the opinion of the county. For the reporters were at work, and every soul present knew that not a word said would escape publication in the county paper.

Mr. Mortoun however was to be worsted within the space of a minute.

"Have you ceased questioning me, gentlemen?" asked the squire.

The coroner bowed, it appeared.

"Then," continued the squire, "before I sit down—and you will allow me to remain in the room until the inquiry is terminated—I will state that of my own free will which I would not submit to make public upon an illegal and a totally uncalled-for attempt at compulsion. Should the jury bring in a verdict of murder against unknown persons, I shall *not* offer a reward for the discovery of those alleged murderers."

"Why not?" asked the coroner, who I learnt afterwards admitted that the question was utterly unpardonable.

"Because," said Squire Petleigh, "it is quite my opinion that no *murder* has been committed."

According to the newspaper report these words were followed by "sensation."

"No murder?" said the coroner.

"No; the death of the deceased was, I am sure, an accident."

"What makes you think that, Mr. Petleigh?"

"The nature of the death. Murders are not committed, I should think, in any such extraordinary manner as that by which my son came to his end. I have no more to say."

"Here," says the report, "the squire took his seat."

The next witness called—the gardener who had discovered the body had already been heard, and simply testified to the finding of the body—was Margaret Quinion, the housekeeper.

Her depositions were totally valueless from my point of view, that of the death of the young squire. She stated simply that she had gone to bed at the usual time (about ten) on the previous night, and that Dinah Yarton retired just previously, and to the same room. She heard no noise during the night, was disturbed in no way whatever until the alarm was given by the gardener.

In her turn Mrs. Quinion was now questioned by the solicitor's clerk, Mr. Mortoun.

"Do you and this—what is her name?—Dinah Yarton; do you and she sleep alone at Petleighcote?"

"Yes—when the family is away."

"Are you not afraid to do so?"

"No."

"Why?"

"Why should I be?"

"Well—most women are afraid to sleep in large lonely houses by themselves. Are you not afraid of burglars?"

"No."

"Why not?"

"Simply because burglars would find so little at Petleighcote to steal that they would be very foolish to break into the house."

"But there is a good deal of plate in the house—isn't there?"

"It all goes up to town with Mr. Petleigh."

"All, ma'am?"

"Every ounce—as a rule."

"You say the girl sleeps in your room?"

"In my room."

"Is she an attractive girl?"

"No."

"Is she unattractive?"

"You will have an opportunity of judging, for she will be called as a witness, sir."

"Oh; you don't think, do you, that there was anything between this young person and your young master?"

"Between Dinah and young Mr. Petleigh?"

"Yes."

"I think there could hardly be any affair between them, for [here she smiled] they have never seen each other—the girl having come to Petleighcote from the next county only three weeks since, and three months after the family had gone to town."

"Oh; pray have you not expected your master's son home recently?"

"I have not expected young Mr. Petleigh home recently—he never comes home when the family is away."

"Was he not in the habit of coming to Petleighcote unexpectedly?"

"No."

"You know that for a fact?"

"I know that for a fact."

"Was the deceased kept without money?"

"I know nothing of the money arrangements between the father and son."

"Well—do you know that often he wanted money?"

"Really—I decline to answer that question."

"Well—did he borrow money habitually from you?"

"I decline also to answer that question."

"You say you heard nothing in the night?"

"Not anything."

"What did you do when you were alarmed by the gardener in the morning?"

"I am at a loss to understand your question."

"It is very plain, nevertheless. What was your first act after hearing the catastrophe?"

[After some consideration] "It is really almost impossible, I should say, upon such terrible occasions as was that, to be able distinctly to say what is one's first act or words, but I believe the first thing I did, or the first I remember, was to look after Dinah."

"And why could she not look after herself?"

"Simply because she had fallen into a sort of epileptic fit—to which she is subject—upon seeing the body."

"Then you can throw no light upon this mysterious affair?"

"No light: all I know of it was the recognition of the body of Mr. Petleigh, junior, in the morning."

The girl Dinah Yarton was now called, but no sooner did the unfortunate young woman, waiting in the hall of the public-house at which the inquest was held, hear her name, than she swooped into a fit which totally precluded her from giving any evidence "except," as the county paper facetiously remarked, "the proof by her screams that her lungs were in a very enviable condition."

"She will soon recover," said Mrs. Quinion, "and will be able to give what evidence she can."

"And what will that be, Mrs. Quinion?" asked the solicitor's clerk.

"I am not able to say, Mr. Mortoun," she replied.

The next witness called (and here as an old police-constable I may remark upon the unbusiness-like way in which the witnesses were arranged)—the next witness called was the doctor.

His evidence was as follows, omitting the purely professional points. "I was called to the deceased on Tuesday morning, at near upon six in the morning. I recognized the body as that of Mr. Petleigh junior. Life was quite extinct. He had been dead about seven or eight hours, as well as I could judge. That would bring his death about ten or eleven on the previous night. Death had been caused by a stab, which had penetrated the left lung. The deceased had bled inwardly. The instrument which had caused death had remained in the wound, and stopped what little effusion of blood there would otherwise have been. Deceased literally died from suffocation, the blood leaking into the lungs and filling them. All the other organs of the body were in a healthy condition. The instrument by which death was produced is one with which I have no acquaintance. It is a kind of iron arrow, very roughly made, and with a shaft. It must have been fixed in some kind of handle when it was used, and which must have yielded and loosed the barb when an attempt was made to withdraw it—an attempt which had been made, because I found that one of the flanges of the arrow had caught behind a rib. I repeat that I am totally unacquainted with the instrument with which death was effected. It is remarkably coarse and rough. The deceased might have lived a quarter of a minute after the wound had been inflicted. He would not in all probability have called out. There is no evidence of the least struggle having taken place—not a particle of evidence can I find to show that the deceased had exhibited even any knowledge of danger. And yet, nevertheless, supposing the deceased not to have been asleep at the time of the murder, for murder it undoubtedly was, or man-slaughter, he must have seen his assailant, who, from the position of the weapon, must have been more before than behind him. Assuredly the death was the result of either murder or accident, and not the result of suicide, because I will stake my professional reputation that it would be quite impossible for any man to thrust such an instrument into his body with such a force as in this case has been used, as is proved by the cutting of a true bone-formed rib. Nor could a suicide, under such circumstances as those of the present catastrophe, have thrust the dart in the direction which this took. To sum up, it is my opinion that the deceased was murdered without, on his part, any knowledge of the murderer."

Mr. Mortoun cross-examined the doctor:

To this gentleman's inquiries he answered willingly.

"Do you think, Dr. Pitcherley, that no blood flowed externally?"

"Of that I am quite sure."

"How?"

"There were no marks of blood on the clothes."

"Then the inference stands that no blood stained the place of the murder?"

"Certainly."

"Then the body may have been brought an immense way, and no spots of blood would form a clue to the road?"

"Not one."

"Is it your impression that the murder was committed far away from the spot, or near the place where the body was found?"

"This question is one which it is quite out of my power to answer, Mr. Mortoun, my duty here being to give evidence as to my being called to the deceased, and as to the cause of death. But I need not tell you that I have formed my own theory of the catastrophe, and if the jury desire to have it, I am ready to offer it for their consideration."

Here there was a consultation, from which it resulted that the jury expressed themselves very desirous of obtaining the doctor's impression.

[I have no doubt the following words led the jury to their decision.]

The medical gentleman said:—

"It is my impression that this death resulted out of a poaching—I will not say affray—but accident. It is thoroughly well-known in these districts, and at such a juncture as the present I need feel no false delicacy, Mr. Petleigh, in making this statement, that young Petleigh was much given to poaching. I believe that he and his companions were out poaching—I myself on two separate occasions, being called out to night-cases, saw the young gentleman under very suspicious circumstances— and that one of the party was armed with the weapon which caused the death, and which may have been carried at the end of such a heavy stick as is frequently used for flinging at rabbits. I suppose that by some frightful accident—we all know how dreadful are the surgical accidents which frequently arise when weapons are in use— the young man was wounded mortally, and so died, after the frightened companion had hurriedly attempted to withdraw the arrow, only to leave the barb sticking in the body and hooked behind a rib, while the force used in the resistance of the bone caused the weapon to part company from the haft. The discovery of the body outside the father's house can then readily be accounted for. His companions knowing who he was, and dreading their identification with an act which could but result in their own condemnation of character, carried the body to the threshold of his father's house, and there left it. This," the doctor concluded, "appears to me the most rational mode I can find of accounting for the circumstances of this remarkable and deplorable case. I apologize to Mr. Petlcigh for the slur to which I may have committed myself in referring to the character of that gentleman's son, the deceased, but my excuse must rest in this fact, that where a crime or catastrophe is so obscure that the criminal, or guilty person, may be in one of many directions, it is but just to narrow the circle of inquiry as much as possible, in order to avoid the resting of suspicion upon the greater number of individuals. If, however, any one can suggest a more lucid explanation of the catastrophe than mine, I shall indeed be glad to admit I was wrong."

[There can be little question, I repeat, that Dr. Pitcherley's analysis fitted in very satisfactorily and plausibly with the facts of the case.]

Mr. Mortoun asked Dr. Pitcherley no more questions.

The next witness called was the police-constable of Tram, a stupid, hopeless dolt, as I found to my cost, who was good at a rustic public-house row, but who as a detective was not worth my dog Dart.

It appeared that he gave his flat evidence with a stupidity which called even for the rebuke of the coroner.

All he could say was, that he was called, and that he went, and that he saw whose body it "be'd." That was "arl" he could say.

Mr. Mortoun took him in hand, but even he could I do nothing with the man.

"Had many persons been on the spot where the body was found before he arrived?"

"Noa."

"How was that?"

"Whoy, 'cos Toom Broown, the gard'ner, 'coomed t'him at wuncet, and 'cos Toom Broown coomed t'him furst, 'cas he's cot wur furst coomed too."

This was so, as I found when I went down to Tram. The gardener, Brown, panic-stricken, after calling to, and obtaining the attention of the housekeeper, had rushed off to the village for that needless help which all panic-stricken people will seek, and the constable's cottage happening to be the first dwelling he reached the constable obtained the first alarm. Now, had the case been conducted properly, the constable being the first man to get the alarm, would have obtained such evidence as would at once have put the detectives on the right scent.

The first two questions put by the lawyerlike juryman showed that he saw how important the evidence might have been which this witness, Joseph Higgins by name, should have given had he but known his business.

The first question was—

"It had rained, hadn't it, on the Monday night?"

[That previous to the catastrophe]

"Ye-es t'had rained," Higgins replied.

Then followed this important question:

"You were on the spot one of the very first. Did you notice if there were any foot-steps about?"

It appears to me very clear that Mr. Mortoun was here following up the theory of the catastrophe offered by the doctor. It would be clear that if several poaching companions had carried the young squire, after death, to the hall-door, that, as rain had fallen during the night, there would inevitably be many boot-marks on the soft ground.

This question put, the witness asked, "Wh-a-at?"

The question was repeated.

"Noa," he replied; "ah didn't see noa foot ma-arks."

"Did you look for any?"

"Noa; ah didn't look for any."

"Then you don't know your business," said Mr. Mortoun.

And the juryman was right; for I may tell the reader that boot-marks have sent more men to the gallows, as parts of circumstantial evidence, than any other proof whatever; indeed, the evidence of the boot-mark is terrible. A nail fallen out, or two or three put very close together, a broken nail, or all the nails perfect, have, times out of number, identified the boot of the suspected man with the boot-mark near the murdered, and has been the first link of the chain of evidence which has dragged a murderer to the gallows, or a minor felon to the hulks.

Indeed, if I were advising evildoers on the best means of avoiding detection, I would say by all means take a second pair of boots in your pocket, and when you near the scene of your work change those you have on for those you have in your pocket, and do your wickedness in these latter; flee from the scene in these latter, and when you have "made" some distance, why return to your other boots, and carefully hide the tell-tale pair. Then the boots you wear will rather be a proof of your innocence than presumable evidence of your guilt.

Nor let any one be shocked at this public advice to rascals; for I flatter myself I have a counter-mode of foiling such a felonious arrangement as this one of two pairs of boots. And as I have disseminated the mode amongst the police, any attempt to put the suggestions I have offered actually into action, would be attended with greater chances of detection than would be incurred by running the ordinary risk.

To return to the subject in hand.

The constable of Tram, the only human being in the town, Mortoun apart perhaps, who should have known, in the ordinary course of his duty, the value of every footmark near the dead body, had totally neglected a precaution which, had he observed it, must have led to a discovery (and an immediate one), which in consequence of his dullness was never publicly made.

Nothing could be more certain than this, that what is called foot-mark evidence was totally wanting.

The constable taking no observations, not the cutest detective in existence could have obtained any evidence of this character, for the news of the catastrophe spreading, as news only spreads in villages, the rustics trumped up in scores, and so obliterated what footmarks might have existed.

To be brief, Mr. Josh. Higgins could give no evidence worth hearing.

And now the only depositions which remained to be given were those of Dinah Yarton.

She came into court "much reduced," said the paper from which I gain these particulars, "from the effects of the succession of fits which she had fallen into and struggled out of."

She was so stupid that every question had to be repeated in half-a-dozen shapes before she could offer a single reply. It took four inquiries to get at her name, three to know where she lived, five to know what she was; while the coroner and the jury, after a score of questions, gave over trying to ascertain whether she knew the nature of an oath. However, as she stated that she was quite sure she would go to a "bad place" if she did not speak the truth, she was declared to be a perfectly competent witness, and I have no doubt she was badgered accordingly.

And as Mr. Mortoun got more particulars out of her than all the rest of the questioners put together, perhaps it will not be amiss, as upon her evidence turned the whole of my actions so far as I was concerned, to give that gentleman's questions and her answers in full, precisely as they were quoted in the greedy county paper, which doubtless looked upon the whole case as a publishing godsend, the proprietors heartily wishing that the inquest might be adjourned a score of times for further evidence.

"Well now, Dinah," said Mr. Mortoun, "what time did you go to bed on Monday?"

[The answers were generally get after much hammering in on the part of the inquirist. I will simply return them at once as ultimately given.]

"Ten."

"Did you go to sleep?"

"Noa—Ise didunt goa to sleep."

"Why not?"

"Caize Ise couldn't."

"But why?"

"Ise wur thinkin'."

"What of?"

"Arl manner o' thing'."

"Tell us one of them?"

[No answer—except symptoms of another fit.]

"Tut—tut! Well, did you go to sleep at last?"

"Ise did."

"Well, when did you wake?"

"Ise woke when missus ca'd I."

"What time?"

"Doant know clock."

"Was it daylight?"

"E-es, it wur day."

"Did you wake during the night?"

"E-es, wuncet."

"How did that happen?"

"Doant knaw."

"Did you hear anything?"

"Noa."

"Did you think you heard anything?"

"E-es."

"What?"

"Whoy, it movin'."

"What was moving?"

"W'hoy, the box."

"Box—tut, tut," said the lawyer, "answer me properly."

Now here he raised his voice, and I have no doubt Dinah had to thank the juryman for the return of her fits.

"Do you hear?—answer me properly."

"E-es."

"When you woke up did you hear any noise?"

"Noa."

"But you thought you heard a noise?"

"E-es, in the—"

"Tut, tut. Never mind the box—where was it?"

"Ter box? In t'hall!"

"No—no, the noise."

"In t'hall, zur!"

"What—the noise was?"

"Noa, zur, ter box."

"There, my good girl," says the Tram oracle, "never mind the box, I want you to think of this—did you hear any noise *outside the house?*"

"Noa."

"But you said you heard a noise?"

"No, zur, I didunt."

"Well, but you said you thought you heard a noise?"

"E-es."

"Well—where?"

"In ter box—"

Here, said the county paper, the lawyer, shaking his hand on the table before him, continued—

"Speak of the box once more, my girl, and to prison you go."

"Prizun!" says the luckless witness.

"Yes, jail and bread and water!"

And thereupon the unhappy witness without any further remarks plunged into a fit, and had to be carried out, battling with that strength which convulsions appear to bring with them, and in the arms of three men, who had quite their work to do to keep her moderately quiet.

"I don't think, gentlemen," said the coroner, "that this witness is material. In the first place, it seems doubtful to me whether she is capable of giving evidence; and, in the second, I believe she has little evidence to give—so little that I doubt the policy of adjourning the inquest till her recovery. It appears to me that it would be cruelty to force this poor young woman again into the position she has just endured, unless you are satisfied that she is a material witness. I think she has said enough to show that she is not. It appears certain, from her own statement, that she retired to rest with Mrs. Quinion, and knows nothing more of what occurred till the housekeeper awoke her in the morning, after she herself had received the alarm. I suggest, therefore, that what evidence she could give is included in that already before the jury, and given by the housekeeper."

The jury coincided in the remarks made by the coroner, Mr. Mortoun, however, adding that he was at a loss to comprehend the girl's frequent reference to the box. Perhaps Mrs. Quinion could help to elucidate the mystery.

The housekeeper immediately rose.

"Mrs. Quinion," said Mr. Mortoun, "can you give any explanation as to what the young person meant by referring to a box?"

"No."

"There are of course boxes at Petleighcote?"

"Beyond all question."

"Any box in particular?"

"No box in particular."

"No box which is spoken of as *the* box?"

"Not any."

"The girl said it was in the hall. Is there a box in the hall?"

"Yes, several."

"What are they?"

"There is a clog and boot box, a box on the table in which letters for the post are placed when the family is at home, and from which they are removed every day at four; and also a box fixed to the wall, the use of which I have never been able to discover, and of the removal of which I have several times spoken to Mr. Petleigh."

"How large is it?"

"About a foot-and-a-half square and three feet deep."

"Locked?"

"No, the flap is always open."

"Has the young woman ever betrayed any fear of this box?"

"Never."

"You have no idea to what box in the hall she referred in her evidence?"

"Not the least idea."

"Do you consider the young woman weak in her head?"

"She is decidedly not of strong intellect."

"And you suppose this box idea a mere fancy?"

"Of course."

"And a recent one?"

"I never heard her refer to a box before."

"That will do."

The paper whence I take my evidence describes Mrs. Quinion as a woman of very great self-possession, who gave what she had to say with perfect calmness and slowness of speech.

This being all the evidence, the coroner was about to sum up, when the Constable Higgins remembered that he had forgotten something, and came forward in a great hurry to repair his error.

He had not produced the articles found on the deceased.

These articles were a key and a *black crape mask*.

The squire being recalled, and the key shown to him, he identified the key as (he believed) one of his "household keys." It was of no particular value, and it did not matter if it remained in the hands of the police.

The report continued: "The key is now in the custody of the constable."

With regard to the crape mask the squire could offer no explanation concerning it.

The coroner then proceeded to sum up, and in doing so he paid many well-termed compliments to the doctor for that gentleman's view of the matter (which I have no doubt threw off all interest in the matter on the part of the public, and slackened the watchfulness of the detective force, many of whom, though very clever, are equally simple, and accept a plain and straightforward statement with extreme willingness)—and urged that the discovery of the black crape mask appeared to be very much like corroborative proof of the doctor's suggestion. "The young man," said the coroner, "would, if poaching, be exceedingly desirous of hiding his face, considering his position in the county, and then the finding of this black crape mask upon the body would, if the poaching explanation were accepted, be a very natural discovery. But—"

And then the coroner proceeded to explain to the jury that they had to decide not upon suppositions' but facts. They might all be convinced that Dr. Pitcherley's explanation was the true one, but in law it could not be accepted. Their verdict must be in accordance with facts, and the simple facts of the case were these:—A man was found dead, and the causes of his death were such that it was impossible to believe that the deceased had been guilty of suicide. They would therefore under the circumstances feel it was their duty to return an open verdict of murder.

The jury did not retire, but at the expiration of a consultation of three minutes, in which (I learnt) the foreman, Mr. Mortoun, had all the talking to himself, the jury gave in a verdict of wilful murder against some person or persons unknown.

Thus ended the inquest.

And I have little hesitation in saying it was one of the weakest inquiries of that kind which had ever taken place. It was characterized by no order, no comprehension, no common sense.

The facts of the case made some little stir, but the plausible explanations offered by the doctor, and the several coinciding circumstances, deprived the affair of much of its interest, both to the public and the detective force; to the former, because they had little room for ordinary conjecture; to the latter, because I need not say the general, the chief motive power in the detective is gain, and here the probabilities of profit were almost annihilated by the possibility that a true explanation of the facts of this affair had been offered, while it was such as promised little hope of substantial reward.

But the mere fact of my here writing this narrative will be sufficient to show that *I* did not coincide with the general view taken of the business.

That I was right the following pages will I think prove.

Of course the Government offered the usual reward, £100, of which proclamation is published in all cases of death where presumably foul play has taken place.

But it was not the ordinary reward which tempted me to choose this case for investigation. It was several peculiar circumstances which attracted me.

They were as follows:—

(1) Why did the father refuse to offer a reward?
(2) Why did the deceased have one of the household keys with him at the time of his death, and how came he to have it at all?
(3) What did the box mean?

    (1) It seemed to me that the refusal by the father to offer a reward must arise from one of three sources. Either he did not believe a murder had been committed, and therefore felt the offer was needless; or he knew murder was committed, and did not wish to accelerate the action of the police; or, thirdly, whether he believed or disbelieved in the murder, knew or did not know it to be a murder, that he was too sordid to offer a reward by the payment of which he would lose without gaining any corresponding benefit.

    (2) How came the deceased to have one of the keys of his father's establishment in his pocket? Such a possession was extremely unusual, and more inexplicable. How came he to possess it? Why did he possess it? What was he going to do with it?

    (3) What did the box mean? Did the unhappy girl Dinah Yarton refer to any ordinary or extraordinary box? It appeared to me that if she referred to any ordinary box it must be an ordinary box under extraordinary circumstances. But fools have very rarely any imagination, and knowing this I was not disposed to accredit Dinah with any ability to invest the box ordinary with any extraordinary attributes. And then remembering that there was nobody in the house to play tricks with her but a grave house-keeper who would not be given to that kind of thing, I came to the conclusion that the box in question was an extraordinary box. "*It was in the hall.*" Now if the box were no familiar box, and it was in

the hall, the inference stood that it had just arrived there. Did I at this time associate the box intimately with the ease? I think not.

At all events I determined to go down to Tram and investigate the case, and as with us detectives action is as nearly simultaneous with determination to act as it can be, I need not say that, making up my mind to visit Tram, I was soon nearing that station by the first train which started after I had so determined.

Going down I arranged mentally the process with which I was to go through.

Firstly, I must see the constable.

Secondly, I must talk to the girl Dinah.

Thirdly, I must examine the place of the murder.

All this would be easy work.

But what followed would be more difficult.

This was to apply what I should discover to any persons whom my discoveries might implicate, and see what I could make of it all.

Arrived at Tram at once I found out the constable, and I am constrained to say—a greater fool I never indeed did meet.

He was too stupid to be anything else than utterly, though idiotically, honest.

Under my corkscrew-like qualities as a detective he had no more chance than a tender young cork with a corkscrew proper. I believe that to the end of the chapter he never comprehended that I was a detective. His mind could not grasp the idea of a police officer in petticoats.

I questioned him as the shortest way of managing him, smoothing his suspicions and his English with shillings of the coin of this realm.

Directly I came face to face with him I knew what I had to do. I had simply to question him. And here I set out my questions and his answers as closely as I can recollect them, together with a narrative of the actions which resulted out of both.

I told him at once I was curious to know all I could about the affair; and as I illustrated this statement with the exhibition of the first shilling, in a moment I had the opportunity of seeing every tooth he had in his head—thirty-two. Not one was missing.

"There was found on the body a key and a mask—where are they?"

"War be they—why, in my box, sin' I be coonstubble!"

"Will you show them to me?"

"Oh, Ise show they ye!"

And thereupon he went to a box in the corner of the room, and unlocked it solemnly.

As the constable of Tram it was perfectly natural that he should keep possession of these objects, since a verdict of wilful murder had been given, and at any time, therefore, inquiries might have to be made.

From this box he took out a bundle; this opened, a suit of clothes came to view, and from the middle of these he produced a key and a mask.

I examined the key first. It was a well-made—a beautifully-made key, and very complicated. We constables learn in the course of our experience a good deal about keys, and therefore I saw at a glance that it was the key to a complicated and more than ordinarily valuable lock.

On the highly-polished loop of the key a carefully-cut number was engraved— No. 13.

Beyond all question this key was no ordinary key to an ordinary lock.

Now, extraordinary locks and keys guard extraordinary treasures.

The first inference I arrived at, therefore, from my interview with the Tram constable was this—that the key found upon the body opened a look put upon something valuable.

Then I examined the mask.

It was of black crape, stretched upon silver wire. I had never seen anything like it before, although as a detective I had been much mixed up with people who wore masks, both at masquerades and on other occasions even less satisfactory.

I therefore inferred that the mask was of foreign manufacture.

[I learnt ultimately that I was right, and no great credit to me either, for that which is not white may fairly be guessed to be of some other colour. The mask was what is called abroad a *masque de luxe*, a mask which, while it changes the countenance sufficiently to prevent recognition, is made so delicately that the material, crape, admits of free perspiration—a condition which inferior masks will not admit.]

"Anything else found on the body?"

"Noa."

"No skeleton keys?"

"Noa; on'y wan key."

So, if the constable were right, and *if the body had remained as it fell*, when found by the gardener, Brown, the only materials found were a key and mask.

But, surely, there was something else in the pockets.

"'Was there no purse found?" I asked.

"Noa; noa poorse."

"No handkerchief?"

"Ooh, 'ees; thar war a kerchiefer."

"Where is it?"

He went immediately to the bundle.

"Are these the clothes in which he was found?"

"Ees, they be."

So far, so good, I felt.

The constable, stupid and honest as he appeared, and as he existed, was very suspicious, and therefore I felt that he had to be managed most carefully.

Having hooked the handkerchief out from some recess in the bundle with the flattest forefinger I think I ever remarked, he handed it to me.

It was a woman's handkerchief.

It was new; had apparently never been used; there was no crease nor dirt upon it, as there would have been had it been carried long in the pocket; and it was marked in the corner "Freddy"—undoubtedly the diminution for Frederica.

"Was the 'kerchiefer,'" I asked, using the word the constable had used—"was it wrapped in anything?"

"Noa."

"What pocket was it in?"

"Noa poockut."

"Where was it, then?"

"In's weskit, agin 's hart, an' joost aboove th' ole made in 'um."

Now, what was the inference of the handkerchief.

It was a woman's; it was not soiled; it had not been worn long; it was thrust in his breast; it was marked.

The inference stood thus:

This handkerchief belonged to a woman, in all probability young, whose Christian name was Frederica; as it was not soiled, and as it was not blackened by wear, it had recently been given to, or taken, by him; and as the handkerchief was found in the breast of his shirt, it appeared to have been looked upon with favour. Suppose then we say that it was a gift by a young woman to the deceased about the time when he was setting out on his expedition?

Now, the deceased had left London within eighteen hours of his death; had the handkerchief been given him in London or after he left town?

Again, had the mask anything to do with this woman?

Taking it up again and re-examining it, the delicacy of the fabric struck me more than before, and raising it close to my eyes to make a still narrower examination I found that it was scented.

The inference stood, upon the whole, that this mask had belonged to a woman.

Again I began to question Joseph Higgins, constable.

"I should be glad to look at the clothes," I said.

"Lard, thee may look," said the constable.

They were an ordinary suit of clothes, such as a middle-class man would wear of a morning, but not so good or fashionable as one might have expected to find in wear by the son of a wealthy squire.

[This apparent incongruity was soon explained away by my learning, as I did in the evening of my arrival, that the squire was mean and even parsimonious.]

There was nothing in the pockets, but my attention was called to the *fluffy* state of the cloth, which was a dark grey, and which therefore in a great measure hid this fluffiness.

"You have not been taking care of these clothes, I am afraid."

"They be joost as they coomed arf him!"

"What, was all this fluff about the cloth?"

"Yoa."

[Yoa was a new version of "e-es," and both meant "yes."]

"They look as though they had been rolled about a bed."

"Noa."

The clothes in question were stained on their under side with gravel-marks, and they were still damp on these parts.

The remarking of this fact, recalled to my mind something which came out at the inquest, and which now I remembered and kept in mind while examining the state of the clothes.

On the Monday night, as the body was discovered on the Tuesday morning, it had rained.

Now the clothes were not damp all over, for the fluff was quite wavy, and flew about in the air. It was necessary to know what time it left off raining on the Monday night, or Tuesday morning.

It was very evident that the clothes had not been exposed to rain between the time of their obtaining the fluffiness and the discovery of the body. Therefore ascertain at what hour the rain ceased, and I had the space of time (the hour at which the body was discovered being half-past five) within which the body had been deposited.

The constable knew nothing about the rain, and I believe it was at this point, in spite of the shillings, that the officer began to show rustic signs of impatience.

I may add here that I found the rain had only ceased at three o'clock on the Tuesday morning. It was therefore clear that the body had been deposited between three and half-past five—*two hours and a-half.*

This discovery I made that same evening of my landlady, a most useful person.

Now, does it not strike the reader that three o'clock on a May morning, and when the morning had almost come, was an extraordinarily late hour at which to be poaching?

This indisputable fact, taken into consideration with the needlessness of the mask (for poachers do not wear masks), and the state of the clothes, to say nothing of the kind of clothes found on the deceased, led me to throw over Mr. Martoun's theory that the young squire had met his death in a poaching affray, or rather while out on a poaching expedition.

I took a little of the fluff from the clothes and carefully put it away in my pocket-book.

The last thing I examined was the barb which had caused the death.

And here I admit I was utterly foiled—completely, positively foiled. I had never seen anything of the kind before—never.

It was a very coarse iron barb, shaped something like a queen's broad arrow, only that the flanges widened from their point, so that each appeared in shape like the blade of a much-worn penknife. The shaft was irregular and perhaps even coarser than the rest of the work. The weapon was made of very poor iron, for I turned its point by driving it, not by any means heavily, against the frame of the window—to the intense disgust of the constable, whose exclamation, I remember thoroughly well, was "Woa."

Now what did I gain by my visit to the constable? This series of suppositions:—

That the deceased was placed where he was found between three and half-past five A.M. on the Tuesday; that he was not killed from any result of a poaching expedition; and that he had visited a youngish woman named Frederica a few hours before death, and of whom he had received a handkerchief and possibly a mask.

The only troublesome point was the key, which, by the way, had been found in a small fob-pocket in the waist of the coat.

While taking my tea at the inn at which I had set down, I need not say I asked plenty of questions, and hearing a Mrs. Green frequently referred to, I surmised she was a busybody, and getting her address, as that of a pleasant body who let lodgings, I may at once add that that night I slept in the best room of the pleasant body's house.

She was the most incorrigible talker ever I encountered. Nor was she devoid of sharpness; indeed, with more circumspection than she possessed, or let me say, with ordinary circumspection, she would have made a good ordinary police-officer, and had she possessed that qualification I might have done something for her. As it was the idea could not be entertained for any part of a moment.

She was wonderful, this Mrs. Green.

You only had to put a question on any point, and she abandoned the subject in which she had been indulging, and sped away on a totally new tack.

She was ravenous to talk of the murder; for it was her foregone conclusion that murder had been committed.

In a few words, all the information afforded to this point, which has not arisen out of my own seeking, or came by copy from the county newspaper (and much of that information which is to follow) all proceeded from the same gushing source— Mrs. Green.

All I had to do was to put another question when I thought we had exhausted the previous one, and away she went again at score, and so we continued from seven to eleven. It was half-past eight for nine before she cleared away the long-since cold and sloppy tea-things.

"And what has become of Mrs. Quinion?" I asked, in the course of this to me valuable entertainment on the part of Mrs. Green, throughout the whole of which she never asked me my business in these parts (though I felt quite sure so perfect a busybody was dying to know my affairs), because any inquiry would have called for a reply, and this was what she could not endure while I was willing to listen to her. Hence she chose the less of two evils.

"And what became of the girl?"

"What gal?"

"Dinah."

"Dinah Yarton?"

"Yes. I believe that *was* her name."

"Lor' bless 'ee! it's as good and as long as a blessed big book to tell 'ee all about Dinah Yarton. She left two days after, and they not having a bed for she at the Lamb and Flag, and I having a bed, her came here—the Lamb and Flag people always sending me their over beds, bless 'em, bless 'ee! and that's how I comes to know arl about it, bless 'ee, and the big box!"

[The box—now this was certainly what I did want Mrs. Green to come to. The reader will remember that I laid some stress upon the girl's frequent reference to the trunk.]

"Bless 'ee! the big box caused arl the row, because Mrs. Quinion said she were a fool to have been frightened by a big box; but so Dinah would be, and so her did, being probable in the nex' county at this time, at Little Pocklington, where her mother lives making lace, and her father a farmer, and where her was born —Dinah, and not her mother—on the 1st o' April, 1835, being new twenty years old. What art thee doing! bless 'ee!"

[I was making a note of Little Pocklington.]

Nor will I here make any further verbatim notes of Mrs. Green's remarks, but use them as they are required in my own way, and as in actuality really I did turn them to account.

I determined to see the girl at once; that is, after I had had a night's rest. And therefore next morning, after carefully seeing my box and bag were locked, I made a quick breakfast, and sallied out. Reaching the station, there was Mrs. Green. She had obviously got the start of me by crossing Goose Green fields, as in fact she told me.

She said she thought I must have dropped that, and had come to see.

"That" was a purse so old that it was a curiosity.

"Bless 'ee!" she says, "isn't yourn? Odd, beant it? But, bless 'ee! ye'll have to wait an hour for a train. There beant a train to anywhere for arl an hour."

"Then I'll take a walk," said I.

"Shall I come, and tark pleasant to 'ee?" asked Mrs. Green.

"No," I replied; "I've some business to transact."

I had an hour to spare, and remembering that I had seen the things at Higgins's by a failing evening light, I thought I would again visit that worthy, and make a second inspection.

It was perhaps well I did so.

Not that I discovered anything of further importance, but the atom of novelty of which I made myself master, helped to confirm me in my belief that the deceased had visited a young woman, probably a lady, a very short time before his death.

Higgins, a saddler by trade, was not at all delighted at my re-appearance, and really I was afraid I should have to state what I was in order to get my way, and then civilly bully him into secrecy. But happily his belief in me as a mild mad woman overcame his surliness, and so with the help of a few more shillings I examined once more the clothes found on the unfortunate young squire.

And now, in the full blazing spring morning sunlight, I saw what had missed my view on the previous evening. This was nothing less than a bright crimson scrap of silk braid, such as ladies use in prosecuting their embroidery studies.

This bit of braid had been wound round and round a breast button, and then tied in a nutty bow at the top.

"She is a lady," I thought; "and she was resting her head against his breast when she tied that bit of braid there. She is innocent, I should think, or she never would have done such a childish action as that."

Higgins put away the dead youth's clothes with a discontented air.

"Look ye yere—do'ee think ye'l want 'em wuncet more?"

"No."

"Wull, if ee do, 'ee wunt have 'un."

"Oh, very well," I said, and went back to the station. Of course there was Mrs. Green on the watch, though in the morning I had seen about the house symptoms of the day being devoted to what I have heard comic Londoners describe as "a water party"—in other words, a grand wash.

That wash Mrs. Green had deserted.

"Bless 'ee, I'm waitin' for a dear fren'!"

"Oh, indeed, Mrs. Green."

"Shall I take ticket for 'ee, dear?"

"Yes, if you like. Take it for Stokeley," said I.

"Four mile away," says Mrs. Green. "*I've* got a fren' at Stokeley. I wounds if your fren' be *my* fren'! Who *be* your fren', bless 'ee?"

"Mrs. Blotchley."

"What, her as lives near th' peump?" (pump)

"Yes."

"Oh, I don't know *she*."

It seemed to me Mrs. Green was awed—I never learnt by what, because as I never knew Mrs. Blotchley, and dropped upon her name by chance, and indeed never visited Stokeley, why Green had all the benefit of the discovery.

"And, Mrs. Green, if I am not home by nine, do not sit up for me."

"*Oh!*—goin' maybe to sleep at *her* hoose?"

"Very likely."

"*Oh!*"

And as Mrs. Green here dropped me a curtsey I have remained under the impression that Mrs. B. was a lady of consequence whose grandeur Mrs. Green saw reflected upon me.

I have no doubt the information she put at once in circulation helped to screen the actual purpose for which I had arrived at Tram from leaking out.

When the train reached Stokeley I procured another ticket on to Little Pocklington, and reached that town about two in the afternoon. It was not more than sixty miles from Tram.

The father of this Dinah Yarton was one of those small few-acre farmers who throughout the country are gradually but as certainly vanishing.

I may perhaps at once say that the poor girl Dinah had no less than three fits over the cross-examination to which I submitted her, and here (to the honour of rustic human nature) let it be recorded that actually I had to use my last resource, and show myself to be a police-officer, by the production of my warrant in the presence of the Little Pocklington constable, who was brought into the affair, before I could overcome the objections of the girl's father. He with much justifiable reason urged that the "darned" business had already half-killed his wench, and he would be "darned" if I should altogether send her out of the "warld."

As I have said, the unhappy girl had three fits, and I have no doubt the family were heartily glad when I had turned my back upon the premises.

The unhappy young woman had to make twenty struggles before she could find one reply.

Here I need not repeat her evidence to that point past which it was not carried when she stood before the coroner and jury, but I will commence from that point.

"Dinah," I inquired in a quiet tone, and I believe the fussiness betrayed by the girl's mother tended as much to the fits as the girl's own nervousness—"Dinah, what was all that about the big box?"

"Darn the box," said the mother.

And here it was that the unfortunate girl took her second fit.

"There, she's killed my Dinah now," said the old woman, and it must he confessed Dinah was horribly convulsed, and indeed looked frightful in the extreme. The poor creature was quite an hour fighting with the fit, and when she came to and opened her eyes, the first object they met made her shut them again, for that object was myself.

However, I had my duty to perform, and therein lies the excuse for my torture.

"What—oh——o-o-oh wha-at did thee say?"

"What about the big box?"

"Doa noa." [This was the mode in those parts of saying "I do not know."]

"Where was it?"

"In th' hall."

"Where did it come from?"

"Doa noa."

"How long had it been there?"

"Sin' the day afore."

"Who brought it?"

"Doa noa."

"Was it a man?"

"Noa."

"What then?"

"Two men."

"How did they come?"

"They coomed in a great big waggoon."

"And did they bring the box in the waggon?"

"Yoa." [This already I knew meant "Yes."]

"And they left the box at the hall?"

"Yoa."

"What then?"

"Whoa?" [This I guessed meant "What."]

"What did they say?"

"Zed box wur for squoire."

"Did they both carry it?"

"Yoa."

"How?"

"Carefool loike." [Here there were symptoms of an other convulsion]

"What became of the big box?"

"Doa noa."

"Did they come for it again?"

"Doa noa."

"Is it there now?"

"Noa."

"Then it went away again?"

"Yoa."

"You did not see it taken away?"

"Noa."

"Then how do you know it is not there now?"

"Doa noa."

"But you say it is not at the hall—how do you know that?"

"Mrs. Quanyan (Quinion) told I men had been for it."

"When was that?"

"After I'd been garne to bed."

"Was it there the next morning?"

"Whoa?"

"Was it there the morning when they found the young squire dead outside the door?"

And now "Diney," as her mother called her, plunged into the third fit, and in the early throes of that convulsion I was forced to leave her, for her father, an honest fellow, told me to leave his house, "arficer or no arficer," and that if I did not do so he would give me what he called a "sta-a-art."

Under the circumstances I thought that perhaps it was wise to go, and did depart accordingly.

That night I remained in Little Pocklington in the hope, in which I was so grievously disappointed, of discovering further particulars which the girl might have divulged to her companions. But in the first place Diney had no companions, and in the second all attempts to draw people out, for the case had been copied into that county paper which held sway at Little Pocklington, all attempts signally failed.

Upon my return to Tram, Mrs. Green received me with all the honours, clearly as a person who had visited Mrs. Blotchley, and I noticed that the parlour fire-place was decorated with a new stove-ornament in paper of a fiery and flaring description.

I thanked Mrs. Green, and in answer to that lady's inquiries I was happy to say Mrs. Blotchley was well—except a slight cold. Yes, I had slept there. What did I have for dinner at Mrs. Blotchley's? Well, really I had forgotten. "Dear heart," said Mrs. Green, "'ow unfortnet."

After seeing "Diney," and in coming home by the train (and indeed I can always think well while travelling), I turned over all that I had pinched out of Dinah Yarton in reference to the big box.

Did that box, or did it not, in any way relate to the death?

It was large; it had been carried by two men; and according to Dinah's information it had been removed again from the hall.

At all events I must find out what the box meant.

The whole affair was still so warm—not much more than a fortnight had passed since the occurrence—that I still felt sure all particulars about that date which had been noticed would be remembered.

I set Mrs. Green to work, for nobody could better suit my purpose.

"Mrs. Green, can you find out whether any strange carrier's cart or waggon, containing a very big box, was seen in Tram on the Monday, and the day before young Mr. Petleigh's body was found?"

I saw happiness in Mrs. Green's face; and having thus set her to work, I put myself in the best order, and went up to Petleighcote Hall.

The door was opened (with suspicious slowness) by a servant-woman, who closed it again before she took my message and a card to Mrs. Quinion. The message consisted of a statement that I had come after the character of a servant.

A few moments passed, and I was introduced into the housekeeper's presence.

I found her a calm-looking, fine, portly woman, with much quiet determination in her countenance. She was by no means badly featured.

She was quite self-possessed.

The following conversation took place between us. The reader will see that not the least reference was made by me to the real object of my visit—the prosecution of an inquiry as to the mode by which young Mr. Petleigh had met his death. And if the reader complains that there is much falsity in what I state, I would urge that as evil-doing is a kind of lie levelled at society, if it is to be conquered it must be met on the side of society, through its employés, by similar false action.

Here is the conversation.

"Mrs. Quinion, I believe?"

"Yes, as I am usually termed—but let that pass. You wish to see me?"

"Yes; I have called about the character of a servant."

"Indeed—who?"

"I was passing through Tram, where I shall remain some days, on my way from town to York, and I thought it would be wise to make a personal inquiry, which I find much the best plan in all affairs relating to my servants."

"A capital plan; but as you came from town, why did you not apply to the town housekeeper, since I have no doubt you take the young person from the town house?"

"There is the difficulty. I should take the young person, if her character were to answer, from a sort of charity. She has never been in town, and here's my doubt. However, if you give me any hope of the young person—"

"What is her name?"

"Dinah—Dinah—you will allow me to refer to my pocket-book."

"Don't take that trouble," said she, and I thought she looked pale; but her pallor might have been owing, I thought at the time, to the deep mourning she was wearing; "you mean Dinah Yarton."

"Yarton—that is the name. Do you think she will suit?"

"Much depends upon what she is wanted for."

"An under nurserymaid."

"Your own family?"

"Oh, dear no—a sister's."

"In town?"

[She asked this question most calmly.]

"No—abroad."

"Abroad?" and I remarked that she uttered the word with an energy which, though faint in itself, spoke volumes when compared with her previous serenity.

"Yes," I said, "my sister's family are about leaving England for Italy, where they will remain for years. Do you think this girl would do?"

"Well—yes. She is not very bright, it is true, but she is wonderfully clean, honest, and extremely fond of children."

Now, it struck me then and there that the experience of the housekeeper at childless Petleighcote as to Dinah's love of children must have been extremely limited.

"What I most liked in Dinah," continued Mrs. Quinion, "was her frankness and trustworthiness. There can be no doubt of her gentleness with children."

"May I ask why you parted with her?"

"She left me of her own free will. We had, two or three weeks since, a very sad affair here. It operated much upon her; she wished to get away from the place; and indeed I was glad she determined to go."

"Has she good health?"

"Very fair health."

Not a word about the fits.

It struck me Mrs. Quinion relished the idea of Dinah Yarton's going abroad.

"I think I will recommend her to my sister. She tells me she would have no objection to go abroad."

"Oh! you have seen her?"

"Yes—the day before yesterday, and before leaving for town, whence I came here. I will recommend the girl. Good morning."

"Good morning, ma'am; but before you go, will you allow me to take the liberty of asking you, since you are from London, if you can recommend me a town servant, or at all events a young person who comes from a distance. When the family is away I require only one servant here, and I am not able to obtain this one now that the hall has got amongst the scandal-mongers, owing to the catastrophe to which I have already referred. The young person I have with me is intolerable; she has only been here four days, and I am quite sure she must not remain fourteen."

"Well, I think I can recommend you a young person, strong and willing to please, and who only left my sister's household on the score of followers. Shall I write to my sister's housekeeper and see what is to be done?"

"I should he most obliged," said Mrs. Quinion; "but where may I address a letter to you in event of my having to write?"

"Oh?" I replied, "I shall remain at Tram quite a week. I have received a telegraphic message which makes my journey to the north needless; and as I have met here in Tram with a person who is a friend of an humble friend of mine, I am in no hurry to quit the place."

"Indeed! may I ask who?"

"Old Mrs. Green, at the corner of the Market Place, and her friend is Mrs. Blotchley of Stokeley."

"Oh, thank you. I know neither party."

"I may possibly see you again," I continued.

"Most obliged," continued Mrs. Quinion; "shall be most happy."

"Good morning."

She returned the salute, and there was an end of the visit.

And then it came about that upon returning to the house of old Mrs. Green, I said in the most innocent manner in the world, and in order to make all my acts and words in the place as consistent as possible, for in a small country town if you do not do your falsehood deftly you will very quickly be discovered—I said to that willing gossip—

"Why, Mrs. Green, I find you are a friend of Mrs. Blotchley of Stokeley!"

"E-es," she said in a startled manner, "Ise her fren', bless 'ee."

"And I'm gratified to hear it, for as her friend you are mine, Mrs. Green."

And here I took her hand.

No wonder after our interview was over that she went out in her best bonnet, though it was only Wednesday. I felt sure it was quite out of honour to Mrs. Blotchley and her friend, who had claimed her friendship, and the history of which she was taking out to tea with her.

Of the interview with Mrs. Green I must say a few words, and in her own expressions.

"Well, Mrs. Green, have you heard of any unusual cart having been seen in Tram on the day before Mr. Petleigh was found dead?"

"Lardy, lardy, e-es," said Mrs. Green; "but bless 'ee, whaty want to know for?"

"I want to know if it was Mrs. Blotchley's brother's cart, that's all."

"Des say it war. I've been arl over toon speering shoot that waggoon. I went to Jones the baker, and Willmott, who married Mary Sprinters—which wur on'y fair; the grocer, an' him knowed nought about it; an' the bootcher in froont street, and bootcher in back street; and Mrs. Macnab, her as mangles, and no noos, bless 'ee, not even of Tom Hatt the milkman, but, lardy, lardy! when Ise tarking for a fren' o' my fren's Ise tark till never. 'Twur draper told I arl shoot the ca-art."

"What?" I said, I am afraid too eagerly for a detective who knew her business thoroughly.

"Why, draper White wur oot for stroll loike, an' looking about past turning to the harl (hall), and then he sees coming aloong a cart him guessed wur coming to him's shop; but, bless 'ee, 'twarnt comin' to his shop at ARL!"

"Where was it going?"

"Why the cart turned roight arf to harl, and that moost ha' been wher they cart went to; and, bless 'ee, that's arl."

Then Mrs. Green, talking like machinery to the very threshold, went, and I guess put on her new bonnet instanter, for she wore it before she went out, and when she brought in my chop and potatoes.

Meanwhile I was ruminating the news of the box, if I may be allowed the figure, and piecing it together.

It was pretty clear to me that a box had been taken to the hall, for the evidence of the girl Dinah and that which Mrs. Green brought together coincided in supporting a supposition to that effect.

The girl said a big box (which must have been large, seeing it took two men to carry it) had been brought to the hall in a large cart on the day previous to the finding of the body.

It was on that day the draper, presumably, had seen a large cart turn out of the main road towards Petleighcote.

Did that cart contain the box the girl Dinah referred to?

If so, had it anything to do with the death?

If so, where was it?

If hidden, who had hidden it?

These were the questions which flooded my mind, and which the reader will see were sufficiently important and equally embarrassing.

The first question to be decided was this,—

Had the big box anything to do with the matter?

I first wrote my letter to head quarters putting things in train to plant one of our people as serving woman at Petleighcote, and then I sallied out to visit Mr. White, the draper.

He was what men would call a "jolly" man, one who took a good deal of gin-and-water, and the world as it came. He was a man to be hail met with the world, but to find it rather a thirsty sphere, and diligently to spirit-and-water that portion of it contained within his own suit of clothes.

He was a man to be rushed at and tilted over with confidence.

"Mr. White," said I, "I want an umbrella, and also a few words with you."

"Both, mum," said he; and I would have bet, for though a woman I am fond of a little wager now and then,—yes, I would have bet that before his fourth sentence he would drop the "mum."

"Here are what we have in umberellers, mum."

"Thank you. Do you remember meeting a strange cart on the day, a Monday, before Mr. Petleigh—Petleigh—what was his name?—was found dead outside the hall? I mention that horrid circumstance to recall the day to your mind."

"Well, yes, I do, mum. I've been hearing of this from Mary Green."

"What kind of cart was it?"

"Well, mum, it was a wholesale fancy article manufacturer's van."

"Ah, such as travel from drapers to drapers with samples, and sometimes things for sale."

"Yes; that were it."

[He dropped the mum at the fourth sentence]

"A very large van, in which a man could almost stand upright?"

"A man, my dear!" He was just the kind of man to "my dear" a customer, though by so doing he should offend her for life. "Half-a-dozen of 'em, and filled with boxes of samples, in each of which you might stow away a long—what's the matter, eh? What do you want to find out about the van for, eh?"

"Oh, pray don't ask me, White," said I, knowing the way to such a man's confidence is the road of familiarity. "Don't, don't inquire what. But tell me, how many men were there on the van?"

"Two, my dear."

"What were they like?"

"Well, I didn't notice."

"Did you know them, or either of them?"

"Ha! *I* see," said White; and I am afraid I allowed him to infer that he had surprised a personal secret. "No; I knew neither of 'em, if *I* know it. Strangers to me. Of course *I* thought they were coming with samples to *my* shop; for I am the only one in the village. But they DIDN'T."

"No; they went to the hall, I believe?"

"Yes. *I* thought they had turned wrong, and I hollered after them, but it was no use. I wish I could describe them for you, my dear, but I can't. How; ever, I believe they looked like gentlemen. Do you think *that* description will answer?"

"Did they afterwards come into the town, Mr. White?"

"Well, my dear, they did, and baited at the White Horse, and then it was I was so surprised they did not call. And then—in fact, my dear, if you would like to know all—"

"Oh, don't keep anything from me, White."

"Well, then, my dear, I went over as they were making ready to go, and I asked them if they were looking for a party or the name of White? And then—"

"Oh, pray, pray continue."

"Well, then, one of them told me to go to a place, to repeat which before you, my dear, I would not; from which it seemed to me that they did *not* want a person of the name of White."

"And, Mr. White, did they quit Tram by the same road as that by which they entered it?"

"No, they did *not*; they drove out at the other end of the town."

"Is it possible? And tell me, Mr. White, if they wanted to get back to the hall, could they have done so by any other means than by returning through the village?"

"No, not without—let me see, my dear—not without going thirty miles round by the heath, which," added Mr. White, "and no offence, my dear, I am bound to submit they were not men who seemed likely to take any unnecessary trouble; or why—why in fact did they tell me to go to where in fact they told me to go to?"

"True; but they may have returned, and you not know anything about it, Mr. White."

"There you have it, my dear. You go to the gateman, and as it's only three weeks since, you take his word, for Tom remembers every vehicle that passes his 'pike—there are not many of them, for business is woundily slack. Tom remembers 'em all for a good quarter."

"Oh, thank you, Mr. White. I think I'll take the green umbrella. How much is it?"

"Now look here, my dear," the draper continued, leaning over the counter, and dropping his voice; "I know the umbereller is the excuse, and though business *is* bad. I'm sure I don't want you to take it; unless, indeed, you want it," he added, the commercial spirit struggling with the spirit proper of the man.

"Thank you," said I. "I'll take the green—you will kindly let me call upon you again?"

"With pleasure, my dear; as often as you like; the more the better. And look here, you need not buy any more umberellers or things. You just drop in in a friendly way, you know. *I* see it all."

"Thank you," I said; and making an escape I was rather desirous of obtaining, I left the shop, which, I regret to say, I was ungrateful enough not to revisit. But, on the other hand, I met White several and at most inconvenient times.

Tom the 'pikeman's memory for vehicles was, I found, a proverb in the place; and when I went to him, he remembered the vehicle almost before I could explain its appearance to him.

As for the question—"Did the van return?"—he treated the "Are you sure of it?" with which I met his shake of the head—he treated my doubt with such violent decision that I became confident he was right.

Unless he was bribed to secrecy?

But the doubt was ridiculous; for could all the town be bribed to secrecy?

I determined that doubt at once. And indeed it is the great gain and drawback to our profession that we have to doubt so imperiously. To believe every man to be honest till he is found out to be a thief, is a motto most self-respecting men cling to; but we detectives on the contrary would not gain salt to our bread, much less the bread itself, if we adopted such a belief. We have to believe every man a rogue till, after turning all sorts of evidence inside out, we can only discover that he is an honest man. And even then I am much afraid we are not quite sure of him.

I am aware this is a very dismal way of looking upon society, but the more thinking amongst my profession console themselves with the knowledge that our system is a necessary one (under the present condition of society), and that therefore in conforming to the melancholy rules of this system, however repulsive we may feel them, we are really doing good to our brother men.

Returning home after I left the 'pikeman——from whom I ascertained that the van had passed his gate at half-past eight in the evening, I turned over all my new information in my mind.

The girl Dinah must have seen the box in the hall as she went to bed. Say this was half-past nine; at half-past five, at the time the alarm was given, the box was gone.

This made eight hours.

Now, the van had left Tram at half-past eight, and to get round to the hall it had to go thirty miles by night over a heath. (By a reference to my almanack I found there was no moon that night.) Now, take it that a heavy van travelling by night-time could not go more than five miles an hour, and allowing the horse an hour's rest when half the journey was accomplished, we find that seven hours would be required to accomplish that distance.

This would bring the earliest time at which the van could arrive at the hall at half-past three, assuming no impediments to arise.

There would be then just two hours before the body was discovered, and actually as the dawn was breaking.

Such a venture was preposterous even in the contemplation.

In the first place, why should the box be left if it were to be called for again?

In the second, why should it be called for so early in the morning as half-past three?

And yet at half-past five it had vanished, and Mrs. Qninion had said to the girl (I assumed the girl's evidence to be true) that the box had been taken away again.

From my investigation of these facts I inferred——firstly:

That the van which brought the box had not taken it away.

Secondly: That Mrs. Quinion, for some as yet unexplained purpose, had wished the girl to suppose the box had been removed.

Thirdly: That the box was still in the house.

Fourthly: That as Mrs. Quinion had stated the box was gone, while it was still on the premises, she had some purpose (surely important) in stating that it had been taken away.

It was late, but I wanted to complete my day's work as far as it lay in my power.

I had two things to do.

Firstly, to send the "fluff" which I had gathered from the clothes to a microscopic chemist; and secondly, to make some inquiry at the inn where the van attendants had baited, and ascertain what they were.

Therefore I put the "fluff" in a tin box, and directed it to the gentleman who is good enough to control these kind of investigations for me, and going out I posted my communication. Then I made for the tavern, with the name of which Mrs. Green had readily furnished me, and asked for the landlady.

The interest she exhibited showed me in a moment that Mrs. Green's little remarks and Mr. White's frank observations had got round to that quarter.

And here let me break off for a moment to show how nicely people will gull themselves. I had plainly made no admission which personally identified me with the van, and yet people had already got up a very sentimental feeling in my favour in reference to that vehicle.

For this arrangement I was unfeignedly glad. It furnished a motive for my remaining in Tram, which was just what I wanted.

And furthermore, the tale I told Mrs. Quinion about my remaining in Tram because I had found a friend of my own friend, would, if it spread (which it did not, from which I inferred that Mrs. Quinion had no confidences with the Tram maiden at that hour with her, and that this latter did not habitually listen) do me no harm, as I might ostensibly be supposed to invent a fib which might cover my supposed tribulation. Here is a condensation of the conversation I had with the landlady.

"Ah! I know; I'm glad to see you. Pray sit down. Take that chair—it's the easiest. And how are you, my poor dear?"

"Not strong," I had to say.

"Ah! and well you may not be."

"I came to ask, did two persons, driving a van—a large black van, picked out with pale blue (this description I had got from the 'pikeman)—stop here on the day before Mr.—I've forgotten his name—the young squire's death?"

"Yes, my poor dear, an' a tall gentleman with auburn whiskers, and the other shorter, without whiskers."

"Dear me; did you notice anything peculiar in the tall gentleman?"

"Well, my poor dear, I noticed that every now and then his upper lip twitched a bit, like a dog's asleep will sometimes go."

Here I sighed.

"And the other?" I continued.

"Oh! all that seemed odd in him was that he broke out into bits of song, something like birds more nor English Christian singing; which the words, if words there were, I could not understand."

"Italian scraps," I thought; and immediately I associated this evidence of the man with the foreign mask.

If they were commercial travellers, one of them was certainly an unusual one, operatic accomplishments not being usually one of the tendencies of commercial men.

"Were they nice people?"

"Oh!" says the landlady, concessively and hurriedly; "they were every inch gentlemen; and I said to mine, said I—'they aint like most o' the commercial travellers that stop here'; and mine answers me back, 'No,' says he, 'for commercials prefers beers to sherries, and whiskies after dinner to both!'"

"Oh! did they only drink wine?"

"Nothing but sherry, my dear; and says they to mine—'Very good wine,'—those were their very words—'whatever you do, bring it dry'; and said mine—I saying his very words—'Gents, I will.'"

Some more conversation ensued, with which I need not trouble the reader, though I elicited several points which were of minor importance.

I was not permitted to leave the hotel without "partaking,"—I use the landlady's own verb—without partaking of a warmer and stronger comfort than is to be found in mere words.

And the last inference I drew, before satisfactorily I went to bed that night, was to the effect that the apparent commercial travellers were not commercial travellers, but men leading the lives of gentlemen.

And now as I have set out a dozen inferences which rest upon very good evidence, before I go to the history of the work of the following days, I must recapitulate these inferences—if I may use so pompous a word.

They are as follow:—

1. That the key found on the body opened a receptacle containing treasure.
2. That the mask found on the body was of foreign manufacture.

3. That the handkerchief found on the body had very recently belonged to a young lady named Frederica, and to whom the deceased was probably deeply attached.

4. That the circumstances surrounding the deceased showed that he had been engaged in no poaching expedition, nor in any house-breaking attempt, notwithstanding the presence of the mask, because no house-breaking implements were found upon him.

5. That the young lady was innocent of participation in whatever evil work the deceased may have been engaged upon. [This inference, however, was solely based upon the discovery of the embroidery braid round the button of the deceased's coat. This inference is the least supported by evidence of the whole dozen.]

6. That a big box had been taken to the hall on the day previous to that on which the deceased was found dead outside the hall.

7. That the box was not removed again in the van in which it had been brought to the house.

8. That whatever the box contained that something was heavy, as it took the two men to carry it into the house.

9. That Mrs. Quinion, for some so far unexplainable reason, had endeavoured to make the witness Dinah Yarton believe that the box had been removed; while, in fact, the box was still in the house.

10. That as Mrs. Quinion had stated the box was gone while it was still on the premises, she had some important motive for saying it had been taken away.

11. That the van-attendants, who were apparent commercial travellers, were not commercial travellers, and were in the habit of living the lives of gentlemen.

And what was the condensed inference of all these inferences?

Why—THAT THE FIRST PROBABLE MEANS BY WHICH THE SOLUTION OF THE MYSTERY WAS TO BE ARRIVED AT WAS THE FINDING OF THE BOX.

To hunt for this box it was necessary that I should obtain free admission to Petleighcote, and by the most extraordinary chance Mrs. Quinion had herself thrown the opportunity in my way by asking me to recommend her a town servant.

Of course, beyond any question, she had made this request with the idea of obtaining a servant who, being a stranger to the district, would have little or not any of that interest in the catastrophe of the young squire's death which all felt who, by belonging to the neighbourhood, had more or less known him.

I had now to wait two days before I could move in the matter—those two days being consumed in the arrival of the woman police-officer who was to play the part of servant up at the hall, and in her being accepted and installed at that place.

On the morning of that second day the report came from my microscopic chemist. He stated that the fluff forwarded him for inspection consisted of two different substances; one, fragments of feathers, the other, atoms of nap from some linen material, made of black and white stuff, and which, from its connexion with the atoms of feather, he should take to be the fluff of a bed-tick.

For a time this report convinced me that the clothes had been covered with this substance, in consequence of the deceased having lain down in his clothes to sleep at a very recent time before he was found dead.

And now came the time to consider the question— "What was my own impression regarding the conduct of the deceased immediately preceding the death?"

My impression was this—that he was about to commit some illegal action, but that he had met with his death before he could put his intention into execution.

This impression arose from the fact that the mask showed a secret intention, while the sound state of the clothes suggested that no struggle had preceded the bloody death—struggle, however brief, generally resulting in clothes more or less damaged, as any soldier who has been in action will tell you (and perhaps tell you wonderingly), to the effect that though he himself may have come out of the fight without a scratch, his clothes were one vast rip.

The question that chiefly referred to the body was, who placed it where it was found between three o'clock (the time when the rain ceased, before which hour the body could not have been deposited, since the clothes, where they did not touch the ground, were dry) and half-past five?

Had it been brought from a distance?

Had it been brought from a vicinity?

The argument against distance was this one, which bears in all cases of the removal of dead bodies—that if it is dangerous to move them a yard, it is a hundred times more dangerous to move them a hundred yards.

Granted the removal of young Petleigh's body, in a state which would at once excite suspicion, and it is clear that a great risk was run by those who carried that burden.

But was there any apparent advantage to compensate that risk?

No, there was not.

The only rational way of accounting for the deposition of the body where it was found, lay in the supposition that those who were mixed up with his death were just enough to carry the body to a spot where it would at once be recognised and cared for.

But against this argument it might be held, the risk was so great that the ordinary instinct of self-preservation natural to man would prevent such a risk being encountered. And this impression becomes all the deeper when it is remembered that the identification of the body could have been secured by the slipping of a piece of paper in the pocket bearing his address.

Then, when it is remembered that it must have been quite dawn at the time of the assumed conveyance, the improbability becomes the greater that the body was brought any great distance.

Then this probability became the greater, that the young man had died in the vicinity of the spot where he was found.

Then followed the question, how close?

And in considering this point, it must not be forgotten that if it were dangerous to bring the body to the hall, it would be equally dangerous to remove the body *from the hall; supposing* the murder (if murder it were) had been committed within the hall.

Could this be the case?

Beyond all question, the only people known to be at the hall on the night of the death were Mrs. Quinion and Dinah.

Now we have closed in the space within which the murder (as we will call it) had been done, as narrowly circumscribing the hall. Now was the place any other than the hall, and yet near it?

The only buildings near the hall, within a quarter of a mile, were the gardener's cottage, and the cottage of the keeper.

The keeper was ill at the time, and it was the gardener who had discovered the body. To consider the keeper as implicated in the affair, was quite out of the question; while as to the gardener, an old man, and older servant of the family (for he had entered the service of the family as a boy), it must be remembered that he was the discoverer of the dead body.

Now is it likely that if he was implicated in the affair that he would have identified himself with the discovery? Such a supposition is hardly holdable.

Very well; then, as the doctor at six A.M. declared death had taken place from six to eight hours; and as the body, from the dry state of the clothes, had *not* been exposed during the night's rain, which ceased at three, it was clear either that the murder had been committed within doors, or that the body had been sheltered for some hours after death beneath a roof of some kind.

Where was that roof?

Apart from the gardener's cottage and the keeper's, there was no building nearer than a quarter of a mile; and if therefore the body had been carried after three to where it was found, it was evident that those cognizant of the affair had carried it a furlong at or after dawn.

To suppose such an amount of moral courage in evil-doers was to suppose an improbability, against which a detective, man or woman, cannot too thoroughly be on his or her guard.

But what of the supposition that the body had been removed from the hall, and placed where it was found?

So far, all the external evidences of the case leant in favour of this theory.

But the theory was at total variance with the ordinary experience of life.

In the first place, what apparent motive could Mrs. Quinion have for taking the young heir's life? Not any apparently.

What motive had the girl?

She had not sufficient strength of mind to hold a fierce motive. I doubt if the poor creature could ever have imagined active evil.

I may here add I depended very much upon what that girl said, because it was consistent, was told under great distress of mind, and was in many particulars borne out by other evidence.

I left Dinah Yarton quite out of my list of suspects.

But in accepting her evidence I committed myself to the belief that no one had been at Petleighcote on the night of the catastrophe beyond the girl and the housekeeper.

Then how could I support the supposition that the young man had passed the night and met his death at the hall?

Very easily.

Because a weak-headed woman like Dinah did not know of the presence of the heir at Petleighcote, it did not follow he could not be there—his presence being known only to the housekeeper.

But was there any need for such secrecy?

Yes.

I found out that fact before the town servant arrived.

Mrs. Quinion's express orders were not to allow the heir to remain at the hall while the family were in town.

Then here was a good reason why the housekeeper should maintain his presence a secret from a stupid blurting servant maid.

But I have said motive for murder on the part of the housekeeper could scarcely be present.

Then suppose the death was accidental (though certainly no circumstance of the catastrophe justified such a supposition), and suppose Mrs. Quinion the perpetratress, what was the object in exposing the body outside the house?

Such an action was most unwomanly, especially where an accident had happened.

I confess that at this point of the case (and up to the time when my confederate arrived) I was completely foiled. All the material evidence was in favour of the murder or manslaughter having been committed under the roof of Petleighcote Hall, while the mass of the evidence of probability opposed any such belief.

Up to this time I had "In no way identified the death with the "big box," although I identified that box with the clearing up of the mystery. This identification was the result of an ordinary detective law.

The law in question is as follows:—

In all cases which are being followed up by the profession, a lie is a suspicious act, whether it has relation or no relation, apparent or beyond question, with the matter in hand. As a lie it must be followed to its source, its meaning cleared up, and its value or want of value decided upon. The probability stands good always that a lie is part of a plot.

So as Mrs. Quinion had in all probability lied in reference to the removal of the box, it became necessary to find out all about it, and hence my first directions to Martha—as she was always called (she is now in Australia and doing well) at our office, and I doubt if her surname was known to any of us—hence my final; instruction to Martha was to look about for a big box.

"What kind of box?"

"That I don't know," said I.

"Well there will be plenty of boxes in a big house—is it a new box?"

"I can't tell; but keep an eye upon boxes, and tell me if you find one that is more like a new one than the rest."

Martha nodded.

But by the date of our first interview after her instruction at Petleighcote, and when Quinion sent her down upon a message to a tradesman, I had learnt from the polished Mr. White that boxes such as drapers' travelers travelled with were invariably painted black.

This information I gave her. Martha had not any for me in return—that is of any importance. I heard, what I had already inferred, that Quinion was a very calm, self-possessed woman, "whom it would take," said Martha, "one or two good collisions to drive off the rails."

"You mark my words," said Matty, "she'd face a judge as cool as she faces herself in the looking-glass, and that I can tell you she does face cool, for I've seen her do it twice."

Martha's opinion was, that the housekeeper was all right, and I am bound to say that I was unable to suppose that she was all wrong, for the suspicion against her was of the faintest character.

She visited me the day after Martha's arrival, thanked me coolly enough for what I had done, said she believed the young person would do, and respectfully asked me up to the hall.

Three days passed, and in that time I had heard nothing of value from my aide-de-camp, who used to put her written reports twice a day in a hollow tree upon which we had decided.

It was on the fourth day that I got a fresh clue to feel my way by.

Mrs. Lamb, the publican's wife, who had shown such a tender interest in my welfare on the night when I had inquired as to the appearance of the two persons who baited the van-horses at their stables on the night of the death—Mrs. Lamb in reluctantly letting me leave her (she was a most sentimental woman, who I much fear increased her tendencies by a too ready patronage of her own liquors) intreated me to return, "like a poor dear as I was"—for I had said I should remain at Tram—"and come and take a nice cup of tea" with her.

In all probability I never should have taken that nice cup of tea, had I not learnt from my Mrs. Green that young Petleigh had been in the habit of smoking and drinking at Lamb's house.

That information decided me.

I "dropped in" at Mrs. Lamb's that same afternoon, and I am bound to say it was a nice cup of tea.

During that refreshment I brought the conversation round to young Petleigh, and thus I heard much of him told to his credit from a publican's point of view, but which did not say much for him from a social standing-place.

"And this, my poor dear, is the very book he would sit in this very parlour and read from for an hour together, and—coming!"

For here there was a tap-tap on the metal counter with a couple of halfpence.

Not thinking much of the book, for it was a volume of a very ordinary publication, which has been in vogue for many years amongst cheap literature devotees, I let it fall open, rather than opened it, and I have no doubt that I did not once cast my eyes upon the page during the spirting of the beer-engine and the return of Mrs. Lamb.

"Bless me!" said she, in moved voice, for she was one of the most sentimental persons ever I encountered. "Now that's very odd!—poor dear."

"What's odd, Mrs. Lamb?" I asked.

"Why if you haven't got the book open at his fav'rite tale!"

"Whose, Mrs. Lamb?"

"Why that poor dear young Graham Petleigh."

I need not say I became interested directly.

"Oh! did he read this tale?"

"Often; and very odd it is, my own dear, as you should be about to read it too; though true it is that that there book do always open at that same place, which I take to be his reading it so often the place is worn and—coming!"

Here Mrs. Lamb shot away once more, while I, it need not be said, looked upon the pages before me.

And if I say that, before Mrs. Lamb had done smacking at the beer-engine, and ending her long gossip with the customer, I had got the case by the throat—I suppose I should astonish most of my readers.

And yet there is nothing extraordinary in the matter.

Examine most of the great detected cases on record, and you will find a little accident has generally been the clue to success.

So with great discoveries. One of the greatest improvements in the grinding of flour, and by which the patentee has made many thousands of pounds, was discovered by seeing a miller blow some flour out of a nook; and all the world knows that the cause which led the great Newton to discover the great laws of the universe was the fall of an apple.

So it frequently happens in these days of numberless newspapers that a chance view of a man will identify him with the description of a murderer.

Chance!

In the history of crime and its detection chance plays the chief character.

Why, as I am writing a newspaper is near me, in which there is the report of a trial for attempt to murder, where the woman who was shot at was only saved by the intervention of a piece of a ploughshare, which was under her shawl, and which she had *stolen* only a few minutes before the bullet struck the iron!

Why, compared with that instance of chance, what was mine when; by reading a tale which had been pointed out to me as one frequently read by the dead young man, I discovered the mystery which was puzzling me?

The tale told of how, in the north of England, a pedlar had left a pack at a house, and how a boy saw the top of it rise up and down; how they supposed a man must be in it who intended to rob the house; and how the boy shot at the pack, and killed a man.

I say, before Mrs. Lamb returned to her "poor dear" I had the mystery by heart.

The young man had been attracted by the tale, remembered it, and put it in form for some purpose. What?

In a moment I recalled the mania of the squire for plate, and, remembering how niggardly he was to the boy, it flashed upon me that the youth had in all probability formed a plan for robbing his father of a portion of his plate.

It stood true that it was understood the plate went up to town with the family. But was this so?

Now see how well the probabilities of the case would tell in with such a theory.

The youth was venturesome and daring, as his poaching affrays proved.

He was kept poor.

He knew his father to possess plate.

He was not allowed to be at Petleighcote when the father was away.

He had read a tale which coincided with my theory.

A large box had been left by strangers at the hall.

The young squire's body had been found under such circumstances, that the most probable way of accounting for its presence where it was found was by supposing that it had been removed there from the hall itself.

Such a plot explained the presence of the mask.

Finally, there was the key, a key opening, beyond all question, an important receptacle—a supposition very clear, seeing the character of the key.

Indeed, by this key might be traced the belief of treasure in the house.

Could this treasure really exist?

Before Mrs. Lamb had said "Good night, dear," to a female customer who had come for a pint of small beer and a gallon of more strongly brewed scandal, I had come to the conclusion that plate might be in the house.

For miserly men are notoriously suspicious and greedy. What if there were some of the family plate which was not required at the town house then at Petleighcote, and which the squire, relying for its security upon the habitual report of his taking all his plate to town, had not lodged at the county bank, because of that natural suspiciousness which might lead him to believe more in his own strong room than a banker's?

Accept this supposition, and the youth's motive was evident.

Accept young Petleigh's presence in the house under these circumstances, and then we have to account for the death.

Here, of course, I was still at fault.

If Mrs. Quinion and the girl only were in the house, and the girl was innocent, then the housekeeper alone was guilty.

Guilty—what of? Murder or manslaughter?

Had the tale young Petleigh used to read been carried out to the end?

Had he been killed without any knowledge of who he was?

That I should have discovered the real state of the case without Mrs. Lamb's aid I have little doubt, for even that very evening, after leaving Mrs. Lamb, and promising to bear in mind the entreaty to "come again, you *dear* dear," my confederate brought me a piece of information which must have put me on the track.

It appeared that morning Mrs. Quinion had received a letter which much discomposed her. She went out directly after breakfast, came down to the village. and returned in about an hour. My confederate had picked the pocket (for, alas! we police officers have sometimes to turn thieves—for the good of society of course) of the housekeeper while she slept that afternoon, and while the new maid was supposed to be putting Mrs. Quinion's stockings in wearable order, and she had made a mental copy of that communication. It was from a Joseph Spencer, and ran as follows:—

MY DEAR MARGARET,—For God's sake look all over the place for key 13. There's such a lot of 'em I never missed it; and if the governor finds it out I'm as good as ruined. It must be somewhere about. I can't tell how it ever come orf the ring. So no more at present. It's post time. With dear love, from your own

Joseph Spencer

Key 13!

Why, it was the same number as that on the key found on the dead man.

A letter was despatched that night to town, directing the police to find out who Joseph Spencer was, and giving the address heading the letter—a printed one.

Mrs. Green then came into operation.

No, she could not tell who lived at the address I mentioned. Thank the blessed stars *she* knowed nought o' Lunnon. What! Where had Mrs. Quinion been that morning? Why, to Joe Higgins's. What for? Why, to look at the young squire's clothes and things. What did she want with them? Why, she "actially" Wanted to take 'em "arl oop" to the Hall. No, Joe Higgins wouldn't.

Of course I now surmised that Joseph Spencer was the butler.

And my information from town showed I was right.

Now, certain as to my preliminaries, I knew that my work lay within the walls of the Hall.

But how was I to reach that place?

Alas! the tricks of detective police officers are infinite. I am afraid many a kindly-disposed advertisement hides the hoof of detection. At all events I know mine did.

It appeared in the second column of the *Times*, and here is an exact copy of it. By the way, I had received the *Times* daily, as do most detectives, during the time I had been in Tram:—

"Wanted, to hear of Margaret Quinion, or her heirs-at-law. She was known to have left the South of England (that she was a Southener I had learnt by her accent) about the year 1830 to become housekeeper to a married foster-sister, who settled in a midland county (this information, and especially the date, Mrs. Green had to answer for). Address, ——" Here followed that of my own solicitors, who had their instructions to keep the lady hanging about the office several days, and until they heard from me.

I am very much afraid I intended that should the case appear as black against her as I feared it would, she was to be arrested at the offices of the gentlemen to whom she was to apply in order to hear of something to her advantage. And furthermore, I am quite sure that many an unfortunate has been arrested who has been enticed to an office under the promise of something to his or her special benefit.

For of such misrepresentations is this deplorable world.

When this advertisement came out, the least acute reader is already aware of the use I made of it.

I pointed out the news to Mrs. Green, and I have no doubt she digited the intelligence to every soul she met, or rather overtook, in the course of the day. And indeed before evening (when I was honoured with a visit from Mrs. Quinion herself), it was stated with absolute assurance that Mrs. Quinion had come in for a good twenty-two thousand pounds, and a house in Dyot Street, Bloomsbury Square, Lunnun.

It was odd, and yet natural, that Mrs. Quinion should seek me out. I was the only stranger with whom she was possibly acquainted in the district, and my strangeness to the neighbourhood she had already, from her point of view, turned to account. Therefore (human nature considered) I did not wonder that she tried to turn me to account again. My space is getting contracted, but as the following is the last conversation I had with Mrs. Quinion, I may perhaps be pardoned for here quoting it. Of course I abridge it very considerably. After the usual salutations, and an assurance that Martha suited very fairly, she said,—

"I have a favour to ask you."

"Indeed; pray what is it?"

"I have received some news which necessarily takes me from home."

"I think," said I, smiling, "I know what that news is," and I related how I had myself seen the advertisement in the morning.

I am afraid I adopted this course the more readily to attract her confidence.

I succeeded.

"Indeed," said she, "then since you have identified yourself with that news, I can the more readily ask you the favour I am about to—"

"And what is that?"

"I am desirous of going up to town—to London—for a few hours, to see what this affair of the advertisement means, but I hesitate to leave Martha alone in the house. You have started, and perhaps you feel offended that I should ask a stranger such a favour, but the fact is, I do not care to let anyone belonging to the neighbourhood know that I have left the Hall—it will be for only twenty-four hours. The news might reach Mr. Petleigh's ears, and I desire that he should hear nothing about it. You see the position in which I am placed. If, my dear lady, you can oblige me I shall be most grateful; and, as you are staying here, it seemed—to—me—"

Here she trailed off into silence.

The cunning creature! How well she hid her real motive—the desire to keep those who knew of the catastrophe out of the Hall, because she feared their curiosity.

Started! Yes, indeed I had started. At best I had expected that I should have to divulge who I was to the person whom she would leave in the place did the advertisement take, and here by the act of what she thought was her forethought, she was actually placing herself at my mercy, while I still remained screened in all my actions referring to her. For I need not say that had I had to declare who I was, and had I failed, all further slow-trapping in this affair would have been at an end—the "game" would have taken the alarm, and there would have been an end to the business.

To curtail here needless particulars, that same evening at nine I was installed in the housekeeper's parlour, and she had set out for the first station past Tram, to which she was going to walk across the fields in order to avoid all suspicion.

She had not got a hundred yards away from the house, before I had turned up my cuffs, and I and Martha, (a couple of detectives,) were hard at work, trying to find that box.

Her keys we soon found, in a work-basket, and lightly covered with a handkerchief.

Now, this mode of hiding should have given me a clue.

But it did not.

For three hours—from nine till midnight, we hunted for that box, and unsuccessfully.

In every room that, from the absence of certain dusty evidences, we knew must have been recently opened—in every passage, cellar, corridor, and hall we hunted.

No box.

I am afraid that we even looked in places where it could not have gone—such as under beds.

But we found it at last, and then the turret-clock had gone twelve about a quarter of an hour.

It was in her bed-room; and what is more, it formed her dressing-table.

And I have no doubt I should have missed it had it not been that she had been imperfect in her concealment.

Apparently she comprehended the value of what I may call "audacity hiding"— that is, such concealment that an ordinary person searching would never dream of looking for the object where it was to be found.

For instance, the safest hiding-place in a drawing-room for a bank note, would be the bottom of a loosely-filled card-basket. Nobody would dream of looking for it in such a place.

The great enigma-novelist, Edgar Poe, illustrates this style of concealment where he makes the holder of a letter place it in a card-rack over the mantelpiece, when he knows his house will be ransacked, and every inch of it gone over to find the document.

Mrs. Quinion was evidently acquainted with this mode of concealment.

Indeed, I believe I should not have found the box had it not been that she had overdone her unconcealed-concealment. For she had used a bright pink slip with a white flounce over it to complete the appearance of a dressing-table, having set the box up on one side.

And therefore the table attracted my notice each time I passed and saw it. As it was Martha, in passing between me and the box, swept the drapery away with her Petticoats, and showed a *black corner*.

The next moment the box was discovered.

I have no doubt that being a strong-minded woman she could not endure to have the box out of her sight while waiting for an opportunity to get rid of it.

It was now evident that my explanation of the case, to the effect that young Petleigh had been imitating the action of the tale, was correct.

The box was quite large enough to contain a man lying with his legs somewhat up; there was room to turn in the box; and, finally, there were about two dozen holes round the box, about the size of a crown piece, and which were hidden by the coarse black canvas with which the box was covered.

Furthermore, the box was closeable from within by means of a bolt, and therefore openable from within by the same means.

Furthermore, if any further evidence were wanting, there was a pillow at the bottom of the box (obviously for the head to rest on), and from a hole the feathers had escaped over the bottom of the box, which was lined with black and white striped linen bed-tick, this material being cut away from the holes.

I was now at no loss to comprehend the fluff upon the unhappy young man's coat.

And, finally, there was the most damnifying evidence of all.

For in the black canvas over one of the holes *there was a jagged cut.*

"Lie down, Martha," said I, "in the box, with your head at this end."

"Why, whatever—"

"Tut—tut,—girl; do as I tell you."

She did; and using the stick of a parasol which lay on the dressing-table, I found that by passing it through the hole its end reached the officer in exactly the region by a wound in which young Mr. Petleigh had been killed.

Of course the case was now clear.

After the young woman, Dinah, had gone to bed, the housekeeper must have had her doubts about the chest, and have inspected it.

Beyond all question, the young man knew the hour at which the housekeeper retired, and was waiting perhaps for eleven o'clock to strike by the old turret clock before he ventured out—to commit what?

It appeared, to me clear, bearing in mind the butler's letter, to rob the plate-chest No. 13, which I inferred had been left behind, a fact of which the young fellow might naturally be aware.

The plan doubtless was to secure the plate without any alarm, to let himself out of the Hall by some mode long-since well-known to him, and then to meet his confederates, and share with them the plunder, leaving the chest to tell the tale of the robbery, and to exculpate the housekeeper.

It struck me as a well-executed scheme, and one far beyond the ordinary run of robbery plots.

What had caused that scheme to fail?

I could readily comprehend that a strong-minded woman like Quinion would rely rather upon her own than any other assistance.

I could comprehend her discovery; perhaps a low-muttered blasphemy on the part of the young man; or maybe she may have heard his breathing.

Then, following out her action, I could readily suppose that once aware of the danger near her she would prepare to meet it.

I could follow her, silent and self-possessed, in the hall, asking herself what she should do.

I could mark her coming to the conclusion that there must be holes in the box through which the evil-doer could breathe, and I apprehended readily enough that she had little need to persuade herself that she had a right to kill one who might be there to kill her.

Then in my mind's eye I could follow her seeking the weapon, and feeling all about the box for a hole.

She finds it.

She fixes the point for a thrust.

A movement—and the manslaughter is committed.

That the unhappy wretch had time to open the box is certain, and doubtless it was at that moment the fierce woman, still clutching the shaft of the arrow, or barb—call it what you will—leant back, and so withdrew the shaft from the rankling iron.

Did the youth recognise her? Had he tried to do so?

From the peacefulness of the face, as described at the inquest, I imagined that he had, after naturally unbolting the lid, fallen back, and in a few moments died.

Then must have followed her awful discovery, succeeded by her equally awful determination to hide the fault of her master's, and perhaps of her own sister's son.

And so it came to pass that she dragged the youth's dead body out into the cold morning atmosphere, as the bleak dawn was filling the air, and the birds were fretfully awaking.

No doubt, had a sharp detective been at once employed, she would not have escaped detection.

As it was she had so far avoided discovery.

And I could easily comprehend that a powerfully-brained woman like herself would feel no compunction and little grief for what she had done—no compunction, because the act was an accident; little grief, because she must have felt she had saved the youth from a life of misery—for a son who at twenty robs a father, however had, is rarely at forty, if he lives so long, an honest man.

But though I had made this discovery I could do nothing so far against the house-keeper, whom of course it was my duty to arrest, if I could convince myself she had committed manslaughter. I was not to be ruled by any feeling of screening the family—the motive indirectly which had actuated Quinion, for, strong-minded as she was, it appeared to me that she would not have hesitated to admit the commission of the act which she had completed had the burglar, as I may call the young man, been an ordinary felon, and unknown to her.

No, the box had no identification with the death, because it exhibited no unanswerable signs of its connexion with that catastrophe.

So far, how was it identifiable (beyond my own circumstantial evidence, known only to myself,) with the murder?

The only particle of evidence was that given by the girl, who could or could not swear to the box having been brought on the previous day, and to the housekeeper saying that it had been taken away again—a suspicious circumstance certainly, but one which, without corroborative evidence, was of little or indeed no value.

As to the jagged cut in the air-hole, in the absence of all blood-stain it was not mentionable.

Corroborative evidence I must have, and that corroborative evidence would best take the shape of the discovery of the shaft of the weapon which had caused death, or a weapon of similar character.

This, the box being found, was now my work.

"Is there any armory in the house, Martha?"

"No; but there's lots of arms in the library."

We had not searched in the library for the box, because I had taken Martha's assurance that no boxes were there.

When we reached the place, I remarked immediately—"What a damp place."

As I said so I observed that there were windows on each side of the room, and that the end of the chamber was circular.

"Well it may be," said Martha, "for there's water all round it—a kind of fountain-pond, with gold fish in it. The library," continued Martha, who was more sharp than educated, "butts out of the house."

Between each couple of book-cases there was fixed a handsome stand of arms, very picturesque and taking to the eyes.

There were modern arms, antique armour, and foreign arms of many kinds; but I saw no arrows, though in the eagerness of my search I had the chandelier, which still held some old yellow wax-candles, lighted up.

No arrow.

But my guardian angel, if there be such good creatures, held tight on to my shoulder that night, and by a strange chance, yet not a tithe so wonderful as that accident by which the woman was saved from a bullet by a piece of just stolen iron, the origin of the weapon used by Quinion came to light.

We had been searching amongst the stands of arms for some minutes, when I had occasion suddenly to cry—

"Hu-u-sh! what are you about?"

For my confederate had knocked off its hook a large drum, which I had noticed very coquettishly finished off a group of flags, and cymbals, and pikes.

"I'm very sorry," she said, as I ran to pick up the still reverberating drum with that caution which, even when useless, generally stands by the detective, when—

There, sticking through the drum, and hooked by its barbs, was the point of such a weapon—the exact counterpart—as had been used to kill young Petleigh.

Had a ghost, were there such a thing, appeared I had not been more astounded.

The drum was ripped open in a moment, and there came to light an iron arrow with a wooden shaft about eighteen inches long, this shaft being gaily covered with bits of tinsel and coloured paper.

[I may here at once state, what I ultimately found out—for in spite of our danger I kept hold of my prize and brought it out of battle with me—that this barb was one of such as are used by picadors in Spanish bull-fights for exciting the bull. The barbs cause the darts to stick in the flesh and skin. The cause of the decoration of the haft can now readily be comprehended. Beyond all doubt the arrow used by Quinion and the one found by me were a couple placed as curiosities amongst the other arms. The remaining one the determined housekeeper had used as suiting best her purpose, the other (which I found) had doubtless at some past time been used by an amateur picador, perhaps the poor dead youth himself, with the drum for an imaginary bull, and within it the dart had remained till it was to reappear as a witness against the guilty and yet guiltless housekeeper.

I had barely grasped my prize when Martha said—"What a smell of burning!"

"Good God!" I cried, "we have set the house on fire!"

The house was on fire, but we were not to blame.

We ran to the door.

We were locked in!

What brought her back I never learnt, for I never saw or heard of her again. I guess that the motion of the train quickened her thought (it does mine), that she suspected—that she got out at the station some distance from Tram, and that she took a post-chaise back to Petleighcote.

All this, however, is conjecture.

But if not she, who locked us in? We could not have done it ourselves.

We were locked in, and I attribute the act to her though how she entered the house I never learnt.

The house was on fire, and we were surrounded by water.

This tale is the story of the "Unknown Weapon," and therefore I cannot logically here go into any full explanation of our escape. Suffice it to our honour as detectives to say, that we did not lose our presence of mind, and that by the aid of the library tables, chairs, big books, &c., we made a point of support on one side the narrow pond for the library ladder to rest on, while the other end reached shallow water.

Having made known the history of the "Unknown Weapon," my tale is done; but my reader might fancy my work incomplete did I not add a few more words.

I have no doubt that Quinion returning, her quick mind in but a few moments came to the conclusion that the only way to save her master's honour was the burning of the box by the incendiarism of the Hall.

The Petleighs were an old family, I learnt, with almost Spanish notions of family honour.

Effectually did she complete her work.

I acknowledge she conquered me. She might have burnt the same person to a cinder into the bargain; and, upon my word, I think she would have grieved little had she achieved that purpose.

For my part in the matter—I carried it no further.

At the inquiry, I appeared as the lady who had taken care of the house while Mrs. Quinion went to look after her good fortune; and I have no doubt her disappearance was unendingly connected with my advertisement in the *Times*.

I need not say that had I found Quinion I would have done my best to make her tremble.

I have only one more fact to relate—and it is an important one. It is this—

The squire had the ruins carefully examined, and two thousand ounces of gold and silver plate, melted into shapelessness of course, were taken out of the rubbish.

From this fact it is pretty evident that the key No. 13, found upon the poor, unhappy, ill-bred, and neglected boy, was the "Open Sesamè" to the treasure which was afterwards taken from the ruins—perhaps worth £4000, gold and silver together.

Beyond question he had stolen the key from the butler, gone into a plot with his confederates—and the whole had resulted in his death and the conflagration of Petleighcote, one of the oldest, most picturesque, and it must be admitted dampest seats in the midland counties.

And, indeed, I may add that I found out who was the "tall gentleman with the auburn whiskers and the twitching of the face"; I discovered who was the short gentleman with no whiskers at all; and finally I have seen the young lady (she was very beautiful) called Frederica, and for whose innocent sake I have no doubt the unhappy young man acted as he did.

As for me, I carried the case no further.

I had no desire to do so—had I had, I doubt if I possessed any further evidence than would have sufficed to bring me into ridicule.

I left the case where it stood.

THE DIARY OF ANNE RODWAY

Wilkie Collins

I

March 3rd, 1840. A long letter to-day from Robert, which surprised and vexed and fluttered me so, that I have been sadly behind-hand with my work ever since. He writes in worse spirits than last time, and absolutely declares that he is poorer even than when he went to America, and that he has made up his mind to come home to London. How happy I should be at this news, if he only returned to me a prosperous man! As it is, though I love him dearly, I cannot look forward to the meeting him again, disappointed and broken down and poorer than ever, without a feeling almost of dread for both of us. I was twenty-six last birthday and he was thirty-three; and there seems less chance now than ever of our being married. It is all I can do to keep myself by my needle; and his prospects, since he failed in the small stationery business three years ago, are worse, if possible, than mine. Not that I mind so much for myself; women, in all ways of life, and especially in my dress-making way, learn, I think, to be more patient than men. What I dread is Robert's despondency, and the hard struggle he will have in this cruel city to get his bread—let alone making money enough to marry me. So little as poor people want to set up in housekeeping and be happy together, it seems hard that they can't get it when they are honest and hearty, and willing to work. The clergyman said in his sermon, last Sunday evening, that all things were ordered for the best, and we are all put into the stations in life that are properest for us. I suppose he was right, being a very clever gentleman who fills the church to crowding; but I think I should have understood him better if I had not been very hungry at the time, in consequence of my own station in life being nothing but Plain Needlewoman.

March 4th. Mary Mallinson came down to my room to take a cup of tea with me. I read her bits of Robert's letter, to show her that if she has her troubles, I have mine too; but I could not succeed in cheering her. She says she is born to misfortune, and that, as long back as she can remember, she has never had the least morsel of luck to be thankful for. I told her to go and look in my glass, and to say if she had nothing to be thankful for then; for Mary is a very pretty girl, and would look still prettier if she could be more cheerful and dress neater. However, my compliment did no good. She rattled her spoon impatiently in her tea-cup, and said, "If I was only as good a hand at needlework as you are, Anne, I would change faces with the ugliest girl in London." "Not you!" says I, laughing. She looked at me for a moment, and shook her head, and was out of the room before I could get up and stop her. She always runs off in that way when she is going to cry, having a kind of pride about letting other people see her in tears.

March 5th. —A fright about Mary. I had not seen her all day, as she does not work at the same place where I do; and in the evening she never came down to have tea with me, or sent me word to go to her. So just before I went to bed I ran up-stairs to say good-night. She did not answer when I knocked; and when I stepped softly into the room I saw her in bed, asleep, with her work not half done, lying about the room in the untidiest way. There was nothing remarkable in that, and I was just going away on tip-toe, when a tiny bottle and wine-glass on the chair by her bed-side caught my eye. I thought she was ill and had been taking physio, and looked at the bottle. It was marked in large letters, "Laudanum—Poison." My heart gave a jump as if it was going to fly out of me. I laid hold of her with both hands, and shook her with all my might. She was sleeping heavily, and woke slowly, as it seemed to me—but still she did wake. I tried to pull her out of bed, having heard that people ought to be always walked up and down when they have taken laudanum; but she resisted, and pushed me away violently.

"Anne!" says she in a fright. "For gracious sake, what's come to you! Are you out of your senses?"

"O, Mary! Mary!" says I, holding up the bottle before her, "If I hadn't come in when I did—" And I laid hold of her to shake her again.

She looked puzzled at me for a moment—then smiled (the first time I had seen her do so for many a long day)—then put her arms round my neck.

"Don't be frightened about me, Anne," she says, "I am not worth it, and there is no need."

"No need!" says I, out of breath. "No need, when the bottle has got Poison marked on it!"

"Poison, dear, if you take it all," says Mary, looking at me very tenderly; "and a night's rest if you only take a little."

I watched her for a moment; doubtful whether I ought to believe what she said, or to alarm the house. But there was no sleepiness now in her eyes, and nothing drowsy in her voice; and she sat up in bed quite easily without anything to support her.

"You have given me a dreadful fright, Mary," says I, sitting down by her in the chair, and beginning, by this time, to feel rather faint after being startled so.

She jumped out of bed to get me a drop of water; and kissed me, and said how sorry she was, and how undeserving of so much interest being taken in her. At the same time, she tried to possess herself of the laudanum-bottle which I still kept cuddled up tight in my own hands.

"No," says I. "You have got into a low-spirited despairing way. I won't trust you with it."

"I am afraid I can't do without it," says Mary, in her usual quiet, hopeless voice. "What with work that I can't get through as I ought, and troubles that I can't help thinking of, sleep won't come to me unless I take a few drops out of that bottle. Don't keep it away from me, Anne; it's the only thing in the world that makes me forget myself."

"Forget yourself!" says I. "You have no right to talk in that way, at your age. There's something horrible in the notion of a girl of eighteen sleeping with a bottle of laudanum by her bedside every night. We all of us have our troubles. Haven't I got mine?"

"You can do twice the work I can, twice as well as me," says Mary. "You are never scolded and rated at for awkwardness with your needle; and I always am. You can pay for your room every week; and I am three weeks in debt for mine."

"A little more practice," says I, "and a little more courage, and you will soon do better. You have got all your life before you —"

"I wish I was at the end of it," says she, breaking in. "I'm alone in the world, and my life's no good to me."

"You ought to be ashamed of yourself for saying so," says I. "Haven't you got me for a friend. Didn't I take a fancy to you when first you left your stepmother, and came to lodge in this house? And haven't I been sisters with you ever since? Suppose you are alone in the world, am I much better off? I'm an orphan, like you. I've almost as many things in pawn as you; and, if your pockets are empty, mine have only got ninepence in them, to last me for all the rest of the week."

"Your father and mother were honest people," says Mary, obstinately. "My mother ran away from home, and died in a hospital. My father was always drunk, and always beating me. My stepmother is as good as dead, for all she cares about me. My only brother is thousands of miles away in foreign parts, and never writes to me, and never helps me with a farthing. My sweetheart—"

She stopped, and the red flew into her face. I knew, if she went on that way, she would only get to the saddest part of her sad story, and give both herself and me unnecessary pain.

"My sweetheart is too poor to marry me, Mary," I said. "So I'm not so much to be envied, even there. But let's give over disputing which is worst off. Lie down in bed, and let me tuck you up. I'll put a stitch or two into that work of yours while you go to sleep."

Instead of doing what I told her, she burst out crying (being very like a child in some of her ways), and hugged me so tight round the neck, that she quite hurt me. I let her go on, till she had worn herself out, and was obliged to lie down. Even then, her last few words, before she dropped off to sleep, were such as I was half-sorry, half-frightened, to hear.

"I won't plague you long, Anne," she said. "I haven't courage to go out of the world as you seem to fear I shall. But I began my life wretchedly, and wretchedly I am sentenced to end it."

It was of no use lecturing her again, for she closed her eyes. I tucked her up as neatly as I could, and put her petticoat over her; for the bed-clothes were scanty, and her hands felt cold. She looked so pretty and delicate as she fell asleep, that it quite made my heart ache to see her, after such talk as we had held together. I just waited long enough to be quite sure that she was in the land of dreams; then emptied the horrible laudanum-bottle into the grate, took up her half-done work, and, going out softly, left her for that night.

March 6th. Sent off a long letter to Robert, begging and entreating him not to be so down-hearted, and not to leave America without making another effort. I told him I could bear any trial except the wretchedness of seeing him come back a helpless broken-down man, trying uselessly to begin life again, when too old for a change. It was not till after I had posted my own letter, and read over parts of Robert's again, that the suspicion suddenly floated across me, for the first time, that he might have sailed for England immediately after writing to me. There were expressions in the letter which seemed to indicate that he had some such headlong project in his mind. And yet, surely if it were so, I ought to have noticed them at the first reading. I can only hope I am wrong in my present interpretation of much of what he has written to me—hope it earnestly for both our sakes.

This has been a doleful day for me. I have been uneasy about Robert, and uneasy about Mary. My mind is haunted by those last words of hers: "I began my life wretchedly, and wretchedly I am sentenced to end it." Her usual melancholy way of talking never produced the same impression on me that I feel now. Perhaps the discovery of the laudanum-bottle is the cause of this. I would give many a hard day's work to know what to do for Mary's good. My heart warmed to her when we first met in the same lodging-house, two years ago; and, although I am not one of the over-affectionate sort myself, I feel as if I could go to the world's end to serve that girl. Yet, strange to say, if I was asked why I was so fond of her, I don't think I should know how to answer the question.

March 7th. I am almost ashamed to write it down, even in this journal, which no eyes but mine ever look on; yet I must honestly confess to myself, that here I am, at nearly one in the morning, sitting up in a state of serious uneasiness, because Mary has not yet come home. I walked with her, this morning, to the place where she works, and tried to lead her into talking of the relations she has got who are still alive. My motive in doing this was to see if she dropped anything in the course of conversation which might suggest a way of helping her interests with those who are bound to give her all reasonable assistance. But the little I could get her to say to me led to nothing. Instead of answering my questions about her stepmother and her brother, she persisted at first, in the strangest way, in talking of her father, who was dead and gone, and of one Noah Truscott, who had been the worst of all the bad friends he had, and had taught him to drink and game. When I did get her to speak of her brother, she only knew that he had gone out to a place called Assam, where they grew tea. How he was doing, or whether he was there still, she did not seem to know, never having heard a word from him for years and years past. As for her stepmother, Mary, not unnaturally, flew into a passion the moment I spoke of her. She keeps an eating-house at Hammersmith, and could have given Mary good employment in it; but she seems always to have hated her, and to have made her life so wretched with abuse and ill-usage, that she had no refuge left but to go away from home, and do her best to make a living for herself. Her husband (Mary's father) appears to have behaved badly to her; and, after his death, she took the wicked course of revenging herself on her step-daughter. I felt, after this, that it was impossible Mary could go back, and that it was the hard necessity of her position, as it is of mine, that she should struggle on to make a decent livelihood without assistance from any of her relations. I confessed as much as this to her; but I added that I would try to get her employment with the persons for whom I work, who pay higher wages, and show a little more indulgence to those under them, than the people to whom she is now obliged to look for support. I spoke much more confidently than I felt, about being able to do this; and left her, as I thought, in better spirits than usual. She promised to be back to-night to tea, at nine o'clock, and now it is nearly one in the morning, and she is not home yet. If it was any other girl I should not feel uneasy, for I should make up my mind that there was extra work to be done in a hurry, and that they were keeping her late, and I should go to bed. But Mary is so unfortunate in everything that happens to her, and her own melancholy talk about herself keeps hanging on my mind so, that I have fears on her account which would not distress me about any one else. It seems inexcusably silly to think such a thing, much more to write it down; but I have a kind of nervous dread upon me that some accident—

What does that loud knocking at the street door mean? And those voices and heavy footsteps outside? Some lodger who has lost his key, I suppose. And yet, my heart— What a coward I have become all of a sudden!

More knocking and louder voices. I must run to the door and see what it is. O, Mary! Mary! I hope I am not going to have another fright about you; but I feel sadly like it.

March 8th.

March 9th.

March 10th.

March 11th. O, me! all the troubles I have ever had in my life are as nothing to the trouble I am in now. For three days I have not been able to write a single line in this journal, which I have kept so regularly, ever since I was a girl. For three days I have not once thought of Robert—I, who am always thinking of him at other times. My poor, dear, unhappy Mary, the worst I feared for you on that night when I sat up alone was far below the dreadful calamity that has really happened. How can I write about it, with my eyes full of tears and my hand all of a tremble? I don't even know why I am sitting down at my desk now, unless it is habit that keeps me to my old everyday task, in spite of all the grief and fear which seem to unfit me entirely for performing it.

The people of the house were asleep and lazy on that dreadful night, and I was the first to open the door. Never, never, could I describe in writing, or even say in plain talk, though it is so much easier, what I felt when I saw two policemen come in, carrying between them what seemed to me to be a dead girl, and that girl Mary! I caught hold of her and gave a scream that must have alarmed the whole house; for, frightened people came crowding down-stairs in their night-dresses. There was a dreadful confusion and noise of loud talking, but I heard nothing, and saw nothing, till I had got her in to my room, and laid on my bed. I stooped down, frantic-like, to kiss her, and saw an awful mark of a blow on her left temple, and felt, at the same time, a feeble flutter of her breath on my cheek. The discovery that she was not dead seemed to give me back my senses again. I told one of the policemen where the nearest doctor was to be found, and sat down by the bedside while he was gone, and bathed her poor head with cold water. She never opened her eyes, or moved, or spoke; but she breathed, and that was enough for me, because it was enough for life.

The policeman left in the room was a big, thick-voiced, pompous man, with a horrible unfeeling pleasure in hearing himself talk before an assembly of frightened, silent people. He told us how he had found her, as if he had been telling a story in a taproom, and began with saying, "I don't think the young woman was drunk." Drunk! My Mary, who might have been a born lady for all the spirits she ever touched—drunk! I could have struck the man for uttering the word, with her lying, poor suffering angel, so white and still and helpless before him. As it was, I gave him a look; but he was too stupid to understand it, and went droning on, saying the same thing over and over again in the same words. And yet the story of how they found her was, like all the sad stories I have ever heard told in real life, so very, very short. They had just seen her lying along on the kerb-stone, a few streets off, and had taken her to the station-house. There she had been searched, and one of my cards, that I give to ladies who promise me employment, had been found in her pocket, and so they had brought her to our house. This was all the man really had to tell. There was nobody near her when she was found, and no evidence to show how the blow on her temple had been inflicted.

What a time it was before the doctor came, and how dreadful to hear him say, after he had looked at her, that he was afraid all the medical men in the world could be of no use here! He could not get her to swallow anything; and the more he tried to bring her back to her senses, the less chance there seemed of his succeeding. He examined the blow on her temple, and said he thought she must have fallen down in a fit of some sort, and struck her head against the pavement, and so have given her brain what he was afraid was a fatal shake. I asked what was to be done if she showed any return to sense in the night. He said, "Send for me directly"; and stopped for a little while afterwards stroking her head gently with his hand, and whispering to himself, "Poor girl, so young and so pretty!" I had felt, some minutes before, as if I could have struck the policeman; and I felt now as if I could have thrown my arms round the doctor's neck and kissed him. I did put out my hand, when he took up his hat, and he shook it in the friendliest way. "Don't hope, my dear," he said, and went out.

The rest of the lodgers followed him, all silent and shocked, except the inhuman wretch who owns the house, and lives in idleness on the high rents he wrings from poor people like us. "She's three weeks in my debt," says he, with a frown and an oath. "Where the devil is my money to come from now?" Brute! brute!

I had a long cry alone with her that seemed to ease my heart a little. She was not the least changed for the better when I had wiped away the tears, and could see her clearly again. I took up her right hand, which lay nearest to me. It was tight clenched. I tried to unclasp the fingers, and succeeded after a little time. Something dark fell out of the palm of her hand as I straightened it. I picked the thing up, and smoothed it out, and saw that it was an end of a man's cravat.

A very old, rotten, dingy strip of black silk, with thin lilac lines, all blurred and deadened with dirt, running across and across the stuff in a sort of trelliswork pattern. The small end of the cravat was hemmed in the usual way, but the other end was all jagged, as if the morsel then in my hands had been torn off violently from the rest of the stuff. A chill ran all over me as I looked at it; for that poor, stained, crumpled end of a cravat seemed to be saying to me, as though it had been in plain words, "If she dies, she has come to her death by foul means, and I am the witness of it."

I had been frightened enough before, lest she should die suddenly and quietly without my knowing it, while we were alone together; but I got into a perfect agony now for fear this last worst affliction should take me by surprise. I don't suppose five minutes passed all that woeful night through, without my getting up and putting my cheek close to her mouth, to feel if the faint breaths still fluttered out of it. They came and went just the same as at first, though the fright I was in often made me fancy they were stilled for ever. Just as the church clocks were striking four, I was startled by seeing the room door open. It was only Dusty Sal (as they call her in the house) the maid-of-all-work. She was wrapped up in the blanket off her bed; her hair was all tumbled over her face; and her eyes were heavy with sleep, as she came up to the bedside where I was sitting.

"I've two hours good before I begin to work," says she, in her hoarse, drowsy voice, "and I've come to sit up and take my turn at watching her. You lay down and get some sleep on the rug. Here's my blanket for you—I don't mind the cold—it will keep me awake."

"You are very kind—very, very kind and thoughtful, Sally," says I, "but I am too wretched in my mind to want sleep, or rest, or to do anything but wait where I am, and try and hope for the best."

"Then I'll wait, too," says Sally. "I must do something; if there's nothing to do but waiting, I'll wait."

And she sat down opposite me at the foot of the bed, and drew the blanket close round her with a shiver.

"After working so hard as you do, I'm sure you must want all the little rest you can get," says I.

"Excepting only you," says Sally, putting her heavy arm very clumsily, but very gently at the same time, round Mary's feet, and looking hard at the pale, still face on the pillow. "Excepting you, she's the only soul in this house as never swore at me, or give me a hard word that I can remember. When you made puddings on Sundays, and give her half, she always give me a bit. The rest of 'em calls me Dusty Sal. Excepting only you, again, she always called me Sally, as if she knowed me in a friendly way. I ain't no good here, but I ain't no harm neither; and I shall take my turn at the sitting up—that's what I shall do!"

She nestled her head down close at Mary's feet as she spoke those words, and said no more. I once or twice thought she had fallen asleep, but whenever I looked at her, her heavy eyes were always wide open. She never changed her position an inch till the church clocks struck six; then she gave one little squeeze to Mary's feet with her arm, and shuffled out of the room without a word. A minute or two after, I heard her down below, lighting the kitchen fire just as usual.

A little later, the doctor stepped over before his breakfast time, to see if there had been any change in the night. He only shook his head when he looked at her, as if there was no hope. Having nobody else to consult that I could put trust in, I showed him the end of the cravat, and told him of the dreadful suspicion that had arisen in my mind, when I found it in her hand.

"You must keep it carefully, and produce it at the inquest," he said. "I don't know though, that it is likely to lead to anything. The bit of stuff may have been lying on the pavement near her, and her hand may have unconsciously clutched it when she fell. Was she subject to fainting fits?"

"Not more so, sir, than other young girls who are hard-worked and anxious, and weakly from poor living," I answered.

"I can't say that she may not have got that blow from a fall," the doctor went on, looking at her temple again. "I can't say that it presents any positive appearance of having been inflicted by another person. It will be important, however, to ascertain what state of health she was in last night. Have you any idea where she was yesterday evening?"

I told him where she was employed at work, and said I imagined she must have been kept there later than usual.

"I shall pass the place this morning," said the doctor, "in going my rounds among my patients, and I'll just step in and make some inquiries."

I thanked him, and we parted. Just as he was closing the door, he looked in again.

"Was she your sister?" he asked.

"No, sir, only my dear friend."

He said nothing more; but I heard him sigh, as he shut the door softly. Perhaps he once had a sister of his own, and lost her? Perhaps she was like Mary in the face?

The doctor was hours gone away. I began to feel unspeakably forlorn and helpless. So much so, as even to wish selfishly that Robert might really have sailed from America, and might get to London in time to assist and console me. No living creature came into the room but Sally. The first time she brought me some tea; the second and third times she only looked in to see if there was any change, and glanced her eye towards the bed. I had never known her so silent before; it seemed almost as if this dreadful accident had struck her dumb. I ought to have spoken to her, perhaps, but there was something in her face that daunted me; and, besides, the fever of anxiety I was in began to dry up my lips as if they would never be able to shape any words again. I was still tormented by that frightful apprehension of the past night, that she would die without my knowing it—die without saying one word to clear up the awful mystery of this blow, and set the suspicions at rest for ever which I still felt whenever my eyes fell on the end of the old cravat.

At last the doctor came back.

"I think you may safely clear your mind of any doubts to which that bit of stuff may have given rise," he said. "She was, as you supposed, detained late by her employers, and she fainted in the work-room. They most unwisely and unkindly let her go home alone, without giving her any stimulant, as soon as she came to her senses again. Nothing is more probable, under these circumstances, than that she should faint a second time on her way here. A fall on the pavement, without any friendly arm to break it, might have produced even a worse injury than the injury we see. I believe that the only ill-usage to which the poor girl was exposed was the neglect she met with in the work-room."

"You speak very reasonably, I own, sir," said I, not yet quite convinced. "Still, perhaps she may——"

"My poor girl, I told you not to hope," said the doctor, interrupting me. He went to Mary, and lifted up her eyelids, and looked at her eyes while he spoke, then added: "If you still doubt how she came by that blow, do not encourage the idea that any words of hers will ever enlighten you. She will never speak again."

"Not dead! O, sir, don't say she's dead!"

"She is dead to pain and sorrow—dead to speech and recognition. There is more animation in the life of the feeblest insect that flies, than in the life that is left in her. When you look at her now, try to think that she is in Heaven. That is the best comfort I can give you, after telling the hard truth."

I did not believe him. I could not believe him. So long as she breathed at all, so long I was resolved to hope. Soon after the doctor was gone, Sally came in again, and found me listening (if I may call it so) at Mary's lips. She went to where my little hand-glass hangs against the wall, took it down, and gave it to me.

"See if the breath marks it," she said.

Yes; her breath did mark it, but very faintly. Sally cleaned the glass with her apron, and gave it back to me. As she did so, she half stretched out her hand to Mary's face but drew it in again suddenly, as if she was afraid of soiling Mary's delicate skin with her hard, horny fingers. Going out, she stopped at the foot of the bed, and scraped away a little patch of mud that was on one of Mary's shoes.

"I always used to clean 'em for her," said Sally, "to save her hands from getting blacked. May I take 'em off now, and clean 'em again?"

I nodded my head, for my heart was too heavy to speak. Sally took the shoes off with a slow, awkward tenderness, and went out.

An hour or more must have passed, when, putting the glass over her lips again, I saw no mark on it. I held it closer and closer. I dulled it accidentally with my own breath, and cleaned it. I held it over her again. O, Mary, Mary, the doctor was right! I ought to have only thought of you in Heaven!

Dead, without a word, without a sign,—without even a look to tell the true story of the blow that killed her! I could not call to anybody, I could not cry, I could not so much as put the glass down and give her a kiss for the last time. I don't know how long I had sat there with my eyes burning, and my hands deadly cold, when Sally came in with the shoes cleaned, and carried carefully in her apron for fear of a soil touching them. At the sight of that—

I can write no more. My tears drop so fast on the paper that I can see nothing.

March 12th. She died on the afternoon of the eighth. On the morning of the ninth, I wrote, as in duty bound, to her stepmother, at Hammersmith. There was no answer. I wrote again: my letter was returned to me this morning, unopened. For all that woman cares, Mary might be buried with a pauper's funeral. But this shall never be, if I pawn everything about me, down to the very gown that is on my back. The bare thought of Mary being buried by the workhouse gave me the spirit to dry my eyes, and go to the undertaker's, and tell him how I was placed. I said, if he would get me an estimate of all that would have to be paid, from first to last, for the cheapest decent funeral that could be had, I would undertake to raise the money. He gave me the estimate, written in this way, like a common bill:

A walking funeral complete 1		13	8
Vestry..0		4	4
Rector...0		4	4
Clerk 0		1	0
Sexton..0		1	0
Beadle..0		1	0
Bell..0		1	0
Six feet of ground 0		2	0
TOTAL............... £2		8	4

If I had the heart to give any thought to it, I should be inclined to wish that the Church could afford to do without so many small charges for burying poor people, to whose friends even shillings are of consequence. But it is useless to complain; the money must be raised at once. The charitable doctor—a poor man himself, or he would not be living in our neighbourhood—has subscribed ten shillings towards the expenses; and the coroner, when the inquest was over, added five more. Perhaps others may assist me. If not, I have fortunately clothes and furniture of my own to pawn. And I must set about parting with them without delay; for the funeral is to be to-morrow, the thirteenth. The funeral—Mary's funeral! It is well that the straits and difficulties I am in, keep my mind on the stretch. If I had leisure to grieve, where should I find the courage to face to-morrow?

Thank God, they did not want me at the inquest. The verdict given—with the doctor, the policeman, and two persons from the place where she worked, for witnesses—was Accidental Death. The end of the cravat was produced, and the coroner said that it was certainly enough to suggest suspicion; but the jury, in the absence of any positive evidence, held to the doctor's notion that she had fainted and fallen down, and so got the blow on her temple. They reproved the people where Mary worked for letting her go home alone, without so much as a drop of brandy to support her, after she had fallen into a swoon from exhaustion before their eyes. The coroner added, on his own account, that he thought the reproof was thoroughly deserved. After that, the cravat-end was given back to me, by my own desire; the police saying that they could make no investigations with such a slight clue to guide them. They may think so, and the coroner, and doctor, and jury may think so; but, in spite of all that has passed, I am now more firmly persuaded than ever that there is some dreadful mystery in connection with that blow on my poor lost Mary's temple which has yet to be revealed, and which may come to be discovered through this very fragment of a cravat that I found in her hand. I cannot give any good reason for why I think so; but I know that if I had been one of the jury at the inquest, nothing should have induced me to consent to such a verdict as Accidental Death.

II

1840. March 12th (continued). After I had pawned my things, and had begged a small advance of wages at the place where I work, to make up what was still wanting to pay for Mary's funeral, I thought I might have had a little quiet time to prepare myself as I best could for to-morrow. But this was not to be. When I got home, the landlord met me in the passage. He was in liquor, and more brutal and pitiless in his way of looking and speaking than ever I saw him before.

"So you're going to be fool enough to pay for her funeral, are you?" were his first words to me.

I was too weary and heart-sick to answer—I only tried to get by him to my own door.

"If you can pay for burying her," he went on, putting himself in front of me, "You can pay her lawful debts. She owes me three weeks' rent. Suppose you raise the money for that next, and hand it over to me? I'm not joking, I can promise you. I mean to have my rent; and if somebody don't pay it, I'll have her body seized and sent to the workhouse!"

Between terror and disgust, I thought I should have dropped to the floor at his feet. But I determined not to let him see how he had horrified me, if I could possibly control myself. So I mustered resolution enough to answer that I did not believe the law gave him any such wicked power over the dead.

"I'll teach you what the law is!" he broke in; "you'll raise money to bury her like a born lady, when she died in my debt, will you? And you think I'll let my rights be trampled upon like that, do you? See if I do! I give you till to-night to think about it. If I don't have the three weeks she owes before to-morrow, dead or alive, she shall go to the workhouse!"

This time I managed to push by him, and get to my own room, and lock the door in his face. As soon as I was alone, I fell into a breathless, suffocating fit of crying that seemed to be shaking me to pieces. But there was no good and no help in tears; I did my best to calm myself, after a little while, and tried to think who I should run to for help and protection. The doctor was the first friend I thought of; but I knew he was always out seeing his patients of an afternoon. The beadle was the next person who came into my head. He had the look of being a very dignified, unapproachable kind of man when he came about the inquest; but he talked to me a little then, and said I was a good girl, and seemed, I really thought, to pity me. So to him I determined to apply in my great danger and distress.

Most fortunately I found him at home. When I told him of the landlord's infamous threats, and of the misery I was in consequence of them, he rose up with a stamp of his foot, and sent for his gold-laced cocked-hat that he wears on Sundays, and his long cane with the ivory top to it.

"I'll give it him," said the beadle. "Come along with me, my dear. I think I told you you were a good girl at the inquest—if I didn't, I tell you so now. I'll give it to him! Come along with me."

And he went out, striding on with his cocked-hat and his great cane, and I followed him.

"Landlord!" he cries the moment he gets into the passage, with a thump of his cane on the floor. "Landlord!" with a look all round him as if he was king of England calling to a beast, "come out!"

The moment the landlord came out and saw who it was, his eye fixed on the cockedhat and he turned as pale as ashes.

"How dare you frighten this poor girl?" said the beadle. "How dare you bully her at this sorrowful time with threatening to do what you know you can't do? How dare you be a cowardly, bullying, braggadocio of an unmanly landlord? Don't talk to me— I won't hear you! I'll pull you up, sir! If you say another word to the young woman, I'll pull you up before the authorities of this metropolitan parish! I've had my eye on you, and the authorities have had their eye on you, and the rector has had his eye on you. We don't like the look of your small shop round the corner; we don't like the look of some of the customers who deal at it; we don't like disorderly characters; and we don't by any manner of means like you. Go away! Leave the young woman alone! Hold your tongue, or I'll pull you up! If he says another word, or interferes with you again, my dear, come and tell me; and, as sure as he's a bullying, unmanly braggadocio of a landlord, I'll pull him up!"

With those words, the beadle gave a loud cough to clear his throat, and another thump of his cane on the floor—and so went striding out again before I could open my lips to thank him. The landlord slunk back into his room without a word. I was left alone and unmolested at last, to strengthen myself for the hard trial of my poor love's funeral to-morrow.

March 13th. It is all over. A week ago, her head rested on my bosom. It is laid in the churchyard now—the fresh earth lies heavy over her grave. I and my dearest friend, the sister of my love, are parted in this world forever.

I followed her funeral alone through the cruel, bustling streets. Sally, I thought, might have offered to go with me; but she never so much as came into my room. I did not like to think badly of her for this, and I am glad I restrained myself—for, when we got into the churchyard, among the two or three people who were standing by the open grave, I saw Sally, in her ragged grey shawl and her patched black bonnet. She did not seem to notice me till the last words of the service had been read, and the clergyman had gone away. Then she came up and spoke to me.

"I couldn't follow along with you," she said, looking at her ragged shawl; "for I haven't a decent suit of clothes to walk in. I wish I could get vent in crying for her, like you; but I can't; all the crying's been drudged and starved out of me, long ago. Don't you think about lighting your fire when you get home. I'll do that, and get you a drop of tea to comfort you."

She seemed on the point of saying a kind word or two more, when, seeing the Beadle coming towards me, she drew back, as if she was afraid of him, and left the churchyard.

"Here's my subscription towards the funeral," said the Beadle, giving me back his shilling fee. "Don't say anything about it, for it mightn't be approved of in a business point of view, if it came to some people's ears. Has the landlord said anything more to you? No, I thought not. He's too polite a man to give me the trouble of pulling him up. Don't stop here crying, my dear. Take the advice of a man familiar with funerals, and go home."

I tried to take his advice; but it seemed like deserting Mary to go away when all the rest forsook her. I waited about till the earth was thrown in, and the man had left the place—then I returned to the grave. O, how bare and cruel it was, without so much as a bit of green turf to soften it! O, how much harder it seemed to live than to die, when I stood alone, looking at the heavy piled-up lumps of clay, and thinking of what was hidden beneath them!

I was driven home by my own despairing thoughts. The sight of Sally lighting the fire in my room eased my heart a little. When she was gone, I took up Robert's letter again to keep my mind employed on the only subject in the world that has any interest for it now. This fresh reading increased the doubts I had already felt relative to his having remained in America after writing to me. My grief and forlornness have made a strange alteration in my former feelings about his coming back. I seem to have lost all my prudence and self-denial, and to care so little about his poverty, and so much about himself, that the prospect of his return is really the only comforting thought I have now to support me. I know this is weak in me, and that his coming back poor can lead to no good result for either of us. But he is the only living being left me to love, and—I can't explain it—but I want to put my arms round his neck and tell him about Mary.

March 14th. I locked up the end of the cravat in my writing-desk. No change in the dreadful suspicions that the bare sight of it rouses in me. I tremble if I so much as touch it.

March 15th, 16th, 17th. Work, work, work. If I don't knock up, I shall be able to pay back the advance in another week; and then, with a little more pinching in my daily expenses, I may succeed in saving a shilling or two to get some turf to put over Mary's grave—and perhaps even a few flowers besides, to grow round it.

March 18th. Thinking of Robert all day long. Does this mean that he is really coming back? If it does, reckoning the distance he is at from New York, and the time ships take to get to England, I might see him by the end of April or the beginning of May.

March 19th. I don't remember my mind running once on the end of the cravat yesterday, and I am certain I never looked at it. Yet I had the strangest dream concerning it at night. I thought it was lengthened into a long clue, like the silken thread that led to Rosamond's Bower. I thought I took hold of it, and followed it a little way, and then got frightened and tried to go back, but found that I was obliged, in spite of myself, to go on. It led me through a place like the Valley of the Shadow of Death, in an old print I remember in my mother's copy of the Pilgrim's Progress. I seemed to be months and months following it, without any respite, till at last it brought me, on a sudden, face to face with an angel whose eyes were like Mary's. He said to me, "Go on, still; the truth is at the end, waiting for you to find it." I burst out crying, for the angel had Mary's voice as well as Mary's eyes, and woke with ray heart throbbing and my cheeks all wet. What is the meaning of this? Is it always superstitious, I wonder, to believe that dreams may come true?

April 30th. I have found it! God knows to what results it may lead; but it is as certain as that I am sitting here before my journal, that I have found the cravat from which the end in Mary's hand was torn! I discovered it last night; but the flutter I was in, and the nervousness and uncertainty I felt, prevented me from noting down this most extraordinary and most unexpected event at the time when it happened. Let me try if I can preserve the memory of it in writing now.

I was going home rather late from where I work, when I suddenly remembered that I had forgotten to buy myself any candles the evening before, and that I should be left in the dark if I did not manage to rectify this mistake in some way. The shop close to me, at which I usually deal, would be shut up, I knew, before I could get to it; so I determined to go into the first place I passed where candles were sold. This turned out to be a small shop with two counters, which did business on one side in the general grocery way, and on the other in the rag and bottle and old iron line. There were several customers on the grocery side when I went in, so I waited on the empty rag side till I could be served. Glancing about me here at the worthless-looking things by which I was surrounded, my eye was caught by a bundle of rags lying on the counter, as if they had just been brought in and left there. From mere idle curiosity, I looked at the rags, and saw among them something like an old cravat. I took it up directly, and held it under a gas-light. The pattern was blurred lilac lines, running across and across the dingy black ground in a trellis-work form. I looked at the ends: one of them was torn off.

How I managed to hide the breathless surprise into which this discovery threw me, I cannot say; but I certainly contrived to steady my voice somehow, and to ask for my candles calmly, when the man and woman serving in the shop, having disposed of their other customers, inquired of me what I wanted. As the man took down the candles, my brain was all in a whirl with trying to think how I could get possession of the old cravat without exciting any suspicion. Chance, and a little quickness on my part in taking advantage of it, put the object within my reach in a moment. The man, having counted out the candles, asked the woman for some paper to wrap them in. She produced a piece much too small and flimsy for the purpose, and declared, when he called for something better, that the day's supply of stout paper was all exhausted. He flew into a rage her for managing so badly. Just as they were beginning to quarrel violently, I stepped back to the rag-counter, took the old cravat carelessly out of the bundle, and said, in as light a tone as I could possibly assume—

"Come, come! don't let my candles be the cause of hard words between you. Tie this ragged old thing round them with a bit of string, and I shall carry them home quite comfortably."

The man seemed disposed to insist on the stout paper being produced; but the woman, as if she was glad of an opportunity of spiting him, snatched the candles away, and tied them up in a moment in the torn old cravat. I was afraid he would have struck her before my face, he seemed in such a fury; but, fortunately, another customer came in, and obliged him to put his hands to peaceable and proper uses.

"Quite a bundle of all-sorts on the opposite counter there," I said to the woman, as I paid her for the candles.

"Yes, and all hoarded up for sale by a poor creature with a lazy brute of a husband, who lets his wife do all the work while he spends all the money," answered the woman, with a malicious look at the man by her side.

"He can't surely have much money to spend, if his wife has no better work to do than picking up rags," said I.

"It isn't her fault if she hasn't got no better," says the woman," rather angrily. "She's ready to turn her hand to anything. Charing, washing, laying-out, keeping empty houses—nothing comes amiss to her. She's my half-sister; and I think I ought to know."

"Did you say she went out charing?" I asked, making believe as if I knew of some-body who might employ her.

"Yes, of course I did," answered the woman; "and if you can put a job into her hands, you'll be doing a good turn to a poor hard-working creature as wants it. She lives down the Mews here to the right—name of Horlick, and as honest a woman as ever stood in shoe-leather. Now then, ma'am, what for you?"

Another customer came in just then, and occupied her attention. I left the shop, passed the turning that led down to the Mews, looked up at the name of the street, so as to know how to find it again, and then ran home as fast as I could. Perhaps it was the remembrance of my strange dream striking me on a sudden, or perhaps it was the shock of the discovery I had just made, but I began to feel frightened without knowing why, and anxious to be under shelter in my own room.

If Robert should come back! O, what a relief and help it would be now if Robert should come back!

May 1st. On getting in-doors last night, the first thing I did, after striking a light, was to take the ragged cravat off the candles and smooth it out on the table. I then took the end that had been in poor Mary's hand out of my writing-desk, and smoothed that out too. It matched the torn side of the cravat exactly. I put them together, and satisfied myself that there was not a doubt of it.

Not once did I close my eyes that night. A kind of fever got possession of me—a vehement yearning to go on from this first discovery and find out more, no matter what the risk might be. The cravat now really became, to my mind, the clue that I thought I saw in my dream—the clue that I was resolved to follow. I determined to go to Mrs. Horlick this evening on my return from work.

I found the Mews easily. A crook-backed dwarf of a man was lounging at the corner of it smoking his pipe. Not liking his looks, I did not enquire of him where Mrs. Horlick lived, but went down the Mews till I met with a woman, and asked her. She directed me to the right number. I knocked at the door, and Mrs. Horlick herself—a lean, ill-tempered, miserable-looking woman—answered it. I told her at once that I had come to ask what her terms were for charing. She stared at me for a moment, then answered my question civilly enough.

"You look surprised at a stranger like me finding you out," I said. "I first came to hear of you last night from a relation of yours, in rather an odd way." And I told her all that had happened in the chandler's shop, bringing in the bundle of rags, and the circumstance of my carrying home the candles in the old torn cravat, as often as possible.

"It's the first time I've heard of anything belonging to him turning out any use," said Mrs. Horlick, bitterly.

"What, the spoilt old neck-handkerchief belonged to your husband, did it?" said I at a venture.

"Yes; I pitched his rotten rag of a neck-'andkercher into the bundle along with the rest; and I wish I could have pitched him in after it," said Mrs. Horlick. "I'd sell him cheap at any rag-shop. There he stands, smoking his pipe at the end of the Mews, out of work for weeks past, the idlest hump-backed pig in all London!"

She pointed to the man whom I had passed on entering the Mews. My cheeks began to burn and my knees to tremble; for I knew that in tracing the cravat to its owner I was advancing a step towards a fresh discovery. I wished Mrs. Horlick good evening, and said I would write and mention the day on which I wanted her.

What I had just been told put thought into my mind that I was afraid to follow out. I have heard people talk of being light-headed, and I felt as I have heard them say they felt, when I retraced my steps up the Mews. My head got giddy, and my eyes seemed able to see nothing but the figure of the little crook-back man still smoking his pipe in his former place. I could see nothing but that; I could think of nothing but the mark of the blow on my poor lost Mary's temple. I know that I must have been light-headed, for as I came close to the crook-backed man, I stopped without meaning it. The minute before, there had been no idea in me of speaking to him. I did not know how to speak, or in what way it would be safest to begin. And yet, the moment I came face to face with him something out of myself seemed to stop me, and to make me speak, without considering before-hand, without thinking of consequences, without knowing, I may almost say, what words I was uttering till the instant when they rose to my lips.

"When your old neck-tie was torn, did you know that one end of it went to the rag-shop and the other fell into my hands?" I said these bold words to him suddenly, and, as it seemed, without my own will taking any part in them.

He started, stared, changed colour. He was too much amazed by my sudden speaking to find an answer for me. When he did open his lips it was to say rather to himself than me:

"You're not the girl."

"No," I said, with a strange choaking at my heart. "I'm her friend."

By this time he had recovered his surprise and he seemed to be aware that he had let out more than he ought.

"You may be anybody's friend you like," he said brutally, "so long as you don't come jabbering nonsense here. I don't know you, I don't understand your jokes." He turned quickly away from me when he had said the last words. He had never once looked fairly at me since I first spoke to him.

Was it his hand that struck the blow?

I had only sixpence in my pocket, but I took it out and followed him. If it had been a five-pound note, I should have done the same in the state I was in then.

"Would a pot of beer help you to understand me?" I said, and offered him the sixpence.

"A pot ain't no great things," he answered, taking the sixpence doubtfully.

"It may lead to something better," I said.

His eyes began to twinkle, and he came close to me. Oh, how my legs trembled!— how my head swam!

"This is all in a friendly way, is it?" he asked in a whisper.

I nodded my head. At that moment, I could not have spoken for worlds.

"Friendly, of course," he went on to himself, "or there would have been a police-man in it. She told you, I suppose, that I wasn't the man?"

I nodded my head again. It was all I could do to keep myself standing upright.

"I suppose it's a case of threatening to have him up, and making him settle it quietly for a pound or two? How much for me if you lay hold of him?"

"Half." I began to be afraid that he would suspect something if I was still silent. The wretch's eyes twinkled again, and he came yet closer.

"I drove him to the Red Lion, corner of Dodd Street and Rudgely Street. The house was shut up, but he was let in at the Jug-and-Bottle-door, like a man who was known to the landlord. That's as much as I can tell you, and I'm certain I'm right. He was the last fare I took up at night. The next morning master gave me the sack. Said I cribbed his corn and his fares. I wish I had!"

I gathered from this that the crook-backed man had been a cab-driver.

"Why don't you speak," he asked suspiciously. "Has she been telling you a pack of lies about me? What did she say when she came home?"

"What ought she to have said?"

"She ought to have said my fare was drunk, and she came in the way as he was going to get into the cab. That's what she ought to have said to begin with."

"But, after?"

"Well, after, my fare by way of larking with her, puts out his leg for to trip her up, and she stumbles and catches at me for to save herself, and tears off one of the limp ends of my rotten old tie. 'What do you mean by that, you brute,' says she, turning round as soon as she was steady on her legs, again, to my fare. Says my fare to her, 'I means to teach you to keep a civil tongue in your head.' And he ups with his fist, and— What's come to you, now? What are you looking at me like that, for? How do you think a man of my size was to take her part, against a man big enough to have eaten me up? Look as much as you like, in my place you would have done what I done—drew off when he shook his fist at you, and swore he'd be the death of you if you didn't start your horse in no time."

I saw he was working himself into a rage; but I could not, if my life had depended on it, have stood near him, or looked at him any longer. I just managed to stammer out that I had been walking a long way, and that, not being used to much exercise, I felt faint and giddy with fatigue. He only changed from angry to sulky, when I made that excuse. I got a little further away from him, and then added, that if he would be at the Mews entrance the next evening, I should have something more to say and something more to give him. He grumbled a few suspicious words in answer, about doubting whether he should trust me to come back. Fortunately, at that moment, a policeman passed on the opposite side of the way, he slunk down the Mews immediately, and I was free to make my escape.

How I got home I can't say, except that I think I ran the greater part of the way. Sally opened the door, and asked if anything was the matter the moment she saw my face. I answered, "Nothing! nothing!" She stopped me as I was going into my room, and said,

"Smooth your hair a bit, and put your collar straight. There's a gentleman in there waiting for you."

My heart gave one great bound—I knew who it was in an instant, and rushed into the room like a mad woman.

"Oh, Robert! Robert!"

All my heart went out to him in those two little words.

"Good God, Anne! has anything happened? Are you ill?"

"Mary! my poor, lost, murdered, dear, dear Mary!"

That was all I could say before I fell on his breast.

May 2nd. Misfortunes and disappointments have saddened him a little; but towards me he is unaltered. He is as good, as kind, as gently and truly affectionate as ever. I believe no other man in the world could have listened to the story of Mary's death with such tenderness and pity as he. Instead of cutting me short anywhere, he drew me on to tell more than I had intended; and his first generous words, when I had done, were to assure me that he would see himself to the grass being laid and the flowers planted on Mary's grave. I could have almost gone on my knees and worshipped him when he made me that promise.

Surely, this best, and kindest, and noblest of men cannot always be unfortunate! My cheeks burn when I think that he has come back with only a few pounds in his pocket, after all his hard and honest struggles to do well in America. They must be bad people there when such a man as Robert cannot get on among them. He now talks calmly and resignedly of trying for any one of the lowest employments by which a man can earn his bread honestly in this great city—he, who knows French, who can write so beautifully! Oh, if the people who have places to give away only knew Robert as well as I do, what a salary he would have, what a post he would be chosen to occupy!

I am writing these lines alone, while he has gone to the Mews to treat with the dastardly, heartless wretch with whom I spoke yesterday. He says the creature—I won't call him a man—must be humoured and kept deceived about poor Mary's end, in order that we may discover and bring to justice the monster whose drunken blow was the death of her. I shall know no ease of mind till her murderer is secured, and till I am certain that he will be made to suffer for his crimes. I wanted to go with Robert to the Mews; but he said it was best that he should carry out the rest of the investigation alone; for my strength and resolution had been too hardly taxed already. He said more words in praise of me for what I have been able to do up to this time, which I am almost ashamed to write down with my own pen. Besides, there is no need—praise from his lips is one of the things that I can trust my memory to preserve to the latest day of my life.

May 3rd. Robert very long last night before he came back to tell me what he had done. He easily recognised the hunchback at the corner of the mews by my description of him; but he found it a hard matter, even with the help of money, to overcome the cowardly wretch's distrust of him as a stranger and a man. However, when this had been accomplished, the main difficulty was conquered. The hunchback, excited by the promise of more money, went at once to the Red Lion to enquire about the person whom he had driven there in his cab. Robert followed him, and waited at the corner of the street. The tidings brought by the cabman were of the most unexpected kind. The murderer—I can write of him by no other name—had fallen ill on the very night when he was driven to the Red Lion, had taken to his bed there and then, and was still confined to it at that very moment. His disease was of a kind that is brought on by excessive drinking, and that affects the mind as well as the body. The people at the public-house called it the Horrors. Hearing these things, Robert determined to see if he could not find out something more for himself, by going and enquiring at the public-house, in the character of one of the friends of the sick man in bed up-stairs. He made two important discoveries. First, he found out the name and address of the doctor in attendance. Secondly, he entrapped the barman into mentioning the murderous wretch by his name. This last discovery adds an unspeakably fearful interest to the dreadful catastrophe of Mary's death. Noah Truscott, as she told me herself in the last conversation I ever had with her, was the name of the man whose drunken example ruined her father, and Noah Truscott is also the name of the man whose drunken fury killed her. There is something that makes one shudder, something fatal and supernatural in this awful fact. Robert agrees with me that the hand of Providence must have guided my steps to that shop from which all the discoveries since made took their rise. He says he believes we are the instruments of effecting a righteous retribution; and, if he spends his last farthing, he will have the investigation brought to its full end in a court of justice.

May 4th. Robert went to-day to consult a lawyer whom he knew in former times. The lawyer was much interested, though not so seriously impressed as he ought to have been, by the story of Mary's death and of the events that have followed it. He gave Robert a confidential letter to take to the doctor in attendance on the double-dyed villain at the Red Lion. Robert left the letter, and called again and saw the doctor, who said his patient was getting better, and would most likely be up again in ten days or a fortnight. This statement Robert communicated to the lawyer, and the lawyer has undertaken to have the public-house properly watched, and the hunchback (who is the most important witness) sharply looked after for the next fortnight, or longer if necessary. Here, then, the progress of this dreadful business stops for awhile.

May 5th. Robert has got a little temporary employment in copying for his friend the lawyer. I am working harder than ever at my needle to make up for the time that has been lost lately.

May 6th. To-day was Sunday, and Robert proposed that we should go and look at Mary's grave. He, who forgets nothing where a kindness is to be done, has found time to perform the promise he made to me on the night when we first met. The grave is already, by his orders, covered with turf, and planted round with shrubs. Some flowers, and a low headstone, are to be added to make the place look worthier of my poor lost darling who is beneath it. Oh, I hope I shall live long after I am married to Robert! I want so much time to show him all my gratitude!

May 20th. A hard trial to my courage to-day. I have given evidence at the police-office, and have seen the monster who murdered her.

I could only look at him once. I could just see that he was a giant in size, and that he kept his dull, lowering, bestial face turned towards the witness-box, and his bloodshot, vacant eyes staring on me. For an instant I tried to confront that look; for an instant I kept my attention fixed on him—on his blotched face, on the short grizzled hair above it—on his knotty, murderous right hand hanging loose over the bar in front of him, like the paw of a wild beast over the edge of his den. Then the horror of him—the double horror of confronting him, in the first place, and afterwards of seeing that he was an old man—overcame me; and I turned away faint, sick, and shuddering. I never faced him again; and at the end of my evidence, Robert considerately took me out.

When we met once more at the end of the examination, Robert told me that the prisoner never spoke, and never changed his position. He was either fortified by the cruel composure of the savage, or his faculties had not yet thoroughly recovered from the disease that had so lately shaken them. The magistrate seemed to doubt if he was in his right mind; but the evidence of the medical man relieved his uncertainty, and the prisoner was committed for trial on a charge of manslaughter.

Why not on a charge of murder? Robert explained the law to me when I asked that question. I accepted the explanation, but it did not satisfy me. Mary Mallinson was killed by a blow from the hand of Noah Truscott. That is murder in the sight of God. Why not murder in the sight of the law also?

June 18th. To-morrow is the day appointed for the trial at the Old Bailey. Before sunset this evening I went to look at Mary's grave. The turf has grown so green since I saw it last; and the flowers are springing up so prettily. A bird was perched dressing his feathers, on the low white headstone that bears the inscription of her name and age. I did not go near enough to disturb the little creature. He looked innocent and pretty on the grave, as Mary herself was in her life-time. When he flew away, I went and sat for a little by the headstone, and read the mournful lines on it. Oh, my love, my love! what harm or wrong had you ever done in this world, that you should die at eighteen by a blow from a drunkard's hand?

June 19th. The trial. My experience of what happened at it is limited, like my experience of the examination at the police-office, to the time occupied in giving my own evidence. They made me say much more than I said before the magistrate. Between examination and cross-examination, I had to go into almost all the particulars about poor Mary and her funeral that I have written in this journal; the jury listening to every word I spoke with the most anxious attention. At the end, the judge said a few words to me approving of my conduct, and then there was a clapping of hands among the people in court. I was so agitated and excited that I trembled all over when they let me go out into the air again. I looked at the prisoner both when I entered the witness-box and when I left it. The lowering brutality of his face was unchanged, but his faculties seemed to be more alive and observant than they were at the police-office. A frightful blue change passed over his face, and he drew his breath so heavily that the gasps were distinctly audible, while I mentioned Mary by name, and described the mark of the blow on her temple. When they asked me if I knew anything of the prisoner, and I answered that I only knew what Mary herself had told me about his having been her father's ruin, he gave a kind of groan, and struck both his hands heavily on the dock. And when I passed beneath him on my way out of the court, he leaned over suddenly, whether to speak to me or to strike me I can't say, for he was immediately made to stand upright again by the turnkeys on either side of him. While the evidence proceeded (as Robert described it to me), the signs that he was suffering under superstitious terror became more and more apparent; until, at last, just as the lawyer appointed to defend him was rising to speak, he suddenly cried out, in a voice that startled every one, up to the very judge on the bench, "Stop!" There was a pause, and all eyes looked at him. The perspiration was pouring over his face like water, and he made strange, uncouth signs with his hands to the judge opposite. "Stop all this!" he cried again; "I've been the ruin of the father and the death of the child. Hang me before I do more harm! Hang me, for God's sake, out of the way!" As soon as the shock produced by this extraordinary interruption had subsided, he was removed, and there followed a long discussion about whether he was of sound mind or not. The point was left to the jury to decide by their verdict. They found him guilty of the charge of manslaughter, without the excuse of insanity. He was brought up again, and condemned to transportation for life. All he did on hearing the sentence was to reiterate his desperate words, "Hang me before I do more harm! Hang me, for God's sake, out of the way!"

June 20th. I made yesterday's entry in sadness of heart, and I have not been better in my spirits to-day. It is something to have brought the murderer to the punishment that he deserves. But the knowledge that this most righteous act of retribution is accomplished, brings no consolation with it. The law does indeed punish Noah Truscott for his crime; but can it raise up Mary Mallinson from her last resting-place in the churchyard?

While writing of the law, I ought to record that the heartless wretch who allowed Mary to be struck down in his presence without making any attempt to defend her, is not likely to escape with perfect impunity. The policeman who looked after him to insure his attendance at the trial, discovered that he had committed past offences, for which the law can make him answer. A summons was executed upon him, and he was taken before the magistrate the moment he left the court after giving his evidence.

I had just written these few lines, and was closing my journal, when there came a knock at the door. I answered it, thinking Robert had called in his way home to say good-night, and found myself face to face with a strange gentleman, who immediately asked for Anne Rodway. On hearing that I was the person inquired for, he requested five minutes' conversation with me. I showed him into the little empty room at the back of the house, and waited, rather surprised and fluttered, to hear what he had to say.

He was a dark man, with a serious manner, and a short stern way of speaking. I was certain that he was a stranger, and yet there seemed something in his face not unfamiliar to me. He began by taking a newspaper from his pocket, and asking me if I was the person who had given evidence at the trial of Noah Truscott on a charge of man-slaughter. I answered immediately that I was.

"I have been for nearly two years in London seeking Mary Mallinson, and always seeking her in vain," he said. "The first and only news I have had of her I found in the newspaper report of the trial yesterday."

He still spoke calmly, but there was something in the look of his eyes which showed me that he was suffering in spirit. A sudden nervousness overcame me, and I was obliged to sit down.

"You knew Mary Mallinson, sir?" I asked, as quietly as I could.

"I am her brother."

I clasped my hands and hid my face in despair. O! the bitterness of heart with which I heard him say those simple words!

"You were very kind to her," said the calm, tearless man. "In her name and for her sake, I thank you."

"O! sir," I said, "why did you never write to her when you were in foreign parts?"

"I wrote often," he answered, "but each of my letters contained a remittance of money. Did Mary tell you she had a step-mother? If she did, you may guess why none of my letters were allowed to reach her. I now know that this woman robbed my sister. Has she lied in telling me that she was never informed of Mary's place of abode?"

I remembered that Mary had never communicated with her step-mother after the separation, and could therefore assure him that the woman had spoken the truth.

He paused for a moment, after that, and sighed. Then he took out a pocket-book and said:

"I have already arranged for the payment of any legal expenses that may have been incurred by the trial; but I have still to reimburse you for the funeral charges which you so generously defrayed. Excuse my speaking bluntly on this subject, I am accustomed to look on all matters where money is concerned purely as matters of business."

I saw that he was taking several bank-notes out of the pocket-book, and stopped him.

"I will gratefully receive back the little money I actually paid, sir, because I am not well off, and it would be an ungracious act of pride in me to refuse it from you," I said. "But I see you handling bank-notes, any one of which is far beyond the amount you have to repay me. Pray put them back, sir. What I did for your poor lost sister, I did from my love and fondness for her. You have thanked me for that; and your thanks are all I can receive."

He had hitherto concealed his feelings, but I saw them now begin to get the better of him. His eyes softened, and he took my hand and squeezed it hard.

"I beg your pardon," he said. "I beg your pardon, with all my heart."

There was silence between us, for I was crying; and I believe, at heart, he was crying too. At last, he dropped my hand, and seemed to change back, by an effort, to his former calmness.

"Is there no one belonging to you to whom I can be of service?" he asked. "I see among the witnesses on the trial the name of a young man who appears to have assisted you in the inquiries which led to the prisoner's conviction. Is he a relation?"

"No, sir—at least, not now—but I hope—"

"What?"

"I hope that he may, one day, be the nearest and dearest relation to me that a woman can have." I said those words boldly, because I was afraid of his otherwise taking some wrong view of the connection between Robert and me.

"One day?" he repeated. "One day may be a long time hence."

"We are neither of us well off, sir," I said. "One day, means the day when we are a little richer than we are now."

"Is the young man educated? Can he produce testimonials to his character? Oblige me by writing his name and address down on the back of that card."

When I had obeyed, in a handwriting which I am afraid did me no credit, he took out another card, and gave it to me.

"I shall leave England to-morrow," he said. "There is nothing now to keep me in my own country. If you are ever in any difficulty or distress (which, I pray God, you may never be), apply to my London agent, whose address you have there." He stopped, and looked at me attentively—then took my hand again. "Where is she buried?" he said suddenly, in a quick whisper, turning his head away.

I told him, and added that we had made the grave as beautiful as we could with grass and flowers.

I saw his lips whiten and tremble.

"God bless and reward you!" he said, and drew me towards him quickly and kissed my forehead. I was quite overcome, and sank down and hid my face on the table. When I looked up again he was gone.

June 25th, 1841. I write these lines on my wedding morning, when little more than a year has passed since Robert returned to England.

His salary was increased yesterday to one hundred and fifty pounds a-year. If I only knew where Mr. Mallinson was, I would write and tell him of our present happiness. But for the situation which his kindness procured for Robert, we might still have been waiting vainly for the day that has now come.

I am to work at home for the future, and Sally is to help us in our new abode. If Mary could have lived to see this day! I am not ungrateful for my blessings; but, oh, how I miss that sweet face, on this morning of all others!

I got up to-day early enough to go alone to the grave, and to gather the nosegay that now lies before me from the flowers that grow round it. I shall put it in my bosom when Robert comes to fetch me to the church. Mary would have been my brides-maid if she had lived; and I can't forget Mary, even on my wedding-day.

HOW HE CUT HIS STICK

M. McDonnell Bodkin

H E BREATHED FREELY AT LAST AS HE LIFTED THE SMALL BLACK GLADSTONE bag of stout calfskin, and set it carefully on the seat of the empty railways carriage close beside him.

He lifted the bag with a manifest effort. Yet he was a big powerfully built young fellow; handsome too in a way; with straw-coloured hair and moustache and a round face, placid, honest-looking but not too clever. His light blue eyes had an anxious, worried look. No wonder, poor chap! He was weighted with a heavy responsibility. That unobtrusive black bag held £5,000 in gold and notes which he—a junior clerk in the famous banking house of Gower and Grant—was taking from the head office in London to a branch two hundred miles down the line.

The older and more experienced clerk whose ordinary duty it was to convey the gold had been taken strangely and suddenly ill at the last moment.

"There's Jim Pollock," said the bank manager, looking round for a substitute, "he'll do. He is big enough to knock the head off anyone that interferes with him."

So Jim Pollock had the heavy responsibility thrust upon him. The big fellow who would tackle any man in England in a football rush without a thought of fear was as nervous as a two-year-old child. All the way down to this point his watchful eyes and strong right hand had never left the bag for a moment. But here at Eddiscombe Junction he had got locked in alone to a single first-class carriage, and there was a clear run of forty-seven miles to the next stoppage.

So with a sigh and shrug of relief, he threw away his anxiety, lay back on the soft seat, lit a pipe, drew a sporting paper from his pocket, and was speedily absorbed in the account of the Rugby International Championship match, for Jim himself was not without hopes of his "cap" in the near future.

The train rattled out of the station and settled down to it smooth easy stride—a good fifty miles an hour through the open country.

Still absorbed in his paper he did not notice the gleam of two stealthy keen eyes that watched him from the dark shadows under the opposite seat. He did not see that long lithe wiry figure uncoil and creep out, silently as a snake, across the floor of the carriage.

He saw nothing, and felt nothing till he felt two murderous hands clutching at his throat and a knee crushing his chest in.

Jim was strong, but before his sleeping strength had time to waken, he was down on his back on the carriage floor with a handkerchief soaked in chloroform jammed close to his mouth and nostrils.

He struggled desperately for a moment or so, half rose and almost flung his clinging assailant. But even as he struggled the dreamy drug stole strength and sense away; he fell back heavily and lay like a log on the carriage floor.

The faithful fellow's last thought as his senses left him was "The gold is gone." It was his first thought as he awoke with dizzy pain and racked brain from the deathlike swoon. The train was still at full speed; the carriage doors were still locked; but the carriage empty and the bag gone.

He searched despairingly in the racks, under the seats—all empty. Jim let the window down with a clash and bellowed.

The train began to slacken speed and rumble into the station. Half a dozen porters ran together—the station-master followed more leisurely as beseemed his dignity. Speedily a crowd gathered round the door.

"I have been robbed," Jim shouted, "of a black bag with £5,000 in it!"

Then the superintendent pushed his way through the crowd.

"Where were you robbed, sir?" he said with a suspicious look at the disheveled and excited Jim.

"Between this and Eddiscomb Junction."

"Impossible, sir, there is not stoppage between this and Eddiscombe, and the carriage is empty."

"I thought it was empty at Eddiscombe, but there must have been a man under the seat."

"There is no man under the seat now," retorted the superintendent curtly, "you had better tell your story to the police. There is a detective on the platform."

Jim told his story to the detective, who listened gravely and told him that he must consider himself in custody pending inquiries.

A telegram was sent to Eddiscombe and it was found that communication had been stopped. This must have happened quite recently, for a telegram had gone through less than an hour before. The breakage was quickly located about nine miles outside Eddiscombe. Some of the wires had been pulled down half way to the ground, and the insulators smashed to pieces on one of the poles. All round the place the ground was trampled with heavy footprints which passed through a couple of fields out on the high road and were lost. No other clue of any kind was forthcoming.

The next day but one a card with the name "Sir Gregory Grant," was handed to Dora Myrl as she sat hard at work in the little drawing-room which she called her study. A portly, middle-aged, benevolent gentleman followed the card into the room.

"Miss Myrl?" he said, extending his hand, "I have heard of you from my friend, Lord Millicent. I have come to entreat your assistance. I am the senior partner of the banking firm of Gower and Grant. You have heard of the railway robbery, I suppose?"

"I have heard all the papers had to tell me."

"There is little more to tell. I have called on your personally, Miss Myrl, because, personally, I am deeply interested in the case. It is not so much the money— though the amount is, of course, serious. But the honour of the bank is at stake. We have always prided ourselves on treating our clerks well, and heretofore we have reaped the reward. For nearly a century there has not been a single case of fraud or dishonesty amongst them. It is a proud record for our bank, and we should like to keep it unbroken if possible. Suspicion is heavy on young James Pollock. I want him punished, of course, if he is guilty, but I want him cleared if he is innocent. That's why I came to you."

"The police think?"

"Oh, they think there can be no doubt about his guilt. They have their theory pat. No one was in the carriage—no one could leave it. Pollock threw out the bag to an accomplice along the line. They even pretend to find the mark in the ground where the heavy bag fell—a few hundred yards nearer to Eddiscombe than where the wires were pulled down."

"What has been done?"

"They have arrested the lad and sent out the 'Hue and Cry' for a man with a very heavy calfskin bag—that's all. They are quite sure they have caught the principal thief anyway."

"And you?"

"I will be frank with you, Miss Myrl. I have my doubts. The case *seems* conclusive. It is impossible that anybody could have got out of that train at full speed. But I have seen the lad, and I have my doubts."

"Can I see him?"

"I would be very glad if you did."

After five minutes conversation with Jim Pollock, Dora drew Sir Gregory aside.

"I think I see my way," she said, "I will undertake the case on one condition."

"Any fee that . . ."

"It's not the fee. I never talk of the fee until the case is over. I will undertake the case if you give me Mr. Pollock to help me. You instinct was right, Sir Gregory: the boy is innocent."

There was much grumbling amongst the police when a *nolle prosequi* was entered on behalf of the bank, and Pollock was discharged from custody, and it was plainly hinted the Crown would interpose.

Meanwhle Pollock was off by a morning train with Miss Dora Myrl, from London to Eddiscombe. He was brimming over with gratitude and devotion. Of course they talked of the robbery on the way down.

"The bag was very heavy, Mr. Pollock?" Dora asked.

"I'd sooner carry it one mile than ten, Miss Myrl."

"Yet you are pretty strong, I should think."

She touched his protruding biceps professionally with her finger tips, and he coloured to the roots of his hair.

"Would you know the man that robbed you if you saw him again?" Dora asked.

"Not from Adam. He had his hands on my throat, the chloroform crammed in my mouth before I knew where I was. It was about nine or ten miles outside Eddiscombe. You believe there *was* a man—don't you, Miss Myrl? You are about the only person that does. I don't blame them, for how did the chap get out of the train going at the rate of sixty miles an hour—that's what fetches me, 'pon my word," he concluded incoherently; "if I was any other chap I'd believe myself guilty on the evidence. Can you tell me how the trick was done, Miss Myrl?"

"That's my secret for the present, Mr. Pollock, but I may tell you this much, when we get to the pretty little town of Eddiscombe I will look out for a stranger with a crooked stick instead of a black bag."

There were three hotels in Eddiscombe, but Mr. Mark Brown and his sister were hard to please. They tried the three in succession, keeping their eyes about them for a stranger with a crooked stick, and spending their leisure time in exploring the town and country on a pair of capital bicycles, which they hired by the week.

As Miss Brown (alias Dora Myrl) was going down the stairs of the third hotel one sunshiny afternoon a week after their arrival, she met midway, face to face, a tall middle-aged man limping a little, a very little, and leaning on a stout oak stick, with a dark shiny varnish, and a crooked handle. She passed him without a second glance. But that evening she gossiped with the chambermaid, and learned that the stranger was a commercial traveller—Mr. McCrowder—who had been staying some weeks at the hotel, with an occasional run up to London in the train, and run round the country on his bicycle, a "nice, easily-pleased, pleasant-spoken gentleman," the chambermaid added on her own account.

Next day Dora Myrl met the stranger again in the same place on the stairs. Was it her awkwardness or his? As she moved aside to let him pass, her little foot caught in the stick, jerked it from his hand, and sent it clattering down the stairs into the hall.

She ran swiftly down the stairs in pursuit, and carried it back with a pretty apology to the owner. But not before she had seen on the inside of the crook a deep notch, cutting through the varnish into the wood.

At dinner that day their table adjoined Mr. McCrowder's. Half way through the meal she asked Jim to tell her what the hour was, as her watch had stopped. It was a curious request, for she sat facing the clock, and he had to turn round to see it. But Jim turned obediently, and came face to face with Mr. McCrowder, who started and stared at the sight of him as though he had seen a ghost. Jim stared back stolidly without a trace of recognition in his face, and Mr. McCrowder, after a moment, resumed his dinner. Then Dora set, or seemed to set and wind, her watch, and so the curious little incident closed.

That evening Dora played a musical little jingle on the piano in their private sitting room, toughing the notes abstractedly and apparently deep in thought. Suddenly she closed the piano with a bang.

"Mr. Pollock?"

"Well, Miss Myrl," said Jim, who had been watching her with the patient, honest, stupid admiration of a big Newfoundland dog.

"We will take a ride together on our bicycles to-morrow. I cannot say what hour, but have them ready when I call for them."

"Yes, Miss Myrl."

"And bring a ball of stout twine in your pocket."

"Yes, Miss Myrl."

"By the way, have you a revolver?"

"Never had such a thing in my life."

"Could you use it if you got it?"

"I hardly know the butt from the muzzle, but"—modestly—"I can fight a little bit with my fists if that's any use."

"Not the least in this case. An ounce of lead can stop a fourteen-stone champion. Besides one six-shooter is enough and I'm not too bad a shot."

"You don't mean to say, Miss Myrl, that you . . ."

"I don't mean to say one more word at present, Mr. Pollock, only have the bicycles ready when I want them and the twine."

Next morning, after an exceptionally early breakfast, Dora took her place with a book in her hand coiled up on a sofa in a bow-window of the empty drawing room that looked out on the street. She kept one eye on her book and the other on the window from which the steps of the hotel were visible.

About half-past nine o'clock she saw Mr. McCrowder go down the steps, not limping at all, but carrying his bicycle with a big canvas bicycle-bag strapped to the handle bar.

In a moment she was down the hall where the bicycles stood ready; in another she and Pollock were in the saddle sailing swiftly and smoothly along the street just as the tall figure of Mr. McCrowder was vanishing round a distant corner.

"We have got to keep him in sight," Dora whispered to her companions as they sped along, "or rather I have got to keep him and you to keep me in sight. Now let me go to the front; hold as far back as you can without losing me, and the moment I was a white handkerchief—scorch!"

Pollock nodded and fell back, and in this order—each about half a mile apart—the three riders swept out of the town into the open country.

The man in front was doing a strong steady twelve miles an hour, but the roads were good and Dora kept her distance without an effort, while Pollock held himself back. For a full hour this game of follow-my-leader was played without a change. Mr. McCrowder had left the town at the opposite direction to the railway, but now he began to wheel round towards the line. Once he glanced behind and saw only a single girl cycling in the distance on the deserted road. The next time he saw no one, for Dora road close to the inner curve.

They were now a mile or so from the place where the telegraph wires had been broken down, and Dora, who knew the lie of the land, felt sure their little bicycle trip was drawing to a close.

The road climbed a long easy winding slope thickly wooded on either side. The man in front put on a spurt; Dora answered it with another, and Pollock behind sprinted fiercely, lessening his distance from Dora. The leader crossed the top bend of the slope, turned a sharp curve, and went swiftly down a smooth decline, shaded by the interlacing branches of great trees.

Half a mile at the bottom of the slope, he leaped suddenly away from his bicycle and with one quick glance back at the way he had come. There was no one in view, for Dora held back at the turn. He ran his bicycle close to the wall on the left hand side where a deep trench hid it from the casual passers by; unstrapped the bag from the handle bar, and clambered over the wall with an agility that was surprising in one of his (apparent) age.

Dora was just around the corner in time to see him leap from the top of the wall into the thick wood. At once she drew out and waved her white handkerchief, then settled herself in the saddle and made her bicycle fly through the rush of a sudden wind, down the slope.

Pollock saw the signal; bent down over his handle bar and pedaled uphill like the piston rods of a steam engine.

The man's bicycle by the roadside was finger post for Dora. She, in her turn, over-perched the wall as lightly as a bird. Gathering her tailor-made skirt tightly around her, she peered and listened intently. She could see nothing but, but a little way in front a slight rustling of the branches caught her quick ears. Moving in the underwood, stealthily and silently as a rabbit, she caught a glimpse through the leaves of a dark grey tweed suit fifteen or twenty yards off. A few steps more and she had a clear view. The man was on his knees; he had drawn a black leather bag from a thick tangle of ferns at the foot of a great old beech tree, and was busy cramming a number of small canvas sacks into his bicycle bag.

Dora moved cautiously forward till she stood in a little opening, clear of the undergrowth, free to use her right arm.

"Good morning, Mr. McCrowder!" she cried sharply.

The man started, and turned and saw a girl a half dozen yards off standing clear in the sunlight, with a mocking smile on her face.

His lips growled out a curse; his right hand left the bags and stole to his side pocket.

"Stop that!" The command came clear and sharp. "Throw up your hands!"

He looked again. The sunlight glinted on the barrel of a revolver, pointed straight at his head, with a steady hand.

"Up with your hands, or I fire!" and his hands went up over his head. The next instant Jim Pollock came crashing through the underwood, like an elephant through the jungle.

He stopped short of a cry of amazement.

"Steady!" came Dora's quiet voice; "don't get in my line of fire. Round there to the left—that's the way. Take away his revolver. It's in his right-hand coat pocket. Now tie his hands!"

Jim Pollock did his work stolidly as directed. But while he wound the strong cord round the wrists and arms of Mr. McCrowder, he remembered the railway carriage and the strangling grip at his throat, and the chloroform and the disgrace that followed, and if he strained the knots extra tight it's hard to blame him.

"Now," said Dora, "finish his packing," and Jim crammed the remainder of the canvas sacks into the big bicycle bag.

"You don't mind the weight?"

He gave a delighted grin for answer, as he swung both bags in his hands.

"Get up!" said Dora to the thief, and he stumbled to his feet sulkily. "Walk in front. I mean to take you back to Eddiscombe with me."

When they got on the road-side Pollock strapped the bicycle bag to his own handle bar.

"May I trouble you, Mr. Pollock, to unscrew one of the pedals of this gentleman's bicycle?" said Dora.

It was done in a twinkling. "Now give him a lift up," she said to Jim, "he is going to ride back with one pedal."

The abject thief held up his bound hands imploringly.

"Oh, that's all right. I noticed you held the middle of your handle-bar from choice coming out. You'll do it from necessity going back. We'll look after you. Don't whine; you've played a bold game and lost the odd trick, and you've got to pay up, that's all."

There was a wild sensation in Eddiscombe when, in broad noon, the bank thief was brought in riding on a one-pedalled machine to the police barrack and handed into custody. Dora rode on through the cheering crowd to the hotel.

A wire brought Sir Gregory Grant down by the afternoon train, and the three dined together that night at his cost; the best dinner and wine the hotel could supply. Sir Gregory was brimming over with delight, like the bubbling champagne in his wine glass.

"Your health, Mr. Pollock," said the banker to the junior clerk. "We will make up in the bank to you for the annoyance you have had. You shall fix your own fee, Miss Myrl—or, rather, I'll fix it for you if you allow me. Shall we say half the salvage? But I'm dying with curiosity to know how you managed to find the money and the thief."

"It was easy enough when you come to think of it, Sir Gregory. The man would have been a fool to tramp across the country with a black bag full of gold while the 'Hue and Cry' was hot on him. His game was to hide it and lie low, and he did so. The sight of Mr. Pollock at the hotel hurried him up as I hoped it would; that's the whole story."

"Oh, that's not all. How did you find the man? How did the man get out of the train going at the rate of sixty miles an hour? But I suppose I'd best ask that question of Mr. Pollock, who was there?"

"Don't ask me any questions, sir," said Jim, with a look of profound admiration in Dora's direction. "She played the game off her own bat. All I know is that the chap cut his stick after he had done for me. I cannot in the least tell how."

"Will you have pity on my curiosity, Miss Myrl."

"With pleasure, Sir Gregory. You must have noticed, as I did, that where the telegraph line was broken down the line was embanked and the wires ran quite close to the railway carriage. It is easy for an active man to slip a crooked spoke like this" (she held up Mr. McCrowder's stick as she spoke) "over the two or three wires and so swing himself into the air clear of the train. The acquired motion would carry him along the wires to the post and give him a chance of breaking down the insulators."

"By Jove! you're right, Miss Myrl. It's quite simple when one comes to think of it. But I still don't understand how . . ."

"The friction of the wire," Dora went on in even tone of a lecturer, "with a man's weight on it, would bite deep into the wood of the stick, like that!" Again, she held out the crook of the dark thick oak stick for Sir Gregory to examine, and he peered at it through his gold spectacles.

"The moment I saw that notch," Dora added quietly, "I knew how Mr. McCrowder had '*Cut his stick.*'"

THE MAN WITH THE WILD EYES

George R. Sims

WHEN I FIRST KNEW DORCAS DENE, SHE WAS DORCAS LESTER. SHE CAME to me with a letter from a theatrical agent, and wanted one of the small parts in a play we were rehearsing at a West End Theatre.

She was quite unknown in the profession. She told me that she wanted to act, and would I give her a chance? She was engaged for a maid-servant who had about two lines to speak. She spoke them exceedingly well, and remained at the theatre for nearly twelve months, never getting beyond "small parts," but always playing them exceedingly well.

The last part she had played was that of an old hag. We were all astonished when she asked to be allowed to play it, as she was a young and handsome woman, and handsome young women on the stage generally like to make the most of their appearance.

As the hag, Dorcas Lester was a distinct success. Although she was only on the stage for about ten minutes in one act and five minutes in another, everybody talked about her realistic and well-studied impersonation.

In the middle of the run of the play she left, and I understood that she had married and quitted the profession.

It was eight years before I met her again. I had business with a well-known West End solicitor. The clerk, thinking his employer was alone, ushered me at once into his room. Mr. —— was engaged in earnest conversation with a lady. I apologised. "It's all right," said Mr. ——, "the lady is just going." The lady, taking the hint, rose, and went out.

I saw her features as she passed me, for she had not then lowered her veil, and they seemed familiar to me.

"Who do you think that was?" said Mr. —— mysteriously, as the door closed behind his visitor.

"I don't know," I said; "but I think I've seen her before somewhere. Who is she?"

"That, my dear fellow, is Dorcas Dene, the famous lady detective. *You* may not have hear of her; but with our profession and with the police, she has a great reputation."

"Oh! I she a private inquiry agent, or a female member of the Criminal Investigation Department?"

"She holds no official position," replied my friend, "but works entirely on her own account. She has been mixed up in some of the most remarkable cases of the day—cases that sometimes comes into court but which are far more frequently settled in a solicitor's office."

"If it isn't an indiscreet question, what is she doing for you? You are not in the criminal business."

"No, I am only an old-fashioned, humdrum family solicitor, but I have a very peculiar case in hand just now for one of my clients. I am not revealing a professional secret when I tell you that young Lord Helsham, who has recently come of age, has mysteriously disappeared. The matter has already been guardedly referred to in the gossip column of the society papers. His mother, Lady Helsham, who is a client of mine, has been to me in greatest distress of mind. She is satisfied that her boy is alive and well. The poor lady is convinced that it is a case of *cherchez le femme*, and she is desperately afraid that her son, perhaps in the toils of some unprincipled woman, may be induced to contract a disastrous *mésalliance*. That is the only reason she can suggest to me for his extraordinary conduct."

"And the famous lady detective who has just left your office is to unravel the mystery—is that it?"

"Yes. All our own inquiries having failed, I yesterday decided to place it in her hands, as it was Lady Helsham's earnest desire that that no communication should be made to the police. She is most anxious that the scandal shall not be made a public one. To-day Dorcas Dene has all the facts in her possession, and she has just gone to see Lady Helsham. And now, my dear fellow, what can I do for you?"

My business was a very trifling matter. It was soon discussed and settled, and then Mr. —— invited me to lunch with him at a neighbourhood restaurant. After lunch I strolled back with him as far as his office. As we approached, a cab drove up to the door and a lady alighted.

"By Jove! it's your lady detective again," I exclaimed.

The lady detective saw us, and came towards us.

"Excuse me," she said to Mr. ——, "I want just a word or two with you."

Something in her voice struck me then, and I suddenly remembered where I had seen her before.

"I beg your pardon," I said, "but are we not old friends?"

"Oh, yes," replied the lady detective with a smile; "I knew you at once, but thought you had forgotten me. I have changed a good deal since I left the theatre."

"You have changed your name and your profession, but hardly your appearance—I ought to have known you at once. May I wait for you here while you discuss your business with Mr. ———? I should like to have a few minutes' chat with you about old times."

Dorcas Lester—or rather Dorcas Dene as I must call her now—gave a little nod of assent, and I walked up and down the street smoking my cigar for fully a quarter of an hour before she reappeared.

"I'm afraid I've kept you waiting a long time," she said pleasantly, "and now if you want to talk to me you will have to come home with me. I'll introduce you to my husband. You needn't hesitate or think you'll be in the way, because, as a matter of fact, directly I saw you I made up my mind you could be exceedingly useful to me."

She raised her umbrella and stopped a taxi, and before I quite appreciated the situation, we were making our way to St. John's Wood.

On the journey Dorcas Dene was confidential. She told me that she had taken to the stage because her father, an artist, had died suddenly and left her and her nothing not but a few unremarkable pictures.

"Poor dad!" she said. "He was very clever, and he loved us dearly, but he was only a great big boy to the last. When he was doing well he spent everything he made, and enjoyed life—when he was doing badly he did bills and pawned things, and thought it was rather fun. At one time he would be treating us to dinner at the Café Royal and the theatre afterwards, and at another time he would be showing us how to live as cheaply as used to in his old Paris days in the Quartier Latin, and cooking our meals himself at the studio fire.

"Well, when he died I got on to the stage, and at last—as I daresay you remember—I was earning two guineas a week. On that my mother and I lived in two rooms in St. Paul's Road, Camden Town.

"Then, a young artist, a Mr. Paul Dene, who had been our friend and constant visitor in my father's lifetime, fell in love with me. He had risen rapidly in his profession, and was making money. He had no relatives, and his income was seven or eight hundred a year, and promised to be much larger. Paul proposed to me, and I accepted him. He insisted that I should leave the stage, and he would take a pretty little house, and mother should come and live with us, and we could all be happy together.

"We took the house we are going to now—a sweet little place with a lovely garden in Elm Tree Road, St. John's Wood—and for two years we were very happy. Then a terrible misfortune happened. Paul had an illness and became blind. He would never be able too paint again.

"When I had nursed him back to health I found that the interest of what we had saved would barely pay the rent of our house. I did not want to break up our home— what was to be done? I thought of the stage again, and I had just made up my mind to see if I could not get an engagement, when chance settled my future for me and gave me a start in a very different profession.

"In the next house to us there lived a gentleman, a Mr. Johnson, who was a retired superintendent of police. Since his retirement he had been conducting a high-class inquiry business, and was employed in many delicate family matters by a well-known firm of solicitors who are supposed to have the secrets of half the aristocracy locked away in their strong room.

"Mr. Johnson had been a frequent visitor of ours, and there was nothing which delighted Paul more in our quit evenings than a chat and a pipe with the genial, good-hearted ex-superintendent of police. Many a time have I and my husband sat till the small hours by our cosy fireside listening to the strange tales of crime, and the unravelling of mysteries which our kind neighbour had to tell. There was something fascinating to us in following the slow and cautious steps with which our friend—who looked more like a jolly sea captain than a detective—had threaded his way through the Hampton Court maze in the centre of which lay the truth which it was his business to discover.

He must have thought a good deal of Paul's opinion, for after a time he would come in and talk over cases which he had in hand—without mentioning names when the business was confidential—and the view which Paul took of the mystery more than once turned out to be the correct one. From this constant association with a private detective we began to take a kind of interest in his work, and there was a great case in the papers which seemed to defy the efforts of Scotland Yard, Paul and I would talk it over together, and discuss it and build up our own theories around it.

After my poor Paul lost his sight Mr. Johnson, who was a widower, would come in whenever he was at home—many of his cases took him out of London for weeks together—and help to cheer my poor boy up by telling him all abut the latest romance or scandal in which he had been engaged.

"On these occasions my mother, who is a dear, old-fashioned simple-minded woman, would soon make an excuse to leave us. She declared that to listen to Mr. Johnson's stories made her nervous. She would soon begin to believe that every man and woman she met had a guilty secret, and the world was one great Chamber of Horrors with living figures instead of waxwork ones like those of Madame Tussaud's.

"I had told Mr. Johnson of our position when I found that it would be necessary for me to do something to supplement the hundred a year which was all that Paul's money would bring us in, and he had agreed with me that the stage afforded the best opening.

"One morning I made up my mind to go to the agent's. I had dressed myself in my best and had anxiously consulted my looking-glass. I was afraid that my worries and the long strain of my husband's illness might have left their mark upon my features and spoilt my 'market value' in the managerial eye.

"I had taken such pains with myself, and my mind was so concentrated upon the object I had in view, that when I was quite satisfied with my appearance I ran into our little sitting-room and, without thinking, said to my husband, 'Now I'm off! How do you think I look dear?'"

"My poor Paul turned his sightless eyes towards me, and his lip quivered. Instantly I saw what my thoughtlessness had done. I flung my arms around him and kissed him, and then, the tears in my eyes, I ran out of the room and went down the front garden. When I opened the door Mr. Johnson was outside with his hand on the bell.

"'Where are you going?' he said.

"'To the agent to see about an engagement.'

"'Come back; I want to talk to you.'

"I led the way into the house, and we went into the dining-room, which was empty.

"'What do you think you could get on the stage?' he said.

"'Oh, if I'm lucky I may get what I had before—two guineas a week.'

"'Well, then, put off the stage for a little and I can give you something that will pay you a great deal better. I've just got a case in which I must have the assistance of a lady. The lady who has worked for me the last two years has been idiot enough to get married, with the usual consequences, and I'm in a fix.'

"'You—you want me to be a lady detective—to watch people?' I gasped. 'Oh, I couldn't!'

"'My dear Mrs. Dene,' Mr. Johnson said gently, 'I have too much respect for you and your husband to offer you anything that you need be fearful of accepting. I want you to help me to rescue an unhappy man who is being so brutally blackmailed that he has run away from his broken-hearted wife and his sorrowing children. That is surely a business transaction in which an angel could engage without soiling its wings.'

"'But I'm not clever at—at that sort of thing!'

"'You are cleverer than you think. I have formed a very high opinion of your qualifications for our business. You have plenty of shrewd common sense, you are a keen observer, and you have been an actress. Come, the wife's family are rich, and I am to have a good round sum if I save the poor fellow and get him home again. I can give you a guinea a day and your expenses, and you have only to do what I tell you.'

"I thought everything over, and then I accepted—on one condition. I was to see how I got on before Paul was told anything about it. If I found that being a lady detective was repugnant to me—if I found that it involved any sacrifice of my womanly instincts—I should resign, and then my husband would never know that I had done anything of the sort.

"Mr. Johnson agreed, and we left together for his office.

"That was how I first became a lady detective. I found that the work interested me, and that I was not so awkward as I had expected to be. I was successful in my first undertaking, and Mr. Johnston insisted on my remaining with him and eventually we became partners. A year ago he retired, strongly recommending me to all his clients, and that is how you find me to-day a professional lady detective."

"And one of the best in England," I said with a bow. "My friend Mr. —— has told me of your great reputation."

"Never mind about my reputation," she said. "Here we are at my house—now you've got to come in and be introduced to my husband and to my mother and to Toddlekins."

"Toddlekins—I beg pardon—that's the baby, I suppose."

"No—we have no family. Toddlekins is a dog."

I had become a constant visitor at Elm Tree Road. I had conceived a great admiration for the brave yet womanly woman who, when her artist husband was stricken with blindness, and the future look dark for both of them, had gallantly made the best of her special gifts and opportunities and nobly undertaken a profession which was not only a harassing exhausting one for a woman, but by no means free from grave personal risks.

Dorcas Dene was always glad to welcome me for her husband's sake. "Paul has taken to you immensely," she said to me one afternoon, "and I hope you will call in and spend an hour or two with him whenever you can. My cases take me away from home so much—he cannot read, and my mother, with the best intentions in the world, can never converse with him for more than five minutes without irritating him. Her terribly matter of fact views of life are, to use his own expression, absolutely 'rasping' to his dreamy, artistic temperament."

I had plenty of spare time on my hands, and so it became my custom to drop in two or three times a week, and smoke a pipe, and chat with Paul. His conversation was always interesting, and the gentle resignation with which he bore his terrible affliction won my heart. But I am not ashamed confess that my frequent journeys to Elm Tree Road were also largely influenced by my desire to see Dorcas Dene, and hear more of her strange adventures and experiences.

From the moment she knew that her husband valued my companionship she treat me as one of the family, and when I was fortunate enough to find her at home, she discussed her professional affairs openly before me. I was grateful for this confidence, and I was sometimes able to assist her by going about with her in cases where the presence of a male companion was a material advantage to her. I had upon one occasion laughingly dubbed myself her "assistant," and by that name I was afterwards generally known. There was only one drawback to the pleasure I felt being associated with Dorcas Dene in her detective work. I saw that it would be quite impossible for me to avoid reproducing my experience in some form or other. One day I broached the subject to her cautiously.

"Are you not afraid of the assistant one day revealing the professional secrets of his chief?" I said.

"Not at all," replied Dorcas—everybody called her Dorcas, and I fell into the habit when I found that she and her husband preferred it to the formal "Mrs. Dene"—"I am quite sure that you will not be able to resist the temptation."

"And you don't object?"

"Oh, no, but with this stipulation, that you will use the material in such a way as not to identify any of the cases with the real parties concerned."

That lifted a great responsibility from my shoulders, and made me more eager than ever to prove myself a valuable "assistant" to the charming lady who honoured me with her confidence.

We were sitting in the dining-room one evening after dinner. Mrs. Lester was looking contemptuously over the last number of the *Tatler*, and wondering out lout what on earth young women were coming to. Paul was smoking the old briar-root pipe which had been his constant companion in the studio when he was able to paint, poor fellow, and Dorcas was lying down on the sofa. Toddlekins, nestled up close to her, was snoring gently after the manner of his kind.

Dorcas had had a hard and exciting week, and had not been ashamed to confess that she had felt a little played out. She had just succeeded in rescuing a young lady of fortune from the toils of an unprincipled Russian adventurer, and stopping the marriage almost at the altar rails by the timely production of the record of the would-be bridegroom, which she obtained with the assistance of the head of the French detective police. It was a return compliment. Dorcas had only a short time previously undertaken for the Chef de Sureté a delicate investigation, in which the son of one of the noblest houses in France was involved, and had nipped in the bud a scandal which would have kept the Boulevards chattering for a month.

Paul and I were conversing below our voices, for Dorcas's measured breathing showed us she had fallen into a doze.

Suddenly Toddlekins opened his eyes and uttered an angry growl. He had heard the front gate bell.

A minute later the servant entered and had a card to her mistress, who, with her eyes still half closed, was sitting up on the sofa.

"The gentleman says he must see you at once, ma'am, on business of the greatest importance."

Dorcas looked at the card. "Show the gentleman into the dining-room," she said to the servant, "and say that I will be with him directly."

Then she went to the mantel-glass and smoothed away the evidence of her recent forty winks. "Do you know him at all?" she said, handing me the card.

"Colonel Hargreaves, Orley Park, near Godalming." I shook my head, and Dorcas, with a little tired sigh, went to see her visitor.

A few minutes later the dining-room bell rang, and presently the servant came into the drawing-room. "Please, sir," she said, addressing me, "mistress says will you kindly come to her at once?"

When I entered the dining room I was astonished to see an elderly, soldierly looking man lying back unconscious in the easy chair, and Dorcas Dene bending over him.

I don't think it's anything but a faint," she said. "He's very excited and over-wrought, but if you'll stay here I'll go and get some brandy. You had better loosen his collar—or shall we send for a doctor?"

"No, I don't think it is anything serious," I said, after a hasty glance at the invalid.

As soon as Dorcas had gone I began to loosen the Colonel's collar, but I had hardly commenced before, with a deep sigh, he opened his eyes and came to himself.

"You're better now," I said. "Come—that's all right."

The Colonel stared about him for a moment, and then said, "I—I—where is the lady?"

"She'll be here in a moment. She's gone to get some brandy."

"Oh, I'm all right now, thank you. I suppose it was the excitement, and I've been travelling, had nothing to eat, and I'm so terribly upset. I do often do this sort of thing, I assure you."

Dorcas returned with the brandy. The Colonel brightened up directly she came into the room. He took the glass she offered him and drained the contents.

"I'm all right now," he said. "Pray, let me get on with my story. I hope you will be able to take up the case at once. Let me see—where was I?"

He gave a little uneasy glance in my direction. "You can speak without reserve before this gentleman," said Dorcas. "It is possible he may be able to assist us if you wish me to come to Orley Park at once. So far you have told me that your only daughter, who is five-and-twenty, and lives with you, was found last night on the edge of the lake in your grounds, half in the water and half out. She was quite insensible, and was carried into the house and put to bed. You were in London at the time, and return to Orley Park this morning in consequence of a telegram you received. That is as far as you had got when you became ill."

"Yes—yes!" exclaimed the Colonel, "but I am quite well again now. When I arrived at home this morning shortly before noon I was relieved to find that Maud— that is my poor girl's name—was quite conscious, and the doctor had left a message that I was not to be alarmed, and that he would return and see me early in the afternoon.

"I went at once to my daughter's room and found her naturally in a very low, distressed state. I asked her how it had happened, and I couldn't understand it, and she told me that she had gone out in the grounds after dinner and must have turned giddy when by the edge of the lake and fallen in."

"Is it a deep lake?" asked Dorcas.

"Yes, in the middle, but shallow near the edge. It is a largish lake, with a small fowl island in the centre, and we have a boat upon it."

"Probably it was a sudden fainting fit—such as you yourself have had just now. Your daughter may be subject to them."

"No, she is a thoroughly strong, healthy girl."

"I am sorry to have interrupted you," said Dorcas; "pray go on, for I presume there is something more than a fainting fit behind this accident, or you would not have come to engage my services in the matter."

"There is a great deal more behind it," replied Colonel Hargreaves, pulling nervously at his grey moustache. "I left my daughter's bedside devoutly thankful that Providence had preserved her from such a dreadful death, but when the doctor arrived he gave me a piece of information which caused me the greatest uneasiness and alarm."

"He didn't believe in the fainting fit?" said Dorcas, who had been closely watching the Colonel's features.

The Colonel looked at Dorcas Dene in astonishment. "I don't know how you have divined that," he said, "but your surmise is correct. The doctor told me that he had questioned Maud himself, and she had told him the same story—sudden giddiness and a fall into the water. But he had observed that on her throat there were certain marks, and that her wrists were bruised.

"When he told me this I did not at first grasp his meaning. "It must have been the violence of the fall," I said.

"The doctor shook his head and assured me that no accident would account for the marks his experience eyes had detected. The marks round the throat must have been caused by the clutch of an assailant. The wrists could only have been bruised in the manner they were by being held in a violent brutal grip."

Dorcas Dene, who had been listening apparently without much interest, bent forward as the Colonel made his extraordinary statement. "I see," she said. "Your daughter told you she had fallen into the lake, and the doctor assures you that she must have told you an untruth. She had been pushed or flung in by some one else after a severe struggle."

"Yes!"

"And the young lady, when you question her further, with this information in your possession, what did she say?"

"She appeared very much excited and burst into tears. When I referred to the marks on her throat, which were now beginning to show discoloration more distinctly, she declared that she had invented the story of the faint in order not to alarm me—that she had been attacked by a tramp who must have got into the grounds, and that he had tried to rob her, and that in the struggle, which took place near the edge of the lake, he had thrown her down at the water's edge and then made his escape."

"And that explanation you *do* accept?" said Dorcas, looking at the Colonel keenly.

"How can I? Why should my daughter try to screen a tramp? Why did she tell the doctor an untruth? Surely the first impulse of a terrified woman rescued from a terrible death would have been to have described her assailant in order that he might have been searched for and brought to justice."

"And the police, have they made any inquiries? Have they learned if any suspicious persons were seen about that evening?"

"I have not been to the police. I talked the matter over with the doctor. He says the police inquiries would make the whole thing public property, and it would be known everywhere that my daughter's story, which has now gone all over the neighbourhood, was untrue. But the whole affair is so mysterious, and to me so alarming, that I could not leave it where it is. It was the doctor who advised me to come to you and let the inquiry be a private one."

"You need employ no one if your daughter can be persuaded to tell the truth? Have you tried?"

"Yes. But she insists it was tramp, and declares that until the bruises betrayed her she kept to the fainting-fit story in order to make the affair as little alarming to me as possible."

Dorcas Dene rose. "What time does the last train leave for Godalming?"

"In an hour," said the Colonel, looking at his watch. "At the station my carriage will be waiting to take us to Orley Court. I want you to stay at the Court until you have discovered the key to the mystery."

"No," said Dorcas, after a minute's thought. "I could do no good to-night, and my arrival with you would cause talk among the servants. Go back by yourself. Call on the doctor. Tell him to say his patient requires constant care during the next few days, and that he has sent for a trained nurse from London. The trained nurse will arrive about noon to-morrow."

"And you?" exclaimed the Colonel. "Won't you come?"

Dorcas smiled. "Oh, yes; I shall be the trained nurse."

The Colonel rose. "If you can discover the truth and let me know what it is my daughter is concealing from me I shall be eternally grateful," he said. "I shall expect you to-morrow at noon."

To-morrow at noon you will expect the trained nurse for whom the doctor has telegraphed. Good evening."

I went to the door with Colonel Hargreaves, and saw him down the garden to the front gate.

When I went back to the house Dorcas Dene was waiting for me in the hall. "Are you busy for the next few days?" she said.

"No—I have practically nothing to do."

"Then come to Godalming with me tomorrow. You are an artist and I must get you permission to sketch that lake while I am nursing my patient indoors."

It was past noon when the fly, hired from the station, stopped at the lodge gates of Orley Park, and the lodge-keeper's wife opened them to let us in.

"You are the nurse for Miss Maud, I suppose, miss?" she said, glancing at Dorcas's neat hospital nurse's costume.

"Yes."

"The Colonel and the doctor are both expecting you, miss—I hope it isn't serious with the poor young lady."

"I hope not," said Dorcas, with a pleasant smile.

A minute or two later the fly pulled up to the door of a picturesque old Elizabethan mansion. The Colonel, who had seen the fly from the window, was on the steps waiting for us, and at once conducted us into the library. Dorcas explained my presence in a few words. I was her assistant, and through me she would be able to make all necessary inquiries in the neighbourhood.

"To your people Mr. Saxon will be an artist to whom you have given permission to sketch the house and the grounds—I think that will be best."

The Colonel promised that I should have free access at all hours to the grounds, and it was arranged that I should stay at a pretty little inn which was about a half mile from the park. Having received full instructions on the way down from Dorcas, I knew exactly what to do, and bade her good-bye until the evening, when I was to call at the house to see her.

The doctor came into the room to conduct the new nurse to the patient's bedside, and I left to fulfil my instructions.

At "The Chequers," which was the name of the inn, it was no sooner known that I was an artist, and had permission to sketch in the grounds of Orley Park, than the landlady commenced to entertain me with accounts of the accident which had nearly cost Miss Hargreaves her life.

The fainting-fit story, which was the only one that had got about, had been accepted in perfect faith.

"It's a lonely place, that lake, and there's nobody about the grounds, you see, at night, sir—it was a wonder the poor young lady was found so soon."

"Who found her?" I asked.

"One of the gardeners who lives in a cottage in the park. He'd been to Godalming for the evening, and was going home past the lake."

"What time was it?"

"Nearly ten o'clock. It was lucky he saw her, for it had been dark nearly an hour then, and there was no moon."

"What did he think when he found her?"

"Well, sir, to tell you the truth, he thought at first it was suicide, and that the young lady hadn't gone far enough in and had lost her senses."

"Of course, he couldn't have thought it was murder or anything of that sort," I said, "because nobody could get in at night—without coming through the lodge gates."

"Oh! yes, they could at one place, but it 'ud have to be somebody who knew the dogs or was with some one who did. There's a couple of big mastiffs have got a good run there, and no stranger 'ud try to clamber over—it's a side gate used by the family, sir—after they'd started barking."

"Did they bark that night at all, do you know?"

"Well, yes," said the landlady. "Now I come to think of it, Mr. Peters—that's the lodge-keeper—heard 'em, but they was quiet in a minute, so he took no more notice."

That afternoon, the first place I made up my mind to sketch was the Lodge. I found Mr. Peters at home, and my pass from the Colonel secured his good graces at one. His wife told him of the strange gentleman who had arrived with the nurse, and I explained that there being only one fly at the station and our destination the same, the nurse had kindly allowed me to share the vehicle with her.

I made elaborate pencil marks and notes in my new sketching book, telling Mr. Peters I was only doing something preliminary and rough, in order to conceal the amateurish nature of my efforts, and keep the worthy man gossiping about the "accident" to his young mistress.

I referred to the landlady's statement that he had heard dogs bark that night.

"Oh, yes, but they were quiet directly."

"Probably some stranger passing down by the side gate, eh?"

"Most likely, sir. I was a bit uneasy at first, but when they quieted down I thought it was all right."

"Why were you uneasy?"

"Well, there'd been a queer sort of a looking man hanging about that evening. My missus saw him peering in at the lodge gates about seven o'clock."

"A tramp?"

"No, a gentlemanly sort of man, but he gave my missus a turn, he had such wild, staring eyes. But he spoke all right. My missus asked him what he wanted, and he asked her what was the name of the big house he could see, and who lived there. She told him it was Orley Park, and Colonel Hargreaves lived there, and he thanked her and went away. A tourist, maybe, sir, or perhaps an artist gentleman like yourself."

"Staying in the neighborhood and studying its beauties, perhaps."

"No; when I spoke about it the next day in the town I heard as he'd come by train that afternoon; the porters had noticed him, he seemed so odd."

I finished my rough sketch and then asked Mr. Peters to take me to the scene of the accident. It was a large lake and answered the description given by the Colonel.

"That there's the place where Miss Maud was found," said Mr. Peters. "You see it's shallow there, and her head was just on the bank here out of the water."

"Thank you. That's a delightful little island in the middle. I'll smoke a pipe here and sketch. Don't let me detain you."

The lodge-keeper retired, and obeying the instructions received from Dorcas Dene, I examined the spot carefully.

The marks of hobnailed boots were distinctly visible in the mud at the side, near the place where the struggle, admitted by Miss Hargreaves, had taken place. They might be the tramp's—they might be the gardener's; I was not skilled enough in the art of footprints to determine. But I had obtained a certain amount of information, and with that, at seven o'clock, I went to the house and asked for the Colonel.

I had, of course, nothing to say to him, except to ask him to let Dorcas Dene know that I was there. In a few minutes Dorcas Dene came to me with her bonnet and cloak on.

"I'm going to a walk while it is light," she said; "come with me."

Directly we were outside I gave her my information, and she at once decided to visit the lake.

She examined the scene of the accident carefully, and I pointed out the hobnailed boot marks.

"Yes," she said, those are the gardener's probably—I'm looking for some one else's."

"Whose?"

"These," she said, suddenly stooping and pointing to a series of impressions in the soil at the edge. "Look—here are a woman's footprints, and here are larger ones beside them—now close to—now a little way apart—now crossing each other. Do you see anything particular in these footprints?"

"No—except that there are no nails in them."

"Exactly—the footprints are smaller, but larger than Miss Hargreaves'—the shape is an elegant one: you see the toes are pointed, and the sole is a narrow one. No tramp would have boots like those. Where did you say Mrs. Peters saw that strange-looking gentleman?"

"Peering through the lodge gates."

"Let us go there at once."

Mrs. Peters came out and opened the gates for us.

"What a lovely evening," said Dorcas. "Is the town very far?"

"Two miles, miss."

"Oh, that's too far for me to-night."

She took out her purse and selected some silver.

"Will you please send down the first thing in the morning and buy me a bottle of Wood Violet scent at the chemist's. I always use it, and I've come away without any."

She was just going to hand some silver to Mrs. Peters, when she dropped her purse in the roadway, and the money rolled in every direction.

We picked most of it up, but Dorcas declared there was another half-sovereign. For fully a quarter of an hour she peered about in every direction outside the lodge gates for that missing half-sovereign, and I assisted her. She searched for quite ten minutes in one particular spot, a piece of sodden, loose roadway close against the right-hand gate.

Suddenly she exclaimed she had found it, and, slipping her hand into her pocket, rose, handed Mrs. Peters a five-shilling piece for the scent, beckoned me to follow her, and strolled down the road.

"How came you to drop your purse? Are you nervous to-night?" I said.

"Not at all," replied Dorcas, with a smile. "I dropped my purse that the money might roll around and give me an opportunity of closely examining the ground outside the gates."

"Did you really find your half-sovereign?"

"I never lost one; but I found what I wanted."

"And that was?"

"The footprints of the man who stood outside the gates that night. They are exactly the same shape as those by the side of the lake. The person Maud Hargreaves struggled with that night, the person who flung her into the lake and whose guilt she endeavoured to conceal by declaring she had met with an accident, was the man who wanted to know the name of the place, and asked who lived there—*the man with the wild eye*s."

"You are absolutely certain that the footprints of the man with the wild eyes, who frightened Mrs. Peters at the gate, and the footprints which are mixed up with those of Miss Hargreaves by the side of the lake, are the same?" I said to Dorcas Dene.

"Absolutely certain."

"Then perhaps, if you describe him, the Colonel may be able to recognize him."

"No," said Dorcas Dene, "I have already asked him if he knew any one who could possible bear his daughter a grudge, and he declares that there is no one to his knowledge. Miss Hargreaves has scarcely any acquaintances."

"And has had no love affair?" I asked.

"None, her father says, but of course he can only answer for the last three years. Previous to that he was in India, and Maud—who was sent home at the age of fourteen, when her mother died—had lived with an aunt at Norwood."

"Who do you think this man was who managed to get into the grounds and meet or surprise Miss Hargreaves by the lake—a stranger to her?"

"No; had he been a stranger, she would not have shielded him by inventing the fainting-fit story."

We had walked some distance from the house, when an empty station fly passed us. We got in, Dorcas telling the man to drive us to the station.

When we got there, she told me to go and interview the porter and try to find out if a man of the description of our suspect had left on the night of the "accident."

I found the man who had told Mr. Peters that he had seen such a person arrive, and had noticed the peculiar expression of his eyes. This man assured me that no such person had left from that station. He had told his mates about him, and some of them would be sure to have seen him. The stranger brought no luggage, and gave up a single ticket from Waterloo.

Dorcas was waiting for me outside, and I gave her my information.

"No luggage," she said; "then he wasn't going to an hotel or to stay at a private house."

"But he might be living somewhere about."

"No; the porter would have recognized him if he had been in the habit of coming here."

"But he must have gone away after flinging Miss Hargreaves into the water. He might have got out of the grounds again and walked to another train station, and caught a train back to London."

"Yes, he might," said Dorcas, "but I don't think he did. Come, we'll take the fly back to Orley Park."

Just before we reached the park Dorcas stopped the driver, and we got out and dismissed the man.

"Whereabouts are those dogs—near the private wooden door in the wall used by the family, aren't they?" she said to me.

"Yes, Peters pointed the spot out to me this afternoon."

"Very well, I'm going in. Meet me by the lake to-morrow morning about nine. But watch me now as far as the gates. I'll wait outside five minutes before ringing. When you see I'm there, go to that portion of the wall near the private door. Clamber up and peer over. When the dogs begin to bark, and come at you, notice if you could possibly drop over and escape them without someone they knew called them off. Then jump again and go back to the inn."

I obeyed Dorcas's instructions, and when I had succeeded in climbing to the top of the wall, the dogs flew out of their kennel, and commenced to bark furiously. Had I dropped I must have fallen straight into their grip. Suddenly I heard a shout, and I recognized the voice—it was the lodge-keeper. I dropped back into the road and crept along in the shadow of the wall. In the distance I could hear Peters talking to some one, and I knew what had happened. In the act of letting Dorcas in, he had heard the dogs and had hurried off to see what was the matter. Dorcas had followed him.

At nine o'clock the next morning I found Dorcas waiting for me.

"You did your work admirably last night," she said. "Peters was in a terrible state of alarm. He was very glad for me to come with him. He quieted the dogs, and we searched about everywhere in the shrubbery to see if anyone was in hiding. That man wasn't let in at the door that night by Miss Hargreaves; he dropped over. I found the impression of two deep footprints close together, exactly as they would be made by a drop or jump down from a height."

"Did he go back that way—*were there return footsteps?*"

I thought I had made a clever suggestion, but Dorcas smiled, and shook her head. "I didn't look. How could he return past the dogs when Miss Hargreaves was lying in the lake? They'd have torn him to pieces."

"And you still think this man with the wild eyes is guilty! Who can he have been?"

"His name was Victor."

"You have discovered that!" I exclaimed. "Has Miss Hargreaves been talking to you?"

"Last night I tried a little experiment. When she was asleep, and evidently dreaming, I went quietly in the dark and stood just behind the bed, and in the gruffest voice I could assume, I said, bending down to her ear, 'Maud!'

"She started up and cried out 'Victor!'

"In a moment I was by her side, and found her trembling violently. 'What's the matter, dear?' I said, 'have you been dreaming?'

"'Yes—yes,' she said. 'I—I was dreaming.'

"I soothed her, and talked to her a little while, and finally she lay down again and fell asleep."

"That's something," I said, "to have got the man's Christian name."

"Yes, it's a little, but I think we shall have the surname to-day. You must go up to town and do a little commission for me presently. In the meantime, pull that boat in and row me across to the fowl island. I want to search it."

"Pull me over," said Dorcas, getting into the boat.

I obeyed, and presently we were on the little island.

Dorcas carefully surveyed the lake in every direction. Then she walked round and examined the foliage and the reeds that were at the end and drooping into the water.

Suddenly pushing a mass of close over-hanging growth aside, she thrust her hand deep down under it into the water and drew out a black, saturated, soft felt hat.

"I thought if anything drifted that night, this is where it would get caught and entangled," said Dorcas.

"If it is the man's hat, he must have gone away bareheaded."

"Quite so," replied Dorcas, "but first let us ascertain if it is his. Row ashore at once."

She wrung the water from the hat, squeezed it together and wrapped it up in her pocket-handkerchief and put it under her cloak.

When we were ashore, I went to the lodge and got Mrs. Peters on to the subject of the man with the wild eyes. Then I asked what sort of hat he had on, and Mrs. Peters said it was a soft felt hat with a dent in the middle, and I knew that our find was a good one.

When I told Dorcas she gave a little smile of satisfaction.

"We've got his Christian name and his hat," she said; "now we want the rest of him. You can catch the 11:20 easily."

"Yes."

She drew an envelope from her pocket and took a small photograph from it.

"That's the portrait of the handsome young fellow," she said. "By the style and size I should think t was taken four or five years ago. The photographers are the London Stereoscopic Company—the number of the negative is 111,492. If you go to them, they will search their books and give you the name and address of the original. Get it, and come back here."

"Is that the man?" I said.

"I think so."

"How on earth did you get it?"

"I amused myself while Miss Hargreaves was asleep by looking over the album in her boudoir. It was an old album, and filled with portraits of relatives and friends. I should say there were over fifty, some of them being probably her schoolfellows. I thought I *might* find something, you know. People have portraits given them, put them in an album, and almost forget they are there. I fancied Miss Hargreaves might have forgotten.

"But how did you select this from fifty? There were other male portraits, I suppose?"

"Oh, yes, but I took every portrait and examined the back and the margin."

I took the photo from Dorcas and looked at it. I noticed that a portion of the back had been rubbed away and was rough.

"That's been done with an ink eraser," said Dorcas. "That made me concentrate on this particular photo. There has been a name written there or some word the recipient didn't want other eyes to see.

"That is only surmise."

"Quite so—but there's a certainty in the photo itself. Look closely at that little diamond scarf-pin in the necktie. What shape is it?

"It looks like a small V."

"Exactly. It was fashionable a few years ago for gentlemen to wear a small initial pin. V stands for Victor—take that and the erasure together, and I think it's worth a return fare to town to find out what name and address are opposite the negative number in the books of the London Stereoscopic Company."

*   *   *   *   *

Before two o'clock I was interviewing the manager of the Stereoscopic Company, and he readily referred to the books. The photograph had been taken six years previously, and the name and the address of the sitter were "Mr. Victor Dubois, Anerley Road, Norwood."

Following Dorcas Dene's instructions, I proceeded at once to the address given, and made inquiries for a Mr. Victor Dubois. No one of that name resided there. The present tenants had been in possession for three years.

As I was walking back along the road I met an old postman. I thought I would ask him if he knew the name anywhere in the neighbourhood. He thought a minute, then said, "Yes—now I come to think of it, there was a Dubois here at No. —, but that was five years ago or more. He was an oldish, white-haired gentleman."

"An old gentleman—Victor Dubois!"

"Ah, no—the old gentleman's name was Mounseer Dubois, but there was a Victor. I suppose that must have been his son as lived with him. I know the name. There used to be letters addressed there for Victor most every day—sometimes twice a day—always in the same hand-writing, a lady's—that's what made me notice it."

"And you don't know where M. Dubois and his son went to?"

"No, I did hear as the old gentleman went off his head, and was put in a lunatic asylum; but they went out o' my round."

"You don't know what he was, I suppose?"

"Oh, it said on the brass plate, 'Professor of Languages.' "

I went back to town and took the first train to Godalming, and hastened to Orley Court to report the result of my inquiries to Dorcas.

She was evidently pleased, for she complimented me. Then she rang the bell—we were in the dining room—and the servant entered.

"Will you let the Colonel know that I should like to see him?" said Dorcas, and the servant went to deliver the message.

"Are you going to tell him everything?" I said.

"I am going to tell him nothing yet," replied Dorcas. "I want him to tell me something."

The Colonel entered. His face was worn, and he was evidently worrying himself a great deal.

"Have you anything to tell me?" he said eagerly. "Have you found out what my poor girl is hiding from me."

"I'm afraid I cannot tell you yet. But I want to ask you a few questions."

"I have given you all the information I can already," replied the Colonel a little bitterly.

"All you recollect, but now try and think. Your daughter, before you came back from India, was with her aunt at Norwood. Where was she educated from the time she left India?"

"She went to school at Brighton at first, but from the time she was sixteen she had private instruction at home."

"She had professors, I suppose, for music, French, etc.?"

"Yes, I believe so. I paid bills for that sort of thing. My sister sent them out to me in India."

"Can you remember the name of Dubois?"

The Colonel thought a little while.

"Dubois? Dubois? Dubois?" he said. "I have an idea there was such a name among the accounts my sister sent to me, but whether it was a dressmaker or a French master I really can't say."

"Then I think we will take it that your daughter had lessons at Norwood from a French professor named Dubois. Now, in any letters that your late sister wrote you to India, did she ever mention anything that caused her uneasiness on Maud's account?"

"Only once," replied the Colonel, "and everything was satisfactorily explained afterwards. She left home one day at nine o'clock in the morning, and did not return until four in the afternoon. Her aunt was exceedingly angry, and Maud explained that she had met some friends at the Crystal Palace—she attended drawing class there—and had gone to see one of her fellow students off at the station, and sitting in the carriage, the train had started before she could get out and she had to go on to London. I expect my sister told me to show me how thoroughly I might reply upon her as my daughter's guardian."

"Went on to London?" said Dorcas to me under her voice, "and she could have got out in three minutes at the next station to Norwood!" Then turning to the Colonel, she said, "Now, Colonel, when your wife died, what did you do with her wedding ring?"

"Good heavens, madam!" exclaimed the Colonel, rising and pacing the room. "What can my poor wife's wedding ring have to do with my daughter's being flung into the lake yonder?"

"I am sorry if my question appears absurd," replied Dorcas quietly, "but will you kindly answer it?"

"My wife's wedding ring is on my dead wife's finger in her coffin in the graveyard at Simla," exclaimed the Colonel, "and now perhaps you'll tell me what all this means!"

"Tomorrow," said Dorcas. "Now, if you'll excuse me, I'll take a walk with Mr. Saxon. Miss Hargreaves' maid is with her, and she will be all right until I return."

"Very well, very well!" exclaimed the Colonel, "but I beg—I pray of you to tell me what you know as soon as you can. I am setting spies upon my own child, and to me it is monstrous—and yet—and yet—what can I do?" She won't tell me, and for her sake I must know—I must know."

The old Colonel grasped the proffered hand of Dorcas Dene.

"Thank you," he said, his lips quivering.

Directly we were in the grounds Dorcas Dene turned eagerly to me.

"I'm treating you very badly," she said, "but our task is nearly over. You must go back to town tonight. The first thing tomorrow morning go to Somerset House. You will find an old fellow named Daddy Green, a searcher in the inquiry room. Tell him you come from me, and give him this paper. When he has searched, telegraph the result to me, and come back by the next train."

I looked at the paper, and found written on it in Dorcas's hand:

Search wanted.

Marriage—Victor Dubois and Maud Eleanor Hargreaves—probably between the years 1905 and 1908—London.

I looked up from the paper at Dorcas Dene.

"Whatever makes you think she is a married woman?" I said.

"This," exclaimed Dorcas, drawing an unworn wedding-ring from her purse. "I found it among a lot of trinkets at the bottom of a box her maid told me was her jewel case. I took the liberty of trying all her keys till I opened it. A jewel-box tells many secrets to those who know how to read them."

"And you concluded from that—?"

"That she wouldn't keep a wedding-ring without it had belonged to someone dear to her or had been placed on her own finger. It is quite unworn, you see, so it was taken off immediately after the ceremony. It was only to make doubly sure that I asked the Colonel where his wife's was."

I duly repaired to Somerset House, and soon after midday the searcher brought a paper and handed it to me. It was a copy of the certificate of the marriage of Victor Dubois, bachelor, aged twenty-six, and Maud Eleanor Hargreaves, aged twenty-one, in London, in the year 1906. I telegraphed the news, wording the message simply, "Yes," and the date, and I followed my wire by the first train.

When I arrived at Orley Park I rang several times before anyone came. Presently Mrs. Peters, looking very white and excited, came from the grounds and apologized for keeping me waiting.

"Oh, sir—such a dreadful thing!" she said—"a body in the lake!"

"A body!"

"Yes, sir—a man. The nurse as came with you here that day, she was rowing herself on the lake, and she must have stirred it pushing with her oar, for it come up all tangled with weeds. It's a man, sir, and I do believe it's the man I saw at the gate that night."

"*The man with the wild eyes!*" I exclaimed.

"Yes, sir! Oh, it is dreadful—Mis Maud first, and then this. Oh, what can it mean!"

I found Dorcas standing at the edge of the lake, and Peters and two of the gardeners lifting the drowned body of a man into the boat which was alongside.

Dorcas was giving instructions. "Lay it in the boat, and cover it with a tarpaulin," she said. "Mind, nothing is to be touched till the police come. I will go and find the Colonel."

As she turned away I met her.

"What a terrible thing! Is it Dubois?"

"Yes," replied Dorcas. "I suspected he was there yesterday, but I wanted to find him myself instead of having the lake dragged."

"Why?"

"Well, I didn't want anyone else to search the pockets. There might have been papers or letters, you now, which would have been read at the inquest, and might have compromised Miss Hargreaves. But there was nothing—"

"What—you searched!"

"Yes, after I'd brought the poor fellow to the surface with the oars."

"But how do you think he got in?"

"Suicide—insanity. The father was taken to a lunatic asylum—you learned that at Norwood yesterday. Son doubtless inherited tendency. Looks like a case of homicidal mania—he attack Miss Hargreaves, whom he probably tracked after years of separation, and after he had as he thought killed her, he drowned himself. At any rate, Miss Hargreaves is a free woman. She was evidently terrified of her husband when he was alive, and so—"

I guess what Dorcas was thinking as we went together to the house. At the door she held out her hand. "You had better go to the inn and return to town to-night," she said. "You can do no more good, and had better keep out of it. I shall be home to-morrow. Come to Elm Tree Road in the evening."

The next evening Dorcas told me all that had happened after I left. Paul had already heard it, and when I arrived was profuse in his thanks for the assistance I had rendered his wife. Mrs. Lester, however, felt compelled to remark that she never felt a daughter of hers would go gadding about the country fishing up corpses for a living.

Dorcas had gone to the Colonel and told him everything. The Colonel was in a terrible state, but Dorcas told him that the only way in which to ascertain the truth was for them to go to the unhappy girls together, and attempt, with the facts in their possession, to persuade her to divulge the rest.

When the Colonel told his daughter that the man she had married had flung her into the lake that night, she was dumbfounded, and became hysterical, but when she learned that Dubois had been found in the lake she became alarmed and instantly told all she knew.

She had been in the habit of meeting Victor Dubois constantly when she was at Norwood, at first with his father—her French master—and afterwards alone. He was handsome, young, romantic, and they fell madly in love. He was going away for some time to an appointment abroad, and he urged her to marry him secretly. She foolishly consented, and they parted at the church, she returning to her home and he going abroad the same evening.

She received letters from him clandestinely from time to time. Then he wrote that his father had become insane and he had to be removed to a lunatic asylum, and he was returning. He had only time to see his father's removal and return to his appointment. She did not hear from him for a long time, and then through a friend at Norwood who knew the Dubois and their relatives she made inquiries. Victor had returned to England, and met with an accident which had injured his head severely. He had become insane and had been taken to the lunatic asylum.

Then the poor girl resolved to keep her marriage a secret for ever, especially as her father had returned from India, and she knew how bitterly it would distress him to learn that his daughter was the wife of a madman.

On the night of the affair Maud was in the grounds by herself. She was strolling by the lake after dinner, when she heard a sound, and the dogs began to bark. Looking up, she saw Victor Dubois scaling the wall. Fearful that the dogs would bring Peters or some one on the scene, she ran to them and silenced them, and her husband leapt down and stood by her.

"Come away!" she said, fearing the dogs might attack him or begin to bark again, and she led him round by the lake which was out of sight of the house and lodge.

She forgot for the moment in her excitement that he had been mad. At first he was gentle and kind. He told her he had been ill and in an asylum, but had recently been discharged cured. Directly he regained his liberty he set out in search of his wife, and ascertained from an old Norwood acquaintance that Miss Hargreaves was now living with her father at Orley Park, near Godalming.

Maud begged him to go away quietly, and she would write to him. He tried to take her in his arms and kiss her, but instinctively she shrank from him. Instantly he became furious. Seized with a sudden mania he grasped her by the throat. She struggled and freed herself.

They were at the edge of the lake. Suddenly the maniac got her by the throat again, and hurled her down into the water. She fell in up to her waist, but managed to drag herself towards the edge, but before she emerged she fell senseless—fortunately with her head on the bank just out of the water.

The murderer, probably thinking that she was dead, must have waded out in the deep water and drowned himself.

Before she left Orley Park Dorcas advised the Colonel to let the inquest be held without any light being thrown on the affair by him. Only he was to take care that the police received information that a man answering the description of the suicide had recently been discharged from a lunatic asylum.

We heard later that at the inquest an official from the asylum attended, and the local jury found that Victor Dubois, a lunatic, got into the grounds in some way, and drowned himself in the lake while temporarily insane. It was suggested by the coroner that probably Miss Hargreaves, who was too unwell to attend, had not seen the man, but might have been alarmed by the sound of his footsteps, and that this would account for her fainting away near the water's edge. At any rate, the inquest ended in a satisfactory verdict, and the Colonel shortly afterwards took his daughter abroad with him on a Continental tour for the benefit of her health.

But of this, of course, we knew nothing on the evening after the eventful discovery, when I met Dorcas once beneath her own roof-tree.

Paul was delighted to have his wife back again, and she devoted herself to him, and that evening had eyes and ears for no one else—not even for her faithful "assistant."

THE GOLDEN SLIPPER

Anna Katherine Green

S HE'S HERE! I THOUGHT SHE WOULD BE. SHE'S ONE OF THE THREE YOUNG ladies you see in the right-hand box near the proscenium."

The gentleman thus addressed—a man of middle age and a member of the most exclusive clubs—turned his opera glass toward the spot designated, and in some astonishment retorted:

"She? Why those are the Misses Pratt and—

"Miss Violet Strange; no other."

"And do you mean to say—"

"I do—"

"That yon silly little chit, whose father I know, whose fortune I know, who is seen everywhere, and who is called one of the season's belles is an agent of yours; a—a—"

"No names here, please. You want a mystery solved. It is not a matter for the police—that is, as yet,—and so you come to me, and when I ask for the facts, I find that women and only women are involved, and that these women are not only young but one and all of the highest society. Is it a man's work to go to the bottom of a combination like this? No. Sex against sex, and, if possible, youth against youth. Happily, I know such a person—a girl of gifts and extraordinarily well placed for the purpose. Why she uses her talents in this direction—why, with means enough to play the part natural to her as a successful debutante, she consents to occupy herself with social and other mysteries, you must ask her, not me. Enough that I promise you her aid if you want it. That is, if you can interest her. She will not work otherwise."

Mr. Driscoll again raised his opera glass.

"But it's a comedy face," he commented. "It's hard to associate intellectuality with such quaintness of expression. Are you sure of her discretion?"

"Whom is she with?"

"Abner Pratt, his wife, and daughters."

"Is he a man to entrust his affairs unadvisedly?"

"Abner Pratt! Do you mean to say that she is anything more to him than his daughters' guest?"

"Judge. You see how merry they are. They were in deep trouble yesterday. You are witness to a celebration."

"And she?"

"Don't you observe how they are loading her with attentions? She's too young to rouse such interest in a family of notably unsympathetic temperament for any other reason than that of gratitude."

"It's hard to believe. But if what you hint is true, secure me an opportunity at once of talking to this youthful marvel. My affair is serious. The dinner I have mentioned comes off in three days and—"

"I know. I recognize your need; but I think you had better enter Mr. Pratt's box without my intervention. Miss Strange's value to us will be impaired the moment her connection with us is discovered."

"Ah, there's Ruthven! He will take me to Mr. Pratt's box," remarked Driscoll as the curtain fell on the second act. "Any suggestions before I go?"

"Yes, and an important one. When you make your bow, touch your left shoulder with your right hand. It is a signal. She may respond to it; but if she does not, do not be discouraged. One of her idiosyncrasies is a theoretical dislike of her work. But once she gets interested, nothing will hold her back. That's all, except this. In no event give away her secret. That's part of the compact, you remember."

Driscoll nodded and left his seat for Ruthven's box. When the curtain rose for the third time he could be seen sitting with the Misses Pratt and their vivacious young friend. A widower and still on the right side of fifty, his presence there did not pass unnoted, and curiosity was rife among certain onlookers as to which of the twin belles was responsible for this change in his well-known habits. Unfortunately, no opportunity was given him for showing. Other and younger men had followed his lead into the box, and they saw him forced upon the good graces of the fascinating but inconsequent Miss Strange whose rapid fire of talk he was hardly of a temperament to appreciate.

Did he appear dissatisfied? Yes; but only one person in the opera house knew why. Miss Strange had shown no comprehension of or sympathy with his errand. Though she chatted amiably enough between duets and trios, she gave him no opportunity to express his wishes though she knew them well enough, owing to the signal he had given her.

This might be in character but it hardly suited his views; and, being a man of resolution, he took advantage of an absorbing minute on the stage to lean forward and whisper in her ear:

"It's my daughter for whom I request your services; as fine a girl as any in this house. Give me a hearing. You certainly can manage it."

She was a small, slight woman whose naturally quaint appearance was accentuated by the extreme simplicity of her attire. In the tier upon tier of boxes rising before his eyes, no other personality could vie with hers in strangeness, or in the illusive quality of her ever-changing expression. She was vivacity incarnate and, to the ordinary observer, light as thistledown in fibre and in feeling. But not to all. To those who watched her long, there came moments—say when the music rose to heights of greatness—when the mouth so given over to laughter took on curves of the rarest sensibility, and a woman's lofty soul shone through her odd, bewildering features.

Driscoll had noted this, and consequently awaited her reply in secret hope.

It came in the form of a question and only after an instant's display of displeasure or possibly of pure nervous irritability.

"What has she done?"

"Nothing. But slander is in the air, and any day it may ripen into public accusation."

"Accusation of what?" Her tone was almost pettish.

"Of—of *theft*," he murmured. "On a great scale," he emphasized, as the music rose to a crash. "Jewels?"

"Inestimable ones. They are always returned by somebody. People say, by me."

"Ah!" The little lady's hands grew steady,—they had been fluttering all over her lap. "I will see you to-morrow morning at my father's house," she presently observed; and turned her full attention to the stage.

Some three days after this Mr. Driscoll opened his house on the Hudson to notable guests. He had not desired the publicity of such an event, nor the opportunity it gave for an increase of the scandal secretly in circulation against his daughter. But the Ambassador and his wife were foreign and any evasion of the promised hospitality would be sure to be misunderstood; so the scheme was carried forward though with less *éclat* than possibly was expected.

Among the lesser guests, who were mostly young and well acquainted with the house and its hospitality, there was one unique figure,—that of the lively Miss Strange, who, if personally unknown to Miss Driscoll, was so gifted with the qualities which tell on an occasion of this kind, that the stately young hostess hailed her presence with very obvious gratitude.

The manner of their first meeting was singular, and of great interest to one of them at least. Miss Strange had come in an automobile and had been shown her room; but there was nobody to accompany her down-stairs afterward, and, finding herself alone in the great hall, she naturally moved toward the library, the door of which stood ajar. She had pushed this door half open before she noticed that the room was already occupied. As a consequence, she was made the unexpected observer of a beautiful picture of youth and love.

A young man and a young woman were standing together in the glow of a blazing wood-fire. No word was to be heard, but in their faces, eloquent with passion, there shone something so deep and true that the chance intruder hesitated on the threshold, eager to lay this picture away in her mind with the other lovely and tragic memories now fast accumulating there. Then she drew back, and readvancing with a less noiseless foot, came into the full presence of Captain Holliday drawn up in all the pride of his military rank beside Alicia, the accomplished daughter of the house, who, if under a shadow as many whispered, wore that shadow as some women wear a crown.

Miss Strange was struck with admiration, and turned upon them the brightest facet of her vivacious nature all the time she was saying to herself: "Does she know why I am here? Or does she look upon me only as an additional guest foisted upon her by a thoughtless parent?"

There was nothing in the manner of her cordial but composed young hostess to show, and Miss Strange, with but one thought in mind since she had caught the light of feeling on the two faces confronting her, took the first opportunity that offered of running over the facts given her by Mr. Driscoll, to see if any reconcilement were possible between them and an innocence in which she must henceforth believe.

They were certainly of a most damaging nature.

Miss Driscoll and four other young ladies of her own station in life had formed themselves, some two years before, into a coterie of five, called The Inseparables. They lunched together, rode together, visited together. So close was the bond and their mutual dependence so evident, that it came to be the custom to invite the whole five whenever the size of the function warranted it. In fact, it was far from an uncommon occurrence to see them grouped at receptions or following one another down the aisles of churches or through the mazes of the dance at balls or assemblies. And no one demurred at this, for they were all handsome and attractive girls, till it began to be noticed that, coincident with their presence, some article of value was found missing from the dressing-room or from the tables where wedding gifts were displayed. Nothing was safe where they went, and though, in the course of time, each article found its way back to its owner in a manner as mysterious as its previous abstraction, the scandal grew and, whether with good reason or bad, finally settled about the person of Miss Driscoll, who was the showiest, least pecuniarily tempted, and most dignified in manner and speech of them all.

Some instances had been given by way of further enlightenment. This is one: A theatre party was in progress. There were twelve in the party, five of whom were Inseparables. In the course of the last act, another lady—in fact, their chaperon— missed her handkerchief, an almost priceless bit of lace. Positive that she had brought it with her into the box, she caused a careful search, but without the least success.

Recalling certain whispers she had heard, she noted which of the five girls were with her in the box. They were Miss Driscoll, Miss Hughson, Miss Yates, and Miss Benedict. Miss West sat in the box adjoining.

A fortnight later this handkerchief reappeared— and where? Among the cushions of a yellow satin couch in her own drawing-room. The Inseparables had just made their call and the three who had sat on the couch were Miss Driscoll, Miss Hughson, and Miss Benedict.

The next instance seemed to point still more insistently toward the lady already named. Miss Yates had an expensive present to buy, and the whole five Inseparables went in an imposing group to Tiffany's. A tray of rings was set before them. All examined and eagerly fingered the stock out of which Miss Yates presently chose a finely set emerald. She was leading her friends away when the clerk suddenly whispered in her ear, "I miss one of the rings." Dismayed beyond speech, she turned and consulted the faces of her four companions who stared back at her with immovable serenity. But one of them was paler than usual, and this lady (it was Miss Driscoll) held her hands in her muff and did not offer to take them out. Miss Yates, whose father had completed a big "deal" the week before, wheeled round upon the clerk. "Charge it! charge it at its full value," said she. "I buy both the rings."

And in three weeks the purloined ring came back to her, in a box of violets with no name attached.

The third instance was a recent one, and had come to Mr. Driscoll's ears directly from the lady suffering the loss. She was a woman of uncompromising integrity, who felt it her duty to make known to this gentleman the following facts: She had just left a studio reception, and was standing at the curb waiting for a taxicab to draw up, when a small boy—a street arab—darted toward her from the other side of the street, and thrusting into her hand something small and hard, cried breathlessly as he slipped away, "It's yours, ma'am; you dropped it." Astonished, for she had not been conscious of any loss, she looked down at her treasure trove and found it to be a small medallion which she sometimes wore on a chain at her belt. But she had not worn it that day, nor any day for weeks. Then she remembered. She had worn it a month before to a similar reception at this same studio. A number of young girls had stood about her admiring it—she remembered well who they were; the Inseparables, of course, and to please them she had slipped it from its chain. Then something had happened—something which diverted her attention entirely,—and she had gone home without the medallion; had, in fact, forgotten it, only to recall its loss now. Placing it in her bag, she looked hastily about her. A crowd was at her back; nothing to be distinguished there. But in front, on the opposite side of the street, stood a club-house, and in one of its windows she perceived a solitary figure looking out. It was that of Miss Driscoll's father. He could imagine her conclusion.

In vain he denied all knowledge of the matter. She told him other stories which had come to her ears of thefts as mysterious, followed by restorations as peculiar as this one, finishing with, "It is your daughter, and people are beginning to say so."

And Miss Strange, brooding over these instances, would have said the same, but for Miss Driscoll's absolute serenity of demeanour and complete abandonment to love. These seemed incompatible with guilt; these, whatever the appearances, proclaimed innocence—an innocence she was here to prove if fortune favoured and the really guilty person's madness should again break forth.

For madness it would be and nothing less, for any hand, even the most experienced, to draw attention to itself by a repetition of old tricks on an occasion so marked. Yet because it would take madness, and madness knows no law, she prepared herself for the contingency under a mask of girlish smiles which made her at once the delight and astonishment of her watchful and uneasy host.

With the exception of the diamonds worn by the Ambassadress, there was but one jewel of consequence to be seen at the dinner that night; but how great was that consequence and with what splendour it invested the snowy neck it adorned!

Miss Strange, in compliment to the noble foreigners, had put on one of her family heirlooms—a filigree pendant of extraordinary sapphires which had once belonged to Marie Antoinette. As its beauty flashed upon the women, and its value struck the host, the latter could not restrain himself from casting an anxious eye about the board in search of some token of the cupidity with which one person there must welcome this unexpected sight.

Naturally his first glance fell upon Alicia, seated opposite to him at the other end of the table. But her eyes were elsewhere, and her smile for Captain Holliday, and the father's gaze travelled on, taking up each young girl's face in turn. All were contemplating Miss Strange and her jewels, and the cheeks of one were flushed and those of the others pale, but whether with dread or longing who could tell. Struck with foreboding, but alive to his duty as host, he forced his glances away, and did not even allow himself to question the motive or the wisdom of the temptation thus offered.

Two hours later and the girls were all in one room. It was a custom of the Inseparables to meet for a chat before retiring, but always alone and in the room of one of their number. But this was a night of innovations; Violet was not only included, but the meeting was held in her room. Her way with girls was even more fruitful of result than her way with men. They might laugh at her, criticize her or even call her names significant of disdain, but they never left her long to herself or missed an opportunity to make the most of her irrepressible chatter.

Her satisfaction at entering this charmed circle did not take from her piquancy, and story after story fell from her lips, as she fluttered about, now here now there, in her endless preparations for retirement. She had taken off her historic pendant after it had been duly admired and handled by all present, and, with the careless confidence of an assured ownership, thrown it down upon the end of her dresser, which, by the way, projected very close to the open window.

"Are you going to leave your jewel *there*?" whispered a voice in her ear as a burst of laughter rang out in response to one of her sallies.

Turning, with a simulation of round-eyed wonder, she met Miss Hughson's earnest gaze with the careless rejoinder, "What's the harm?" and went on with her story with all the reckless ease of a perfectly thoughtless nature.

Miss Hughson abandoned her protest. How could she explain her reasons for it to one apparently uninitiated in the scandal associated with their especial clique.

Yes, she left the jewel there; but she locked her door and quickly, so that they must all have heard her before reaching their rooms. Then she crossed to the window, which, like all on this side, opened on a balcony running the length of the house. She was aware of this balcony, also of the fact that only young ladies slept in the corridor communicating with it. But she was not quite sure that this one corridor accommodated them all. If one of them should room elsewhere! (Miss Driscoll, for instance.) But no! the anxiety displayed for the safety of her jewel precluded that supposition. Their hostess, if none of the others, was within access of this room and its open window. But how about the rest? Perhaps the lights would tell. Eagerly the little schemer looked forth, and let her glances travel down the full length of the balcony. Two separate beams of light shot across it as she looked, and presently another, and, after some waiting, a fourth. But the fifth failed to appear. This troubled her, but not seriously. Two of the girls might be sleeping in one bed.

Drawing her shade, she finished her preparations for the night; then with her kimono on, lifted the pendant and thrust it into a small box she had taken from her trunk. A curious smile, very unlike any she had shown to man or woman that day, gave a sarcastic lift to her lips, as with a slow and thoughtful manipulation of her dainty fingers she moved the jewel about in this small receptacle and then returned it, after one quick examining glance, to the very spot on the dresser from which she had taken it. "If only the madness is great enough!" that smile seemed to say. Truly, it was much to hope for, but a chance is a chance; and comforting herself with the thought, Miss Strange put out her light, and, with a hasty raising of the shade she had previously pulled down, took a final look at the prospect.

Its aspect made her shudder. A low fog was rising from the meadows in the far distance, and its ghostliness under the moon woke all sorts of uncanny images in her excited mind. To escape them she crept into bed where she lay with her eyes on the end of her dresser. She had closed that half of the French window over which she had drawn the shade; but she had left ajar the one giving free access to the jewels; and when she was not watching the scintillation of her sapphires in the moonlight, she was dwelling in fixed attention on this narrow opening.

But nothing happened, and two o'clock, then three o'clock struck, without a dimming of the blue scintillations on the end of her dresser. Then she suddenly sat up. Not that she heard anything new, but that a thought had come to her. "If an attempt is made," so she murmured softly to herself, "it will be by—" She did not finish. Something—she could not call it sound—set her heart beating tumultuously, and listening—listening—watching—watching—she followed in her imagination the approach down the balcony of an almost inaudible step, not daring to move herself, it seemed so near, but waiting with eyes fixed, for the shadow which must fall across the shade she had failed to raise over that half of the swinging window she had so carefully left shut.

At length she saw it projecting slowly across the slightly illuminated surface. Formless, save for the outreaching hand, it passed the casement's edge, nearing with pauses and hesitations the open gap beyond through which the neglected sapphires beamed with steady lustre. Would she ever see the hand itself appear between the dresser and the window frame? Yes, there it comes,—small, delicate, and startlingly white, threading that gap— darting with the suddenness of a serpent's tongue toward the dresser and disappearing again with the pendant in its clutch.

As she realizes this,—she is but young, you know,—as she sees her bait taken and the hardly expected event fulfilled, her pent-up breath sped forth in a sigh which sent the intruder flying, and so startled herself that she sank back in terror on her pillow.

The breakfast-call had sounded its musical chimes through the halls. The Ambassador and his wife had responded, so had most of the young gentlemen and ladies, but the daughter of the house was not amongst them, nor Miss Strange, whom one would naturally expect to see down first of all.

These two absences puzzled Mr. Driscoll. What might they not portend? But his suspense, at least in one regard, was short. Before his guests were well seated, Miss Driscoll entered from the terrace in company with Captain Holliday. In her arms she carried a huge bunch of roses and was looking very beautiful. Her father's heart warmed at the sight. No shadow from the night rested upon her.

But Miss Strange!—where was she? He could not feel quite easy till he knew.

"Have any of you seen Miss Strange?" he asked, as they sat down at table. And his eyes sought the Inseparables.

Five lovely heads were shaken, some carelessly, some wonderingly, and one, with a quick, forced smile. But he was in no mood to discriminate, and he had beckoned one of the servants to him, when a step was heard at the door and the delinquent slid in and took her place, in a shamefaced manner suggestive of a cause deeper than mere tardiness. In fact, she had what might be called a frightened air, and stared into her plate, avoiding every eye, which was certainly not natural to her. What did it mean? and why, as she made a poor attempt at eating, did four of the Inseparables exchange glances of doubt and dismay and then concentrate their looks upon his daughter? That Alicia failed to notice this, but sat abloom above her roses now fastened in a great bunch upon her breast, offered him some comfort, yet, for all the volubility of his chief guests, the meal was a great trial to his patience, as well as a poor preparation for the hour when, the noble pair gone, he stepped into the library to find Miss Strange awaiting him with one hand behind her back and a piteous look on her infantile features.

"O, Mr. Driscoll," she began,—and then he saw that a group of anxious girls hovered in her rear—"my pendant! my beautiful pendant! It is gone! Somebody reached in from the balcony and took it from my dresser in the night. Of course, it was to frighten me; all of the girls told me not to leave it there. But I—I cannot make them give it back, and papa is so particular about this jewel that I'm afraid to go home. Won't you tell them it's no joke, and see that I get it again. I won't be so careless another time."

Hardly believing his eyes, hardly believing his ears,—she was so perfectly the spoiled child detected in a fault—he looked sternly about upon the girls and bade them end the jest and produce the gems at once.

But not one of them spoke, and not one of them moved; only his daughter grew pale until the roses seemed a mockery, and the steady stare of her large eyes was almost too much for him to bear.

The anguish of this gave asperity to his manner, and in a strange, hoarse tone he loudly cried:

"One of you did this. Which? If it was you, Alicia, speak. I am in no mood for nonsense. I want to know whose foot traversed the balcony and whose hand abstracted these jewels."

A continued silence, deepening into painful embarrassment for all. Mr. Driscoll eyed them in ill-concealed anguish, then turning to Miss Strange was still further thrown off his balance by seeing her pretty head droop and her gaze fall in confusion.

"Oh! it's easy enough to tell whose foot traversed the balcony," she murmured. "It left *this* behind." And drawing forward her hand, she held out to view a small gold-coloured slipper. "I found it outside my window," she explained. "I hoped I should not have to show it."

A gasp of uncontrollable feeling from the surrounding group of girls, then absolute stillness.

"I fail to recognize it," observed Mr. Driscoll, taking it in his hand. "Whose slipper is this?" he asked in a manner not to be gainsaid.

Still no reply, then as he continued to eye the girls one after another a voice—the last he expected to hear—spoke and his daughter cried:

"It is mine. But it was not I who walked in it down the balcony."

"Alicia!"

A month's apprehension was in that cry. The silence, the pent-up emotion brooding in the air was intolerable. A fresh young laugh broke it.

"Oh," exclaimed a roguish voice, "I knew that you were all in it! But the especial one who wore the slipper and grabbed the pendant cannot hope to hide herself. Her finger-tips will give her away."

Amazement on every face and a convulsive movement in one half-hidden hand.

"You see," the airy little being went on, in her light way, "I have some awfully funny tricks. I am always being scolded for them, but somehow I don't improve. One is to keep my jewelry bright with a strange foreign paste an old Frenchwoman once gave me in Paris. It's of a vivid red, and stains the fingers dreadfully if you don't take care. Not even water will take it off, see mine. I used that paste on my pendant last night just after you left me, and being awfully sleepy I didn't stop to rub it off. If your finger-tips are not red, you never touched the pendant, Miss Driscoll. Oh, see! They are as white as milk.

"But some one took the sapphires, and I owe that person a scolding, as well as myself. Was it you, Miss Hughson? You, Miss Yates? or—" and here she paused before Miss West, "Oh, you have your gloves on! You are the guilty one!" and her laugh rang out like a peal of bells, robbing her next sentence of even a suggestion of sarcasm. "Oh, what a sly-boots!" she cried. "How you have deceived me! Whoever would have thought you to be the one to play the mischief!"

Who indeed! Of all the five, she was the one who was considered absolutely immune from suspicion ever since the night Mrs. Barnum's handkerchief had been taken, and she not in the box. Eyes which had surveyed Miss Driscoll askance now rose in wonder toward hers, and failed to fall again because of the stoniness into which her delicately-carved features had settled.

"Miss West, I know you will be glad to remove your gloves; Miss Strange certainly has a right to know her special tormentor," spoke up her host in as natural a voice as his great relief would allow.

But the cold, half-frozen woman remained without a movement. She was not deceived by the banter of the moment. She knew that to all of the others, if not to Peter Strange's odd little daughter, it was the thief who was being spotted and brought thus hilariously to light. And her eyes grew hard, and her lips grey, and she failed to unglove the hands upon which all glances were concentrated.

"You do not need to see my hands; I confess to taking the pendant."

"Caroline!"

A heart overcome by shock had thrown up this cry. Miss West eyed her bosom-friend disdainfully.

"Miss Strange has called it a jest," she coldly commented. "Why should you suggest anything of a graver character?"

Alicia brought thus to bay, and by one she had trusted most, stepped quickly forward, and quivering with vague doubts, aghast before unheard-of possibilities, she tremulously remarked:

"We did not sleep together last night. You had to come into my room to get my slippers. Why did you do this? What was in your mind, Caroline?"

A steady look, a low laugh choked with many emotions answered her.

"Do you want me to reply, Alicia? Or shall we let it pass?"

"Answer!"

It was Mr. Driscoll who spoke. Alicia had shrunk back, almost to where a little figure was cowering with wide eyes fixed in something like terror on the aroused father's face.

"Then hear me," murmured the girl, entrapped and suddenly desperate. "I wore Alicia's slippers and I took the jewels, because it was time that an end should come to your mutual dissimulation. The love I once felt for her she has herself deliberately killed. I had a lover—she took him. I had faith in life, in honour, and in friendship. She destroyed all. A thief—she has dared to aspire to *him*! And *you* condoned her fault. You, with your craven restoration of her booty, thought the matter cleared and her a fit mate for a man of highest honour."

"Miss West,"—no one had ever heard that tone in Mr. Driscoll's voice before, "before you say another word calculated to mislead these ladies, let me say that this hand never returned any one's booty or had anything to do with the restoration of any abstracted article. You have been caught in a net, Miss West, from which you cannot escape by slandering my innocent daughter."

"Innocent!" All the tragedy latent in this peculiar girl's nature blazed forth in the word. "Alicia, face me. Are you innocent? Who took the Dempsey corals, and that diamond from the Tiffany tray?"

"It is not necessary for Alicia to answer," the father interposed with not unnatural heat. "Miss West stands self-convicted."

"How about Lady Paget's scarf? I was not there that night."

"You are a woman of wiles. That could be managed by one bent on an elaborate scheme of revenge."

"And so could the abstraction of Mrs. Barnum's five-hundred-dollar handkerchief by one who sat in the next box," chimed in Miss Hughson, edging away from the friend to whose honour she would have pinned her faith an hour before. "I remember now seeing her lean over the railing to adjust the old lady's shawl."

With a start, Caroline West turned a tragic gaze upon the speaker.

"You think me guilty of all because of what I did last night?"

"Why shouldn't I."

"And you, Anna?"

"Alicia has my sympathy," murmured Miss Benedict.

Yet the wild girl persisted.

"But I have told you my provocation. You cannot believe that I am guilty of her sin; not if you look at her as I am looking now."

But their glances hardly followed her pointing finger. Her friends—the comrades of her youth, the Inseparables with their secret oath—one and all held themselves aloof, struck by the perfidy they were only just beginning to take in. Smitten with despair, for these girls were her life, she gave one wild leap and sank on her knees before Alicia.

"O speak!" she began. "Forgive me, and—"

A tremble seized her throat; she ceased to speak and let fall her partially uplifted hands. The cheery sound of men's voices had drifted in from the terrace, and the figure of Captain Holliday could be seen passing by. The shudder which shook Caroline West communicated itself to Alicia Driscoll, and the former rising quickly, the two women surveyed each other, possibly for the first time, with open soul and a complete understanding.

"Caroline!" murmured the one.

"Alicia!" pleaded the other.

"Caroline, trust me," said Alicia Driscoll in that moving voice of hers, which more than her beauty caught and retained all hearts. "You have served me ill, but it was not all undeserved. Girls," she went on, eyeing both them and her father with the wistfulness of a breaking heart, "neither Caroline nor myself are worthy of Captain Holliday's love. Caroline has told you her fault, but mine is perhaps a worse one. The ring—the scarf—the diamond pins—I took them all—took them if I did not retain them. A curse has been over my life—the curse of a longing I could not combat. But love was working a change in me. Since I have known Captain Holliday—but that's all over. I was mad to think I could be happy with such memories in my life. I shall never marry now—or touch jewels again—my own or another's. Father, father, you won't go back on your girl! I couldn't see Caroline suffer for what I have done. You will pardon me and help—help—"

Her voice choked. She flung herself into her father's arms; his head bent over hers, and for an instant not a soul in the room moved. Then Miss Hughson gave a spring and caught her by the hand.

"We are inseparable," said she, and kissed the hand, murmuring, "Now is our time to show it."

Then other lips fell upon those cold and trembling fingers, which seemed to warm under these embraces. And then a tear. It came from the hard eye of Caroline, and remained a sacred secret between the two.

"You have your pendant?"

Mr. Driscoll's suffering eye shone down on Violet Strange's uplifted face as she advanced to say good-bye preparatory to departure.

"Yes," she acknowledged, "but hardly, I fear, your gratitude."

And the answer astonished her.

"I am not sure that the real Alicia will not make her father happier than the unreal one has ever done."

"And Captain Holliday?"

"He may come to feel the same."

"Then I do not quit in disgrace?"

"You depart with my thanks."

When a certain personage was told of the success of Miss Strange's latest manœuvre, he remarked:

"The little one progresses. We shall have to give her a case of prime importance next."

MANDRAGORA

Richard Marsh

I HAD RETURNED FROM WEEK-ENDING WITH A FRIEND, AND WAS HAVING LUNCH AT the railway station dining room before returning to my work. Just as the waiter had brought me what I had ordered two men, coming hurriedly in, took the only vacant seats in sight—at a little table next to mine. Something in their appearance attracted my attention. One was about 30: tall, dark, square faced; the other was possibly nearly twice that age, a little white-haired man who looked as if his health was failing. What caught my attention chiefly was that he seemed to be in such a curious state of nervousness; watching him gave one the jumps. At last his companion commented on it—they were sitting sideways to me, so that I could see both their faces.

"If I were you, Hutton, I should take some thing for it."

"Ah, Walker, I wish I could take some thing for it; but—who can minister to a mind diseased? Mandragora would have no effect on me."

An unpleasant look came upon the others face as he said:

"I wish you wouldn't talk such nonsense. What do you suppose is the good of it?"

"For one thing I am nearer the grave than you are; perhaps that's why I'm so much more disposed than you to think of what's beyond it. I never thought that I would go to the judgment seat with such a crime to answer for."

"If you don't stop talking like that, taking up that pose, you and I will quarrel."

"I'm not afraid of that, Walker; I'm inclined to wish that you and I had quarreled before. Rather Dartmoor with Young than torment with you."

"Hutton, I can't think what's come to you. You'll worry yourself into actual illness if you don't look out."

"I'm a sick man already—sick unto death."

"Of course, if it pleases you to feel like that, I can't help it, can I? Only let me give you a tip. You played a trick on George Young: don't you try to play it a second on me. It won't benefit you to go to the judgment seat with two crimes to answer for."

"That's true. Don't I know it? I'd have made a clean breast of things before this if I were the only one who would suffer."

The young man regarded his companion fixedly, a savage some thing coming into the expression in his face.

"Hutton, we did this thing together, but the first suggestion came from you. If I thought that because of any sophistical nonsense, or because your digestion was out of order, you were meditating putting me where we put him, I'm not sure that I wouldn't kill you."

"I wish you would kill me, Tom."

His sincerity seemed to impress his younger companion, who looked at him as if seeking words with which to answer; then, as if finding none, he summoned the waiter, paid their joint bill and rose from his chair.

They went out. They had got through their lunch in a very few minutes. Since their entry I barely touched mine. I had, before I knew it, become a confidante in a tragedy in circumstances, which had deprived me of the little appetite I had had.

For days afterward I kept asking myself what was the nature of the tragedy which had made that old gentleman so willing that his companion should kill him.

In the late summer of that year I went to a seaside town, which I will call Easthampton. I believed it to be an obscure hamlet, until on getting there I found it impossible to rent a bed and sitting room, either for love or money. When I had received the same answer for about the twentieth time, I asked the fly man, who was taking me from one likely house to another, if there was still another he could think of.

"I can't say, miss, that there is—at least, there is a cottage in the fields about half a mile along the shore in which you might find accommodation; but I can't say that I know much in its favor."

I told him to drive me to that cottage. It turned out to have just the accommodation I was looking for, and to be quite a charming cottage in itself. Then I liked the landlady; she was quite a pretty woman, possibly not more than 26 years old. She told me she had one child, a girl of six, and kept no servant, but did all the work herself.

I was never in more comfortable quarters. And my landlady was a most charming person; no make-believe lady, but a real one. She told me that her name was Mrs. Vinton, and that she was a widow; her husband had been dead three years. Since she was practically my sole companion, I saw a good deal of her.

I never met a woman who had a finer gift of silence. She would sit for hours and say nothing. What cause she had for silence I could not tell.

One evening as I was going to my room to change my blouse for dinner, the door of the bed-room which she shared with her small child was wide open. She was putting the maid to bed. The child, kneeling at her mother's knee, was about to say her prayers, and the mother, bending over, said to her:

"I want you, Nellie, to pray for papa tonight very especially indeed; it's his birthday."

Tears fell from her eyes to the child's fair hair. I had left my walking shoes downstairs and was moving very quietly; I suppose that was why she had not heard me come.

The very next day some thing else occurred. I had made another intrusion on her confidence—I protest, quite unwillingly. It was where I was passing the kitchen window, which like the bed-room door on the previous evening, was wide open. I could not help seeing that Mrs. Vinton was on her knees beside the kitchen table, that she had a photograph in her hands, that tears were streaming down her cheeks, and that her lips were forming words.

"My dear, my dear! May the Lord God bless and keep you, and send you back to me before my heart is quite broken."

Plainly there was a skeleton in this lady's cupboard. Why did she say her husband was dead, if she prayed the Lord God to send him back to her?

It was the following evening, after dinner. We were at my sitting room window, looking out across the wheat-field which divided us from the sea. Although she had done her best to hide it, I felt pretty certain that she had been crying nearly all day long.

"If you are not careful, Mrs. Vinton, you will make yourself ill."

With this remark I broke a silence which was becoming almost painful. She started and her cheeks flushed.

"Why do you say that?" she asked with startled eyes.

"Because it is so obvious. I wonder if you'll forgive me if I say something? Do you know that each of us has been keeping a secret from the other?"

"What do you mean?" Her surprise seemed to increase.

"The secret I have kept from you is that I have the gift of seeing what people say merely by watching their lips, even if they are speaking to themselves."

"I don't understand. How can you possibly do that?" Her eyes seemed to grow larger; they were very pretty eyes.

"The secret you have been keeping from me is that your husband is still alive."

I had done it then. She got off her chair with quite a jump.

"Miss Lee."

What she actually did was to collapse in a sort of heap on the floor, pillow her head on the seat of the chair on which she had been sitting, and burst into tears. It was my turn to be startled. Kneeling beside her on the floor I put my hands on her shoulders, whispering:

"I am so sorry to have intruded on your sufferings, but I could not help it."

She stood up, the tears still streaming down her cheeks.

"I am ashamed of myself, Miss Lee. I suppose some one has been telling you something?"

"Not a word; all I know you have told me yourself."

I explained to her how that was. Her tears ceased to fall; the expression on her face was like a note of exclamation.

"You see, it is because of this gift I have of reading people's most secret thoughts—sometimes, as in your case, even against my will—that I thought I might be of some little help to you."

"I don't see how you can be of help to me. It's quite true, as you say, that my husband is alive: but he might as well be dead, because he's in prison."

"I beg your pardon, Mrs. Vinton; I did not guess it was that way. Please forgive me. Still, perhaps I can be of help to you."

"My husband was sentenced to 14 years' penal servitude; he has served three. In those circumstances, I don't see what help you, a perfect stranger, can be to me."

"I might at least be able to send you some lodgers."

"Do you think people will come and lodge with me when they know who I am? I don't suppose anyone knows the whole truth about me. I have done my best to hide it but even as it is they shun me as if I were the plague."

I was at a loss for things to say, the situation being one for which I was so utterly unprepared. Presently she gave me unlooked-for help, while inflicting on me what was very like a snub.

"This is a subject, Miss Lee, on which you have forced my confidence—I am not sure quite fairly. Whether you go or stay, on one point there must be no misunderstanding; it is a subject on which you must never speak to me again. But before quitting it forever, I should like to make myself clear to you on one matter; the jury found him guilty, the judge sent him to prison for 14 years, the world thinks that punishment well merited—but I know that my husband is innocent."

She turned to leave the room, but something made it impossible for me to let her go.

"Mrs. Vinton? One moment, please? Don't you see that if your husband is innocent that is just the point on which I might be able to help you?"

Again her manner was not encouraging.

"Help me? You? How can you help me?"

"I have sufficient confidence in your judgment, Mrs. Vinton—"

"My name is not Vinton; nor is my husband's—his name is George Young." I suppose it was because I started that she added: "Now you will probably adopt a different tone, in common with all the world, you held my husband to be guilty."

"I know nothing either of your husband's innocence or guilt. Nearly four years ago I left England for a long tour around the world. Your husband's trial must have taken place while I was away."

"I saw you start when I said my husband's name was George Young. If you did not know it, why start as you did?"

Her tone was suspicious, even resentful.

"You have heard how the mouse helped the lion," I said. "I honestly think it is within range of possibility that I may be able to help you. You say your husband's name is George Young. Tell me about him. With what was he charged?"

Abandoning her intention of quitting the room, she had sunk upon a chair. Her words limped a little.

"My husband was managing clerk to a group of solicitors. There was a trust fund of rather more than 20,000 pounds of which they were custodians; when the trustees wanted the money it was gone. They charged George with taking it. Other charges were made against him in the course of the trial, but it was on that charge that he was found guilty and sentenced to 14 years penal servitude."

"What was the name of the firm by which your husband was employed?"

"Hutton, Hutton and Walker. Young Mr. Hutton had died some time before the discoveries were made. The firm consisted of Mr. Hutton, the senior partner, and Mr. Walker."

"Was his name Thomas Walker, and did Mr. Hutton sometimes call him Tom?"

"You know the firm—or do you know Tom Walker? His name was Tom. I was almost engaged to him once, and should have been quite if George had not—well, you know."

A faint flush tinged her white cheeks. I wondered if that had anything to do with the position Mr. Walker had taken up."

"Is Mr. Hutton a little man, all a bundle of nerves?"

"His nerves were strong enough before the trouble began; he was a very able man. Now he is ill. Once he found out where I was and came to see me; he was so changed that I hardly knew him. I cannot help thinking that he has my movements watched, because when I came here I not only concealed my address, but I changed my name. Yet the other day he wrote to me a curious, rambling letter, parts of which almost suggested that he was in his second childhood. He is at Torquay, and hints that he does not expect to leave it again alive."

"What is his address at Torquay? It is just possible that I may go and see him."

When she had given me old Mr. Hutton's address at Torquay, and had gone to bed that night, I was convinced that some thing like a gleam of hope had come into her life, the responsibility for which lay on me.

I went to Torquay the very next day, and a tedious journey it was. On arrival I put up at a hotel on the Strand, dined, spent a very dull evening, and went to bed. The next morning, when, waking up, I remembered where I was and what I was there for. I asked myself what on earth I was to do. However, I dressed and had breakfast, then went into the public gardens on the other side of the road, armed with a book and newspaper. After I had enough of reading I began to walk about. There were not many people in the gardens. There was an old gentleman—

I stopped as I was approaching that old gentleman, suddenly conscious of a little catching of the breath. I had seen that old gentleman before—once; it was to see him a second time that I was there. He looked to me like a very sick man indeed—smaller than when I had seen him first, as if he had lost both flesh and vitality.

I was wondering whether or not to address him, and what method of address to employ, when I had another little shock of surprise. Some one else had entered the gardens—a tall, upstanding quite young man. It was the square-faced man who had sat with the other at the adjoining table. He eyed me as we passed each other, as if my face was not entirely unfamiliar, as if he were asking himself where he had seen it before.

He went one way, I the other. I had no doubt that he was making for the old man on the seat. Turning into a side path upon the left, I turned again into another narrower path which ran parallel with the broad one I had left. I retraced my steps along it. Between the intervening shrubs and trees I could see the seats on the broader walk. When I came abreast of the one on which the old man had been sitting he was talking to the newcomer. A clump of rhododendrons was between us, high enough, unless particular search was made for a suspected presence, to serve as a screen. Standing as far back as I could without losing sight of the two men's faces, I made it serve as a screen for me, and I watched, so far as I could, what was being said between the two.

The younger man came up while the elder still had his eyes closed. He stood for a moment observing him, then he greeted him, "Good morning."

The old man opened his eyes, looking up at him as if he were not quite sure who he was; then he said:

"It will never be a good morning to me again—never—never!"

I could see from the look on the younger man's face that he sneered.

"Aren't you slightly melodramatic? Didn't you sleep well?"

"I have not slept well since the day on which George Young went to jail; his going murdered sleep. All night I lie in agony."

"You were saying the other day how you longed for some thing to give you sleep; here is some thing."

"The speaker took out of a waistcoat pocket a small blue vial, offering it to the old man on his open palm. The old man looked at the vial, and then up at the face of the person who offered it.

"What is it?"

"Mandragora."

"Will it give me sleep?"

"If you choose, sleep which will know no waking."

The two men exchanged looks—such strange ones; then the older took with tremulous fingers the vial off the other's palm. The younger, without another word, left the gardens.

I waited. If I could help it I was not going to lose sight of the vial which was in the old man's hand. Presently I followed. They stopped at what I recognized to be the house in Belgrave rd., which Mrs. Young had given me as Mr. Hutton's address. The old man entered the house leaning on the chairman's arm. I walked up the road, then back again.

Twenty minutes had elapsed since the old man entered. It was like one of those lodging houses in which the hall door proper is never closed in the daytime. Turning the handle, I passed into the hall. I had noticed that the bath chairman had led the old gentleman into a room on the left. After momentary hesitation I turned the handle of that room and, without any sort of ceremony, passed in. It was, as I had expected, a sitting room. There was a big armchair on one side. On this, propped up by cushions, was the old man. He had a small blue vial in his hand; the cork was out; he was in the very act of raising it to his lips. I crossed the room and it was in my hand almost before he knew it. There was no label on the vial, but one sniff of its contents was enough to tell me what it was.

"Do you imagine, Mr. Hutton, that by committing suicide you'll escape the consequences of crime?"

He stared at me as if I were some supernatural visitant; his jaw dropped open; his head fell back, he was one great tremble. I went on:

"When you allowed George Young to be sent to prison for the crime of which you were guilty, you practically committed murder: Conscience has you by the throat; God punishes in this world as well as the next. Do you think this will save you from the wrath to come?"

I alluded to the vial. He stammered out a question:

"Who are you?"

"I am the voice of the avenging angel, calling you to account for this evil you have done and still would do. Repent—there is still time—and God's infinite mercy will give you peace at last."

He gasped; I thought every moment he would collapse.

"I do not know who you are, where you come from, what you want with me; but—but if only I could believe that by doing what you say—I could be at peace again with God and man!"

He did believe before I had done with him, or if his faith were not so perfect as it might have been, he did as I wished. He made a complete confession of the whole painful business. I wrote down every word he said. Then I read over to him what I had written; the landlady was called in, and in her presence and mine he signed it.

His son had been the thief, his only child. When detection threatened, to escape punishment he had poisoned himself. How he had obtained the poison remained a mystery. And not only so, the tragedy had been handled in such a fashion as to make it appear that George Young had been to blame for it. At the trial certain evidence was produced that made it seem that he had been Young's victim; that he was of such a sensitive nature that, rather than face what must be the result of George Young's villainy, he preferred to die. As I heard this part of the tale I thought of the vial which had been given to the old man, and I drew my own conclusions.

When I left Mr. Hutton I returned to my hotel, to find a telegram awaiting me. It was in answer to one I sent while I had been following that bath chair. I smiled as I read it; I glanced at the clock—and I thought I learned from Mr. Hutton where Mr. Thomas Walker was staying; he was in a house on the higher part of the town, which belonged to a relative of his, and of which, in his relative's absence, he was with the exception of some sort of servant, the only occupant. About a quarter to four, at which time the London express reaches Torquay, I went to call at Mr. Thomas Walker's, leaving at my hotel a note for a person whom I told them I presently expected.

The address the old man had given me was Tormohan, Ilsham rd. Any idea I had of introducing myself to Mr. Walker as I had done to Mr. Hutton vanished directly I saw what kind of place Tormohan was. It was shut off from the main road on which I had stood by a high wall. Admission was gained by a gate which opened on what was presumably some sort of passage. The way to get that gate open was to pull at the old-fashioned bell which hung beside it. I pulled; when nothing particular happened I pulled again. I pulled four times before the door was opened a few inches, and the square-faced man looked through the opening. Rather an odd dialogue took place, which I commenced:

"Mr. Thomas Walker?"

"Who are you? What do you want?"

"I wish to see you on very important business, and my name is Judith Lee."

"Haven't I seen you somewhere before?"

"It is possible; but I think I shall be able to satisfy you when you have allowed me to enter."

He opened the door just wide enough to let me enter, and I went in. The moment I was in he closed it. We were, as I had expected, in a sort of passage covered with a glass roof. He led the way to the house; I followed. We passed through another door, which this time was opened by turning a handle. We went into a dark hall, and then into a room at the back which was shadowed by a big tree, which grew nearly up to the window. When we were in the room he eyed me with what I felt were inquiring glances.

"Did I understand you to say that you are Miss Lee? On what business, which is of such great importance, do you wish to see me?"

"The business which has brought me here is to tell you that you are a contemptible, cowardly, murderous scoundrel, and that the hour is struck in which your sins are going to find you out. That, in the first place."

He stared as if he wondered if I were mad; then he smiled oddly.

"That, in the first place. And in the second?"

"In the second, I am going to enter into details, by way of calling certain facts to your recollection." Then I jumped at my fences without stopping to consider what was on the other side. "How many years ago is it since you began to incite young Frank Hutton to rob his father?"

At that he did change countenance; I had found a safe landing on the other side of the fence.

"What on earth are you talking about? Who are you, and what do you want with me?"

"You taught Frank Hutton to be a thief; in a small way at the beginning, on a large scale later on. You shared his ill-gotten spoils; yet when detection threatened, you played so upon his fears that you induced him to commit suicide, in order to escape the consequences of what were more your misdeeds than his. Did you, a lawyer, forget that when A assists B in committing suicide A is guilty of murder? When you put poison within Frank Hutton's reach, knowing perfectly well the use he was about to make of it, you committed murder; for that murder the law is presently going to call you to account."

The way in which he looked at me! I already began to suspect that his fingers were itching to take me by the throat.

"Not content with destroying young Frank Hutton, soul and body, to cover your own offenses, you proceeded to wreck his father's happiness and to lead him into crime. You lied to him about his son; you were so skillful as to make him believe that his boy was the sole offender, and then, pretending that it was your desire to spare him shame, you put it into his head to lay the burden upon an innocent man. You were so skillful as to make it seem that the suggestion came from himself and not from you. You unutterable thing!"

When I paused, he said nothing. I was aware that he was all the more dangerous on this account.

"You made black seem white; you manufactured false evidence; you lied, and lied, and lied—and George Young was sentenced to 14 years' penal servitude. Thief, murderer, liar, you have succeeded in doing that! I have no doubt you hoped that you were safe at last, you short-sighted fool! The mills of God grind slowly, but they grind exceeding fine—your sort they grind to powder. You are already being slipped between the stones; your course has run."

The grimace which distorted his face was rather a grin than a smile as he asked:

"In the name of all that's marvelous, from what madhouse have you been permitted to escape?"

When you planned that grand coup, putting the onus of all your guilt upon an innocent man and shutting him up for 14 awful years, you overlooked one small point; that all men are not devils, that to some is given the saving grace of repenting their sins. And so poor a judge of character are you that you were unaware that your own partner, your first victim's unhappy father, was one of them."

He interrupted me, speaking for the first time, savagely.

"Have you been talking to old Hutton? Has he been coaching you in this issue of nonsense?"

As before, I left his questions unanswered; I simply went on.

"Fortunately for himself, your partner was one of those who cannot know happiness unless his conscience is clear and he is at peace with God. You had his son in your mind. By inciting him to self-murder you believed yourself to have escaped one danger. You hoped, by inducing the father to imitate his son, you would escape another. Today—only a very little while ago—you murdered him."

His skin became livid, his lips trembled, words stuck in his throat, fear touched his heart.

"What—what do you mean?"

I believe he meant to say more, but could not. He shrank back from me as if in physical terror. I gave him no quarter. I held out my right hand, palm uppermost. On it was the small blue vial.

"Do you recognize that?"

He looked at it as if it were some dreadful thing; again he stammered his question:

"What—what do you mean?"

"This morning I saw you give that vial to your partner, Michael Hutton. I saw you give him this vial a few hours ago, in the public gardens. He said to you, 'What is it?' You replied 'Mandragora.' He asked, 'Will it give me sleep?' You said, 'If you choose, sleep which will know no waking.' You let him take the vial between his shaking fingers, and you walked off, knowing that you had left death behind you."

Suddenly, I realized that he was eyeing the tiny glass bottle with a new expression in his glance.

"I don't believe it's empty." He said it almost as if he were speaking to himself. He drew closer. "I don't believe the contents have been touched."

He made a sudden grab at the vial. I withdrew it just in the nick of time. There was the sound of an unmusical bell.

"Who's that?" he asked.

I said: "Had you better not go to the door and see?"

He looked at me. I suppose he saw some thing in my face which set his own thoughts traveling.

"Is it some one for you?"

"It is some one for you—at last!"

"Is that so? Some one for me—at last."

He stopped; there was silence. The bell rang again. I was just about to suggest that he should go and see who was the outer door when—he leaped at me. And I was unprepared. He had me by the throat before I had even realized that danger threatened.

I am a woman, but no weakling. I have always felt it my duty to keep my body in proper condition, trying to learn all that physical culture can teach me. I only recently had been having lessons in jiu-jitsu—the Japanese art of self-defense. I had been diligently practicing a trick which was intended to be used when a frontal attack was made upon the throat. Even as, I dare say, he was thinking that I was already as good as done for, I tried that trick. His fingers released my throat, and he was on the floor, without, I fancy, understanding how he got there. I doubt if there ever was a more amazed man. When he began to realize what had happened he gasped up at me—he was still on the floor: "You—you—"

While he was still endeavoring to find adjectives sufficiently strong to fit the occasion the inspector for whose attendance I had telegraphed to Scotland Yard came into the room. In the note I had left at the hotel I told him to follow me at once, and if he was not able to obtain instant admission to the house, then he was to use means of his own to get in quickly. The inspector had some skeleton keys in his pocket which had once been part of a skillful burglar's outfit: when there came no answer to his ringing he promptly opened the front door with them.

Mr. Thomas Walker understood what the newcomer's presence meant; he needed no explanation. In the struggle I had dropped the blue vial, a fact which he realized quicker than I did. Before I knew it had fallen he, still on the floor, had snatched it, had the cork out, and was putting the bottle to his lips.

"Stop him!" I cried. "It's poison!"

I cried too late; before we could reach him he had emptied the vial. He was dead, as quickly as if he had been struck by lightning. The vial had contained sufficient cyanide of potassium to kill 50 men. The death he had meant for his partner was his instead.

Representations were made to the authorities. Michael Hutton's confession was placed before them, together with certain facts which came to light when examination was made of Thomas Walker's papers. George Young was pardoned—for what he had never done. Old Mr. Hutton was arrested; he died before the magistrate's examination was concluded. It was found that he had made a will by which he possessed was left to the man he had so cruelly injured.

THE MURDER AT TROYTE'S HILL

C. L. Pirkis

G RIFFITHS, OF THE NEWCASTLE CONSTABULARY, HAS THE CASE IN HAND," said Mr. Dyer; "those Newcastle men are keen-witted, shrewd fellows, and very jealous of outside interference. They only sent to me under protest, as it were, because they wanted your sharp wits at work inside the house."

"I suppose throughout I am to work with Griffiths, not with you?" said Miss Brooke.

"Yes; when I have given you in outline the facts of the case, I simply have nothing more to do with it, and you must depend on Griffiths for any assistance of any sort that you may require."

Here, with a swing, Mr. Dyer opened his big ledger and turned rapidly over its leaves till he came to the heading "Troyte's Hill" and the date "September 6th."

"I'm all attention," said Loveday, leaning back in her chair in the attitude of a listener.

"The murdered man," resumed Mr. Dyer, "is a certain Alexander Henderson— usually known as old Sandy—lodge-keeper to Mr. Craven, of Troyte's Hill, Cumberland. The lodge consists merely of two rooms on the ground floor, a bed-room and a sitting-room; these Sandy occupied alone, having neither kith nor kin of any degree. On the morning of September 6th, some children going up to the house with milk from the farm, noticed that Sandy's bed-room window stood wide open. Curiosity prompted them to peep in; and then, to their horror, they saw old Sandy, in his night-shirt, lying dead on the floor, as if he had fallen backwards from the window. They raised an alarm; and on examination, it was found that death had ensued from a heavy blow on the temple, given either by a strong fist or some blunt instrument. The room, on being entered, presented a curious appearance. It was as if a herd of monkeys had been turned into it and allowed to work their impish will. Not an article of furniture remained in its place: the bed-clothes had been rolled into a bundle and stuffed into the chimney; the bedstead—a small iron one—lay on its side; the one chair in the room stood on the top of the table; fender and fire-irons lay across the washstand, whose basin was to be found in a farther corner, holding bolster and pillow. The clock stood on its head in the middle of the mantelpiece; and the small vases and ornaments, which flanked it on either side, were walking, as it were, in a straight line towards the door. The old man's clothes had been rolled into a ball and thrown on the top of a high cupboard in which he kept his savings and whatever valuables he had. This cupboard, however, had not been meddled with, and its contents remained intact, so it was evident that robbery was not the motive for the crime. At the inquest, subsequently held, a verdict of 'willful murder' against some person or persons unknown was returned. The local police are diligently investigating the affair, but, as yet, no arrests have been made. The opinion that at present prevails in the neighbourhood is that the crime has been perpetrated by some lunatic, escaped or otherwise and enquiries are being made at the local asylums as to missing or lately released inmates. Griffiths, however, tells me that his suspicions set in another direction."

"Did anything of importance transpire at the inquest?"

"Nothing specially important. Mr. Craven broke down in giving his evidence when he alluded to the confidential relations that had always subsisted between Sandy and himself, and spoke of the last time that he had seen him alive. The evidence of the butler, and one or two of the female servants, seems clear enough, and they let fall something of a hint that Sandy was not altogether a favourite among them, on account of the overbearing manner in which he used his influence with his master. Young Mr. Craven, a youth of about nineteen, home from Oxford for the long vacation, was not present at the inquest; a doctor's certificate was put in stating that he was suffering from typhoid fever, and could not leave his bed without risk to his life. Now this young man is a thoroughly bad sort, and as much a gentleman-blackleg as it is possible for such a young fellow to be. It seems to Griffiths that there is something suspicious about this illness of his. He came back from Oxford on the verge of delirium tremens, pulled round from that, and then suddenly, on the day after the murder, Mrs. Craven rings the bell, announces that he has developed typhoid fever and orders a doctor to be sent for."

"What sort of man is Mr. Craven senior?"

"He seems to be a quiet old fellow, a scholar and learned philologist. Neither his neighbours nor his family see much of him; he almost lives in his study, writing a treatise, in seven or eight volumes, on comparative philology. He is not a rich man. Troyte's Hill, though it carries position in the county, is not a paying property, and Mr. Craven is unable to keep it up properly. I am told he has had to cut down expenses in all directions in order to send his son to college, and his daughter from first to last has been entirely educated by her mother. Mr. Craven was originally intended for the church, but for some reason or other, when his college career came to an end, he did not present himself for ordination—went out to Natal instead, where he obtained some civil appointment and where he remained for about fifteen years. Henderson was his servant during the latter portion of his Oxford career, and must have been greatly respected by him, for although the remuneration derived from his appointment at Natal was small, he paid Sandy a regular yearly allowance out of it. When, about ten years ago, he succeeded to Troyte's Hill, on the death of his elder brother, and returned home with his family, Sandy was immediately installed as lodge-keeper, and at so high a rate of pay that the butler's wages were cut down to meet it."

"Ah, that wouldn't improve the butler's feelings towards him," ejaculated Loveday.

Mr. Dyer went on: "But, in spite of his high wages, he doesn't appear to have troubled much about his duties as lodge-keeper, for they were performed, as a rule, by the gardener's boy, while he took his meals and passed his time at the house, and, speaking generally, put his finger into every pie. You know the old adage respecting the servant of twenty-one years' standing: 'Seven years my servant, seven years my equal, seven years my master.' Well, it appears to have held good in the case of Mr. Craven and Sandy. The old gentleman, absorbed in his philological studies, evidently let the reins slip through his fingers, and Sandy seems to have taken easy possession of them. The servants frequently had to go to him for orders, and he carried things, as a rule, with a high hand."

"Did Mrs. Craven never have a word to say on the matter?"

"I've not heard much about her. She seems to be a quiet sort of person. She is a Scotch missionary's daughter; perhaps she spends her time working for the Cape mission and that sort of thing."

"And young Mr. Craven: did he knock under to Sandy's rule?"

"Ah, now you're hitting the bull's eye and we come to Griffiths' theory. The young man and Sandy appear to have been at loggerheads ever since the Cravens took possession of Troyte's Hill. As a schoolboy Master Harry defied Sandy and threatened him with his hunting-crop; and subsequently, as a young man, has used strenuous endeavours to put the old servant in his place. On the day before the murder, Griffiths says, there was a terrible scene between the two, in which the young gentleman, in the presence of several witnesses, made use of strong language and threatened the old man's life. Now, Miss Brooke, I have told you all the circumstances of the case so far as I know them. For fuller particulars I must refer you to Griffiths. He, no doubt, will meet you at Grenfell—the nearest station to Troyte's Hill, and tell you in what capacity he has procured for you an entrance into the house. By-the-way, he has wired to me this morning that he hopes you will be able to save the Scotch express to-night."

Loveday expressed her readiness to comply with Mr. Griffiths' wishes.

"I shall be glad," said Mr. Dyer, as he shook hands with her at the office door, "to see you immediately on your return—that, however, I suppose, will not be yet awhile. This promises, I fancy, to be a longish affair?" This was said interrogatively.

"I haven't the least idea on the matter," answered Loveday. "I start on my work without theory of any sort—in fact, I may say, with my mind a perfect blank."

And anyone who had caught a glimpse of her blank, expressionless features, as she said this, would have taken her at her word.

Grenfell, the nearest post-town to Troyte's Hill, is a fairly busy, populous little town—looking south towards the black country, and northwards to low, barren hills. Pre-eminent among these stands Troyte's Hill, famed in the old days as a border keep, and possibly at a still earlier date as a Druid stronghold.

At a small inn at Grenfell, dignified by the title of "The Station Hotel," Mr. Griffiths, of the Newcastle constabulary, met Loveday and still further initiated her into the mysteries of the Troyte's Hill murder.

"A little of the first excitement has subsided," he said, after preliminary greetings had been exchanged; "but still the wildest rumours are flying about and repeated as solemnly as if they were Gospel truths. My chief here and my colleagues generally adhere to their first conviction, that the criminal is some suddenly crazed tramp or else an escaped lunatic, and they are confident that sooner or later we shall come upon his traces. Their theory is that Sandy, hearing some strange noise at the Park Gates, put his head out of the window to ascertain the cause and immediately had his death blow dealt him; then they suppose that the lunatic scrambled into the room through the window and exhausted his frenzy by turning things generally upside down. They refuse altogether to share my suspicions respecting young Mr. Craven."

Mr. Griffiths was a tall, thin-featured man, with iron-grey hair, but so close to his head that it refused to do anything but stand on end. This gave a somewhat comic expression to the upper portion of his face and clashed oddly with the melancholy look that his mouth habitually wore.

"I have made all smooth for you at Troyte's Hill," he presently went on. "Mr. Craven is not wealthy enough to allow himself the luxury of a family lawyer, so he occasionally employs the services of Messrs. Wells and Sugden, lawyers in this place, and who, as it happens, have, off and on, done a good deal of business for me. It was through them I heard that Mr. Craven was anxious to secure the assistance of an amanuensis. I immediately offered your services, stating that you were a friend of mine, a lady of impoverished means, who would gladly undertake the duties for the munificent sum of a guinea a month, with board and lodging. The old gentleman at once jumped at the offer, and is anxious for you to be at Troyte's Hill at once."

Loveday expressed her satisfaction with the programme that Mr. Griffiths had sketched for her, then she had a few questions to ask.

"Tell me," she said, "what led you, in the first instance, to suspect young Mr. Craven of the crime?"

"The footing on which he and Sandy stood towards each other, and the terrible scene that occurred between them only the day before the murder," answered Griffiths, promptly. "Nothing of this, however, was elicited at the inquest, where a very fair face was put on Sandy's relations with the whole of the Craven family. I have subsequently unearthed a good deal respecting the private life of Mr. Harry Craven, and, among other things, I have found out that on the night of the murder he left the house shortly after ten o'clock, and no one, so far as I have been able to ascertain, knows at what hour he returned. Now I must draw your attention, Miss Brooke, to the fact that at the inquest the medical evidence went to prove that the murder had been committed between ten and eleven at night."

"Do you surmise, then, that the murder was a planned thing on the part of this young man?"

"I do. I believe that he wandered about the grounds until Sandy shut himself in for the night, then aroused him by some outside noise, and, when the old man looked out to ascertain the cause, dealt him a blow with a bludgeon or loaded stick, that caused his death."

"A cold-blooded crime that, for a boy of nineteen?"

"Yes. He's a good-looking, gentlemanly youngster, too, with manners as mild as milk, but from all accounts is as full of wickedness as an egg is full of meat. Now, to come to another point—if, in connection with these ugly facts, you take into consideration the suddenness of his illness, I think you'll admit that it bears a suspicious appearance and might reasonably give rise to the surmise that it was a plant on his part, in order to get out of the inquest."

"Who is the doctor attending him?"

"A man called Waters; not much of a practitioner, from all accounts, and no doubt he feels himself highly honoured in being summoned to Troyte's Hill. The Cravens, it seems, have no family doctor. Mrs. Craven, with her missionary experience, is half a doctor herself, and never calls in one except in a serious emergency."

"The certificate was in order, I suppose?"

"Undoubtedly. And, as if to give colour to the gravity of the case, Mrs. Craven sent a message down to the servants, that if any of them were afraid of the infection they could at once go to their homes. Several of the maids, I believe, took advantage of her permission, and packed their boxes. Miss Craven, who is a delicate girl, was sent away with her maid to stay with friends at Newcastle, and Mrs. Craven isolated herself with her patient in one of the disused wings of the house."

"Has anyone ascertained whether Miss Craven arrived at her destination at Newcastle?"

Griffiths drew his brows together in thought.

"I did not see any necessity for such a thing," he answered. "I don't quite follow you. What do you mean to imply?"

"Oh, nothing. I don't suppose it matters much: it might have been interesting as a side-issue." She broke off for a moment, then added:

"Now tell me a little about the butler, the man whose wages were cut down to increase Sandy's pay."

"Old John Hales? He's a thoroughly worthy, respectable man; he was butler for five or six years to Mr. Craven's brother, when he was master of Troyte's Hill, and then took duty under this Mr. Craven. There's no ground for suspicion in that quarter. Hales's exclamation when he heard of the murder is quite enough to stamp him as an innocent man: 'Serve the old idiot right,' he cried: 'I couldn't pump up a tear for him if I tried for a month of Sundays!' Now I take it, Miss Brooke, a guilty man wouldn't dare make such a speech as that!"

"You think not?"

Griffiths stared at her. "I'm a little disappointed in her," he thought. "I'm afraid her powers have been slightly exaggerated if she can't see such a straight-forward thing as that."

Aloud he said, a little sharply, "Well, I don't stand alone in my thinking. No one yet has breathed a word against Hales, and if they did, I've no doubt he could prove an *alibi* without any trouble, for he lives in the house, and everyone has a good word for him."

"I suppose Sandy's lodge has been put into order by this time?"

"Yes; after the inquest, and when all possible evidence had been taken, everything was put straight."

"At the inquest it was stated that no marks of footsteps could be traced in any direction?"

"The long drought we've had would render such a thing impossible, let alone the fact that Sandy's lodge stands right on the graveled drive, without flower-beds or grass borders of any sort around it. But look here, Miss Brooke, don't you be wasting your time over the lodge and its surroundings. Every iota of fact on that matter has been gone through over and over again by me and my chief. What we want you to do is to go straight into the house and concentrate attention on Master Harry's sick-room, and find out what's going on there. What he did outside the house on the night of the 6th,

I've no doubt I shall be able to find out for myself. Now, Miss Brooke, you've asked me no end of questions, to which I have replied as fully as it was in my power to do; will you be good enough to answer one question that I wish to put, as straightforwardly as I have answered yours? You have had fullest particulars given you of the condition of Sandy's room when the police entered it on the morning after the murder. No doubt, at the present moment, you can see it all in your mind's eye—the bedstead on its side, the clock on its head, the bed-clothes half-way up the chimney, the little vases and ornaments walking in a straight line towards the door?"

Loveday bowed her head.

"Very well. Now will you be good enough to tell me what this scene of confusion recalls to your mind before anything else?"

"The room of an unpopular Oxford freshman after a raid upon it by undergrads," answered Loveday promptly.

Mr. Griffiths rubbed his hands.

"Quite so!" he ejaculated. "I see, after all, we are one at heart in this matter, in spite of a little surface disagreement of ideas. Depend upon it, by-and-bye, like the engineers tunneling from different quarters under the Alps, we shall meet at the same point and shake hands. By-the-way, I have arranged for daily communication between us through the postboy who takes the letters to Troyte's Hill. He is trustworthy, and any letter you give him for me will find its way into my hands within the hour."

It was about three o'clock in the afternoon when Loveday drove in through the park gates of Troyte's Hill, past the lodge where old Sandy had met with his death. It was a pretty little cottage, covered with Virginia creeper and wild honeysuckle, and showing no outward sign of the tragedy that had been enacted within.

The park and pleasure-grounds of Troyte's Hill were extensive, and the house itself was a somewhat imposing red brick structure, built, possibly, at the time when Dutch William's taste had grown popular in the country. Its frontage presented a somewhat forlorn appearance, its centre windows—a square of eight—alone seeming to show signs of occupation. With the exception of two windows at the extreme end of the bed-room floor of the north wing, where, possibly, the invalid and his mother were located, and two windows at the extreme end of the ground floor of the south wing, which Loveday ascertained subsequently were those of Mr. Craven's study, not a single window in either wing owned blind or curtain. The wings were extensive, and it was easy to understand that at the extreme end of the one the fever patient would be isolated from the rest of the household, and that at the extreme end of the other Mr. Craven could secure the quiet and freedom from interruption which, no doubt, were essential to the due prosecution of his philological studies.

Alike on the house and ill-kept grounds were present the stamp of the smallness of the income of the master and owner of the place. The terrace, which ran the length of the house in front, and on to which every window on the ground floor opened, was miserably out of repair: not a lintel or door-post, window-ledge or balcony but what seemed to cry aloud for the touch of the painter. "Pity me! I have seen better days," Loveday could fancy written as a legend across the red-brick porch that gave entrance to the old house.

The butler, John Hales, admitted Loveday, shouldered her portmanteau and told her he would show her to her room. He was a tall, powerfully-built man, with a ruddy face and dogged expression of countenance. It was easy to understand that, off and on, there must have been many a sharp encounter between him and old Sandy. He treated Loveday in an easy, familiar fashion, evidently considering that an amanuensis took much the same rank as a nursery governess—that is to say, a little below a lady's maid and a little above a house-maid.

"We're short of hands, just now," he said, in broad Cumberland dialect, as he led the way up the wide stair case. "Some of the lasses downstairs took fright at the fever and went home. Cook and I are single-handed, for Moggie, the only maid left, has been told off to wait on Madam and Master Harry. I hope you're not afeared of fever?"

Loveday explained that she was not, and asked if the room at the extreme end of the north wing was the one assigned to "Madam and Master Harry."

"Yes," said the man; "it's convenient for sick nursing; there's a flight of stairs runs straight down from it to the kitchen quarters. We put all Madam wants at the foot of those stairs and Moggie herself never enters the sick-room. I take it you'll not be seeing Madam for many a day, yet awhile."

"When shall I see Mr. Craven? At dinner to-night?"

"That's what naebody could say," answered Hales. "He may not come out of his study till past midnight; sometimes he sits there till two or three in the morning. Shouldn't advise you to wait till he wants his dinner—better have a cup of tea and a chop sent up to you. Madam never waits for him at any meal."

As he finished speaking he deposited the portmanteau outside one of the many doors opening into the gallery.

"This is Miss Craven's room," he went on; "cook and me thought you'd better have it, as it would want less getting ready than the other rooms, and work is work when there are so few hands to do it. Oh, my stars! I do declare there is cook putting it straight for you now." The last sentence was added as the opened door laid bare to view, the cook, with a duster in her hand, polishing a mirror; the bed had been made, it is true, but otherwise the room must have been much as Miss Craven left it, after a hurried packing up.

To the surprise of the two servants Loveday took the matter very lightly.

"I have a special talent for arranging rooms and would prefer getting this one straight for myself," she said. "Now, if you will go and get ready that chop and cup of tea we were talking about just now, I shall think it much kinder than if you stayed here doing what I can so easily do for myself."

When, however, the cook and butler had departed in company, Loveday showed no disposition to exercise the "special talent" of which she had boasted.

She first carefully turned the key in the lock and then proceeded to make a thorough and minute investigation of every corner of the room. Not an article of furniture, not an ornament or toilet accessory, but what was lifted from its place and carefully scrutinized. Even the ashes in the grate, the debris of the last fire made there, were raked over and well looked through.

This careful investigation of Miss Craven's late surroundings occupied in all about three quarters of an hour, and Loveday, with her hat in her hand, descended the stairs to see Hales crossing the hall to the dining-room with the promised cup of tea and chop.

In silence and solitude she partook of the simple repast in a dining-hall that could with ease have banqueted a hundred and fifty guests.

"Now for the grounds before it gets dark," she said to herself, as she noted that already the outside shadows were beginning to slant.

The dining-hall was at the back of the house; and here, as in the front, the windows, reaching to the ground, presented easy means of egress. The flower-garden was on this side of the house and sloped downhill to a pretty stretch of well-wooded country.

Loveday did not linger here even to admire, but passed at once round the south corner of the house to the windows which she had ascertained, by a careless question to the butler, were those of Mr. Craven's study.

Very cautiously she drew near them, for the blinds were up, the curtains drawn back. A side glance, however, relieved her apprehensions, for it showed her the occupant of the room, seated in an easy-chair, with his back to the windows. From the length of his outstretched limbs he was evidently a tall man. His hair was silvery and curly, the lower part of his face was hidden from her view by the chair, but she could see one hand was pressed tightly across his eyes and brows. The whole attitude was that of a man absorbed in deep thought. The room was comfortably furnished, but presented an appearance of disorder from the books and manuscripts scattered in all directions. A whole pile of torn fragments of foolscap sheets, overflowing from a waste-paper basket beside the writing-table, seemed to proclaim the fact that the scholar had of late grown weary of, or else dissatisfied with his work, and had condemned it freely.

Although Loveday stood looking in at this window for over five minutes, not the faintest sign of life did that tall, reclining figure give, and it would have been as easy to believe him locked in sleep as in thought.

From here she turned her steps in the direction of Sandy's lodge. As Griffiths had said, it was graveled up to its doorstep. The blinds were closely drawn, and it presented the ordinary appearance of a disused cottage.

A narrow path beneath over-arching boughs of cherry-laurel and arbutus, immediately facing the lodge, caught her eye, and down this she at once turned her footsteps.

This path led, with many a wind and turn, through a belt of shrubbery that skirted the frontage of Mr. Craven's grounds, and eventually, after much zig-zagging, ended in close proximity to the stables. As Loveday entered it, she seemed literally to leave daylight behind her.

"I feel as if I were following the course of a circuitous mind," she said to herself as the shadows closed around her. "I could not fancy Sir Isaac Newton or Bacon planning or delighting in such a wind-about-alley as this!"

The path showed greyly in front of her out of the dimness. On and on she followed it; here and there the roots of the old laurels, struggling out of the ground, threatened to trip her up. Her eyes, however, had now grown accustomed to the half-gloom, and not a detail of her surroundings escaped her as she went along.

A bird flew from out the thicket on her right hand with a startled cry. A dainty little frog leaped out of her way into the shriveled leaves lying below the laurels. Following the movements of this frog, her eye was caught by something black and solid among those leaves. What was it? A bundle—a shiny black coat? Loveday knelt down, and using her hands to assist her eyes, found that they came into contact with the dead, stiffened body of a beautiful black retriever. She parted, as well as she was able, the lower boughs of the evergreens, and minutely examined the poor animal. Its eyes were still open, though glazed and bleared, and its death had, undoubtedly, been caused by the blow of some blunt, heavy instrument, for on one side its skull was almost battered in.

"Exactly the death that was dealt to Sandy," she thought, as she groped hither and thither beneath the trees in hopes of lighting upon the weapon of destruction.

She searched until increasing darkness warned her that search was useless. Then, still following the zig-zagging path, she made her way out by the stables and thence back to the house.

She went to bed that night without having spoken to a soul beyond the cook and butler. The next morning, however, Mr. Craven introduced himself to her across the breakfast-table. He was a man of really handsome personal appearance, with a fine carriage of the head and shoulders, and eyes that had a forlorn, appealing look in them. He entered the room with an air of great energy, apologized to Loveday for the absence of his wife, and for his own remissness in not being in the way to receive her on the previous day. Then he bade her make herself at home at the breakfast-table, and expressed his delight in having found a coadjutor in his work.

"I hope you understand what a great—a stupendous work it is?" he added, as he sank into a chair. "It is a work that will leave its impress upon thought in all the ages to come. Only a man who has studied comparative philology as I have for the past thirty years, could gauge the magnitude of the task I have set myself."

With the last remark, his energy seemed spent, and he sank back in his chair, covering his eyes with his hand in precisely the same attitude as that in which Loveday had seen him over-night, and utterly oblivious of the fact that breakfast was before him and a stranger-guest seated at table. The butler entered with another dish. "Better go on with your breakfast," he whispered to Loveday, "he may sit like that for another hour."

He placed his dish in front of his master.

"Captain hasn't come back yet, sir," he said, making an effort to arouse him from his reverie.

"Eh, what?" said Mr. Craven, for a moment lifting his hand from his eyes.

"Captain, sir—the black retriever," repeated the man.

The pathetic look in Mr. Craven's eyes deepened.

"Ah, poor Captain!" he murmured; "the best dog I ever had."

Then he again sank back in his chair, putting his hand to his forehead.

The butler made one more effort to arouse him.

"Madam sent you down a newspaper, sir, that she thought you would like to see," he shouted almost into his master's ear, and at the same time laid the morning's paper on the table beside his plate.

"Confound you! leave it there," said Mr. Craven irritably. "Fools! dolts that you all are! With your trivialities and interruptions you are sending me out of the world with my work undone!"

And again he sank back in his chair, closed his eyes and became lost to his surroundings.

Loveday went on with her breakfast. She changed her place at table to one on Mr. Craven's right hand, so that the newspaper sent down for his perusal lay between his plate and hers. It was folded into an oblong shape, as if it were wished to direct attention to a certain portion of a certain column.

A clock in a corner of the room struck the hour with a loud, resonant stroke. Mr. Craven gave a start and rubbed his eyes.

"Eh, what's this?" he said. "What meal are we at?" He looked around with a bewildered air. "Eh!—who are you?" he went on, staring hard at Loveday. "What are you doing here? Where's Nina?—Where's Harry?"

Loveday began to explain, and gradually recollection seemed to come back to him.

"Ah, yes, yes," he said. "I remember; you've come to assist me with my great work. You promised, you know, to help me out of the hole I've got into. Very enthusiastic, I remember they said you were, on certain abstruse points in comparative philology. Now, Miss—Miss—I've forgotten your name—tell me a little of what you know about the elemental sounds of speech that are common to all languages. Now, to how many would you reduce those elemental sounds—to six, eight, nine? No, we won't discuss the matter here, the cups and saucers distract me. Come into my den at the other end of the house; we'll have perfect quiet there."

And utterly ignoring the fact that he had not as yet broken his fast, he rose from the table, seized Loveday by the wrist, and led her out of the room and down the long corridor that led through the south wing to his study.

But seated in that study his energy once more speedily exhausted itself.

He placed Loveday in a comfortable chair at his writing-table, consulted her taste as to pens, and spread a sheet of foolscap before her. Then he settled himself in his easy-chair, with his back to the light, as if he were about to dictate folios to her.

In a loud, distinct voice he repeated the title of his learned work, then its subdivision, then the number and heading of the chapter that was at present engaging his attention. Then he put his hand to his head. "It's the elemental sounds that are my stumbling-block," he said. "Now, how on earth is it possible to get a notion of a sound of agony that is not in part a sound of terror? or a sound of surprise that is not in part a sound of either joy or sorrow?"

With this his energies were spent, and although Loveday remained seated in that study from early morning till daylight began to fade, she had not ten sentences to show for her day's work as amanuensis.

Loveday in all spent only two clear days at Troyte's Hill.

On the evening of the first of those days Detective Griffiths received, through the trustworthy post-boy, the following brief note from her:

> I have found out that Hales owed Sandy close upon a hundred pounds, which
> he had borrowed at various times. I don't know whether you will think this
> fact of any importance.—L. B.

Mr. Griffiths repeated the last sentence blankly. "If Harry Craven were put upon his defence, his counsel, I take it, would consider the fact of first importance," he muttered. And for the remainder of that day Mr. Griffiths went about his work in a perturbed state of mind, doubtful whether to hold or to let go his theory concerning Harry Craven's guilt.

The next morning there came another brief note from Loveday which ran thus:

As a matter of collateral interest, find out if a person, calling himself Harold Cousins, sailed two days ago from London Docks for Natal in the *Bonnie Dundee?*

To this missive Loveday received, in reply, the following somewhat lengthy dispatch:

I do not quite see the drift of your last note, but have wired to our agents in London to carry out its suggestion. On my part, I have important news to communicate. I have found out what Harry Craven's business out of doors was on the night of the murder, and at my instance a warrant has been issued for his arrest. This warrant it will be my duty to serve on him in the course of to-day. Things are beginning to look very black against him, and I am convinced his illness is all a sham. I have seen Waters, the man who is supposed to be attending him, and have driven him into a corner and made him admit that he has only seen young Craven once—on the first day of his illness—and that he gave his certificate entirely on the strength of what Mrs. Craven told him of her son's condition. On the occasion of this, his first and only visit, the lady, it seems, also told him that it would not be necessary for him to continue his attendance, as she quite felt herself competent to treat the case, having had so much experience in fever cases among the blacks at Natal.

As I left Waters's house, after eliciting this important information, I was accosted by a man who keeps a low-class inn in the place, McQueen by name. He said that he wished to speak to me on a matter of importance. To make a long story short, this McQueen stated that on the night of the sixth, shortly after eleven o'clock, Harry Craven came to his house, bringing with him a valuable piece of plate—a handsome epergne—and requested him to lend him a hundred pounds on it, as he hadn't a penny in his pocket. McQueen complied with his request to the extent of ten sovereigns, and now, in a fit of nervous terror, comes to me to confess himself a receiver of stolen goods and play the honest man! He says he noticed that the young gentleman was very much agitated as he made the request, and he also begged him to mention his visit to no one. Now, I am curious to learn how Master Harry will get over the fact that he passed the lodge at the hour at which the murder was most probably committed; or how he will get out of the dilemma of having repassed the lodge on his way back to the house, and not noticed the wide-open window with the full moon shining down on it?

Another word! Keep out of the way when I arrive at the house, somewhere between two and three in the afternoon, to serve the warrant. I do not wish your professional capacity to get wind, for you will most likely yet be of some use to us in the house.

S. G.

Loveday read this note, seated at Mr. Craven's writing-table, with the old gentleman himself reclining motionless beside her in his easy-chair. A little smile played about the corners of her mouth as she read over again the words—"for you will most likely yet be of some use to us in the house."

Loveday's second day in Mr. Craven's study promised to be as unfruitful as the first. For fully an hour after she had received Griffiths' note, she sat at the writing-table with her pen in her hand, ready to transcribe Mr. Craven's inspirations. Beyond, however, the phrase, muttered with closed eyes—"It's all here, in my brain, but I can't put it into words"—not a half-syllable escaped his lips.

At the end of that hour the sound of footsteps on the outside gravel made her turn her head towards the window. It was Griffiths approaching with two constables. She heard the hall door opened to admit them, but, beyond that, not a sound reached her ear, and she realized how fully she was cut off from communication with the rest of the household at the farther end of this unoccupied wing.

Mr. Craven, still reclining in his semi-trance, evidently had not the faintest suspicion that so important an event as the arrest of his only son on a charge of murder was about to be enacted in the house.

Meantime, Griffiths and his constables had mounted the stairs leading to the north wing, and were being guided through the corridors to the sick-room by the flying figure of Moggie, the maid.

"Hoot, mistress!" cried the girl, "here are three men coming up the stairs—policemen, every one of them—will ye come and ask them what they be wanting?"

Outside the door of the sick-room stood Mrs. Craven—a tall, sharp-featured woman with sandy hair going rapidly grey.

"What is the meaning of this? What is your business here?" she said haughtily, addressing Griffiths, who headed the party.

Griffiths respectfully explained what his business was, and requested her to stand on one side that he might enter her son's room.

"This is my daughter's room; satisfy yourself of the fact," said the lady, throwing back the door as she spoke.

And Griffiths and his confrères entered, to find pretty Miss Craven, looking very white and scared, seated beside a fire in a long flowing robe de chambre.

Griffiths departed in haste and confusion, without the chance of a professional talk with Loveday. That afternoon saw him telegraphing wildly in all directions, and dispatching messengers in all quarters. Finally he spent over an hour drawing up an elaborate report to his chief at Newcastle, assuring him of the identity of one, Harold Cousins, who had sailed in the *Bonnie Dundee* for Natal, with Harry Craven, of Troyte's Hill, and advising that the police authorities in that far-away district should be immediately communicated with.

The ink had not dried on the pen with which this report was written before a note, in Loveday's writing, was put into his hand.

Loveday evidently had had some difficulty in finding a messenger for this note, for it was brought by a gardener's boy, who informed Griffiths that the lady had said he would receive a gold sovereign if he delivered the letter all right.

Griffiths paid the boy and dismissed him, and then proceeded to read Loveday's communication.

It was written hurriedly in pencil, and ran as follows:

Things are getting critical here. Directly you receive this, come up to the house with two of your men, and post yourselves anywhere in the grounds where you can see and not be seen. There will be no difficulty in this, for it will be dark by the time you are able to get there. I am not sure whether I shall want your aid to-night, but you had better keep in the grounds until morning, in case of need; and above all, never once lose sight of the study windows. (This was underscored.) If I put a lamp with a green shade in one of those windows, do not lose a moment in entering by that window, which I will contrive to keep unlocked.

Detective Griffiths rubbed his forehead—rubbed his eyes, as he finished reading this.

"Well, I daresay it's all right," he said, "but I'm bothered, that's all, and for the life of me I can't see one step of the way she is going."

He looked at his watch: the hands pointed to a quarter past six. The short September day was drawing rapidly to a close. A good five miles lay between him and Troyte's Hill—there was evidently not a moment to lose.

At the very moment that Griffiths, with his two constables, were once more starting along the Grenfell High Road behind the best horse they could procure, Mr. Craven was rousing himself from his long slumber, and beginning to look around him. That slumber, however, though long, had not been a peaceful one, and it was sundry of the old gentleman's muttered exclamations, as he had started uneasily in his sleep, that had caused Loveday to open, and then to creep out of the room to dispatch, her hurried note.

What effect the occurrence of the morning had had upon the household generally, Loveday, in her isolated corner of the house, had no means of ascertaining. She only noted that when Hales brought in her tea, as he did precisely at five o'clock, he wore a particularly ill-tempered expression of countenance, and she heard him mutter, as he set down the tea-tray with a clatter, something about being a respectable man, and not used to such "goings on."

It was not until nearly an hour and a half after this that Mr. Craven had awakened with a sudden start, and, looking wildly around him, had questioned Loveday who had entered the room.

Loveday explained that the butler had brought in lunch at one, and tea at five, but that since then no one had come in.

"Now that's false," said Mr. Craven, in a sharp, unnatural sort of voice; "I saw him sneaking round the room, the whining, canting hypocrite, and you must have seen him, too! Didn't you hear him say, in his squeaky old voice: 'Master, I knows your secret—'" He broke off abruptly, looking wildly round. "Eh, what's this?" he cried. "No, no, I'm all wrong—Sandy is dead and buried—they held an inquest on him, and we all praised him up as if he were a saint."

"He must have been a bad man, that old Sandy," said Loveday sympathetically.

"You're right! you're right!" cried Mr. Craven, springing up excitedly from his chair and seizing her by the hand. "If ever a man deserved his death, he did. For thirty years he held that rod over my head, and then—ah where was I?"

He put his hand to his head and again sank, as if exhausted, into his chair.

"I suppose it was some early indiscretion of yours at college that he knew of?" said Loveday, eager to get at as much of the truth as possible while the mood for confidence held sway in the feeble brain.

"That was it! I was fool enough to marry a disreputable girl—a barmaid in the town—and Sandy was present at the wedding, and then—" Here his eyes closed again and his mutterings became incoherent.

For ten minutes he lay back in his chair, muttering thus; "A yelp—a groan," were the only words Loveday could distinguish among those mutterings, then suddenly, slowly and distinctly, he said, as if answering some plainly-put question: "A good blow with the hammer and the thing was done."

"I should like amazingly to see that hammer," said Loveday; "do you keep it anywhere at hand?"

His eyes opened with a wild, cunning look in them.

"Who's talking about a hammer? I did not say I had one. If anyone says I did it with a hammer, they're telling a lie."

"Oh, you've spoken to me about the hammer two or three times," said Loveday calmly; "the one that killed your dog, Captain, and I should like to see it, that's all."

The look of cunning died out of the old man's eye—"Ah, poor Captain! splendid dog that! Well, now, where were we? Where did we leave off? Ah, I remember, it was the elemental sounds of speech that bothered me so that night. Were you here then? Ah, no! I remember. I had been trying all day to assimilate a dog's yelp of pain to a human groan, and I couldn't do it. The idea haunted me—followed me about wherever I went. If they were both elemental sounds, they must have something in common, but the link between them I could not find; then it occurred to me, would a well-bred, well-trained dog like my Captain in the stables, there, at the moment of death give an unmitigated currish yelp; would there not be something of a human note in his death-cry? The thing was worth putting to the test. If I could hand down in my treatise a fragment of fact on the matter, it would be worth a dozen dogs' lives. so I went out into the moonlight—ah, but you know all about it—now, don't you?"

"Yes. Poor Captain! did he yelp or groan?"

"Why, he gave one loud, long, hideous yelp, just as if he had been a common cur. I might just as well have let him alone; it only set that other brute opening his window and spying out on me, and saying in his cracked old voice: 'Master, what are you doing out here at this time of night?'"

Again he sank back in his chair, muttering incoherently with half-closed eyes.

Loveday let him alone for a minute or so; then she had another question to ask.

"And that other brute—did he yelp or groan when you dealt him his blow?"

"What, old Sandy—the brute? he fell back— Ah, I remember, you said you would like to see the hammer that stopped his babbling old tongue—now didn't you?"

He rose a little unsteadily from his chair, and seemed to drag his long limbs with an effort across the room to a cabinet at the farther end. Opening a drawer in this cabinet, he produced, from amidst some specimens of strata and fossils, a large-sized geological hammer.

He brandished it for a moment over his head, then paused with his finger on his lip.

"Hush!" he said, "we shall have the fools creeping in to peep at us if we don't take care." And to Loveday's horror he suddenly made for the door, turned the key in the lock, withdrew it and put it into his pocket.

She looked at the clock; the hands pointed to half-past seven. Had Griffiths received her note at the proper time, and were the men now in the grounds? She could only pray that they were.

"The light is too strong for my eyes," she said, and rising from her chair, she lifted the green-shaded lamp and placed it on a table that stood at the window.

"No, no, that won't do," said Mr. Craven; "that would show everyone outside what we're doing in here." He crossed to the window as he spoke and removed the lamp thence to the mantelpiece.

Loveday could only hope that in the few seconds it had remained in the window it had caught the eye of the outside watchers.

The old man beckoned to Loveday to come near and examine his deadly weapon. "Give it a good swing round," he said, suiting the action to the word, "and down it comes with a splendid crash." He brought the hammer round within an inch of Loveday's forehead.

She started back.

"Ha, ha," he laughed harshly and unnaturally, with the light of madness dancing in his eyes now; "did I frighten you? I wonder what sort of sound you would make if I were to give you a little tap just there." Here he lightly touched her forehead with the hammer. "Elemental, of course, it would be, and—"

Loveday steadied her nerves with difficulty. Locked in with this lunatic, her only chance lay in gaining time for the detectives to reach the house and enter through the window.

"Wait a minute," she said, striving to divert his attention; "you have not yet told me what sort of an elemental sound old Sandy made when he fell. If you'll give me pen and ink, I'll write down a full account of it all, and you can incorporate it afterwards in your treatise."

For a moment a look of real pleasure flitted across the old man's face, then it faded. "The brute fell back dead without a sound," he answered; "it was all for nothing, that night's work; yet not altogether for nothing. No, I don't mind owning I would do it all over again to get the wild thrill of joy at my heart that I had when I looked down into that old man's dead face and felt myself free at last! Free at last!" his voice rang out excitedly—once more he brought his hammer round with an ugly swing.

"For a moment I was a young man again; I leaped into his room—the moon was shining full in through the window—I thought of my old college days, and the fun we used to have at Pembroke—topsy turvey I turned everything—" He broke off abruptly, and drew a step nearer to Loveday. "The pity of it all was," he said, suddenly dropping from his high, excited tone to a low, pathetic one, "that he fell without a sound of any sort." Here he drew another step nearer. "I wonder—" he said, then broke off again, and came close to Loveday's side. "It has only this moment occurred to me," he said, now with his lips close to Loveday's ear, "that a woman, in her death agony, would be much more likely to give utterance to an elemental sound than a man."

He raised his hammer, and Loveday fled to the window, and was lifted from the outside by three pairs of strong arms.

"I thought I was conducting my very last case—I never had such a narrow escape before!" said Loveday, as she stood talking with Mr. Griffiths on the Grenfell platform, awaiting the train to carry her back to London. "It seems strange that no one before suspected the old gentleman's sanity—I suppose, however, people were so used to his eccentricities that they did not notice how they had deepened into positive lunacy. His cunning evidently stood him in good stead at the inquest."

"It is possible," said Griffiths thoughtfully, "that he did not absolutely cross the very slender line that divided eccentricity from madness until after the murder. The excitement consequent upon the discovery of the crime may just have pushed him over the border. Now, Miss Brooke, we have exactly ten minutes before your train comes in. I should feel greatly obliged to you if you would explain one or two things that have a professional interest for me."

"With pleasure," said Loveday. "Put your questions in categorical order and I will answer them."

"Well, then, in the first place, what suggested to your mind the old man's guilt?"

"The relations that subsisted between him and Sandy seemed to me to savour too much of fear on the one side and power on the other. Also the income paid to Sandy during Mr. Craven's absence in Natal bore, to my mind, an unpleasant resemblance to hush-money."

"Poor wretched being! And I hear that, after all, the woman he married in his wild young days died soon afterwards of drink. I have no doubt, however, that Sandy sedulously kept up the fiction of her existence, even after his master's second marriage. Now for another question: how was it you knew that Miss Craven had taken her brother's place in the sick-room?"

"On the evening of my arrival I discovered a rather long lock of fair hair in the unswept fireplace of my room, which, as it happened, was usually occupied by

Miss Craven. It at once occurred to me that the young lady had been cutting off her hair and that there must be some powerful motive to induce such a sacrifice. The suspicious circumstances attending her brother's illness soon supplied me with such a motive."

"Ah! that typhoid fever business was very cleverly done. Not a servant in the house, I verily believe, but who thought Master Harry was upstairs, ill in bed, and Miss Craven away at her friends' in Newcastle. The young fellow must have got a clear start off within an hour of the murder. His sister, sent away the next day to Newcastle, dismissed her maid there, I hear, on the plea of no accommodation at her friends' house—sent the girl to her own home for a holiday and herself returned to Troyte's Hill in the middle of the night, having walked the five miles from Grenfell. No doubt her mother admitted her through one of those easily-opened front windows, cut her hair and put her to bed to personate her brother without delay. With Miss Craven's strong likeness to Master Harry, and in a darkened room, it is easy to understand that the eyes of a doctor, personally unacquainted with the family, might easily be deceived. Now, Miss Brooke, you must admit that with all this elaborate chicanery and double dealing going on, it was only natural that my suspicions should set in strongly in that quarter."

"I read it all in another light, you see," said Loveday. "It seemed to me that the mother, knowing her son's evil proclivities, believed in his guilt, in spite, possibly, of his assertions of innocence. The son, most likely, on his way back to the house after pledging the family plate, had met old Mr. Craven with the hammer in his hand. Seeing, no doubt, how impossible it would be for him to clear himself without incriminating his father, he preferred flight to Natal to giving evidence at the inquest."

"Now about his alias?" said Mr. Griffiths briskly, for the train was at that moment steaming into the station. "How did you know that Harold Cousins was identical with Harry Craven, and had sailed in the *Bonnie Dundee*?"

"Oh, that was easy enough," said Loveday, as she stepped into the train; "a newspaper sent down to Mr. Craven by his wife, was folded so as to direct his attention to the shipping list. In it I saw that the *Bonnie Dundee* had sailed two days previously for Natal. Now it was only natural to connect Natal with Mrs. Craven, who had passed the greater part of her life there; and it was easy to understand her wish to get her scapegrace son among her early friends. The alias under which he sailed came readily enough to light. I found it scribbled all over one of Mr. Craven's writing pads in his study; evidently it had been drummed into his ears by his wife as his son's alias, and the old gentleman had taken this method of fixing it in his memory. We'll hope that the young fellow, under his new name, will make a new reputation for himself—at any rate, he'll have a better chance of doing so with the ocean between him and his evil companions. Now it's good-bye, I think."

"No," said Mr. Griffiths; "it's au revoir, for you'll have to come back again for the assizes, and give the evidence that will shut old Mr. Craven in an asylum for the rest of his life."

SHERLOCKIAN SATIRES AND HOMAGES

THE GREAT PEGRAM MYSTERY

Robert Barr

I DROPPED IN ON MY FRIEND, SHERLAW KOMBS, TO HEAR WHAT HE HAD TO SAY about the Pegram mystery, as it had come to be called in the newspapers. I found him playing the violin with a look of sweet peace and serenity on his face, which I never noticed on the countenances of those within hearing distance. I knew this expression of seraphic calm indicated that Kombs had been deeply annoyed about something. Such, indeed, proved to be the case, for one of the morning papers had contained an article eulogizing the alertness and general competence of Scotland Yard. So great was Sherlaw Kombs's contempt for Scotland Yard that he never would visit Scotland during his vacations, nor would he ever admit that a Scotchman was fit for anything but export.

He generously put away his violin, for he had a sincere liking for me, and greeted me with his usual kindness.

"I have come," I began, plunging at once into the matter on my mind, "to hear what you think of the great Pegram mystery."

"I haven't heard of it," he said quietly, just as if all London were not talking of that very thing. Kombs was curiously ignorant on some subjects, and abnormally learned on others. I found, for instance, that political discussion with him was impossible, because he did not know who Salisbury and Gladstone were. This made his friendship a great boon. "The Pegram mystery has baffled even Gregory, of Scotland Yard."

"I can well believe it," said my friend, calmly. "Perpetual motion, or squaring the circle, would baffle Gregory. He's an infant, is Gregory."

This was one of the things I always liked about Kombs. There was no professional jealousy in him, such as characterizes so many other men.

He filled his pipe, threw himself into his deep-seated arm-chair, placed his feet on the mantel, and clasped his hands behind his head.

"Tell me about it," he said simply.

"Old Barrie Kipson," I began, "was a stock-broker in the City. He lived in Pegram, and it was his custom to——"

"COME IN!" shouted Kombs, without changing his position, but with a suddenness that startled me. I had heard no knock.

"Excuse me," said my friend, laughing, "my invitation to enter was a trifle pre-mature. I was really so interested in your recital that I spoke before I thought, which a detective should never do. The fact is, a man will be here in a moment who will tell me all about this crime, and so you will be spared further effort in that line."

"Ah, you have an appointment. In that case I will not intrude," I said, rising.

"Sit down; I have no appointment. I did not know until I spoke that he was coming."

I gazed at him in amazement. Accustomed as I was to his extraordinary talents, the man was a perpetual surprise to me. He continued to smoke quietly, but evidently enjoyed my consternation.

"I see you are surprised. It is really too simple to talk about, but, from my position opposite the mirror, I can see the reflection of objects in the street. A man stopped, looked at one of my cards, and then glanced across the street. I recognized my card, because, as you know, they are all in scarlet. If, as you say, London is talking of this mystery, it naturally follows that *he* will talk of it, and the chances are he wished to consult with me upon it. Anyone can see that, besides there is always—*Come* in!"

There was a rap at the door this time.

A stranger entered. Sherlaw Kombs did not change his lounging attitude.

"I wish to see Mr. Sherlaw Kombs, the detective," said the stranger, coming within the range of the smoker's vision.

"This is Mr. Kombs," I remarked at last, as my friend smoked quietly, and seemed half-asleep.

"Allow me to introduce myself," continued the stranger, fumbling for a card.

"There is no need. You are a journalist," said Kombs.

"Ah," said the stranger, somewhat taken aback, "you know me, then."

"Never saw or heard of you in my life before."

"Then how in the world—"

"Nothing simpler. You write for an evening paper. You have written an article condemning the book of a friend. He will feel bad about it, and you will condole with him. He will never know who stabbed him unless I tell him."

"The devil!" cried the journalist, sinking into a chair and mopping his brow, while his face became livid.

"Yes," drawled Kombs, "it is a devil of a shame that such things are done. But what would you, as we say in France."

When the journalist had recovered his second wind he pulled himself together somewhat. "Would you object to telling me how you know these particulars about a man you say you have never seen?"

"I rarely talk about these things," said Kombs with great composure. "But as the cultivation of the habit of observation may help you in your profession, and thus in a remote degree benefit me by making your paper less deadly dull, I will tell you. Your first and second fingers are smeared with ink, which shows that you write a great deal. This smeared class embraces two subclasses, clerks or accountants, and journalists. Clerks have to be neat in their work. The ink smear is slight in their case. Your fingers are badly and carelessly smeared; therefore, you are a journalist. You have an evening paper in your pocket. Anyone might have any evening paper, but yours is a Special Edition, which will not be on the streets for half an hour yet. You must have obtained it before you left the office, and to do this you must be on the staff. A book notice is marked with a blue pencil. A journalist always despises every article in his own paper not written by himself; therefore, you wrote the article you have marked, and doubtless are about to send it to the author oi the book referred to. Your paper makes a speciality of abusing all books not written by some member of its own staff. That the author is a friend of yours, I merely surmised. It is all a trivial example of ordinary observation."

"Really, Mr. Kombs, you are the most wonderful man on earth. You are the equal of Gregory, by Jove, you are."

A frown marred the brow of my friend as he placed his pipe or the sideboard and drew his self-cocking six-shooter.

"Do you mean to insult me, sir?"

"I do not—I—I assure you. You are fit to take charge of Scotland Yard to-morrow—I am in earnest, indeed I am, sir."

"Then heaven help you," cried Kombs, slowly raising his right arm.

I sprang between them.

"Don't shoot!" I cried. "You will spoil the carpet. Besides, Sherlaw, don't you see the man means well. He actually thinks it is a compliment!"

"Perhaps you are right," remarked the detective, flinging his revolver carelessly beside his pipe, much to the relief of the third party. Then, turning to the journalist, he said, with his customary bland courtesy—

"You wanted to see me, I think you said. What can I do for you, Mr. Wilber Scribbings?"

The journalist started.

"How do you know my name?" he gasped.

Kombs waved his hand impatiently.

"Look inside your hat if you doubt your own name."

I then noticed for the first time that the name was plainly to be seen inside the top-hat Scribbings held upside down in his hands.

"You have heard, of course, of the Pegram mystery—"

"Tush," cried the detective; "do not, I beg of you, call it a mystery. There is no such thing. Life would become more tolerable if there ever *was* a mystery. Nothing is original. Everything has been done before. What about the Pegram affair?"

"The Pegram—ah—case has baffled everyone. The *Evening Blade* wishes you to investigate, so that it may publish the result. It will pay you well. Will you accept the commission?"

"Possibly. Tell me about the case."

"I thought everybody knew the particulars. Mr. Barrie Kipson lived at Pegram. He carried a first-class season ticket between the terminus and that station. It was his custom to leave for Pegram on the 5:30 train each evening. Some weeks ago, Mr. Kipson was brought down by the influenza. On his first visit to the City after his recovery, he drew something like £300 in notes, and left the office at his usual hour to catch the 5:30. He was never seen again alive, as far as the public have been able to learn. He was found at Brewster in a first-class compartment on the Scotch Express, which does not stop between London and Brewster. There was a bullet in his head, and his money was gone, pointing plainly to murder and robbery."

"And where is the mystery, might I ask?"

"There are several unexplainable things about the case. First, how came he on the Scotch Express, which leaves at six, and does not stop at Pegram? Second, the ticket examiners at the terminus would have turned him out if he showed his season ticket; and all the tickets sold for the Scotch Express on the 21st are accounted for. Third, how could the murderer have escaped? Fourth, the passengers in two compartments on each side of the one where the body was found heard no scuffle and no shot fired."

"Are you sure the Scotch Express on the 21st did not stop between London and Brewster?"

"Now that you mention the fact, it did. It was stopped by signal just outside of Pegram. There was a few moments' pause, when the line was reported clear, and it went on again. This frequently happens, as there is a branch line beyond Pegram."

Mr. Sherlaw Kombs pondered for a few moments, smoking his pipe silently.

"I presume you wish the solution in time for to-morrow's paper?"

"Bless my soul, no. The editor thought if you evolved a theory in a month you would do well."

"My dear sir, I do not deal with theories, but with facts. If you can make it convenient to call here to-morrow at 8 A.M. I will give you the full particulars early enough for the first edition. There is no sense in taking up much time over so simple an affair as the Pegram case. Good afternoon, sir."

Mr. Scribbings was too much astonished to return the greeting. He left in a speechless condition, and I saw him go up the street with his hat still in his hand.

Sherlaw Kombs relapsed into his old lounging attitude, with his hands clasped behind his head. The smoke came from his lips in quick puffs at first, then at longer intervals. I saw he was coming to a conclusion, so I said nothing.

Finally he spoke in his most dreamy manner. "I do not wish to seem to be rushing things at all, Whatson, but I am going out to-night on the Scotch Express. Would you care to accompany me?"

"Bless me!" I cried, glancing at the clock. "You haven't time, it is after five now."

"Ample time, Whatson—ample," he murmured, without changing his position. "I give myself a minute and a half to change slippers and dressing-gown for boots and coat, three seconds for hat, twenty-five seconds to the street, forty-two seconds waiting for a hansom, and then seven minutes at the terminus before the express starts. I shall be glad of your company."

I was only too happy to have the privilege of going with him. It was most interesting to watch the workings of so inscrutable a mind. As we drove under the lofty iron roof of the terminus I noticed a look of annoyance pass over his face.

"We are fifteen seconds ahead of our time," he remarked, looking at the big clock. "I dislike having a miscalculation of that sort occur."

The great Scotch Express stood ready for its long journey. The detective tapped one of the guards on the shoulder.

"You have heard of the so-called Pegram mystery, I presume?"

"Certainly, sir. It happened on this very train, sir."

"Really? Is the same carriage still on the train?"

"Well, yes, sir, it is," replied the guard, lowering his voice, "but of course, sir, we have to keep very quiet about it. People wouldn't travel in it, else, sir."

"Doubtless. Do you happen to know if anybody occupies the compartment in which the body was found?"

"A lady and gentleman, sir; I put 'em in myself, sir."

"Would you further oblige me," said the detective, deftly slipping half a sovereign into the hand of the guard, "by going to the window and informing them in an offhand casual sort of way that the tragedy took place in that compartment?"

"Certainly, sir."

We followed the guard, and the moment he had imparted his news there was a suppressed scream in the carriage. Instantly a lady came out, followed by a florid-faced gentleman, who scowled at the guard. We entered the now empty compartment, and Kombs said:

"We would like to be alone here until we reach Brewster."

"I'll see to that, sir," answered the guard, locking the door.

When the official moved away, I asked my friend what he expected to find in the carriage that would cast any light on the case.

"Nothing," was his brief reply.

"Then why do you come?"

"Merely to corroborate the conclusions I have already arrived at."

"And might I ask what those conclusions are?"

"Certainly," replied the detective, with a touch of lassitude in his voice. "I beg to call your attention, first, to the fact that this train stands between two platforms, and can be entered from either side. Any man familiar with the station for years would be aware of that fact. This shows how Mr. Kipson entered the train just before it started."

"But the door on this side is locked," I objected, trying it.

"Of course. But every season ticket holder carries a key. This accounts for the guard not seeing him, and for the absence of a ticket. Now let me give you some information about the influenza. The patient's temperature rises several degrees above normal, and he has a fever. When the malady has run its course, the temperature falls to three quarters of a degree below normal. These facts are unknown to you, I imagine, because you are a doctor."

I admitted such was the case.

"Well, the consequence of this fall in temperature is that the convalescent's mind turns towards thoughts of suicide. Then is the time he should be watched by his friends. Then was the time Mr. Barrie Kipson's friends did *not* watch him. You remember the 21st, of course. No? It was a most depressing day. Fog all around and mud under foot. Very good. He resolves on suicide. He wishes to be unidentified, if possible, but forgets his season ticket. My experience is that a man about to commit a crime always forgets something."

"But how do you account for the disappearance of the money?"

"The money has nothing to do with the matter. If he was a deep man, and knew the stupidity of Scotland Yard, he probably sent the notes to an enemy. If not, they may have been given to a friend. Nothing is more calculated to prepare the mind for self-destruction than the prospect of a night ride on the Scotch Express, and the view from the windows of the train as it passes through the northern part of London is particularly conducive to thoughts of annihilation."

"What became of the weapon?"

"That is just the point on which I wish to satisfy myself. Excuse me for a moment."

Mr. Sherlaw Kombs drew down the window on the right-hand side, and examined the top of the casing minutely with a magnifying glass. Presently he heaved a sigh of relief, and drew up the sash.

"Just as I expected," he remarked, speaking more to himself than to me. "There is a slight dent on the top of the window frame. It is of such a nature as to be made only by the trigger of a pistol falling from the nerveless hand of a suicide. He intended to throw the weapon far out of the window, but had not the strength. It might have fallen into the carriage. As a matter of fact, it bounced away from the line and lies among the grass about ten feet six inches from the outside rail. The only question that now remains is where the deed was committed, and the exact present position of the pistol reckoned in miles from London, but that, fortunately, is too simple even to need explanation."

"Great heavens, Sherlaw!" I cried. "How can you call that simple? It seems to me impossible to compute."

We were now flying over northern London, and the great detective leaned back with every sign of *ennui*, closing his eyes. At last he spoke wearily:

"It is really too elementary, Whatson, but I am always willing to oblige a friend. I shall be relieved, however, when you are able to work out the A B C of detection for yourself, although I shall never object to helping you with the words of more than three syllables. Having made up his mind to commit suicide, Kipson naturally intended to do it before he reached Brewster, because tickets are again examined at that point. When the train began to stop at the signal near Pegram, he came to the false conclusion that it was stopping at Brewster. The fact that the shot was not heard is accounted for by the screech of the air-brake, added to the noise of the train. Probably the whistle was also sounding at the same moment. The train being a fast express would stop as near the signal as possible. The air-brake will stop a train in twice its own length. Call it three times in this case. Very well. At three times the length of this train from the signal-post towards London, deducting half the length of the train, as this carriage is in the middle, you will find the pistol."

"Wonderful!" I exclaimed.

"Commonplace," he murmured.

At this moment the whistle sounded shrilly, and we felt the grind of the air-brakes.

"The Pegram signal again," cried Kombs, with something almost like enthusiasm. "This is indeed luck. We will get out here, Whatson, and test the matter."

As the train stopped, we got out on the right-hand side of the line. The engine stood panting impatiently under the red light, which changed to green as I looked at it. As the train moved on with in- creasing speed, the detective counted the carriages, and noted down the number. It was now dark, with the thin crescent of the moon hanging in the western sky throwing a weird half-light on the shining metals. The rear lamps of the train disappeared around a curve, and the signal stood at baleful red again. The black magic of the lonesome night in that strange place impressed me, but the detective was a most practical man. He placed his back against the signal-post, and paced up the line with even strides, counting his steps. I walked along the permanent way beside him silently. At last he stopped, and took a tape-line from his pocket. He ran it out until the ten feet six inches were unrolled, scanning the figures in the wan light of the new moon. Giving me the end, he placed his knuckles on the metals, motioning me to proceed down the embankment. I stretched out the line, and then sank my hand in the damp grass to mark the spot.

"Good God!" I cried, aghast. "What is this?"

"It is the pistol," said Kombs quietly.

It was!

Journalistic London will not soon forget the sensation that was caused by the record of the investigations of Sherlaw Kombs, as printed at length in the next day's *Evening Blade*. Would that my story ended here. Alas! Kombs contemptuously turned over the pistol to Scotland Yard. The meddlesome officials, actuated, as I always hold, by jealousy, found the name of the seller upon it. They investigated. The seller testified that it had never been in the possession of Mr. Kipson, as far as he knew. It was sold to a man whose description tallied with that of a criminal long watched by the police. He was arrested, and turned Queen's evidence in the hope of hanging his pal. It seemed that Mr. Kipson, who was a gloomy, taciturn man, and usually came home in a compartment by himself, thus escaping observation, had been murdered in the lane leading to his house. After robbing him, the miscreants turned their thoughts towards the disposal of the body—a subject that always occupies a first-class criminal mind after the deed is done. They agreed to place it on the line, and have it mangled by the Scotch Express, then nearly due. Before they got the body half-way up the embankment the express came along and stopped. The guard got out and walked along the other side to speak with the engineer. The thought of putting the body into an empty first-class carriage instantly occurred to the murderers. They opened the door with the deceased's key. It is supposed that the pistol dropped when they were hoisting the body in the carriage.

The Queen's evidence dodge didn't work, and Scotland Yard ignobly insulted my friend Sherlaw Kombs by sending him a pass to see the villains hanged.

THE ADVENTURE OF THE CLOTHES-LINE

Carolyn Wells

THE MEMBERS OF THE SOCIETY OF INFALLIBLE DETECTIVES WERE JUST sitting around and being socially infallible, in their rooms in Fakir Street, when President Holmes strode in. He was much saturniner than usual, and the others at once deduced there was something toward.

"And it's this," said Holmes, perceiving that they had perceived it. "A reward is offered for the solution of a great mystery—so great, my colleagues, that I fear none of you will be able to solve it, or even to help me in the marvelous work I shall do when ferreting it out."

"Humph!" grunted the Thinking Machine, riveting his steel-blue eyes upon the speaker.

"He voices all our sentiments," said Raffles, with his winning smile. "Fire away, Holmes. What's the prob?"

"To explain a most mysterious proceeding down on the East Side."

Though a tall man, Holmes spoke shortly, for he was peeved at the inattentive attitude of his collection of colleagues. But of course he still had his Watson, so he put up with the indifference of the rest of the cold world.

"Aren't all proceedings down on the East Side mysterious?" asked Arsène Lupin, with an aristocratic look.

Holmes passed his brow wearily under his hand.

"Inspector Spyer," he said, "was riding on the Elevated Road—one of the small numbered Avenues—when, as he passed a tenement-house district, he saw a clothes-line strung from one high window to another across a courtyard."

"Was it Monday?" asked the Thinking Machine, who for the moment was thinking he was a washing machine.

"That doesn't matter. About the middle of the line was suspended—"

"By clothes-pins?" asked two or three of the Infallibles at once.

"Was suspended a beautiful woman."

"Hanged?"

"No. *Do listen!* She hung by her hands, and was evidently trying to cross from one house to the other. By her exhausted and agonized face, the inspector feared she could not hold on much longer. He sprang from his seat to rush to her assistance, but the train had already started, and he was too late to get off."

"What was she doing there?" "Did she fall?" "What did she look like?" and various similar nonsensical queries fell from the lips of the great detectives.

"Be silent, and I will tell you all the known facts. She was a society woman, it is clear, for she was robed in a chiffon evening gown, one of those roll-top things. She wore rich jewelry and dainty slippers with jeweled buckles. Her hair, unloosed from its moorings, hung in heavy masses far down her back."

"How extraordinary! What does it all mean?" asked M. Dupin, ever straightforward of speech.

"I don't know yet," answered Holmes, honestly. "I've studied the matter only a few months. But I will find out, if I have to raze the whole tenement block. There *must* be a clue somewhere."

"Marvelous! Holmes, marvelous!" said a phonograph in the corner, which Watson had fixed up, as he had to go out.

"The police have asked us to take up the case and have offered a reward for its solution. Find out who was the lady, what she was doing, and why she did it."

"Are there any clues?" asked M. Vidocq, while M. Lecoq said simultaneously, "Any footprints?"

"There is one footprint; no other clue."

"Where is the footprint?"

"On the ground, right under where the lady was hanging."

"But you said the rope was high from the ground."

"More than a hundred feet."

"And she stepped down and made a single footprint. Strange! Quite strange!" and the Thinking Machine shook his yellow old head.

"She did nothing of the sort," said Holmes, petulantly. "If you fellows would listen, you might hear something. The occupants of the tenement houses have been questioned. But, as it turns out, none of them chanced to be at home at the time of the occurrence. There was a parade in the next street, and they had all gone to see it."

"Had a light snow fallen the night before?" asked Lecoq, eagerly.

"Yes, of course," answered Holmes. "How could we know anything, else? Well, the lady had dropped her slipper, and although the slipper was not found, it having been annexed by the tenement people who came home first, I had a chance to study the footprint. The slipper was a two and a half D. It was too small for her."

"How do you know?"

"Women always wear slippers too small for them."

"Then how did she come to drop it off?" This from Raffles, triumphantly.

Holmes looked at him pityingly.

"She kicked it off because it was too tight. Women always kick off their slippers when playing bridge or in an opera box or at a dinner."

"And always when they're crossing a clothes-line?" This in Lupin's most sarcastic vein.

"Naturally," said Holmes, with a taciturnine frown. "The footprint clearly denotes a lady of wealth and fashion, somewhat short of stature, and weighing about one hundred and sixty. She was of an animated nature—"

"Suspended animation," put in Luther Trant, wittily, and Scientific Sprague added, "Like the Coffin of Damocles, or whoever it was."

But Holmes frowned on their light-headedness.

"We must find out what it all means," he said in his gloomiest way. "I have a tracing of the footprint."

"I wonder if my seismospygmograph would work on it," mused Trant.

"I am the Prince of Footprints," declared Lecoq, pompously. "*I* will solve the mystery."

"Do your best, all of you," said their illustrious president. "I fear you can do little; these things are unintelligible to the unintelligent. But study on it, and meet here again one week from tonight, with your answers neatly typewritten on one side of the paper."

The Infallible Detectives started off, each affecting a jaunty sanguineness of demeanor, which did not in the least impress their president, who was used to sanguinary impressions.

They spent their allotted seven days in the study of the problem; and a lot of the seven nights, too, for they wanted to delve into the baffling secret by sun or candlelight, as dear Mrs. Browning so poetically puts it.

And when the week had fled, the Infallibles again gathered in the Fakir Street sanctum, each face wearing the smug smirk and smile of one who had quested a successful quest and was about to accept his just reward.

"And now," said President Holmes, "as nothing can be hid from the Infallible Detectives, I assume we have all discovered why the lady hung from the clothes-line above that deep and dangerous chasm of a tenement courtyard."

"We have," replied his colleagues, in varying tones of pride, conceit, and mock modesty.

"I cannot think," went on the hawk-like voice, "that you have, any of you, stumbled upon the real solution of the mystery; but I will listen to your amateur attempts."

"As the oldest member of our organization, I will tell my solution first," said Vidocq, calmly. "I have not been able to find the lady, but I am convinced that she was merely an expert trapezist or tight-rope walker, practising a new trick to amaze her Coney Island audiences."

"Nonsense!" cried Holmes. "In that case the lady would have worn tights or fleshings. We are told she was in full evening dress of the smartest set."

Arsène Lupin spoke next.

"It's too easy," he said boredly; "she was a typist or stenographer who had been annoyed by attentions from her employer, and was trying to escape from the brute."

"Again I call your attention to her costume," said Holmes, with a look of intolerance on his finely cold-chiseled face.

"That's all right," returned Lupin, easily. "Those girls dress every old way! I've seen 'em. They don't think anything of evening clothes at their work."

"Humph!" said the Thinking Machine, and the others all agreed with him.

"Next," said Holmes, sternly.

"I'm next," said Lecoq. "I submit that the lady escaped from a near-by lunatic asylum. She had the illusion that she was an old overcoat and the moths had got at her. So of course she hung herself on the clothes-line. This theory of lunacy also accounts for the fact that the lady's hair was down—like *Ophelia's*, you know."

"It would have been easier for her to swallow a few good moth balls," said Holmes, looking at Lecoq in stormy silence. "Mr. Gryce, you are an experienced deducer; what did *you* conclude?"

Mr. Gryce glued his eyes to his right boot toe, after his celebrated habit. "I make out she was a-slumming. You know, all the best ladies are keen about it. And I feel that she belonged to the Cult for the Betterment of Clothes-lines. She was by way of being a tester. She had to go across them hand over hand, and if they bore her weight, they were passed by the censor."

"And if they didn't?"

"Apparently that predicament had not occurred at the time of our problem, and so cannot be considered."

"I think Gryce is right about the slumming," remarked Luther Trant, "but the reason for the lady hanging from the clothes-line is the imperative necessity she felt for a thorough airing, after her tenemental visitations; there is a certain tenement scent, if I may express it, that requires ozone in quantities."

"You're too material," said the Thinking Machine, with a faraway look in his weak, blue eyes. "This lady was a disciple of New Thought. She had to go into the silence, or concentrate, or whatever they call it. And they always choose strange places for these thinking spells. They have to have solitude, and, as I understand it, the clothes-line was not crowded?"

Rouletabille laughed right out.

"You're way off, Thinky," he said. "What ailed that dame was just that she wanted to reduce. I've read about it in the women's journals. They all want to reduce. They take all sorts of crazy exercises, and this crossing clothes-lines hand over hand is the latest. I'll bet it took off twenty of those avoirdupois with which old Sherly credited her."

"Pish and a few tushes!" remarked Raffles, in his smart society jargon. "You don't fool me. That clever little bear was making up a new dance to thrill society next winter. You'll see. Sunday-paper headlines: STUNNING NEW DANCE! THE CLOTHES-LINE CLING! CAUGHT ON LIKE WILDFIRE! *That's* what it's all about. What do you know, eh?"

"Go take a walk, Raffles," said Holmes, not unkindly; "you re sleepy yet. Scientific Sprague, you sometimes put over an abstruse theory, what do you say?"

"I didn't need science," said Sprague, carelessly. "As soon as I heard she had her hair down, I jumped to the correct conclusion. She had been washing her hair, and was drying it. My sister always sticks her head out of the skylight; but this lady's plan is, I should judge, a more all-round success."

As they had now all voiced their theories, President Holmes rose to give them the inestimable benefit of his own views.

"Your ideas are not without some merit," he conceded, "but you have overlooked the eternal-feminine element in the problem. As soon as I tell you the real solution, you will each wonder why it escaped your notice. The lady thought she heard a mouse, so she scrambled out of the window, preferring to risk her life on the perilous clothes-line rather than stay in the dwelling where the mouse was also. It is all very simple. She was doing her hair, threw her head over forward to twist it, as they always do, and so espied the mouse sitting in the corner."

"Marvelous! Holmes, marvelous!" exclaimed Watson, who had just come back from his errand.

Even as they were all pondering on Holmes's superior wisdom, the telephone bell rang.

"Are you there?" said President Holmes, for he was ever English of speech.

"Yes, yes," returned the impatient voice of the chief of police. "Call off your detective workers. We have discovered who the lady was who crossed the clothes-line, and why she did it."

"I can't imagine you really know," said Holmes into the transmitter; "but tell me what you think."

"A-r-r-rh! Of course I know! It was just one of those confounded moving-picture stunts!"

"Indeed! And why did the lady kick off her slipper?"

"A-r-r-r-h! It was part of the fool plot. She's Miss Flossy Flicker of the Flim-Flam Film Company, doin' the six-reel thriller, 'At the End of Her Rope.'"

"Ah," said Holmes, suavely, "my compliments to Miss Flicker on her good work."

"Marvelous, Holmes, marvelous!" said Watson.

"And where could you find better?" I said enthusiastically. "I should say the cigar case is as good as recovered already."

"I shall remind you of that again," he said lightly. "And now, to show you my confidence in your judgment, in spite of my determination to pursue this alone, I am willing to listen to any suggestions from you."

He drew a memorandum book from his pocket and, with a grave smile, took up his pencil.

I could scarcely believe my senses. He, the great Hemlock Jones, accepting suggestions from a humble individual like myself! I kissed his hand reverently, and began in a joyous tone:

"First, I should advertise, offering a reward; I should give the same intimation in handbills, distributed at the 'pubs' and the pastry cooks'. I should next visit the different pawnbrokers; I should give notice at the police station. I should examine the servants. I should thoroughly search the house and my own pockets. I speak relatively," I added, with a laugh. "Of course I mean *your* own."

He gravely made an entry of these details.

"Perhaps," I added, "you have already done this?"

"Perhaps," he returned enigmatically. "Now, my dear friend," he continued, putting the notebook in his pocket and rising, "would you excuse me for a few moments? Make yourself perfectly at home until I return; there may be some things," he added with a sweep of his hand toward his heterogeneously filled shelves, "that may interest you and while away the time. There are pipes and tobacco in that corner."

Then nodding to me with the same inscrutable face he left the room. I was too well accustomed to his methods to think much of his unceremonious withdrawal, and made no doubt he was off to investigate some clue which had suddenly occurred to his active intelligence.

Left to myself I cast a cursory glance over his shelves. There were a number of small glass jars containing earthy substances, labeled PAVEMENT AND ROAD SWEEPINGS, from the principal thoroughfares and suburbs of London, with the subdirections FOR IDENTIFYING FOOT TRACKS. There were several other jars, labeled FLUFF FROM OMNIBUS AND ROAD-CAR SEATS, COCONUT FIBER AND ROPE STRANDS FROM MATTINGS IN PUBLIC PLACES, CIGARETTE STUMPS AND MATCH ENDS FROM FLOOR OF PALACE THEATRE, ROW A, 1 TO 50. Everywhere were evidences of this wonderful man's system and perspicacity.

I was thus engaged when I heard the slight creaking of a door, and I looked up as a stranger entered. He was a rough-looking man, with a shabby overcoat and a still more disreputable muffler around his throat and the lower part of his face.

Considerably annoyed at his intrusion, I turned upon him rather sharply, when, with a mumbled, growling apology for mistaking the room, he shuffled out again and closed the door. I followed him quickly to the landing and saw that he disappeared down the stairs. With my mind full of the robbery, the incident made a singular impression upon me. I knew my friend's habit of hasty absences from his room in his moments of deep inspiration; it was only too probable that, with his powerful intellect and magnificent perceptive genius concentrated on one subject, he should be careless of his own belongings, and no doubt even forget to take the ordinary precaution of locking up his drawers. I tried one or two and found that I was right, although for some reason I was unable to open one to its fullest extent. The handles were sticky, as if someone had opened it with dirty fingers. Knowing Hemlock's fastidious cleanliness, I resolved to inform him of this circumstance, but I forgot it, alas! until—but I am anticipating my story.

His absence was strangely prolonged. I at last seated myself by the fire and, lulled by warmth and the patter of the rain, fell asleep. I may have dreamt, for during my sleep I had a vague semiconsciousness as of hands being softly pressed on my pockets —no doubt induced by the story of the robbery. When I came fully to my senses, I found Hemlock Jones sitting on the other side of the hearth, his deeply concentrated gaze fixed on the fire.

"I found you so comfortably asleep that I could not bear to awaken you," he said with a smile.

"I rubbed my eyes. "And what news?" I asked. "How have you succeeded?"

"Better than I expected," he said, "and I think," he added, tapping his notebook, "I owe much to *you*."

Deeply gratified, I awaited more. But in vain. I ought to have remembered that in his moods Hemlock Jones was reticence itself. I told him simply of the strange intrusion, but he only laughed.

Later, when I arose to go, he looked at me playfully. "If you were a married man," he said, "I would advise you not to go home until you had brushed your sleeve. There are a few short brown sealskin hairs on the inner side of your forearm just where they would have adhered if your arm had encircled a sealskin coat with some pressure!"

"For once you are at fault," I said triumphantly; "the hair is my own, as you will perceive; I have just had it cut at the barber shop, and no doubt this arm projected beyond the apron."

He frowned slightly yet nevertheless, on my turning to go, he embraced me warmly—a rare exhibition in that man of ice. He even helped me on with my overcoat and pulled out and smoothed down the flaps of my pockets. He was particular, too, in fitting my arm in my overcoat sleeve, shaking the sleeve down from the armhole to the cuff with his deft fingers. "Come again soon! he said, clapping me on the back.

"At any and all times," I said enthusiastically; "I only ask then minutes twice a day to eat a crust at my office, and four hours' sleep at night, and the rest of my time is devoted to you always, as you know."

"It is indeed," he said, with his impenetrable smile.

Nevertheless, I did not find him at home when I next called. One afternoon, when nearing my own home, I met him in one of his favorite disguises—a long blue swallow-tailed coat, striped cotton trousers, large turn-over collar, blacked face, and white hat, carrying a tambourine. Of course to others the disguise was perfect, although it was known to myself , and I passed him—according to an old understanding between us—without the slightest recognition, trusting later to an explanation. At another time, as I was making a professional visit to the wife of a publican at the East End, I saw him, in the disguise of a broken-down artisan, looking into the window of an adjacent pawnshop. I was delighted to see that he was evidently following my suggestions, and in my joy I ventured to tip him a wink; it was abstractedly returned.

Two days later I received a note appointing a meeting at his lodgings that night. That meeting, alas! was the one memorable occurrence of my life, and the last meeting I ever had with Hemlock Jones! I will try to set it down calmly, though my pulses still throb with the recollection of it.

I found him standing before the fire, with that look upon his face which I had seen only once or twice—a look which I may call an absolute concatenation of inductive and deductive ratiocination—from which all that was human, tender, or sympathetic was absolutely discharged. He was simply an icy algebraic symbol!

After I had entered he locked the doors, fastened the window, and even placed a chair before the chimney. As I watched these significant precautions with absorbing interest, he suddenly drew a revolver and, presenting it to my temple, said in low, icy tones:

"Hand over that cigar case!"

Even in my bewilderment my reply was truthful, spontaneous, and involuntary. "I haven't got it," I said.

He smiled bitterly, and threw down his revolver. "I expected that reply! Then let me now confront you with something more awful, more deadly, more relentless and convincing than that mere lethal weapon—the damning inductive and deductive proofs of your guilt!" He drew from his pocket a roll of paper and a notebook.

"But surely," I gasped, "you are joking! You could not believe— "

"Silence! Sit down!"

I obeyed.

"You have condemned yourself," he went on pitilessly. "Condemned yourself on my processes—processes familiar to you, applauded by you, accepted by you for years! We will go back to the time when you first saw the cigar case. Your expressions," he said in cold, deliberate tones, consulting his paper, "were, 'How beautiful! I wish it were mine.' This was your first step in crime—and my first indication. From 'I *wish* it were mine' to 'I *will* have it mine,' and the mere detail, '*How can* I make it mine?' the advance was obvious. Silence! But as in my methods it was necessary that there should be an overwhelming inducement to the crime, that unholy admiration of yours for the mere trinket itself was not enough. You are a smoker of cigars."

"But," I burst out passionately, "I told you I had given up smoking cigars."

"Fool!" he said coldly. "That is the *second* time you have committed yourself. Of course you told me! What more natural than for you to blazon forth that prepared and unsolicited statement to *prevent* accusation. Yet, as I said before, even that wretched attempt to cover up your tracks was not enough. I still had to find that overwhelming, impelling motive necessary to affect a man like you. That motive I found in the strongest of all impulses—love, I suppose you would call it—" he added bitterly—"that night you called! You had brought the most conclusive proofs of it on your sleeve."

"But—" I almost screamed.

"Silence!" he thundered. "I know what you would say. You would say that even if you had embraced some Young Person in a sealskin coat what had that to do with the robbery? Let me tell you then, that that sealskin coat represented the quality and character of your fatal entanglement! You bartered your honor for it—that stolen cigar case was the purchaser of the sealskin coat!

"Silence! Having thoroughly established your motive I now proceed to the commission of the crime itself. Ordinary people would have begun with that—with an attempt to discover the whereabouts of the missing object. These are not *my* methods."

So overpowering was his penetration that, although I knew myself innocent, I licked my lips with avidity to hear the further details of this lucid exposition of my crime.

"You committed that theft the night I showed you the cigar case, and after I had carelessly thrown it in that drawer You were sitting in that chair, and I had arisen to take something from that shelf, that instant you secured your booty without rising. Silence! Do you remember when I helped you on with your overcoat the other night? I was particular about fitting your arm in. While doing so I measured your arm with a spring tape measure, from the shoulder to the cuff. A later visit to your tailor confirmed that measurement. It proved to be *the exact distance between your chair and that drawer!* I sat stunned.

"The rest are mere corroborative details! You were again tampering with the drawer when I discovered you doing so! Do not start! The stranger that blundered into the room with a muffler on was myself! More, I had placed a little soap on the drawer handles when I purposely left you alone. The soap was on your hand when I shook it at parting. I softly felt your pockets, when you were asleep, for further developments. I embraced you when you left—that I might feel if you had the cigar case or any other articles hidden on your body. This confirmed me in the belief that you had already disposed of it in the manner and for the purpose I have shown you. As I still believed you capable of remorse and confession, I twice allowed you to see I was on your track: once in the garb of an itinerant Negro minstrel, and the second time as a workman looking in the window of the pawnshop where you pledged your booty."

"But," I burst out, "if you had asked the pawnbroker, you would have seen how unjust—"

"Fool!" he hissed. "Do you suppose I followed any of your suggestions, the suggestions of the thief? On the contrary, they told me what to avoid."

"And I suppose," I said bitterly, "you have not even searched your drawer."

"No," he said calmly.

I was for the first time really vexed. I went to the nearest drawer and pulled it out sharply. It stuck as it had before, leaving a section of the drawer unopened. By working it, however, I discovered that it was impeded by some obstacle that had slipped to the upper part of the drawer, and held it firmly fast. Inserting my hand, I pulled out the impeding object. It was the missing cigar case! I turned to him with a cry of joy.

But I was appalled at his expression. A look of contempt was now added to his acute, penetrating gaze. "I have been mistaken," he said slowly. "I had not allowed for your weakness and cowardice! I thought too highly of you even in your guilt! But I see now why you tampered with that drawer the other night. By some inexplicable means—possibly another theft—you took the cigar case out of pawn and, liked a whipped hound, restored it to me in this feeble, clumsy fashion. You thought to deceive me, Hemlock Jones! More, you thought to destroy my infallibility. Go! I give you your liberty. I shall not summon the three policemen who wait in the adjoining room—but out of my sight forever!"

As I stood once more dazed and petrified, he took me firmly by the ear and led me into the hall, closing the door behind him. This reopened presently, wide enough to permit him to thrust out my hat, overcoat, umbrella, and overshoes, and then closed against me forever!

I never saw him again. I am bound to say, however, that thereafter my business increased, I recovered much of my old practice, and a few of my patients recovered also. I became rich. I had a brougham and a house in the West End. But I often wondered, if, in some lapse of consciousness, I had not really stolen his cigar case!

THE ADVENTURES OF SHAMROCK JOLNES

O. Henry

I AM SO FORTUNATE AS TO COUNT SHAMROCK JOLNES, THE GREAT NEW YORK detective, among my muster of friends. Jolnes is what is called the "inside man" of the city detective force. He is an expert in the use of the typewriter, and it is his duty, whenever there is a "murder mystery" to be solved, to sit at a desk telephone at Headquarters and take down the messages of "cranks" who phone in their confessions to having committed the crime.

But on certain "off" days when confessions are coming in slowly and three or four newspapers have run to earth as many different guilty persons, Jolnes will knock about the town with me, exhibiting, to my great delight and instruction, his marvelous powers of observation and deduction.

The other day I dropped in at Headquarters and found the great detective gazing thoughtfully at a string that was tied tightly around his little finger.

"Good morning, Whatsup," he said, without turning his head. "I'm glad to notice that you've had your house fitted up with electric lights at last."

"Will you please tell me," I said, in surprise, "how you knew that; I am sure that I never mentioned the fact to anyone, and the wiring was a rush order not completed until this morning."

"Nothing easier," said Jolnes, genially. "As you came in I caught the odor of the cigar you are smoking. I know an expensive cigar; and I know that not more than three men in New York can afford to smoke cigars and pay gas bills too at the present time. That was an easy one. But I am working just now on a little problem of my own."

"Why have you that string on your finger?" I asked.

"That's the problem," said Jolnes. "My wife tied that on this morning to remind me of something I was to send up to the house. Sit down, Whatsup, and excuse me for a few moments."

The distinguished detective went to a wall telephone, and stood with the receiver to his ear for probably ten minutes.

"Were you listening to a confession?" I asked, when he had returned to his chair.

"Perhaps," said Jolnes, with a smile, "it might be called something of the sort. To be frank with you, Whatsup, I've cut out the dope. I've been increasing the quantity for so long that morphine doesn't have much effect on me any more. I've got to have something more powerful. That telephone I just went to is connected with a room in the Waldorf where there's an author's reading in progress. Now, to get at the solution of this string."

After five minutes of silent pondering, Jolnes looked at me, with a smile, and nodded his head.

"Wonderful man!" I exclaimed. "Already?"

"It is quite simple," he said, holding up his finger. "You see that knot? That is to prevent my forgetting. It is, therefore, a forget-me-knot. A forget-me-not is a flower. It was a sack of flour that I was to send home!"

"Beautiful!" I could not help crying out in admiration.

"Suppose we go out for a ramble," suggested Jolnes.

"There is only one case of importance on hand just now. Old man McCarty, one hundred and four years old, died from eating too many bananas. The evidence points so strongly to the Mafia that the police have surrounded the Second Avenue Katzenjammer Gambrinus Club No. 2, and the capture of the assassin is only the matter of a few hours. The detective force has not yet been called on for assistance."

Jolnes and I went out and up the street toward the corner, where we were to catch a surface car.

Halfway up the block we met Rheingelder, an acquaintance of ours, who held a City Hall position.

"Good morning, Rheingelder," said Jolnes, halting. "Nice breakfast that was you had this morning."

Always on the look-out for the detective's remarkable feats of deduction, I saw Jolnes's eyes flash for an instant upon a long yellow splash on the shirt bosom and a smaller one upon the chin of Rheingelder both undoubtedly made by the yolk of an egg.

"Oh, dot is some of your detectiveness," said Rheingelder, shaking all over with a smile. "Vell, I pet you trinks und cigars all round dot you cannot tell vot I haf eaten for breakfast."

"Done," said Jolnes. "Sausage, pumpernickel and coffee."

Rheingelder admitted the correctness of the surmise and paid the bet. When we had proceeded on our way I said to Jolnes:

"I thought you looked at the egg spilled on his chin and shirt front."

"I did," said Jolnes. "That is where I began my deduction. Rheingelder is a very economical, saving man. Yesterday eggs dropped in the market to twenty-eight cents per dozen. Today they are quoted at forty-two. Rheingelder ate eggs yesterday, and today he went back to his usual fare. A little thing like this isn't anything, Whatsup; it belongs to the primary arithmetic class."

When we boarded the streetcar we found the seats all occupied—principally by ladies. Jolnes and I stood on the rear platform.

About the middle of the car there sat an elderly man with a short gray beard, who looked to be the typical well-dressed New Yorker. At successive corners other ladies climbed aboard, and soon three or four of them were standing over the man, clinging to straps and glaring meaningly at the man who occupied the coveted seat. But he resolutely retained his place.

"We New Yorkers," I remarked to Jolnes, "have about lost our manners, as far as the exercise of them in public goes."

"Perhaps so," said Jolnes, lightly, "but the man you evidently refer to happens to be a very chivalrous and courteous gentleman from Old Virginia. He is spending a few days in New York with his wife and two daughters, and he leaves for the South tonight."

"You know him, then?" I said, in amazement.

"I never saw him before we stepped on the car," declared the detective, smilingly.

"By the gold tooth of the Witch of Endor," I cried, "if you can construe all that from his appearance you are dealing in nothing else than black art."

"The habit of observation—nothing more," said Jolnes. "If the old gentleman gets off the car before we do, I think I can demonstrate to you the accuracy of my deduction."

Three blocks farther along the gentleman rose to leave the car. Jolnes addressed him at the door:

"Pardon me, sir, but are you not Colonel Hunter, of Norfolk, Virginia?"

"No, suh," was the extremely courteous answer. "My name, suh, is Ellison—Major Winfield R. Ellison, from Fairfax County, in the same state. I know a good many people, suh, in Norfolk—the Goodriches, the Tollivers, and the Crabtrees, suh, but I never had the pleasure of meeting yo' friend Colonel Hunter. I am happy to say, suh, that I am going back to Virginia tonight, after having spent a week in yo' city with my wife and three daughters. I shall be in Norfolk in about ten days, and if you will give me yo' name, suh, I will take pleasure in looking up Colonel Hunter and telling him that you inquired after him, suh."

"Thank you," said Jolnes. "Tell him that Reynolds sent his regards, if you will be so kind."

I glanced at the great New York detective and saw that a look of intense chagrin had come upon his clear-cut features. Failure in the slightest point always galled Shamrock Jolnes.

"Did you say your *three* daughters?" he asked of the Virginia gentleman.

"Yes, suh, my three daughters, all as fine girls as there are in Fairfax County," was the answer. With that Major Ellison stopped the car and began to descend the step.

Shamrock Jolnes clutched his arm.

"One moment, sir—" he begged, in an urbane voice in which I alone detected the anxiety—"am I not right in believing that one of the young ladies is an *adopted* daughter?"

"You are, suh," admitted the major, from the ground, "but how the devil you knew it, suh, is mo' than I can tell."

"And mo' than I can tell, too," I said, as the car went on.

Jolnes was restored to his calm, observant serenity by having wrested victory from his apparent failure; so after we got off the car he invited me into a café, promising to reveal the process of his latest wonderful feat.

"In the first place," he began after we were comfortably seated, "I knew the gentleman was no New Yorker because he was flushed and uneasy and restless on account of the ladies that were standing, although he did not rise and give them his seat. I decided from his appearance that he was a Southerner rather than a Westerner.

"Next I began to figure out his reason for not relinquishing his seat to a lady when he evidently felt strongly, but not overpoweringly, impelled to do so. I very quickly decided upon that. I noticed that one of his eyes had received a severe jab in one corner, which was red and inflamed, and that all over his face were tiny round marks about the size of the end of an uncut lead pencil. Also upon both of his patent-leather shoes were a number of deep imprints shaped like ovals cut oft square at one end.

"Now, there is only one district in New York City where a man is bound to receive scars and wounds and indentations of that sort—and that is along the sidewalks of Twenty-third Street and a portion of Sixth Avenue south of there. I knew from the imprints of trampling French heels on his feet and the marks of countless jabs in the face from umbrellas and parasols carried by women in the shopping district that he had been in conflict with the Amazonian troops. And as he was a man of intelligent appearance, I knew he would not have braved such dangers unless he had been dragged thither by his own womenfolk. Therefore, when he got on the car his anger at the treatment he had received was sufficient to make him keep his seat in spite of his traditions of Southern chivalry."

"That is all very well," I said, "but why did you insist upon daughters—and especially two daughters? Why couldn't a wife alone have taken him shopping?"

"There had to be daughters," said Jolnes, calmly. "If he had only a wife, and she near his own age, he could have bluffed her into going alone. If he had a young wife she would prefer to go alone. So there you are."

"I'll admit that," I said; "but, now, why two daughters? And how, in the name of all the prophets, did you guess that one was adopted when he told you he had three?"

"Don't say guess," said Jolnes, with a touch of pride in his air; "there is no such word in the lexicon of ratiocination. In Major Ellison's buttonhole there was a carnation and a rosebud backed by a geranium leaf. No woman ever combined a carnation and a rosebud into a boutonniere. Close your eyes, Whatsup, and give the logic of your imagination a chance. Cannot you see the lovely Adele fastening the carnation to the lapel so that Papa may be gay upon the street? And then the romping Edith May dancing up with sisterly jealousy to add her rosebud to the adornment?"

"And then," I cried, beginning to feel enthusiasm, "when he declared that he had three daughters—"

"I could see," said Jolnes, "one in the background who added no flower; and I knew that she must be—"

"Adopted!" I broke in. "I give you every credit; but how did you know he was leaving for the South tonight?"

"In his breast pocket," said the great detective, "something large and oval made a protuberance. Good liquor is scarce on trains, and it is a long journey from New York to Fairfax County."

"Again I must bow to you," I said. "And tell me this, so that my last shred of doubt will be cleared away; why did you decide that he was from Virginia?"

"It was very faint, I admit," answered Shamrock Jolnes, "but no trained observer could have failed to detect the odor of mint in the car."

THE UMBROSA BURGLARY

R. C. Lehmann

D URING ONE OF MY SHORT SUMMER HOLIDAYS I HAPPENED TO BE SPENDING A few days at the delightful riverside residence of my friend James Silver, the extent of whose hospitality is only to be measured by the excellence of the fare that he sets before his guests, or by the varied amusements that he provides for them. The beauties of Umbrosa (for that is the attractive name of his house) are known to all those who during the summer months pass up (or down) the winding reaches of the Upper Thames. It was there that I witnessed as series of startling events which threw the whole county into a temporary turmoil. Had it not been for the unparalleled coolness and sagacity of Picklock Holes the results might have been fraught with disaster to many distinguished families, but the acumen of Holes saved the situation and the family plate, and restored the peace of mind of one of the best fellows in the world.

The party at Umbrosa consisted of the various members of the Silver family, including, besides Mr. and Mrs. Silver, three high-spirited and unmarried youths and two charming girls. Picklock Holes was of course one of the guests. In fact, it had long since come to be an understood thing that wherever I went Holes should accompany me in the character of a professional detective on the look-out for business; and James Silver, though he may have at first resented the calm unmuscularity of my marvellous friend's immovable face, would have been the last man in the world to spoil any chance of sport or excitement by refraining from offering a cordial invitation to Holes. The party was completed by Peter Bowman, a lad of eighteen, who to an extraordinary capacity for mischief added an imperturbable cheerfulness of manner. He was generally known as Shockheaded Peter, in allusion to the brush-like appearance of his delicate auburn hair, but his intimate friends sometimes addressed him as Venus, a nickname which he thoroughly deserved by the almost classic irregularity of his Saxon features.

We were all sitting, I remember, on the riverbank, watching the countless craft go past, and enjoying that pleasant industrious indolence which is one of the chief charms of life on the Thames. A punt had just skimmed by, propelled by an athletic young fellow in boating costume. Suddenly Holes spoke.

"It is strange," he said, "that the man should be still at large."

"What man? Where? How?" we all exclaimed breathlessly.

"The young puntsman," said Holes, with an almost aggravating coolness. "He is a bigamist, and has murdered his great aunt."

"It cannot be," said Mr. Silver, with evident distress. "I know the lad well, and a better fellow never breathed."

"I speak the truth," said Holes, unemotionally. "The induction is perfect. He is wearing a red tie. That tie was not always red. It was, therefore, stained by something. Blood is red. It was, therefore, stained by blood. Now it is well known that the blood of great aunts is of a lighter shade, and the colour of that tie has a lighter shade. The blood that stained it was, therefore, the blood of his great aunt. As for the bigamy, you will have noticed that as he passed he blew two rings of cigarette smoke, and they both floated in the air *at the same time*. A ring is a symbol of matrimony. Two rings together mean bigamy. He is, therefore, a bigamist."

For a moment we were silent, struck with horror at this dreadful, this convincing revelation of criminal infamy. Then I broke out:

"Holes," I said, "you deserve the thanks of the whole community. You will of course communicate with the police."

"No," said Holes, "they are fools, and I do not care to mix myself up with them. Besides, I have other fish to fry."

Saying this, he led me to a secluded part of the grounds, and whispered in my ear.

"Not a word of what I am about to tell you. There will be a burglary here to-night."

"But Holes," I said, startled in spite of myself at the calm omniscience of my friend, "had we not better do something; arm the servants, warn the police, bolt the doors and bar the windows, and sit up with blunderbusses anything would be better than this state of dreadful expectancy. May I not tell Mr. Silver?"

"Potson, you are amiable, but you will never learn my methods." And with that enigmatic reply I had to be content in the meantime.

The evening had passed as pleasantly as evenings at Umbrosa always pass. There had been music; the Umbrosa choir, composed of members of the family and guests, had performed in the drawing-room, and Peter had drawn tears from the eyes of every one by his touching rendering of the well-known songs of "The Dutiful Son" and "The Cartridge-bearer." Shortly afterwards, the ladies retired to bed, and the gentlemen, after the customary interval in the smoking-room, followed. We were in high good-humour, and had made many plans for the morrow. Only Holes seemed preoccupied.

I had been sleeping for about an hour, when I was suddenly awakened with a start. In the passage outside I heard the voices of the youngest Silver boy and of Peter.

"Peter, old chap," said Johnny Silver, "I believe there's burglars in the house. Isn't it a lark?"

"Ripping," said Peter. "Have you told your people?"

"Oh, it's no use waking the governor and the mater; we'll do the job ourselves. I told the girls, and they've all locked themselves in and got under their beds, so they're safe. Are you ready?"

"Yes."

"Come on then."

With that they went along the passage and down the stairs. My mind was made up, and my trousers and boots were on in less time than it takes to tell it. I went to Holes's room and entered. He was lying on his bed, fully awake, dressed in his best detective suit, with his fingers meditatively extended, and touching one another.

"They're here," I said.

"Who?"

"The burglars."

"As I thought," said Holes, selecting his best basket-hiked life-preserver from a heap in the middle of the room. "Follow me silently."

I did so. No sooner had we reached the landing, however, than the silence was broken by a series of blood-curdling screams.

"Good heavens!" was all I could say.

"Hush," said Holes. I obeyed him. The screams subsided, and I heard the voices of my two young friends, evidently in great triumph.

"Lie still, you brute," said Peter, "or I'll punch your blooming head. Give the rope another twist, Johnny. That's it. Now you cut and tell your governor and old Holes that we've nabbed the beggar."

By this time the household was thoroughly roused. Agitated females and inquisitive males streamed downstairs. Lights were lit, and a remarkable sight met our eyes. In the middle of the drawing-room lay an undersized burglar, securely bound, with Peter sitting on his head.

"Johnny and I collared the beggar," said Peter, "and bowled him over. Thanks, I think I could do a ginger-beer."

The man was of course tried and convicted, and Holes received the thanks of the County Council.

"That fellow," said the great detective to me, "was the best and cleverest of my tame team of country-house burglars. Through him and his associates I have fostered and foiled more thefts than I care to count. Those infernal boys nearly spoilt everything. Potson, take my advice, never attempt a master-stroke in a houseful of boys. They can't understand scientific induction. Had they not interfered I should have caught the fellow myself. He had wired to tell me where I should find him."

AN IRREDUCIBLE DETECTIVE STORY

Stephen Leacock

THE MYSTERY HAD NOW REACHED ITS CLIMAX. FIRST, THE MAN HAD BEEN undoubtedly murdered. Second, it was absolutely certain that no conceivable person had done it.

It was therefore time to call in the great detective.

He gave one searching glance at the corpse. In a moment he whipped out a microscope.

"Ha! Ha!" he said, as he picked a hair off the lapel of the dead man's coat. "The mystery is now solved."

He held up the hair.

"Listen," he said, "we have only to find the man who lost this hair and the criminal is in our hands." The inexorable chain of logic was complete. The detective set himself to the search.

For four days and nights he moved, unobserved, through the streets, of New York scanning closely every face he passed, looking for a man who had lost a hair.

On the fifth day he discovered a man, disguised as a tourist, his head enveloped in a steamer cap that reached below his ears.

The man was about to go on board the *Gloritania*.

The detective followed him on board.

"Arrest him!" he said, and then drawing himself to his full height, he brandished aloft the hair.

"This is his," said the great detective. "It proves his guilt."

Remove his hat," said the ship's captain sternly.

They did so.

The man was entirely bald.

"Ha!" said the great detective, without a moment of hesitation. "He has committed not *one* murder but about a million."

BIOGRAPHICAL NOTES

Grant Allen (1848–1899) was a Canadian science writer and novelist. His crime fiction includes *An African Millionaire* (1897), which features his gentleman thief, Colonel Clay, and two books featuring female detectives, *Miss Cayley's Adventures* (1899) and *Hilda Wade* (1900).

Robert Barr (1849–1912) was a journalist and writer of popular fiction who spent most of his early life in Canada before moving to England in 1881. His books include *The Triumphs of Eugene Valmont* (1906), a collection of satirical detective stories, and *The O'Ruddy* (1903), a collaboration with Stephen Crane.

M(atthias) McDonnell Bodkin (1850–1933) was an Irish politician and journalist who also wrote in a wide variety of fiction genres. He created the detectives Paul Beck in *Paul Beck: The Rule of Thumb Detective* (1899) and Dora Myrl in *Dora Myrl: The Lady Detective* (1900), and had them marry in *The Quests of Paul Beck* (1910). Their detective son appeared in *Paul Beck: A Chip Off the Old Block* (1912).

Guy Boothby (1867–1905) was a prolific Australian writer who wrote in a variety of popular fiction genres. His most popular crime novels featured series character Dr. Nikola, an occultist and criminal mastermind, who first appeared in *A Bid for Fortune; or Dr. Nikola's Vendetta* (1895).

Mary Elizabeth Braddon (1835–1915) was a British writer whose novel *Lady Audley's Secret* (1862) was one of the bestselling mystery novels published in the nineteenth century.

Ernest Bramah (1868–1942) was a British humorist and writer of popular fiction. He published four books featuring his blind detective, Max Carrados: *Max Carrados* (1914), *The Eyes of Max Carrados* (1922), *Max Carrados Mysteries* (1927), and *The Bravo of London* (1934).

Ellis Parker Butler (1869–1937) was an American humorist and writer of popular fiction. He wrote forty stories featuring detective Philo Gubb, several of which are collected in *Philo Gubb: Correspondence School Detective* (1918).

G(ilbert) K(eith) Chesterton (1874–1936) was a British writer, intellectual, and Christian apologist. He published more than fifty stories featuring his Roman Catholic priest detective Father Brown, between 1910 and 1936.

Wilkie Collins (1824–1889) was a British writer of novels, short stories, and plays, and a frequent collaborator with Charles Dickens. His influential novel *The Moonstone* (1868) is considered the first detective novel written in the English language.

Richard Harding Davis (1864–1916) was an American journalist, war correspondent, and writer of popular fiction. His detective fiction was collected in a number of different volumes, including *Gallegher and Other Stories* (1891), which relates the adventures of a newsboy detective.

Charles Dickens (1812–1870) was a British novelist and social critic and one of the bestselling writers in the English language. His pioneering works of detective fiction include his novel *Bleak House* (1852–53), whose character Inspector Bucket is considered to be the first police detective in fiction.

Dick Donovan (1842–1934) was the pseudonym of Joyce Emmerson Preston Muddock, as well as the name of the character in his most popular detective series. Donovan's other fictional detectives include Vincent Trill, Tyler Tatlock, and forensic criminologist Fabian Field.

Robert Eustace (1854–1943) was the pen name of Eustace Robert Barton, a British physician who also wrote crime fiction. His books written with frequent collaborator L. T. Meade include *A Master of Mysteries* (1898), a collection of rationalized macabre mysteries.

J(oseph) S(mith) Fletcher (1863–1935) was a British journalist and mystery writer whose best-known novel is *The Middle Temple Murder* (1918). His adventures of serial detective Archer Dawe were collected in *The Adventures of Archer Dawe: Sleuth Hound* (1909).

Andrew Forrester (1832–c. 1909) was the pseudonym of James Redding Ware, a British novelist and playwright. His collection *The Female Detective: The Original Lady Detective* (1864), "edited by A. F.," is one of the earliest books to feature a female detective.

R. Austin Freeman (1862–1943) was a British writer of mystery fiction. In his tales of medicolegal forensic investigator Dr. Thorndyke, collected in *The Singing Bone* (1912) and other volumes, he pioneered the "inverted" detective story, in which a crime and its perpetrator are known to the reader, and the detective must examine evidence and clues to solve it.

Jacques Futrelle (1875–1912) was an American journalist and writer of mystery fiction. The title of his book *The Thinking Machine* (1907) is the nickname given to his series detective Augustus S. F. X. Van Dusen, who applies his superior intellectual skills to the solving seemingly insoluble crimes.

Émile Gaboriau (1832–1873) was a French novelist and journalist. His novel *L'Affaire Lerouge* (1866) introduced thief-turned-detective Monsieur Lecoq, one of the most popular detectives in fiction before the emergence of Sherlock Holmes.

Anna Katherine Green (1846–1935) was an American poet and bestselling mystery writer whose best-known novel is *The Leavenworth Case* (1878). She introduced her series detective Violet Strange in her short-fiction collection *The Golden Slipper, and Other Problems for Violet Strange* (1915).

T. W. Hanshew (1857–1914) was an American actor and writer. His best-known fictional creation was detective Hamilton Cleek, a master of disguise, whose adventures were collected in *The Man of Forty Faces* (1910) and other volumes.

Bret Harte (1836–1902) was an American writer who specialized in stories featuring settings and characters from the American West. He served as editor of the *Overland Monthly* and the *Atlantic Monthly*.

W(illiam) S(tephens) Hayward (1835-1870) was a British writer of sensation stories and penny dreadfuls. Hayward frequently published his fiction under a female pseudonym, or anonymously, as he did for *Revelations of a Lady Detective* (1864).

O. Henry (1862–1910) was the pseudonym of William Sydney Porter, one of the most popular American writers of short fiction in the late-nineteenth and early-twentieth centuries. "The Adventures of Shamrock Jolnes" was one of three stories that he wrote spoofing Sherlock Holmes.

Fergus Hume (1859–1932) was a British novelist whose book *The Mystery of a Hansom Cab* was one of the bestselling mystery novels of the nineteenth century.

C(harles) J(ohn) Cutcliffe Hyne (1865–1944) was a British novelist who wrote in a variety genres. He is best known for his novel about Atlantis, *The Lost Continent* (1899), and his adventures of seafaring thief Captain Kettle.

Stephen Leacock (1869–1944) was a Canadian writer and humorist.

R. C. Lehmann (1856–1929) was a British writer and politician who contributed regularly to the magazine *Punch*.

Francis Lynde (1856–1930) was an American writer whose collection *Scientific Sprague* (1912) featured a scientific detective who solves mysteries set against a railroad background in the American West.

Richard Marsh (1857-1914) was the pseudonym of British writer Richard Bernhard Hellmann, who wrote in a variety of popular fiction genres. He is best-known for his supernatural thriller *The Beetle* (1897).

L. T. Meade (1844–1914) was the pseudonym of Elizabeth Thomasina Meade Smith, a prolific writer of novels for young women. Her more than 300 books include scores of novels of mystery and detection, several written in collaboration with Robert Eustace. Arthur Morrison (1863–1945) was a British writer and journalist. His stories featuring detective Martin Hewitt are collected in *Martin Hewitt, Investigator* (1994), *Chronicles of Martin Hewitt* (1895) and *Adventures of Martin Hewitt* (1896).

Rodrigues Ottolengui (1861–1937) was an American dentist and writer of crime fiction. The stories he collected as *The Final Proof* (1898) features his series characters Detective Barnes and Robert Leroy Mitchel, who also appeared in the novels *An Artist in Crime* (1892) and *The Crime of the Century* (1896).

Charles Felton Pidgin (1844–1923) was an American statistician and writer. His tales of attorney detective Quincy Adams Sawyer were collected in several volumes, including *The Chronicles of Quincy Adams Sawyer, Detective* (1912), and adapted as a movie in 1922.

C(atherine) L(ouisa) Pirkis (1841–1910) was a British writer best known for the detective tales collected in *The Experiences of Loveday Brooke, Lady Detective* (1894).

Edgar Allan Poe (1809–1849) was an American writer, essayist, and critic. His three tales featuring C. August Dupin—"Murders in the Rue Morgue," "The Mystery of Marie Rogêt," and "The Purloined Letter"—laid the foundations for the modern detective story.

Melville Davisson Post (1869–1930) was an American writer who specialized in crime fiction. He is best known for his series of stories featuring Randolph Mason, an unscrupulous lawyer who exploits legal loopholes for the benefit of his clients, and his historical tales of Uncle Abner, a rural detective whose adventures are set in the years before the American Civil War.

Hesketh Prichard (1876–1922) was a British writer who is best known for his tales of psychic detective Flaxman Low (written in collaboration with his mother under the joint pseudonyms E. and H. Heron) and his adventures of backwoods Canadian November Joe, collected in *November Joe* (1913).

Arthur B. Reeve (1880–1936) was an American fiction writer and journalist. His tales of series detective Craig Kennedy, dubbed "the American Sherlock Holmes," helped to inaugurate the scientific detective subgenre.

George R. Sims (1847–1922) was an English journalist and dramatist. The adventures of his series character Dorcas Dene, a female detective who works to support herself and her blind artist husband, were collected in 1897 and 1898.

Carolyn Wells (1870–1942) was an American mystery writer and parodist, best known for her novels featuring series detective Fleming Stone.

Victor L. Whitechurch (1868–1933) was a British clergyman and writer whose tales of railroad detective Thorpe Hazell were collected in *Thrilling Stories of the Railway* (1912).

SOURCES

Allen, Grant. "The Great Ruby Robbery," *The Strand Magazine*, September 1892.

Barr, Robert. "The Great Pegram Mystery," *The Face and the Mask*. New York: Frederick A. Stokes Company Publishers, 1895.

Bodkin, M. McDonnell. "How He Cut His Stick," *Dora Myrl, The Lady Detective*. London: Chatto & Windus, 1890.

Boothby, Guy. "The Duchess of Wiltshire's Diamonds," *The Viceroy's Protégé; or, A Prince of Swindlers*. New York: New Amsterdam Book Co., 1903.

Braddon, Mary Elizabeth. " 'Thou Art the Man,' " *Flower and Weed; and Other Tales*. London: Simpkin, Marshall, Hamilton, Kent, & Co., 1891.

Bramah, Ernest. "The Coin of Dionysius," *Max Carrados*. London: Methuen & Co., 1914.

Butler, Ellis Parker. "Philo Gubb's Greatest Case," *Philo Gubb: Correspondence School Detective*. Boston: Houghton Mifflin Company, 1914.

Chesterton, G. K. "The Hammer of God," *The Innocence of Father Brown*. London: John Lane Company, 1911.

Collins, Wilkie. "The Diary of Anne Rodway," *Novels and Tales Reprinted from Household Words*. Leipzig: Bernhard Tauchnitz, 1856.

Davis, Richard Harding. "The Amateur," *The Bar Sinister*. New York: Charles Scribner's Sons, 1916.

Dickens, Charles. "Three "Detective" Anecdotes," *The Lamplighters Story; Hunted Down; The Detective Police; and Other Nouvellettes*. Philadelphia: T. B. Peterson & Brothers, 1861.

Donovan, Dick. "A Hunt for a Murderer," *Caught at Last! Leaves from the Note-Book of a Detective*. London: Chatto & Windus, 1889.

Fletcher, J. S. "The Contents of the Coffin," *The Adventures of Arthur Dawe, Sleuth-Hound*. London: Digby, Long & Co., 1909.

Forrester, Andrew. "The Unknown Weapon," *Tales of a Female Detective*. London: Ward, Lock, and Tyler, 1868.

Freeman, R. Austin. "The Case of Oscar Brodski," *The Singing Bone*. London: Hodder & Stoughton, 1912.

Futrelle, Jacques. "Problem of Cell 13," *The Thinking Machine*. New York: Dodd, Mead, 1907.

Gaboriau, Émile. "The Little Old Man of Batignolle," *The Little Old Man of Batignolle and Other Stories*. London: Vizetelly & Co., 1886.

Green, Anna Katherine. "The Golden Slipper," *The Golden Slipper and other Problems for Violet Dare*. New York: G.P. Putnam's, 1915.

Hanshew, T. W. "The Riddle of the 5:28," *Cleek the Master Detective*. New York: Doubleday, Page & Company, 1918.

Harte, Bret. "The Stolen Cigar Case," *Condensed Novels, Second Series*. Boston: Houghton, Mifflin and Company, 1902.

Hayward, W. S. "The Lost Diamonds," *Revelations of a Lady Detective*. London: George Vickers, 1864.

Henry, O. "The Adventures of Shamrock Jolnes," *Sixes and Sevens*. New York: Doubleday, Page & Company, 1911.

Hume, Fergus. "The Green-Stone God and the Stockbroker," *The Dwarf's Chamber and Other Stories*. London: Ward, Lock & Bowden, Limited, 1896.

Hyne, C. J. Cutcliffe. "The Tragedy of a Third Smoker," *The Harmsworth Monthly Pictorial Magazine*, October 1898.

Leacock, Stephen. "An Irreducible Detective Story," *Further Foolishness: Sketches and Satires on the Follies of the Day*. New York: John Lane Company, 1916.

Lehmann, R. C. "The Umbrosa Burglary," *Punch*, November 4, 1893.

Lynde, Francis. "The Wire-Devil," *Scientific Sprague*. New York: Charles Scribner's Sons, 1912.

Marsh, Richard. "Mandragora," *The Adventures of Judith Lee*. London: Methuen, 1916.

Meade, L. T. and Eustace, Robert. "The Mystery of the Felwyn Tunnel," *A Master of Mysteries*. London: Ward Lock & Co., 1898.

Morrison, Arthur. "The Lenton Croft Robberies," *Martin Hewitt: Investigator*. New York: Harper & Brothers Publishers, 1907.

Ottolengui, Rodrigues. "The Art of Forgery," *Ainslee's Magazine*, August 1901.

Pidgin, Charles Felton. "The Affair of the Double Thumb Print," *The Chronicles of Quincy Adams Sawyer, Detective*. New York: Grosset & Dunlap, 1912.

Pirkis, C. L. "The Murder at Troyte's Hill," *The Experiences of Loveday Brooke: Lady Detective*, Hutchinson & Co., 1894.

Poe, Edgar Allan. "The Purloined Letter," *Tales*. New York: Wiley & Putnam, 1845.

Post, Melville Davisson. "The Angel of the Lord," *Uncle Abner, Master of Mysteries*. New York: D. Appleton and Company, 1919.

Prichard, Hesketh. "The Hundred Thousand Dollar Robbery," *November Joe, Detective of the Woods*. Boston: Houghton Mifflin, 1913.

Reeve, Arthur B. "The Case of Helen Bond," *Cosmopolitan*, December 1910.

Sims, George R. "The Man with the Wild Eyes," *Dorcas Dene, Detective*. London: F. V. White & Co., 1897.

Wells, Carolyn. "The Adventure of the Clothes-Line," *The Century Magazine*, May 15, 1893.

Whitechurch, Victor L. "Sir Gilbert Murrell's Picture," *Thrilling Stories of the Railway*, London: C. Arthur Pearson Ltd., 1912.